Craig Thomas was educated at University College, Cardiff, where he gained his M.A. in 1967. His bestselling novels, include *Firefox* and most recently, *Winter Hawk, Emerald Decision, The Last Raven, All the Grey Cats, A Hooded Crow* and *A Wild Justice*, all of which spring from his interest in geopolitical tensions and conflicts.

Craig Thomas is married and lives with his wife and two tortoiseshell cats in Staffordshire. His interests include cricket, gardening and music, especially classical music and jazz. He is also interested in philosophy and political theory.

CRAIG THOMAS

PLAYING WITH COBRAS

SEA LEOPARD

Grafton

This omnibus edition published in 1998 by
HarperCollins*Publishers*

Reprinted 2003

HarperCollins*Publishers*
77-85 Fulham Palace Road,
Hammersmith, London W6 8JB

ISBN 0 007 68305 7

Printed and bound in Great Britain by
Mackays of Chatham Ltd, Chatham, Kent

for
Gethyn and Phyll

and for
Ed and Lynn

with love

'The old, most populous, wealthiest of earth's lands
The streams of the Indus and the Ganges and their
many affluents . . .

On the one side China and on the other side
Persia and Arabia,
To the south the great seas and the bay of Bengal . . .

Doubts to be solv'd, the map incognita, blanks
to be fill'd.'

Walt Whitman: *Passage to India*, 6

PRELUDE

'. . . it is perhaps only with him that
the real question mark is posed for
the first time . . . the hand moves
forward, the tragedy *begins*.'

Nietzsche: *The Gay Science*, V

Philip Cass nudged the Japanese 4WD out from behind the sight-seeing bus wheezing up the road, and slid carefully past it. The road dropped away to his left, into the smeared, scented dark-ness of pines. Pines loomed above, too, marching down towards the twisting, dusty track wriggling tiredly up towards Gulmarg. The bus, its asthmatic engine belching exhaust fumes, dis-appeared from the mirror as he rounded a twist of the road. Nanga Parbat, for a moment, hunched to the north, snow-peaked. The Kashmir Valley's orchards and ricefields, in the haze of late summer, spread out to his left then behind him as the road climbed and twisted again.

The smell of the pines. He sighed. Not long now, not much of such things left, unless he came back as a tourist. The steering wheel struggled in his hands against the potholes and stones of the road, before his vehicle levelled and confronted the old hill-station of Gulmarg. New ski-lifts against the sky, new hotels and bungalows beached amid grass and wild flowers. The sen-sation of imminent departure not only from Kashmir but from India suddenly hurt him, like emotions he might have felt beside a terminal sickbed. He passed two backpacked trekkers, utensils rattling at their shoulders above the noise of the vehicle's engine. Bright shirts and slacks on the highest golf course in the world. A necklace of tourists mounted on ponies emerged from the crowding pines. They paused to appreciate their first glimpse of the resort afloat in its meadow, with the Pir Panjal range pushing up to the south and the outriders of the Himalayas to the north,

11

cupping the place in a great rock embrace. Cass smiled with something approaching bitterness. He spoke Hindi, Urdu, a smattering of Punjabi, could stumblingly read Sanskrit – all of which meant that his tour of duty in India was over and that SIS would probably send him to Washington or Moscow, where the last four years would immediately be redundant.

He tossed his head. He had another couple of months, why so sad already? He sniffed like a hound at the clean, sharp air. Delhi was still like a cauldron, even Srinagar behind him in the valley had been sticky, oppressive – but up here . . .

Up here was the real source of his melancholy, and it was human. Sereena. Waiting for him in her husband's bungalow just behind Gulmarg, perched on the edge of a cliff and facing north towards Pakistani Kashmir and the great mountain, Nanga Parbat. Sereena the Indian film star and the wife of the Minister of Tourism and Civil Aviation, V. K. Sharmar. He rubbed his hand through his breeze-blown hair as if embarrassed, grinning at the awakened sense of danger, the effrontery of their months-long liaison, the locales of their encounters in Delhi or here in Kashmir. The dangerous, exhilarating joke of it, the added earnestness that risk gave to their lovemaking. When he left India, he'd leave her behind, too.

The resort trickled tourists along its main street. There was noise from cafés, music blaring from open-topped cars and flung-open doors. Then he was climbing the short, winding, narrow track up towards the long wooden bungalow that once had housed, beneath elaborately carved eaves and in scented-wood rooms, memsahibs for each summer of the Raj. He slowed the vehicle and dragged on the brake, disappointed that she was not posed in the shadow of the verandah, then at once pleased in anticipation of her waiting for him in the minister's kingsize bed in the long, low-beamed main bedroom. The fan would be turning coolly above her, its arms waving in encouragement rather than reproach. He cocked his head, listening. The hi-fi was playing some of the American country rock Sereena incongruously enjoyed; even as he preferred ragas and the sitar. She was, because of her status as one of the Hindu deities of the cinema, more Western than he, sometimes. She was in bed, then. It would all be done with titillating, cinematic cliché; the iced champagne, the silk sheets, the seductive underwear, the acted whore– everything. He smiled, rubbing his cheeks. He *was* in the intelligence service, after all; Sereena had merely changed his name to Bond, glamorising their relationship within the conventions of celluloid.

And, if it was a fantasy, then he enjoyed that too . . . it was *every* man's sexual fantasy, after all. Experienced Asian beauty, exotic settings, the delicious-lubricious, the element of risk. Enough to make him all but rub his hands in anticipation.

Or remember that she'd become more than a fantasy, an appetite. Awkwardly, he had begun to love her. At least, to want to be with her, and to want not to end it. He climbed out of the vehicle and breathed deeply, slowly. He could just see the spray of a fountain at the rear of the bungalow. Jesus, it was close enough to paradise, every aspect of the situation. He dragged his overnight bag out of the 4WD and hurried into the cool, purple shadow of the verandah. Maybe, just maybe, he'd wangle another extension to his tour of duty . . . trouble was, with Aubrey gone, there was no one who would just OK it with a slight smile. Pete Shelley was stuffed to the gills with pompous rectitude since taking over the Director-General's job. He might well not give him an extension –

Sod that for the moment, anyway. He called out: 'Sereena – it's me! The flight was on time.'

She must be teasing, some new game. Wanted him to go straight into the bedroom, be surprised by what she was wearing, or the way her body was posed in the bed or perhaps against the late afternoon light from the window, the mountains behind her. He hurried, dropped his overnight bag and cotton jacket on the living-room sofa. Scented woods, carved cornicing, heavy old furniture, deep, complex rugs. He plucked up a glass of still-bubbling champagne from a small table, sipping it as he grinned. Sipped again, the drink's coldness tightening his throat pleasurably. A broken champagne glass crackled into shards beneath his shoe as he approached the bedroom door. He could smell, above the usual scents and incenses of the bungalow, the Chanel he'd bought for her last birthday –

He looked down at the broken glass beneath his feet. She was getting careless in her eagerness – perhaps she'd heard his engine note approaching and dropped it in her hurry. He stepped through the open door of the bedroom, rubbing his temple against a sudden dizziness. She was lying on the silk sheets – saried though, as if she'd flung herself on the bed in a modelling pose, her hair strayed out like a black cloud across the pillows. There was a great deal of blood, a great deal. It had soaked into the sheets and the pillows, there was even a splash of it on the wall behind the elaborate carving of the headboard. Blood everywhere . . .

The room whirled, even before he could vomit in horror, the smear of blood on the wall spinning like a firework, fiery in the slanting sunlight coming through the window . . . window, which was moving, circling the room, then floating above him as he fell into the darkness.

Window . . . He realised the opaque area of dull light was the window. It was unmoving, but not where . . . He was lying on the bed. The window was where it should be, if he was lying on the bed. Nanga Parbat's flanks were goldened as the sun began to go down. His hand and forearm, stretched out to where she would be across the bed, were sticky. His fingers – he wriggled them – were weblike, stuck to one another. His head lurched like a loosely-stowed cargo as he attempted to sit up and look at his – *red*? – hand – why red, *sticky*? Flies buzzed in the room beneath the revolving, slow fan. He turned. Her body was covered with them, feasting on the drying blood that covered her, covered the sheets – his hand, his shirt, the knife that lay on the bed between them. He lurched across her body, waggling his arms, beating at the air around the flies, his head aching, his stomach revolted. His mind seemed pierced by a silent scream attempting to bully itself into his awareness. He stared at the gashes in the glowing, bloodstained sari, then at his reddened hands. He was stilled with shock, unable to move, his throat fighting back the bitter vomit he could taste. The flies settled on her again, advantaged by his paralysis.

The hi-fi continued its drool of country rock from the living room, the noise pressing against his throbbing temples. Then, gradually loudening as it approached from Gulmarg, the noise of the police siren drowned the music as Cass continued to stare, immobile, at the woman's body.

PART ONE

Casual Labour

'He has an angry wrenlike vigilance,
a greyhound's gentle tautness;
he seems to wince at pleasure . . .

He is out of bounds now.'
        Robert Lowell: *For the Union Dead*

ONE

the burning

'I can't oblige you – you see how I'm fixed,' Hyde responded mockingly, even though he had never intended it to come out as a flip excuse.

As if in disappointment at suspected compromise, the leggy Burmese cat walked away from him. The tortoiseshell, meanwhile, quizzically bent her masked features to one side as she sat outside on the sunblocked windowsill overlooking the scrappy garden. They were probably right to be disappointed. He had wanted to say, *You don't employ me any more. I'm a free agent. Bugger off, Shelley.*

Shelley was seated across the lounge, the unexplained videotape he had brought with him beside him on the sofa. The late summer sun fell across the carpet with the beginnings of reluctance. There was, seemingly, a third human presence in the room with them, even though the Burmese had joined Ros in the bedroom, where she was noisily packing. Aubrey was there, as usual reproving Hyde, on this occasion in fragments of the long, maundering, confessional letter he had written to Hyde only days after resigning from the Cabinet Office. The phrases flicked in Hyde's thoughts with the remonstrance of cuffing hands. *Only theories offer freedom of action. Other people offer nothing but endless obligations, the very opposite of freedom . . .* Aubrey, explaining why he had bent or broken every cardinal rule in order to pursue Paulus Malan to his death. Aubrey, to square his vigorous conscience, had been apologising for the predominance of personal motives over duty and the priorities of the operation.

Hyde shook his head and then rubbed his hands through his curling hair. He was instantly angry, recalling Aubrey – recalling *obligation*.

'I can't do it, Shelley,' he burst out. 'I don't have to do it. You don't *pay* me to do things like that any more. I resigned because of Aubrey. So, don't look for terminal boredom that'll make me do *anything* slightly interesting or dangerous.'

Even that hadn't come out as he intended. Obligation. As Shelley had already put it – assuming the irresistible force of any new D-G – he *owed Cass his life. Cass saved you in Delhi, put you on the right plane to the safe place. They'd have killed you, if not.* Because of the baldness of the statement, what he really wanted to say – *oh, sod Cass* – kept whimpering away in his thoughts, like a puppy dismissed for weeing on the new carpet; or like one of the cats caught stropping at the brocade covering of the suite. *Oh, fuck Cass* . . . It didn't work, not really, because in the darkness at the back of his mind Cass howled and whimpered like all dogs and cats.

'It's no *big* deal, Patrick,' Shelley soothed. 'What I'm asking.'

Shelley was there on his own initiative. The paint that emblazoned his name and new title on his office door in Century House wasn't yet dry. Director-General of the Secret Intelligence Service. Shelley could at last recite it to himself every morning as he looked out over the slate-grey river. Aubrey's dauphin had got the top job, but the old man must have pulled the last of the strings he held very hard to ensure the appointment.

To deflect Shelley, he said: 'How's the old bugger? I don't hear gossip any more.' *I'm an outsider.*

'What? Oh . . . Sir Kenneth.' Shelley smiled with genuine affection. 'I hear he's in Vienna, staying with Frau Elsenreith.'

'His only *old* true love,' Hyde scoffed. 'After that? Winter in the Bahamas – memoirs should be worth a bit.'

'I think he's happier than his former political mistress, at the least,' Shelley replied.

Probably true. Aubrey had waddled away overburdened with honours and praise.

In the bedroom, Ros was making ostentatious noises as she opened and closed drawers, shut suitcases. As if cued, Shelley murmured:

'What will you do with the cats?'

'What —? Oh, the cattery.'

'And you'll be gone . . . ?'

'A couple of months. It depends how long it takes Ros to sort out her uncle's estate.' A wardrobe door slid shut with an exasperated noise. Both cats had now disappeared from the windowsill, the Burmese having returned from the bedroom, inspected Shelley's trousers, then joined the tortoiseshell outside. The Earl's Court afternoon seeped the scent of petrol and dust into the bright room. Hyde shrugged. 'You see why I can't help.'

Ros clicked suitcase locks firmly shut, then, to Shelley's evident discomfort, her large shadow hovered at the door of the lounge. Discomforted, he was, of course, anyway. It wasn't acted, either. Not only did he no longer know how to ask, but he didn't really know the question he wanted answered.

Curious, Hyde murmured: 'What's on the tape? Snuff video?'

'Well — someone who appears in it *is* dead. May I put it on?'

Hyde shrugged, and Shelley moved towards the VCR beneath the TV set, inserting the cassette as Hyde felt himself burrowing mentally back into the room, noticing details – the glimpse of the tortoiseshell's features above the windowsill before it ran off, as if warned; then the slow slippage of the sunlight across the carpet, and the warmth it gave to the furniture and drapes. As if, he realised, he needed reassurance. Shelley flicked on the television set, using the remote control.

At once, a struggling mass of humanity.

'This is a film star's funeral, Indian style,' Shelley remarked drily, passing some photographic enlargements to Hyde. Hyde leant forward to take them. The screen showed the vast crowd

21

from the vantage of a high window, as it seethed and struggled like the grubs in a fisherman's plastic box before being flung into a canal. Then, unedited, the scene was registered from ground level, amid the struggle for breath and glimpse. 'They seem quite keen,' Shelley added.

Hyde tossed his head and glanced down at the snapshots.

'Cass was giving *this* one?' he muttered.

'The affair had been in progress for some months.'

'I can't really blame him.'

Hyde glanced up from the spread snapshots to encounter the screen, where the camera swayed and wriggled through the pressing undergrowth of upraised arms and bent heads and waved scarves and handkerchiefs. He saw a distant funeral pyre – for a film star? In India, yes.

'That's the minister, her husband,' Shelley remarked, as Hyde watched a slick-haired and prosperous man circle the pyre. The soundtrack was poor, but the susurrations of the crowd, the collective orgasm of grief, was mounting. The sunlight gleamed into the camera for a moment, then the picture cleared. Foreign, hot, threatening, was how the scene appeared to Hyde – who allowed his senses to dictate, despite their catching Ros' exhalations of dislike coming from the bedroom. 'That's his brother, to his left.'

Hyde merely nodded. The minister, Sharmar – whom he recognised at once – was dignified and somehow aloof, despite the evident scandal of his wife having been murdered by an English lover. Perhaps the exigencies of the Indian cinema required decorum for a film star's burial, whatever the circumstances. Surreptitiously, he watched Shelley watching him watching the television screen. The husband's family gathered closer to the pyre, before the flames became too intense, while the crowd lamented in gusts of grief in the evening glow which managed to ridicule the flickers of flame from the scented wood surrounding –

He glanced down. *Her*.

'And Cass was giving her one, was he?'

22

'Apparently,' Shelley replied.

The crowd drew nearer to the updraught of flames from the pyre. The white-shrouded figure was further shrouded by blue and orange and the enveloping gleam of the early evening. The crowd seemed to press on like pilgrims towards an instantaneous miracle.

'What does *he* say?'

The afternoon, palely-English, reentered the lounge at the coat-tails of the Burmese, who had dropped like a large, dusky leaf through the open window. The scene on the television screen appeared exotically unreal.

'He won't say anything – that's the problem. Not to Head of Station or anyone else. He keeps –' Shelley spread his hands in supplication and then added: 'Direct contact with D-G, or nothing.'

'I would have thought he'd be screaming for help.'

As the flames leapt higher and the nearest and dearest moved aside, the wailing and – yes, rage – of the crowd swelled like a chorus. Last night of the Indian Proms.

'He is, in a way.'

'And you think he *might* have something to say for himself,' Hyde challenged, 'but really you'd prefer to believe the salacious little story the Indian papers are reciting.' He grinned sourly. 'Go on, you would really, wouldn't you? No diplomatic immunity, just a sordid sexual quarrel that became very nasty in the final round – head-butting, whips-and-scorpions, buggery, then murder,' he goaded. 'What does Delhi say?'

'They're not surprised.' It was evident that Shelley had arrived at the rock in the road which halted him. Hyde vaguely recalled Dickson and the others.

'What would they know? Bunch of tossers, Delhi Station.'

Immediately, as if Hyde had mismanoéuvred, Shelley became supplicatory, his hands stretched outwards, forearms resting on his thighs, white wrists protruding from shirtcuffs, cuffs protruding from a light-grey suit.

'That's why I have to be certain, Patrick –' He grinned. 'Why I'm trying to blackmail you into assisting.'

'Because you can't trust those second-rate buggers? You should sort them out, *Peter*.'

The Burmese passed regally towards Ros – who had again become an unacknowledged shadow in the doorway, arms undoubtedly folded, chins defiant, nostrils wide. Shelley appeared to flinch back into his chair at what Hyde gratifyingly sensed was one of Ros' very best glares.

'Cass was sending back some puzzling material. He was playing things close to his chest,' Shelley announced cathartically, clearing his throat. The distance between him and Hyde was evident to both of them, as was the required favour that hung over them like a weapon. 'He thought –' He glanced towards the still-running videotape picture. Sharmar, the minister, was grief-laden upon some relative's whiteclad shoulder. His family crowded as if to hungrily eat grief or share its televisual benefits. '– thought Sharmar was engaged in something.'

'His excuse for bonking the wife?' Hyde mocked.

'Perhaps,' Shelley replied, disconcerted. 'We didn't think so. But we're not sure. People are inclined to disbelieve it now – in the circumstances.' He shrugged once more like a reluctant moneylender.

'What was it – this excuse for poking Mrs Sharmar?'

'Drugs. At least, that's the story. Sharmar owns great tracts of land in the Kashmir Valley. Cass seemed to think it was being used to grow the poppy. The harvest moves mainly in this direction.' He looked up from his hands. 'Before you say that isn't really the service's business, I'd just interpose that everything seems to be our business these days – for the want of our old objectives.' He smiled tiredly, appeared younger and as if he still stood at Aubrey's shoulder. It was a clever trick, if trick it was. 'Therefore, it's possible –'

'– Cass was set up.' Hyde looked down at the photographs on the sofa beside him, then up at the swimming, smeared images

24

on the screen where the fire was dying down, as was the sun, and the crowd alone seemed vigorous – swelled with assumed grief and anger. 'Was he? Do you believe Cass? Or do you just want to make certain it *can't* be true? Sharmar's supposed to be our friend, isn't he? I imagine he would be, if he was making a fortune over here out of drugs.'

'I don't know – that's what I need to discover . . .' Shelley shrugged, as if a mild wave of nausea had shuddered through him. 'I don't want to sign my *first* termination order – a Black Page – unless it's necessary. I mean *really* necessary.'

In Cass' case, it meant slightly less than termination. Just being left to the mercy of local justice. No deals, no rescue.

Swallowing, Hyde said: 'I didn't know you *suddenly* became a psychopath. I thought you always were.'

'You mean the attack on the woman?'

'Did she say she had a headache?' He glanced towards the source of the indrawn breath at the doorway. 'Ros does it all the time. I haven't done her in yet.'

'Fat chance,' Ros offered, startling and embarrassing Shelley, but suggesting she was prepared to continue to monitor the situation.

'I'd like *your* assessment, Patrick.'

'Ask Aubrey to go – he's doing bugger all just now. I really want sod all to do with it. Why me?'

'Because you'll tell me the truth – at least as you see it.'

'So – JIC has Cass in the dustbin, and that makes *you* squeamish, so you come round here to do the same to me? You sure you don't want me to knock him off for you? Otherwise, you need an interrogator, not me.'

Ros' breathing was harsh. She did, after all, know almost all the routines and devices – so that she could, if it had ever happened to him, write to *The Times* or appear on *World in Action* and tell the truth in retrospect. She seemed annoyed with *him*; surprisingly.

'No, I don't,' Shelley asserted, as if he had only then reached

25

that decision. Then he blurted: 'Look, Cass sent word to me – bribed someone, I think, but it came via unsafe channels – *get me out – I didn't do it. They want my head.*'

'Doesn't trust Delhi Station? Paranoia – or good sense?' Hyde laughed. 'Got you jumping, though, Peter.'

Ros said, from the doorway: 'You're so bloody *childish*, Hyde!' She moved into the room with the span and deliberation of a treasure galleon, plumping herself next to Hyde as if to diminish him. 'What are you up to, Mr Shelley? You want *him* to talk to this bloke Cass. So – why? Is Cass going into the dustbin – a trial, long sentence, and then eventually he can serve it out over here, at Ford Open or somewhere nice? Is that it?'

'Gerald Ronson's old quarters,' Hyde smirked. 'Cass would like the two-inch pile on the carpet and the quality of the hi-fi. The Queen Mum might even come and visit him.'

Shelley shifted uncomfortably in his chair. Once more his hands came out of his sleeves in supplication. Hyde could not quite mock him. There was that trick of the genuine, that glimpse of the real, that Aubrey had retained and Shelley still possessed.

'I need to know!' he snapped. 'Sharmar, the widower, is the next leader of Congress – the country's next leader-but-one, maybe even the next leader. Cass is suggesting he's a drug-baron. Might I ask you to enquire as to the truth of the accusation, and perhaps help Cass at the same time –?' He glanced at Ros, then pressed on: 'Cass *insists* it's true – but he won't say *anything* to Delhi Station.' He clamped his fist on his thigh. 'I need to know! One interview – one bloody interview is all I'm asking – and we'll pay rank rates!'

'And a bonus, and expenses – you can pay our fares to Oz, while you're at it,' Hyde murmured. Ros, at his side, seemed to silently moralise.

'Patrick – find out what he has to say. It'll be a day, two days out of your trip – it's practically en route.' He rubbed a hand through his thinning hair. It was grey at the temples. Burden of office, Hyde thought mockingly. 'Unless I have something – anything – to show JIC, they may be prepared to go along with the current wisdom, which is that Cass be left to the mercy of Indian justice. Unless he becomes an *embarrassment* . . .'

'In which case, he might wake up one day to find he's hanged himself in his cell?'

Shelley nodded.

'The old order changeth – but do you think I want to change it *that* much? To see Cass off the end of an approved and authorised gangplank. If Sharmar wants it, if he insists – then HMG might just agree it be done. So – *now* will you bloody well go and see him and ask him what the hell is on his mind?'

Hyde clenched his hands on his thighs. The tortoiseshell – wisely, he thought – had withdrawn from the window overlooking the garden with a flick of ears and tail. The problem, the *real* problem – apart from his awakened curiosity, his reformed alcoholic's thirst – was that Shelley wasn't acting. He was genuinely bemused and reluctant. Sharmar was a powerful friend, a rising star. His actress wife was dead. He might want Cass to *pay* . . . if he wasn't a drug-producer, in which case the setup would have to end in Cass' neat death. A remorseful suicide, shot while attempting to escape – so sorry, sahib, these things happen.

Then Ros dug her elbow into his side, prompting compliance.

'So, JIC are prepared to let him go, turn the poor sod's diplomatic iron lung off?' Shelley nodded his head. 'And I just have to talk to him – report back?' Another nod. Ros nudged him impatiently, harder, as if it was nothing more than a child's game, a child's version of honour. *Dib dib dib* . . .

'Oh, ballocks,' he sighed. 'The things I do for England!'

She was still shaking as she stepped onto the deck of the houseboat, her hand quivering even as she waved aside the servant and passed into the sitting room. Her stomach revolted once more at the recalled images. A small child's legless body, an old man thrust through a window, glass-stippled and bloody, hanging across the sill — other things. A dead dog, noticeable because it had been flung onto a shop's torn awning. She glanced through the window as she noisily poured herself a large whisky and wiped at the sweat and monsoon dampness of her forehead and hair. There was a glow beyond the Hari Parbat fort, towards the centre of Srinagar, where fires started by the explosion and the subsequent rioting were still burning. She could faintly catch the noise of sirens — ambulances, fire-trucks, the police and the army.

She swallowed at the drink, coughed and all but retched, then stared down at her leg. The streak of blood caused by flying glass was muddied from the streets. She had run in the panic everyone had shared, fled the place in the torrents of rain from one of the last outbursts of the monsoon season. She continued to stare at her leg, her quivering tumbler at the corner of eyesight seen foggily as if through a cataract. The early evening sun splashed across the threshold of the houseboat's verandah and a kingfisher flashed through it.

A Moslem shop had been blown up, in a crowded market street, without advance warning. Hindu terrorists — that's what they would say, twisting the thong of tension tighter around Srinagar. The sirens wailed in the distance. Her cook's slight form appeared in the rear doorway for an instant, then flicked away. She lifted her head and stared at the intricate carving of the ceiling, then the panelling of the walls, the complex rugs, the old-fashioned English furniture. The room did not close around her, there was too much light coming into it through the net curtains, so that it appeared fragilely unable to protect her. She finished her drink and poured another before crossing to the telephone, on a table beneath the chandelier. A film set from the 1930s, the room repelled her now. As she picked up the receiver, she heard the cookboy padding barefoot along the catwalk that girdled the boat. From the neighbouring houseboat — one of her hotel boats — she heard the excited cawing of returning, unnerved tourists. Two more days of bombs and the bloody Foreign Office would be advising all the Brits to leave Kashmir! Business was bad as it was . . . Concentrating on stilling her index finger, she dialled a long-distance number and waited as the phone rang out, gripping her drying blouse across her breasts with her free hand, her hair, smelling of rain and fear, plastered to her cheeks.

He answered, and she blurted out: 'You bastard! You bloody nearly *killed* me!'

'What is the matter?' he replied, unbalanced. 'Are you hurt?'

'Scratch on my leg. I was luckier than a lot –! There are a dozen, two dozen *dead* –!'

'What would you expect?' he enquired levelly. 'Pull yourself together, Sara. It is all *necessary*, as you know, and as you believe yourself.'

'There were so *many* of them –' she began, swallowing bile and something else that clotted in her throat.

'Then there need be fewer in the future – fewer explosions. Now, pull yourself together. You did know this would happen. If you don't wish to see the evidence, stay indoors. Where you will be safer.' There was a distant, aloof concern, almost that of a doctor prescribing lack of stress and a stricter regimen to someone with a heart condition. *Heart condition?* Too late for *heart* now, she thought bitterly. She was angry with herself, heatedly so, because she appeared weak and stupid – *womanish*, having the bloody vapours!

'I – I might have been killed,' she repeated, cowed.

'I'll be there at the weekend, Sara. Meanwhile, be careful. I'm glad that you were not badly hurt. I must hurry now –' The phone rather than he seemed to pause, then the connection was broken. She put down the receiver with an angry thrust of the bakelite; unclenched her drying, creased blouse, saw another kingfisher flash across the sunlit doorway, and walked out onto the verandah, keeping in the shadow of the carved awning. Across the still water the vegetable and grocery boats plied with small, insignificant dips of oars, and tourists were poled under awnings across Nagin Lake and Dal Lake in gaudy shikaras. The glow from the city was fading like the sunlight. She looked at the hills cupping the lakes and the town and breathed deeply, slowly.

She should go across to the hotel boats and calm the bloody tourists, she supposed – before they tried to cross to her mooring and complain or ensconce themselves. In a minute, then – in a minute or two. There was a slight, fresh breeze off the lake, the putter of small outboard motors, louder now than the faded sirens, the cries of vendors and the responses of cooks and other servants; the cheekiness of cookboys. She avoided detailing any more of the human noises, since they failed to calm, drew her instead back into the crowded market and the first screams.

Instead she watched the boats as *boats*, as shadowy, silhouette cutouts, pieces of a mosaic or painting. Clouds persisted around the mountains, but wispily. The smell of drying grass. Lotuses clumped near her boat – there was a large, opened lotus-flower in a tall vase on the verandah table, alongside the two-days-old copy of *The Times*. She glanced at the foreign news, where she had opened the paper before her shopping –

Forget that. The headline, however, read – *Kashmir approaches boiling point* – and she could not, therefore, forget. A second, smaller headline – *New election probable*. Not in Kashmir or the Punjab, she acknowledged. But there will be an election soon. A quarter-column near the bottom of the page – *Bus massacre in Punjab*.

Savagely, she brushed at the newspaper, so that it fluttered over the rail of the verandah and down to the darkening water. It floated as if in threat towards the nearest clump of lotuses, which suddenly seemed to be the foam of pollution rather than a garland of flowers. She rubbed her forehead. It had become too real – much too real.

'You see the problem, don't you, Phil? I mean, it's all political from now on – not just murder.'

Cass looked up slowly, focusing on Miles' face, which flabbily betrayed a piquant sense of amusement, even a satiated revenge. As if Miles was responsible for his incarceration, the setup, the charge of murder and the demonstrating mob that surged and moaned every day outside the prison. Cass rubbed his unshaven cheek, which seemed deadened, like grafted skin from a less sensitive part of his body.

'Political, is it? Even if I didn't do it?' he sneered. 'I'm to be left in the shit, is that really it? Shelley and London are leaving me where I've been dropped – they don't like the smell!'

He tapped the cigarette Dickson had given him against the cheap tin ashtray that advertised Hindu beer. The prison warder stood at attention in baggy shorts and a peaked cap beside the interview room's door.

Dickson, less of a gourmand of Cass' situation, cleared his throat and murmured:

'It does seem to be the way things are moving, Cass. I'm sorry about it, Lord knows . . . I'm not getting much feedback or cooperation from London. Sharmar's playing the grieving husband for all the part's worth, and the FO really would like to make it up to him –'

'What with? A resurrection?'

'Your bitterness isn't helping.'

'Miles is enjoying it. It's helping *him.*'

'You're bound to be angry – but there's no *evidence* you were set up. Yours are the prints on the knife, there's no drugged drink and no trace of one, and there's the passing witness who heard your voice as well as hers . . . *before* the screams started.'

Cass glared.

'Then bloody get me out as a fucking murderer with diplomatic immunity – let's sort it out in London, for Christ's sake!'

Dickson shook his head gravely. It was the action of a dignified marionette, a hollow body suspended from strings. Dickson, as Head of Station, looked good at garden parties.

Miles scoffed: 'The best offer you're going to get, mate, is to eat your porridge here for a respectable time, then hope to get shipped back to Millionaire's Row in Ford Open prison after all the fuss has died down and Sharmar's forgotten about you.'

Dickson demurred by clearing his throat once more, then he said, leaning forward on his creaking chair: 'Cass, there was cocaine in your pockets. There were traces of it – '

'– up your nose, Phil.'

Cass clenched his hands into fists on the wooden table and snapped: 'You think coke makes you into a homicidal maniac? Someone *else* did it, I tell you!'

'Who? *Why?*'

'To stitch me *up*, bugger you!'

The room was hotter. From a high window, the pearly light fell wearily into the room, laden with dust. Cass rubbed his face once more, then gripped the edge of the table with whitening fingertips.

'Why would they do that, Phil? For poking his missis?'

'If there is anything, Cass – *anything*,' Dickson soothed, 'then tell us. Anything that justifies us making a special plea to Century House, reinvoking your diplomatic status. We'll get straight onto it – '

'What are you holding back, Phil?' Miles mocked him. 'That Sharmar bumped off his old woman, found you in bed together? London won't wear that. It looks much more likely that – '

'I don't care what it *looks* like, Miles, you dim little prick! I'm telling you I didn't do it. Get me *out* of here . . .' Dickson was embarrassed by the plea in his roughened, dry voice. Miles continued to smirk with evident, enduring satisfaction. Cass felt all optimism slump like a drunk against his ribs. Why the hell wouldn't Shelley listen? Send someone, or come himself? Fear sidled to his shoulder and he glanced nervously towards the warder. Staying in India – Christ, not like *this*!

He looked at his hands as if he could still see Sereena's blood.

What use was Shelley, anyway? SIS was being run by people Aubrey wouldn't have employed to make the fucking tea! Oh, shit, what a bloody mess . . . He looked up, avoiding the bland certitude of Miles' features. The interview room was hot. Flies had got in – as if looking for a promised carcase – and made the room small, noisy. They were hovering near the bucket that served as a toilet. He was alone in the cell, twenty-four hours a day. For his own safety. Almost anyone in the prison would knife the murderer of Sereena Sharmar, given an opportunity. He pressed his fingertips whiter around the edge of the table, confining the tremor of fear to his arms and legs.

Shelley was going to leave him in the shit. That much was obvious, the bastard. He couldn't tell Miles or Dickson what he knew, what more he suspected. They'd blab it around and then someone *would* come looking for him with a knife or an invitation to stage his own suicide. He shuddered, as if hands were on his sides and thighs lifting him into a noose. Jesus Christ . . .

Dickson stood up and said awkwardly: 'Is there anything we can send in for you?'

'Besides a hacksaw blade, of course,' Miles added.

Cass ignored him, watching the livid, hypnotised disbelief and repulsion spread on Dickson's dignified, stereotypically-diplomatic features. Distaste mingled with the disbelief, and an incapacity to cope. Dickson had realised that he might, simply by assuming a soothing manner, have offered his hand towards something alien and malevolent. Then Dickson re-captured common sense, and seemed to disapprove Miles' remark much as he would have done a wind emission at the dinner table.

'Chin up, Cass,' Miles added. 'You'll get home – eventually.'

The guard let them out of the cramped room, and Cass turned greedily to the last of the cigarette. The smoke threatened to choke him, gagging his throat. His exhalations sounded fearful, ragged – God, they *were* . . . He began to shiver. Dickson's momentary admission of the nature of his supposed crime placed him in SIS' outer darkness. He *was* out there, beyond *any* pale. It had been so *clever*, the setup – so horrible and so clever. Who'd rescue a sex-killer, who'd speak up for him, who *wouldn't* let him go hang?

Therefore, the consequences were now political, diplomatic; a question of appeasement – *this* lamb to the slaughter.

He swept his hand across the table, as if to brush spiders or beetles from it. The tin ashtray rattled, with a pitiful little protest, into the corner of the room. He looked up, with a frightened glare, at the high window and its pearly light. It seemed that all India was rushing away from it, retreating.

He could see from where he was seated at his desk, if he looked out through the tall windows, all of Connaught Place and the hub and spokes of government. It was a dazzling pattern of grand buildings, dominated by the Parliamentary Rotunda, but it was called New Delhi – it perpetuated the Raj. *Oh, thank you, sahib, you will send Sir Edwin Lutyens here to redesign our city – thank you, sahib.* The Hindu had always been capable of thanking their oppressors, living as they did inside, and clinging to, some net-curtain Nirvana to compensate them for the unpleasantness of the present. When he looked down, there was little or no retinal afterimage of the city that remained stubbornly, ineffaceably British – the parliament, the war memorial, Parliament Street, Queen Victoria Road, the rectangular, tamed stretches of water and the neat, alien gardens.

On his desk were the first sketchy reports of the midair explosion of the Indian Airlines jet and the assumed deaths of more than eighty people. On the other side of his desk, his brother sat smoking a cigarette, patient and assured. Above them both, the traditional, British fans moved their huge arms stiffly against the soupy air.

As he looked through the windows once more, the sun, moving lower, illuminated the temples of Lakshmi, Kali and the Buddha, surrounding them with hazy gold. Then the Rotunda and the India Gate emplaced him firmly within the inheritance of the Raj. He gestured angrily at the report of the airliner crash, and said:

'*This* I could have done without.'

His brother, taller and slimmer in his chair than himself, smiled back. 'You must attend – you must be at the crash site. The publicity value is too great to ignore.'

'But there is a Party caucus tonight which I should attend, Prakesh! Some of those old fools are not to be trusted with decisions of any importance whatsoever!'

'Then you will have to trust me, V.K., to look after your interests –'

'If only that damned old Chopri would sign his letter of resignation –!'

'Our respected Prime Minister is hanging on to more than life, V.K. – but, brother, how could he sign? He's in a coma.'

'Then the President should call an election at once. Why wait for Chopri to die – or wake up just long enough to write his name?'

'Calm down, V.K. A few days, that's all – just a few days. Everything is proceeding very nicely. *You* get off to Punjab and look solemnly at the cameras. Leave the caucus to me.'

V. K. Sharmar looked down at his desk, his glance catching the personal letter of condolence from Peter Shelley that had been delivered by someone from the British High Commission an hour earlier. He clenched his hand and burst out:

'When I think of what that loose-mouthed woman may have told him –!'

Prakesh Sharmar clicked his tongue against his teeth in mild exasperation, then murmured soothingly:

'Whatever she told him, V.K., he has said nothing. Stop worrying. Cass is believed only as a sex-murderer –' Sharmar winced against his brother's casualness. 'You have that letter from Peter Shelley to prove the point. Do you think he would have written such a guileless letter if any word of what Cass thought he had begun to learn had reached London and been believed?' He gestured with a dismissive sweep, wiping a smear of cigarette smoke across his features before stubbing out the butt in an ornate wooden ashtray.

'But that *whore* could have told him so much!'

'Perhaps she did not – or Cass forgot to ask. Or didn't even believe what he was told . . . ?'

'Then we needn't have –?'

'Oh, yes, V.K. Sereena was too dangerous alive – in love with Cass. She was unreliable. On the way to recklessness.' Prakesh sighed and raised his eyes to the high ceiling, then glanced towards the windows where, Sharmar sensed acutely, all India seemed to press for admittance – or waited as a prize. The sunlight slanted across the room, and the temples and domes were oranged by the dying light. Prakesh insisted: 'We can be sure – after a week – that Cass knew nothing of any significance. He may have begun the affair to investigate you . . . he continued it for the pleasure it gave. His own people at the High Commission believe he is guilty. You heard the tape from their meeting with him in prison, V.K., what could be more reassuring than that? Shelley will be told Cass is a murderer.'

Sharmar nodded. 'Yes, yes –' He indicated the letter of condolence. 'Peter's embarrassment is evident here – oh, very well, Prakesh, very well!' Most of the buttons on the telephone console to his right were now lit from the pressure of calls which he had not answered. Perhaps Chopri had even died in his coma? Unlikely. They would have interrupted him and Prakesh had that been the case.

But there were urgent matters to be settled in Delhi. He did not need the inconvenience of inspecting the remains of an airliner and scattered bodies and luggage and metal in Punjab. Damned Sikh terrorists, they had no sense of timing!

'You're worrying again, V.K.,' Prakesh mocked, lighting another cigarette. 'That frown of yours. I can handle the caucus.'

'I am thinking, Prakesh – thinking. Not just about Congress, not just about the election. I am thinking that I would rather this man Cass never came to trial, here or in England, now or in the future. Do you understand?'

Prakesh Sharmar inspected his fingernails. Eventually, he said: 'An accident could be arranged easily enough – but not *yet*. Not for the moment. The timing isn't right just now. Cass is being watched. It's unlikely he will have any more visitors, other than his colleagues. So, when attention is lulled, perhaps then he can meet with an accident. One of Sereena's devoted fans, maddened by grief and a desire for revenge.'

'Good.'

'Now, go and make your press statement about this airliner. Put on your most lugubrious face, my dear brother, and forget about drugs and land deals in Kashmir – all those niggling little details Cass evidently knows nothing about after all!'

'Are you trying to irritate me, Prakesh? You think I would prefer it if she was still alive?'

'No. I know that's not true, V.K. You wished her dead from the moment of her first infidelity.' He spread his hands on the edge of the desk, as if it were a keyboard.

Sharmar stood up and walked to the window. The traffic was clogged along Parliament Street and into Connaught Place. His gaze followed the dusty lawns of Raj Path towards the arch of India Gate, then moved north once more to the hazed highrise blocks around Connaught Place. Domes and towers receded into the dusty evening haze beyond the modern blocks. The city teemed homewards.

It was true, of course. Prakesh could handle the Party caucus meeting – perhaps even more skilfully than himself, he admitted without bitterness. He would argue, subtly, quietly and without apparent drama or self-advertisement, the case for an election. Chopri's tired old heart would give out at any time, and an election would be expected, even if it was not mandatory. They must have the election, however – since now was the time when another and even weaker minority government would be elected. And *before* the Janata fundamentalists become stronger than ever, strong enough to take power away from Congress. He rubbed his forehead soothingly with this thumb and fore finger. They had to have a minority government and a weak one with reliable partners. Only *then* did the strategy have a certain chance . . . the time was right, *so* right –!

That much they had always agreed, and for that they had worked, getting a sick man like old Chopri in as PM, knowing the pressures would bring about the final collapse of his health and leave his office door open for . . .

He clenched his hand against his temple, as if holding a gun to it – then rubbed his knuckles against the vein that throbbed there. Damned old Chopri, just like him to refuse to die right away!

As if reading his thoughts, Prakesh murmured: 'It will work V.K. – it will. There is time for it to work.'

'Yes, yes!' Sharmar snapped.

Then the intercom buzzed and he whirled round, hurrying to answer it. Pray God the old fool is dead, he thought. Dead *now*.

'Oh, sorry to have got you out of the *shower*, darling!' Hyde grumbled into the telephone receiver as he lay back on the creased sheets and stared at the cracked ceiling. A large spider was patrolling the plaster, presumably in search of something to eat. Flies droned and circled in the room's hot, thick air-lessness. The thin curtains at the window hung unmoving. 'Nice suite, is it?' He grinned in contrast to the sourness of his tone. Ros was installed in one of the largest suites in Claridges on Aurangzeb Road, south of the Raj Path. He'd wangled that out of Shelley to compensate for the seedy place he needed as a cover.

'Lovely. What's yours like?'

'A dump – listen to the noise.' He held the receiver towards the window. The decayed, dusty hotel was in the Paharganj district, near the main railway station. 'Hear it?' he asked, forcing the hot bakelite against his ear. He was sweating, as if the noise from outside was kinetic energy. It pressed against him, a bellow of traffic and voices and animals. Unburned petrol was thick and nauseously sweet on the air, visible as the dust.

'Christ,' he heard Ros murmur.

'Feel sorry for me, do you? Your bloody fault we're here — I'm where *I* am, anyway.'

'Hyde, you could always have said no.'

'With the long moral face you were pulling from the doorway? You must be joking.'

'When are you going to see him?'

'Tomorrow morning — if I can't get a pass, I'll have to buy one. His cousin Pat has come a bloody long way, after all. He should have got the letter from home by now, setting the cover up . . . Listen, it's too bloody hot to talk. Just so long as you're comfortable, darling, I can stop worrying about you. Have a nice dinner — got the tablets? Don't drink the water, there's a sensible girl.'

'I have been here before, Patrick. Before I met you. If I get stomach trouble this time, it'll be you causing it, not India.' There was a pause, and Hyde tensed against the anticipated remark. As if aware of his dislike, Ros merely mumbled: 'Be careful,' then, almost at once, 'See you, Hyde,' in her brusquest tone and put down the phone.

Hyde studied the receiver for a moment, then rolled across the creaking bed's sagging middle and replaced it. Then he swung his legs off the bed and crossed the narrow room to the window. Eighty rupees a day, fleas inclusive. Christ, what a dump — just the place for someone like Cass' schoolteacher cousin, his closest relative, to stay as cheaply as possible in Delhi. Just in case anyone enquired after Cass' unexpected visitor . . . He rubbed his hands through his hair, yawned, scratched his stubbled cheeks, then thrust his hands into the pockets of his denims. The flight, shoehorned into Economy while Ros lived it up in

Business Class, had been cool and noiseless by comparison with this.

Beneath the window, the narrow street between Main Bazaar and Panchkuin Marg moved with the slow struggle of a snake sloughing an old skin. People wriggled in opposing skeins and queues through each other and the dense scrapyard of vehicles and rickshaws – autos and the peddled variety – and old, fume-coughing buses. Spices and hot food scents penetrated the haze of petrol. Saris, grubby white shirts, the bright plumage of tourists, dhotis, turbans, the pyjamalike lenga trousers of bemused country people stunned by proximity, traffic and the sun. Inky, purple shadows. Out of one of them, a Moslem woman in an enveloping burka moved, her dark costume confronted by heaped dishes of spices in front of a shop – red, green, purple, orange mounds.

Hyde watched the street, fascinated and deafened, hands still in his pockets. He was detached, a spectator. An ex-field agent approaching forty, half a stone out of condition, reactions too slow for an endgame situation – for any operation, really. Pensioned off by his own choice, fit – just about – to be some Arab prince's bodyguard for the rest of his useful life. And someone to whom the most pressing question was whether Ros had some unconveyed idea of staying in Oz, once they got there. He suspected it – and was almost certain he didn't want it.

Eventually, wearying of the struggle of the street, its stink of ordure, sweat, petrol, dust and spicy food, he returned to the bed and sat beside the rucksack he had collected from the luggage locker at New Delhi station. He re-checked its contents merely to occupy himself before he waded into the breakers of the street in search of food. Apart from the pills and the alternative cover-papers and the maps and addresses, there was the gun. Heckler & Koch, as he preferred. Krauts make good, accurate weapons. Spare ammo, the knife, and the tablet – though not for him. Shelley was calling the tune, and Hyde understood the unspoken. If Cass proved likely to embarrass the service or if the Indians, intelligence or just police, decided it might be useful to take an abandoned agent apart to find out what he knew . . . then kill him.

That was the bit Ros neither knew nor suspected.

home thoughts from abroad

Hyde shrugged himself back into the T-shirt blazoned with Mozart's profile that they had made him remove, then tugged on his denims. The body search had been polite, even delicate, but thorough. He zipped up the small rucksack – paperbacks, shaving gel, cigarettes for Cass – and then followed the prison officer along hot, wearying corridors, past blank doors whose peepholes stared at him with Cyclops' eyes. There was singing from behind one door, moaning from another cell, but after the streets the prison across the Yamuna River was orderly, quiet. The door of a small, cramped interview room stood open. Hyde saw Cass' grubby hands clenched together as if confronting a mean fire on the plain table, then the door was closed behind him. The officer stood beside it, at once impassive.

Cass' reactions were confused, muddy – relief, a sense of contrast between Hyde and himself, as if Hyde still bore the scents of the streets and the air on his clothes ... and the almost immediate nervousness because it was he, *Hyde*, who was good at one thing above all – seeing people off the end of the plank. Cass was, irrefutably, aware of that possible solution to his situation. Immediately, Hyde said, holding out his hand:

'Phil! Christ, mate, I got out here as soon as I heard! You got my letter?' Awkwardly, as if slowly remembering behaviour, Cass nodded and mumbled a reply. 'A guy from the Foreign Office rang me at school. The secretary took the message 'cause I was teaching – 3W, what a bunch of spastics!' He sat down, adjusting the clear-glass spectacles with his forefinger, having released Cass' clammy, shivery grip. 'I had to check back with them – couldn't believe it, Phil! Bloody hell, mate, there must be a mistake –? How are they treating you, though?' His accent was somewhat Midlands, his tone breathless. He was amused by Cass' continuing suspicion as he assessed him, and recognised the erosions of shock and incarceration. Cass' face was stubbled, his eyes red-rimmed, his attention vague and selfish. A *civilian* going to pieces under pressure. 'This was such a cushy little billet,' he pursued sharply.

Cass' gaze flickered brightly with dislike for an instant, then clouded again, narrowing only on his fear of Hyde. His eyes inspected the table, as if fleas hopped and skittered on it. Open-eyed dreaming – Cass was in poor shape. Too poor to play the memory game the letter had set up?

At least he didn't look ill-treated, just worn down from the inside. Hyde rubbed his hand through his hair and fiddled with the spectacles, then unzipped the rucksack at his feet. He pulled the paperbacks out and put them on the table, neatening them in a little heap with fussy movements. He pointed at the top of the pile.

'That's good, that one – sorry it's a bit tatty, I read it on the plane. I wasn't sure you liked Conrad –?'

'Yes,' Cass replied tiredly. Had he consented to the game or not? *Nostromo* – our man. It was supposed to reassure.

Hyde's finger tapped the spines of the books, one by one. Cass would be looking for *The Great Escape*, or another Conrad, *The Rescue*. Neither was there. *Our Mutual Friend* was, though, meaning Century House. He hadn't been abandoned – at least, not entirely. *All's Well That Ends Well* would have made him happier, but that was missing, too. Cass studied the titles of the books glumly, his head slightly on one side, his eyes staring. Jane Austen's *Persuasion* was at the bottom of the pile. *Tell me about it, it's in the balance but we want to believe you . . . Pilgrim's Progress –?*

Hyde reached down into the open-mouthed rucksack and fished out Bunyan's allegory.

'Forget this one,' he muttered, smiling. 'Remembered it was a favourite –'

After what seemed an interminable silence, Cass said quietly: 'Good of you to come, Patrick.' He was injected with the stimulant of the possibility of rescue signalled by the Bunyan. He might get out of this place, eventually. 'Bit of a mess, all this.' He spread his arms apologetically.

'You're not joking, mate! Uncle Peter's really down about it. I had to tell him, but no one else in the family. He sends his best –'

Cass blinked, and his gaze was clearer, more focused.

'I brought some pills, too –' Hyde began, and Cass sat bolt upright, stung and frightened. 'Left them at the hotel, though . . .' *Tell me as carefully as you can, tell me the truth, and there won't be any need for a cyanide pill . . .*

. . . if I believe you.

Cass swallowed audibly, a creaking, dry sound like that of old wood cracking.

'I don't – don't need pills. They're all right to me in here.' He looked at the patient, still warder.

'They mentioned drugs – you'd been taking drugs,' Hyde said, leaning forward across the table, his eyes round and surprised. 'You never touched drugs before –'

'You can – they're easy to get hold of here, Pat. Too easy. Grow the poppy everywhere . . .' He glanced at the guard and then seemed to surrender to lethargy and laid his forehead on his hands as they gripped one another on the table. He shook his head. 'I didn't know what I was doing,' he murmured, so softly that Hyde leaned closer to him, after shrugging at the warder, who seemed politely indifferent, staring at the opposite wall. If the room was bugged – it probably was, even though there was no sign of a video camera – Cass' voice would be barely decipherable. Good.

'Try to make the best of it, Phil,' he offered with studied naivety. 'It can't be as bad –'

Cass' words dribbled on.

'. . . Kashmir, mostly – top people own land up there, own the peasants to grow the crop . . . didn't think it would end like this, not her and me, that is. Not like *that* –' His voice had altered, and he looked up, his eyes wet, surprising Hyde. Cass rubbed at his eyes angrily, then at his loose, wet mouth. 'Christ, there was blood everywhere, but *I* didn't do it!' he snarled breathily. 'I'd never have . . .' He shrugged exaggeratedly. '*Would* I?'

Hyde sat stiffly, silently. It wasn't acted. Unless Cass was in the Gielgud class, his distress was real – grief hard as stone looked through the shivering cheeks and the welling eyes. Christ, the bugger had been in love with her!

'They – I mean, they're saying you went . . . you know, berserk. A quarrel –'

'*No.*'

Then he was silent. Hyde nodded slowly and Cass, sniffing noisily, understood and lowered his head onto his knuckles once more, sighing loudly. Hyde patted his forearm, bending forward. As if accidentally, he touched *Nostromo* with his fingers. Cass saw the gesture and swallowed wetly. *Our man.*

Cass murmured: 'Drugged – drink . . . woke up, she was dead.' His voice was barely audible. Hyde glanced at the door. If they were suspicious or interested, they'd be in before long to break it up – even tell them not to whisper. 'Husband owns . . . his family –' Cass sat upright suddenly, wiping at his face. 'Enough about me,' he announced. 'Feeling sorry for myself. Christ, thanks for coming, Pat – it's good to see you, even under the circumstances. Pity you had to tell Uncle Peter. Has he still got that allotment of his?'

After a moment, Hyde said: 'Oh, that – yes. You know what he's like. Up on it all the time. What he grows I don't know –'

'I do.' Cass lit a cigarette, the last in the packet, and crushed it in his fist, leaving the small crumpled ball on the table. Hyde said:

45

'I've got some more for you — bought them on the plane. Rothman's — like them, I remember.' The crumpled packet was Silk Cut. Hyde seemed disappointed.

Cass laughed. 'Thanks, Pat.' He smiled at the warder as he opened the pack of two hundred, then offered him one. 'Jawal here got the Silk Cut for me. Here, Jawal, one for you —'

'Thank you, Mr Cass.'

The warder moved back to his position beside the door, still smiling. Hyde took his hand from his pocket, leaving the crumpled Silk Cut packet inside. He then cleared the cellophane Cass had removed from the duty-free pack and thrust it into the rucksack.

Hyde relaxed on his chair as Cass smoked greedily, with a somehow greater, healthier appetite for whatever future he now envisaged.

'Is there anything else I can bring in — if they let me come back?'

'Some stuff at my flat — if they'll let you in.'

'Is there anyone I can see — at the High Commission?' Cass shook his head. 'Anyone else? Have you got a solicitor?' Cass nodded. 'He all right?' Again, he nodded.

Jawal coughed politely.

'Time's up, Pat,' Cass explained. He swallowed, and the skin over his jaw and cheeks tightened. 'Thanks again, mate. You're a good'un, coming all this way.' He stood up and thrust out his hand. There was a slight tremor. His shirt-cuff was grubby. 'Hotel all right?' he asked with forced casualness.

'A dump,' Hyde replied, grinning innocently. 'Still, I don't mind — in the circumstances. Look, I'll call Uncle Peter and tell him you're bearing up — and all the news. Blow the expense of the phone call, eh? And I'll see if I can get permission to bring a few things from your flat — what, clothes and that, eh?'

'Change of underwear — pity you can't bring the telly and the VCR.' Cass clicked his fingers theatrically. 'If you can get in there, see if I turned off the stopcock, will you?'

'Pipes won't freeze here, will they? OK, I'll look. I know people worry in — well, your sort of ... yes. I'll come back tomorrow — OK?'

'Yes. Thanks again, Patrick — *thanks*.'

His eyes were sparkling wetly once more, and there was a catch in his voice. Hyde turned away and followed Jawal down the corridor as another warder appeared to collect Cass and take him back to his cell.

He hadn't killed her. Instead, it was drugs and Sharmar was involved at least as a producer and that was how it had begun. Then Cass had got careless because he fell in love and they'd had the opportunity to stitch him up. Sharmar — the Minister for Tourism and Civil Aviation, the next leader of Congress, and just maybe the next Prime Minister of India ... ?

Interesting that —

— and worth killing one film star for, even if she was your wife, if it shut her up and banged up her boyfriend from British Intelligence.

Hyde was almost blithe as he stepped out into the blind sunlight of midmorning and looked across the brown river towards the hazy city that, even at that distance, hummed like a nest of insects.

Sharmar could have been — probably had been — a very naughty boy. Grinning to himself, he thrust his hands into his pockets, slouching beneath the smear of the rucksack across his back, beginning to sweat as he walked towards the nearest bus stop. He felt his knuckles touch the crumpled cigarette packet.

Read whatever Cass had written inside it on the bus, he told himself. Don't be impatient ... then go to his flat, check for surveillance, and try to get inside. In the VCR, or on tape, hidden in the back of the telly, or under the sink. Something on Sharmar ...

The wreckage was spread over hundreds of acres of farmland. Only the larger pieces of the fuselage of the medium-haul Boeing jutted above green wheat already springing up. The tailplane, like a great abandoned ploughshare, still evidenced the logo of Indian Airlines. Its scorched, sloping letters – IA – glowered like a message of great distress, a phonetic cry. Sharmar shivered at the idea. Glass crunched under his feet – or something did – as he waded through the new wheat, shaking his head lugubriously for the cameras, saluting Hindu and Sikh appropriately with the small hand-signals of sorrow and sympathy.

The flight deck lay on its side – like the broken egg in that Bosch painting, he thought; his imagination affected as if by some nervous tic rather than horror at the scene. It was hundreds of yards away, cordoned off, surrounded by the ants of the accident investigators and the police. Sikh turbans seemed inappropriately gay above the green wheat, alongside the wreckage.

'Yes, yes – terrible,' he must have murmured again and again. 'Such a tragedy.'

The domestic news services were already filled with speculation. Sikh separatists, was the consensus – and, no doubt, the truth. The plane had been en route from Amritsar to Delhi, and most of the passengers, it had been established, had been Hindu. Only months before, it had been buses, and a small suburban train. Only dozens dead. Now, it was eighty people, an entire passenger list – the innocent. The anger raged in his stomach. There was no space for guilt or reflection, only for the sense of outrage at the killing of –

People like that. The unwound length of a sari weighing down the new wheat, blue threaded with gold, and at the end of it a body. A young woman, broken like a rabbit dropped from on high by a hawk. He shivered, despite the heat. Always, he remembered that from his childhood, finding the rabbit, so loose as to be boneless yet its fur hardly ruffled. Staring up near the sun, he had seen the speck of the hawk that had been clumsy enough to lose its victim.

He paused a little past the body, where the field remained

untrampled and ungouged, and looked around him. Punjab. The granary of India that wished, with most of its unsettled hearts, to become Khalistan, an independent Sikh state. There were military vehicles on the nearest road, parked in a line, and soldiers near and about him. Martial law, even when it was only the dead they had come to see. TV cameras bobbed on shoulders like black water-pitchers through the fields and around the wreckage of the tailplane and the flight deck. V. K. Sharmar wiped his forehead, then his palms, on the grubby ball of his handkerchief. A helicopter, noisy as a wasp, droned high above the disaster site.

Then a pink-faced Englishman with wispy blond hair was beside him and he was staring into a shoulder-held camera. A microphone appeared. He did not catch the reporter's name, merely the initials that followed it.

'— BBC,' then, 'television news, Minister Sharmar.'

'Yes, yes.' He appeared, he realised, suitably abstracted. He *was*; it was no pretence.

'Minister, can you confirm . . . ?'

Sikh terrorists — oh, yes, quite certainly.

'Our investigations are proceeding,' he murmured. 'There are eye-witness reports of an explosion —' The reporter already appeared bored, he knew this much. '— and preliminary evidence that the explosion occurred in the main cabin. An item of hand luggage has been removed for forensic examination. All further speculation is merely that, at the moment.'

'No one has claimed responsibility, Minister? None of the separatist groups?'

He shook his head gravely. The object after all was terror, not publicity — to make the Punjab *untenable*, even under martial law.

'No. No one has claimed responsibility. We should not jump to conclusions —'

'Even in the light of recent atrocities, Minister?'

'I'm afraid that *I*, at least, as a minister of the government, cannot afford to speculate.'

49

He turned slightly aside, reassuming his sorrowful countenance. The reporter seemed compliantly bored, then the camera was at once beside him again as he walked forward with the senior army officer and the managing director of Indian Airlines. The microphone and the blond reporter, sun-pinked, thrust themselves in front of him.

'Could we do a short piece for tomorrow's main news on Prime Minister Chopri's health and your own future, Minister?'

Temptation for an instant that did not even reach his eyes. Instead, he scowled in affront.

'At the scene of this tragedy, I think that subject would be inappropriate. Now, if you will excuse me –'

He moved on towards the wreckage of the flight deck. This close, he could see the gouged earth and chlorophyll that stained its livery. Behind him, the reporter was performing his piece to camera which would introduce the careful, anodyne sympathy Sharmar had presented for a British audience. Strange that they referred to themselves as English while, more correctly, India had always known them as the *British*. The British . . . even *this*, this *here*, was part of their damned legacy to India. British India – Himalaya to Tamil Nadu, the mouths of the Indus to the mouths of the Ganges – had still only *begun* to fragment. This, in front of him now, this broken egg that had cracked off the main fuselage, spilling the yolk and albumen of passengers into the air – *this* kind of thing would happen again and again, perhaps forever . . . He clenched his hands in the pockets of his suit in rage. For the foreseeable future, into a new *millennium*, what had been *British India* would continue to tear itself to pieces!

'Yes, yes,' he murmured to the forensic investigators presented to him, the severed flight deck looming over them all. 'Yes, I understand – yes, of course . . .'

Sunlight glowed on the wreckage, glistening like dew on fragments of glass, plastic, metal, gilding the flank of the flight deck. The fields were dark green in the afternoon light. The attempt to make the scene innocent was at once illusory and touching. India, attempting to heal itself –

Ridiculous – poetry, he exclaimed against his thoughts. It can only be done by *effort*.

'Yes, yes,' he continued to murmur as he shook hands or listened with apparent absorption.

The cameras whirred nearer and the reporters gabbled into their microphones, louder than the flies that filled the wreckage and settled on dried patches of what had been human blood.

Cass' flat was in a low, modern block on the fringe of the Chanakyapuri Diplomatic Enclave, near the High Commission. Everyone lived either above or next door to the shop if they had diplomatic status in Delhi – and Cass' cover was diplomatic. He might, just might, need to go in, but it was under surveillance and probably bugged. The surveillance was discreet. It had taken Hyde an hour to establish its presence. On the other hand, here in a narrow street off the Chandni Chowk, he'd never have confirmed surveillance. The place was just a tributary pouring people into the main shopping bazaar, day and night.

Cass had scribbled two addresses on a sliver of crumpled paper Hyde had found inside the crushed Silk Cut packet. Contacts, though of what kind and quality Hyde had no notion. Unofficials – natives – who knew at least something about V. K. Sharmar's links with heroin poppies in Kashmir. He paused amid the evening crowd, jostled and buffeted by their slow, strong tide. Murmured apologies were a continuous hum. He looked up at the first-floor windows of a verandahed wooden building, crushed between a handicrafts shop and a grocer's. Below the first floor, a narrow, grubby window displayed shawls and bright cloth. A dog lifted its thin leg against the building, urinated and moved on, slipping awkwardly through the crowd's legs in constant anticipation of being kicked. Hyde scratched his head, then drew the tourist map of the city from his back pocket. The rucksack was jostled continually as it hung over his shoulder.

He looked up and down the street, not nervous, merely disorientated. Behind a long barrow untidily heaped with limp vegetables, he saw the face he anticipated. He had made little or no attempt to shake off the tail – it was his city, after all, not Hyde's. And it was idle curiosity, for the moment. He hadn't done anything other than visit Cass and tour the city, gawping and apparently unaware; fascinated. There were only two of them and they took it in turns to drive the battered Ford and follow him on foot. He thrust forward against the crowd and gained the shadows beneath the verandah. He bent to study the bright lengths and rolls of cloth in the shop window. Tourist buys Indian cloth for wife or girlfriend. The man who lived in a flat above the shop worked as a messenger – that was all the information Cass had minutely scribbled next to his name and address – *messenger*. The stairs up to the flat would be through the shop. Just so long as he wasn't followed inside, he'd have no problems . . .

He adjusted the clear-glass spectacles, sensed the little bulge of his stomach over his belt, the creased denims, the cheap trainers – reestablishing his cover, the harmless, bumbling teacher from the Midlands whose part was easy to play since it was probably close to his future . . . The sense of an operation refused to gather as closely about him as the flies did in the shadows near the shop window. Unconcerned with surveillance, he rubbed his hand nervously through his hair, as if expecting a current of static electricity to enliven unpractised instincts.

Two men are following you, and they know the old car-and-on-foot routine . . . you barely noticed, until now, how well they'd got their act together.

He felt a slight and surprising chill fall down his back like the slow descent of cold air from the opened door of a freezer –

He straightened, sighing audibly and shaking his head, even as the shopkeeper appeared in the narrow doorway and he was nudged towards the man by another push of the crowded street. He waved his hands, palms outwards, in embarrassed refusal

52

of the sales-pitch, and shuffled away from the window, out into the evening light and the swimming motions of the crowd against their own mass, knowing more clearly now and with what intent the man on foot would have moved out with him.

He came to the corner of the street and its aquatic junction with Chandni Chowk, where the stream flowed more broadly and even slower. His skin tickled across his back and shoulders, reassuringly. The sun was an orange, muddy-haze ball behind the roofs of the bazaar, and Chandni Chowk was vociferous with insistence against the sunset. Gobbets of bright spices lying spread out – the smell was sharp under his hitherto unconscious nose. Shops and stalls, bullock-carts and buses and ancient taxis, into which the occasional Mercedes attempted to intrude, seemed to belong in a film set retelling some poignant-satiric tale of the Raj's last days –

Awakened.

He sniffed the air greedily, at once repelled and enlivened by the spices of ordure, crammed bodies, petrol and food. He controlled the twitches of muscles and nerves; ducked casually behind a stall of silk bales and balloons as the man on foot came into Chandni Chowk and at once betrayed nervousness – had he lost the subject? His head began to twitch and rotate more quickly. Hyde all but rubbed his hands. The old game. The Heckler & Koch was in the rucksack, a round in the chamber. But this wasn't even close to offensive action. He stayed pressed against a shop window where strips of unidentifiable meat stared at his back from the vantage of hooks. The battered Ford attempted, like a too-young salmon, to nose against the flow of people along the street, failing halfway through its turn out of the sidestreet. Hyde suppressed his grin of satisfaction. Then waited.

The man on foot began to move back towards the car. Hyde was in an alleyway now – the houses were shallow, there were noisome back yards, crowded alleys filled with refuse and rats and dogs. He found it, and began numbering back from the corner – there? No, next door, that one, where the eaves leaned drunkenly and wooden tiles had slipped like a minor avalanche. He shouldered the hanging gate aside and walked carefully across the strewn yard, where a child seemed as deposited as the rubbish sacks and the broken cardboard boxes.

He walked through an open door and into a narrow hallway of cracked linoleum over packed earth, his nerves twitching now. He calmed himself by touching the rucksack over his shoulder. Gun – old habits, old friend. He paused at the foot of a confined staircase, listening towards the shop and its customers and the breeze of street noise blown through it. He listened, too, towards the head of the stairs and a radio playing and the chatter of a small child. The voice of a man. Good, he was home from work. He stepped quietly upwards.

He'd seen Ros once, fleetingly, during the day, the bulkiest member of a party being towed by a tall, supremely beautiful Indian woman around the circumference of the Parliament House – while he had been dragging the two men around on another, more innocuous tour of the city, before plunging into Old Delhi like a nervous diver from a high board.

Now, it was nice to be back, even if it was only turning out for the Third Eleven in a limited-overs game. Enough evidence to get Cass off the hook, get Shelley interested in rescuing the poor sod –

– if there *was* evidence. He knocked politely on a thin plywood door at the head of the stairs. The radio or television was immediately turned down and the door was opened by a large, middle-aged Indian who was at once shocked at the sight of a white man, before he declined into practised cunning. It was as if he expected that sometime, somehow, *someone* would come and would have to be answered in a certain manner.

'You speak English?'

The man cleared his throat, as if assuming the language, then merely nodded.

'Oh, good,' Hyde said, fiddling with his spectacles, shuffling the rucksack, aware of the stairs behind him and his exposed back. 'You see I – I'm Philip Cass' cousin – well, half-brother, really . . .' He realised he was going through the motions *expected*. The noise of the street came through an open window somewhere behind the Indian, whose presence in the doorway had darkened because of the lowering sun. Hyde was suddenly aware that he was *expected*. Not feared, as he might have been by someone unofficial; but *anticipated*. Something was wrong and becoming *very* wrong. Hyde persisted with his cover.

'You see, Mr Banerjee –'

'I am afraid you have the wrong name – what address are you looking for, Mr –?'

Time to leave –

'Oh – you're not Mr Banerjee? You see, my half-brother mentioned you, he said, in fact, that you were someone who might be prepared to act as a character witness.'

The Indian was shaking his head.

'Oh, no, I do not understand.'

'My half-brother, Philip Cass – he mentioned your name.' Hyde shrugged with disorientation. Fiddled with the disarming spectacles. 'You see, I'm only out here because of him – I don't really know my way around. Phil asked me to look you up.'

'I do not think so.' *Professional* dismissal. He was sure of it now. Sure the man was planted, *in place*. Poor fucking Banerjee, whoever he *used* to be.

'You're not Mr Banerjee – does he live here?'

'No Mr Banerjee here.'

They'd closed it off . . . Cass' contact was known to them, or had been dug up like any ordinary mole, and they'd put someone here in his place – Banerjee was on a rubbish dump somewhere outside the city, slowly decaying. But they'd sent a professional, and that meant the intelligence services were involved. So the tailmen were intelligence, looking for another professional, not his assumed amateur . . . *But they'd acted to shut Cass out,* that was the point. *Minister* Sharmar had control. Not only of the setup – which was what it was now, for certain – but of the possible consequences. Anyone who might be coming round like the thin dog with the cocked leg, sniffing after the event. Hyde felt the adrenalin hurry through him like the dry, hot wind from a railway tunnel.

'Oh, I see. I must have got the address wrong, or the name.' Fiddling with the spectacles, shuffling the rucksack on his back, the stoop of the shoulders that confirmed the harmless anonymity of the caller. 'I'm sorry to have troubled you.'

The Indian dismissed him with a shrug, and Hyde at once turned away with an additional apology and began descending the creaking, narrow stairs. He heard the plywood door shut confidently behind him.

A man paused at the foot of the stairs, and the plywood door opened once more behind him. The man's gaze was beyond Hyde's shoulder, looking up, and then there was a glaze to the eyes – not dangerous. Hyde smiled innocuously at the man on foot who had been tailing him and the man moved aside to let him pass. He controlled his nerves and went out into the yard, where the child had been rescued by a magnificent young woman in a sari whose eyes fell as his glance moved over her. He slipped through the awry gate and huddled along the alley into Chandni Chowk and the crowd. The battered Ford's driver was at once alert, then was evidently calmed by a signal from behind Hyde . . . deep breath. He passed on, beginning to gaze up at the buildings, around at the still-massing crowds –

– shivering, nonetheless, from the aftershock of the encounter, which buffeted against him more palpably than the throng. The tailmen had responded to orders from the man occupying Banerjee's flat. They'd placed someone fairly senior there. Cass' contact had been identified and silenced – any family he might have had were also missing.

But *he* remained uncompromised. His fumbling, incoherent

56

sketch of a cover-story had convinced the man at the head of the stairs and wouldn't be scrutinised. He'd persuaded them that Cass had sent him in all innocence.

Hyde struggled through the evening shoppers, their noise and heat glutinously restraining him. He paused a number of times, apparently abstracted by stalls and shop windows. The battered Ford slipped farther and farther behind him, loitering out of boredom.

Sharmar wanted this buried deep. And, the deeper the hole, the bigger the guilt. The old adage in all probability applied here. And, for Cass, it was profoundly real. Shelley had better get Cass out – quickly. Sharmar was into drugs – growing, harvesting, refining most probably, even shipping . . . most likely along the Balkan lorry route through Yugoslavia. Neither Croats, Serbs or Slovenians stopped *that* traffic – there was a slice off the top for everyone. And Cass had blundered like a child into the game, and was right in the mire.

He rubbed his chin. Shelley had to get him out, or he'd be shipped home in a box.

Prakesh was standing beside the window in the last of the daylight as Sharmar hurried into the anteroom, closing the door on the Congress party caucus meeting from which he had been summoned. Prakesh's features were uninterpretable in the dusk. Beyond the window, an ornamental pool glowed and its fountain spray glittered in the last of the light. Sharmar hurried to his brother.

'What is it, Prakesh – what is it?'

Prakesh turned, smiling.

'It is *it*, V.K. That old goat, Chopri – he's dead. I've just come from the hospital.'

It was difficult to speak, for a moment. He stared beyond the pillars supporting the great dome of the rotunda's roof, beyond the pool, to the city stretching away into the darkness to the north. His breathing was noisy, as if attempting to blow words from his tight throat. The city blazed with lights. His hand moved like that of a nerveless old man, clutching at his brother's sleeve.

'Who – who knows? Who else knows?'

'His widow, the children. I hurried here from the hospital. It is advantageous for *you* to inform the President.'

Sharmar glanced towards the door he had closed on the meeting.

'What about –?'

'Call the President first – at once, V.K.' He hurried Sharmar across the room towards the littered desk and the telephone and all but thrust it against his cheek, then dialled the number for him. 'Very grave, V.K. – solemn sadness.'

Prakesh wandered to the window once more, his head cocked as if listening like a curious bird. V.K. paused, then was evidently talking to Namal Singh. Prakesh smiled. His brother was really so *good* at that kind of thing, fluid as an actor, a sinuous dancer of the personality, the adopter of masks and costumes that were always appropriate. Beside his brother, he knew himself to be clumsily arrogant, aloof, uningratiating. Merely the complete manager.

He lit a cigarette and stared out of the window at the darkened, broad paths surrounding the Parliament. A few figures, many of them slackly dressed tourists, the occasional more purposeful walk of a politician or civil servant. There would be much hurrying in an hour, perhaps less –

'I think you must announce it on the television this evening, Mr President,' his brother was saying. He rarely needed to be briefed. He found the words as he found the tone and the facial expression.

Prakesh looked down at his tightly curled hand. Not a fist clenched in threat, but a grip that was triumphant. The old women and the young and ambitious in the next-door room would not oppose V.K.'s elevation to the leadership of Congress. To persuade them to risk their possession of power in a sudden general election would be more difficult. They had to have one

in the next six months, and by that time the Hindu fundamentalists would be much stronger . . . He rubbed his bottom lip with
the fingers that held the cigarette, hardly attending to his
brother's words. V.K.'s performance would be, as always,
faultless.

Bharatiya Janata had a leader almost more persuasive than
V.K., even more charismatic. A damned film star! Anand Mehta,
heartthrob, action man, national dream-made-flesh. He could
sweep V.K., himself and all of Congress aside. Prakesh smiled
sourly, listening to his brother conclude his call to the President.
Mehta wasn't as good an actor as V.K., but V.K. wasn't a damned
film star, either!

He turned as his brother put down the receiver.

'Good,' he said, then: 'How is the caucus, the Party's mood?'

V. K. Sharmar waggled his hand, then shrugged.

'Worried – by Bharatiya Janata and Anand Mehta.
Worried . . .'

'Then they must be made to see that an election now is less
dangerous than one in six months' time. Are you ready, V.K.?'

'What –? Oh, yes.' Sharmar composed his features to solemn
grief. Only his clenching and unclenching hands betrayed his
sense of the moment. He took a handkerchief from his pocket
and dabbed it as carefully as a makeup girl along his hairline,
removing the slight sheen of perspiration. *Two* actors, Prakesh
thought for a moment – it would be an election campaign
between two consummate actors. Except that V.K. wanted to *do*
while Anand Mehta merely wanted to *be*, to continue as adored
as ever but on a larger screen. 'Are we ready?' Sharmar asked.

'Strike hard, V.K. – be very positive.' Sharmar nodded in
acquiescence.

It was a risky strategy. Sereena would have been a great deal
of help in the campaign, one film star offsetting another. But *that*
would have been unthinkable. Had her affair with an *Englishman*
become public, Mehta would have exploited it fatally against
Congress. Dead, she might have the status of an invisible, minor

deity, hovering over the Party. Mehta's own background was vulgar, murky, tasteless, financially often illegal. To exploit it to the advantage of Congress was, however, difficult. Hardly anything could dent Mehta – he was a living god of the screen. Only his political ineptitude could be used against him, and even then carefully and soon. They could not afford to wait until the beginning of the year for an election – it must be held before that star of Curry Westerns and cops-and-robbers fantasies became unassailable.

Sharmar was already at the door, his features suitably composed. Prakesh nodded, then crossed to his side and opened the door on the caucus meeting.

He sat behind the wheel of the Hertz-rented Ford and adjusted his tie and damp collar. The suit was uncomfortably warm, the Delhi night close and humid. Beside him, on the passenger seat, lay a briefcase, a further contribution to his cover. Hyde sighed, tuning the car radio to the BBC World Service and its hastily assembled voices discussing the death of Prime Minister Chopri. The well-lit, orderly street hurried with figures and limousines. Chopri's death had been a poked stick, stirring up the termite-mound of the Diplomatic Enclave.

'. . . of course Sharmar is the favoured successor – he and his family have the machine to manufacture the desired result,' someone pontificated in a light, trilling Indian voice from the radio. And the machinery to operate a drugs cartel, sport, he added silently. And have irritations like wives and British agents taken care of . . . *and* poor sods like Banerjee. 'I expect the announcement within a matter of hours . . .' the voice from the radio continued, lulling Hyde as much as the night and the purposeful, distanced hurry of figures and cars.

Cass' block of flats was at the end of the street. So was the surveillance car, a black Peugeot. There was a man on foot, too, patrolling near the entrance to the flats. He fiddled with his tie once more.

He'd called Shelley. Alison, the wife, had told him Shelley

wasn't home. Nor was he at Century House. This wasn't an operation, there was no board and no lines of communication. If he couldn't reach Shelley, there was no one else. Banging down the telephone in frustration, he'd switched on the radio, to pick up the news of Chopri's death. An hour earlier.

'– question of an early election?' someone posed from the radio.

'Possibly. Support among millions of Hindus is slipping away from Congress to the Bharatiya Janata Party and its charismatic, film-star leader –' Hyde switched off the car radio. Sharmar was about to become PM, was he? Cass' situation had become, as euphemism would describe it, *untenable*. And Shelley was out!

Hyde had slipped out of the hotel's rear entrance, through the noisome yard and its rubbish, wearing a sober suit. Hired the necessary car to deflect attention, bought the briefcase. If Banerjee was dead, so would be the possessor of the other name Cass had scribbled on the crumpled fragment of paper in the fag packet. Waste of time checking him out. Whatever material or product Cass had was inside his telly or VCR, or shoved up behind the sink, near the stopcock Cass had asked him to turn off. Get it, and he might attract Shelley's serious attention before Cass stopped waving and began drowning.

He raised the small, monocular nightsight to his eye and studied the entrance to the flats, where street-lighting fell silver through the branches of saplings. Activity, just the thing, diplomatic staff coming and going, busied with Chopri's death and its consequences for Congress, India – and most of all, their own piddling concerns and the guest-lists for immediate cocktail receptions and ambassadorial invitations and calls. A young woman emerged from the flats in the company of two smooth, ghost-grey young men and they moved towards a stretched Granada that drew up outside the block. A uniformed driver ushered them into it and the car pulled away, slipping past him moments later with tinted, diplomatic windows revealing nothing. Putting the nightsight in his pocket, he checked the toolkit in the briefcase. He slipped the gun into his waistband. Nodding, he opened the door of the Ford and got out, locking the car and walking with studied purpose towards the flats.

He passed the surveillance car. The man on foot was on the other side of the block. He felt tensed against the opening of a car door, a voice raised in question or recognition. The lights were bright at the entrance to the flats, so that even his back and shoulders might be familiar, recognisable. He paused, fishing in his pockets for a keycard he did not have. The foyer beyond the reinforced glass doors was empty. The entryphone invited and mocked. A keycard and a personal code number. Easy when you –

Ten seconds. He opened the briefcase, clutching it against his chest. Sweat was damp beneath his arms and against his sides. The humid air pressed like a soft, clinging towel. The image of the middle-aged Indian at the head of the narrow staircase, denying he was Banerjee, was very distinct. He raised his hand after closing the briefcase, to scratch his head, hover with some semblance of conviction.

The flat's doubtless been searched, anything there would have already been found . . . you should have gone via the solicitor, even the embassy . . .

'Thanks!' he blurted. 'Lost my bloody card or something!'

The woman, forty, precise, hurried and unsuspicious, nodded her thanks as he held open one of the doors for her as she left the building. She cradled a sheaf of files in the crook of her arm. Hyde closed the door behind him. Oh, easy when you know how –

Cass' flat was on the top floor, the fourth. He took the lift, chilly in the air-conditioning after the humidity of the street and the heat of his tension. The door of the lift opened onto a quiet, carpeted corridor – any office building anywhere; utterly anonymous. He heard a child singing beyond one of the doors, then an adult voice grumbled it into silence. For a moment. As he reached the door of Cass' flat, the singing began again. He smiled. The woman's arrival in the foyer had been more convenient than using the entryphone, pretending he was some diplomatic messenger looking for one of the names ... entry, yes, but his non-arrival at whichever door he had selected would have aroused curiosity.

He looked down at the doormat, then along the corridor. There were doormats outside other flats. He knelt down, peeling the mat back like cut turf. Tut, tut ... The pressure pad lay like an envelope left beneath the mat. Straddling it with his feet, he leaned gently towards the door; inserted the stiff plastic card, slipping it, forcing it ... yes, it would go. He reached up, feeling along the top of the door frame. No wires. No sign of an alarm rigged from outside.

He employed the card once more, hearing the lock click back. Gently, he pushed the door open, studying the floor of the darkened hallway. No mat. He flicked on the pencil-thin beam of a torch he drew from his pocket, running the finger of pale light along the skirting. No sign that the carpet had been lifted, then replaced. He heard the child continue its nursery rhyme like a tape-loop and the predictable grumbles of its mother, and his own magnified breathing. Cass' flat smelt unused, already mildewed by the heat. He stepped through the doorway and shut the door behind him, locking it on the latch. The only sound now was that of his steady, loud breathing.

He flicked the torchbeam into a small bedroom, a bathroom, then he entered the main living room. The beam wiped assuredly over furniture, the television, hi-fi, bookshelves, a complexly patterned rug. They didn't use infra-red detectors in Indian alarm systems — legitimate or covert. Too hot. Here, if the flat had been bugged against intrusion by the people who'd tipped Banerjee off the end of the gangplank, then it would be noise-activated bugs and pressure-pads. Which way does the window look out? North-east, towards the illuminated wedding cakes of Parliament House and the Secretariat. Beyond them, the domes and minarets and towers of mosques and temples and forts jutted into their floodlighting. He needed to risk crossing the living room, which had to be bugged, to draw the curtains.

The thin beam from the torch preceded like the gently feeling enquiries of a blind man's stick. He avoided the rug, the chairs, the low table, a standard lamp set beside one curtain. Found the cord and softly drew the curtains. Then he flicked the torchbeam around the room's walls, skirting, corners, before he returned to the doorway and switched on the room's lights. Dimmer switch. He lowered the brightness. Kneeling, he peeled back the rug. Another pressure pad, its lead disappearing like a snail-trail under the sofa. Pads under the cushions, doubtless — don't sit down on the job, sport . . . He squatted on his haunches, absorbing the room. Where are the bugs? He looked up. Not in the lampshade suspended from the ceiling. He stood up and crossed to the standard lamp — hello, old friend. There'd be others, but perhaps not too many. Any hidden cameras? The furniture was functional, uncrowded. It hadn't been moved to accommodate sightlines or angles. He eased open the single sideboard. Nothing.

He knelt beside the television set, the VCR on a shelf beneath it, and felt its surface and angles and leads. Inspected his fingers. The TV hadn't been fiddled with — the dust on the back of the set only now disturbed. Opening the briefcase, he took the screwdriver from the toolkit and removed the back of the set, placing the breastplate-like board on the carpet beside him. Then he flashed the torch into the set.

Masking tape. Two miniature tape cassettes from a mini-recorder. Gently, he unpeeled the tape, grinning. He placed the tapes in the briefcase and judged the size of the video recorder. It would go into the case, no need to take it to pieces here. He unplugged the aerial and the lead and lifted the recorder into the briefcase. *They always pinch the video recorder, sir, first thing they go for.*

Stopcock. Was that just a general reference to the plumbing, or was whatever-it-was actually beneath the kitchen sink? He stood up, glancing around the living room. There were no photographs in the room. The place seemed self-contained, sufficient. Books everywhere, and an immodest collection of records and CDs. The sky had fallen in on a contented man. Pieces of jade, statuettes of Shiva and Parvati, the Lord Krishna, a bulging image of the Buddha. On a desk in the corner, opened books, notes, and a sheet of paper in a small electronic typewriter.

Shaking his head, he moved to the kitchen and switched on the light after lowering the blind. He opened the cupboard beneath the sink, and found the stopcock, then fingered his way along the copper pipework. He leant forward on his knees. The smell of detergent and the unemptied wastebin. He felt behind the belly of the sink. Masking tape. He tugged at it –

– too late realising that he had pulled away a fine electronic wire, broken a contact placed there just to be broken. No audible alarm sounded in the building or outside it. The wiring shook in his hand as he inspected it. He'd set off some alarm, somewhere –

THREE

diplomatic presence

Hyde switched off the kitchen light, as if to return the narrow room to a state of innocence, then stood hesitantly in the doorway of the lounge. The back of the television set lay on the fawn carpet like the shell of a dead turtle. *Put the bloody back on the telly or they'll ask Cass what was hidden there.* The idea's urgent clarity was its conviction. He hurried to the set, fumbling the casing and its screws into place, scratching his forefinger with the screwdriver, dropping one of the screws, snatching it up, pressing it home – then the second, the third, fourth –

– tightening it, he heard the noise of the lift from the corridor. *Oh, Jesus, not yet –*

He snatched up the briefcase. Then, swallowing, deliberately stood on the pressure pad beneath the bright subtle rug, scuffing the rug into shapelessness. Opened drawers in the sideboard, tugged books from the wall shelves and the bookcases. No time for the bedroom, it would have to do. The lift had stopped.

How the hell could they have responded so fast? He turned wildly towards the main window. Metal frames, lever-catches – no locks. He opened one window on the damply-clinging night air and looked down, then back towards the hallway as he heard the door handle tried. They'd informed the surveillance car and they'd been across the street like dogs out of traps. He swung one leg over the windowsill, clinging on to the briefcase with one hand, the other gripping the window frame above his head.

A key was tried gently in the lock, a small scratching sound as if a dog wanted to gain entry. *Drop the bloody case, the VCR doesn't have to work.* The briefcase fell dully onto a grass verge and was lost in shadow. He thrust himself over the sill, clinging to it as his feet searched for purchase on a jutting concrete sill above the windows of the flat below. He felt it through the toes of his shoes and let himself slide away from his grip, pressing himself to balance against the concrete of the wall. Pebble-dash scraped at his cheek and palms. Then he edged himself along the narrow outcrop towards the closest drainpipe. Above his head, he heard no sounds from Cass' flat. They were trying to catch an agent, a professional who'd been searching the flat, not someone who'd just waltz off with the video to flog it in Chandni Chowk tomorrow morning. They needed surprise, an edge. Reinforcements.

He tested the drainpipe. It moved – unsafe. Had to suffice. He looked down. A grass verge hard as concrete below him, shadow, a fall of light at the corner of the block, no one moving. He swallowed and began sliding as hurriedly as he dared down the drainpipe, hearing the small tears of screws from fixings, the grumble of metal against concrete. Dropped the last eight or ten feet, jolting himself.

Running footsteps – where the hell was the briefcase? He gripped it in the dark and thrust it under his arm. Then moved along the wall of the building until he reached its angle and the spill of light from the street.

Looking up, he saw a dark head leaning from the window through which he had escaped. Then a voice called with exaggerated and redundant caution. The running footsteps had halted. The man patrolling on foot was shrugging up at the man in the window. Go now –

He walked as steadily and unconcernedly as he could towards the streetlamps and the wide pavement and the neat saplings and the passing limousines, then crossed the street towards the rented Ford. He unlocked the door and got in, throwing the briefcase into the rear of the car. Despite the temperature of the night, his tension clouded the windscreen. Jesus. His hands slipped sweatily on the wheel. He started the engine and pulled away from the kerb. As he passed the surveillance car, he saw that it was empty, but one of them was standing at the glass doors of the flats, using an R/T. He glanced up at the passing Ford, and then ignored it as Hyde turned the car towards Satya Marg and the perimeter of the Enclave. Ahead of him, suspended but moving in the darkness, a light aircraft was coming into Safdarjang aerodrome. Then, heading in the direction from which he had come, a car at high speed. He grinned shakily. The backup was too late – just . . .

'Look, the sleek bastard's grinning all over his face!' Hyde snorted, towelling his hair as he slumped, bathrobed, into one of the cane armchairs that littered Ros' suite.

On the screen – Hindi newsreader's voice turned down – V. K. Sharmar was receiving the adulation of a crowd, waving his hands above his head, then presenting them folded time and again in the gesture of returned greeting which always appeared that of prayer or service. Apt in this instance. Garlands were placed around his neck, almost obscuring his broad, continuous grin. Unlike the late Rajiv, he did not remove them as soon as they bedecked him.

Ros' head appeared at the bedroom door.

'I thought your cover involved you keeping miles away from me,' she remarked.

'I heard there was some middle-aged biddy staying here looking for a toy boy.'

'*Toy*, maybe. *Not* a model steam loco whose clockwork's buggered.' She wandered forward into the suite's sitting room, wrapping a bright, sari-like housecoat around her and tying it at the waist. She tugged her hair to a semblance of order. 'You'd better bugger off into the bedroom when the waiter brings the breakfast up. I've got my reputation to consider.'

'He'll understand – you're Australian.'

'*Don't* make any observations that the amount of breakfast

you made me order won't arouse suspicion, on account of my size – will you?' She tugged at Hyde's hair, sharply. 'That's him, is it?' she continued. 'You think he killed his wife – or had her killed?'

'Had to be behind it.'

'Christ – they don't play about here, do they? Why, though?'

Hyde gestured towards the screen. The same image of Sharmar, in frozen, beaming monochrome, decorated the front page of the English-language daily, *Indian Express*, that had been left outside the door of the suite. *V.K. to lead Congress*, was a sober-enough headline, but it seemed to sussurate with adulation. There was a photograph of Anand Mehta on the same front page in a scene from his latest movie.

'Cass was a danger to him – the woman was a danger. Cass did start off by using her, after all.'

'Why didn't they kill Cass?'

'That might have aroused our interest. Though I doubt it!'

'Haven't got hold of Shelley yet?' Hyde shook his head. 'You can't get Cass out on your own – you're *not* going to try, are you?'

Ros' features were suspiciously concerned. Again, he shook his head. She stared hard at him for perhaps ten seconds, then nodded slowly.

'I haven't got the resources. And with the buggers at the High Commission telling Shelley there's nothing to worry his blond head about, I can't get hold of any. Shelley's either got to trade, or threaten. But is he going to do that to someone he used to be at Oxford with – I ask in all innocence?'

'Was he?'

'Weren't they all, darlin'?'

'There wasn't anything in that video recorder, was there?'

'I didn't have time to search through the tapes – perhaps they were what he meant? Though I didn't see a video camera anywhere. All I've got out of it is those two cassettes – a lot of hoarse breathing from Cass, a couple of voices mostly speaking

Hindi, Cass' jumbled jottings and meanderings. A lot of the stuff's got to be translated and I can't do it.'

'So? Apart from moving in here and trying to turn this into a dirty weekend, what *can* you do, Hyde?' She lit a cigarette and moved to the window. Beyond her, the morning heat made the scene indistinct, the towers of Connaught Place and the business area fragile and merely decorative in the haze; the government buildings and the Supreme Court were lightened, made less massive – galleys rather than great, monumental warships. The brown river was almost invisibly sand-coloured. 'Well, my bright, shining boy – what *are* you going to do?'

'If I can't get Shelley by the time I've finished my tucker, Ros*alind* –' Ros scowled at him and he grinned. ' – then I'm off to see Cass again. I need to know more, in case.'

'In case of what?'

'In case they decide he's better off out of the way.'

'Would they –?'

Hyde jabbed his finger towards the television. 'He's playing in a very big game. What's Cass to him, that he should weep for him? If Sharmar gets the slightest twitch because of Cass, then the poor bloke's going straight into the dark. *That*'s why Shelley needs to be at the other end of a phone!'

Ros turned back to the view from the window, blowing smoke across it, masking the slender minarets and towers beyond the office blocks. Then she said:

'How dangerous is this?'

'Not that much. My cover's still intact. Cass' diplomatic status could give Shelley leverage . . . ?' The observation became a question, and Hyde rubbed his chin. Ros' glance pounced on him with accusatory concern. He raised his hands, palms outwards. 'Not *that* dangerous. More a job of convincing Shelley than anything else. It's not going to degenerate into a punch-up – I'm just the wood-and-water joey in this. For once, I'm not left on my ace with the arse hanging out of my pants.' The colloquialisms were intended to diminish the situation. Ros' large features remained suspicious. 'Look, I'll go and see the poor sod *once* more, *get* something out of him to forklift Shelley out of his chair. OK?'

'Right. When do we leave, in that case?'

'Tomorrow – or the day after. Promise.'

There was a knock on the door. Ros was plucking at her lower lip with thumb and forefinger, ignoring the polite noise, even as Hyde nodded towards the door. She was staring at the front page of the newspaper.

'I don't like it,' she said. 'That bugger's got *everything* to lose.'

'Answer the door, Ros – I'm hungry,' Hyde said, grinning, as he disappeared into the bedroom.

Cass had become paranoid; sullen, grubby, withdrawn, his shoulders hunched like the frill of a carapace. Hyde rubbed his hands through his hair. The interview room was stifling, airless. Jawal stood deferentially silent beside the door. Cass had replied to his greeting and enquiries monosyllabically; he was disgruntled, fearful. Desperation had cultivated cunning.

Hyde leant forward, pushing more cigarettes towards Cass. 'Did you enjoy the Jane Austen?' Hyde asked. *Persuasion*. I'm interested, make it more convincing . . .

'What?' Cass' reddened eyes were ferally alert, like those of a rat caught by a sudden light. The mind behind them seemed to scuttle away from Hyde. 'Not much.'

'Pity.' Hyde controlled his quick anger. He had dressed as the Midlands teacher before leaving Ros' hotel, reentered his own hotel via the back yard, found that his room had not been searched. The awkward drawer of the rickety chest in the room had remained opened to just the extent he had left it. 'Pity,' he sighed. There was, as yet, no connection between the man in the suit at Cass' flat and himself. He'd been tailed out to the prison this time, however. The same blue Ford, the same team. 'Want me to bring you some more books, Phil?'

Cass shook his head, his hair flopping over his forehead in

greasy licks. He rubbed it back with one hand. Hyde quelled his impatience. This sort of thing wasn't his game. What the hell was Shelley doing, for God's sake? He still wasn't home – middle of the bloody night in London.

Clearing his throat, he murmured: 'You know, pity you can't have the telly in here, since you speak the local lingo. I've got one – but its only use to me would be with a VCR. But then, who wants to watch Indian films? A VCR would be useless.'

Cass appeared startled, then at once wizened with cunning, his eyes darting and hot with realisations and dangers.

'You – did the stopcock?'

'Already done.' Hyde stared until he perceived that Cass understood, then waited for him to weigh the implications of the information, hoping he would respond.

The silence continued. Hyde's temperature rose. His mouth was arid. He heard a large insect blundering slowly through the soupy air. Cass stared at the burning cigarette in his fingers, intent as if he had heard of the death of a close relative, Hyde thought. Shit. He's going to close up altogether. He's the *only* source of information now. He knows there's not much on those tapes, it's mostly still in his head.

Finally, Cass shook his head, and looked up at Hyde. His face was pale beneath the stubble, and drawn around what had become a very young man's eyes, expressing pique, adolescent defiance.

'Thanks for coming,' he muttered sullenly.

'I'm willing to help,' Hyde insisted. 'But really, Phil, I do need some information from you.'

'I've told my story too many times – *Patrick*,' he added. 'Too many people know my story.' He swallowed and his hands clenched together on the scratched table, stilling each other.

'That makes it all the more important *I* know.' Again, Cass shook his head.

'*No*,' he announced emphatically. 'Not here.'

'Tell me.'

The adolescent had vanished and the cunning, exhausted man had returned, with his rat's eyes. Cass' mouth was loose and wet, he smelt of dirt and fear, but his paranoid terror at being abandoned – even his terror of Hyde – silenced him.

'Uncle Peter – how do I explain it to him?'

'I'll tell him, when I –' he swallowed noisily. Hyde's throat remained dry. 'I get out of this place. Don't want to go over it now, not *again*. Not here.'

'Christ, Phil – don't be so upset!' Hyde urged. 'It might help, you know. You say you didn't do it –?' He glanced towards the guard. Jawal seemed uncomprehending. Was there any point in this furtive half-dialogue any more?

Except that it might keep his own cover intact – and keep him alive.

'Phil,' he murmured, leaning forward. 'I *understand* the chip on your shoulder. The High Commission doesn't seem to be doing much – but if *I* could talk to someone in London, create a stink at *home*, then things might get better. But, I'd need to be able to convince them with something. You know, what really happened, what you were doing there . . . ?'

Cass prodded his own chest, as if inviting attack. The small room now seemed further diminished by the tension within him, the clash of desperation and paranoia. The prodding became a feeble tapping, as if he were attempting to transmit in a morse code he had largely forgotten. Hyde felt the perspiration as a line across his forehead. Cass opened his lips, but said nothing.

Hyde persisted: 'You don't want to spend more time here than you have to, Phil – you need help. *I* need help with London.' Cass was shaking his head. 'Uncle Peter was a bit shocked – you having a mistress, an affair. You know how old-fashioned he is in some ways.' Hyde searched for some word or idea that would act like a cattle-prod. No good frightening Cass, he'd already done that to himself. His paranoia at least prevented him from asking about Banerjee. No good just coaxing him. He'd already lost interest, perhaps even forgotten he'd smuggled the two names to Hyde. Everything had hinged on the tapes and whatever else –

– hadn't really. Cass had collapsed of his own accord. Caved in. Abandoned, isolated – expecting to be cheated.

The cunning was back in his eyes, as was the palsied, ceaseless shaking of his head. He pointed to his chest, then to the door, still silent. You bloody stupid bastard, Hyde thought, and said:

'You're *wrong*, Phil – *dead* wrong.' The head continued with its palsy and the eyes glittered with held-back tears. The room, the prison, were as small as the enclosure of Cass' temples. Hyde had to make him believe they *had* to get him out, that they knew he had a great, priceless secret. He wasn't really in touch any longer, merely crawling towards the mirage of an oasis. 'Phil.' Nothing short of shock therapy would awaken Cass. Strangely, he was safe inside his terror. His secret was keeping him alive. Hyde stood up.

For a moment, there was a new horror of being abandoned in Cass' eyes, but it faded almost immediately. A weak and cunning smirk possessed his mouth. Jawal opened the door.

Hyde went out into the corridor, tugging the rucksack onto his shoulder. Cass' silence pressed at his back like the fear of a terminal illness. The stupid, *stupid* bastard . . . but there was no vigour in his condemnation. Cass had retreated to his only place of safety – the den of his secret. He'd been alone too long. Nothing had been done for him with enough *urgency* –!

Right, *Uncle* Peter – be there, on the other end of the line.

The security guard seemed disdainful of him, the effect of his appearance combined with the scent of the tandoori meal he had bought and eaten at a stall near his hotel. His lips were probably still stained from the food. It was a pleasant little confrontation at the gate of the High Commission on Shantipath, the porticoed Edwardian building looming behind the uniformed man. He trumped the guard's reluctance with his ID card, drawing it from the lining of the rucksack with a small flourish. Midday pressed down on them, hazily burning.

'Now you know,' Hyde remarked with a smirk designed to irritate.

The security guard's disdain seemed unchipped. Having presented his ID, he had declared himself one of a species thought extinct; a coelacanth brought up in a fisherman's net, a dinosaur bone excavated on the site of a new office block.

'I want to see Dickson – now.'

The guard, stiffly refusing to perspire in the glass booth parked beside the open gates of the High Commission, picked up a telephone. Behind him, in the grounds, a fountain was displayed in a peacock's tail by a momentary puff of breeze. Dark privet hedges, English lawns being continuously watered. The place seemed more archaic than his ID card. Shelley would be peeved by his self-declaration, but there wasn't time any more. The midday editions of the English language newspapers were speculating with what seemed worshipful, obsessive ferocity on Sharmar calling an early election. Photographs of the new PM, the President, the dead Chopri and the magnetic Mehta littered the newsstands. There wasn't time now for a quiet chat, a teasing-out of Cass' story. Shelley had to promise the Indians whatever they demanded for Cass' transfer to London – or for a transfer to diplomatic custody, pending his trial.

The guard put down the receiver.

'With a certain reluctance, you're to be let in,' he announced.

'So kind.'

He crunched along the weedless gravel drive towards the marble steps up to the main doors. Another puff of hot breeze splashed droplets pleasantly from the fountain's spray against his arm and cheek. He all but rubbed his hands as he mounted the steps and passed the raised eyebrows of another security man. Then he paused.

'Where's Dickson's office?'

'*Mr* Dickson's office is on the second floor. Room 221. You the new punkah-wallah?'

'Your bovine mate at the gate told you who I am.' The foyer was as cool as its marble, less frosty than the security man's glance. 'Cheers.'

He climbed the grand staircase. Whitehall-among-the-Darkies, the Raj lives, OK? He turned and reached the first floor, then climbed to the second, passing secretaries and attachés and even cleaners who regarded him with the same blank incomprehension. Long windows overlooked the careful, ordered gardens around the Commission. India remained at a respectful distance beyond an imitation of Sussex. Delhi, to the north, squatted patiently in its own heat. He checked the numbers on the doors, and when he reached 221 simply opened it and walked in, sniffing loudly to announce his presence in an amalgam of haste and mockery.

'Mr *Hyde*?' a youngish woman asked, rising from her chair behind a desk. He nodded. She moved hesitantly from the desk towards the other door in the room. Air-conditioning grumbled against the enormity of its task and a small fan on the woman's desk turned with a bemused buzzing noise. 'I'll see if he can see you now –'

Hyde passed her at the door, opening it on a larger office that was scented with cigar smoke. He recognised Dickson behind the desk, haloed by the light from tall windows. Other embassies, mirror-images of the High Commission, echoed away in the windows' perspective. A game of mirrors. Dickson was immediately angry, bridling to a squatting position above his chair, hands gripping its arms. The other man in the room may have been Miles, or another of the SIS complement. It had no bearing. Dickson nodded at the secretary, who remained behind Hyde, then lowered himself into his chair and immediate imperturbability. His features composed themselves diplomatically; aloof, certain, half-amused.

'Hyde, isn't it?' he asked, the slightest trace of Edinburgh in his voice, his mistrust evident. The other man grinned, even mockingly held his nose.

'Who's the monkey?' Hyde asked, nudging an elbow towards Dickson's companion. 'You're obviously the organ-grinder.'

'Miles – Hyde . . . Hyde – *Mr* Miles. Your senior, I'd say.'

'You mean he's reached pensionable age?'

Miles scowled.

'Why are you here – or needn't I ask?' Dickson remarked equably, gesturing towards a leather chair after Hyde had dragged it closer to the desk and sat down. 'We were a little puzzled when Jackson at the gate rang through, saying he'd got someone with one of *our* type of ID cards down there.'

'Right scruffbag, he said,' Miles offered.

'I heard him, and he didn't.' He slapped his hands on the edge of the desk, and said: 'I haven't got time to waste. I want fully independent use of the Code Room now, full signals with Shelley. No one else, just Shelley.'

'I was about to ask who might have sent you into our neck of the woods. It doesn't seem necessary any longer, does it?'

'Or have you just run out of traveller's cheques, Hyde?' Miles sneered.

'Look, neither of you are any good at this stuff. I've had it from the best, Sir Kenneth of sainted memory. Now, stop pissing about and give me the key to the Code Room.' His voice was level, even amused. He realised that he was enjoying himself.

'Did the D-G send you – why?' Dickson asked.

'That's it. Watch your arse, it might be on fire. You don't know *what* authority I have, do you?'

'You're not here about the Cass business, are you, Hyde?'

'Someone has to be, Miles – you don't give a stuff, that's obvious. Look, Dickson, you're Head of Station. Just get me into signals with Shelley. No skin off your nose.'

A giant fan windmilled above their heads. The room was comfortable with cigar smoke, leather, bookcases, rugs – the view from the window of a safe, surrounding diplomatic world. Delhi was a good posting for anyone – for the SIS personnel, it was a glimpse of Nirvana. It had made Cass careless and soft; and endangered.

'You don't believe Cass' story, do you? I took you for a cynic, not a soppy girl.'

'Miles, why don't you piss off?' He only then turned to Miles, and added: 'If I was Shelley, I'd want to know why you *want* to believe Cass killed the woman.' He turned to Dickson, squinting into the noon, pearled light from the windows. 'Both of you.'

Dickson's face narrowed on the acid of Hyde's tone, then he said equably: 'All – *all* the evidence points to that fact, Hyde. We've been over it, again and again. Hence our report to Shelley. You've got *other* information?' There was a tiny tremor of worry in his voice.

'Cass is a *mate* of his, sir,' Miles offered with obsequious sarcasm. 'I doubt very much whether the D-G sent him out here. We'd have heard –'

'Will you put me in signals with Shelley or not? I haven't got time to waste.' He paused, then something about the room, its occupants or the hermetic view from its windows angered him. He caught the scent of perspiration and fear and the prison interview room from his clothing. He clenched his right hand into a fist and banged it down on the desk. Dickson's cheeks flinched. 'I haven't got time to waste on you pair of wankers! Sharmar *framed* Cass – or someone did on his behalf. Sharmar, in case you don't read the papers, is the new Prime Minister – Sharmar is into heroin. Cass *knows* – at least, Sharmar thinks he knows! QED – Cass' life isn't worth a fart after a vindaloo! Now, do I get into signals with Shelley or not?'

Dickson's features glowed with affront. Miles' face had whitened as if with flour, and his eyes moved with a fierce cunning that reminded Hyde of Cass. Hyde saw him nod at Dickson from the corner of eyesight. Collapse of less-than-stout parties. Parties were as much as they were good for, these buggers who'd been prepared to hand him over to Harrell and his *Carpetbaggers* the last time he was in Delhi. Just as they were prepared to let Cass go into the dark now. And Cass had saved him from Harrell, smuggled him out of the airport under their noses . . . he owed Cass a bit of outrage on his behalf and half a chance to go on living.

As if mind-reading, Miles sneered: 'You owe Cass one, don't you, Hyde? He saved your skin a couple of years ago.'

'Just remember whose side *you* were on, Miles. I didn't hear that Harrell got the Congressional Medal of Honour post-humously – did you?'

Dickson stood up. 'I shall report your manner, Hyde. I am effectively your senior – you know the rules. This is *my* bailiwick. However, I'd be interested to observe the D-G's reaction to your claims that he sent you out and that Cass is innocent of murder. I think we can accommodate you.'

'Good!' Miles appeared relieved, and then angry that he experienced a sense of relief; angry mostly against Hyde – perhaps even against Cass. It had been so easy to ignore Cass, even enjoy his predicament. Even Shelley only wanted to be *sure*, just in case something blew up in his face. Bunch of fucking time-servers and cocktail-party spies. 'Let's go, then.'

Clearing his throat, Dickson announced like a butler at a door: 'Jim, would *you* take Hyde down to the Code Room – and *stay* with him, please?'

'Sir.'

Miles hurried after Hyde through the outer office. Hyde glimpsed a flash of amusement at Miles' heightened colour and evident haste on the secretary's face. Then they were passing the tall windows with their view of the gardens and formal, regimented hedges set out for a chessgame that had been assumed to be eternal. Alices, all of them, unaware they were about to stumble upon the Queen of Hearts behind one of the hedges. Miles and Dickson were as stupid as anyone who had

ever Rajed it out here. Sharmar was going to have Cass killed —
— and he had to convince Shelley . . .
. . . not easy.

Miles, at his side on the staircase, exhibited an edge of fretful anxiety and a contempt for Hyde that was masked by caution. He was handling a wild animal. The business of the High Commission passed them with careful accents, wearing white shirts and bright blouses. Then they were in the marbled, pillared foyer, and Miles nudged him towards a narrower set of stairs leading down to the building's basement.

'Shelley's not going to like you calling him,' Miles offered.

'Too bad,' Hyde murmured casually. The air was cooler and musty in the corridor they entered, the walls cream-coloured, drab and unornamented.

'Things are changing rapidly. Cass is a bloody great *embarrassment* now,' Miles insisted. There was a shirt-sleeved security man seated on an upright chair at the end of the corridor, beside a blank door. Hyde saw the shoulder holster beneath his armpit. 'Sharmar's PM now. Big Friend status — and did you know that he was at Oxford with the D-G? Quite pally they were, I believe.'

'I knew.'

'The boat isn't going to be allowed to rock, Hyde. You ought to realise that. Not for Cass, anyway. Sending you, mind — I'd have thought that was to do Cass in. Sure you got your orders right?'

Miles' broad pink forehead was greasy with perspiration as he exuded gratuitous well-being, as if after a satisfying meal. He was no more than an inch taller than Hyde. The temptation to headbutt the obsequious, crowing little pillock was all but irresistible. Especially because there was an element of truth in his supercilious confidence. Hyde clenched his hands in his pockets.

'What's the matter with you, Miles? Home comforts been withdrawn until you lose weight, or something?' He turned to the security man, who was on his feet. 'Get him to open the door, will you?' Miles wasn't certain, but his confidence was enraging. Most of the man *did* believe Shelley would hang Cass out to dry, just as Dickson evidently did.

'Rogers, open the door.'

'Yes, Mr Miles.'

The Code Room was like an exhibit in a theme park museum. Secure Room for Cold War Purposes, c.1960–1990. A bored young man with a designer stubble climbed languidly to his feet as the door was relocked behind them. Plastic coffee cups and old newspapers littered his desk. The screen of his most immediate VDU was turned away from him. He had been reading a paperback on the English Civil War – probably doing an Open University degree on the quiet. Hyde felt like a maiden aunt inspecting dust along mantels and table-edges.

'This is Geoff,' Miles said. 'Hyde here wants full signals with home, D-G personally.' Geoff seemed as much bemused as impressed. Hyde's name evidently meant nothing to him.

Cass had gone the same way as Geoff – private study, a nice little billet, very little to do.

'Mr Hyde – ?'

'Don't bother with the *Mister*,' Miles smirked.

'Just get on with it, sport. I want high-speed voice contact. Get it set up. Should take you two minutes, if you're in training.'

Hyde wandered away from the banks of equipment and especially from Miles. Geoff was already signalling London, while Miles idled his way through a days-old newspaper he had found on one of the work stations. Then he remembered Cass' face, during the first encounter. The bemusement, the stunned horror of any hostage, any victim. Why me? *How* me? Knowing he was trapped in the nightmare, while people like Miles smirked and then ignored him and read old newspapers. It was as if Miles had, indeed, held the English tabloid up as a deliberate insult. A ghastly footballer with vacant eyes and his tongue protruding grimaced at Hyde like something from Bedlam. Cass *was* in Bedlam, his appalled, horrified sense of innocence like a torment, more violent and incarcerating than the prison. *You overweight bastard, Miles,* he thought.

'You through yet?' he snapped at Geoff, hunched at tape-spools and a microphone. Geoff glanced round, his features filled with alarm, as if his competence had been challenged by a remote, aloof professor. 'They're getting Mr Shelley down to their Code Room now – er, Mr Hyde. Won't be a minute,' he added with a tepid grin. His fingers dabbled nervously near the high-speed tapes.

Hyde drew a typist's chair towards the central console. High-speed voice transmission and reception was old-fashioned now – and redundant, by and large. It was associated with operations and urgencies and men and women's lives – and the past. It was quick, covert, almost romantic. He experienced a mild tension merely confronting the electronics. Then a light came on near Geoff's sallow cheek and the tapes whirled, momentarily stopped, rewound at the same speed, then began playing. Shelley's voice, prim, hurried, slightly breathless.

'Patrick? Why have you broken your cover and involved the High Commission? What's wrong?'

The other tape deck waited for Hyde to speak. Voice-activated, no buttons to press. Hyde leant forward almost eagerly towards the microphone. The air-conditioning's soughing was the only sound in the room for a moment, except for Miles' turning of the newspaper's pages. Beside him, Geoff's face wore a childish, uncomprehending excitement.

'Cass needs to be got out soonest. He's in poor shape, he's *innocent*, and he has a story to tell.' He nodded, and Geoff transmitted his words. The tape noise was the brief rush of wings of an unseen bird. Shelley's tape began working almost immediately. Hyde felt his own excitement.

'Who's with you there?'

Hyde's tape seemed to spit back his reply. 'What the bloody hell does that matter – I'm the one who saw Cass.'

A few moments later, into which intervening silence Miles

had dropped a snigger like a pebble; 'This business has taken on a different dimension, Patrick. I have a full report on the Sharmar family from Delhi Station on my desk – I have a long fax from Sharmar himself. It's been analysed, of course – the distress is quite affecting, very genuine. Sharmar has been deeply grieved by his wife's murder. He is not, however, vindictive. Cass will receive justice.'

The voice had become more impersonal than the machinery rendered it. It seemed to echo out into the corridors and rooms of the embassy, and have nothing to do with secrecy; it had become diplomatic.

'Cass is *innocent* – he *didn't do it*,' Hyde enunciated with cold anger. 'Sharmar is in the heroin business.'

'We checked all that,' Miles offered snickeringly, with assumed boredom. 'Cass disagreed with us, went off on his own.'

Then Shelley, before Hyde could reply: 'Cass might just *want* you to believe him, Patrick. There's no corroboration. Sharmar is a force for stability –' Again, the words seemed directed beyond Hyde, out into the legitimate air of the High Commission. Having been absorbed by Shelley from other corridors and vaulted rooms in London. Cass' features did not need to return to fuel Hyde's corrosive anger, though they were there in the dark at the back of his head. '– as PM and leader of Congress, he is now in a position, as a staunch friend of HMG –'

Hyde gripped his microphone. 'You sound like a bloody Foreign Office communiqué, Shelley!' he snapped. 'Just because you were up at Oxford with the bugger, that doesn't make him squeaky-clean. *Howard Marks* went to Oxford, and *he* had his hand in the drugs till! Get Cass out of prison – get him here, into diplomatic custody to await trial. Don't leave him where they can reach him.'

Eventually, Shelley's tapes stilled after rewind, and began to play back soothing assurances.

'My room for manoeuvre is limited. But we have reassurances regarding Cass. Just so long as he pleads guilty on a reduced charge of manslaughter, even diminished responsibility —'

'I don't believe I'm hearing this, Shelley.' Hyde heard his own breathing rustling like hoarse autumn leaves around the foam-capped microphone. Heard Geoff's embarrassment signalled through his fingertips on the desk; heard Miles' theatrical, dismissive sighs.

Heard Shelley.

'— fundamentalist parties getting in because of a scandal involving Sharmar. To put it bluntly, Patrick, the game has gone beyond Cass in the past forty-eight hours.' Beyond me, too . . . Hyde watched his hand curl and uncurl on the grey surface of the desk, like that of a child constantly wishing to inspect a bright insect it had caught. Cass wasn't going to fly away, there was no open hand here. Shelley had paused in the basement of Century House, expecting another outburst. He continued: 'Tell Cass that everything will be conducted through normal channels. Tell him —' It must have been embarrassment that provoked another pause. '— tell him there's nothing to worry about. That he's in no danger.'

'Tell him the committee that sat all day and most of the night in Whitehall don't give a shit about what happens to him as long as he keeps his trap shut,' Hyde offered cynically, and waited. Miles was behind him now, as if looking over his shoulder at a letter he had difficulty in composing; a letter explaining to parents that their son was missing in action. *Missing through inaction* . . .

Shelley's absence the previous day had been at that bloody cookery school in the Foreign Office where they concocted elaborate sauces to disguise the flavour of rotten meat. The Foreign Secretary and his smarmy Permanent Secretary and probably the Cabinet Secretary had all signed Cass off.

And there was no Aubrey to cut through the crap, not any more. It was all assessments, weighings; the Foreign Office's futures market. Sharmar was flavour of the month, and Cass was a nasty smell from the drains.

'Patrick, I understand your — concern. Tell Cass simply to plead guilty when offered a lesser charge. We have certain assurances —'

'He'll be killed trying to escape, Shelley — is that what you'd *like*?'

'Thank you for your help in this matter, Patrick. There's nothing more you can do. If you'd like to leave matters in the hands of the High Commission . . .'

Hyde stood up abruptly, thrusting his hands into the pockets of his denims. He snatched up the rucksack from the floor, and glowered at Miles, who found the outcome immensely satisfying.

At once, Hyde barked: 'It's in your hands, Miles. I'm dumping it all on *you*.'

He allowed his face to be inspected. Miles' gaze crawled on his skin like the sensation of moving ants. Shelley was reprimanding Hyde for breaking cover, but only Geoff and Miles were listening now. He jerked open the door of the Code Room, and slammed it shut again on Miles' parting:

'Have a good flight, Hyde. Enjoy retirement —'

Hyde passed the security man, bestowing a meaningless glare, then mounted the basement stairs to the foyer. Coolness, elaborate cornices and ceiling roses, great, intricate chandeliers. The export department of the Foreign Office. He went through the doors and down the marble steps to the gravel drive. A small flock of black Mercedes limousines was waddling sedately in through the open wrought-iron gates. He had hardly noticed the red carpet spilling down the marble steps. He stepped onto the grass as tinted, unrevealing windows slid past him. The High Commissioner was on the steps. Hyde had noticed nothing in preparation inside the place as he had stormed through the foyer. Business as usual, Praise the Lord and pass nothing more dangerous than the port decanter.

The security man at the gate seemed, by his expression, to lift him in mental fingertips and deposit him like a speck of ash on the other side of the High Commission's walls. As he paused, the embassies and consulates receded from him like great, secure ships in line astern, marshalled for some meaningless review. White and cream, basking like walruses in the early afternoon.

You just didn't do it . . . it could be me, he thought. You didn't leave agents hanging out to dry because it was *politic*. You just didn't do it – and if Shelley didn't understand that, then he understood *nothing*!

'Don't come the old soldier, Hyde,' Ros warned as he threw the rucksack across the sitting room of her hotel suite. He was shivering suddenly, because of the air-conditioning or because of the journey on the crowded, sweating bus; or because Delhi had clamped upon him like a straitjacket, heat and noise imprisoning him as certainly as Cass was incarcerated. He poured beer into a glass with shaking hands, and gulped most of it in a single swallow. 'What do we do now, Hyde? Never mind the tantrum.'

He glowered at her, rubbing his free hand through his dust-dry hair then across his stubbled face, before pouring himself a second beer snatched angrily from the minibar.

'Oh, bugger off, Ros! I've had it up to *here* –!' The flat of his hand chopped at his forehead. 'They're leaving the poor sod to drown in his own vomit!'

After a moment's silence, Ros asked: 'Better now?' Her features fluttered with a muscular tic, and her brown eyes were dark with premonitions. 'You're not giving it up, then?' she said quietly. Then her effort at calm erupted, and her slim hands slapped her thighs and she burst out: 'Why *you*, Hyde? Why do *you* have to care so bloody much?'

Hyde's gaze roamed the sitting room, glancing across the windows onto the alien city. On the table were curling sheets of paper covered with Ros' hastiest handwriting. The mini-recorder sat there, too. As he'd asked her, she had transcribed the contents of the tapes from Cass' flat.

'About Cass, you mean? I don't, really. Except it might have been me, some time, any place. They're just ditching him because the Foreign Office doesn't want Sharmar's nice white suit to get stained.'

'You can't do anything.'

'Maybe not.' He'd lost the tail in the crowded streets, leading them the old dance through crowded alleys and across vast, governmental squares and into the main bazaar. Dropped them one by one. If they knew anything, they knew he was professional. But then, they could have guessed that already. They had no way to Ros – they'd be waiting at his hotel. 'Christ, I don't know what to do, Ros! But no other bugger's going to try – what's on those tapes? Cass' bits and the other bits in English?'

'Liquorice allsorts. Some names, places, dates . . .' The information seemed dragged from her, as if she were being interrogated and was already guilty of betraying colleagues and friends. 'Look, Hyde, I don't want you to go on with this – let's get out of here. Let's just –' She hesitated, her feet shuffling against each other. Then she violently smoothed the full, flower-vivid skirt, and added: ' – get out of here, get on the plane and carry on . . .' Her voice faded, as if something inside, rather than Hyde's eyes, cautioned her.

He waved his arms dismissively as he crossed to the window. Then he turned to face her.

'I am pissed *off* with that attitude, Ros! Not from you, from Shelley and Century House and Whitehall! The *big* picture. It's all *bullshit*, when it comes to it. Diplomacy means don't rock the boat, policy means doing sod all to upset anyone.' He waved his arms again, as if raging at the city beyond the window. He couldn't see the river from here, only the solidly complacent ships and wedding cakes of government. 'Cass is like John McCarthy and Terry Waite and Jacky Mann and all the others – stuffed by a bunch of *bandits* and abandoned by a bunch of wankers wearing Old School ties!' He turned back to her once more, leaning heavily on the table, his knuckles curled hard on her transcription of Cass' tapes. 'Nobody gives a *toss* about *one* poor sod with the shaft stuck up his backside!' He licked the spittle from his lips. The table trembled beneath the pressure of his outburst. 'Cass didn't kill the woman, he was set up for it. Sharmar is into heroin, but that doesn't matter if you've recently become Prime Minister of India and went to Oxford with Peter-bloody-Shelley! They'll kill Cass now, just *because* Sharmar's got the foreman's job at last. Cass is on the way out and no one wants to hear the bad news!'

He turned away from her, poured himself another beer, and faced the far wall of the sitting room as if exiled there for misbehaviour.

Eventually, Ros murmured: 'Are you sure you're not making this your grand exit, Hyde?'

He turned, enraged, then felt the violent frustration lessen. He said, quite calmly: 'No – I don't think so . . .' Shook his head after a brief pause. 'No, I'm not making it my cause. Any more than any other cause. Sharmar's dealing in filth and now he's hoping to run India. Should I be *pleased*?'

'No. But you're usually just a complainer, not a campaigner.' She raised her hands in almost comic defence. 'OK, I apologise.' Hyde saw accommodation of a kind, however reluctant, and said:

'You're always on bloody marches, signing petitions, making covenants all over the place. This is just charity on the move, Ros – *practical* charity.'

'They're on to you!'

'Not quite – not completely.' He grinned shakily. 'Look, now isn't the time to show you the size of the gap someone like me needs to slip in and out of things.'

'What can you *do*, you stupid bugger? I saw you when you came out of Tadjikistan, mate. *Remember?*'

'And getting blind drunk to forget and not sleeping because of the nightmares – I know, Ros. As to what I can *do* . . . there's nothing in those transcriptions that'll convince anyone?' Ros shook her head reluctantly. Her hands fidgeted in her lap and along the edge of the table, as if they were attempting to dig her out from beneath some fallen weight of soil.

Hyde crossed to the table and sat down.

'Let's see what there is, then. Something – some links, clues . . .' He shuffled the sheets busily, then slyly looked up at her face. 'Are you in, Ros?'

Eventually, she shrugged.

'I'm not leaving you here on your own, mate – not bloody likely.'

He smiled at her, but she tugged her hand quickly away from his as he reached for it.

'OK, then – let's see what we've got . . .' His finger began tracing across Ros' handwriting, his head nodding as he did so. Then he murmured: 'Order some sandwiches or something, will you? More beer.' Her shadow moved on the page as she got up from her seat. He sensed her tension, and her compliance. She'd be getting angry soon, too. Her voice on the telephone to room service faded to the buzzing of an insect.

His hand, curled against his chest as he leaned over the page, was happily clammy. The tracing forefinger occasionally smudged Ros' handwriting.

He picked up a felt-tip pen and began linking material, taking it into the bedroom when the lunch order arrived, bringing it back to the table immediately the uniformed waiter had been tipped and had left. Cass had used the tapes as rough notes, nothing more, bits of breathless speculation and snatches of interview and passed-on information. He noted the name of *Banerjee* – late and lamented, poor sod – and of someone called *Lal* . . . the other name on the crumpled piece of cigarette paper. He hadn't checked Lal – perhaps he should. Ros placed a plate of sandwiches beside his hand and a glass of beer. He nodded his thanks.

There were two other voices, neither of which was identified, neither of which Cass had mentioned – their words were in

Hindi, anyway. The city beat against the window and his cheek, strong as the sunlight. It was the sense of the cool, ordered Diplomatic Enclave, however, that irritated his skin like a rash, rather than the towers and minarets and office buildings. That and the Lutyens Raj now to be controlled by a drug producer. A woman's name, curiously English – no one Cass knew . . . ? No. *Sara*. He scribbled on Ros' pad. *Sara Mallowby. Kashmir – houseboat hotel. Srinagar.* Had Cass been mixing the white sugar and the brown –? No, he didn't know her, not from his first comments. He'd sent whoever *Lal* was, up to Kashmir . . . oh, yes, Lal was the *reporter* – on what, who for?

He heard the cork of a wine bottle being removed, and liquid falling into a glass as if in a slowed-down recording. Almost at once, it seemed, Ros was refilling her glass. His glass was empty, so was his plate. The afternoon was older beyond the window. Eventually he underlined the name of the newspaper, which seemed like the freesheet Delhi equivalent of the *National Enquirer* – no, it appeared to be some radical rag that preferred to work from scandal rather than ideology. Lal had . . . yes, gone up to Srinagar on Cass' advice, to check on Sara Mallowby – when? Two months ago . . . dead end? He sipped at another beer Ros poured him. Sara Mallowby owned some houseboats on Dal Lake. Sara Mallowby –

Shit . . .

He stifled his grin. Crossed to the rucksack and drew out a map, crackling it open as he returned to the table, then spreading it like a cloth. The city intruded at that moment, its afternoon haze deceptive. He bent over the map. Cass had been found with the dead woman . . . there. The resort outside Srinagar. His finger jabbed on Dal Lake's blue smear on the map, while his thumb stretched towards Gulmarg. Sharmar's bungalow –

– shit again . . . Because what he had read was once more under his hand, pierced by the tip of the pen. Sharmar *knew* Sara Mallowby. Sharmar had hosted a party on one of her –

Feverishly, he snatched up the recorder.

'Which tape was this on – about the woman Mallowby and Sharmar?' He looked down. 'Tape two, counter mark one-seven-four – the one that's in here now – yes.' Ros remained seated, forking the last of her salad and sipping her wine. He ran the tape back to the counter mark. He wanted to *hear* Lal's words, not just read them.

'. . . recognised one Pakistani general . . . another of them was the Sikh leader, Khushwan Singh . . .' He let the tape run as if cold water were running against his beating temple. 'The Englishwoman is Sharmar's mistress, I am sure . . .' Finally: 'I will keep the pictures, Mr Cass – they may be useful to *us* – indeed, they belong to us . . .' He switched off the tape and sat heavily down, sighing. Grinning, which became chuckling.

'Oh, shit – what a bloody neat arrangement. They're *all* in it, the Pakis, the Sikhs and the Sharmar family. They're *all* shovelling that shit into Europe – and a different sort of shit all over Cass!' He clasped his hands behind his head as Ros waited with an expectant face. He swallowed carefully, so that she would not remark his guilt, then he said:

'You know Kashmir, don't you, Ros? Know Srinagar and Dal Lake quite well. From your old hippy days . . .'

God forgive me, I'm not risking your life, he thought. Say yes, Ros – please . . . I'll join you just as soon as I've found Lal, wherever he is. Oh, Lal – what a tale you can tell. Ros, say *yes* – I promise I'll watch out for you.

It sounded hollow, as if he were promising into a tunnel that had opened ahead of them.

in harm's way

'You are certain of this, Colonel?'

The light of the afternoon fell heavily across the room. The heat was almost kept at bay by the air-conditioning. Prakesh Sharmar rubbed at his cheek below the earpiece of the telephone, where perspiration threatened. His office overlooked Connaught Place and its receding ripples of the modern which stretched out like a whirlpool that might, eventually, suck in the old city and the Red Fort, the temples, mosques and stupas. Every spoke of its wheel was labelled with numbers and the birth-name of Radial Road.

He listened to the colonel in Intelligence with what might have been consternation. It was tight-reined still, but the sweat seemed to break out like little signals of fever around his throat, across his forehead, behind the ear pressed to the telephone.

'The man's name is Hyde?' he repeated. 'He is a British agent – *resigned*? Then what, I ask you, Colonel, is he doing interfering in our business?' It was as if he expected a reduction in price on some item in a bazaar, and he despised the tone of his voice. 'Yes, yes –' he said urgently, the scribbled words on the pad heavily underscored, the whorls and loops of indecision curling away and around the Englishman's name – Australian, the Colonel was explaining . . . 'Yes, yes – I know of Sir Kenneth Aubrey. I also know, Colonel, that he has retired from British Intelligence! You assume that this man Hyde was the thief who broke into Cass' apartment –? You do . . .'

Connaught Place, revealed again as one of his assistants

moved away from the broad window on the sixteenth floor of a building owned by a foreign bank, was ringed with high, modern buildings and thronged with crowds as he carried the telephone to the window. To the south, the government buildings and then the Diplomatic Enclave were all but lost in the heat haze. For a moment, it was as if the scene – or just perhaps the altitude of the office – made him dizzy; he was disorientated between the irreconcilable images of India that forced themselves upon him.

'Yes, then,' he admitted to the colonel, the scene and himself, 'the man must be taken care of at once. If you are certain of his identity, and therefore he has masqueraded as a relative of Cass, he is here for some other purpose.' Perhaps, we should not have taken Peter Shelley for the fool he appeared to V.K. at Oxford . . . ? 'No, I think as soon as is practicable. And the other matter – Cass – they must not meet again. That can be taken care of today. Thank you, Colonel. Goodbye.'

Prakesh put down the telephone and then returned it to his desk. He lit another cigarette. It was amateurish, he instructed himself, a case of just-in-case. It was nothing to do with Aubrey, nothing important. The colonel would understand that it must be made to look accidental –

He'd seen Ros onto the Srinagar flight, watching her in a detached way. A fat white woman, travel bag hitched over one shoulder, walking through the Departures door, which slid back like glass lips to swallow her. Then the sense of her on the other side of the glass and her large figure diminishing along the moving walkway suggested her danger and his guilt. He was – *could be* – risking Ros' life, and that was unforgivable –

But he needed information. Shelley would make no move against Sharmar because they were up at Oxford together! Sharmar was untouchable – he grimaced. His eminence was a matter of policy, and Cass – and even himself – had become an embarrassment.

Hyde sighed and stared at the ceiling, listening to the radio news in English and the newest atrocities in the Punjab and Kashmir. He was uncomfortable. Ros was flying into a war zone. The Pakistani army, the woman newsreader's voice informed him, was strengthening its positions along sections of the Cease-fire Line that amputated Indian Kashmir from what they referred to as Azad – free – Kashmir. Sharmar was on the news, of course, soothing and promising. The evening slid across the cracks in the ceiling as if investing a tumbled landscape viewed from a high satellite. A tiny lizard in search of insects followed the dusk across the ceiling.

He'd reentered the hotel without encountering surveillance. If the room had been searched, it had been expertly done. He felt unsettled, itchy to move on, find an even more anonymous hotel somewhere in the Chandni Chowk. But Ros and Cass weighed; restraining him like bonds. He needed to find Lal, the reporter for a scandalous radical rag, wherever he had gone. He was not at home – but his family didn't behave as if he'd been arrested. He'd hovered near the house on his way from the airport. It wasn't under surveillance – didn't *they* know about Lal? A young woman in traditional dress and an incongruous knitted cardigan had left the house and returned with shopping. A child had played in front of the house. It was either a clever come-on, or it was innocent.

He had to get up to Srinagar and Ros soonest. It was a crazy imperative to have created.

He rolled off the bed and twisted the cap on the bottle of Evian water – the one with the French-applied seal that distinguished it from the fakes that induced immediate gut-ache. Sipped the tepid liquid. The travel bag was packed. The Midlands teacher was ready to leave, bill paid. He wandered to the window. There was no way *he* could get Cass out, unaided. It would require pressure, leverage. *We know you're a snowman, a horsebreaker, V.K. – sorry about it, but would you let our man out in exchange for our silence . . . ?* In exchange for *mine*, Shelley. *This chap Hyde threatens to tell the papers if you don't let our chap go . . .*

Hyde grinned and watched the changing of the guard in the hot, crowded, inkily-shadowed street below. His phone call to the rag Lal worked on had produced a *Mr Lal is on holiday* response which was almost certainly untrue. Another phone call had proven it was. A woman's nervous answers, abruptly ended. Lal was on the run, or in hiding. Tonight, he'd make certain.

There they go. Even the surveillance men seemed animated by an Indian courtesy towards one another as they changed duties . . . old team wandering off, new team more alert, selecting new shadows and doorways and innocent occupations. He watched the outgoing team slide away through the crowds –
– coming back. He raised the Evian bottle to his lips with slow, calming deliberation, even as he stepped slightly further to one side, out of sight but still able to monitor the street. The three men who had been watching the hotel had doubled back, reinforcing the new surveillance team. Six of them now –

He looked down at the sweatshirt he was wearing, as if to accuse it of ineffectuality. Its blazon for some real ale made in the Black Country had become a transparent mockery of a disguise, like the dirty trainers and the denims. He had been seen through. His forearm, tilting the bottle to his lips, was stringy with the muscular tension of his grip; the skin quivered as if on entering a cold store. His ears caught the first of the sirens and the men below him moved immediately. He'd be arrested and the inevitable drugs, or some unlicensed weapon, would be found in his baggage – anything to put him in the cell next to Cass for long enough to make the right decision about the burial plot.

He placed the bottle of water on the rickety table with exaggerated care. Pulled the gun from the travel bag, slid a round into the chamber, then tucked it into his waistband, pulling the sweatshirt loosely outside it. Returned for an instant to the window. The siren was muddy, its noise struggling through the crowd. There was one man left on the street. There'd be another at the rear of the hotel, perhaps two. The others would come bolting up the stairs and through the door of his room within –

Time to go.

There were two uniformed policemen in the evening street now, close to the surveillance man.

He opened the door of the room, slinging his travel bag to comfort on his shoulders. The corridor creaked with his steps and with heat and age. Noises of radios from rooms, like the radio he had left on in his own room; the murmur of conversations. He leant over the balcony. Swift, purposeful voices from the hotel desk. Only seconds now. The back exit through the kitchen was out. He returned to his own door, then moved to the end of the corridor and climbed the last rickety, twisted flight up to the attic rooms where the staff slept. Bare floors, paintwork all but vanished, the smell of a urinal despite the open skylight above the tiny-waisted passageway. He reached up. Low ceiling, low skylight. He gripped the wooden frame. The wood powdered and his fingers were gritty with old flaked paint. Just strong enough. He pulled himself up until his head was through the skylight and the evening struck as hot as the hotel passageway against his cheeks. He levered his body through the gap, pushing back the skylight, struggling like an exhausted swimmer on the shore of the sloping roof. His feet came through the opening and he clung to the wooden tiles, his chest thudding against the roof.

He crouched, and closed the skylight. Hardly the world's greatest bluff. Looked around him. Two big-eyed children were watching him, squatting beside a narrow cage in which pigeons chuckled. A goat munched some dry and yellow grass on the flat roof of an adjacent building. The low sun made him squint against its red glare. The occasional television aerial, the odd petrol-tin or cardboard shack erected on flat roofs to house relatives from the country, friends, dependants. Chickens being fed with corn scattered by a woman's hand which glowed with bangles in the sunset.

He reached the edge of the roof. He could cross other roofs, but it would be like moving through open country, and already the curiosity of the roof-dwellers was aroused because he was white. He looked down into a shadowy, noisome alley at the side of the hotel. A sacred cow wandered along it, defecating complacently. A cart with a broken wheel lay on its side, there was the smell of decaying fruit, rotting flesh, and a thin, nosing dog. And two forms slumped in boarded-up doorways which might be those of beggars. Or the dead.

Hyde lowered himself over the edge of the roof until his feet rested on a window ledge. He slid himself down, balanced against the weight of the rucksack, until he squatted on the windowsill like a tame monkey. The darkened room appeared empty. He lowered himself to the next storey, squatting again to regain his breath, then to the ground floor –

Lost patience in a surge of panic aroused by voices on the roof, and dropped the last eight or ten feet into the slither and stench of the alley's mud. He stumbled, righting himself against the bare breezeblock of an outside wall. The smells from the hotel kitchen –

– and then his temple recognised the impression of a gun barrel pressed against it as his neck cringed from the hot breath of the policeman whose triumph was a shiver that communicated itself to Hyde's body.

Cass looked up, slow even to be startled, as they entered his cell. The very last of the sunset was barred redly against the opposite wall. They had arranged themselves on either side of him before he could swing his legs off the cot and sit upright. Two of them in suits. There was no prison officer, no Jawal or any of the other faces with which he had become familiar. His mouth tried to form a protest, but that was difficult because they were almost deferential as they pushed his arms into those of his jacket – just like a couple of express tailors. Their grip on his arms as they marched him from the cell and then along unexpectedly deserted corridors was firm, unshakeable – yet weirdly polite.

He couldn't struggle against them, as if it would be bad manners, a social inelegance. Even though he knew they were removing him from prison on Sharmar's orders, and that those orders certainly, irrefutably, encompassed his murder and the disposal of his body.

Shot while trying to escape . . .

Had he hesitated for another moment after his body recognised the gun and the triumph of the man who held it, it would have been too late. Instead, his hand pushed the gun up and away the involuntary shot deafening him. His assailant hadn't turned his head away and his large brown eyes were blinking and unfocused. Hyde head-butted the man, and he staggered back, leaving the gun in Hyde's hand, his palm and fingers pained by the barrel's heat. As the Indian collapsed onto the ground, holding his broken nose, Hyde turned away without glancing up at the roof and the source of the cry of alarm, skittering along the alley. He turned into another, narrower backstreet where washing draped between the houses on either side as if to cover the embarrassment the filthy alley represented. Then, after another corner, he blundered into a crowded, violently noisy street – and immediate obscurity. Safety.

Flame roared at a cooking stall, the scent of the food overpowering. He brushed against men, women, a progress of apologies amid the crowd's shallows and sandbars. The sky was blue-black above the awnings and verandahs. He glanced back occasionally, but no individual could have been distinguished in the veldt of faces, and the grass of the crowd did not sway or disrupt with the purposeful movement of a hunt.

Slowly, with increasing certainty, he made his way to the railway station. The porticoes of a temple confronted him after the narrow streets and the press of Paharganj. The square before the station seemed alien within the walls and courts and twisting streets of the old city. Something British-oriental. Above the railway station, the crescent moon already gleamed amid warm stars.

In the main concourse, he reached the left-luggage locker and opened it. He removed a travel bag, more affluent than the faded rucksack, and thrust the rucksack into the locker. The new set of papers, clothing, money – a second gun – were all contained in the travel bag with its fashionable logo. He was, he admitted with cynical amusement, about to go upmarket. He required a better sort of hotel, one out near the Interstate bus terminal – a room with air-conditioning and a TV, as befitted the name in the passport and the clothing in the bag. He looked around him, locating the cloakroom. Better change now and put the old clothes in the locker, and appear at his new hotel clean-shaven – what was the cover? Journalist?

The cloakroom was clean, the water that leaked into the basins slightly rust-stained but hot. He began shaving, the travel bag at his feet, the mirror clouding from the water, its temperature stilling, comfortable. Indians moved in and out with grace and humour; Westerners with hurry and purpose and slight but evident disdain, suspicion of the plumbing. A victim of gastro-enteritis groaned in a cubicle, cursing the country and its backwardness. Hyde grinned at the mirror. They tell you to bring the tablets, not to drink the water, no ice in your G and T –

He ducked his head and washed the remaining lather from his cheeks and throat. When he looked up, he realised they'd found him.

Expected him, rather. They knew enough to know that the SIS method had always been left-luggage lockers for guns, papers, changes of identity and clothing. Or Dickson or some other bastard at the High Commission had *supplied* the information – just for a laugh.

The man reflected in the mirror was tall for an Indian, lithe, well-balanced and at his ease. Hyde continued to lave his face with the soapy water in the washbasin, watching him from beneath half-closed lids. Through the slight misting of the mirror, he seemed prepared to wait; confident. He was reading a copy of the *Illustrated Weekly of India* with apparent interest. Nothing was overstated.

The gun would be in a shoulder-holster. He was right-handed as he lit a cigarette before returning to the magazine. There was the bulge of an R/T in his pocket. Its weight drew the jacket down over the bulky silhouette of the holster. He'd have summoned assistance. Slowly, carrying the travel bag, Hyde crossed to the row of roller-towel cabinets on the far wall; tugged down the towel and wiped his face carefully, methodically. They must have Cass already – maybe they'd even done him in? Not necessarily. Taking him into their own custody would do for the moment. They might want to know what he'd told Hyde, whether Hyde might be believed, not quite trusting the Old University tie. But these boys were quick and they were good.

They would be – they were working for the bloody Prime Minister of India.

He'd have to make a move for the door. The Indian was waiting for assistance but ready to act. He wouldn't let him run.

Hyde finished drying his face, sniffing loudly. He picked up the travel bag and wandered as innocently as he could to the door. The Indian carefully folded the magazine and laid it on a chair beside him. His hand began moving towards the inside of his jacket, as if reaching for a wallet or comb. The travel bag drew level with the man, feeling like a dog straining at the leash in Hyde's hands. Then the bag leapt at the man's groin, making him wince, expel breath, making his hand hesitate, want to move to the area of the sudden pain – for long enough. Hyde hit the Indian across the throat with the flat of his hand to silence any cry. Hit him twice in the stomach with quick jabs, then once to the side of the head as he doubled up. Before the first raised voice of alarm or protest, he had vanished through the door into the main concourse, his eyes ferreting in the crowd for recognition, gestures, movements, for R/Ts clamped to cheeks like poultices, for guns.

Nothing — not yet. He hurried between bookstalls, food vendors, the detritus of beggars and passengers returning to the countryside and the tourists debouching into the deceptive familiarity of the station. He glanced back once. A railway official was entering the cloakroom, but there was no crowd yet, and no security men or police thrusting their way through the gawpers.

The night air was as warm as a cloak, making him sweat at once. He must go to ground. Dump the travel bag, get another one, then find a better class of hotel —

But they were good and they were quick and they knew exactly who he was and why he was in Delhi . . . and they doubtless knew he was on his own, without legitimacy. Killing him wouldn't cause a ripple, never mind waves —

If Ros ignored the last sultry smoke from one of the fires started the previous night during a minor riot of Hindus through a Moslem shopping area, then Dal Lake was as beautiful as it had ever been when she was eighteen. The water was still and pearly beneath a slight mist that would burn off in no more than another ten minutes. The shikaras of traders slipped in and out of the mist, startling the occasional duck into flight from clumps of reeds. The mist magnified the songs and murmurs of other birds. Last night's rain pearled in droplets along the carved roof of the verandah at the front of the houseboat. There was, as yet, no scent in the early morning that was not sweet. Breakfast was not yet cooking and the woodsmoke from the boiler had nothing to do with human beings, belonging instead to the scene and to memory.

The early '70s. Her youth. Pot and idleness and sex . . . before she became the fat white woman. She had spent almost three years, on and off, in Srinagar and other, more remote bits of Kashmir. Without a single regret. Recalling her father's unyielding hatred of what she — pretended? — to have become and his apoplexy at her wasting her dead mother's money . . . Now, even all that was long gone. She did not need marijuana or anything else to clear her head of her father, as she had in those long-gone days. Pot, idleness, sex – she smiled cleanly for a moment before the nerves returned at the thought of him. She must recommend it to Hyde . . . but she had hardly completed the thought, when she remembered what she was here to do –

– and Sara Mallowby had just appeared at the square, roofed front of her own houseboat, thirty yards of water away. The woman stood with casual, inbred elegance, slightly pigeon-toed. She saw Ros and waved. Ros returned the gesture as Sara Mallowby called, clear as any of the birds or vendors:

'Good morning. Sleep well?'

'Yes, thanks,' Ros replied, clearing her throat.

The muezzin calling the faithful to prayer . . . in *Hyde's* mosque, where *all* the worshippers were to be regarded with suspicion. It was as if the lake, the hills surrounding it just emerging from the mist and the mountains climbing beyond, all vanished. The illusion that had been herself at eighteen vanished too. She hadn't ever really escaped into Kashmir from Melbourne. She had still had to confront her father and quarrel so violently with him that the next time she had seen him his face was staring sightlessly up at her after the embalmer's work. Nothing she had ever said had touched him. She had always been the *disappointment* registered in her father's hard, forensic glance.

Hyde's work. She stood up. She had the houseboat to herself because it was early in the season, *and anyway*, as Sara Mallowby had explained as they had struggled her suitcases across the causeway to the houseboat in the wobbling light of the English-woman's torch the previous night, *I'll be lucky to see any return this year – people won't come to a war zone, will they?*

Am I doing this because I'm still grateful to Hyde for noticing me? she had wondered, crossing the little causeway behind Sara Mallowby. Because he made me not as plain as Dad always remarked? She brushed the thought aside. Hyde wanted to know about the woman –

– who moved with leggy grace along the shore from her own causeway to the one connecting Ros' houseboat to Srinagar. Behind the boat, the moored cookboat was active and the boy was padding along the catwalk, tugging down the awnings against the sunlight now leaping like a tiger across the lake, so that great claws of gold appeared on the water, having thrust through the remnants of the mist. Sara Mallowby's low shoes clicked on the planking of the houseboat. Ros took off the shawl – reminder of cool nights in Kashmir and a former life – and went through the sitting room and the narrow passageway between the bedrooms to encounter her.

Sara's hand flicked through her long hair, brushing its gold away from her face. The sun caught it for a moment, illuminating it like fire catching at straw. Ros envied her carriage, her waistline – her sophistication. Sara reduced her to her father's dumpy, plain daughter in a silent moment, even though the Englishwoman was engaged in a burst of orders and repartee with the cook and his wife. Then, consciously remembering her role, she allowed Ros to precede her back to the verandah and the noise of the lake lapping against its wooden steps. Even so, Sara sat first, crossing her legs, brushing her hair once more away from her fine cheekbones, smoothing her full skirt. *Memsahib*, Ros thought, her guilt making her vindictive rather than merely envious.

'Good – I'm glad you slept. I think it's for early mornings like this I *live* –! But you – you said you'd lived on a houseboat on Dal before?'

Sara Mallowby watched the fat Australian woman as she nodded in reply. Her face was moonlike – gentle but plain, like so many women in middle-age. She was the pretty girl's fat friend and flattering mirror at school. Sara stretched.

'You mentioned you knew Srinagar. Last night, when you arrived –?' she said.

The Australian woman nodded again, her gaze roaming beyond the houseboat, over Dal Lake and the mountains and temples and great clumps of reeds and water-lilies.

'A long time ago.' The woman seemed displaced, uncertain now that she had returned to somewhere that might have only ever existed in her imagination – or youth, which was much the same species of illusion. There had been hundreds of Australians, English and Americans in Kashmir, cluttering Srinagar and the lake and the villages and towns or scattered like ash over the hills, back in the late '70s when Sara herself had first come. This woman had been fleeing – what? Her plainness, the unbelievable dullness of most of Australia? 'I stayed, off and on, for almost three years. My misspent youth . . .' The woman's smile was striking; warm, almost beatific. Beneath the moon face and the extra stones in weight badly concealed by the loose, flowing frock, the woman was either currently happy or had at least recently known happiness.

'Didn't we all,' Sara replied drily, a sting of dislike evident like a slight headache. 'Old times –' Her sigh quavered and fell below the genuine, becoming a false note. The woman seemed not to remark it.

Old times. Perhaps it had been a better place when the litter of hippies still lay in the streets and on the lake's margins. Better that than the increasingly stifling Moslem atmosphere of the Kashmir that hated, and was hated by, the central government . . .

. . . better than V.K.'s schemes and stratagems for a different India.

Better than seeing the broken and bloodstained bodies after the atrocities of each night – which V.K. allowed, by restraints on the army and his strategic contacts with Kashmiri separatist groups. Because greater and greater turbulence made Kashmir ungovernable and thus easier to let go when the time came. She rubbed her forehead. It was information she now hated being privy to; there was no lingering glamour of the covert, of the emanated power of the men who met on her houseboat. Conspiracy had become an exercise in sense-deprivation; the technique of an interrogator. It maddened her. Why else would she feel so eager to talk to this fat woman from London, seeking obliquely for news of a place she loathed, a country she had abandoned almost twenty years before? *Old times.*

Bloody V.K. had arranged another of his damned meetings with the Pakistani generals and the Sikh and Kashmiri leaders for that weekend –! To plan, arrange, decide – to caution and control. Only *so* much violence, only *so* many dead. Cold, brutal and clever. As clever as the drugs that founded the family fortune of the Sharmars and helped control the separatists. High-risk strategy – *in which I don't believe any more* –! *Cri de coeur*, darling, she told herself at once. Too late for that much honesty.

'It used to be a much more relaxed place,' she observed. 'And more peaceful.' The latter bitterly.

'I almost cancelled,' Ros said. 'Didn't even want to come as far as Delhi, then I thought, what the hell –?' She shrugged. 'I suppose I didn't really believe it. Is it that bad now?'

Sara pointed towards the smoke, which had begun to flatten like stretched grey cloth on the morning breeze.

'Last night wasn't too bad. But you noticed the soldiers at the airport?' Ros nodded. The woman seemed to be wandering in a landscape of the past on which the contemporary hardly impinged. That must be why she had continued her journey; these events were only as real as newspaper reports. 'We haven't had any trouble here. But there's only you on this boat and a couple of elderly Americans now on that one – there, the pink and green one. The others left yesterday.'

'How many boats do you own?'

'Four – oh, and my own, of course.'

'You fell in love with the place, too?'

Sara almost wrinkled her face, as if at an odour or the touch of something slippery. Then felt appalled that she had dismissed her own past so easily. 'Yes,' she replied as if in a foreign language, 'I suppose I did.'

The cookboy appeared in the doorway onto the verandah, the

day's menus in his hand as innocent as his smile. Sara said, before he could speak:

'We'll have the French breakfast, Hamdi,' hardly glancing across for Ros' acquiescence. 'Tell your father *not* to overheat the croissants and not to burn the toast. Coffee?' she aimed at Ros, who nodded at the English word amid the evidently incomprehensible Hindi. The cookboy nodded gravely, then vanished beyond the curtain. Pots rattled only moments later signalling comprehension of her orders.

'You evidently did – fall in love with Kashmir, I mean?'

Again, the woman nodded. It was as if she were visibly regressing to awkward adolescence before Sara's gaze. She was leaning gauchely forward, big hands clasped together on her knees, attaching herself through a sense of inferiority and her own plainness to someone more languid and assured.

Ros watched the woman watching her. It was so bloody *easy* to play the part expected of her – plain, dull, naive, mawkish. Sara Mallowby appeared entirely satisfied that she *knew* her and, in knowing, could afford to dismiss her. There was no mote of suspicion in her eyes.

The woman was tense, resentful, and bored. The voice, beneath the clipped drawl, was quavering and uncertain, like voices Ros had heard before, on the Samaritans' line she periodically manned. Like many voices on that line, except the few who had already abandoned all forms of self-deception and defence, it betrayed a person lumbering around a darkened, enclosed space filled with alien furniture, where nothing was familiar. The woman was already worn and eroded behind habit and manner. None of which Hyde would have noticed, of course.

'How was London when you left?' Sara Mallowby enquired as she leant back in the wicker chair, which creaked gently like the small noises of the houseboat against the water.

'Sticky and full of tourists. Do you ever go back?'

She shook her head. 'Not for years. I prefer New York if I

must have the manmade – or Delhi at the right time of year. Sometimes Tokyo.'

'At times I wonder why I still live in London – what with this here.' A faint police siren sounded above the voices of hawkers in shikaras which made finlike trails on the lake. The siren gradually faded. Ros shivered. 'You know what I mean –'

'Yes, I suppose so.'

The breakfast arrived, served by the cookboy and his father. For the memsahib, Ros thought, the proprietor; Sharmar's mistress, hawsered and roped to the shore of Dal Lake as certainly as her houseboats, and as rudderless as they were. A kingfisher flashed in the rising sun. Sara Mallowby's eyes were caught and held by it as if by some imagined alternative, or even a dream. Ros carefully pretended not to notice the swift, dismissive shake of the Englishwoman's head, then the rough brush of her hand sweeping her hair back. Recomposed, she seemed to stare out from above her high cheekbones as if over some fortress wall. The chains mooring the houseboats to the shore of the lake glittered. The roof of the Hazratbal Mosque gleamed against the backdrop of the mountains.

Ros picked up a small plate, helped herself to a croissant. The cook poured the coffee.

'London must have changed a lot – tell me,' Ros heard Sara murmur. She wiped a flake of croissant from the corner of her mouth before replying. One could begin to sympathise with her –

– and Hyde had said, *Watch out for that. That's like pointing a gun at yourself* . . .

So she smiled as mawkishly as she could manage.

Lal's house, of which the first and second storeys were let out to relatives and assorted tenants, was on Desh Bandhu Gupta Road, north of Main Bazaar in Paharganj. Less than half a mile from the railway station, the point at which the stone of his assault on the Intelligence agent had created the ripples of the search for him. He had found a middle-priced hotel on Ashoka

Road, ten minutes from Connaught Place, booked in, tried to rest – not easy – staring at the bruise spreading on the flat of his hand. He had had to get up from the bed and scout Lal's house twice during the night – an incontinence for action. There were police cars threading the streets, foot patrols, other cars with greater purpose than homegoing or early appointments. No one had stopped him. He was a man in a fashionably shapeless summer suit, loose tie, clear-glass spectacles. A respectable Westerner.

Now, as dawn streaked the sky above the street with pink clouds, delicately coloured and trimmed with orange and gold as roses might have been, he was opposite Lal's narrow house once more. It was imprisoned between a rambling guest house and a tiny mosque. The refuse cart was grinding its jaws outside the guest house and the traffic was already thickening and darkening the air. Further along the road, tapes and the first crowd of the day enclosed the filming of some rubbishy Indian cops-and-robbers movie, screeching cars racing each other along Desh Bhandu and down into Main Bazaar. Hyde had wandered past the filming and the applauding crowd, as he approached Lal's house. It had the necessary earnestness of all movie productions everywhere in the world, and the same unnecessary result.

He had phoned again, in another voice. Lal was not at home, he was *away on assignment*. To his newspaper, he was *on holiday* still.

Then there was the other phone call he had made, before he had picked up the early edition of the *Times of India* and read of Cass' escape from custody. The phone call had resulted in demands as to his identity, a regimented secrecy which had disturbed Hyde. The newspaper had been explicit. *Murderer of Sereena Sharmar escapes*, bellowed the front page. The photograph of Cass – a bad one – had been minuscule by comparison with the glamour shot of the dead film actress. There had been a statement by V. K. Sharmar, and assurances from the Chief of Police. Prison officers were being disciplined for their abominable laxity with regard to a dangerous criminal. Cass' persona was established. When his dead body – drowned, suicide, otherwise discovered – turned up, the case would automatically be closed.

The article was designed to tell him – *him* before the rest of humanity – that it was too late, that Cass had been rendered unreachable. Then to tell Shelley, as a friendly warning and confirmation of his worst nightmare, that Cass *had* done it . . . then to tell India so that there was nowhere Cass could go or be safe.

While they got rid of him.

But they'd want to know – wouldn't they? – what Hyde knew, what Cass had communicated, why Hyde was there, if he'd been sent by Shelley . . . before they killed him? And, if that was to be prevented, then Lal – bloody vanished Lal – would have to come out of the woodwork. Hence, the *urgency*. He'd rung Ros late the previous evening to give her the new hotel number, the new name. She hadn't made contact with the woman, apart from signing the bloody register – he'd checked.

The sky lightened to a washed-out blue, and became less distinct, as the sun dropped heavily into Desh Bandhu. Window blinds had long opened like mouths in the façade of Lal's house and the pavements were already crowded. Lal and his extended family lived on the ground and first-floor front. Faces at the windows, the activity of women. He had asked at a shop on this side of the street, the grocer Lal's wife used. *Yes, Lal's mother, her mother, an aunt, three children, a grandfather* . . . and then the other residents, including a solitary white man who was regarded with tolerant contempt by the shopkeeper. One of those whose head had died years before, courtesy of some permanent drug trip, but who still shambled between the house, the nearest cinema, a bar, and the local mosque, having exchanged an adopted Buddhism for the certainties of the Prophet.

It was after eight when Lal's wife emerged from the house in a violent green and gold sari and a flash of arm jewellery, and turned west along Desh Bandhu. The grocer's description was close enough for Hyde to casually unfurl himself from the wall against which he was leaning. *Haven't seen Lal for years . . . used to work with him before I got transferred back to London. Heard he lived around here . . .*

The same cover would suffice for the wife. He moved like a matador through the traffic to the other side of the street, forty yards or so behind her. Lata. Hyde quickened his pace to overtake her.

The woman paused outside a shop selling locally made clothes. She seemed intent upon men's shirts, and her attention was a small betrayal. Hyde arrived at her side – and startled her, even though he appeared, deliberately, as no more than another window-shopper. She stared wide-eyed into his face. The phone calls enquiring about Lal – the newspaper report of Cass' escape? He closed his hand on her slim, bangled wrist.

'Lata – it is Lata, Lal's wife? I *remember* –!' The little charade was boring and pointless, but necessary to prevent her inviting attention and suspicion from people around her. Did she speak English?

'Yes,' the woman fumbled. 'I do not know you – sir.' It was dropped at the end of the protestation like a curtsey, a racial memory.

'Dave – Dave Holland. No? It's been a long time. We only met briefly . . . I used to work with Lal. Got sent back to London – now out here again. Came to look him up, thought I knew you, you haven't changed –!' Her suspicions remained, but he was now a nuisance, someone who had blundered on a secret, who might cause embarrassment. Good – she knew where Lal was. 'You don't remember me at all, do you? Be honest with me –' His smile was at its most ingratiating. The last vestiges of suspicion disappeared from her fine-boned features, from the huge brown eyes. She shook her head, intending a smile that did not quite break through a small cloud of nerves.

'Mr – Holland? I am so sorry, Mr Holland, but I do not remember. You worked with Lal?'

'Yes, years ago, Before he got onto *Conscience of Delhi* . . . in fact, I was hoping we might work together again. Generous expenses, you know. I could do with local help, you understand? When could I meet him? Is he at home now?'

She glanced fearfully back along Desh Bandhu, shaking her head vigorously. His smile continued, inappropriate and necessary in the atmosphere she had so changed. He was still holding her slim wrist, and sensed the quiver of her arm.

'No, no – he is away, on an assignment. I – he cannot be reached, I am sorry . . .'

'Oh. When will he be back, do you know?'

'He did not say. I will tell him, when he returns. Perhaps you have a telephone number, Mr Holland – ?'

She had remembered the lessons Lal must have drummed into her.

Hyde shrugged reluctantly.

'I suppose so. Don't let him leave it too long. Soon as he gets back – '

'Yes, yes,' she replied urgently, as if she was late for an appointment. Hyde stilled the tremor in his fingers. After a moment, he released her wrist. She snatched her arm away, then her body almost at once, to continue her journey. Then she looked back, nodding. 'Yes, I will tell him, Mr Holland, I will tell him.'

Hyde watched her go, then turned away and slowly crossed the road. She glanced back a number of times, on each occasion more satisfied that he presented no danger. Eventually, she hurried on, oblivious once more.

By that time, Hyde was tailing her on the opposite side of Desh Bandhu, moving coolly, assuredly, through the crowd, weaving between stalls and barrows and sacred cows and ill-parked cars. He was certain that she was on her way to Lal, dragging him unsuspectingly behind.

*

Ros disliked the manner in which she felt she must be imitating Hyde — or, perhaps, the manner in which she was no longer Sara Mallowby's Samaritan at the end of a telephone line replete with intimacies. She was actually spying on the woman. Spying . . . Hyde always referred to himself as an *agent*. She was not an agent, there was no pay cheque and pension scheme to alleviate the sense of unpleasantness and intrusion she experienced, as she trailed the market streets of Srinagar with the Englishwoman.

Especially since she had begun to notice . . .

Sara Mallowby was supervising the purchase of supplies for her four houseboats, for the coming weekend. There was, firstly, the amount, then the selection or variety, and finally the Moslem element. An Urdu-speaking woman accompanied them, together with a Hindu male who seemed to be some kind of head chef and who resented the woman's presence, even though he deferred to Ros as a paying memsahib. A tight flowered cap on her head and a loose, long cotton blouse, her trousers tied at the ankles, the woman was evidently Moslem, passing brightly against the brick and wood of the houses in the narrow streets. Ros knew enough to recognise Urdu — and halal meat ordered at one shop where the butcher's wife wore the full black burka to conceal her form and a chador scarf over her head. Ros had glimpsed her passing across an open doorway at the back of the shop. But the colour of the meat, the language of the customers, were both omnipresent. Was Sara Mallowby expecting strict Moslems, a group of them?

The air was sultry, like a hangover of the retreated monsoon. The narrow streets pressed their crowds against her, and there was a smell of old burning in the atmosphere and a fear of more fires to come. They had passed a patch of dried blood around which insects vainly noised at the corner of the street in which Sara now argued, through the Moslem woman, with the halal butcher. She was evidently known, and respected — the butcher was enjoying the haggling, the selection of meat, the attendance

112

to the ceremonies of slaughter. Ros caught the scent of slow-leaked blood – or an image of it in her mind – and pressed her hand against her lips, swallowing hard. She wanted to distract herself from her thoughts at a papier-mâché artist's shop across the street, but remained obedient to Hyde's strictures. Ingratiation and observation would sum them up. As a compromise, she stared out of the window of the shop, vaguely seeing a grain dealer's sacks beneath broken window-frames and the scorching of fire across the whitewashed brick of the building. Then a woman in spotted robe and headdress squatting outside a greengrocery with a huge basket of carp from the lake.

Eventually, Sara Mallowby had finished with the butcher and, smiling apologetically, guided Ros back into the noise and smells of the street. Which still hemmed her in like thoughts of Hyde and what she was engaged upon. *Pakistani generals,* Hyde had said, repeating Cass' information. *Strict Moslems.*

But it was the amount of meat and vegetables, fish and fruit, that was being ordered when business was slack and no one else occupied the houseboats except herself and the elderly Americans . . . and the *dislike* she felt at the ease with which suspicion came! She smiled disarmingly at Sara as they paused outside a greengrocer's. A rickshaw loaded with produce brushed past them, heavy as a wagon. Srinagar was laden with odours, depressing her. Making her guilt seem enormous. She shook her head, puzzling Sara, but not inviting suspicion. It wasn't the bloody Samaritans, she admitted. Hyde said Cass had been framed, he was in danger – and she had bloody *agreed* to act as Hyde's bookie's runner until he could get here himself! Oh, Hyde, you bugger, you'd better not have thought of me as just the *bloke* for the job –

'Yes,' she murmured, admiring papier-mâché vases and dishes in a greasy shop window as Sara pointed them out. She manned a telephone at the Samaritans, she helped at an animal rescue centre, she had joined Amnesty International, she wrote letters when she couldn't march or protest in person – and all of it was because she was an optimist who didn't really believe in human wickedness! Hyde had accused her of that, and now it stabbed like indigestion, created by her suspicion of Sara and a gaping hole where a shop had been bombed days before. Flies around a dead dog which no one had bothered to remove, its body broken by the blast. 'Yes . . .' she repeated, so that Sara Mallowby glanced narrowly at her. 'Sorry . . . headache,' she explained weakly.

She *was* naive – at least, not a cynic. That was the problem. They turned into a broader street with cleaner, well-lighted shops. The cloudy noon pressed down on the street, but not as formidably as in the narrow gash of the town they had just left. She wanted to help, the world was redeemable . . . unlike Hyde's world, which was peopled by enemies rather than fellow creatures. That was what she hated about his work – and what she was now asked to do. To pounce upon impressions as if they were facts, to interpret moments as if they were God-given and set in stone; to condemn people on a glance or whisper or facial tic.

It would have been so easy, of course, to have dismissed everything Hyde wanted and suspected – and deal only with Sara's upper-middle-class patronage and uneasy compromise with Srinagar – if it was not for the two men. The one outside the greengrocer's as she had looked from the window of the butcher's shop, near the woman with the basket of carp; and the other paused against an old scorching on a whitewashed wall, his head and shoulders darkly haloed by the mark of the fire. Both men had fallen in behind them soon after they had walked the causeway from Sara's houseboat and had trailed fifty yards behind along a new street of lakeside shops deserted of tourists. Sara had promised souvenir shops, but had concentrated slavishly on groceries and meat. But that hadn't been the problem, even though she recognised she had tried to make it such. The problem had been the two men.

They followed, paused, began again in rhythm with the shopping expedition. And they were tall, hook-nosed, suited. Dark-eyed, arrogant. She was afraid to ascribe a country of origin, but could not but think of Pakistan once they were ensconced in the Moslem butcher's shop. And then could not forget the fanciful identification. The men were watching them, but seemed to be their bodyguards. And so Hyde's world closed over her like water, and she was drowning in suspicion and twitchy nerves and tension. The men were still behind them as they avoided donkey carts and rickshaws and fume-belching buses in one of the main shopping streets. Halal-bled carcases in one window, Benetton sweaters in the one next to it; perfumes and spices, Amex symbols and Urdu. She glanced back from a pause outside a leather shop, where made-to-measure suede coats were being offered at 500 rupees and shoes at less. Italian advertisements induced. Get your genuine copy here . . . The men had stopped, one of them smoking a cigarette, the other unfolding a newspaper, perhaps forty yards behind them. There was little effort at concealment, no effort at disguise. She turned, suddenly, to Sara –

– whose eyes were looking beyond Ros, back towards the men. Her eyes narrowed for a moment, then she relaxed. *Fat, dim woman.* Ros had been dismissed.

But Sara knew the men were there – *expected* them to be there.

'The quality never used to be very good,' Ros offered, nodding at the leather shop's window and displayed goods. 'Fell off your back or your feet in the first cold snap – is it any better now?'

Sara laughed exaggeratedly, also shaking her head.

'Not often. If you're serious, I can get something *good* made – but not here.' She moved away, and Ros followed dutifully.

The street opened ahead of them, and there was a glimpse of mountains, and of the lake carved into a slice by the buildings at the end of the street; a wedge of still, gleaming cake rather

115

than water. Then the street closed about them, quivering as if in a heat haze, before beginning to crumble and bulge outwards. The two buildings had begun to collapse into the street as the pressure wave and the first flying glass struck against them and they still hadn't heard the noise of the explosion –

reportage

Lal's wife glided past the tiny mosque and entered her house. From the opposite side of Desh Bhandu, Hyde watched her disappear through the narrow doorway, then glimpsed her pass across one of the windows a few moments later. She paused and bent to kiss an old woman who was presumably either her mother or Lal's. Then the bright sari flitted from the window. The early afternoon sun was like a pressing hand in the busy street and the petrol fumes stirred in the light, hot breeze as visibly as a mist.

Hyde had lost Lata Lal in the lunchtime crowds, in a narrow, twisting street near Chandni Chowk. The Fatehpuri Mosque had glowered down on his frustration, and a cinema's blazons and queue had mocked him. The woman could *not* have suspected she was being followed, it had to have been an accident. Whatever, the result had been the same – she had eluded him when, he was sure, she was close to Lal's hideout. Cars passed, ancient Hindustan Ambassadors looking like old Morris Oxfords, belching fumes, horns continually irritated against inevitable delay. The occasional Mercedes or other imported car, old buses jammed with passengers, bullock carts and rickshaws clotting at the slightest obstacle or opportunity. The waving of arms was a semaphore of distress and anger; part of the ritual of driving in Delhi. Hyde bit into the last of the samosas, savouring the curried vegetables in their pastry triangle. He'd bought them from the cookstall ten yards beyond the alley corner where he had taken up his loungeing surveillance, awaiting the wife's return.

His hotel had been checked. His cover passport had been taken away by the police for examination, so the desk clerk had informed him. It wasn't worrying – the passport would withstand any examination, and besides he had a second should he need to use it – but it meant that the search for him had been stepped up, had become urgent; while he was no nearer Lal then he had been that morning.

He wiped his mouth on a paper napkin and deposited the paper plate in an overflowing bin, then moved further along Desh Bhandu. There was no surveillance of the house, so far as he could tell, but the torpor of the early afternoon heat was twitchy with his nerves. He slid around a legless beggar, dropping some rupee coins into his bowl; they rattled ominously, like the first drops of a thunderstorm's rain on a corrugated roof. The situation was too open, too unprotected. He needed to talk to Shelley, even though he knew the pointlessness of such a conversation. Shelley would, in all probability, have swallowed the official story and order him out of Delhi – all expenses paid.

In the midday edition of one of the English language papers, he saw his own photograph – the passport photograph of the scruffy, anonymous man who had posed as Cass' Midlands cousin. Suspected drug smuggler. Rich that, coming from V. K. Sharmar and his brother. He passed a newspaper vendor. Sharmar stared at him from the front page of a Congress-allied evening paper, his expression slightly surprised, as if he had recognised Hyde as he passed. The same photograph, with an English headline, struck him so much that he paused. Sharmar – a reported speech. *We are a nation of entrepreneurs held down by our outdated nationalised industries and institutions* . . . the state banks, the state businesses. *Other parties represent the past – Congress is the future.* Go for it, sport. The big lie. Maybe the bastard even meant it –

– and if he did, then his own life, that of Cass, Ros' safety . . . all meant *bugger all*. Because the apostate who wanted to get back into the church was ruthless with his past and anyone who lived as a reminder of it. Sharmar had made a fortune in a not very nice but certainly not unusual manner, for India and Pakistan, but now it was a loose cannon on the deck which could crush him against the hull of his own ambition.

Fanciful . . . he already knew his life wasn't worth a damn, so why fill in the background?

He drifted back towards the Lal house. Would the woman see her husband again today – even tomorrow? How long could he hang about? How long before Sharmar, his brother or one of the police or intelligence high-ups they controlled stumbled on Lal's name – a snapshot of Lal with Cass, the recollection of some copper keeping an eye on the radical rag and its employees who remembered an Englishman . . . ? The Lal house's shutters were being closed by the old woman, who threatened to burst from her sari and obligatory, alien cardigan. The shuttered façade seemed final, and pricked memory concerning Ros. He was wasting his time in Delhi and he'd placed her in probable danger. He looked at his watch. Nearly two. He'd give it until evening. That night he had to be on a plane to Srinagar –

Headlines against the wall behind the news-stand, surrounding the grizzled, lined features of the seller. *Bombs in Kashmir, rioting in Srinagar*. The possible price might, at any moment, become too exorbitant. You pillock, sending her up there . . .

He must ring Shelley – get some action –

It was settled, agreed. That much was obvious to Prakesh Sharmar as his brother emerged from the party caucus, waving the draft manifesto for the election like a flag. In V.K.'s walk there was the strut of success and the sweep of ideas communicated. And a gleam of distance in his eyes as he saw Prakesh – who turned aside at once from the Intelligence colonel to move towards his brother. The manifesto would be titled *Golden Bridge*, the path to the next century. It was indeed grandiose, but necessary.

'It went well?' Prakesh murmured, his concerns with the

colonel remaining uppermost. Behind V.K., the senior Congress party members were filing out of the Cabinet Room. Prakesh checked their expressions as if calling their names and their futures. They were persuaded, even enthusiastic. The meeting had gone *very* well. 'Good, good –'

V.K. was looking over his shoulder, as at a small cloud on the horizon. His firmament had expanded and he filled it like a visiting god, Prakesh realised. He was seized by his own ideals, by a sudden, urgent purpose of good works, of *change* and the incessant business of government.

In less than an hour, V.K. had a meeting with senior representatives of the IMF, to attempt to unfreeze the next structural adjustment loan of perhaps three billion dollars. V.K. would be arguing, together with the young, clever economic advisers they had gathered into their fold, that their indebtedness was a better risk than the horrendously large debts of every country in South America and many in Africa. The loans would come – especially since the manifesto offered entrepreneurialism, privatisation, the setting free of the economy and measures against endemic corruption –

– and *there* was V.K.'s sudden distaste for his brother and for the Intelligence colonel who had drifted to a corner of the anteroom. Endemic corruption. The legacy of the family fortune. The expansion of their father's little plots of poppies designed to make their fortune. How else might a middle-caste, middle-income Kashmiri become Prime Minister of India? The Nehru dynasty had been Kashmiri, but they had had money – and the Sharmars would have remained farmers and clerks forever, without the heroin. Nehru had been a *pandit*, an intellectual, educated. Only money could have placed V.K. where he now was and would be – perhaps – for the next decade . . . and their only resource, their *cash crop*, had been the heroin poppy.

Which was now so inconvenient!

Prakesh shook hands with passing caucus members, his enthusiasm imitating their own. Firm gripping of hands, nodding, the few enthusiastic clichés, the assurance of success. V.K. adopted a more backslapping style, but the hand was laid upon the shoulderblades more as a form of blessing, Prakesh noted, than had formerly been the case. V.K. had grown into his role, but now the past threatened like insects at a broken screen, poised to invade his new and future kingdom.

Then the room was empty, except for himself and his brother and the colonel. As if the man's presence stung him, V.K. burst out:

'It could all end in ruin, Prakesh!' *Mea culpa*, as Catholic priests, with whom both of them had had some contact when school-boys, would have claimed. V.K.'s hands made a putting-behind gesture, the putting-away of the past.

'It will not, V.K. – it will not,' he soothed.

'Has this man been found?' Sharmar hissed, taking his brother to the window so that they looked along Raj Path together towards the India Gate; the perspective of power.

'No, V.K. – it is only a matter of time.'

'Has he gone to Srinagar – Cass was in Srinagar!'

'No, he has not gone to Srinagar. Our people are in place, there are more than usual precautions at the houseboats –'

'I wish I did not have to go –!'

'You must, V.K. You must continue to deal with these people . . . no, not just in the old way, but the violence must be con-trolled. Only *you* can ensure that there is just sufficient violence and not too much.' Prakesh squeezed at the expensive shoulder of his brother's suit. 'This is a small matter, V.K. It is being *handled.*'

Sharmar looked into Prakesh's eyes quizzically, and Prakesh despised the weakness he saw in them. He masked his reaction as he murmured:

'The man Lal is still in Delhi. We have someone at that rag he worked for. If Hyde approaches the newspaper, he will be found. Lal's house has been watched. Hyde has not appeared there – as yet. As to – the family *business*, V.K., how could you be in a

121

position to lead the country into the next century, without it? We were not the Nehrus. We had to have money. There was only *that* way –'

'That damned woman! Why did Sereena ever get herself involved with Cass?'

'She was a whore when you married her, V.K. – for the sake of your political career . . .' His brother flinched under the quiet whip of words, then subsided into nodding. 'As you were rid of her, you will be rid of this man Hyde. You *are* the PM, V.K. – unreachable now. *You* do the work you must do – I will do the rest of it.' He sighed theatrically, holding his brother's sleeve.

'Yes, yes. The Pakistani generals are necessary. They must hold back at the Ceasefire Line while Kashmir goes into decline – they must prevent the hotheads in Islamabad from taking advantage. Yes, I must go up to Srinagar and placate them over again.' He leaned forward fiercely. 'But, the drugs, Prakesh –! If anyone found out, I would have to resign. Not just the fundamentalists – the West, America, the IMF and the World Bank. The moral tones in which they would condemn me!'

'Be damned to them, V.K.! I am your brother. We are family. Do you think I would let this happen now?' Sharmar seemed reassured, stiffened – just like a straw doll, Prakesh thought, with a metal rod thrust into it in place of a backbone. 'The manifesto is agreed. You call the election next week, surprising the other parties and that damned film star who is your only rival. I *know* the stakes are the highest, V.K. No one knows that better than myself. Except you.'

'Thank you, Prakesh. But what did Cass tell this British agent?' He smiled disarmingly. 'Just this *last* question,' he added.

'So far, we have got nothing out of Cass. But it won't be long. The prison officer who was present is frightened enough to be telling the truth. He says nothing was said, nothing was passed –'

'Then I won't worry.' V. K. Sharmar looked at his watch, consciously ignoring the retreated presence of the colonel.

Staring instead along the broad Raj Path, scanning the offices of government. 'Better bring in our experts!' he announced heartily, the past forgotten like a dream.

V.K., Prakesh observed, had awoken into his future. He was still in the present but winking in and out of it like a star, really existing in the time after the election; the remainder of the decade and beyond. 'You have no need to worry, V.K.'

They embraced briefly, and then Prakesh, nodding to the colonel that he must exit and wait until their conversation might be concluded, went to a set of doors leading to another anteroom. Prakesh thought of the *corridors of power*. But he knew that the real power was in *rooms*. The occupation of rooms by right, the coming into them as into an inheritance. That was power.

And power was also the colonel and his people, the ability to mobilise steam hammers to crack betel-nuts, to take a huge machinery under control to destroy mere mosquitoes. The man Hyde would be found, and anyone else who might, or might not, be a small obstacle to ownership of these rooms. Lal, for example; a smell from the drains, nothing more.

He smiled as he opened the double doors on the eager young faces of their economics team, some of whom all but bolted from their chairs to begin the changing of India. The slight danger, which periodically unnerved V.K., was to him, enjoyable. A spice. India was, above all, famed for its spices. His smile broadened, to welcome the new recruits into an inner circle.

As the young men filed past him and the colonel slipped into the room they had occupied and sat himself like patient machinery near a tall window, Prakesh Sharmar nodded to himself. V.K. could take on the great work, he would deal with the little problem. A couple, even a few, deaths –

– all that was required.

Ros stared at the gash along her left forearm in the same mood of disbelief as when she had come round in the devastated street. Now, hunched in a cane chair on the verandah of Sara

123

Mallowby's houseboat, there was further incredulity at the tall man's words, spoken in Urdu, and Sara's contemptuous, pained reply.

'The woman is – *nothing*. It is *not* important – do you understand me?'

He was one of the two men who had formed their bodyguard or prisoners' escort. The other had been blinded in one eye by flying glass. This one, standing between Ros and the afternoon light, his arms working like the blades of a windmill, was protecting –

– an area. Not people, just the place. Ros knew she was *the woman*; inconvenient, possibly dangerous. Then she caught *others*, and the respectful tone. Superiors. Others were coming, Ros was an object of suspicion. Beyond the carnage in the street, the moans of the injured and dying, it was Ros that concerned the tall Pakistani.

A doctor wound a careful bandage around the cleaned and stitched gash along her arm. It puckered like an elongated smirk, as if taunting her memory with the explosion, the bloodied forms on the ground and the helpless screams and waving limbs of the injured. *This* place was alien now, unnerving. Who were the *others* – his superiors? The tone of respect was more immediate than the rusty dribble of Urdu she was able to recall from twenty years before. He had left his companion lying blinded and screaming in pain in the street, commandeered a taxi and driven himself and Sara back to the houseboats. Sara had, despite her own shock, ordered him to remember Ros. She nodded her thanks to the silent, efficient doctor, who moved away. He was watching the tall Pakistani carefully, awaiting his dismissal – with a nod that came almost immediately.

As she pretended ignorance of Urdu and lack of interest in Sara's clipped conversation, she was aware of guests on the other houseboats. The turban of a Sikh on the one next to hers, a bulky, self-important figure posed with binoculars on another. The binoculars seemed trained on Sara's boat, and she realised that some of the tall man's gestures might have been made in the direction of that boat, that man. She shivered.

'All right?' Sara asked with surprising concern, disconcerting the Pakistani. Kashmiri Moslem would explain the Urdu. Though he was *official* in some way, a man used to the currency of orders, discipline. And enough of a stranger to Sara, even though permitted on her boat, to convince Ros that he was not Indian. 'All right, Ros?' Sara persisted with an effort that strangely suggested guilt.

'What –? Oh, yes, thanks . . . Sorry, just a bit dazed still, I expect. The arm hardly hurts at all.' The man watched her with gleaming eyes, at a loss as to how to deal with her. 'God, what a bloody awful thing –!'

'I know,' Sara murmured. She was leaning back against the brass rail that surrounded the verandah, one arm stretched behind her as if trailing her fingers from a punt. 'God, I know.' She was staring at the Pakistani with a hard glare. Then, jerkily, she stood up, and swayed as if dizzy, before holding out her hand to the man. 'Thank you very much for your help. We were very lucky you were there, just at that moment.'

Moonface, moonface, Ros instructed herself, holding her bandaged arm with her hand, seemingly slightly giddy herself as she stared at the lake. Sara's face had been full of instruction to the man; she knows nothing, she's not a problem. It had all been there, and in the pressure of her grip on the man's hand. Finally, he nodded in acquiescence. Ros controlled her relief as the man turned away without again glancing in her direction. Moonface – play dumb. He passed through the curtain towards the rear of the houseboat and the causeway to the lake shore. Sara at once relaxed. Ros swallowed carefully. The dull, plain-girl charade had succeeded. Suddenly, Sara was shivering, rubbing her bare arms as if a cold breeze had sprung up, dispelling the hot afternoon.

'*You* all right?' Ros asked. Sara's features at once bridled against sympathy.

'Yes,' she replied sharply. 'Fine.'

'I see some more guests –' She gestured with a movement of her head.

'Some kind of business meeting, I gather. They've just asked for a meeting room and dinner.' The explanation was pat, tidily clear. 'Bit of a nuisance, actually, but beggars can't be choosers.' She smiled, confident that the thin fiction was accepted. Shareholders' meeting of Poppies for Export, Ros thought. 'They're staying in the area but this is good *local colour*, or something. I didn't take a lot of interest.'

'Bit of an intrusion.'

'What? Oh, yes – it'll have to be my boat. Biggest sitting room –' She laughed. 'I shouldn't say that to paying guests, should I?' Then her features clouded almost at once, as if she was staring – but where? Not across the glittering water towards the tall Pakistani and the man on the other houseboat he had now joined, and with whom he was engaged in an urgent, deferential conversation. Not even towards the meeting soon to occur on her boat . . . Towards something further away; an instruction against laughter that had been issued a long time ago. Sara sighed. 'Scraps from the rich man's table – that's all there is in this business until things settle down. You're sure you're all right? I wouldn't blame you if you left.'

It was not an enquiry or a nudge.

'I might stay close to the lake,' Ros replied. 'I *was* enjoying myself.' She settled back into her cushions as Sara's cook solicitously brought coffee. Sara nodded him away. 'Yes, please,' she added to Sara's gesture with the silver coffee pot. 'Lucky that chap was there, and recognised you,' she murmured, eyes half-closed.

'Yes.' The noise of coffee slight as that of a shikara moving lazily through the water. The birdsong was muted in the heat and the mountains were hazy and distant. Sirens wailed from the town. 'Yes.' She passed Ros her cup.

'My backside's going to be black and blue,' Ros announced,

shifting uncomfortably in her chair. 'Too much weight to bounce,' she added. Then she stood up, shakily. 'Could I use your loo before I drink this?'

'Of course. Same location as your boat. Excuse the mess.'

'Ta.'

Ros forced unreliable legs to move her through the curtain, along the short passageway and into the large, ornately panelled sitting room. The furniture was Edwardian rather than the usual '30s or '40s copies, the drapes heavy at the screened windows. The wood was richly scented. A long dining table occupied half the room, a suite of big chairs and a sofa gathered heavily around the long, inlaid coffee table. Crystal glittered in cabinets. A few oil paintings on the panelling – English landscapes or French ones, Impressionist in execution. They might even have been valuable.

Get on with it –

She knelt heavily by the dining table, as if a bout of angina had doubled her up. Her head rested on the tablecloth that diamonded the centre of the table. She searched with her fingers, then transferred the small metal object from her handbag to the underside of the table, tucking it adhesively into the inner side of the table's carved fringe, a polished pelmet of flowers and birds. One of the birds stared at her with bright suspicion. Then she rose to her feet like someone with arthritic joints. Done –

She had brought the bug, hoping to plant it, not anticipating its almost immediate use. Hyde had told her where, how – and how to monitor what it picked up.

And told her to be careful –

As she thrust herself, quaking, towards the bathroom, she tasted sweet, fearful nausea rise at the back of her throat. If they found it, they'd *know* at once –

The Overseas Communications Service office on Bangla Shahib was under surveillance. It had taken him a wasted hour to be certain of it. On Market Road nearby, they were watching the Post Restante. Tightening the noose, or hauling back on a dog-lead he hadn't until then noticed. Were they following him, rather than just waiting for him to fall into their arms? Once or twice, Hyde had thought so, catching suspicious movement like grit at the corner of eyesight. But his instincts wouldn't confirm how close they were.

He had decided he could not go back to the hotel, now his passport had been taken for scrutiny. They might just think of putting someone in the hotel lobby to wait for him. If he went back, it wouldn't be until he had flushed Lal out.

The Telephone Office on Janpath, which ran south from Con-naught Place towards Raj Path, was opposite a hotel, and the banks of telephones, though near the broad expanse of the main window, were masked by the hawkers and stalls selling the overflow of India's garment export trade at knockdown prices. And the Tibetan refugees selling carpets, the trinket stalls, the junk jewellery . . . It had taken a great deal of careful time to decide that the Telephone Office was clear of surveillance, then to enter it and place his call to Shelley at Century House. Insecure phone – tut.

He loosened his tie further, wiping his forefinger around the dampness of his collar. The heat in the streets was stifling, the air-conditioning suddenly chilly, even if inefficient. The perspir-ation sprang in cold droplets along his hairline. It was taking too long, they were too interested in finding him, they held all the cards. He watched the broad glass like a crowded movie-screen for the first signs of intent against him. The gun pressed into the small of his back as he perched on the narrow, folding seat in the telephone booth. Shelley's new secretary was having diffi-culty in interesting herself in his call, seeming resentfully puzzled that he should have the office number.

'Just tell him it's good old Patrick – telephoning from Delhi, will you, *dear*? What . . . ? He's only being briefed at your time in the morning, dear – nothing he can't break off from. Please do as I ask – *dear*.' The venom calmed his itchy nerves. For a few seconds. 'Shelley?' he eventually blurted out, aware at once that the tone was stretched thin – aware that Shelley, too, would be mindful.

'What is it, Patrick?' he heard asked urgently.

'Cass' escape. Don't believe it.'

'I – must,' Shelley eventually replied. 'I have been given assurances. It's become official, Patrick. The truth.' Shelley's clipped constraint was enervating, at once wearying him. Bright bales of cloth and brighter finished garments were wielded like matadors' capes beyond the window, almost disorientating him. 'You understand me?'

There was reluctance in the voice, a flinch against any accusation Hyde might make. Hyde understood. *Nostromo* was being abandoned. *Without a net*, it had been called – or *Kiss of the Spiderwoman* if you felt anything for the agent who was being disowned. It had happened, though not with Aubrey. The old man would never have –

'I understand,' he replied woodenly.

'Everything points to Cass' guilt – of murder, I mean.'

'Yes, doesn't it? He didn't do it, though.'

'You believe he's been removed?'

'He has. Article of my faith – *Pete*, old mate.'

'But you have no contact – ?'

'No.'

'Then give it up.'

'No.'

The pause was filled with the hypnotic, calming swirl of clothing beyond the window, the glitter of jewellery, the somnolent, surging passage of the constant crowd. Finally, Shelley murmured:

'What can you do?'

'Not much.'

'Delhi Station would be of no help, I'm afraid.'

'That bunch of tossers? I wouldn't ask them to look after

my Auntie Glad. Listen, Shelley – will you use *leverage*? In an *exchange*?'

Another lengthy pause, then, tightly and small-toned: 'Yes.'

Hyde sighed with relief. The old vacillator had come down, finally, as he usually came down, on the right side. Shelley wouldn't lift a finger until there was leverage, something to use. Shelley arrived at the good by way of the broad avenues of career and pension, knighthood and high office. Aubrey had always travelled the narrow path of loyalty, personal probity. More overgrown, harder on the feet, but quicker to action.

'Good. I'll get it for you.'

'Usual *Schedule D* strictures apply.' You're on your own if anything goes wrong. No trades, no official status. 'You think they *are* running drugs?'

'Cass does.'

'Hard to believe – almost impossible.'

'Sure. But they were boys from the village, not the Nehrus or the inheritedly rich. They needed a fortune, and now they've got one.'

'They weren't *quite* boys from the village.'

'Still two generations too close to it – for India.' Hyde relaxed. Shelley had given his word. He would keep it.

'You *can* get something?'

'I hope so. One chance. But quickly or not at all.'

'Then, I'll instruct my secretary to deal with you more respectfully, and man a line for you with someone who'll understand cryptic remarks and your misplaced sense of humour. Right, go quickly and in safety.'

Hyde put the phone down. The imitation of the old man's grave and theatrical concern was intentional, deliberate. I mean what I say. He watched the window, the foyer of the Telephone Office, the row of heads bent or raised, impassive or emotional, along the line of glass-sided booths. No one was interested in him. He looked at his watch. Four. The glass of the window was slightly tinted towards the top, like a car windscreen. The smoky effect was a line of threatening cloud along his horizon of action. He left the hot, enclosing booth, shutting the glass door behind him, then reopening it for a small, plump, saried woman to enter. Ringing Bradford? he wondered. Or Southall?

The cramped, ramshackle façade of the offices of *Conscience of Delhi* was farther along Janpath. He'd call in, see if he could talk to someone who'd worked with Lal, might know or suspect where he was.

What you really have to do, sport, is to flush his wife out, good old Lata Lal who threw off your tail. Con her into going to Lal – today.

Easier said than done . . .

Janpath boomed with noise. Cycle-rickshaws, taxis, old Harley Davidson four- and six-seater auto-rickshaws on their usual routes. Long Mercedes and American limousines, ancient cars tottering like the fragile aged on the pavements. Hands in his pockets, he nudged his way through the crowd. It was impossible to spot a tail – all but impossible to maintain one. A crowded bus debouched its passengers through one door, devoured a new queue of them through another. He passed jewellery shops, statues of the Buddha crammed into niches, beggars, lame dogs, the screams of parrots from a petshop. Then crossed the broad street at the next junction towards the narrow front of the decaying building that housed the radical freesheet for which Lal worked. His hands clenched in his pockets. Lal had – and had kept – information. Lal wasn't a dummy. He had to be found before others found him, and his wife had to accustom herself to a lodger from Intelligence who waited like a spider for seekers-after-Lal to innocently turn up.

He enquired at the reception desk. Behind a flimsy, temporary door, he heard the babble of the newspaper staff. One of the windows had been boarded up, too, which probably indicated someone had attacked the newspaper offices recently.

'Dave Holland – that's H-o-l-l –' The girl seemed insulted,

131

and her handwriting hurried to overtake his spelling. Then she picked up her telephone and dialled an extension, speaking rapidly in Hindi almost at once.

As she put down the receiver, she said: 'Someone will come to answer your enquiry, Mr *Holland*.' Upper-caste girl with a social conscience? Not prepared merely to decorate an Air India office or a bank counter while she waited for her marriage to be arranged. She indicated a dusty plastic-covered bench, and Hyde sat down near a large tear in the material and two cigarette burns.

He waited for fifteen minutes, increasingly aware of the narrow corridor in which he sat, the cool, distant girl behind the scuffed desk, the front door, and the inner door behind which was a layout he could not begin to imagine – should he need to bolt that way. Then a short, slim young man, bespectacled and sharp-glanced, came through the flimsy door and studied him as he approached, hand extended. Hyde took the cool grip for a moment.

'Dave Holland,' he persisted. 'I'm looking for Lal. He and I have worked together in the past.'

'You are a foreign correspondent?'

'Right. Press Association. I need a runner –' It was intentionally demeaning to Lal and *Conscience of Delhi*. The young man duly bridled.

'I don't think Lal is looking for such work.'

'I'd like to ask him. Generous expenses, all that. Where is he?'

'He is – on holiday.'

'Lata says he's on an assignment.'

'You know Lata?'

'Used to. Which is it – assignment or holiday?'

'Whichever you prefer, Mr Holland.'

'Look, I'm not trying to make trouble – just offer the guy a job. Is that a crime?'

'No. I'm afraid that Lal's whereabouts are a matter for the newspaper.'

A young woman in Western dress, accompanied by a man of around thirty in grey slacks and a white shirt, came through the inner door and edged past them. The girl looked sharply at Hyde as the Indian mentioned Lal's name.

'– coffee break,' Hyde caught from the girl before they went outside and the street's noise bullied in. Hyde shrugged.

'OK, I don't want to spoil a good story. Sorry to have bothered you.' He looked around the narrow corridor with undisguised superiority. 'Just tell him I called. When you talk to him. I'll call again.'

He waved a hand loosely and drifted back into the street. His shoulders sloped casually, his hands were in his pockets. He saw the girl in the cream suit and the shirtsleeved man forty yards or so along Janpath. They had paused at a stall selling fruit. The girl had been almost stung by Lal's name. She might know where he was.

He hurried after them as they turned into an ice-cream parlour decorated in black and white, patronised by bodies in Western clothes with loud voices. Hyde saw the girl wave to various tables, then she and the man sat at the window. The Indian waitress who took their order, might have been uniformed for McDonald's. The girl saw Hyde at once as he entered the tiled, chromed room, its fan turning slowly as if mixing the air into a paste rather than cooling it. The air-conditioning struck chill after the street. He approached their table at once and sat down, holding out his hand, which neither of them took.

'Dave Holland. You two work for *Conscience of Delhi*, right?'

'Obviously,' the girl replied, her eyes warning her companion. 'Who are you, Mr Holland?'

'Press Association.' The girl seemed to disbelieve him. 'Look, I've worked the Delhi beat before, now I'm just back after a spell in the UK. I worked with Lal – you know Lal. I just wanted to look him up, offer him some work. Can't get hold of him anywhere.'

The girl held up a cigarette and the man snatched out his lighter. Hyde banished amusement from his face. The crowds flowed sludgily past the windows in the late afternoon light.

'He's not in the office. At the moment.' She brushed lustrous dark hair away from her heavily made-up cheeks. Her huge eyes were highlighted by makeup and the curve of her nose. 'Don't know when he'll be back.'

Hyde turned to the man. 'Look, last I heard Lal was doing some work with a pal of mine, Phil Cass —? Name mean anything?' It did. Would they admit it? The man glanced at the woman, who glared at his incontinence of expression. 'Phil Cass? He and Lal were onto something in Kashmir. Some government scandal — the sort your paper revels in. Do you know anything about it?'

'Are you looking for ready-made headlines, Mr Holland?'

Hyde grinned. 'Not quite. Sharp question, though. Look, Phil Cass has passed stuff to me before now, stuff he couldn't hand on or wasn't being given the prominence — listen, you do *know* Cass is British High Commission, yes?' The girl evidently did. It didn't matter now, his risk of exposure. Risk was inevitable, the foot on the accelerator. 'OK — Phil had me fired up with some dark hints about government high-ups and Kashmir, right? I come out prepared to take up the story, but no Phil and no Lal. I can't find either of them.'

The man was prepared to trust him, that much was obvious. The girl *might* have delusions of grandeur, a sense of the big story. He wasn't sure. Neither of them seemed other than wary of him. They were clean, in that sense. The man said, with the woman's voiceless permission:

'Can you describe Mr Cass?'

'What?' He grinned again. 'Oh, Phil — how much do you know about him? Six foot, fair hair, the skin under his eyes is crinkled like crepe paper — you know what crepe paper is? Speaks Hindi like a native — sorry. Been posted out here for about three years

134

now, went to school –' The woman's glance allowed him to pause. Then she said suddenly:

'We know what Mr Cass is. Do you? *Are* you –?'

'Not in that game, love. Phil was a spook. I got that impression a long time ago. Glad we agree. So – where is he?' He leant forward conspiratorially as he said it. The woman's eyes flickered with something that might have been success, as she said:

'Your NUJ card?' Clever girl – the trouble was, she was too clever. Hyde produced his wallet, then the crumpled NUJ membership card.

'Sorry about the state of it.'

The girl didn't believe the card. It was suddenly a situation that required containment – simply keeping these two at that table until he could exit. The man hadn't graduated to this level of the game, he was just what he appeared to be. But, the woman –

The man blurted, satisfied: 'The police raided us a week ago. They searched Lal's desk and locker, asked questions about him –' The woman's rite of passage to indifference was momentary, but there had been an instant's hard, squinting glare, as if into the sun.

'What were they looking for? Did they find anything?'

'They took a lot of material away, Mr Holland. We lodged a protest, produced a vigorous editorial –' And the woman couldn't have given a stuff, apparently. Oh, yes – she knew the game as it really was. One move to the bog and I'm off, sport. She'd be ringing police HQ or Intelligence at the first opportunity. And she knew what he looked like, his present cover. He prompted the man, even as he watched the woman's eyes watching the windows of the ice-cream parlour. The gun in the small of his back was present in an insistent manner, like someone calling loudly for a debt that was outstanding. She wasn't yet sure. She obviously hadn't a good photograph of him, she hadn't recognised him. Was just suspicious.

'What do you think Lal was working on?' Come on, catch the

scent – *you* could get in on the act, the London expenses.

The man shrugged. 'Something involving the Sharmar family, I believe. I'm not sure –'

'But you don't know *where* Lal is now?' The man shook his head, attempting cunning and honesty in a single, awkward moment. He didn't know, bugger it . . . nor did the woman, that much was obvious. It was becoming a waste of time at a great rate of knots. 'Shame. And Phil's done a runner, too. They must be together, wouldn't you think?' he asked, turning to the woman.

'I didn't know Lal's business very well,' she managed. She lit a second cigarette, but her disguise of calm and haughty indifference wasn't as convincing this time. 'The police were very interested –' The radical journalist had to emerge now, or her cover was snapped. 'He could be dead.' The man shivered. 'Or imprisoned. It happens here –'

'Do the Sharmars go in for that kind of thing?'

'How would I know? Perhaps Lal does?' The contempt was undisguised for a moment. 'I hope not,' she added perfunctorily. The man was nodding in more fervent hope.

'OK, thanks.' He stood up quickly. 'I'll keep looking.'

'Have a coffee,' the woman offered. He shook his head.

'Must dash.' And bloody how.

He turned back after his plunge into the tide of the street. The woman was already on her feet and making her way towards the row of helmetlike phone booths at the rear of the ice-cream parlour. Hyde allowed himself to be drowned in the crowd, taking him instantly away from the man's gaze.

Right, darling – you're the inside-job on the paper, but you don't know where Cass or Lal can have got to. You know me, though. Time to get on with it, then. Back to Lal's place and get the wife stirred up. Some message, some sudden intrusion of danger into the woman's imagination that would drag her out, send her rushing off to where Lal was hiding –

*

It was him, Ros thought, her confirmatory nods making the night-glasses wobble, causing the small, tight group of men crossing the short causeway, to dissolve as if behind oil. Then she stilled her head and the men's faces reassembled in the grey half-light of the binoculars. It *was* V. K. Sharmar, and that was his brother, Prakesh, if their newspaper photographs were anything like. Bodyguards, presumably, around them.

She took the glasses away from her eyes to rest them for a moment, as the Sharmars entered at one end of the tunnel of Sara's houseboat, evidently to emerge at the other end, where a group of men were knotted in quiet conversations on the verandah. The moonlight silvered the lake and the carved wood around her. She pulled the shawl closer around her shoulders and breathed deeply – but softly, as if the bug was capable of two-way transmission and they might easily hear her breathing. The recorder was at her feet as she rested against cushions in the darkest shadows of her verandah, its tape sighing regularly as it turned. The headphones lay in her lap ready for use. Voice-activated, Hyde had explained. Just leave the tape on, it'll collect the info . . . don't listen if you don't want to. She put on the headphones and was startled by the greetings exploding from them. Yes, *Prime Minister*, was an instant reply. It *was* the Sharmars.

Half an hour before, the setting sun had still gilded the water and drawn the mosquitoes, and she had been nervous of appearing on the verandah and attracting their notice. Now, the mountains in the distance were ghostly with moonlight and the lake appeared as if that silvery light was melting into the water, staining it.

Sharmar and his brother passed through the sitting room and beyond the range of the bug, which was picking up no more than distant murmurs now. She raised the glasses. Yes, there they were, amid a tight group of Pakistani Urdu-speakers and a small knot of turbanned Sikhs; perhaps no more than eight – maybe nine, if she hadn't counted in one of the houseboat's servants.

She shivered. The temperature was falling, but it was more than that. She looked down at the recorder at her feet. It was working again, but in the headphones it was only the casual intercourse of security men and orders to the servants. She left the equipment where it lay and retreated into the houseboat, picking up the telephone from its ornate table against one wall. The old-fashioned black bakelite was now a tourist attraction. She felt her body decline into the armchair with heavy tension as she began dialling the number of Hyde's hotel. Talking to him would be enough – she didn't need him there, not yet, she was coping. Even if her fingers did drum out more than mere impatience as she waited for the connection to be made through the slow Srinagar exchange. *Holland* –

'Mr Holland's room, please.'

There was a pause, and the woman's light voice and practised manner were replaced with a peremptory and demanding bark.

'Who is this calling, please? Mr Holland is not available at the moment. Who is this, please?'

She stared, horrified, at the receiver, brandishing it in the air like a rat she had caught attempting to bite her in her sleep. 'Who is this, please? Why do you wish to speak to Mr Holland? Can I take a message for Mr Holland?' Then she thrust it away from her, back onto its rest. The voice had flickered in and out of politeness and threat, cover and reality.

Oh, dear *Jesus* – the bloody police! They knew who Hyde was, they . . .

. . . had Hyde –

The room swirled, as with drunkenness, changing its proportions and form. She could hear her heart in the silence.

Eventually, the room slowed.

Knew – but didn't *have*. They'd have been less eager, a lot more cocky, if Hyde was in their hands. But he'd been Holland for a day, no more, and they knew who Holland really was.

Her forehead was cold with perspiration and her arm throbbed with adrenalin and the stitches. She couldn't warn him, she had no means of contacting him. How could they know about him? Her chest heaved, as if she were being asthmatically assaulted. Her heart sounded louder, yet more feeble and uncontrolled. Jesus, they were waiting for him to turn up at the bloody hotel –!

'Ros?'

She heard the call before she heard the footsteps end their passage across the causeway from the shore. Sara Mallowby's voice.

'Ros? Can you stand some company? *Ros?*'

Ros stared towards the verandah and the recorder lying on the planking of the deck and the night-glasses resting where she had left them.

lord of the dance

The urchin had been easy to find, easier to coach after the lubrication of bright, high-denomination rupee notes. He was already, at perhaps twelve, undersized and beyond small change. Huge-eyed, their darkness almost entirely cataracted with cunning and street wisdom, except where there was concern for the even younger sister who accompanied him and the three-legged dog that had attached itself to them. Ros would never, in a million years or fear of her life, have been able to exploit them. *Employ.* It sounded better.

The message was simple and seemed to cover all anticipated objections – just so long as Lata Lal had met Cass, knew as much as Hyde believed she did, it would work. *Mr Cass has come to me. Do not call, the telephone is intercepted. We are being watched. Be careful. Bring money.* Yes, son, it's crooked. The boy probably wouldn't have done it if he couldn't feel it was criminal, something to boast of later.

After returning across the street, the boy winked at him in the quick dusk, his teeth gleaming bright as his eyes as he passed him. In another moment, he and his sister and the limping dog had disappeared down a narrow alleyway and turned out of sight. Hyde put them out of mind and concentrated on Lal's house; the lights gleaming through the shutters on the windows, the slow passage of time being marked by the door not opening. The thinner crowds offered no chance of missing someone slipping through that door – there was no easy back entrance, he'd checked that. The drug-aged hippie returned from one of his shambling journeys and let himself into the house. The father of the family from the country appeared at one unshuttered window and called to a passer-by he knew. Lata Lal was *not* taken in, was not going to come out –

Half an hour, and darkness, the soft night flaring with sodium lamps, electric bulbs, candles and butter lamps. She's called Lal, he told himself, again and again. She knows it was a bluff . . . Forty minutes. A woman smaller and more rotund than Lata Lal emerged, carrying a shopping bag and a child slung in a tiny hammock across her breasts. The woman from the country. He all but started after her, especially since he had not seen the door open as a crowded bus passed, only seen the woman close it . . . but she wouldn't be undertaking the journey for Lal's wife, carrying her youngest child. Forty-seven minutes –

She was on the doorstep, furtive, it seemed to his stretched nerves. She turned the way she had gone that morning, her face scarved as if to conceal her identity. Hyde crossed the street and fell in behind her, twenty yards back. There was no evidence of other purposeful movement on either side of Desh Bhandu as he passed the tiny mosque and the first of the shops. Ahead of him, her bright-scarved head bobbed and wended through the shoulders of the crowd. Then she turned into Qutab Road. As Hyde reached the corner, the lit windows of a train flashed along the tracks towards Old Delhi station. The line was raised above the brow of houses and shops and the lights of the train made the scene strangely wintry, despite the warmth of the night. Hyde closed to ten yards behind her as she hurried across the street in a surge of pedestrians loosed by a change of traffic lights. It was the same route as before. She wasn't aware or even suspicious of being followed, since she never looked round. The delay might have been the money, or a lack of nerve – anything. Hyde clenched his teeth. Her house wasn't being watched – he was certain of it. Almost.

He'd done as much to change his appearance as he could.

Walk, posture, taking off the jacket of the suit, cigarettes – anything he could do that wasn't makeup or dye that needed an expert. A new tie, red braces. An absolute prick, he admitted, catching sight of himself in a dingy shop window where lizards, snakes and frogs lingered in glass tanks too small for their comfort.

He hurried after Lata Lal, feeling his teeth grinding together in increasing tension, his jaw begin to ache with the pressure. He was fifteen yards behind her as she climbed the steps of a wooden bridge that crossed the main railway tracks as daringly as if over a chasm, fragile and unlit in the night. Still the same route. Her pace had increased. The smell of food from a stall perched precariously above the descent to the other side of the tracks, the exhalation of steam and smoke as a train passed beneath, a vast adapted Russian or American locomotive hauling packed carriages. Already, there were passengers on the roof. He paused to remark its passage, watching sidelong the way he had come. Amid the pedestrians, there seemed no one interested in him. If the operation – if operation there were – were big enough, he'd never see them, they'd waste manpower handing him back and forth between front and rear tails like a ball. Too late now –

He hurried down the steps and caught up to within ten yards of the woman. The train's sparks, lights and smoke moved away into the night as they turned north, then quickly east into Chandni Chowk. His teeth gritted again. It was here he had lost her that morning, at this junction of the Chowk and three other crowded streets. Almost at once, in the darkness and the pools between the sodium flares and the lights from cafés and shops, he thought he had lost her again. Immediate rage of frustration. Then he realised she was still in sight, he was merely dazzled by the lights. The Fatehpuri Mosque gloomed over her. He closed to six or seven yards behind her – he'd hung back too far that morning, the bazaar had been too crowded. Books, jewellery, parrots filled the windows of the nearest shops. Stalls crowded the pavements as if suggesting fraternity with more legitimate businesses. He pressed on behind her, past a cinema queue, past the ugly, garish hoardings. One of the films of Anand Mehta, the new leader of the fundamentalists. A cops-and-robbers spectacular. Above the cinema's entrance, two huge, badly-painted, idealised Indians — Mehta and his leading lady — embraced passionately. It might, a year ago, have been Sereena Sharmar . . . then he realised it was —

— and that he had lost Lata Lal.

Oh, *Jesus* —!

Mehta and the woman's stylised, high-coloured portraits stared down at him as he stood, hands on hips, as if to indulge a bout of temper as the queue shuffled into the interior of the dilapidated cinema. A sitar and tabla boomed, together with a high-pitched Indian voice, from a loudspeaker, unseductive but effective. Sereena Sharmar seemed to mock him, her broad red lips pressed against those of her co-star. Where the hell had she gone? His head twitched angrily to and fro —

— so that she passed all but unnoticed in front of him, oblivious to him, beyond the pay-booth and into the cinema. He stared after her in an effort to convince himself, as if following her was impossible. Then he lurched to the cashier's window, ahead of good-natured protest, paid in loose change and pressed into the flock-papered, red-lit interior, past the betel-nut sellers and hawkers and the saried usherette, into the hot dark.

Lights sprang up for the interval. The cinema buzzed like a hornets' nest and the whole audience seemed at once on its feet, engaged in another element of the ritual of cinema-going. He watched in a moment of calm that was little more than orientation. He had Lata Lal in sight as she swayed down one of the sloping aisles then paused in confusion.

Then she looked up towards the balcony. She seemed the only still figure, besides himself, in the auditorium. The screen flickered with pale images of Indian products. In front of it, she was posed in stylised, intense bewilderment.

Hyde realised, as her head began turning almost mechanically, like some searching, unimaginative radar dish, that this was the meeting place – that she expected him to meet her . . .

. . . but the summons was Hyde's. Lal wouldn't show up. He didn't know his wife was here. He wouldn't show –

'You must be just a little bored?' Sara asked in a desultory tone. 'Sitting in the dark, listening to your Walkman.' Ros saw her smile in the moonlight, her face tiredly paled by the silvery night as it reflected from the lake. Rose looked down guiltily at the recorder and the headphones she had bundled onto the cushions.

The glasses were under her chair.

'What –? Oh, no . . . time to think. You know.' Hyde had said once, on one of the few occasions he indulged in description, that *running for your life was the easy bit. Sitting still and telling porky pies to save your skin was a lot harder*.

God, I hope not, Hyde, I really hope not . . . 'Time to think.'

Sara arranged herself on one of the chairs with unstudied, languid grace. The upper classes must be born with suppler bones –

'Is that why you came? Running away?' she asked. There was an edge to her voice as she touched intimacy then withdrew herself like a child's hand encountering a new pet with teeth.

'Not really . . .' *Making up a cover story as you go along is the worst* . . . 'Well, yes, I suppose so,' Ros added confessionally. Sara leaned forward with what might have been eagerness. 'Just a bit sick of things. At home – wherever that is.'

Sara was silent for a time, brushing her hand through her hair, then she said:

'You came to find yourself the first time – lose yourself the second, mm?'

'Something like that.'

'Some man, I suppose? Tell me if I'm prying –'

'No, it's all right.' Ros settled in her chair, her bandaged arm across her lap, her other hand against her forehead with spread

144

fingertips. She could feel a tremor in her legs and hear the palpitation of her heart. 'Not fundamentally, I suppose – not really his fault.'

'You had someone? A long time?' It was as if she was an anorexic of the emotions attempting to swallow what had become alien to her. Ros was puzzled by the woman. She seemed to have been hollowed out from inside, not just worn. 'Men are buggers,' she added, glaring across the moonlit water towards her houseboat. There was an edge of fear in her voice, quarrelling with contempt.

'He wasn't so much of a bugger,' Ros replied, thinking of Hyde and amused at the pretence. The one thing she did *not* share with her younger self who had first met Hyde was the fear of losing him. She was sometimes – perhaps too often – his mother or his elder sister, but he needed her in all sorts of ways. Even if it had taken years for her to believe it. 'He was a clerk in an office. Not very exciting, but he was a decent bloke –'

Her voice broke, aware that they knew Hyde's new cover, were waiting for him at his hotel, that she couldn't warn him. The sudden rush of renewed awareness made her shiver. Her response was misinterpreted.

'Sorry,' Sara muttered. 'Being on one's own makes one just a little insensitive. Wounds still not healed?'

'Just about.' She gestured with her hands at the bulk of her body. 'Can't blame him, can you? Not much of a catch for any bloke, even a clerk, am I?' She sniffed loudly. 'Don't worry, I've been through the self-pity stage. I only came away while the estate agent tries to sell the flat. I don't think it would be a good idea to go on living there, for either of us.' Again, her voice had caught. There was something cathartic, however, in maintaining the pretence. Her fears for Hyde could be channelled and disguised. 'You said men are buggers – you sound as if you've been handed the shitty end of the stick, at some time?'

People don't notice you when it's themselves they're talking about . . . That wasn't Hyde, that was the Samaritans. It helped now,

145

though, in a way that Hyde would appreciate. Sara began staring at her low-shod feet shuffling on the planking of the deck. Near the concealed night-glasses.

Across the water, the murmur of voices, the subdued lighting of Sara's sitting room showing through the drawn curtains and the mosquito screens. The night was turning chilly. Ros thought she could hear the slow, interrupted susurrations of the tape.

'I've rehearsed the story so many times – for shrinks, lovers, guests, it sounds very pat now, and rather dead.' Sara's smile was ironic, bitter. She brushed angrily at her hair, sweeping it away from her face. 'I wouldn't want to hear it if I were you.'

'Anyone in particular, or just men in general?' Ros prompted.

Sara grinned. 'I did warn you.'

'You did. *Men are buggers*, you began . . . ?'

'How were you with your father, Ros? I ask everyone that. Hoping to find out I'm not a freak, I suppose –'

'Don't ask about the old man!'

'Ah, but the trick is – did you fail him.' Sara observed, her eyes gleaming, her hands picking at the stuff of her full skirt. 'Or did he fail you?'

The lights dimmed quickly, and Hyde squeezed onto a narrow, hard aisle seat three rows from Lata Lal. She seemed similarly disorientated by the communal sigh and the ensuing silence as the film's credits began to roll, superimposed upon a shot of a speeding car. It might have been the movie he had seen being filmed in Desh Bhandu early that morning. The woman hovered against the technicolour images. Latecomers passed across the screen, eager to be seated. The auditorium's temperature rose with feverish anticipation. Dustbins and a fruit stall were sent careering and spilling by the impact of the car, to the unalloyed delight of the audience. Lata La remained standing. At a loss.

Hyde knew he wouldn't get her out of the house again on any similar pretext – it was blown for that night. Blown for good. The hotel was effectively barred to him, his only option was Srinagar. Imperative, not option. Ros couldn't be left on her own any longer. His guilt and sense of her danger nagged more than a decaying tooth, continually present.

The appearance of the movie's hero, played by Anand Mehta, immediately swinging a fist at a scowling, scar-faced Indian, was greeted with a sigh and a great cheer. Sharmar could lose the election to this celluloid hero . . . he'd have to, wouldn't he, *you* can't do anything about bloody Sharmar. At once, Sereena Sharmar – welcomed with almost mystical, revelatory responses from the audience, entered, to rush into Mehta's arms. Sharmar shouldn't have had her killed, she was an election asset . . .

Lata Lal hovered on the edge of another aisle seat, four rows in front of him. She was hunched, her shoulders stiff with fears and dislocated nerves. Sereena Sharmar and Mehta continued their embrace. Cass had had an affair with *her* – lucky sod. Yet it was weirdly unreal, looking at a dead woman on the screen, relating her to Cass and to heroin production and to the woman in front of him, and Ros . . . He hesitated for a moment between the unreality of the appalling movie and the unreality of the situation he had muddied and let slip.

Then Lata Lal got up and hurried up the aisle, to the curiosity of a few patrons before they at once returned their mesmerised attention to the incredulities of the screen. Mehta was swinging from a rope which had been let down from a high window – Christ, I couldn't manage half that without drugs. Sereena gazed enraptured from the window at his spinning, descending figure. Vote for a real hero. Hyde got up and scurried after the woman, who had already reached the heavy curtains on her way to the foyer. The usherette seemed offended that he was capable of walking out.

Lal's wife had paused again, then she began climbing the narrow staircase to the balcony. Hyde followed. If Lal was here, if he was only *here*, he kept repeating. She couldn't just be changing her seat, surely. He swallowed the lump of hope that had risen into his throat. He passed a toilet's odour, then paused at another curtain through which she had slipped. Behind it, a cramped, uncarpeted staircase. He glanced at the splay of light, smoke-roiled, from the projection equipment, then down at the screen, where Mehta, to the evident absorption of the audience, was engaged in another fist fight. Probably beating up Sharmar —

He closed the curtain behind him and ascended the stairs as he heard the sigh and click of a door shutting. In the light of the single weak, dusty bulb, he had momentarily been aware of a gleam of light surrounded by darkness through the open door. The projection room? He reached the door and edged it open a couple of inches. The whirr of the projector, the murmur of voices. A door closing at the other end of the projection room, cutting off the light of another weak bulb. He could see the outline of two heads, smell food. He eased himself into the hot dark of the room. The two outlined heads turned incuriously towards him, and he was surprised by their lack of interest and continued silence. The narrow staircase behind him was vivid in his imagination, then the staircase to the foyer and the corridor to the street, all as if he had walked into a trap. Was that the delay before Lata Lal left her home? That she had been acting on instructions, that the setup had to be put in place?

He opened the other door and slipped through it. A grubby corridor with a door at the far end. The smell of another toilet. The door claimed *Manager*, in English and Hindi. He touched the gun in the small of his back, as if at a talisman, then knocked and quickly opened the door. Lata Lal looked round at him, afraid, while the Indian who was presumably the manager of the cinema rose to his feet in mid-gesture — waving his arms in denial or panic or both. The other man had a gun in his hand and paused in the act of shouting at Lata to waggle it fiercely and amateurishly at Hyde. Christ, it was just like the bloody movie!

The woman's expression was one of recognition and immediate fear. The two men appeared sufficiently alike to be brothers. They had been sharing a curry when Lata arrived.

'Oh, my stupid wife –!' the man with the gun cried out in English, as Hyde raised his hands to the level of his shoulders. 'Who is this man? He has followed you here, you silly woman!'

The manager's forehead was greasy with the situation. Lal's face was vivid with consternation, anger, a growing sense of the gun. Amateurs killed out of panic. Lal would be aware of the room as narrow, cramped, of Hyde's form as something between himself and the door. Hyde waggled his hands.

'Lal?' he said quietly. 'You don't need the gun, Mr Lal. I'm a friend of Phil Cass. You know Phil . . . I'm a mate of his – *really*. And we need to talk – I just came to talk.' On the manager's desk, beneath the debris of the curry, lay the evening paper. 'You must have read he escaped, right? I don't think he did. We *need* to talk.'

The woman was making the room edgy now, she and the manager. Lal himself seemed like an actor off-set, not playing his part, divorced from the imagery and plot of whatever he had been doing with Cass. Just a freesheet radical who knew how serious the police could become, now he'd had hiding-time to think about it. Looking for money or a story, he'd found the shitty world where people disappeared, were no longer a joke but had become a threat to the powerful.

'What damned trouble have you brought me *now*?' the manager protested, glaring at Lal. 'Oh my brother, you have been a damned bloody *fool*!'

'Be quiet, Prem!' Lal snapped back. 'He is alone. You are alone, friend of Mr Cass?' The gun waved, not quite with a life of its own, but nor was it entirely subdued.

'I'm alone.' There was no satisfaction, no edge of nerves that suggested they had only to keep him immobile for a matter of minutes before others arrived. He hadn't been led into a blind alley. 'Can we talk?'

He moved forward very slowly, almost deferential to the gun, and gradually drew a chair from the wall and placed it innocently beside the chair on which Lata Lal perched. He placed his hands, fingers spread, on the table.

'Can we talk, Mr Lal? There isn't a lot of time —'

'What do you mean?'

Hyde raised his hands in innocence. 'For Phil Cass, there's not much time. That's what I meant. They've removed him from prison, he didn't escape. You didn't suppose he had, did you?'

Lal shook his head. 'He would have contacted Lata.'

'Or *me*, Mr Lal.'

'What kind of friend are you to Mr Cass?'

'The kind he needs. Are *you*, Mr Lal?'

Ros sat on, staring at the moonflecked ripples on the lake as they reached the hull of the houseboat and gently touched it. Sara had finished her second whisky and excused herself — to *supervise the servants. These people require extra deference*. Ros listened to her footsteps, quite clear against the hum from the town and the night-noises from the reeds, crossing her own short causeway in the silence after a passing car. Their conversation had been as hypnotic as the landscape under the moon and the noises of Srinagar.

The problem had been absurdly simple ... Christ, don't I know how simple. Her father, carrying the burden of exposure of his shady business deals by a left-wing Labour MP, had collapsed into self-pity and feet of clay and eventual decline to the moment of suicide. War hero, magistrate, kind father, all gone in an instant. The instant had been England as well as a shotgun cartridge. The easy partnership in property development, the easy money, the easy guilt when the frauds and the exploitations had been illuminated by one self-righteous torch. Sara Mallowby had left England in the late '60s and had never been back to what had become a place without heroes. A place that destroyed heroes. And because there had been no one to turn to, no other close family, no husband or lover. And spent more than twenty years blaming England, politics . . . and her father for not being a continuing hero in unpropitious times.

Enter Sharmar?

Eventually, yes . . . Sharmar, another hero. Dominating, attractive, charismatic, uxorious. Sara had fallen in with him, fallen *for* him, been taken up by him. And had eventually discovered the nastiness under the stones. Ros guessed that she knew it all, or at least most of it, and feasted on the past as a means of dieting with the truth in the present. Sharmar was an idol she couldn't afford to let fall.

Shaking her head, she absent-mindedly picked up the headphones and slipped them over her hair. The tape had wheezed only intermittently during the last half-hour, while the group of men appeared once more on the verandah of Sara's houseboat, breaking off the discussion she had not overheard.

Walkman . . . She smiled. It was well enough disguised. Good job Sara didn't want to share her guest's taste in music. Then, at once, the brief exchange between Sara and the voice she knew to be V. K. Sharmar's mesmerised her. She recognised an excess of guilt as Sara confronted her lover. Their voices were punctuated by her own sharp breaths, heard from beyond the headphones like the cries of a distressed bird somewhere in the lakeshore reeds.

'You seem worried – tired –?' Politic sex, a stroking operation.

'No, it's nothing.'

'What is the matter? Where have you been?' Diplomatic nostrils and the scent of trouble.

'It's nothing. I need a drink. That depressing woman –'

'What woman?'

'The one on the boat, the one I told you about.'

'Who is she?'

'No one, I told you. How's your meeting –?'

'Sara, never mind about the meeting.' Political nerves heightened by the situation and declining into suspicion. Pouncing on it. 'Sara, what has upset you?' The stroking gesture again.

151

Ros stared across at the other houseboat from the shadows of her verandah. She was intrigued, fascinated, just as she was by glimpses into Hyde's world whenever he came back, shagged-out from wherever his orders and his own personality defects had taken him. Her own danger struck like melted ice, hardly cold.

'Oh, nothing. You know me.'

'Yes. I do. This woman has been upsetting you, that much I understand.'

'No, she hasn't –! Thanks.' Ros thought she detected the clink of ice, but that had to be her heightened nerves. 'Oh, she's a sad case –' Thanks, darling. '– oh, how long are these people going to be here, V.K.? Can't you get rid of them tonight?'

'Perhaps. You've been talking to this woman?'

'Not about you. Don't be stupid, V.K. – sorry.' The last word was hurried, as if he had glared at her, even raised his hand. 'Just about old times . . . the long-dead past. I'm tired, V.K.'

'Yes. You're sure about this woman? You seem upset by her presence. Can't you get rid of her?'

'She's *paid*, V.K.' An audible sigh. 'She *is* peculiar, though.'

'How?'

'Perhaps it's just a clever person inside a fat body.'

'How clever?'

'Just insight, V.K. Just insight.'

'Into what?'

'Anything she turned her attention to, I shouldn't wonder.' The extra drink had made her mocking, and as rebellious as a teenager. You profoundly silly *cow*, Ros added. 'Goodnight, V.K. Tell them not to make a noise as they leave, would you?'

'She'd better be watched, Sara. Just as a precaution.'

Snatching off the headphones in no measure diminished her sudden, uncontrollable fear. Her coat of bluff, which had been so warm around her as she talked to Sara, had vanished.

Dal Lake spread out friendlessly before her, and the town's murmur was like that of a disturbed wasps' nest. And Hyde's hotel was being watched and she couldn't warn him – couldn't tell him about her own situation, closing over her head like deep water.

'I will not stay, brother.'

The manager got out of his chair, shiftily afraid and very sensible, and motioned Lata Lal to accompany him to the door. Lal laid his free hand on hers and nodded.

'I'm quite safe with this man, Lata. I do not think he means us any harm.' He smiled at Hyde. 'Anyway, he is alone. As stupid –' His features darkened quickly, as if dyed. '– as Mr Cass, walking about unprotected, thinking they can blunder in anywhere!' His eyes glittered. 'As stupid as I have been, my wife, in bringing us all to this!' The gun ground at the cartons the curry had come in, at the sheets of the evening newspaper and the ledger in which Lal's brother had been entering the receipts for the afternoon. Old-fashioned cloth bank bags on the desk.

Lata Lal held her husband's hand imploringly as her brother-in-law waited at the door with undisguised impatience. He held it slightly ajar, and the gunfire from the movie intruded, startling Lal and unnerving his wife.

'It's all right,' Hyde soothed. 'It won't take long. I'll have come and gone before the big picture's finished.' He grinned disarmingly. Lal nodded his wife's dismissal.

As the door closed behind them, Hyde said: 'Thanks. For believing me.'

Lal, surprisingly, put down the gun.

'Lata said someone approached her this morning. Mr *Holland*?' Hyde nodded. 'I thought so. Mr Cass told me that journalism was often a disguise for – his friends. I wondered – indeed, Mr Holland, I hoped –'

'I'm here. The entire US Cavalry – and I mean *entire*. What I *can* do for Phil Cass is to acquire leverage. Understand, Mr Lal? *Evidence*. You have some.'

'You are certain of it?'

'Oh, yes, I'm certain. It was your story, after all. Once Cass had picked the bones out of it, the rest was yours.'

'I warned him about that woman, Sereena Sharmar!'

'Trouble was, he fell for her.'

'Yes, I realised that. I was more cautious from that moment, Mr Holland. Of necessity.'

'So? What have you got?'

'What have *you* got?'

'A couple of tapes Cass had hidden in his flat – which led me to you. The other bloke – I forget his name – he's disappeared. Not like you, though. I think he's dead –'

'I – had heard that, too.'

Lal hesitated now, and stared frequently at the gun, then at Hyde, then at the cracked and peeling walls of the cramped office. Even at the curry's remains. He did not seem lost, simply miserly with what had created his predicament and which might still save him. Why spend it on Cass or Mr Holland? Hoard it until it *had* to be spent –

'It's now,' Hyde said, startling Lal. 'It's now. This is the last chance for Cass – and for you, if you're thinking of bargaining with the Sharmars. The lady down there on the screen is *dead*, Lal. Even you don't believe Cass killed her, do you?'

Lal shook his head.

'I don't think it was possible for Mr Cass –'

'Neither do I. So, where do we go from here? You point the gun at me, and I leave. You shoot me and I'm dead. And so is Cass, and so, probably, are you.'

'The British government will save *me*?' Lal asked scornfully.

'*I* will.' Keep your hands on the table, keep smiling, let's have utmost sincerity in the eyes, shall we? '*I* will,' he repeated. I will, too, if I can. But that isn't good enough for belief. A little cinematic heroism is what is required. Believe me, Mr Lal – come on, *believe me*!

Eventually: 'Very well. I was beginning to hate this place,

anyway. My brother has the most awful films here, week after week!' He smiled, but touched the gun's butt.

Hyde sat back on his chair. 'Good. That's settled. Can't say I'm sorry.' Conspiratorial grin. 'They're into drugs, correct? Their whole fortune is founded on drugs. That's what you two found out.'

'We found *evidence*, Mr Holland. We had photographs – of Prakesh Sharmar in the middle of a poppy field, for example. Of V.K. and his brother with high ranking Pakistani officers and government officials from Islamabad – with Sikhs, too, it is true, but the Pakistan connection is the important one. That is how it was smuggled out of Kashmir, with the connivance of the Pakistan army. On its way to the West.'

Lal was proud, and afraid, of what he had done. It had been a radical adventure, *Boys' Own Paper* in an honourable cause. Biggles and Algy exposing corrupt politicians instead of just tapping Orientals and Germans on the jaw.

He continued: 'People who would leave each other to die in the gutter, under any normal circumstances, were embracing like brothers in Srinagar –'

'Where?'

'On V.K.'s mistress' houseboat, Mr Holland, where else? Regular meetings, which we both eavesdropped upon.' The fear had dissipated now in the glow of the righteous goal. 'I have the tapes. Much of what *I* discovered I did not tell Mr Cass. It would have made him too afraid. You see, at first, the woman was useful. Then he became attached to her, and I was no longer able to trust him completely. He began to want to save her.'

'He would.'

'There were land deals, of course, buying more and more acreage to grow poppies – but that is a small matter beside the smuggling itself. It would bring them down, all of them, Congress and V.K. together.' His eyes glowed.

Srinagar . . . Christ. Ros . . . on one of the woman's bloody houseboats!

'Where – where would they have taken Cass, do you think, Mr Lal?' The tone was ingratiating, congratulatory.

'To Kashmir. Srinagar. The lake maybe, or one of the houses V.K. and his family own in Kashmir.' He shook his head. 'How much can you do to help?'

'Depends on what you can do to help me.' He tapped his palms lightly on the edge of the desk. His features were bland with confidence and alliance. 'I have to know – *have* – everything. I have to have it now, if I'm to do any good.' Lal was already shaking his head, and the glint of fear had returned to his eyes. 'You haven't got a government you can go to –' He pressed. Neither have I, he thought, all he'd got was Shelley. '– I have. I need proof, to be able to guarantee your safety and that of your wife, brother and anyone else – as well as Cass. I have to get him handed over.'

'Then what will happen to the material I have collected?'

Jesus, the *Sun* or the *News of the Screws* will pay you for it, Hyde thought. Think big, Lal.

'Your story would be worth a fortune in London. Look, it won't be used publicly by my people. It's still yours, in that sense. You'll have made copies?'

Lal hesitated, his forehead creased, for a long time. Eventually, he said: 'I must have time to think about it, Mr Holl –'

'There isn't any time *left*, Lal!' Christ, he had to get to Srinagar and Ros tonight. '*Cass* is in their hands, it's just a matter of time before he tells them where to find *you*. He knows about your brother, I take it?' He did. 'Then get off your arse, get me the stuff, and then lie back and think of all the money the rags will pay you in London, or New York! Now, do it, Lal!'

His reaction must have been subliminal, almost like capturing a moment ahead of the present. His anger was at what he only now seemed consciously to hear. An alarm. Not quite outside, but in the cinema itself. A continuous, old-fashioned ringing. A bloody *fire* alarm.

Lal heard it, too, and appeared wizened as if by the onset of heat and flames. Hyde was already hearing the first distant bells of fire engines thrusting towards the cinema through crowded streets. He rose, hands resting on the table, weight poised – hand on Lal's gun.

'Get the stuff.'

Lal's brother appeared in the doorway, for an instant.

'You must get out now, brother. Lata – I have sent her down the back stairs to the street. I must supervise, and be legitimately evacuated. Hurry, my damned fool brother!' Then he disappeared, his footsteps running along the corridor back towards the projection room. The murmur of the audience, an angry, disappointed hum at first, was now becoming a swell of panic. Hyde crossed to the window, holding Lal's gun by the barrel, and peered down into Chandni Chowk.

Police cars, their lights whirling above their roofs, and the first of the fire engines. A cordon of police and tapes pushing the crowd back, creating a bottleneck into which the audience would be funnelled to be checked. They knew that neither Lal nor himself would come out –

The cordon spread outwards, but there were more police, sifting the audience roughly as it panicked into the wide street. He turned to Lal, who seemed stunted by disbelief, then hurried along the corridor and through the deserted, silent projection room. There was a muffled bellow, as through a megaphone, from the auditorium, and the sound of whistles and orders. He peered, on tiptoe, out of the open flap of the projection window. The lights were on and there were torches sweeping the rows of seats. The noise of boots thudding on strips of carpet and on stairs. They'd be here in moments.

Then he smelt it – the smoke. The bastards were going to have a real fire, one they started. We don't need to interrogate you, sahib, we just want you out of the way, or panicked like a forest animal into our arms. Either way, you're done, sport –

The smoke's scent intensified. He hurried back towards the manager's office. He couldn't go down into the auditorium, probably wouldn't be able to use the fire escape. They had the place sealed off – and now they had it alight.

The office was empty. Lal had gone, neatly, simply, completely. And Hyde realised where. He dragged open the narrow door he had thought must lead to a lavatory, and found behind it a narrow, twisting flight of concrete steps. Lightless, silent. He sniffed.

The fire was approaching. He felt his skin warm and shivered, but that was only imagination. Outside, the sirens of more fire appliances were bullying through the streets. Trapped in the crowds, as he was trapped – oh, *shit* . . .

He closed the door behind him and began climbing the stairs towards the roof of the cinema. It did feel hotter – it *did*.

dark area

There was still no sign of smoke, but it was as if the fumes were already in his head and lungs; choking him, making thought obscure. He dialled the number, watching the door of the manager's office. Lal's gun was on the desk near his dialling hand, a round in the chamber, safety off. This was bloody daft. He had heard Lal moving about in which must be the roof space, heavy-footed and secretive. He had returned to the office – to make a phone call. His action, as much as that of Lal, was stupid beyond belief.

If he didn't call now, when would he? Later would be too late to organise an exit for himself and the man whose stumblings above him settled tiny flakes of plaster on his hair and shoulders and the littered desk.

He rendered his name to the secretary like a threat – then got whoever Shelley had manning the all-hours line.

'Hyde – I want a Dark Area. Understand? Blanket coverage by Delhi Station, active from this moment. Two in the dark. *Two*. Got that? What – location? Tell them a cinema's on fire on the Chandni Chowk. I'm inside –' His nostrils dilated. He could smell the smoke. There were no noises outside the office – yet. The staffer manning the line was clinical, detached – as required. 'No, no ingress. Tell them to wait, then move. Get Miles – say the field agent asked for Miles to command.' He replaced the old-fashioned, heavy receiver with a grimace. The smell of smoke was stronger now –

Wrong composition. He sifted it. The clever bastards, they

were using smoke canisters, just to fill the auditorium and make it look good. *After* the search, the flames. They'd burn the place down if they couldn't find him and Lal, just for the sake of verisimilitude. All the searchers needed were masks and breathing equipment. He strained to listen, but they were being cautious because they had the time. No one was hurrying. He moved to the door and shut it behind him before climbing the lightless stairs towards the roof. Lal had ceased moving, had burrowed into some corner behind inflammable rubbish and believed himself secure.

'Lal?' he whispered hoarsely as he reached the top of the stairs. 'Lal, you pillock, where are you?' The gun was in his hand, his own VP-70 still thrust into his waistband in the small of his back. He listened back down the stairs. Nothing yet. 'Lal, stop playing games!'

There was a small door into the roof space – which was obviously cramped, as only part of the roof sloped. It was mostly flat. The sirens and the noises of the crowd were loud through the thin walls, the broken skylight –

– through which a beam flashed, glaring yellow, stabbing like a finger on an ant. The roar of a helicopter drowned the other noises – he could feel the slightest breeze from its rotors. They'd be putting police down on the roof, or just waiting, marksmen dangling their legs out of the open doors of the chopper like kids sitting on a sea wall at high tide, until he and Lal raised their heads through the skylight or broke through the rotting roof. Neat, encompassing.

'Lal?' he called more loudly as the helicopter's growl threatened to drown his voice. 'Lal?' He pushed at the tiny door, through which Lal must have crawled, unless he was already on the roof –? No. They'd be calling down to him, or shooting at him if he was up there.

He crawled on hands and knees into the roof space. Through dozens of collapses and erosions of the lath and plaster, the helicopter's searchlight seeped and poked. There were patches of damp, and the ceiling between the joists across which he slowly crawled creaked and murmured at his passage.

'Lal – listen, you stupid bastard, they're going to set fire to the whole place! I smelt the smoke before I came up here, for Christ's sake!' There was a whimper of protest, as from a kicked dog, from the darkness away to his right. He turned towards it. 'Lal, I can get us out. I've made the arrangements. It's all laid on. Just come out and let's get moving before we get torched!' There was no need to inject panic, it had already taken up temporary residence in his voice. 'Come on, you bastard! Get off your arse and let's get out of here!'

He still could not see Lal, but could all but smell the man's fear, his retreated self in its den behind what looked like packing cases and old cinema hoardings propped against the far wall. Utensils rattled as Lal shuffled in terror. This had been his bolt hole – still was. Hyde realised, with a sick certainty, that Lal had no intention of moving. *All* safety was here, where he had spent maybe a fortnight or more above his brother's office, emerging for meals like a squirrel in a hard winter. The bad weather's only just beginning, Lal . . . but Lal wouldn't believe that. He was protected, crouched in there behind the garish images of men and women embracing and fighting. The helicopter's searchlight insisted through the roof.

Where the hell was the stuff? In there, behind the leaning, crazed hoardings and the cardboard boxes?

'Can't you smell the bloody smoke, Lal? You'll burn to death if you stay here!'

He *must* be able to catch the scent by now. He wouldn't recognise smoke canisters. He must want to live, or he wouldn't be here in the first place!

Hyde heard the scrabbling of what might have been a large rat, but it grunted with effort and clumsiness like a human in the dark, and then a hand touched his arm and clung to it. Lal's terrified features were caught by a glance of the searchlight. Lal was shivering as he knelt beside Hyde. In his hand he held the straps of a rucksack, then held up the bag as a pitiful offering.

'Come on – keep close to me.'

'Which way can we get out?' Lal began. 'They have a heli copter on the roof.' *I know they have*, don't ask awkward ques tions. The smoke was acrid in his throat, as it seeped up through cracks in the plaster of the ceiling below his knees and through the tiny door into the roof space. 'How can we get out, M Holland? How can we get out?'

The smoke was thick on the stairs, billowing wearily in the rays of light from the helicopter. They'd be coming any moment with their frogs' masks and soughing breaths. He turned back to Lal and saw the glitter of terrified eyes. Then Lal must have knel on the plaster of the ceiling between two joists, and it broke away from beneath his weight, revealing a jagged section of the office below – the littered desk and the strip of threadbare carpe in front of it. The chairs where he and Lata Lal had been seated

Lal cursed and shuffled. More plaster fell, showering the desk opening up the office and making the roof space lighter. Hyde could see Lal staring as if transfixed down into the room.

'Come on!' It was as if the joists and plaster beneath him had turned him to stone. Lal seemed unable to move. The rucksack was hanging limply from his grip, down into the office. Santa's fucking sack and he's stuck up the bloody chimney! Sweat streamed from Hyde's forehead and from beneath his arms; a sweat of panic and rage. *'Come on!'* he screamed at the immobile Lal.

Then there was a frog staring up at the hole in the ceiling, and a second, two-legged frog behind him. Both of them had guns. And there was only a moment of shock before the guns were raised towards Lal, who seemed newly afraid of the appar ition of the security men in breathing apparatus. Hyde made a lunge towards the hand holding the rucksack, but they had already fired twice, both bullets hitting Lal. He slumped forward, deadweight, then toppled through the hole in the rotten joists, tumbling onto the littered, plaster-strewn desk – to roll to stillness at the feet of one of the men who had shot him. The rucksack obligingly obtruded itself by lapping against the man's legs.

Lal was dead and they had everything he had. Everything . . . Hyde couldn't move for the shock of enraged disappointment. The searchlight's streams of light filtered into the cramped space where he knelt, its fingers touching his shoulders as if to arrest him.

The black tube of the Minimodulux night-vision module attached to the SLR camera tapped in nervous accompaniment as she attempted to steady it on the windowsill of her bedroom. Her fingers were damp with perspiration. The image intensifier tube was less than eight inches long and weighed no more than three and a half pounds, yet it felt leaden. She heard the footsteps of the police officer Sharmar had instructed to check on her, crossing the planked causeway from Sara's boat to the shore. Her tension invested the camera and its surveillance lens. The motor whirred, startling her, as if a weapon had accidentally discharged. The Sikh and the Pakistani were together at the blunt prow of Sara's houseboat, posed as if they understood they were being photographed. They were almost the last of Sharmar's guests to be caught by the night-vision tube and the shutter's click – then she would be done.

The footsteps along the shore were masked by the last of Srinagar's nocturnal activity. In a moment, they would sound on the causeway to her boat. Ros blinked away the perspiration that coldly blurred her vision.

She dragged the camera and the Minimodulux back through the window and slumped onto her bed, the betraying apparatus seeming strange and unmanageable in her quivering hands. The first footstep sounded on the planking at the back of the boat, sharp in the gleaming, still night. *A routine check*, she had heard Sharmar instruct – the brother, not the Prime Minister. *Check her papers – say it's for her safety. Get her to think of leaving.*

With what seemed a huge effort, she untwisted the image intensifier from the camera and fumbled a harmless, commercial daytime lens onto the body of the SLR. Folded it, in rhythm to the approaching footsteps, into its case. Surely, he'd wake the cook, wouldn't he, or the cookboy, and pause to explain himself? The Minimodulux lay phallically, full of threat, on her wide lap. The footsteps halted. The sound of the police officer's voice, then the cook's voice. *The memsahib is asleep.* Her terror made her want to giggle at the archaic form of respect. The policeman was not to be deterred. Ros clutched the tube against her breasts, as if intending to flee with it as with some prized possession from a burning house. One of the cats —

Christ, Hyde —!

She blundered across the bedroom, its furniture indistinct in the moonlight filtering through the mosquito screen — banged her right shin against a chair and stifled the exclamation. Then feverishly opened the bedroom door as the door to her left was tapped politely. She lurched across the narrow corridor and dumped her shivering body on the edge of the bath, still clutching the tube against her. The knocking sounded again, a little more peremptorily. The cook's murmur still protested her innocent sleep, which the policeman brushed aside. She stood up, her legs weak, and placed the tube on the lid of the toilet. Bending forward, she felt nauseously dizzy. As quietly as she could, she lifted the top of the cistern and placed the Minimodulux into the tepid water, replacing the lid gently, holding her breath, a terror of perspiration bathing her. Then she sat down on the edge of the bath once more. She stared down at her clothing, hanging in creases and folds. She hadn't changed, she was supposed to be asleep, her light had been out for nearly an hour —!

Christ . . . She held her forehead with her hot, damp palm, and forced her lips to move, rehearsing sound as she cleared her throat. The words seemed farther back than the sweet taste of nausea. She was shivering, and clutched her upper arms with her hands, arms folded tightly across her breasts.

Eventually, after the knocking had occurred once more: 'Yes? Who – is it?' A thin, reedy voice, like an actress playing the radio part of a child. 'I'm – who is it?'

'Ms Woode? I am from the police. It is a routine matter. May I come in?'

'Wait a minute – I'm busy. Hang on.' She had managed to shape her fear into something that approximated irritation. She stood up and deliberately flushed the toilet. Realised, as the cistern noisily emptied, that the Minimodulux tube was audibly moving against the vitreous china. As the flushing noise faded, and the cistern began to fill, there were small, distressed tappings. She stood, frozen, her hand having turned the cold water tap in the basin.

Cold water –

She dabbed the cold water on her face, rubbed at the wetness with a thick white towel. Smoothed her creased frock – *frock*, Christ –! She pulled the bathrobe from its hook behind the door and tugged off her dress, throwing it over the bath. Then she struggled into the too-small robe and tied it across her middle. Untidied her hair as she walked to the outer door and unlocked it.

'Yes?' she snapped, expelling nerves in the pretence of annoyance.

The police officer was dressed in a lightweight suit, was slightly taller than herself, and prepared to be deferentially pleasant – for the moment. The cook hovered apologetically behind his shoulder.

'I am sorry, Ms Woode. I am Inspector Dhanjal, of the Srinagar police. I am ensuring the safety of visitors to our city, in view of the circumstances.' His English was polished, carelessly displayed like a family's accumulated objets d'art. He wasn't any ordinary Kashmiri copper ... drugs? The stitch you up with an illegal substance kind of copper? Ros quailed. She'd heard Sharmar's brother give his instructions, but the conversation had moved about the room like a weak radio signal, wavering into audibility. And there had been a murmured babble from the other guests. 'We would not wish anything to happen to any of our foreign visitors,' Dhanjal added.

'Thanks for the concern,' Ros bridled. 'Does it mean you have to disturb me at this time of night?'

Dhanjal raised his hands apologetically. 'I am sorry for that. Your arrival has only just been processed. I'm sorry. But I would like to ensure you are safe here. Could we call it a security check, perhaps?'

Search. Christ, Hyde – you owe me for this bloody lot!

'I feel safe enough.'

'But – an expert eye, perhaps?'

'The town seemed quiet, tonight.' She was holding onto the door. The bloody cistern hadn't finished filling up yet! 'Is there any cause for alarm?'

'Perhaps not.' His eyes were becoming suspicious, glinting in the moonlight. The air cooled her body beneath the bathrobe, tautened the skin on her cheeks. 'Nevertheless, we of the Srina-gar police –' Blow that for a tale, mate. '– would feel happier if we had made a security check on our visitors. Especially those in such isolated positions as this.'

Just let the bugger in, Ros – just let him in. It was as if Hyde was prompting her. It even sounded like him. He's getting sus-picious, he thinks you should be more frightened by rumours and bangs offstage.

'Yes. I see. Come in, Inspector.'

She held the door wide for him and he squeezed past her. The cook shrugged another of his interminable, silent apologies, and departed towards the cookboat. The lights of Srinagar were a hazy, deceptively peaceful glow. As she turned, Dhanjal was already checking the windows of the lounge, having switched on the lights. At once, there were small explosions of insects against the mosquito screens.

Ros followed him into the lounge. He was determined to make a search, that much was evident.

'Are Ms Mallowby's boats a special target, then?' she asked, disconcerting Dhanjal, who looked up from an apparent inspection of a window lock. Beneath the window, Ros' handbag yawned. The fingers of his hidden right hand had played over it, she guessed.

'Oh, no, I would not wish you to think that.' His English was suddenly more stagily Indian as he, too, deceived. This is going to cost you, Hyde – real money. She seized on the idea. It's adding up, Hyde. Fifty quid for the Cats' Protection League. 'It is wise to be sure, however.'

'OK. Pity you had to wake me up, though.'

'The bedroom windows, please?' He put down the telephone. 'This way.'

With a trepidation she could not entirely suppress, she opened the door to her bedroom.

'Ah, I'd advise you did not sleep with the window open, Ms Woode,' Dhanjal said at once, turning to her. That's another fifty for the Samaritans, Hyde, she announced to herself. In a strange way it calmed and distracted, enabling her to appear off-balance and nervous in a way that was free of guilt and professionalism – which he would be looking for. I *am* a bloody amateur, she told herself.

'I won't.' He closed the window for her. 'Just used to fresh air.'

'In London?' He shook his head. 'Ms Woode, I really do not think that this houseboat is very secure, though it pains me to slander Ms Mallowby.' He smiled. 'But, I would suggest a move to one of the larger hotels – for your own safety.'

Was he there to threaten, or inspect? Suddenly, Ros did not know, and was unnerved. Bugger fifty quid handouts, she calmed herself. This is *really* serious. Two hundred quid for Famine Relief . . .

'I – I take it I can choose?'

He had moved out of the bedroom, having glanced through the window across at Sara's houseboat – and seemed satisfied

167

at the safety of distance. Glanced, too, at the camera, then disregarded it. An unspecialised Japanese 35mm SLR – which it was. *Now*. She controlled her breathing, but felt a tremor in her flesh that made her wrap her arms more closely about her.

Dhanjal peered into the bathroom, hesitated – so that she hovered at the brink of panic for what seemed minutes – then withdrew his head. Then he marched through the lounge once more and opened the doors onto the verandah. He stood with his hands on his hips, staring at Dal Lake like a visitor.

Then he bent and picked up the recorder, turning it in his hand like a nugget of what might only be iron pyrites. The cord of the headphones dangled from the recorder. Smiling at her, he picked up the headphones and pulled them over his head. Ros watched with assumed, taut passivity. He listened for a moment before switching off the recorder. Then he inspected the cassette inside.

'I am, perhaps, too young to remember,' he murmured. Cheeky bastard.

The meeting had declined into huddles and coteries. Some members had even left. She had concealed the tapes in her suitcase and substituted *Blood on the Tracks*. This Kashmiri didn't like Dylan – but felt that Dylan fitted with the image he had acquired of her.

A concept of innocence, of middle-aged prologue to pathos and decline. Fat white woman. Hyde, it's bloody two hundred and fifty to the NSPCC if it's anything!

Dhanjal seemed satisfied; mystified, and irritated that he had been despatched on a pointless little exercise. His self-importance made him intolerant, impatient.

'Thank you, Ms Woode. I would heed my advice, if I were you – but I can do nothing to force you, of course. Good night.'

With a great effort, Ros closed the door slowly behind him, then leaned back against the perfumed wood of the corridor's rich panelling, head lifted to the carved ceiling. Oh, my God –! Oh, my sainted bloody Aunt –!

Hyde, you'd better get here tomorrow – I can't stand any more of this. No more of it. Charity donations or not, *get here!*

Hyde ducked aside from the ragged, gaping hole in the ceiling, uncertain that he remained undetected. The two men in the frog-mask breathing apparatus still had their guns drawn. They seemed mesmerised by the body of Lal lying amid the plaster, his head at a strange angle, the light palm of one hand twisted so that it appeared about to accept a furtive remuneration. They were drawn to the rucksack, which had obligingly spilt folders of snapshots at their feet. Had they seen him? They'd flinched back at Lal's fall, after they'd shot him, and now one of them was kneeling beside the body. He could hear the artificially loud pumping of their breathing inside the masks. There was a leak of dark blood across a wedge of fallen plaster, near the feet of the man who remained standing.

He decided they hadn't seen him. They were in no hurry now, he recognised, peering forward down into the room, balanced on his haunches, hands taking much of his weight. Their magnified breathing was more immediate than the noises of sirens and the continuous, disregarded din of the fire alarm. The helicopter's rotor noise had retreated too, filtered out for the sake of survival.

Feet were dropping onto the roof above him, regular small detonations. The chopper was dropping two – three? – men onto the roof to link up with these two below –

Noise of an R/T, from the room. English rather than Hindi. Official language. He leaned forward, like a monkey about to leap from one branch to another. The snapshots, Lal's papers, the other contents of the rucksack, were spread on the littered, plaster-strewn desk, and were being relayed to whoever had command outside, or in the chopper.

'– the man Lal, confirmed, sir . . . yes, the material is very interesting, sir.' The tone was authoritative. These two, and the men on the roof, must be elite troops. Either army commandos or Intelligence. 'Yes, sir — we'll bring the bag and leave by the roof. Sir —'

Hyde watched, appalled at the idea that they would climb the stairs, pass his hiding place and leave by the door onto the flat roof. He might hide over *there*, in a still-dark corner . . . Forget it, he admitted, as he saw the man with the R/T draw a wedged, bulky pistol from inside his black windcheater and aim it at the sagging sofa. Flame glared at once, dazzlingly bright. A flame-cartridge pistol. He had turned his head away, but his eyesight was flaring with solar images. The acrid smell of the charge, the smoke from the sofa which would choke him —

They'd start other fires now, burn the whole place down. His vision wouldn't clear. The two men moved through smoke and flame and the sunspots on his retinae out of the room towards the stairs. The fumes from the sofa were scratching at the back of his throat. Without conscious decision, he had closed the small door through which he had crawled to find Lal, and listened now as their footsteps climbed towards the roof. R/T voices crackled like flames. They were hurrying now, the rucksack prize enough, the burning cinema a rather definite kind of insurance against having overlooked anything. The roof door banged open, then closed again on the bellowing of the helicopter.

He clasped his handkerchief over his mouth and nose. The whole of the roof space glowed like the interior of a small furnace, and the smoke and fumes rolled upwards. The office was burning a bloody treat. There was nothing left up here, nothing he could see. Lal had had everything in the rucksack, everything that was going to make him rich. His body was obscured by smoke, licked at by flames. Hyde's temperature soared.

The helicopter's rotors moved away into the night, leaving the noise of the alarm and the sirens of fire appliances and ambulances. They'd left, assured of an irrefutable certainty — if the Englishman was inside, he was dying or dead already.

He opened the door. The staircase was blind with smoke. He coughed retchingly against the fumes, more dense now. His lungs felt hot. Something exploded in the office below. He eased his way up the stairs, hand sliding along the wall, and kicked open the door to the roof. He staggered out, his body overwhelmingly relieved yet flinching against an anticipated flurry of shots from someone they might have left on the roof. He dragged air in, his head spinning, his lungs bursting.

Flames gouted from skylights and gaps in the tiles where the roof sloped, like a line of flares laid for the night landing of a small aircraft. He hurried to the edge of the roof and looked over the parapet. His eyes ran with tears, and he brushed them away. The side alley was taped off and empty. He saw firemen passing its opening onto the Chowk, the snake of hoses, the gleam of a ladder reflecting hot flame. There was no drainpipe, no fire escape. He was trapped on the roof, as they had anticipated. He looked up wildly. The lights of the helicopter as it retreated were no bigger than the warm stars. They were bloody certain. He glanced around the roof. There was no escape.

He felt the panic rising. Nothing rational was going to get him out. The panic had to do it or nothing would. He stared at the roof across the alley, and at the barrenness of the cinema's roof. No ladders, no planks, nothing he could use ... distance? Too much.

Alarms and sirens were louder, phantasmagorical. A part of the roof, a whole raft of wooden tiles and joists, fell inward, leaving a volcanic hole through which the fire erupted. Most of the pitched part of the roof had gone, sliding with a terrifying laval noise down into the bowels of the auditorium. The flames glared over him and he was enveloped by smoke. He was gasping and coughing as a shift in the slight breeze moved the fire closer to him. The concrete beneath his knees and feet seemed to be hotter.

He looked longingly across the gap of the alley to the other, smaller roof. It wasn't flat like that of the cinema, but sloped with ill-fitting wooden tiles. There was no lip of guttering. He could see two skylights set like eyes, seductive and mocking. The parapet was a couple of feet high, he'd have to jump onto the parapet and thrust himself off, land flat – it was impossible, but what was the alternative . . . ?

Do it.

He backed away from the low parapet, walking steadily, sensing the heat against his back, feeling his temperature climbing inexorably –

He ran, head down, the parapet jogging towards him. He was as helpless as if he was in a car rushing towards a collision. Images of flame, images of pain and broken limbs, the swallowing sensation of falling, the parapet under the arch of his foot, the last stride and thrust from a powerless leg, the moment above the alley, and then the collision.

The breath was forced out of his body, his chest and stomach ached, his knees were stabbed with pain, his hands hurt as they slapped against the wooden tiles – tile coming away in his right hand, left one loosening, hands scrabbling, his body slipping, so that his feet and ankles were over the edge of the roof, then his shins and knees –

Right hand holding, holding –

– left hand scrabbling, come on, you bloody useless *thing*, get hold of something . . . breath impossible to draw, the blood pounding in his temples, left hand, left hand – legs waggling over the alley, pointlessly seeking purchase against air –

– left hand holding, right hand climbing, stomach and crotch shrugging themselves further up, back onto the roof . . . right foot holding against a gap where a tile had been dislodged.

He lay there until he was certain that there were no noises from the alley other than those funnelled from the Chowk; until he was assured he had broken no ribs or limbs. Until the first ragged gasps had become breathing that was recognisably human. The sirens had died like the anticipation of a crowd that had been watching him. Behind him, another section of the roof of the cinema collapsed and he was bathed in brighter, fiercer light from the fire. There were sparks in the breeze landing beside him, on him. Smell of singed cloth and hair. He beat at his head with one hand. Licks of flame leapt from the wooden roof on which he lay spreadeagled.

Slowly, carefully, unable to suppress a grin that felt like a rictus after cyanide ingestion, he climbed the roof, wriggling his way up like a crippled lizard. He reached the nearest skylight and heaved it open. Old paint flaked. Below him was darkness. He crouched, then lowered himself carefully into the musty scent. A roof space littered with boxes and junk. His feet touched joists and he released his grip on the frame of the skylight. Balanced himself, hearing his breathing magnified by the musty silence, then fished in his pockets for the cigarette lighter whose lid clanged open like a steel door. The wobbly flame was little more illuminating than the reflection of the fire, but he saw the joists –

– and the hatch from the room or stairwell below. Opened it, listening to the gurgle of a water tank and the rusty whirr of a bat. The glow of the fire through windows revealed an office. He dropped into the room.

Then he hurried. Three flights of stairs, the offices and corridors becoming progressively better decorated, more Western and proclamatory. The ground floor was a travel agency.

Through the windows, he could see the play of hoses and the scamper of fire-fighters and the taped-back crowd in the Chowk, the scene played upon by an orange light. He made for the rear of the building, his elbow aching, splinters in his left hand, his knees raw, chest aching with each breath – *no* broken ribs, he reminded himself. He smashed a small window when he found the door locked. A narrow yard, an open gate, then an alley. He paused for a moment, then brushed at his clothes. Pockmarked with the singeing of sparks, greened by the old wooden tiles. You'll do – in the dark, anyway. He coughed again. His throat was raw from fumes and smoke.

Where would they be? On the Chowk – Miles wouldn't have the imagination to look round the back. Casually, after checking the pistol – he'd lost Lal's gun somewhere – he followed the alley until it junctioned with a crowded street, then made for Chandni Chowk. Paused at the corner. The police had long since completed their check on the cinema audience, who had melted into the absorbed, gabbling crowd held back by tapes. Fire appliances and police cars and ambulances littered the street. Glass exploded somewhere in the direction of the cinema.

He waited for ten minutes.

The young man who approached him furtively even glanced at a photograph – presumably of Hyde – before making contact. He seemed more concerned with his form of address than with anything else.

'I – Mr Hyde . . . *sir*?' Was he a sir? Did he have any rank? Hyde saw the young man's eyes bemused by the total significance of his question.

'Don't worry about it.'

Surprised, the young man said: 'Lowell – Hyde.'

'Lowell,' Hyde replied, luxuriating in the nervous shiver of relief that possessed him. 'Where's Miles? Let's get on with it.'

'This way.'

Two more fell in with them as they walked along the Chowk away from the cinema, where the blaze seemed to be slowly falling into the grasp of the fire-fighters. A pall of smoke hung over the street and the smell of burning cloth and wood clung about them. Dark Area. The relief was stronger now, its effect making his legs rubbery and ill-moving. The aches of his impact with the roof nagged. Lal's death – *the loss of what Lal had!* – was a hangover of frustration and anger.

Lowell opened the door of a black, stretched Granada parked two blocks away from the cinema. The street was crowded, its occupants moving, pausing, shopping with strange normality. Hyde glanced behind him, as if to assure himself of the reality of the fire. Miles' features glared up at him from the rear of the Granada.

'Get in!' he snapped. Hyde grinned contemptuously. 'Where's the other one? *Two* in the dark, you claimed.'

'He didn't make it.'

'Come on, for God's sake – don't waste any more of our time!'

'All right, keep your drawers on, Miles – '

He bent to climb into the rear of the car. Sitting beside Miles was an Indian in an expensive grey suit, his hands calmly resting, palms down, on his thighs, his interest in Hyde apparently minimal.

'Come on, Hyde – '

'Who the hell is *he*?'

'You don't need to know. The deal's done, Hyde. You're on your way within the hour – and good bloody riddance! You're guaranteed – '

'This is supposed to be a Dark Area – that doesn't mean black faces, Miles. What the hell have you done?'

'How the hell else could we have done it in the time?' Hyde was aware of Lowell, the others. 'It's a *deal*! You'll be – '

'You prick, Miles! You think Gunga Din here – ' The Indian's face was pinched. ' – is just going to see me off the premises? You *pillock*!' he raged, appearing absorbed in the confrontation, aware of passers-by stopping, off-balanced by his raised voice. Miles' features were puzzled, then enraged. 'You made a deal with Intelligence because you're too bloody idle to organise a Dark Area!'

'You'll be in London tomorrow morning, Hyde – out of my hair! Get in the bloody car!' He was already looking over Hyde's hunched shoulder towards Lowell and whoever else had closed in behind Hyde.

'Tell him where I'll be,' Hyde snapped at the Indian. Calculating eyes alive, mouth a narrow line, a sense of preparation. His people wouldn't be far away – he wouldn't trust Miles either. 'In the morning – bottom of the bloody river!'

'Get him in the car!' Miles barked, but Hyde slammed the door before the order was complete. Miles rocked back in his seat, staring at the hand he had rescued before the door closed on it. The Indian's hand was reaching for his door handle. Hyde's elbow caught Lowell's soft midriff, before he turned and saw the other two of them hesitating as Lowell buckled over, retching.

Hyde moved into the crowd at once, then into the first side street off the Chowk. Dark Area my arse! Miles just wanted the horse manure removed from the street and thought the Indians, nice polite chaps as they were, on our side and all that, would help him put Hyde on a safe flight out of Delhi, back to London. What a dickhead –

He slipped and minced through the thinning crowds without looking back until he reached the Mukherji Marg, north of the Chowk. Heading for the railway station, they'd assume. Having to get out under his own steam. He thought he saw one bobbing head, then a second moving radarlike to locate him. The black Granada, too, ploughing through the crowd as if across a muddy field. The Indian Intelligence officer was out of the car, so was Miles, both of them angry as they bundled themselves in the direction they knew he had taken. He hurried away along Mukherji, then crossed the street towards a rank of decrepit taxis – a few black hackney carriages, ancient Ambassadors, the revenants of old European cars. He scanned the railings of Mahatma Gandhi Park, the portico of the railway station, the town hall. Picked out Lowell, still delicately clutching his stomach, another face he recognised, two purposeful Indians, and the Granada.

Then he bent into the first old taxi at the rank.

'Safdarjang Aerodrome – no haggling, I'll pay what's on the clock.' Twice the price, but then, twice the eagerness.

'Certainly, sahib – into the back, sir!'

Hyde climbed in, raising dust from the ancient upholstery. The Ambassador pulled chuggingly out into the traffic, heading west before it turned into Shradha Nand Marg, paralleling the main railway line towards Connaught Place. He took out his wallet and removed the scrap of paper on which he had scribbled the pilot's name. A two-Cessna operation called Krishna Air

Taxis, flying anywhere – for a price – out of the aerodrome near the racecourse and the polo ground. They'd be watching the trains, Indira Gandhi airport, the bus terminals, but they might not be alert to a small plane taking off from the aerodrome.

Might not. If he was quick.

It had seemed more certain when he'd booked the flight to Srinagar that morning, as a backup. It had seemed much more certain, then –

Ros lay in the darkness, the headphones of the recorder against her ears, her body half-propped on pillows. Her position suggested an uncomfortable sense of hospital, of invalidity, to her frayed, worn nerves. The illuminated dial of her travelling clock showed three-fifteen. Only the Sharmar brothers remained on Sara's houseboat, and awake. She had not heard Sara's voice since she had dismissed herself from Sharmar's presence hours earlier. V. K. Sharmar showed no interest in joining her in bed.

She knew what they were doing. Arranging India's future. Carefully sustaining and controlling the violence in the Punjab and Kashmir, so that both might be surrendered without national outrage at some unspecified time in the future, after they had won a general election.

They had to compromise; they were afraid of Moslem fundamentalism, and the power of Pakistan. They would buy Pakistan's friendship, buy peace with the Indian half of Kashmir . . . because the Soviet Union had shattered into pieces and India's most powerful ally didn't want to hand over money and weapons and support any longer. Couldn't afford to.

What wearied her more than any other element of the situation was the see-saw of relief and tension she experienced. It was listening to the Sharmars as they talked and drank, and waiting for them to finish – or to mention herself. That was it, that anticipation and its disappointment. Being free of suspicion yet aware that suspicion could be expressed at any moment –

Three thirty-two. It was voiced.

'Dhanjal seems convinced. I do not know —' Prakesh Sharmar.

'What?'

'The woman on the next houseboat.'

'Why are you so concerned?'

'Because of what we are *doing* here — because we are here, the others are here.'

'Is she anyone official?'

'I do not know. She will be watched, brother. I *know* she should be watched.'

'Very well, then,' V. K. Sharmar replied wearily. 'If you think so.'

Ros snatched off the headphones, as if they would transmit her coarse, sharp breathing to the Sharmars. Her heart palpitated with great, rapid thudding noises and she pressed her hand against it. It wasn't better knowing — it was worse, much worse.

It was as if her heartbeat was an echo-sounding device to locate metal objects at great depth, where the tapes were, the location of the recorder on the bedside table, the Minimodulux night-lens, the camera, each little tub of exposed film. Knowing that it would take less than a minute for a trained man to find every piece of evidence.

Not knowing where Hyde was — *if* Hyde was, any longer.

She was shivering. Her entire body was chilled and trembling. She had to leave. Had to get away — in the morning — before they *knew* about her.

PART TWO

Full Employment

'Stand now with thine enchantments,
and with the multitude of thy sorceries,
wherein thou hast laboured from thy youth;
if so be, thou shalt be able to profit,
if so be, thou mayest prevail.'

Isaiah: ch. 47, v.12

EIGHT

doubt and certainty

Even the static of the code room seemed musty to Miles as he
shut the door behind himself and Dickson. Shut it on an image
of the High Commission's lawns glistening with the first of the
day's constant watering, the sprays turning slowly like dancers'
skirts. Hyde was more alive to him with the door shut; the
absolute *shithouse*–! Dickson was enraged at him for losing
Hyde, releasing his grip on the loose cannon. As for Shelley –
who knew which way Aubrey's protégé would jump on anything! Shelley could start handing out armfuls of manure, piling
it on . . . That bastard Hyde – the deal was *done*, for Christ's
sake. There was no setup, it was a plain tit-for-tat, a favour. No
questions asked, no names, no pack-drill. Hyde would have been
on the plane to London by now, in sodding Business Class, too,
if he hadn't bolted into the night, cocking up a perfectly well-
organised Dark Area and making *him* look a wanker in Dickson's
eyes and maybe in Shelley's, too – oh, *sod* Hyde!

He eventually murmured: 'Sir? Better get it over with, I
suppose –?' He realised his grin was sickly, undernourished.
Dickson's features were momentarily contemptuous; then the
eyes within the diplomatic Noh mask became more calculating.

'Yes – Jim.' There was a hesitation before Dickson pronounced
his name, as if he were close to having forgotten it.

The room was empty, apart from themselves. Miles checked
the equipment, which had been brought to readiness for full
Signals with Century House. He felt hot – yet it was the thought
of Hyde that was raising his temperature, rather than his

anticipation of any discolouration of his record. Yet perhaps it was better that the bastard had gone haring off. It gave him and Dickson another opportunity to insinuate their disbelief in Cass' story and his innocence. If Hyde chose to believe otherwise, so what.

It did not calm. That was just knowledge. Instinct continued to hate Hyde and raise his temperature accordingly. He wiped at his damp forehead as Dickson seated himself with some ceremony in front of the main console.

'Ready, sir?' Miles asked. Then added: 'Hyde can't really *believe* in Cass' innocence, can he? I mean, Cass was talking rubbish from the start. He was having an affair – *and* he did the woman in after a frenzied quarrel – ?' Even to himself, it sounded as if he were rehearsing a cover story. Dickson, however, after narrowing his nostrils momentarily as at a sudden, unpleasant odour, appeared mollified; the structure of the story, the account of their behaviour and attitude, seemed to satisfy him.

'If the D-G wants any more than we can offer – Jim,' he announced in a warmer tone, 'then he'll have to find Hyde for himself. Or Cass – if the man ever turns up. Very well, Jim, let's get on with it.' The slight impatience was a gesture of confidence.

Perhaps it would be all right. After all, what could Shelley do to them? He sat down beside Dickson. And what, on his complete tod, could Hyde do to upset *any* apple-cart? The bugger had probably started the fire in the cinema, anyway, just as the police suspected . . . not to mention a body they'd found inside. Shot to death. Hyde was a berserker, trying to pay an old debt. Off his trolley –

He switched on the microphones, readied the high-speed tapes. The needles twitched at their breathing in the silent room.

Hyde was just bloody paranoid, that was it – all of it. The needles quivered more violently at his exhalation. It was easy to hate the bastard, hard to remember he wasn't important any more. *Nobody*'s star pupil –

*

182

He had little need of Hyde's file. He *knew* Patrick's psychological profile, service record, peccadilloes, shadows and lights, relationships – everything – almost by heart. To have sent for the file would have implied consideration or reconsideration, neither of which was necessary. And the file would *not* provide further illumination.

Peter Shelley thrust his hands into his pockets and stood at the broad window overlooking the Thames, turning his head from the watercolours and charcoals framed on the buff walls towards the river, glinting with morning sun. The leaves along the embankment hinted at yellow. The air-conditioning purred as if pleased at remaining necessary. Shelley removed one hand and brushed at his hair, then clutched at his narrow chin. What the devil was Patrick playing at now?

Perhaps he'd *over*-prodded his indebtedness, so that he was determined to find something – anything – that would get Cass out safely.

Both hands were again in his pockets, as he nodded sternly towards the river. It must be the answer. Hyde believed this fantastic story about the Sharmars because he must. Driving himself forward with it.

No assistance, hands off, he'd agreed with Dickson and Miles half an hour earlier. Accepted their assurances, which were his own, that the Sharmars were not guilty and that Cass was. How could he believe otherwise, for God's sake? V.K. a drug-dealer? How could there possibly exist any *proof* that V. K. Sharmar, Prime Minister of India, was actively engaged in the growing, refining and smuggling of heroin? Cass must be wrong – and because he was wrong, he was guilty of murder. *Quod erat demonstrandum* – inescapable logic, the one inextricable from the other.

And Patrick was a convert, a zealot after his new faith.

Must be . . .

The Foreign Secretary, the whole of the Foreign Office, was behind Sharmar. Big-friend status. Coming man, right policies, man of the future, just what India needs, what *we* need in India

. . . The whispers seeped along the corridors of the Foreign Office and through Whitehall like a chorus of breezes. Gentle zephyrs, no rough winds shaking any darling buds, not in the Sharmars' case.

Q.E.D. again, then. He was answerable to the Foreign Secretary and could not go against him. So, Patrick was mistaken, abused – just like Cass.

And on his own –

Shelley glanced at the wide desk and its banks of telephones. Then back towards the river and the slow patrol of craft on its wrinkled, glittering light. *Proof?* Even proof would hardly be able to dynamite current thinking into new channels on the subject of V.K. Without proof, nothing whatsoever could be done. If Patrick wouldn't come out when the chance was provided, then there was nothing he could do for him – nothing.

And if what Delhi Station reported was the literal truth, that Hyde had killed an Indian citizen and was being hunted by the police . . . it was a bloody mess all round. If Patrick would only get out of there, it might be smoothed over . . . which meant, if only Cass were dead. It was a bitter, rather shaming thought, but it was a consummation rather fervently to be wished. Whatever was going on, and whatever the truth, Cass' demise would be a clean fracture. If Phil Cass was dead, and Patrick learned that fact, then he would get himself out of Delhi and away. And take Ros with him – the image of her niggled like a splinter beneath some mental nail.

He sniffed. He had erred, it was true, in sending Hyde, in giving the slightest credence to Cass' story. Otherwise, the pressure of the facts was irresistible. Even Kenneth, who was not at his elbow with an admonishing look, would have had to have seen that. Phil Cass killed the woman in some sort of frenzied argument, and the rest was convenient fantasy. A dream that wouldn't persevere in a bright morning –

– must be.

*

She had set out, in a hailed shikara, with a deliberate bravado that had now evaporated. She had crossed the lake through the clinging, chill mist, as if engaged upon some covert enterprise, towards the Nishat Bagh, the Garden of Delight, on the eastern shore. Now the sun was out, the shawl she had clutched about her in the stern of the narrow shikara was dry as it hung over her arm, where her stitches still pulled. On the lake, hearing the noises of waking birds and the cries of vendors and the unseen, slow dip of oar or pole, the shawl had clung as damply as the mist. As the mist dispersed, the mountains had lumbered, alien and high with menace.

None of her admonitions, her self-ridicule, could recapture the initial bravado. Not while she knew she was being followed.

If you can't sit still, then go for a walk. Nowhere quiet. Hyde again, tossing scraps of tradecraft from his dangerous table. Where the hell was the bugger? Terraces, water, dark lilac hedges, flowerbeds, amid which the scene in the now hot morning air was sickly, clinging like too much perfume. Ros paused to take photographs, admire a lattice-windowed pavilion, a fountain erect in the windless air. Dal Lake was diminished, yet she could make out Sara's small group of houseboats like the shadow of a detached retina at the corner of eyesight. Nanga Parbat, the vast mountain, was reflected in the lake. Shikaras and other craft plied the water like insects.

She rubbed her arm where the stitches plucked like a sudden chill. There were two of them. Sharmar must have sent them after her, and Dhanjal probably controlled them. She had seen neither face before – they might be local police. Birdsong littered the bushes and paths, bright plumage flashed into shrubs and trees. The colours of the new flowers were hot, alien, real only as a backcloth against which she posed, out of place. And alone. In her capacious shoulder bag, were the tiny tapes and the tubs of film. She could not risk taking them to be developed – though what else was she to do with them? What *use* were they? She had not dared approach the airport or even call to book a flight. There was an army presence there.

She'd bloody done the bloody job, for Christ's sake —! So, where *was* he?

She felt dizzy, as if her eyes had let in too much of the hot light and the dazzle from the lake and snow-capped peaks. Her broad hand pressed hotly against her forehead. She felt nauseous with fear — not because of the two men who hung back as if respectful or without orders, but because she hadn't heard from Hyde. Because she knew they knew who *Holland* really was — because they must have him; knowledge which had forbidden sleep.

Ros stumbled to a wooden bench and slumped heavily onto it as a sense of all his absences rushed against her like a bully. Sitting offered no relief. The place and its few tourists was autumnal and lonely, the birds mocking. The Sharmars and whoever else had been on Sara's houseboat had gone. She must recover the bug, but hadn't the nerve or any idea how to accomplish it. But that was a pinprick, like the small protests from the new lips of healing skin on her arm. It was Hyde's danger, and its likely outcome, that churned in her head and stomach.

One of the two men following her passed idly by, all but unnoticed. He seemed content at her lack of occupation, alert to the bench as a possible place of contact. With whom, for Christ's sake? The bugger was dead or incarcerated . . .

. . . it was hotter, brighter it seemed, when she finally looked up, wiping her eyes clear, steadying herself on the arm of the bench spotted with bird droppings. With a vast effort, she moved her body onto boneless legs and forced herself to walk towards the gate in the high wall surrounding the gardens. Gravel rustled beneath her flat shoes. Her full skirt clung around her thighs and her blouse constricted her breathing. Ahead of her again was the lake, the purposeful mountain occupying the northern part of its mirror, the small clutter of insects on the far shore that were Sara's houseboats black in the light.

At once, there was a shikara, but she was reluctant to get into it, as if the water churned betrayingly. Then she stepped in and sat down heavily. The boat rocked. The small Indian in a ragged shirt and shorts seemed amused at her bulk, but she had no energy for either resentment or self-mockery. The shikara, poled with a long, knobbly tree branch, slipped out onto the lake, and she glanced behind her, just once. One of the two men was hesitant on the landing stage, then he, too, climbed into a narrow boat which was poled after her in slow pursuit. The slowness of it suggested inexorability, the plod of something she could not avoid or escape. She clutched her arms about her knees, and the strap of the shoulder bag slid to her wrist, as if to suggest its being snatched by another's hand. She shivered. The mountain seemed to press closer, the dark beetles of the houseboats became larger, brightly coloured, like boiled sweets in the sunlight. Then they were low buildings, eerily floating. Kashmir was sullied by the dread of what must have happened to Hyde.

The shikara behind her own glided past as her boat bumped against the steps of her houseboat, its prow knocking as if to alert someone who might be waiting for her. She paid, the tip effusively accepted, and clambered aboard. The narrow boat slid away, now pursuing her pursuer. Srinagar seemed unnaturally quiet. She paused, dizzied again. She must get out of the place, back to –

– well, *where?* London? To Shelley – ?

The cookboy looked up from washing pans, his smile gleaming. Ros ignored him and passed into the cool gloom of the houseboat. The scented wood was sharp to her heightened senses as she all but saw Dhanjal or someone else unfurl themselves from a chair in the lounge –

– empty. Her breathing was loud in the silence. Only motes moved in the sunlight strained through the net curtains and mosquito screens at the windows.

The bedroom door opened. She turned with huge reluctance. '*Christ –*' she breathed. 'Where have you *been*?' she accused him.

Hyde was shocked by her appearance, the signs of strain and tension around her dark-stained eyes, quivering on her mouth. She backed away from him, waving a hand as if to ward off his advance. He grabbed the hand, then her body, which shook against him in mingled relief and anger.

'All right?' he asked insensitively.

'No, I'm *not* all right!' she burst out. 'You've put me through the bloody mangle, you bugger!' The two statements balanced each other, the first angry, the second relieved welcome.

'Sorry.' Her body went on shuddering against him, her eyes and mouth wet against his cheek and neck. He swallowed residual guilt, controlling his own quiver of relief. She was all right. In a bad way, but *there*.

When her shaking had diminished, he sat her in the large settee and perched on its arm, stroking her hair. Her hand rested on his thigh, clamping it firmly as if to test the flesh's reality.

Then she said: 'You stink.'

'Morally or physically, darling?'

'Probably both.' She sniffed. 'Your clothes will do for the moment. I thought you were —' His hands paused on her head, squeezing the back of her skull. She was warned into habitual silence regarding his risks.

'Just think of the size of the gap. I got through it. Not even really close.'

Then they were silent, his silence enforcing hers. Until eventually, she was, by the relaxed pressure of his hand on her hair, allowed to ask: 'How did you get here?'

'On the boat?'

'The lot.'

Ros' debriefing. He could permit that. Only scars, limps, or an uncontrollable shudder required the nastier details. He was exhibiting no physical symptoms of another brush with his diseased world. She'd be satisfied with a timetable, his travel arrangements.

188

'Light aircraft out of Delhi – last night. Then a taxi. I got on board from a shikara or whatever they call them, after having a look at the other houseboats from the lake. Not much doing –'

'Not any more, *no*! she snapped. 'You missed the bloody *party*!'

He suppressed the shiver that threatened to accompany a memory of Lal's body lying on his brother's office floor amid plaster debris, of the frog mask looking up at the gaping ceiling, and the heat and smell of smoke.

'Any good – the party?'

She wasn't ready yet. There was a residue of unused anger and fear.

'I've been *followed*, Hyde –! They're interested in me. I heard it –' She glanced at her shoulder bag, then at the Walkman lying on the table. 'I heard them talking about me, Hyde!'

He started brushing her hair, but the set of her head seemed to resist the gesture as patronising, uncomfortable. Yet she did not shake his hand away, instead she calmed slowly, her hands greeting and reassuring one another in her lap. Oh, Ros, I'm sorry –

Then: 'No one's searched this place.'

'You'd know, of course – having just arrived?'

'I know. Who's interested?'

'The brothers. They were both here last night. Gone now. A copper called Dhanjal has been around. Said it was routine. It wasn't.'

'There's no one out there now – unless you brought them back with you?'

'One followed me across the lake. There were two of them.'

'It's OK, then – for now.'

She turned her head and looked up at him. 'Are we getting out?' She attempted to suppress the plea, but it was nakedly in her eyes.

'What have you got?'

She swallowed in distaste, her eyes flaring angrily before she closed them with pseudo-cunning. She'd seen the way out. Her information was good. She believed he'd be convinced enough to get them out at once.

'Drugs. The easy bit.' Then she asked quickly: 'Did you get anything?' He waggled his hand.

'Yours is what we've got. Anything about Cass?'

'Not that I heard. He must be dead, mustn't he?' she hoped.

'I don't think so.' Her disappointment was evident.

'He's bound to be dead,' she insisted, her cheeks white, her eyes clown-dark in her pale face. Her fingers hurt his thigh. 'They're bloody everywhere, ahead of everything. They'll have done him in – won't they?'

It was strange – stupid to be disappointed, but he was, for a moment – that she felt no spell of safety around her now that he was with her. His monumental sense of self-preservation did not communicate itself to her. Only getting out would help. She was more worn than he – a lot more.

'They could have done. I'll listen to the tapes, though,' he compromised.

She pleaded silently for a moment, then snapped: 'Get back in the bedroom. I'll order some breakfast.'

'Ros, I have to listen to the tapes – have to be sure.'

She glared at him. His presence had meant only escape, not safety.

'This is a *fucking* mess, Hyde –!'

He spread his hands as she halted at the door.

'I can't help that, Ros – I shouldn't have involved you, but it's done now. Shelley and everyone else are being played as a gang of mugs, Ros. Sharmar's flavour of the month. There has to be something on tape or in the snaps you've taken, something I can *trade* for Cass, if I can't find out where they've got him –'

'*Why?*' she all but wailed.

190

'Because I can't leave him, if he's alive – not if I *know* he's here. I can't uninvent Cass.'

She did not reply, merely turned and left the room.

It's out of control, V.K., Sara had said when he had been brought news of the atrocity, the bus that had been bombed. *You have to make an announcement, bring it to an end* – now. He had shaken his head as much in horror at the event as in attempting to refute her demand. The gesture had further angered her, her hair falling across her face as she bent to her toast and coffee and deliberately ignored him and Prakesh as they prepared to leave for Bandipur.

To be flown by helicopter to witness –

– *this*. Beneath the vastness of Nanga Parbat, with Wular Lake's great expanse below the town, this devastation. The morning sun reflected in a million shards of glass, the scattered bodies, the trails of hosepipes. And, central to it all, the wreckage of the crowded bus that had been lifted and flung onto a bus shelter, so that it lay on its side like a scorched, dead lizard of gigantic size.

The noise, the faces of the survivors, the cries of the wounded and the police had maddened him like flies or Furies. So that he had retreated from the medical teams, police, fire officers, his security guards, even Cabinet colleagues who had managed to reach the event before it lost its news value. *The Prime Minister was visibly distressed by the scene*, the newspapers could claim. He sat slumped, with only Prakesh, on the hard bench of a deserted waiting room, through the shattered window of which the wreckage of the bus was visible, were he but to lift his head and turn it through only a few degrees.

He did not.

. . . *bring it to an end*, she had demanded. He could not answer her, since he would have had to say, *Not yet. Closer to the election*, and earn a withering contempt, vivid and unspoken. He curled his hands tightly on his thighs. Fragments of glass glittered amid

191

the dust on his suit, as if it had remained suspended in the air like bright soot, only to fall on him as soon as he arrived. He could not even protest that it had been no more than agreements with the Sikhs and the Kashmiri separatists who had done this, and with Pakistan – it wasn't planned or funded. He was only trying to bring some control, some lessening . . . a sense of slippage, not chaos. He was not to blame for *this*! *Yes, you are*, she would have answered implacably.

Prakesh stood at the window smoking a cigarette, apparently able to look with equanimity across the littered desolation outside. V.K. glanced away from his shadowed form against the light and the wreckage.

Two opinion polls – *only in damned Hindu papers!* Prakesh had snapped back at him above the roar of the helicopter's rotors – put him slightly behind Mehta and his party, the Hindu fundamentalists. Another poll in a government newspaper put Congress and Bharatiya Janata neck-and-neck, and in personal terms he lagged two points behind Mehta, the bloody film actor! How *could* he now make any announcement about the future of Kashmir or the Punjab, with Mehta and his hangers-on calling for retribution and more emergency measures to protect Hindus from Moslem extremists. Of course it could not be done – not yet.

He feared, too, that it was out of hand, that those people with whom he had met only last night had known in advance of this atrocity, that they welcomed it, their impatience battening on his promises like vultures on a carcase. He shivered, attracting the attention of his brother, who studied him sardonically.

'What is it, V.K.?' Sirens wailed behind Prakesh's words; women and men mourned behind them. *Bring it to an end* . . .

'Those – *people*,' he managed. 'Do they want the army down on them once and for all?'

'They can't control everything, V.K. They are trying. It would be worse without your intervention, without the future you have held out –'

'You make it sound like a bonfire of waste paper out there, Prakesh!' he stormed.

'Keep your voice down, V.K.'

V.K. swallowed, lowering his head. 'Will they be satisfied *now* – for a time?' he asked in a small voice.

'Fifty dead, sixty more injured – I imagine so.' He studied his cigarette carefully, then continued. 'I imagine so. The Sikhs have had their airliner, the Kashmiris their bus –'

'How can you be so callous?'

'I was going to add – and they have made you attend both spectacles, to remind you of your promises. I think they want you to win the election, V.K. They must want that. There'll be no hope from Mehta. Things will be quieter after this.'

'First it was Sereena –!' he blurted.

Prakesh turned on him. Even with his face in shadow, his eyes burned.

'*You* wanted Sereena dead! From the first moment – don't shake your head, it is true! – the first moment you discovered she was playing you for a cuckold with the Englishman! Ever since you began to believe she had slept with Mehta when she played Sita to his Rama in the bloody television series!' He had moved closer to his brother, bent forward, the cords in his neck as visible as ropes, his voice a whispered bellow that cowed V.K. 'Or was it when she played Parvati to his Shiva, or moll to his gangster or trollop to his hero in a dozen other movies? When was it, V.K., that you *first* wanted her dead?'

His shaking head was inadmissible denial, a form of perjury, and he knew it was such.

More softly, Prakesh murmured: 'Sereena would not have won you enough extra votes to take hold of all India, V.K. Only *you* can do that.'

'But, Mehta –?'

Something V.K. would have identified as contempt in anyone else's glance flickered in Prakesh's eyes for an instant, then was replaced by a smile, the bestowal of confidence.

'Mehta? When things have died down, you can make your announcement. Promise India her *future*. Mehta will never surrender Kashmir. You can surrender it, and win the votes of everyone in India who is sick of murder. So long as the timing is right . . . in a while. Not just yet –'

Sara's features were contemptuous in his imagination for a moment, then he was able to dismiss her. She did not understand strategy, necessity –

'Find that Australian, Prakesh. How did they let him get away from them? Are we surrounded by incompetents?'

'He was to be handed over, in all innocence, by the British. It was all agreed. They had no suspicion – he did, however. Such people are paranoid. It will not be long –'

'That woman – at Sara's – she's Australian. Are they connected? Is it coincidence?'

'I'm having it checked. In London, at the woman's address. We have their names. I should hear this evening. If so, then we can expect him in Srinagar, no doubt.' He smiled, then added: 'And now, your press conference . . . ? It is time you made an appearance. Father of India must be –'

'I understand, Prakesh,' V.K. replied waspishly. 'I may not be in the movies, like that damned Mehta, but I know which part to play when the cameras are pointed at me!'

Despite his confident tone, his commanding anger, he quailed at his glimpse of the ruined bus as he rose from the bench and brushed at the dust and glass fragments on his suit. The glass pricked and roughened his palms.

Hyde looked at his watch, glancing almost guiltily away from the notes he had transcribed from the tapes. Eleven thirty. Time, time – no that wasn't the bone sticking through the skin of his concentration. He was guilty because he had finally admitted that the Sharmars knew precisely who he was – *what* he was. Patrick Hyde, of Philbeach Gardens, Earl's Court, London. They'd have found out from Miles and Dickson if from no one else. And therefore, they'd know by now, or very soon, precisely *who* Ros was.

He clenched his hand on his thigh, the clutched felt pen marking his denims. He sensed Ros' presence in the lounge press demandingly against the wall of the houseboat's second bedroom, where he sat hunched over the tiny recorder and the miniature tapes, as if fiddling with scale models of something real. He wore the headphones with one earpiece askew, listening for the noises of the cookboy or anyone else. He heard beyond the confines of the boat the sounds of Srinagar, the location of transport – the airport. He had to get Ros out. She had to leave legitimately – now.

The tapes were interesting. The photographs, when they were developed, might be even more incriminating. There were references to drug money, to the distribution of funds which could be damagingly interpreted . . . and the other thing, that Cass had not had any idea of. The Sharmars playing for the future of India . . .

. . . and they might even be right, for God's sake, to let Kashmir and the Punjab go independent, linked to the rest of India only by economic ties. V. K. Sharmar's big idea –

Big, dangerous idea, because there was enough on the tapes to confirm links with Kashmiri and Sikh terrorists. Enough to bring Sharmar down like Lucifer. And the bug that had picked it all up was still on Sara Mallowby's houseboat, just waiting to be found by someone flicking a duster along the underside of the table . . . Hyde shivered.

What about Cass . . . ?

He pressed the Play button and adjusted the sweat-damp earpiece over his left ear. It was *so* incriminating Shelley would merely have to wave it under Sharmar's nose and the smell would make him faint. He'd surrender the family fortune, never mind Cass . . . of whom there was still nothing –

– get out then. Forget him. Get this stuff back to London, stick it in the post, for Christ's sake, and leave before they arrange your disappearance!

And yet he could not. Not even with Ros' tension like an invisible tremor through the boat. Not even with the risk of being stumbled upon, nor the danger of a dark-skinned, polite man from the Indian High Commission calling at Philbeach Gardens, having inspected the electoral register, just to confirm that he and Ros were –

Not even for that. Until he *knew* they'd done the poor bastard in, just like Lal and Banerjee. The tape rolled. He wanted, he admitted, proof that Cass was dead, out of the way, unrequiring of concern, time or effort. One word – he'd missed nothing so far – one word that said *kaput*, one dismissive verb in the past tense in reference to Cass. Then he'd get Ros on the first plane out and himself –

Right, then, this is the last of the tapes, there's no more than twenty minutes of stuff on it. Hurry it up . . .

. . . the unvoiceable – be dead, Cass. I have to save Ros. Be –

He was alive, then . . .

Almost robotically, he rewound a short section of the tape and adjusted both earpieces. Cass alive, in stereo. A half-caught, brief report by Dhanjal to Prakesh Sharmar, late the previous night, the buzz of politics uninteresting as mosquitoes at one of the mesh screens in the background, the occasional rise in volume of V. K. Sharmar's reassurances. Hyde listened intently, feeling the shirt dampen under his arms and perspiration spring coldly along his hairline. He rewound the tape once more.

Alive, then – and uncommunicative, just. But *soon*, Dhanjal promised like a procurer, to Sharmar's evident pleasure. Cass was in bad shape. It would be difficult for him to be rescued, hard to move him if he was got out. He let the tape run on, but there was nothing more. Prakesh Sharmar moved away into the political murmuring. Dhanjal's voice vanished from the room.

Hyde wiped his forefinger along his hairline and inspected its wetness, then rubbed his arms after switching off the tape. He retained the headphones. They kept out – almost – the sense of Ros and the immediate future. The *decided* future. The polite

Indian on the front steps of the house in Philbeach Gardens, inspecting the list of tenants' names. *R. Woode. P. Hyde.* Asking Max or his girlfriend, who occupied the ground floor – *ah, Mr Hyde and Ms Woode are in India . . . on their way to Australia – together. I will call again . . .* Reporting direct to Sharmar or his brother, who would report to Dhanjal.

He breathed carefully and slowly, removed the headphones, unplugging them from the recorder and stowing the recorder and the phones in the travel bag alongside the tubs of undeveloped film and the other tapes. Then placed the travel bag in the wardrobe after zipping its mouth tight. Ros *had* to go, today. The evening flight, at the latest, to Delhi, and then back to London with the tapes and film. See Shelley, be safe.

He straightened, as if from hard physical labour, his hands cradling his back, his face raised to the carved ceiling. Exhaled. It had to be done, she had to go.

She was frightened enough, after all –

He opened the bedroom door and stepped into the corridor, almost colliding with Sara Mallowby, who was entering from the stern, as Ros' shadow darkened the passageway, her form motionless in the lounge doorway.

The Englishwoman's eyes were suspicious. Hyde dropped his shoulders slightly in embarrassment. His smile was deliberately slow and uncertain, puzzled yet aware of incongruity.

'I – er . . .' he stared at Ros rather than Sara, turning away from the tall blonde woman. 'I'll – see you, then . . . uh, thanks for – you know . . .' He shrugged. 'I'd better be off –'

He willed Ros to see his posed form as that of a semi-stranger. Her face was stunned and pale, her body awkwardly still.

'Sara –' Ros began and Hyde hesitated, his hands aching with tension. 'Yes . . . *Max*!' Hyde winked at her, even though she had grasped at her tenant's name too eagerly, plucking it from memory rather than acquaintance. 'Yes – um, thanks, too.'

Hyde waved with a small gesture.

'Excuse me.' He passed Sara, whose face was sardonically amused. Beaut. Just keep up the pretence, Ros – where we met, et cetera. He stepped onto the rear deck, to the shock of the cook, then crossed the planked jetty towards the shops along Houseboats Boulevard. The traffic seemed senselessly loud and the scents of the middle of the day oppressive. He glanced back once, then began to hurry, the inventory of what he needed unrolling in his head like the hard copy of computer-stored information. Ros weighed on him as heavy as the sunlight. The woman was Sharmar's mistress, she was on the payroll. And Ros was frightened and disorientated.

And Cass was alive. That was the worst news –

brief encounters

'Sorry to create embarrassment,' Sara Mallowby offered, her mouth sardonic in expression as soon as the words had been uttered.

Ros shrugged and attempted a grin. 'Doesn't matter ... I – I was hoping he wasn't going to hang around, anyway. You helped shoo him off.'

She gestured Sara to the settee and held the door handle for a moment, steadying herself, before moving into the room behind Sara.

'Where did you meet him?' Sara enquired, arranging the full, brightly flowered skirt around her long legs.

'Oh – the cocktail bar of the Oberoi. I wasn't keen, to tell you the truth –' Her tension was beginning to become absorbed by the fiction, and the amusement of belittling Hyde – however much it was like laughing at fear in a dark house. 'He tried chatting me up ...' Her hand movements conjured at her body, as if to make her bulk vanish. 'He just knocked on the bloody door last night like the Sheik of Araby, full of eastern promise!'

Sara laughed without suspicion.

'And you didn't turn him away.'

'It was charitable, wasn't it?' Ros responded with studied lightness. 'Coffee – or can we share lunch?'

Sara hesitated, then: 'Lunch would be fun. Shall I organise it?'

'Please.'

Sara rose from the settee and left the room. In another moment, she was talking to the cook in Kashmiri. Ros' hands fluttered at her face, then she calmed them in her lap, laving them together. She was so much inside the fiction that she felt her cheeks flush. Then Hyde's absence chilled her, together with images of the Sharmars, Dhanjal, the Pakistanis and Sikhs on Sara's boat. Sara was *dangerous*, she told herself. Why had she come? What did she want?

Lunch stretched ahead of her like an obstacle course, a place of menacing pitfalls.

He'd seen Sara Mallowby leave Ros' houseboat, watching from beneath the awning of a shop whose window spilt furs like frozen streams, bright leather handbags lying amongst them like pebbles. Her movements had been languid, unsuspicious, but he had not dared return to the boat. Then, an hour later, Dhanjal had called briefly on Sara and, on leaving, had paused to study Ros' boat before getting back into his Japanese 4WD. The vehicle's driver was in police uniform. Guiltily, he had begun trailing Dhanjal through Srinagar, the houseboat becoming ever more isolated and unprotected in his imagination as his Land Rover followed the Subaru out of Srinagar and up towards the hills.

Now, in the afternoon's light and warmth, he brought the Land Rover to a halt at the edge of Gulmarg . . . knowing that the bungalow a few hundred yards away belonged to Sharmar, and that Sereena Sharmar had died in it.

Cass must have been brought back to it . . .

He looked at his watch. A little after four. The sun had ignited the lower sky, so the valley burned and Srinagar seemed little more than debris amid the fire. Dal Lake gleamed like a blank window. The flanks of Nanga Parbat glowed to the north. Gulmarg was crowded with trekkers and tourists, with large cars and wealthily dressed children. Ahead of him, the track was a pale, dusty parting in the vivid grass leading towards Sharmar's bungalow, outside which the Subaru and its driver sat impassively.

His mind inventoried once more, as if he was again a child checking obsessively the means of his own safety and reassurance . . . switching off lights six, seven, eight times, walking only on the edge of the rug, pressing the door again and again to ensure that it was shut. He had Ros' ticket for Delhi in his pocket, bought at a travel agency. The Land Rover had been easy to hire, the Sterling Mk 5 sub-machine-gun and the old but operable smoke grenades even easier. No one wanted addresses, credit card numbers in the Srinagar backstreets. The binoculars had been bought in a tourist trap. He studied the bungalow through them. Nothing at the windows or the door. Two men loitered at the rear of the bungalow, amid the fountains and trees.

It would have to be tonight.

He had trailed Dhanjal north to Lake Wular and what he knew to be the Sharmar estates. From there, then, the heroin began its journey, probably west on the first leg to the border with Pakistan. Too close to the Cease Fire Line to be used by tourist traffic – by anyone without passes, authority or influence. Dhanjal was evidently keeping a managerial eye on the family business. A truck was being loaded as Hyde watched. Then the policeman had headed south towards Srinagar, until he had branched off and climbed up to Gulmarg. Hyde did not need to see Cass to know he was there. Scene of the crime.

He studied the bungalow for another hour, as the sun slipped down towards the valley, obscuring it in gold and fire. A late afternoon breeze prickled his bare arms. He saw two more men, but no sign of Dhanjal or Cass. Cass was being turned inside out, imploded on himself in the effort to discover *who, what, how much, when* – and *who is this man Hyde?* It didn't matter now – unless they'd taken the use of his legs away from him and caused him to be incapable of movement. The noiseless bungalow presumably had a cellar or they'd never have taken Cass there; he would have been somewhere more secure.

Having to render Cass the extreme unction of a final bullet would solve a great many problems . . .

The bugger was going to have to walk, even run. To that he could make up his mind the moment Hyde dragged him off the cot or out of the chair in which he found him. Ten past five – time to get back. The shadows were longer, the sun low, Dal Lake's mirror spotted with the flyspecks of places like Ros' houseboat. Lights were already pricking out from Srinagar.

He hoped Ros had had the sense to pack in preparation.

'Cass is alive, you berk – and Sharmar's been a *very* naughty boy. When I call you again, *be* there.'

Hyde slapped the telephone back onto the receiver. The voice of Shelley's wife, Alison, on the answerphone. *You have reached the Shelley household. I'm afraid –*

You're afraid, darling? What about the poor bleeding infantry – how do you think we feel? He glared at Ros, whose whole frame had shuddered at the suggestion of violence that his replacing of the receiver had promised.

'That's that, then,' he said, shaking his head. 'Another two hundred quid on a night at Covent Garden, or whatever that tosser is doing with his time!'

The windows of the houseboat's lounge were dark, the room itself goldenly dim with the light of a single table lamp. Ros stood up stiffly and began pacing the room, her shadow thrown towards the windows and to Sara Mallowby's houseboat. He kept out of the light, hunched on the settee.

'What now, then?' Ros suddenly demanded, turning on him as if he had tried unsuccessfully to steal up on her.

'We're getting out.'

Her relief was immediate; and immediately qualified.

'Without Cass?'

Slowly, Hyde shook his head. 'No.'

202

'We could –' But she could not continue. He had told her where Cass must be held, what they must have been doing to him. She clenched her hands against her breasts like doves, angry at her empathy with a man she had never met, the unregarded debt he had accumulated in Hyde's name, even her own. 'How can you get him out?' she protested.

'That's the easy bit. Out of India –? I'll need Shelley for that.'

'He's not answering your calls, haven't you noticed?'

'He will. When you tell him, show him.'

'Me? I'm not going anywhere on my own, Hyde! I tried it once before and ended up in this bloody mess!'

'You're going to have to. I've –' *Got all my work cut out looking after Cass*, was what he wished to say, but saw that she understood. 'There's your ticket, on the table. There's time to make the flight –' She shook her head. 'You've got to go, Ros – for Christ's sake, you have to let me do my own thing here!'

'*When* you've got Cass. Not before.'

Part of her wanted to escape as easily as waking from a nightmare. Nothing, however, would persuade her to leave him until circumstances permitted or forced her. He spread his hands.

'OK – since you're in, there are rules. If I'm hit, you disappear – *understand?*' He emphasised the point by pressing his hand on the arm of the settee as if squeezing unsupple flesh, to hurt it, to knead it into feeling. 'You just go away from wherever it happens. Also, if I can't move Cass, then I may have to – do the vet's job for him. Understood? That's non-negotiable. He might be too far gone for anything else.'

He listened to her outraged breathing for a few minutes, all but heard her tension thrum in the panelling. Eventually, she sniffed loudly, and announced:

'What a *filthy* bloody job you've got, Hyde.'

'Too true.' He picked up the nightsight from beside him on the settee and sidled to one of the dark windows. 'Too true.' He felt a thrill of nerves, the rush of adrenalin. He was about to attempt to repay his debt to Cass in his best currency, physical action, his gold standard of professional skill. The anticipation was satisfying, and Ros had begun to move to the edge of his mental field of vision.

Through the nightsight, he saw grey figures moving behind the uncurtained windows of Sara's houseboat. A long Mercedes was parked at the end of the jetty, and there were two policemen beside it, smoking, engaged in amused conversation. He returned his attention to the houseboat and saw Sara and Dhanjal, as if mimicking the two policemen – except that he recognised the postures of bullying and outrage. They were quarrelling.

'Get the recorder and the headphones, Ros,' he murmured. Her bags and the suitcase she had brought up for him lay neatly on the bed in the main bedroom, as if awaiting a hotel porter. He heard the zip of the travel bag drawn back like a blade being unsheathed from a heavy scabbard. When she handed it to him, he plugged in the headphones and switched on the recorder. The tape moved, the voices tinnily reaching him. A distant play transmitted from a country thousands of miles away.

'Then *describe* him to me!' Dhanjal.

'He was ordinary. So bloody *ordinary*!' Sara replied. 'A nobody who picked her up –'

He swung the nightsight towards the Mercedes. The two policemen were inattentive, relaxed. The Land Rover was in the underground garage of one of the better hotels.

'Ros – get the bags ready.' He could see the lights of late shikaras, hopeful for tourists or sales, shimmering across the lake like fireflies.

'What?'

'Ros, just do as I tell you. Just what you *need*.'

'What is it –?' she began, but then hurried from the room.

Through the headphones, he heard himself accurately, if disparagingly, described. Dhanjal's murmurs were as precise as if

204

he were studying a photograph to match it to the woman's words. Ros returned to the lounge with one suitcase, the travel bag and his own small case.

'Too much?' she asked, her voice breathy with an exhilarated fear. He shook his head.

'Go and attract the closest shikara – do it quietly.'

'There's a light – Sara showed me.'

'Don't attract her attention.'

'Who's there with her?' Her breath was warm on his scalp and cheek. Her hands touched his shoulders for reassurance.

'Your boy Dhanjal. Quick, Ros –'

On Sara's houseboat, the woman continued to dribble out her description of him. And the fact that he had left at once – *no, she hadn't seen him return* ... Give me credit for a little skill, darling. Was she sure –? Yes – she hadn't seen him again. *He's just a tourist. She can hardly afford to be choosy, can she, Inspector?* Arrogant female. Hyde swallowed nervously.

Come on Ros – hurry up with that bloody shikara and let's get out of here.

'Prakesh has received a report on the man you describe – at least, someone very like him. He's a British agent. He and the woman live together in London – Earl's Court? Do you know it?' Dhanjal asked with mocking anger.

V.K. was confident that he appeared at his most solemn and statesmanlike; a father figure, wise, tolerant – yet now deeply angry, like a god with his recalcitrant people. On the monitor screen, the images of carnage succeeded one another. On the desk, jutting as it were from beneath his formally folded hands, his speech waited. The airliner disaster, the bus station atrocity ... earlier horrors, even the attack on the Golden Temple in Amritsar ... army violence in Kashmir ... rioting, the Tamils –

The sequence was brief, hardly more than two minutes, but it had taken weeks to compile. Its use had been intended very close to the election, but the party's inner caucus had agreed that it should be used well before the nation went to the polls. They had been persuaded by the latest outrage and the calm they suspected would follow – except from Mehta's fundamentalist camp. The exact timing had not yet been decided. This was merely a rehearsal. *A new headline image*, Prakesh had said. The bus station at Bandipur. The sequence rolled back, inexorable as a blood-soaked tank track, through the post-Imperial history of India, to culminate in rioting and murder in monochrome. 1948. Independence – from what? British India's ways and irreconcilables hung about the new nation like a shroud, tormenting her . . .

He would speak as the father of the nation. That, they had decided. The speech would probably be rewritten another dozen times, tinkered with obsessively after that, the images on film juggled, honed, choreographed. As father of the nation, he would ask the people – *is this what you want? Is this really how you see India and yourselves?*

It was a risky strategy – the highest of risks. Mehta wanted this kind of India, one full of dead bodies and old hatreds; self-mutilation, abject, passive suffering. Mehta played with a strong hand of cards – history. But *he*, V. K. Sharmar, offered the future, which was the greater risk . . .

. . . yet they might believe. Soundings were promising. People were almost as tired of murder as they were of poverty. Would they come with him, into the future, or would they choose a movie star and all the other old, weary clichés?

It was very perilous.

Prakesh had hurried away, leaving the Party's studios almost an hour earlier, his features determined, angry. Why? Because of the *other* danger, the one that could bring them down? The greatest risk, that the British agent could not be found, that he would find someone to listen to his story –

His stomach clenched with nerves, as if the broadcast were about to begin in earnest, to be seen by hundreds of millions.

The images had reached the riots of 1948, the country the British had *created* tearing itself in two.

He felt frightened and enraged.

The shikara landed them near Dal Gate, where the glow of Srinagar threw the houseboats along the boulevard into comparative darkness. Hyde paid the owner, tipping him generously, then the shikara was poled silently out onto the glimmering silver mirror of the lake, creating a lengthening scratch on its surface.

'Where's the Land Rover?' Ros asked, her whisper hoarse and exaggerated. Traffic all but swallowed her words.

'In the garage of the Broadway –' He waved his arms. 'On Mandana Azad. Know it? It's not far.' He was squatting on his haunches on the jetty, watching back the way they had travelled, the patrol of traffic along the boulevard, the gleam of shops, the briefer, more discreet lights from the ranks of houseboats.

'What is it?'

'Just watching my back.' He sniffed sweet, unburned petrol on the cool night air, and the scent of open-air cooking. 'Just making sure . . .' He held the small night-scope to his right eye. Grey night, off-white ghosts of people and cars, the lighted windows of the houseboats like a retreating audience of white, square mouths. He found Sara's houseboat, then the one Ros had rented and the long Mercedes – policemen suddenly alert. A figure was waving its arms at them from the jetty to Sara's boat, then they were running towards Ros' boat, tiny figures with bent elbows then freed hands holding what had to be guns.

A siren, nearing, the springing on of headlights along the boulevard. 'Time to go,' he murmured, straightening.

'Are they on to us?'

'They are, my one and only – they are.'

He hefted the travel bag onto his shoulder and picked up the suitcase in his left hand. He was aware of the gun in the small of his back, beneath the cotton jacket. Ros, carrying the smaller suitcase, followed him into the thinning crowds along Azad Road, noise and imbibers spilling gratingly from the garishly neoned clubs and the gleaming hotel foyers. The body of a dog in the gutter, a beggar hunched into a shop doorway. Superstitiously, Hyde scattered coins near the gaunt figure without pausing. His face was grateful in the light that illuminated jewellery behind a security grille.

They entered the Hotel Broadway's carpeted foyer and crossed it to the lifts. Casually dressed tourists, uniformed police, suited, wealthy locals. Then the lift doors closed and opened again on the petrol-scented, dusty air of the underground garage.

'Goodbye to all that,' Ros murmured, shivering despite her heavy sweater.

Hyde grinned at her, realising the expression unnerved her. Too feral, too close to that of an animal scenting prey.

'It's all right, Ros,' he reassured. 'Over there, beyond the pillar.'

Two Mercedes, a Jaguar, a small red Porsche; European saloons and older Indian cars, a few 4WDs. The Land Rover – he bent and looked beneath it, checked the bonnet. It was undisturbed, still locked, its contents unriffled. He dumped the suitcases in the rear, away from the tool box which contained the guns and the locker containing the smoke grenades. His hands hesitated, as if he had come to the wrong vehicle, then he realised that Ros' presence was disorientating him. She hovered like someone waiting for a door to be opened for her, a door to safety or sleep.

'OK?' She nodded, but was not. 'Look, Ros,' he began reluctantly as she climbed into the passenger seat, he remaining beside the driver's door, holding it open. 'I'll take you to the airport now.' He checked his watch to avoid the glare she directed at him. 'You can still make the flight.'

She shook her head, struggling not with his suggestion but with everything in her that wished to acquiesce with it. Then she shook her head more decisively.

'Not without you.' She had decided; he was her responsibility. 'Let's get on with it.'

He knew they must. If Dhanjal was convinced Sara had seen him, that he had been on Ros' boat and had only now vanished, then the city would be cordoned, the roads checkpointed. The police patrols would be increased, and the army woken and forced into its uniforms and vehicles. Anticipating the immediate future, he realised how normal the streets had seemed; without incident, as if Srinagar had exhausted itself, sated on recent violence. The police and army would have no distractions, they could concentrate wholly on him and Ros.

He climbed into the vehicle, fishing the ignition keys from his pocket, gripping the wheel tightly for a moment, as if settling himself into his seat like someone disabled.

'OK. Get that travel bag from the back and sort through the tapes and film. Split it in two – half for me, half for you –' He swallowed, flinching against her realisation of the implications of what he had said.

She did not reply, merely twisted her bulk in the seat and reached the travel bag onto her lap, unzipping it loudly in the garage's silence –

– broken by the firing of a car engine, which made her shudder, and drop the two tubs of film she held in one hand onto the floor of the Land Rover.

'Shit,' she muttered, bending forward to retrieve the tubs.

Hyde watched the small Nissan draw past them, driven by an Indian, a woman innocently in the passenger seat. His gaze followed it towards the ramp up to Azad Road, its headlights glancing off the concrete wall, then fading –

– appearing to return. Headlights enlarging, bucking along the concrete from a still-concealed car ... which became a police car, nosing down the ramp into the garage as if sniffing like a trained dog. Ros straightened up, holding the two tubs of film like a small consolation prize, and, as Hyde glanced sideways, her face changed as she saw the blazon on the approaching car.

Automatically, she dropped the film into the bag and zipped it hurriedly shut. The police car's engine growled off the walls of the underground garage. Ros' hand hesitantly reached towards his arm, but then withdrew itself.

The police car stopped thirty yards away, almost rubbing flanks against a mudstained Japanese 4WD. Both policemen got out of it, their doors slamming shut like echoing explosions in the garage. Hyde held Ros' arm and pulled at it until she imitated him in sliding down in her seat. Delicately, he opened his door, tugging at her sleeve to indicate she was to remain in the Land Rover. The two policemen had already completed their inspection of the Japanese vehicle and had moved routinely and together to the car parked next to it. Procedure.

He shook her sleeve, then slipped out of the vehicle, closing the door to behind him. The policemen's heels clicked echoingly. He resented the sluggishness of his senses, the almost clumsy movements of his body. It must be Ros, acting like a kind of moral multiple sclerosis, insinuating the ailment of ordinary sensibility. The policemen's heels continued to click, pause, click, their voices murmur. He eased himself onto his back and slid under the Land Rover, crabbing beneath it until he reached the passenger side. He climbed upright against a BMW. Cassette tape cases littered its rear seats, nestling in the cobralike folds of a Burberry scarf. The hotel restaurant must be full ... The two policemen had begun a return journey towards their own car, inspecting in little darts and rushes the scattered cars in the garage.

Hyde waited, then skittered on his hands and feet in a caricature of a frightened cat towards the door of the lift. The majority of the cars were parked near the lift, and he remained unseen. Then he stood up, and began walking abstractedly across the garage as if towards a distant car, oblivious of the police car and the two uniforms — who had come to a halt to observe and discuss him. He noticed them, even nodded in the vague, supplicatory manner of a stranger in a strange land. They nodded politely back. He passed on, towards a dusty grey Peugeot that he might have hired from Avis or Hertz, aware that they were still watching him. Then he sensed the moment when they lost interest, before he heard the more rapid click of their heels and the acquiescent murmurs of their mutual boredom and agreement that they had fulfilled their instructions –

– another glare of headlights froze them, as if they were the hunted, and the long black Mercedes that had been parked at the end of the jetty nosed sharklike and implacable into the garage. The policemen, ten yards from their car, remained immobile in the limousine's headlights as the vehicle slowed.

Almost at once, Dhanjal stepped from the rear of the Mercedes and they hurried to him, saluting with a deference greater than mere rank required. Different organisation, close to the Sharmars ... Dhanjal was even more interesting, much more dangerous.

He was interrogating the policemen in Kashmiri, as if to exclude them from the caste of the educated and powerful who continued to regard fluent English as a letter of credit. The policemen shrugged, even at attention, snapped back answers, shook heads. Dhanjal, tall in his well-cut suit, stood with his hands on his hips, inspecting the garage. Hyde glanced towards the Land Rover, and could see no sign of Ros. He crouched behind the bonnet of the Peugeot, his right hand poised behind his back. The police radio crackled and one of the policemen made as if to answer it and was stilled by a gesture from Dhanjal.

It was as if the man *knew* he was in the right place and that he was in time.

Then, as if to confirm Hyde's creeping anxiety, Dhanjal began walking across the stained concrete floor towards the Land Rover. He must have asked them which vehicles they had not inspected. Hyde slipped from behind the Peugeot to the concealment of a rough pillar, then to a hotel minibus, then to a dusty Hindu Ambassador ... Dhanjal continued his leisurely patrol

211

towards the group of vehicles amid which the Land Rover was parked. Hyde was close to the doors of the lift –

– as they sighed open and laughter emerged, tugging an obese Indian behind it and a woman whose legs were uncertain and whose figure was trapped inside gleaming lurex, as if she had been wrapped tightly for the oven. Dhanjal was distracted, the couple surprised into stillness. The doors clattered shut and the lift sighed away. Dhanjal approached the ill-matched, perfectly-mated couple, then halted and nodded in recognition. The obese man in the dinner jacket called Dhanjal's name and rank, drunkenly amused. Dhanjal explained – Hyde heard *drugs*, they were speaking in English now, and the obese man snorted in derision, as if Dhanjal had lost face. He and the woman, propelled now into movement and giggling by the man's tug on her arm, made towards a large American limousine. Dhanjal watched them, then shrugged in irritation and hurried towards the Land Rover and its satellite cars. He glanced into the BMW, then turned to the 4WD, trying the door handle –

His footsteps in the trainers were dull thudding noises that required time to interpret correctly. Too much time for Dhanjal and the policemen, now engaged in conversation with Dhanjal's driver. Hyde's right foot hit the bonnet of the BMW and felt it flex like a disapproving cheek as Dhanjal whirled away from Ros' appalled face at the passenger window. The Indian's expression all but matched hers for an instant before Hyde struck Dhanjal across the side of the head with the pistol as he cannoned into the man and crushed him against the Land Rover. As Hyde hit him again, Ros' face was almost alongside that of Dhanjal, her expression suggesting that she was Hyde's intended victim. Dhanjal slumped to the concrete, curled like a damaged crab. Running footsteps, shouts.

Hyde rounded the Land Rover and thrust himself into the driving seat, slamming the door behind him. Ros' breathing and his own in chorus. The engine caught and he put the vehicle into gear, the tyres screeching as he accelerated towards the two policemen.

Ros' scream of protest, surprised faces, bodies flinging themselves safely aside.

He careened along the side of the Mercedes as he dragged on the steering wheel, the driver's gun hardly emerged from his jacket. The tear of metal sharp as a scream. Then the Land Rover was bolting up the ramp towards the street. He bucked over a speed-restriction bump set with gleaming cats' eyes, then the flimsy arm of the barrier brushed the roof, unable to raise itself in time to avoid the Land Rover's stampede.

A screech of brakes, the wobble of a cycle rickshaw as he swerved to avoid it, then the glaring tunnel of lights of Azad Road, the quick card-riffle of restaurant and café and shop façades before the telegraph office blurred behind them. A queue at a bus stand, then the wide street bore right towards the market and a narrow bridge over a tributary of the Jhelum. The road to Gulmarg. He'd have to bluff them after he crossed it, before they had the centre of the city haltered in a bag.

Behind them, the police car stumbled as if blinded by the lights out of the garage and swung violently as a drunk to pursue them. Ros, beside him, was stiff-bodied, silent.

And with him, whether he wished it or not.

The responsibility for Cass was a debt, a single occasion. Not her, though. The obligation was too great, too continuous; part of him.

'The damned man was *here*, Dhanjal!' Prakesh Sharmar raged. His own anger buzzed in his ears like the noise of the engines of the family plane which had brought him up from Delhi. Summoned by a *confident* Dhanjal! 'He was here and no one realised it!'

Dhanjal occupied a corner of the houseboat's lounge, his long fingers itching through the contents of the suitcase Hyde and the woman had left behind. Her clothes, in the main, some men's clothing. A pristine white bandage decorated Dhanjal's scalp and forehead like an unearned medal.

Prakesh strode about the room, the fingers of his right hand extending and closing, as if he were attempting to reckon a complex sum and take hold of something physical at the same moment.

It was not complex – it was absurdly simple. One man to be silenced – and the woman, of course. Hyde was a British agent – or had once been. Shelley must have sent him, not entirely convinced – although now, from the manner in which his people in Delhi were behaving, Shelley *was* convinced. So, it was remarkably simple, so simple that Dhanjal had managed to make a complete damned *curry* of the whole business!

He turned to Dhanjal, whose features immediately assumed a composed, earnest apology, a sheen of loyalty and self-criticism.

'Where are they now?'

Dhanjal said, hesitantly: 'They cannot have got far. We have the registration of the Land Rover, we know where he hired it. We have –'

'You have *nothing*!' Prakesh stormed back, striding about the room. Then, silkily: 'He must be found and eliminated, Dhanjal. That is your only priority, my good fellow. He has to be eliminated. He must be here because of the man Cass. Do you agree?'

'He can't know where he is.'

'You're certain?' Dhanjal nodded. 'Why?'

'The man must have arrived last night. The woman has been watched since you and V.K. gave the order –'

'You didn't see him arrive, even with the woman under surveillance.'

'He was in Delhi, wasn't he? He couldn't have been here before early today.'

'Quite. So, he doesn't know where Cass is – the woman couldn't know?' Dhanjal shook his head. 'Very well. But you say the woman was entertained on Sara's houseboat? What was our English rose playing at, Dhanjal?' Dhanjal offered neither word nor expression. Dumb machinery, awaiting instructions. Prakesh felt his anger direct itself at Sara Mallowby. That

214

unsacred cow. 'What measures have you taken to apprehend Hyde and the woman?'

'Army and police units. The centre of Srinagar is sealed off. The hotels, good and bad, are all being checked, the houseboats, everywhere they might attempt to hide. The airport is closed to them, the railway station, the buses and the roads. They cannot get out – Prakesh . . .' The name was offered with the greatest respect, like a title; and as a litmus test of favour or displeasure.

'Very well, Dhanjal, very well . . .' Prakesh's anger had been redirected. Dhanjal had been over-confident. He had known Hyde was a British agent, and therefore he should have been a great deal more careful. Just as Sara should have been.

Why was the woman here? he wondered with a sudden urgency. She came up to Srinagar before Hyde, she must have come with a purpose, not as *cover*. Then what has she done, what has she learned –? He felt himself inflate with rage. That damned Sara Mallowby, always feeling sorry for herself, bitter even when V.K. had taken her up, aloof and so bloody *British*! She could have said *anything* –

Damn V.K. for enjoying the kind of patronage she dispensed in bed, the covert humiliation with which she always seemed to treat him – and himself to an even greater degree. Undisguised dislike. Unless V.K. exercised power over her, dominated her, she had always seemed able to ignore him entirely.

'Come with me, Dhanjal – Ravindar.' He added the given name as a small token. Dhanjal gobbled it as eagerly as a hungry dog. 'I want to talk to our hostess.'

They left the houseboat and crossed the jetty to the boulevard. The shops had closed, and the place was strolled only by a handful of people and a few cars. As he had told V.K., the Kashmiris had subsided into quiet. There had been no incidents in Srinagar for two days, and no threat of any. The air smelt of the lake and the mountains, not of smoke and ashes. He knocked violently on the door of Sara's boat and immediately opened it, hurrying through the corridor and into the lounge.

Sara Mallowby was seated languorously – it was the only manner in which he could describe her pose, for that was what it was. Her elbow rested on the arm of the chair, as if she were engaged in inspecting the tumbler of whisky; as if she had anticipated his entrance and upstaged him. He could almost visualise her in some Memsahib's long dress, high at the throat so that it tilted the head back in surprised disdain. She was so damned British he wanted to strike her.

Frighten her, rather . . .

He had left her not fifteen minutes before. The whisky was refreshed, the level in the bottle apprehensibly lower. He did not frighten her, he realised as Dhanjal slipped into the lounge of the houseboat behind him, deferential and stereotyped. She was V.K.'s whore, and that gave her an unseemly, and now, he thought with satisfaction, an unfounded sense of self-assurance. She could be hurt. She could be pricked and she would bleed. What had she told that bloody Australian woman in one of her half-drunk bouts of confidence?

'The woman is the *mistress* –' He emphasised the word. ' – of a British agent. An intelligence agent. Does that surprise you?'

'A *spy*? Do we still have any?' she mocked.

We. We *British.* We stealers of an empire and we runners-away when things get difficult, leaving you *wogs* to get on with it. The British legacy . . .

'Yes, you do. Apparently.' He felt chilled with anticipation. 'What did you and she talk about, Sara?'

'This and that.'

He moved two steps closer to her. She turned her head as if to welcome a blow, but really so that she could exhibit his unimportance.

'What *this*, exactly – and what *that*?'

'Why? Does it matter? I didn't commit any sins of indiscretion, Prakesh, if that's what's worrying you.' She smiled and flicked her hair aside, again as if inviting him to strike her across the face.

He took a further step closer to her and she continued to ignore his presence, sipping meditatively at the whisky as if she still enjoyed it rather than found it necessary. Necessary because she slept with his brother, or because she suddenly found it inconvenient to be privy to their strategy?

'Sara, the woman was sent here, ahead of the man you discovered on her houseboat and conveniently ignored –' Her eyes flashed with contempt. '– obviously to spy on you, V.K., myself, even Dhanjal for all we know. She would have been eager for information, she would have probed.'

Sara snorted in derision. 'I think I would have noticed any *probing*, Prakesh. She was an overweight, middle-aged woman who was desperate –'

'She was not!' he shouted, losing all sense of control. 'She has lived with this man for years, Sara! He is her *lover*! She is sane, well-adjusted – *happy*.' His voice had become softer. 'She is not the sad, pathetic creature you described earlier. Perhaps that figure of pity is yourself? What did you tell her?'

The whisky trembled in the tumbler, as if a breeze had passed across its surface, but he could not divine the motive, whether anger or apprehension.

'Not me,' she replied, tight-lipped. 'Whatever would *I* have to complain of, Prakesh? Except the poor business I'm doing at the moment because of the uncertainty – the atrocities.'

Dhanjal shifted his feet as if having stumbled upon an embarrassing struggle for temporary advantage in some endless marital conflict.

'Exactly. Yet you drink.'

'I drink because I enjoy it, Prakesh. *And* because it contains an ingredient for forgetting.' She smiled, folding one long leg over the other, then smoothing her skirt. She sipped again at her drink.

'Then you told her nothing?' he asked, baffled, his anger returning.

Sara shook her head. 'Not likely, is it, Prakesh? By the way,

Ros, my lover, the Prime Minister, is a drug producer and is engaged in . . . Finish the sentence yourself, Prakesh, I'm going to bed.' She swallowed the whisky and made to get up.

Enraged, he lunged forward, his hands gripping hers on the arms of the chair, his face thrust towards her.

'Do you think I am some sort of idiot?' he yelled. 'Some bloody *cookboy* you can treat like dirt whenever it suits you? A bloody Indian servant who must be watched in case he is making off with the knives and forks, memsahib?' He saw the spittle from his words on her cheek, saw the flinch of genuine fear in her eyes, felt her hands struggle under his grip. 'You bloody bitch! You may please my brother in bed, flatter his vanity, but I am not your servant! You will answer my questions politely, you will listen to me, you will sit in that chair –' He backed away with a lurch that might have been that of a drunk. '– until I have finished with you.' His voice was hoarse, he felt heated and clammy in his suit, his collar tight at his narrow throat.

He lit a cigarette and stifled the initial cough it provoked. The fear in the woman's eyes had faded, but it remained in her voice as she said:

'I won't mention this conversation to V.K.' It was a threat, a bloody threat!

'Do as you like,' he snapped at her. 'Meanwhile, where do you think the woman has gone?'

'Has she disappeared?'

'For the moment.'

'Why do *you* think they came here?' There was something businesslike, controlled and commanding about her now which he tried to dismiss but which made her quite formidable. It reminded him of her early enthusiasm for their ideals *and* their tactics, the dangerous strategy of allowing violence in order to control it. She had enjoyed power then; secret power. 'Well, Prakesh? You had a great deal to say just now.'

'To find the man Cass. That is who Hyde has been seeking. In

218

Delhi and now here. Did you tell them anything – did the woman ask?'

'The woman did not ask. If she is connected with the man, then she's his cover, nothing more. You have my word on that.'

Prakesh Sharmar sat perched on the edge of the table, his hands gripping the carved, pelmetlike wood that fringed beneath it. Birds, flowers, vines curved and flitted beneath his restless hands. Trees, leaves, branches, flowers, small animals. He had always admired the old table. *Indian* craftsmanship merely bought by the British, not inspired or made by them.

'I can, can I? Can I be certain you were always sober, on your guard –?' She tossed her head in contempt.

Birds, flowers – the petals of a wooden lily, the beak of a wooden hoopoe or bulbul, its stiff wings . . . He fingered the table as if poring over a work of history, some national epic. Fanciful –

He looked down at what his fingers had dislodged and which had fallen onto the polished floor near the fringe of a rug. He bent swiftly, outraged yet triumphant, and picked it up. Held it out to Dhanjal, whose face paled, then towards Sara.

'And what is this bloody thing doing in your lounge?' he screamed, his neck taut, his lips wet. 'This is a *bug*, the kind that *spies* use!' The woman's eyes darted, her face gratifyingly ashen. Her fingers played at her lips. 'That woman who was so innocent, so *pathetic* – put it here. When? They have overheard everything! You stupid, damned woman, they know it all!' He lunged at her, striking her across the cheek, then danced away from her as from an opponent in a boxing match. 'They have everything on tape, because you were taken in by that woman. You believed her as stupid and innocent as she wished to be thought!' Sara cowered in the chair, all masks removed and somehow boneless. Prakesh whirled on Dhanjal, shouting: 'You – get up to Gulmarg and have the man Cass killed! Do it now! Kill him and bury the body. *Then* find the other two and dispose of them. Do you understand? *Kill* them!'

As Dhanjal exited, Prakesh at once turned to Sara. He pounced forward on the balls of his feet and struck her twice across the cheek and mouth with his open hand.

hill station

'All right?' he called out softly. The whisper was almost lost in the static of laughter and music floating up from a long, low bungalow perched on a grassy outcrop below the track on which the Land Rover was parked.

'Yes!' She realised there was too much relief in her voice.

Hyde's head and shoulders thrust themselves above the vague edge of the track, where the slope fell away towards the lights of Gulmarg. His slight figure loomed like a shadow against the big stars. Then she could hear the exertions of his breathing and his hand scrabbled on the passenger door. He was grinning in the darkness. She touched his face momentarily and he did not resent the gesture.

'Done,' he murmured. 'How many have you seen?'

'Two more. That's five.'

'Six. There's one inside all the time, by the look of it. They're jumpy. I didn't see Dhanjal – he must be back in Srinagar.'

'Where's the bug?'

'Corner of the living-room window.'

'Did you see – him?' She saw Hyde shake his head vigorously.

'No. I checked the wood store and the garage. Nothing. He's in the house – maybe a bedroom? I couldn't check it all.' To Ros, his voice seemed remote, clinical; as if he were thinking aloud, nothing more. He was, of course, she realised. He was usually alone. 'Where are they now?'

'Same routine.' She indicated the night-glasses in her left hand, then raised them conscientiously to her eyes, sweeping their grey curtain across the site of Sharmar's bungalow. Nodded. 'Round and round the mulberry bush – they are alert, aren't they?' she added, pulling the shawl closely around her shoulders and breasts. The night was cool.

'Jittery. Maybe Cass tried something. We'll wait until they settle down. A lot later.'

Involuntarily, she looked at her watch. Almost midnight. The party in the closer bungalow was raucous, as if someone had opened a door – yes, a spill of light and somebody staggering happily across it as if treading water. Laughter. Loud Western pop music. There were European cars scattered like pebbles around the place. Its noise and vibrancy made the Sharmar bungalow seem deserted, dangerous.

Hyde was riffling his hands through the equipment he had stationed in the rear of the vehicle. She heard the click of metal, small cold sounds that were immensely threatening. The clinking together of what might have been bottles, but weren't. She distracted herself by watching the drunk lunge back through the door, which was closed behind him. The music dimmed. Ros looked down at her hands clutching penitently at the shawl. Then Hyde was back beside her door, wearing the headphones of the recorder, his face intent and disappointed.

'Bugger's snoring,' he murmured. 'Guard passing –?' He glanced down the long, steep slope, and nodded. A shadow flitted across the large, curtained window at the rear of the bungalow. Hyde appeared frustrated.

'What is it?'

'What? Oh, just waiting – and not knowing where they've got him. I *need* to know that . . .'

She reached down beside her feet and hauled up the thermos flask she had filled with tea at a roadside stall on the poorly-lit edge of Srinagar. Scattered street lighting strung on sagging cables at long intervals, the low houses and shacks crouching in the shadows like penned animals; the spurt of an occasional open fire, the smell of ordure and rubbish and incessant cooking.

222

'Want some tea?'

'Why not?' She poured some into the cap of the flask and handed it to him. It was as if there was a charge of electricity between them; cold, unerotic, distancing.

He smiled encouragingly as if he, too, had remarked its passage.

'Don't worry. These boys aren't army and they're not any sort of special forces. Just coppers. You can tell by the exact routine –' He paused, aware she was unconvinced. She sipped her tea from the inner cap of the flask.

'Want something to eat?' she asked, determined to be banal for her own nerves' sake. He shook his head.

'Might make me fart at the wrong moment. Could be fatal.' He paused, his grin frozen. 'No, thanks.'

'What – what do we do, afterwards?'

'Can't go back into Srinagar. Sewn up tight by now.'

The conversation, she realised, belonged in an asylum, some special hospital where the inmates had to have their fantasies drugged into submission. She felt colder, despite the tea, which was no more than a tepid trickle of warmth in her chest. They had missed the patrols by taking dirt tracks, crossing the River Jhelum – slowly, very slowly, across a narrow, swaying bridge, the Land Rover in its lowest gear and four-wheel drive. The creaking of the logs and ropes of the bridge like the collapse of a building in a storm. No headlights, the water below rushing, it seemed, in the starlight. It was all mad, insane, perched above Gulmarg waiting for Hyde to risk his life to *kill* strangers for the sake of someone he hardly knew. Crazy that she continued to attempt desultory, in-front-of-the-telly murmurings. Asking about *cups of tea* and remarking the *price of potatoes in Safeway* while half-observing gunfire and bodies in a piece of news footage. Was he as distanced from it as she was?

She shrugged herself away from reflection, as if moving aside from the glare of sunlight through a window.

'What, then?'

223

'I'll get hold of him first.' There was no impatience in his voice. 'We'll take the track north – like I showed you – up towards Baramula. Then decide. It depends on the state he's in, Ros.'

'I know that –!' she replied too quickly. Then: 'I'm all *right*, Hyde,' anticipating the deception of comfort.

'Sure.' He tugged off the headphones, which he had been wearing askew on his head, one ear listening to the noises from the bungalow. 'Sod all on the radio tonight.'

Ros looked down towards Gulmarg. Occasionally, headlights splashed and bucked towards or away from the resort that had once been a hill station of the Raj. *Cooler for the memsahibs.* The noise of car engines blurted through the night murmurs of the small town. The lights of wealthy houses and bungalows lay scattered like jewels across the sloping meadows. Narrow tracks wound like irregular partings in dark hair. Another set of headlights, spread like two assaulting fingers, swung along the road and stabbed towards the town. Moving quickly. She watched for the sake of another small distraction that promised to last as long as a few minutes. It was past midnight. The headlights splashed hurriedly through the town, emerging from its bowl of light with what seemed renewed urgency, bounding along the track towards –

'Hyde,' she murmured.

'Mm?'

She hesitated; not uncertain, merely reluctant. Then: 'I think –' she began. Hyde still had his back to the headlights and the dark beetle-shape of the vehicle she could now distinguish behind them as it slowed beside the Sharmar bungalow. The headlights disappeared. She thrilled with shock and certainty. 'Someone's arrived – down there. In a hurry –' He had already turned to look, snatching the night-glasses from her lap, focusing them.

'Your eyesight's getting worse,' he murmured with a quiver of excitement. She saw two small figures hurry into the shadow

224

of the building. Hyde said: 'Couldn't make out who they were.' Two of the patrolling guards had followed them into the bungalow. Hyde replaced the headphones and fiddled with the volume control on the tiny recorder. His head was bent, shoulders crouched in concentration. 'Dhanjal,' he murmured in a cold voice.

He began small, jerky, diving movements with his hands and body into the rear of the Land Rover. The clinks and reverberations of metal, the slight, slipper-tread of plastic being moved. She watched him don a shoulder holster and slip a small transceiver into it, then feed a thin lead down the sleeve of his sweater. A small switch nestled in his hand. Under his other shoulder was the pistol. A second pistol was thrust into his waistband.

'Listen to this,' he ordered, handing her the headphones. Then he fitted a tiny earpiece into his left ear. Just as she slipped on the headphones, she heard the slither and kiss of velcro as he adjusted the transceiver's harness. He placed a second transceiver in her lap and she stared at it as at a weapon. 'Well?' he snapped.

'Dhanjal,' she confirmed.

'What's he *want*?'

'He's excited, angry –'

'Where's Cass?' Hyde hissed against her cheek, shrugging himself into a camouflage jacket.

' – bedroom!' she blurted, then in protest: '*No –!*'

'What is it?' His hands gripped her arm fiercely. She shook her head, stunned. 'What? *Ros* – what?'

'Kill him,' she murmured. 'Asking about *you* –' as if that were a more enormous and disabling surprise.

'Shit!' he snapped. She realised he had already known. Instinct. He zipped up the jacket and she saw the smoke grenades go into two big pockets. Then he was at once checking the Sterling sub-machine-gun. 'Made in India – let's hope it bloody works!' He grinned like a savage. Her head whirled with

Dhanjal's tinny words and the other voices speaking English. As they debated where to dispose of Cass' body –

'It's an order from Prakesh Sharmar,' she informed Hyde, who appeared indifferent, distracted by the weapon he turned in his hand. A knife, hardly catching the light. Then he gestured her to remove the headphones, which she did reluctantly because even the details of Cass' murder were less terrifying than confronting Hyde's face and the vulnerability of his body. A respirator dangled on his chest from the straps he had pulled over his head. 'No,' she muttered in a strangled way.

He tuned the transceiver after lifting it from his lap, nodded, then thrust it into her hand, indicating the buttons.

'Transmit – Receive,' he said once. 'We'll test it when I get down the hill a bit. Use the night-glasses. I want to know what happens when it happens – *each* of the guards. Got it? Ros – got it?' She could only nod. 'Good.' He snatched up the headphones of the recorder for a moment, listening to one earpiece. 'Still debating the burial plot and who's going to do the digging.' He grinned, then swallowed, before he said solemnly: 'If anything happens – if I *tell* you or if I can't tell you, then get out. Just *go*. Train or bus. Not Srinagar. OK?' Again she nodded. 'It's what I do best, Ros. I'll be back.'

Then, immediately, he was gone, a small, exposed figure seeming to hop, even bounce, down the dark slope away from the vehicle. She swallowed, then sniffed loudly.

'Quiet, they'll hear you,' came a mutter from her lap, as if his head lay there. She stared in horror at the transceiver, then snatched it up with stiff, icy fingers. Clutching at the source of his voice as if to catch his arm and restrain him. 'What's happening, Ros?' She strained to see him, then, galvanised by fear, pressed the night-glasses hurtingly against her eye-sockets. She could see him now, a grey shadow moving like the drunk who had staggered out of the party, dodging from side to side, crouched and apparently irresolute. 'How many still outside?'

'Two – *three*,' she blurted, then pressed the PTT switch and

226

repeated: 'Three – one on your side, two watching the road. Someone's just told them to do it, by the look –'

'OK. Keep it short.'

'Yes –'

The great peak of Nanga Parbat intruded, gleaming like a vast, suspended curtain in the night-glasses. Cold. Ros shivered and fumbled with one hand at the anorak that lay on the seat beside her.

It was narcotic, in a strange and ugly sense, reporting the movements of the men she could see. Twin grey figures beneath the shadows of enormous pines. She could clearly see the sticks of their rifles. She pulled the anorak around her shoulders, clutching it across her chest, which heaved beneath her hand like a quick tide.

'They're talking, still together in front of the house.' In the headphone pressed against her ear, Dhanjal was berating the guards who had followed him inside. He seemed reluctant to proceed, continuing to debate the location of the burial, not mentioning the act of killing Cass. Hyde's grey form was far down the slope now, past the party bungalow which gleamed with light like an explosion –

She controlled her imagination.

'Still there?' the transceiver asked, as if he sat beside her.

'Still here. Can you – can you see the one on your side?'

'Too much shadow. Where is he?'

'Under the verandah, waiting like a servant.'

'OK.' She heard Hyde's breathing. He had halted behind an outcrop of rock perhaps fifty yards or so from the bungalow. A shadow passed across the lighted, curtained window, waving its arms as if pointing towards Hyde's concealment. 'Listen, Ros. Bring the Land Rover down the track to the bungalow *when* I tell you – *if*. OK?'

'Yes,' she replied in a tiny voice.

'Good –' She sensed he had been about to add some patronising endearment and had thought better of it. She might almost

227

have welcomed it, to fend off the immediate, stifling reality of events. 'You're going to have to listen to everything. Understand, Ros?'

'Yes,' in the same helpless voice.

'You'll hear my breathing, especially once I put on the respirator. Keep listening for it, Ros.' Then, more quietly: 'Fucking sub-machine-guns – I don't trust them. Let's get the silencer on . . .' She strained to hear tiny, betraying sounds, but there were none. As if the transceiver had gone dead.

'Right,' he murmured. 'Where and when, all the time, Ros. Any movement. Don't expect me to reply.'

'Hyde –'

There was no reply, only his breathing. She watched him slip from behind the rocks and continue towards the bungalow, now with exaggerated, cartoonlike caution, literally tiptoeing up on them. Christ, *please* let him be all right . . .

'Then get on with it!' she heard Dhanjal snap in the headphone. 'The two of you. Go on!' The voice was strained.

'Hyde, they're ready to –'

'OK.'

His breathing became quicker through the transceiver, like a rush of static. She forced herself to focus on the guards who remained outside, the two on the track still together, one of them smoking, the other scuffing his foot in the dust as if making some mean confession. The solitary third guard – she heard her own breathing quicken to the pace of Hyde's as she glimpsed his ghostly figure converging on the third man, who had stepped out from beneath the verandah and was gazing towards the looming mountain peak. The two together – oblivious . . . the one – unalert. Hyde had paused, his breathing controlled, coming like the background hum of smooth machinery beside her cheek.

Hyde moved closer. Oh sweet Christ –! She was shivering and could not control the spasms. The man turned –

No . . .

228

Hyde was aware of the six yards of starlit ground between them as the guard turned, bulky in his anorak, the stick of the automatic rifle waving like a wand, conjuring the Indian out of surprise and into action. The moon was nudging over the mountain peak behind the man. Four paces – three, two –

Hyde clashed with the rifle so that it struck his shoulder, numbing it as he thrust his weight upwards, levering the Kalashnikov beneath the man's chin and into his throat, gagging off the voice he had been about to use. Hyde swung the short, folded butt of the sub-machine-gun against the man's head, knocking him off his feet. Then he kicked him heavily on the left temple as he lay on the ground. Glared around him like an animal as he fitted the respirator's mask, its snout jutting into his vision.

'OK,' he announced, knowing she would hear him.

He removed one of the CS smoke grenades from his jacket and weighed it in his hand.

'Hyde,' her voice blurted. 'They've left the room –!'

Now.

There were shadows on the blind at the smaller window to the right, fleeting with ominous purpose. Fifteen yards. The shadows were moving, blurred. Ten yards. Sod the blind, that's going to get in the way. Five yards, then the verandah under his feet, the glass shattering. The blind rolled obligingly up, as if for comic effect. The faces of the two Indians were poised at the bedside, as the pale, frightened features, bruised and crumpled, looked up at them from the white pillows. Then the CS pellets in the submunition burst a second after the grenade exploded. The room was filled with roiling grey smoke within which the blinded, coughing shadows of the two Indians wobbled and gestured like the shadows of hanged men.

Hyde flung the second grenade through the main window and heard it explode, then the pellets burst a second later. He heard cries of shock, warning. He clambered towards the sill of the broken bedroom window as a shadow blundered towards him,

229

arms waving, seeking the window rather than encounter. He squeezed the trigger of the silenced sub-machine-gun. The gases hissed from the casing like a cobra as the Sterling bucked in his hands and against his hip. The body collapsed over the sill as if to gulp air into dead lungs. The second man's shadow was purposeful, looming in the smoke and light over the bed, heaving as it was racked with coughing. Hyde shot towards the shadow, wounding the man, hearing his body hit the floor as he cried out for assistance.

He retreated from the sill as the smoke swirled freshly in a gust from the suddenly opened door of the bedroom. He kicked at the shards of glass jutting from the frame of the lounge window. Something tore at the window frame ahead of the roar of a 9mm pistol.

'Hyde, Hyde —!' It was Ros. 'They're moving towards the front porch, both of them —!'

Hyde fired perhaps ten rounds into the lounge, which was chaotic with smoke and shadows, before he hit the source of the glow from the far side of the room. Larger, dimmer shadows. He ducked beside the window, squatting on his haunches. He heard Dhanjal's voice calling out orders, he thought from the bedroom. The lounge was cavernous with the irritant CS smoke, enlarged too by his sense of imprisonment in the mask of the respirator. He fired in the direction of another glow and immediately there were only the flames of the open fire flickering within the smoke. He heard the front door open and slam shut, and then Dhanjal calling out for it to be left open. The draught of air moved the smoke and began to disperse it. Someone fired towards the window and he fired back at the shadow, hitting nothing except the panelling of the wall. The smoke opened for a moment to reveal the scars on the dark wood. He rolled behind the edge of a long sofa placed at an angle near the window.

The smoke was clearing. There were four — and Dhanjal — unwounded. Someone lumbered from the bedroom and he

230

squeezed off three shots. The grunt was real, not pretended, like the noise of the body slipping on a rug and colliding with the far wall. A gun fell into the firelight. Four in all now. The smoke was thinning. He appeared to be alone in the room. The furniture seemed hunched like waiting men in the flicker from the fire. He fired two more shots – less than twenty left in the magazine now, maybe fewer than fifteen. He fingered the last of the smoke grenades in his jacket, withdrew it, then flung it across the room towards the fire. The ejection charge exploded, flinging fragments of wood and flame into the room, then the CS smoke billowed out of the fireplace.

And then he moved.

Immediately, wood puckered and scarred beside his cheek, splintering him enough to make him gasp. At once he heard in the earpiece:

'Hyde –!'

'OK!' he snarled, huddling into himself as he ran for the bed-room door –

– collision with something soft. Hands tugging more in instinct than purpose at his respirator, heaving on its snout as if to overturn a bullock or a pig. He butted at the man's ribs with the short stock of the Sterling, but his grip did not loosen. His face, as twistedly masklike as Hyde's, thrust itself against the polycarbonate of the facemask, clouding it. Hyde struck again at the man's ribs, making his features snarl silently.

'Hyde – Hyde!' Ros was like a terrified child in a darkened cinema. As he gripped the box magazine of the sub-machine-gun, it pressed against the transmitter switch in the palm of his left hand, leaving the channel to Ros open.

The Indian was reaching into his jacket, struggling with some-thing that would not easily come free, his body thrusting against Hyde, holding him against the door jamb. Then an arm tightened around Hyde's throat, half-blocked by the respirator's bulk. Fingers obscured his vision as the second attacker attempted to rip off the mask. He squeezed the trigger of the Sterling. The

231

hiss of gas like the assailant's surprised last breath. He fell away. Hyde raked his heel down the second man's shin, twice, stamping on the foot. He twisted in the man's grip but lost his balance. The attacker was bigger than he, bulky in a dark anorak. As Hyde was thrust sideways, the man brought his Kalashnikov to bear. CS drifted like incense over a form on the bed, half-propped on one elbow, its pale features sick and stunned.

The Sterling had jammed – or the magazine was empty. Hyde fired through the camouflage jacket without withdrawing the pistol, merely tugging its blunt little barrel from his waistband and squeezing the trigger. The door chipped beside the man's shoulder, then the second shot flung his arm out, making him drop the rifle. He slid into a sitting position in the doorway. Hyde stared at Dhanjal's face, creased with pain, his eyes wide with surprise.

Voices. Smoke that was from burning furniture drifting across the doorway. Someone in the lounge was screaming in agony and terror.

The body of his first assailant lay near his feet as he leant back against the bedroom wall. Dhanjal watched him with hatred from the doorway, as he tore off the respirator. The first to die was still hanging out of the window frame as if vomiting at a party. There was a stillness of shock-response in the bungalow, and the crackling of burning wood. Someone was coughing –

– regrouping? How many? Three dead, one unconscious, two wounded. *Two* others fit – who probably didn't know whether Dhanjal was alive or dead . . . or were cleverer than their panic and would be waiting for him when he came out. Or just waiting for the cavalry.

He moved to the bed and switched off the lamp after a momentary inspection of Cass, who displayed no recognition of him, little sense of time or place. Vacant, drugged shock. The paleness of the features was a false impression. There were bruises and cuts. Blood on the shirt. Needle-marks in his arm. Cass fell back on the bed like an invalid grateful for the darkness.

Smoke drifted through the moonlit room like that from a ciga-rette left burning in an ashtray.

Hyde crossed the room again, fitting a new magazine to the Sterling. Getting sloppy, can't count. It had been empty. He switched the selector to single shot. Gripped the shoulder of Dhanjal's anorak and dragged him to his feet with a vast effort. The man's eyes were still watering violently from the irritant smoke and something that could only be enraged, impotent hatred. Or the pain from his shoulder. There was nothing else for it, he had to keep the bastards from blowing him and Cass away when they stepped through the door. No sense in shooting your superior officer, Pandit Plod . . . Dhanjal struggled until Hyde pressed the muzzle of the sub-machine-gun into his stomach, then moved lamely across the room to the bed.

'Get him up!' he growled.

'Hyde —!' like the sighing relief of the sea.

'Where are they, Ros?' he snapped, remembering her.

He glared back towards the bedroom door, then squeezed off two shots into the motionless lounge. There was no returned fire. Outside, then —

'Three of them —' He hadn't hit the first man hard enough. 'This side of the bungalow — all of them, I think. In the pines to the left —'

'Good girl. I'm all *right*,' to stifle further dialogue. Dhanjal was watching him like a cunning animal, waiting. He snatched the pistol from Dhanjal's waistband as the man's eyes conveyed a sense of advantage, then his features collapsed into defeat. 'Do it. Get him on his feet!'

Dhanjal indicated his shoulder, and Hyde slapped the barrel of the Sterling against his wounded arm, making him cry out.

'Do it.'

Dhanjal struggled with Cass, holding him with his good arm beneath Cass' armpit. Hyde pressed the gun into Dhanjal's side and helped him hoist Cass who protested with the intensity and silence of a dreamer. They got him into a sitting position, then onto feet that immediately parted from one another below rubbery legs. Hyde thrust Cass' deadweight against Dhanjal, then pushed them towards the door. Dhanjal would appear first in the doorway, half-shielding Cass, covering himself. The screams had died, and the fires that had caught at the rugs and the furniture were still hesitant, as if undecided upon destruction.

Hyde pushed them towards the door to the rear of the bungalow. It was open with the hospitality of ambush.

'Tell them we're coming out!' he grunted at Dhanjal. 'I know where they are. Tell them you'll be the first to go – tell them!'

Dhanjal yelled in a pained, frightened voice from well within the shelter of the doorway.

'Do not fire! I am his prisoner! Do not open fire!'

They waited, as if enraged animals trapped together in a sack. Then:

'Yes, sir. We will not open fire!' Shouted from the pines. Good girl.

'OK, Dhanjal – get moving. You're on the right side of our friend to get shot first. Let's go!'

They struggled through the door as in some comic cartoon, then down the verandah steps and across the garden behind the bungalow. The sigh and dribble of water from fountains and the miniature landscapes of pools and rockeries. Their breathing clouded on the cold air. The ground began to slope upwards, towards the –

Bloody kids and their party. The bungalow was brightly lit, people crowded on to its verandah.

'Get on with it, Dhanjal – you're not dying!' Voices called out, questioningly. They struggled up the slope, Cass' left arm draped across Hyde's shoulder, his feet dragging, his voice a continuous mumble now, as if he was imitating the noise of the water in the Sharmars' garden. 'Piss off!' Hyde cried. 'Tell them it's a police operation,' he snarled at Dhanjal.

'Police! Clear the area – we, we require *no* assistance. Nothing has happened here! This is a police operation!'

They were watched by a silenced group from the verandah as they struggled up the slope, leaving the well-lit bungalow behind. Terrorists, drug smugglers – the fictions were too easy for the party-goers to find, too real in Kashmir. As he glanced back, Hyde saw one or two drifting curiously towards the Sharmar bungalow. Spectators, merely interested, excited by the proximity of the covert and dangerous. None of Dhanjal's men had emerged from the pines. No shots – not yet. Couldn't risk killing the officer . . .

'I must rest!' Dhanjal protested.

'Fuck you, sport!' Hyde snarled, forcing them on, stumbling occasionally, dragging either Cass or Dhanjal or himself to his feet again, urging them on, being maddened by Cass' monotone, the dribble of senseless words. Then the noise of music behind them as the party recommenced.

Eventually

'Hyde –!'

Dhanjal, as if recognising their destination before Hyde, slumped to the ground, letting Cass fall into Hyde's embrace. The mumbling had ceased, like a worn-out recording. He lowered Cass to the ground, bereft of feeling – somehow distanced from the slim, now-frail form, as if Cass was a derelict who had slumped against him from the shadows of an alley. Dhanjal nursed his arm as Ros loomed over him, horrified; as if he was the victor about to announce their collective capture.

Hyde looked back down the long slope. Flames flickered behind the broken windows of the Sharmar bungalow, stronger now. Party-goers milled on the lawn, a small knot of people huddled around someone who had collapsed or who they had dragged out of the bungalow. Along the main road leading to Gulmarg, there were no urgent headlights, but there was the distant noise of a siren and a clanging bell from the hill station. Hyde looked down at Cass, feeling the man's weight not as something he had slipped but which insisted into the future. Cass had been beaten –

He opened the shirt and the heart fluttered beneath his hand.

Its sound came clearly through the transceiver Ros held in a dumb hand, and he shook the transmitter switch from his palm. Bruising. Cass groaned as he touched him across the shivery, goose-pimpled skin. One broken rib, perhaps two. He inspected the puckered, punctured arm.

Who gives a sod, anyway, he thought. What could you have told London? Nothing to tell any more . . .

Cass was – a liability, not to put too fine a point on it. Better – dead . . . Dhanjal groaned in a pleading way and Ros' exclamation was pitying.

Hyde stood up and tugged a blanket from the rear of the Land Rover, wrapping it roughly around Cass' shoulders, angry with the purposeless, scrabbling movements of the man's hands and the sick, dead, penitential gratitude that sheened his features. Then he crossed to Dhanjal, the scent of woodsmoke from the bungalow reaching his nostrils, the music of the party in his ears. He stood behind Dhanjal and, like an executioner, so that the Indian's body shuddered itself smaller, more suppliant, thrust the muzzle of the sub-machine-gun against the back of his head. Ros' face abhorred, but he snapped:

'Stick a bloody plaster on his shoulder or arm or wherever.'

Ros quickly, with fumbling inspired by concern rather than nerves, inspected the arm – flesh wound, upper arm, he was in better shape than Cass. Then she brought the first-aid kit from the vehicle and dabbed the wound with iodine. Dhanjal winced back against the pressure of the gun muzzle, then Ros covered the wound with a patch of lint and a crossed plaster like a holy sign on the brown flesh. Dhanjal nodded and pulled his suit jacket and then his anorak over the wound.

Ros got to her feet to confront Hyde, then recalled Cass, his teeth chattering audibly. Hyde shook his head and indicated the Land Rover. Ros followed him. He leant against the vehicle, the Sterling pointed towards the huddled figure of Dhanjal. Ros' breathing might have been a reminder of his own as she had heard it through the transceiver.

'What now?' she demanded.

Nanga Parbat was massive and gilded in the risen moonlight. The bungalow burned as comfortably as a domestic fire. A police car had reached it, and a fire engine was labouring towards it, a second toy vehicle. The party continued, healing over the wound of the interruption.

'Now, we get out.'

'*How?*'

'Keep your voice down, Ros –'

'Why? What about him?' She gestured towards the squatting policeman. 'Or him?' Cass appeared unaware of his surroundings, his voice once more a continuous mumble.

'Drugged up to the eyeballs. And they've duffed him up.'

'Who? The *late* however many?'

'Shut it, Ros.'

'How the bloody hell do we get out of here?' There were other headlights down on the road now, hurrying into and through Gulmarg. Still had to be local. Srinagar was an hour away.

'I'm thinking. *Not* together – not you, anyway.'

'Why not?'

'I told you. Someone's got to make it.' He scraped the barrel of the Sterling on the door of the Land Rover, making Dhanjal twitch, then subside again into his confinement. 'You –' He looked at her. Then back to Dhanjal. 'There are ways out that I *need* to take, you don't. So, just do as I bloody say for once, will you?' He paused, but she said nothing. 'They'll be looking for us now,' he supplied. 'Not for you. You're incidental, now there are bodies. You can get down as far as Jammu in a bloody *taxi* if necessary, or on the bus. But get there you will.'

'This is the plan, is it?' she sneered. Vehicles had collected like moths around the flames of the bungalow. 'The great-bloody-escape, I don't think!'

He turned his head violently towards her.

'Ros – *don't*!' he warned. 'You have half the evidence. Take

237

it, get to Jammu, then down to Delhi on the train – you've got the bloody guide book, for God's sake! They won't be looking for you in Delhi, you're not connected there. Get a plane to Paris, not London . . .' He was dizzied between Dhanjal's suspect somnolence and her disbelief and silent refusal. He was sufficiently enraged almost to want to point the Sterling at her, move it between her and Dhanjal as he shifted his gaze. 'You have to reach Shelley, meet him in Paris, if you can. You have to *convince* him . . .' He subsided for a moment, shielding his calculation and anxiety from her, then he added: '*You* have to give him the price of the trade, the gold charge card that gets Cass and me out.'

Her breathing in the silence, Cass' mumbling like water, the distant, tiny noises of the fire being put out and the search being organised. There'd be a chopper out at first light at the latest, once Prakesh Sharmar was informed. Dhanjal's absence would slow that process down, but the insistence of those still alive would ensure the pursuit. Kashmir stretched away on every side of him, climbing and falling like a vast mural; a mural he would have to enter, learn, use.

'And you? You're just going to hang about until I can get home, are you?'

'Not necessarily. I can't get Cass out by any respectable route. I've got *him* as some kind of insurance. Otherwise, I've got you. I could get killed, so could Cass. If we're out of the game, then I want someone alive and safe who can screw the Sharmars on behalf of both of us. You're elected, Ros.' He glared at her, then added: 'Ros, you're not going to be able to cope – not with anything that comes after this. I'll take you up the track to Baramula and we'll find a bus station or a taxi rank. Pay the bugger over the odds and his car won't break down before you get to Jammu –' He grabbed her arm and pulled her against him. Her flesh quivered as if with sexual excitement. Her hands were icy. 'Listen,' he whispered, 'just get on with your bit, leave me to do mine. I'll get through to Shelley, if necessary – if I'm desperate. *You* get through and I can get on Air India, first class, out of here . . .' He kissed her.

When she drew back from him, he recognised her compliance. She would not be able to cope, but she did have something she could do. She could try to save him. She knew she was being played upon, but accepted the melody.

'Jammu?' she asked. 'How long, by car?'

He masked his relief. And fear.

'Nine or ten hours from Baramula – I guess.'

She nodded. 'All right,' in a small voice.

'Let's get moving, then.' There were headlights thrusting into the garden of the bungalow, party-goers would be questioned at the other bungalow. They'd already stayed too long. The conversation with Ros had been his post-mission relapse. He felt weary now and shook his head to clear it. 'Let's get Nehru here into the back of the vehicle, tied up like a chicken, and then we'll sort out –' He hesitated, watching Cass, crouched like a mystic, staring at the grass just in front of him; oblivious.

Jesus, he was full of drugs – pentathol or something else, maybe just something to keep him quiet. Now, he was concussed with the immediate; the night, the cold, his rescue.

'Christ, Hyde, he's a bloody liability,' Ros whispered against his cheek.

'I know it, darling – I know.'

But *you're* not, he thought. You're getting out, at least –

239

ELEVEN

into the black

The grey light slipped across the unwrinkled surface of Dal Lake like the wake of a boat. The peak of Nanga Parbat became sheened; the other, receding peaks beyond it. A shikara moved as secretly as a fish. Prakesh Sharmar turned on the verandah of Sara Mallowby's houseboat, away from the slight nudge of the water against the bottom step. Srinagar's noises stirred into audibility, soft as the clash of pots from the cookboat. He slapped one arm against the chilly air as if to dissipate the sense of innocuous peace.

He turned to Sara, her long housecoat wrapped about her, her feet cold and slim in slippers. She seemed to have absorbed the peace of the lake like an affront to his sense of urgency.

Prakesh looked at his watch. Where in damnation was the colonel? Now that Dhanjal had allowed himself to become a hostage — his stupidity would be punished — he needed the colonel here to coordinate the hunt for the agent, Hyde. And the *tape recorder* that the man Cass had become, not only when he'd made love to Sereena but since his captivity . . . because to extract information they had had to supply it, albeit in the form of questions. If Cass retained his mind – they grovellingly admitted that he did – then he now knew much more than he had done. And the search of the houseboat on which that fat Australian woman had stayed had revealed scratch marks on a windowsill consistent with the resting of a telephoto lens. And the bug –

It was the most damnable situation! Every moment that they

remained at large, unapprehended, they magnified his danger, the danger to V.K. –

– near her feet – *there* – were the early editions of the newspapers. V.K. and Mehta were neck and neck in some polls; in others, V.K. had moved into a small but dramatic lead. And she sat amid what might symbolise the wreckage of V.K. himself and the whole of Congress, as if she presided over it and approved! He moved his arm again and she flinched, then seemed to despise herself for the reaction. She pulled her housecoat more comfortably about her and gazed sardonically out over the lightening lake, where shikaras now plied in small, busy schools and the noises of ducks and waterfowl rose from the reeds.

It was ready now, everything . . . Poised. In the balance.

Hanging by the merest thread, he admitted. How strong was Dhanjal? What would the British agent do to him, should he need to know more? What would he *promise* Dhanjal? Could Hyde contact Shelley, convince him?

Not over the telephone – he'd never persuade him that way. He had to get Cass out of Kashmir, out of India . . . He listened, his attention suddenly caught and held by the approach of a large-engined car. He leaned like a schoolboy over the rail, feeling her mockery across his shoulders like his father's cane, and saw the black limousine draw to a halt at the end of Sara's jetty. Colonel Rao stepped from it at once. Aides hurried after him onto the houseboat, their heavy footsteps alarming Sara. He saw her look up, as afraid as at a noise that signified immediate arrest. He smiled with deliberate malice and she shivered visibly. Her cheek was bruised and one eye was puffy. Her confidence, all her hauteur, seemed to decline to the condition of her damaged looks. Rao emerged onto the verandah without either pause or knock.

'Colonel,' he acknowledged, stifling his sense of relief.

'Mr Sharmar,' Rao replied formally, with a slight, nodded bow – valedictory, Prakesh sensed. From the moment of his arrival,

241

the operation was entirely his. 'I came as soon as I was able.' It was neither apology nor explanation. The patient piece of machinery who had seemed content to wait in anterooms and back offices was now animate and possessive. 'Your summons explained that they have Dhanjal. That is regrettable. Where are they?'

'There is no trace of them. The helicopters were ordered up as soon as it became light enough.'

'To search what area?' Rao demanded, moving closer to Prakesh, ignoring the tame white woman gazing across the lake. There was something brutally admirable about Rao, something that gave confidence; and discomfiting in its directness, its lack of regard for former niceties, the castes of politics. 'Was that the local army commander in the lounge?' Prakesh nodded. 'Then I must speak with him at once.'

He turned away from Sharmar, and Prakesh had no option, so Sara's mouth and eyes emphasised, but to follow him into the houseboat. The interior still glowed with lamplight, which enlarged Rao's presence, diminished that of his aides and the junior officers who accompanied the army commander. Another colonel was already deferring to Rao's manner and his Intelligence status. He and his aide hovered near a huge map of Kashmir that lay spread on the polished table like a cloth. The soldiers and aides were poised like children awaiting a summons to eat.

Rao began at once, in an interrogatory tone, his hands, joined by other, more supplicatory hands, gliding and gesturing over the map. Occasionally, they appeared tender, as if about to pick up an infant. Rao nodded continually, or shook his head, his large jaw clutched in his right hand, his left arm across his chest. He peered closely at the map like a doctor at the symptoms of a disease; an ailment which had wasted his talents and for which he did not expect payment. The damnable contempt of the *military*. So necessary now, Prakesh admitted. Rao began patrolling the circumference of the table, as if to capture and pen the country portrayed on the map. His power hinted at a dangerous future, even as it made him confident that Hyde and Cass could not escape. The man's disregard for the local commander, his own aides – even himself, unnerved Prakesh.

'Then get equipment installed here – or on another of these houseboats – at once. No, your local headquarters are too insecure, *here* will be best. The centre of the web.' Spiders did build their own webs, of course . . . 'No, only handpicked people involved here –' Rao glanced towards his aides as if to judge their suitability rather than indicate that they were to fill the roles he had suggested.

The telephone rang. The army commander and one of the Intelligence aides looked towards it, but Prakesh felt an irresistible impulse to answer it, if only to prevent it interrupting Rao's concentration. He was no more than a *civilian*, he realised. India's own Raj pertained in the suddenly close atmosphere of the lounge as the day intruded at the net curtains masking the windows. The men in uniform expected, like *England expects* –!

He picked up the telephone. It was V.K., excited and anxious, like a child preparing to come home for his school holidays. He turned his back to the table and Rao, as if embarrassed.

'I am being pressured, Prakesh –' V.K. blurted, then at once: 'What is happening there? Have they been found?'

The connection was secure, there was that fuzz around V.K.'s voice that indicated he had activated the masking unit.

'No, they have not. Rao – Colonel Rao is here and has taken control.' He felt he had had to supply the colonel's rank. He could not subordinate the Intelligence officer. As a result, he added waspishly to V.K.: 'There is no need to panic, brother. Matters are in hand.'

'But your call said that the British agent had Cass!' V.K. protested.

'Is that all you called about?'

'– troops up from Delhi, or units from Pathankot,' he heard Rao announce at the table. The map rustled under his fingers. 'No, your people are *not* suitable, Colonel.'

'No, Prakesh.' V.K. was attempting to win him over with a

243

child's charm. 'I am being pressured by the party. They want us to go on the results of the latest polls.'

'I know that.'

'How can we?'

' – I don't think they would go north, Colonel,' Rao said. 'That is a bottleneck, up towards the Cease Fire Line. There are too many troops –'

'We must, V.K. We have argued this until it is a dead dog. You must take the tide –'

'I'm not certain, Prakesh! Not while we have these people on the loose.'

'Do it, V.K. See the President and have parliament dissolved. *Call* the election.'

'Are you certain that Rao can contain this?'

'Yes –'

Prakesh glanced towards the knot of men intent upon the map of Kashmir. A comforting, assured bulk.

'I read his file on the way up here,' Rao was explaining. 'This agent is experienced, he is lucky. But he does not know this area. Evidently that is why the woman was sent.'

'Yes,' Prakesh confirmed. 'Yes, it is under control. Only a matter of time –'

Rao had looked up at him, his dark eyes blackly intent. He nodded and returned his attention to the map. Sara was a shadow in the doorway, her face as stunned as if she had opened the door of her home on the wreckage of a burglary.

'No, no – that is not sufficient. *This* size of area – see? In a Land Rover, if they set out at one this morning, they might have reached a point anywhere in this large a radius. That means more helicopters. See to it, Mathur.'

An aide left immediately. Prakesh, absorbed in the minutiae that would bring about the recapture and death of Cass and his rescuer, shook himself back to attention to his brother.

'You can announce the election by midday, V.K. Yes, I'm certain.'

'Get these photographs duplicated and circulated,' Rao ordered. 'Find out about the C31 arrangements. I want the command post set up here in one hour.'

'What the hell – ?' It was Sara Mallowby.

Rao turned to her, after a glance towards Prakesh.

'This is the headquarters of an intelligence operation, Miss Mallowby. I take it you agree to cooperate.'

She paused, then nodded dumbly before leaving the doorway. Sunlight spilled warmly on the steps like gold leaf. Prakesh suppressed a smile of pleasure.

'Yes, V.K. I hope to return this evening. What? You have the programme, V.K. No, not *the* speech – you do not need me to arrange your TV appearances, V.K.!' he protested in frustration. 'We have teams of people to do that. Yes, very well . . . Goodbye, V.K. Good luck.'

Prakesh put the receiver down heavily, at once isolated from his brother and Congress and the election, and from the soldiers gathered at the table. An aide entered from the stern of the houseboat, followed by overalled soldiers with the flashes of engineers on their sleeves. They were carrying heavy communications equipment. Leads trailed behind them. He heard a generator start up somewhere, like the purr of a distant motor boat. The whole section of the boulevard where Sara's boats were located would be isolated. There was a comfort in bustle, in the heavy black bulk of the equipment, in the uniforms and Rao's focal, commanding presence. The intimate isolation from the world of a party caucus meeting, any piece of politicking.

It was done, then. The die was cast. V.K. would cope, now that the decision was taken, the necessity of an election obeyed. Parliament would be dissolved, the election announced, the campaign begun.

And Cass and the man Hyde killed –

The taxi had run out of petrol. A shock like a confirmation of cancer. Dread rather than annoyance, a creeping terror that subtly, inexorably increased with each passing minute – with each approaching vehicle, car or bus or truck, until the vehicle passed without slowing or stopping. The dread leaping back into the shallow relief, to create the waves of hot distress and helplessness she experienced.

She obeyed the tic of head and wrist once again and looked at her watch. Nine twenty. They had been on the road for two hours, she had been abandoned in the taxi for another half-hour while the driver walked towards the village of Punch, two miles farther on. He had insisted she not accompany him, had reassured her she was safe . . . The pistol Hyde had given her was in her lap, useless as any piece of machinery she had no idea how to operate. No comfort whatsoever.

The driver had scrambled away down the narrow mountain road as if pursued – more in pursuit of the fare they had agreed. The moment he had disappeared around a twist of the mountain road, the peaks and folds of the Pir Panjal range had threatened her, moving their great shoulders and blank features, already snowcapped, towards her. Dark pine forests, bleak ridges of grey rock, the sheer drop to one side of the road to a dribble of river far below. The isolation and massiveness of the place unnerved her.

Hyde had waved a thick wad of bright notes in front of the taxi driver's nose. The man had been asleep in his seat – his *home*, she had realised. Hyde had given him clear, repeated instructions, pecked at her cold cheek, and waved her off as the first grey light struggled down from the mountains into Baramula. Hyde had issued her instructions with the same measured and distant authority. Dhanjal was trussed up in the rear of the Land Rover, presumably staring at the sleeping form of Cass. A few early workers, children and dogs, the first cooking smells and the drying overnight shower on the deserted streets. There was the scent of snow in the air and a clothing mist on the closest peaks. Even in Baramula's main square, the mountains had seemed to stretch endlessly, disconsolately away, suggesting

246

that there was nowhere to be reached, however far she travelled and in whatever direction. Hyde had instinctively recognised her mood and gripped her hand, but it was nothing but a premonition of this . . .

. . . the sense of unimportance, an imitation of extreme weariness, where nothing mattered. However far the taxi travelled, when its interrupted journey was continued, there would only be more mountains, more dark forests. The landscape anaesthetised like an odourless gas.

The noise of an engine recalled her to her fears. A bus limped past, the driver and the succession of windowed passengers glancing at the taxi while continuing their own journey. Dust from the road rattled against the windows. Then the road was empty again, hemmed by a rock face, threatened by the drop to the narrow river. She fumblingly lit another cigarette and huddled into her anorak.

The train for Delhi left Jammu at six in the evening, arriving in Delhi somewhere around ten the following morning. She had all day to reach Jammu, no more than a hundred and fifty miles away. The pressure of the mountains insisted that it could not be done, and she shivered deeply, the cigarette making her cough. She opened the window and threw it away. The mountain air chilled the taxi, as cloud hovered sombrely along the Pir Panjal. Hyde had been certain she would make the train –

– as certain as she was uncertain of his situation. As she left Baramula, he had made reassuring, empty noises like a relative leaving a terminal sickbed; polite, soothing, finally insulting. If she didn't know anything, she realised, she couldn't tell anyone. He'd reach Shelley somehow . . . or he'd stooge around, waiting for the cavalry . . . he'd hide up somewhere . . . he'd all *all right*, Ros. Then he'd nudged the taxi driver into putting the cab into gear, as if he had slapped the flank of a horse and sent her careering away. She'd watched his retreating figure beside the Land Rover, hand raised as if in warning rather than wishing her well or regretting her departure. Then the creaking, asthmatic taxi lurched around a corner and the rear window was a screen for a travelogue of Kashmir, tiny figures, animals, great peaks watching the town for signals of intent. She had no idea what he would do, where he would go, even though he knew the strain that ignorance would place on her.

She lit another cigarette. The smoke was less rough on her throat, the fugginess of the taxi warm and enclosing. A haze on the windows kept the mountains at bay. The road ahead of the windscreen was empty.

Nine forty . . . two miles there, two miles back, and between them lack of urgency by the driver, except to haggle over the price of the petrol or to pause to eat something. The dread was creeping like cold up through her body again, and once more the cigarette began to nauseate. She persisted with it, however. It was better than opening the window to throw the cigarette away.

She stared instead at her lap, at the litter on the floor of the taxi, at the signs that the driver lived in his vehicle. A portable stove on the rear parcel shelf, clothing, a copy of the Koran, a vase of flowers attached to the dashboard by a large rubber sticker.

Come on, come on, come *on* . . .

A helicopter flashed over the stand of pines and disappeared towards the Cease Fire Line to the north. It wasn't military but that meant nothing. Below him, the scattered village of Kupwara. The road, which had headed due north from Sopore, bent like an elbow as it passed through the low houses and huts, before it slithered like a long brown snake westwards towards Tithwal and the border with Azad Kashmir – and the guards and the Pakistani army.

But it had to be. Had to . . . Didn't it? The faultless logic of his guesswork petered out like the crude huts and refugee tents at the edge of Kupwara. Hindus, presumably, from the other side of the CFL. Moslems from the south the Pakistanis wouldn't let cross into their *free* Kashmir? Pakistanis persecuted for some God-forsaken reason in their own country. It didn't matter. The ragged movements of the tents in the wind were universal symbols of distress and the ignorance or indifference of the world. There was snow in the air, the peaks obscured along the Pangi range. Nanga Parbat was closer, no more than fifty direct miles away. Its bulk was insuperable and unnerving.

But he had to be right . . . this was the route out, the one taken by the heroin shipments from the Sharmar estates around Sopore. This underpopulated part of Kashmir, risky and unsettled, rather than any other route, south or south-west. It had to go out via Pakistan – Pakistan had the experience, the track record. FedEx as far as drugs were concerned, not some mushroom operation only just starting up. And this was the least conspicuous way out of Kashmir – Tithwal and Muzaffarabad – then 'Pindi or whichever distribution centre in Pakistan one had dealings with. He glanced back at the Land Rover. Dhanjal would know. Dhanjal would have crossed the CFL . . .

. . . and could do again.

Frying pan and fire. But the frying pan was hot and getting hotter and the state of the fire was still uncertain, hopefully only smouldering. Crossing the border would give them *time*, the interval of cross-border dealings and collaboration, the spreading of the net until, maybe, it stretched too far. The only way they could even approach the CFL, let alone cross it without papers, was with Dhanjal.

Certainly, Captain Dhanjal – you can cross the CFL with these two Englishmen whose descriptions we have and one of whom has obviously been interrogated . . .

Crazy. But crazier to stay put, let them cast and recast the net, fill Kashmir with the manhunt, get themselves organised, efficient, utterly competent. The Sharmars, through Dhanjal or someone like him, must have the border guards and their Pakistani counterparts on the payroll. It *had* to work – didn't it?

The alternative was down there, the ragged tents between which women trudged to a cold-looking stream, their garments flying in the wind, and men moped on the ground or sulked in tents and children had forgotten everything but hunger. There were no dogs. They'd probably already been eaten. Neither Cass nor he could cope with the mental equivalent of that down there, for however long it took Ros to get back, get Shelley off his bum, get the deal set up – a week? Two –? Before the Sharmars admitted they were on the rack and an exchange was necessary.

Two weeks? They'd find them before that.

In *Kashmir*.

It was already past ten. The helicopter had been the second – or the same one a second time – since Sopore. It had landed briefly on the outskirts of Handwara, but he'd bypassed the village along a deserted track and they'd have received no report of a Land Rover with a pale face behind the windscreen. The search must be concentrated to the south of Sopore, towards Srinagar and south of the city. The city itself would be house-to-housed.

With luck, they'd ignore Ros, even if they assumed she wasn't with him and Cass. It was Cass and Dhanjal they had to silence, and he they had to stop – dead.

He shrugged and hunched against the wind into the camouflage jacket, aware of the ragged hole the two pistol shots from inside had made in the material. His cheeks were blanched and numb. The tents on the edge of the village flapped in distress. He turned back to the Land Rover, pine needles crunching under his hiking boots.

He ripped open the flap of the canvas canopy, startling the Indian, who was tied by his hands to a metal handrail. He was crouched awkwardly on the bench seat. Cass lay in a sleeping bag on the other bench seat, snoring. His features remained as pale and battered and defeated as they had appeared on the pillows of Sharmar's bed. The sleeping bag quivered with the

250

feverish, unregarded movements of his body as the drug-coma receded and the muscles and blood demanded to be returned to silence. That Cass was sleeping through his withdrawal was bad –

Hyde grinned suddenly and alarmingly at Dhanjal, whose anorak, open to the waist, seemed to have breathed in cold air that made him shiver. His eyes were brown and angry. His mouth seemed still aware of the wound to his arm, but there was little sign of real distress.

'Well, Gandhi,' Hyde began insultingly. 'I think it's about time you and I decided your future – don't you?'

Dhanjal was immediately aware of the threat in Hyde's voice, and instantly alarmed. His hands struggled against the rope binding them to the handrail and his left foot stirred against the steel storage box on the floor between him and Cass.

'You've been stupid,' he managed.

'Not bad,' Hyde replied mockingly. 'Not bad. But then, I've left you alone so far, haven't I?' He climbed into the vehicle, his movements deliberate and menacing. Dhanjal flinched as Hyde reached for the rope and untied it. Then he dragged the Indian to the tailgate, gripping the rope that bound his wrists together. Pulled him forward, off balance, and let him sprawl on the rocky ground, stepping back as if to admire his work. 'I'm not leaving you alone any more, though.'

Dhanjal sat up, hunched to protect himself, his eyes watching Hyde's feet rather than his face.

'What do you want with me? I can't help you – as a hostage? I think they want you too much to stop –'

Hyde waited until the self-condemnation brightened like a dark light in Dhanjal's eyes, then he murmured: 'That's it – that's exactly it. You're no fucking use to me, none at all. Are you? You've just admitted as much.' He turned away, hands on his hips, just within the shadow of the pines, staring down at Kupwara. A single wandering cow, a scattering of sheep on poor grass. The few inhabitants he could see seemed slight, insubstantial figures. The weather looked to be worsening to the north, where the mountains crowded beyond Nanga Parbat in what might have been an endless succession.

All the way to Mongolia, given a couple of hiccoughs on the way – Christ . . .

He rubbed his hands eagerly together as he turned back to Dhanjal, whose eyes darted like rats seeking escape from flame. He bent and hoisted the man to his feet, then pushed him more upright against the resinous bole of a pine. He pressed his face close to Dhanjal's.

'Now, you've got nowhere to go unless we cooperate – have you? You can help me, and if you do, I might keep you alive. No one's going to believe you haven't spilt the beans, are they? Prakesh Sharmar isn't known for his generosity or forgiveness, is he?'

Dhanjal was shaking his head.

'They'll believe me.'

'Your first thought was the right one. They want Cass too much – and they want *me* very badly. If the chopper that just passed us by had seen us and was sure who was in the vehicle, what would have happened? Would they have shouted you a warning before they rocketed us or dropped something nicely combustible on the canopy? What do you think, Dhanjal – what do you *really* think?'

He was breathing heavily. The Indian's body against his own was heaving with admissions and denials, with revulsion at his helplessness, at Hyde's threatening pressure against him. He was shaking his head in futile denial –

'Christ –!'

Then the breath was gone from his body and he collapsed to the ground, clutching his groin. Dhanjal's knee had driven between his thighs. Then his hands flew to his head as the Indian aimed out at it with his right foot. Hyde, rolling, snatched at the extended leg but failed to grab it. Dhanjal's shoe caught him in the small of the back, then on the point of the shoulder as he

252

rolled away from the man's frenzied, desperate attack. The breath wouldn't catch in his throat, like an old engine failing to fire, and he was dizzy. His groin stabbed with pain.

You pillock! He's qualified you for the geldings' plate, you overconfident bas –

Dhanjal kicked out again, then turned away, hurrying to the Land Rover and dragging open the driver's door. Hyde, on his knees and still clutching his groin in both hands, stared like a stupefied sleeper suddenly awakened as the engine caught. The vehicle was thrust into reverse and began hurrying towards him, its exhaust pluming smoke, reversing lights gleaming.

He rolled to one side and the Land Rover's brakes were stamped on. The handbrake's rasp. Hyde staggered to his feet, wiping pine needles from his mouth. Beginning to run as he realised the meaning of Dhanjal's hunched shoulder half-turned from the driver's window. Hurried, five paces, three, two –

– jumped for the door, hands outstretched like those of a beggar, fumbled, then grasped the pistol Dhanjal had grabbed from the dashboard locker. Gripped, held on. Explosion. Hyde was deafened, his vision blurred and dazzling from the pistol's discharge into the roof of the Land Rover. Dhanjal grunted in pain, holding onto the gun with his right hand as he worked at something with his left. Hyde jarred his elbows against the sill, his cold hands clammily around the Indian's grip. Then he was jerked off balance as the vehicle was flung into reverse again and rushed backwards. He paddled his legs comically as Dhanjal braked, then flung the Land Rover forward. Hyde saw the narrow pines rush towards him and heaved on the pistol's hot barrel, tugging it free, falling away then rolling on the stone-splintered ground and its carpet of pine needles. He came to his knees as the Land Rover's brakes screeched and the brake lights glowed.

He lumbered to his feet as Dhanjal's wild-looking features stared back at him from the driver's window. Ran as the gears were clashed in desperation and the vehicle rocked backwards towards the narrow track they had turned off to park. He thought he heard Cass groaning in a detached, delirious way from inside. Then the gun was thrust against Dhanjal's temple, hard, as the Indian attempted to swing the Land Rover around to face the track. It teetered as if suggesting the precarious, momentary balance of everything.

'Switch it off! *Switch off the engine!*' Hyde bellowed in a cracked, breathless voice. He dragged the door open and jabbed the gun against the Indian's cheek. 'It's *finished* —!'

A moment, then the ignition was switched off and the hand-brake dragged on. Then only their breathing, like challenges between two struggling animals.

'Out,' Hyde managed, gesturing with the gun.

Dhanjal climbed from the Land Rover. His hands were free, his wrists scored from the struggle which had forced one hand from its bonds. The rope dangled from his left wrist. He shuddered, clutching his wounded arm as if only now reminded of it. Hyde gulped in cold air which the wind seemed determined to deny him.

'Sit!' he coughed, his testicles protesting at a renewed surge of pain which all but doubled him up. He sank to his knees, cradling the pit of his stomach. Dhanjal's hatred was virulent, stinging his cheeks like acid. Hyde aimed the gun at him, stiff-armed, until he dropped his gaze into sullen calculation.

'Right, Pandit-bloody-Nehru —! Christ, you've got bony bloody knees, Dhanjal!' He grinned savagely. 'I ought to kick *your* balls into touch, mate —!' Dhanjal rubbed his wounded arm. There was blood on his fingers. 'Right. *Now*, we're going to have a little talk or you won't be able to stop the bleeding with both hands!' He waggled the gun. The wind rushed through the pines above them with a deep moaning noise. 'We're sitting just south of the Cease Fire Line, correct? The road goes west from here to the Line itself. So do the heroin shipments, right?' It was correct, despite the almost immediate blankness of Dhanjal's features.

He was ashen beneath his racial pallor, exhausted by failure. 'Right? Am I *right*?'

He fished in the breast pocket of the camouflage jacket and removed a silencer, which he fitted to the barrel of the Heckler & Koch. Dhanjal's eyes watched him like those of a cat.

'Get the idea?' Hyde asked, then: 'Am I right?'

Without waiting for a reply, he squeezed the trigger and the bullet flicked up dust a few inches from Dhanjal's right leg. The man flinched away.

'Right, am I?'

He fired again, the shot embedding itself in the pine behind Dhanjal's head; audibly.

'Am I *right*?'

He fired again. The bullet flicked stone chippings onto Dhanjal's hand. He stared at it as if certain of the spurt of blood. Then he nodded violently.

'Yes, yes –!' he shouted. 'Yes – Tithwal, Tithwal –!'

'Then Muzaffarabad, in Pakistan?' Dhanjal nodded, his head bobbing like that of a puppet. Inwardly, Hyde felt relief sink through his rage and weariness like a stone through amber. 'OK. Then you've been across, plenty of times – uh?' Again, the defeated, mechanical nodding. 'Then you're about to take another little trip to Pakistan – aren't you?'

Reluctantly – yet with the return of cunning in his eyes – Dhanjal nodded, just once. Hyde got to his feet.

'Stay put, sport.'

He crossed to the Land Rover, walking crablike, the gun always on the Indian. He glanced into the rear of the vehicle. Cass was staring at him like some inmate of an asylum, wide-eyed at surroundings he could not comprehend. He'd been woken when flung from the bench seat by the violent movements of the vehicle. He struggled feebly with the folds of the sleeping bag, as if his survival depended upon it, with the weakness of someone very old, very dazed.

Hyde glanced at Dhanjal, who had not moved. No, he'd wait

now, hoping for luck and a good moment at the border post. A word, a sign, something that would bring guns to bear and save him.

Christ, an invalid and someone who wants to kill you . . . the brochure didn't mention little drawbacks like that when you booked the holiday —

Sara removed one of her earrings and brushed her hair away from her face. She moved to the telephone Prakesh Sharmar, with a smirking, angering kind of amusement, had invited her to take; his long-cherished humiliation of an opponent. She deliberately turned her back to him, staring out across the lake, the cellular phone bulky and unfamiliar against her cheek. She was repelled by the sense of Prakesh's lips having been against the mouthpiece as hers now were.

'Yes, V.K.?' she murmured hesitantly, looking across the water at her own houseboat which had been commandeered by Rao and his uniformed minions, and was now guarded by the army. As if the place had been animate and now disembowelled; cables and leads trailed to the generator truck, and the other trucks whose roofs sprouted aerials and dishes. 'Yes?' She had been billeted on the boat that bloody Ros had used to spy on V.K. and Prakesh!

'How are you, Sara?'

'Fine, V.K.' Prakesh hovered near her like a doctor, his face lugubriously indicating that she lied about her health. She was *not* fine —

'You heard the announcement?'

'Yes. You came over very well.' She had not intended the edge of irony, but did not regret it. 'It's all hell let loose from now on . . .' It was, and the sentiment was too redolent of her own situation and Prakesh's proximity and malice.

'Perhaps. Sara — I think you should talk to Prakesh about this Australian woman. Don't you?'

'What is there to say, V.K.?' she enquired, her voice carrying

256

a vibrato of nerves that were not customary. The sunlight gleamed off the lake as the clouds opened for a moment. Bad weather. 'I'm sorry . . . I *am* sorry, V.K. How was I to know?' She loathed the apologetic tone, like a verbal hand raised to fend off an anticipated blow.

'Yes. Obviously. But, you talked to her, Sara. You *knew* her. I think you could be more helpful.' His voice purred. It was seductive with threat. She felt her balance become unsettled.

'How, V.K.?' she asked hoarsely. Behind her, Prakesh snorted like an eager horse. 'I don't see what —'

'Sara,' he warned. 'I shall be entirely occupied with the election from now on. This matter must be resolved. Very quickly.' She felt the fear well up from her legs into her stomach, then into her chest, so that breathing was difficult. The uniforms on her boat and along the cordoned-off section of the boulevard insisted she was a prisoner. 'You do understand, Sara.' Now the tone was loftily dismissive; disappointment that had become a resolve to disregard. V.K. blamed her, she was the focus of suppressed rage, all his fears. 'I think you should cooperate with Prakesh — tell him everything you can, assist him in whatever needs to be done.' A silence. The connection hissed like a cobra, then: '*Sara?* You *do* understand?'

She turned and glared at Prakesh. Her cheek stung with the memory of him striking her. She was *consigned* to him now, handed over, her status that of . . . prisoner indeed. Even enemy.

'Yes, V.K.,' she replied heavily. 'I understand very clearly.'

She switched off the phone before he could do so and complete his dismissal of her. She held it out to Prakesh, who took it as insinuatingly as if he had begun to undress her. She shivered, her hands clutching at her forearms, which prickled with cold. The earring she had removed fell from her unregarding fingers and plopped into the water, disappearing immediately. She stared after it in what might have been horror.

257

'Good,' Prakesh announced. 'Very good. Very sensible of you to agree with V.K., Sara.'

'Did I have any choice?' she snapped.

'No.'

'Look, Prakesh — what the hell do you expect me to do? The woman's with the man Hyde, isn't she? Where else could she be? For God's sake, you've appropriated my *home*, you're keeping me here practically under guard —! What the hell do you expect to gain?' There was only anger now, the induced and encouraged heat of argument that kept at bay the cold threatening to well up inside her.

'Sit down, Sara.'

She hesitated, then saw that he wanted her to defy him. She dragged the cardigan closer around her shoulders as she sat down. She looked from him to the lake, and its gunmetal colour under the clouds, now that the sun had once more been swallowed. It now seemed an ominous blank expanse ploughed by small distant boats, a disappointing holiday snapshot of a place that meant nothing. They'd changed it . . . *he'd* changed it. *They*, Prakesh *and* V.K. She shivered and he seemed to enjoy the reaction. His malice was now undisguised. She swallowed.

'I can't *help* you, Prakesh,' she insisted. 'The woman was a guest, I don't *know* her.'

He shrugged, spreading his hands on his thighs as he sat opposite her on a cane chair. It creaked as if the wind was blowing through a dilapidated building.

'Then you must try. For example, Sara, do you *think* she is with the man?'

'How would I know?'

'Think. We know some things about them. They have a long-standing relationship, they inhabit the same house. He, presumably, cares for her — and her safety. Would that make him take her along?'

'I suppose so.'

'But, he has Cass with him —' She shuddered. It was only now

258

that she knew they'd tortured Cass – no, that wasn't true. She'd known they had him at Gulmarg, known *why*, known what the scheme had been from the beginning.

She did not admit as much. Whatever she had gleaned she had been able to lose from consciousness, even from her dreams, even from her bed when she and V.K. inhabited it. She had never admitted that V.K. had had Sereena killed.

'You see,' Prakesh continued. 'Hyde has Cass and Dhanjal with him –'

'He might have killed Dhanjal by now.'

'Perhaps. But, with two of them, would he want the woman, too? Would he risk anything, all his eggs in the one basket?'

'Look, Prakesh, I don't know how a spy thinks. Why ask me?'

'What do you think of this?' He reached into the inside pocket of his jacket and removed a folded piece of paper. Opening it, he passed it across the verandah to her. She took it with an uncertain hand. 'Read it.'

It was a sheet from a message pad, handwritten in English, the letters more certainly and formally shaped than any English-speaker would have produced.

'A woman answering her description paid for petrol at Punch, only two hours ago. The taxi had run out of petrol, apparently. The driver had had to leave a watch, some other things, as a deposit. Then the garage owner agreed only to a full tank at an exorbitant price. Quite scandalous –' He was luxuriating in the description, and in something else she could not discern but which involved her, she suspected. 'It might not have been her, the garage owner's description is vague, a peasant's. He remembers the money more than the payer. If it was her, where would she be heading? Why was she as far west as Punch?'

'It's near Gulmarg.'

'On a very poor road. We haven't located the taxi. The garage peasant remembers nothing about it or the driver.' His features twisted in contempt. 'It may have come from Gulmarg, even from here, perhaps. But from Punch, the taxi continued *south*. What is south of Punch, Sara?'

'Jammu — eventually,' she replied, as if to demonstrate she knew her catechism, or the answers to a geography test at school.

'Exactly. Jammu — buses, trains, aircraft. They couldn't have hoped to get out of Srinagar, so they decided that Jammu was far enough and safe enough.'

Acidly, she remarked: 'See, Prakesh? You didn't need me at all — did you?'

'There you are wrong, dear Sara — very wrong. I have a poor description of a large Englishwoman, nothing more. I did not see her. Colonel Rao has not had the pleasure of an introduction to your *friend*.' He paused. She was bewildered, her head foggy. 'You know her well. *You* can identify her —' She began violently shaking her head, not understanding why she did so. Not merely because he wanted it, nor merely to spite V.K., who apparently no longer required the flattery of her white body beside him . . . she could not comprehend the force or nature of her reaction. Prakesh was nodding. 'Yes, Sara. We will fly you down to Jammu by helicopter — in fifteen minutes. I suggest you prepare —'

'No —!'

'Yes. You will identify her. You will trawl the airport, the bus station, the trains, until you find her.' He stood up. 'I'm wasting valuable time,' he muttered. 'There it is, Sara. If the woman is in Jammu, find her. She will be heading for Delhi, presumably — or Pakistan or Nepal. Delhi, I would think. I haven't time to squander on her, but I would be remiss to forget she might be travelling alone.' He looked down at her. 'I suggest you hurry, Sara.'

He turned away and entered the lounge of the houseboat, murmuring instructions to someone who waited inside.

Oh, *God*, she thought, they want me to point her out so they can kill her . . . and they know I'll do it. I can't do anything else. The grey water surrounding her appeared cold. Nanga Parbat was hidden from view. The mountains to the north and north-west were all masked. Prakesh had removed the veil of self-deception with a single rough gesture. He'd shown her she was their creature, V.K.'s tart and someone to be ordered about at will. What choice did she have? None.

They killed his *wife*, what safety for her?

Or Ros, whom she barely knew. Even though she hoped she was with Hyde, and the taxi passenger was some other fat white woman . . . though she hardly believed it.

The land seemed to have been thrown up into a great barrier across the road, forcing them into the narrowing neck of a valley where Tithwal lay like a small heap of stones fallen from one of the cliff faces. Beyond the village and the border post, the mountains rose again. On the other side of them, north of Muzaffarabad, lay the Kagan Valley and a future he did not want to think about.

He instructed Dhanjal to stop the Land Rover at the side of the road, beneath overhanging rock. There had been little or no traffic on the road, which led only to the Cease Fire Line, the border between Indian and Pakistani Kashmir; a handful of trucks, a couple of army vehicles, two official-looking limousines. The place seemed deserted, quarantined, chilly. Grit was blown off the road by the increased force of the wind, pattering against the canvas hood and the windscreen. Hyde breathed deeply. Dhanjal watched him as a cornered animal might watch a predator. Cass coughed rackingly in the rear of the Land Rover, startling Hyde, encouraging Dhanjal. Leaving the gun pressed into the Indian's ribcage, Hyde turned to inspect Cass.

The face was still vague, like that of a man with very poor eyesight suddenly bereft of his spectacles. White, dead-looking skin on which the stubble of beard appeared like the impregnations of gunpowder. His whole look and posture was that of someone who had been too close to death. He was shivering despite the sweaters and the heavy anorak. He'd drunk a little water and even that had revolted against the drugs still in his system; eaten practically nothing except a few spoonfuls of heated soup. Dhanjal had wolfed his food against some great physical effort he envisaged being called upon to make.

Would Cass pass muster? Could he look *well* enough not to create suspicion?

There'd been no helicopter or unexpected army activity during their journey from Kupwara, just as there'd been no further attempt at escape by Dhanjal. It was just possible that the border guards wouldn't have been alerted. This was the unexpected – wasn't it?

The road wound ahead of them, dropping into the knife-cut of the valley. He raised the glasses to his eyes. The red and white barrier across the road, the guard hut, barbed wire like a fowling net at either side of the dusty, empty road. Bored Indian guards, and a hundred yards beyond them, equally bored Pakistani troops. A parked jeep, a docile army truck. It was as unsuspicious as any trap.

He had no thought but to complicate things for the hunt; confuse them, make them employ a longer, messier chain of command, widen the search area. Talk to Shelley – wait for Ros to get home . . . There were alternatives, but he wanted not to have to choose any of them. Not with Cass, not with Dhanjal, who couldn't be dumped after they crossed the border. He might have to be killed but he didn't want to think about that. Cross-border cooperation to pursue them would have to be carefully conceived and kept secret among the Sharmars' contacts in Islamabad.

None of it made him feel any better.

He lowered the glasses and turned to Dhanjal.

'Your turn now,' he murmured. 'Talk us through those two border posts and I won't kill you.'

'How can I do that?' The disclaimer was almost outraged; nearly genuine. Hyde grinned.

'Oh, you can do it. You've been this way before, and not in

262

another Hindu life either. You're the Sharmars' *boy*, the drug-wallah –' Dhanjal scowled. 'This is the crossing point and you must know the guards. They know you, anyway. They won't question you crossing over.'

'But who are *you*?' Dhanjal spat back with what might have been childish, playground spite.

'Customers. *Representatives* of clients. Whatever you like. You wouldn't explain to border guards, would you – not Captain Dhanjal!' Dhanjal squirmed with anger and impotence against the barrel of the pistol. 'I shouldn't, if I were you,' Hyde added, nudging the muzzle harder against the ribcage.

'If I take you across – what then?' Dhanjal asked, surprising Hyde.

'I said – I won't kill you.'

'Where will you go?' Dhanjal scorned. 'Where *can* you go?'

The wind picked up, as if to emphasise the isolation and friendlessness of the place. Clouds scurried across the mountains like dark, fleeing sheep.

'I could walk into the High Commission –'

'Do you trust them? After Delhi?'

Hyde grinned savagely. 'Is this to make me keep you alive? Respect your value? You have a deal?'

'No. I will just wait, I think.'

'Suits me, sport.' He caught the hollow bravado of his own voice. There weren't any places he and Cass could safely go. Not until Shelley was prepared to intervene. The proof would get lost down the nearest toilet at express speed, *they*'d be down the same toilet inside ten minutes. Unfortunate accident . . . *No one* wanted to know. 'Suits me,' he repeated carefully.

It didn't, of course. Which was why Ros had only half the evidence. Shelley would have an attack of gastroenteritis as soon as he saw the first frame of film, heard the first voices on the tapes. So would HM Secretary of State for Foreign and Commonwealth Affairs . . . so would everyone. And then Ros would tell them there was more, *just like this lot* . . .

. . . and they'd deal because they had to, to keep the lid on. *After* Ros got back, *after* Shelley was convinced. Until then, he and Cass – and Dhanjal – were on their own.

Cass began coughing again. Hyde whirled around as if to berate him. Dhanjal smirked.

'He is rather ill, I think,' he said.

'Then it'll have to be the fucking food that's got to him, or ice in his gin and tonic – won't it? Let's go, Dhanjal!' He prodded the Indian with the pistol's muzzle. 'You know the deal. You know the details. One word in Hindi or Urdu or anything else I don't understand, and this will go off.' He glared at Dhanjal. It wasn't difficult to appear desperate, wildly uncalculating. That was the problem, it was easy.

Dhanjal studied him for a moment, then started the engine. Hyde turned to Cass.

'Just listen to me, Cass,' he announced. The Land Rover pulled out onto the gravel road and began descending towards the Indian side of the Cease Fire Line. Dust blew across the road as if from a high desert. Clouds raced. 'Listen to him. Just keep quiet and *listen*. If he tries saying something in Hindi or Urdu, tell me. Understand?'

There was only the noise of the engine for a time, and the wind against the canvas hood. Then, through chattering teeth, Cass said weakly:

'All right.' The words seemed dredged from some deep place, a discovery by the speaker of sounds he seemed to have little or no use for. Jesus –

They neared the barrier across the road. There were no other vehicles moving in either direction. The valley closed beyond the scattered village, grey flanks of mountains looming until lost in cloud and the gloomy early afternoon light. The Land Rover slowed. Dhanjal's tension was evident through the divining-rod of the pistol's stubby barrel and plastic grip. An officer strolled towards the Land Rover, an armed guard behind him shuffling in new boots; stunted in growth, it seemed, by the helmet he wore.

Dhanjal looked briefly at Hyde, then slid open the window.

The officer, a captain, recognised Dhanjal with a smile that was both conspiratorial and deferential. The cold wind blew the skirts of his greatcoat about his boots, blew grit into the cab of the vehicle. The captain studied Hyde, who tried to appear indifferent, even impatient.

'Captain –'

'Captain.' The two Indians exchanged ranks like codewords. Hyde felt his temperature begin to rise. Cass coughed in the back of the Land Rover, startling the Indian officer.

There was no other way, except to run into this noose. Only Dhanjal could expect to pass across without the necessary, rarely-granted papers. Hyde saw an anti-aircraft battery mounted on a wide ledge of rock above the road only a few hundred yards away. A wrecked, burned-out, rust-enveloped scout car lay in a shallow grave of land a quarter of a mile away. He suppressed a tremor of nerves. The whole place twitched with danger like the filaments of a spider's web.

'We didn't expect you,' the officer remarked.

'No. My friends here –' He gestured and the captain inspected Hyde, peered into the rear of the vehicle. ' – are hoping to understand more of our situation. *Business* friends. Who is on the other side?'

'Husain. No problem. You can go straight through. You're on your way to –?'

'Muzaffarabad, no farther,' Dhanjal replied easily. The voice lied. His body was tense and stiff. His knuckles light-skinned on the steering wheel. 'Not far.'

'One of your passengers seems ill,' the officer remarked. Then spoke rapidly in Hindi, his face casual, even affable. Hyde pressed the pistol against Dhanjal. The flesh was hard as wood, unyielding. The fingers moved on the steering wheel, uncurling as from something he had strangled.

Then Cass mumbled something in Hindi from the back of the Land Rover. The officer laughed and said:

'Your companion is complaining about our food. I apologise. He should be more careful.'

'Yes,' Hyde said. 'Captain Dhanjal, we have a longish journey ahead –'

'Yes,' Dhanjal replied through set teeth. 'We'll go on, then.'

The officer waved his arm and the barrier sprang up. The Land Rover nudged forward beneath it, then accelerated across the no man's land between the two border posts. Hyde felt relief choking in his throat. Dhanjal's features were twisted with rage.

The noise of the engine, the wind, the clunking of the suspension across the rough, pitted gravel – and the other noise. A military helicopter blazoned with green and white and the crescent of Islam dropped like an olive-coloured stone out of the cloud, its downdraught swirling the dust as it settled to land at the Pakistani border post.

the road to the north

The wind tugged open the cloud and sunlight fleeted on the slowing rotor blades of the helicopter as its wheels skipped, then settled. Then the light whisked across the border post, the soldiers and the Land Rover as it came to a halt. Rifles gleamed for a moment before the afternoon became dull and grey once more. Dhanjal's face seemed to retain an illuminated cunning that shone like hope.

A Pakistani officer hesitated between the Land Rover and the Puma helicopter, the sliding cabin door of which remained closed. There was an unhurried certainty about the machine as Hyde heard the upspring of the wind once more. Clouds pursued each other across the grim flanks of the mountains. Then the door opened and two uniformed men jumped down. A few moments later, an officer clambered gingerly from the interior. The border post commander moved towards the Puma, his hand raised in greeting. Hyde nudged Dhanjal, who switched off the engine.

Four more soldiers climbed out of the helicopter, their movements neither urgent nor alert; bored and reluctant, rather. Then Dhanjal said:

'I don't know the officer. They're changing the guards. It happens every two weeks.' Further confirmation as the hut door opened and two soldiers humped with kit and weapons hunchbacked into the wind. 'We won't be allowed through.' He smiled a grim, nervous smile, newly aware of the pistol nudging against his ribs.

'Pity for you,' Hyde managed.

The two officers were conferring, their troops huddled together in greeting and commiseration, the hands of the newcomers flapping arms against the chill wind. The two guards who remained at the barrier seemed eager to be gone, scowling at the Land Rover as if it were a customer banging at the door of a shop that had just closed.

'Get out – *now*!' Hyde hissed. 'Do it. Call him – what's his name, Husain? *Call* him, make sure he knows it's you. They'll let us through. *English.*'

He thrust Dhanjal against the door of the Land Rover and the Indian twisted the handle angrily, as if killing a chicken, then stepped down. He followed the indication of Hyde's gun and came round to the passenger window. Waved to the officers, called out Husain's name.

The man looked up, and appeared startled.

'Cass?' Hyde whispered hoarsely.

A few moments of the wind, into which Dhanjal called again, then:

'Yes?' The croak of a hermit.

'Get the bloody gun out, will you? Get back among the living instead of the undead. We might have a small problem here.' He checked that Dhanjal had left the key in the ignition. If it began to explode, he'd reverse, handbrake turn –

– and go where?

They were stranded between the two border posts, amid a dozen uniformed Pakistanis, all armed.

Husain gabbled something to the relieving officer, then scurried towards Dhanjal, his face pale, his coal-black eyes burning with distress and compromise. This was a small link in the chain, just baksheesh for Husain. His commanding officer might be on a tiny percentage, then *his* senior on a bigger one, then a general or two, like the ones Ros had photographed on the houseboat, lining their pockets – however many it took to keep a nice clear open road for the Sharmars' heroin. Hyde studied Husain and

268

then the relieving officer, who was lighting a cigarette as he hunched against the wind, his troops stamping with cold and silent protest; rifles slung on their shoulders, kitbags at their feet.

'What are you doing here, Captain Dhanjal?' Husain asked in English. 'There was no warning, I did not expect you – you know the guards are changed today!' His knuckles were white as he gripped the windowsill of the Land Rover, his face puzzled by Hyde's unfamiliarity. Dhanjal had known – hoped. All that was needed was that they be turned back.

'A small emergency,' Dhanjal explained levelly, his voice consciously under control. 'Let us through before you go off duty.' There was nothing deceptive about the voice, no sign or gesture to create suspicion.

Because Dhanjal didn't want the other Pakistani officer to know . . . Hyde felt the relief drain him, make his hand quiver as it held the gun out of sight. So, come on then, let's get on with it.

'I can't – you have papers?'

'No,' Dhanjal replied. Then he reached into his breast pocket and removed his wallet. Fictitious papers. 'Pretend to inspect them,' he instructed. Oh, you're good, Dhanjal. You're really good. 'Hurry, Husain – let us through.'

The man looked dubious, and glanced towards the new arrivals. His own men appeared uninterested, eager to collect their kit and climb into the waiting Puma. Then he nodded, and stepped back, gesturing that the barrier be raised. The other officer seemed casually observant, smoke being snatched away from his mouth by the wind. His greatcoat billowed like a skirt. The barrier climbed slowly upright like an arthritic, warning finger. Dhanjal stared for a moment at Husain, as if he had been betrayed, then hurried around the Land Rover and clambered into the cab, slamming the door behind him and switching on the engine with a snatched, enraged movement.

'What shall I tell him?' Husain all but pleaded.

'Intelligence — just say Intelligence. I outranked you!' Dhanjal snapped angrily, as if a child was pestering him.

The Land Rover lurched forward. Husain waved his men towards the hut and they scuttled away to collect their kit. Hyde glanced back. The relieving officer had ordered two of his men to man the barrier and they reluctantly moved forwards as it dropped into its rest.

Dhanjal was grinding his teeth in a fury of frustration. The cover story was thin, but it ought to hold. Back and forth, diplomats, trucks, traders, Intelligence people. No questions asked . . . it should hold.

It had better —

— and Dhanjal? He'd have to be watched like a hawk.

One in the afternoon.

The road dropped away beyond the scattered, gritty-looking village towards a narrow river. Mountains thrust up again ahead of them. Mountains surrounded them. They were in Pakistan, without papers and with no good cover story. Smart move.

It was the heat and dust of another world. Jammu was hot and crowded, alien after Srinagar and the cloud and wind that had seemed to be hurrying her down from the mountains to the plain. The afternoon sun burned through a haze of dust as she looked along the cramped, struggling platform of the railway station. The old town sat on its hillside, its fort and temples lacking identity against the warm sky. She felt her balance go again and leaned her leg against the suitcase beside her, lowering the travel bag to the extent of its strap as she did so. She was exhausted.

The taxi had deposited her at the main railway station in the new town, amid a sudden flurry of bearers and touts and police and passengers. It had been a gauntlet of rucksacks, backpacks, suitcases, tickets offered at cut prices for trains already full, beggars and bright frocks and shirts. She was unprepared for it and without reserves. The station had crowded against her as if to indicate her presence to the uniformed soldiers and policemen.

Then she had queued for an hour for a ticket to Delhi, only to find that there was no sleeping accommodation, no ladies' compartment – just second-class ordinary, as they called it. The long-distance express was as much a chaos of caste and class and confusion as everything else in India – second-class ordinary, second-class sleeper, first-class sleeper *without* air-conditioning, first-class *with* air-conditioning and de luxe with carpets on the floor and the best loos. *Nothing, no, I am so sorry, nothing but second-class ordinary, I am so sorry . . .*

It was not so much disappointing as frightening. She wanted a small, four-berth compartment around her, the comfort of no more than *three* strangers . . . instead, she would have wooden slatted seats, the crowd, heat and halitosis and sweat, luggage racks swaying on chains suspended from the ceiling, iron bars across the windows, the gloomy, soupy air hardly distressed by two inadequate fans. Four or more to a bench –

– why are you worried, you've done it before. When you were eighteen there wasn't any other way . . . It brought back her younger self, the innocent from Melbourne passing around the funny fags with people she hardly knew; sleeping with some of the strangers, sharing food and money with others –

Ros shook her head. She couldn't afford to be that girl any longer. She needed concealment. She was afraid of a crowded carriage filled with strange faces, hers probably the only white one over the age of twenty.

She shook her head, dizzying herself, and remembered she had not eaten since mid-morning; a snatched lump of spicy bread and some vegetable curry from a stall in Rajauri's one shabby street. She glanced towards the rows of cookstalls, then towards the retiring rooms. She should have paid for the use of one, lain there in the hot gloom until it was time to board the train. But that was something you couldn't do if you were travelling second-class ordinary. You had to perch on the

271

platform waiting to pounce on a seat as soon as they blew the whistle to board. She needed luggage space.

Beyond the old town across the river, the mountains of Kashmir were pale, gold-flanked mirages. She swallowed. She was hungry, *that* was the something wrenching at her stomach, she told herself, not the distance between herself and Hyde.

Dragging her suitcase by its dog-lead strap – it moved through legs and bustle like any reluctant animal – and hefting the travel bag, she crossed to one of the cookstalls and chose something unlikely to upset her or cause her to use the loos they provided in second-class ordinary. She chewed on the papadam that came with the *thali* vegetarian dish on its battered metal plate. Her stomach rumbled as she tasted the fruit and nuts rolled in a leaf. Ignoring Hyde was only possible when her own anxieties were inflating in her mind.

She shook her head as another tout offered her a seat in first class – air-conditioning of course – at a discount price. First class was already full. Someone pressing towards the cookstall nudged the travel bag on her shoulder and her temperature jumped for an instant, as she thought the tubs of film and the tapes were being snatched away. The Indian apologised profusely. Longingly, she watched bearers wheeling luggage towards one of the first-class compartments behind a well-dressed Indian and his saried wife. She looked at her watch, balancing the metal plate awkwardly as she rotated her wrist. Another forty minutes before the train left. The lowering sun burned along the platform, its light falling heavily through the dusty glass roof of the station. Pigeons and bright, sparrow-sized birds flicked and waddled around her feet amid the crumbs of dozens of meals.

She finished eating. She must wash. The edge of the platform, along the rank of second-class carriages, was becoming more crowded. She was again aware of herself, white, looked-for, endangered, then she shook her head and hoisted the travel bag to greater comfort. Sod it.

'Ros!' She whirled, unnerved, the travel bag banging a boy, who scuttled away. 'My God, *Ros!*'

Sara Mallowby.

Unbelievable – and immediately threatening, despite the broad smile. Nervousness in her eyes, even though the hand that flicked the blonde hair aside was steady.

'I –'

'You left without a word!' And then she knew it was something acted. The words were uttered in the tone of a chiding hostess welcoming a belated guest. 'What happened?' The eyes were lascivious, mocking. 'Was it your friend? Was he *that* persuasive? But what are you doing in Jammu, of all places?' It was a performance she must have rehearsed over and over, but it still failed to carry conviction. Or was she just over-suspicious, her nerves jumping like fleas between a dog-pack of fears?

'Sentimental journey,' Ros managed, and Sara's glance hesitated between suspicion and what seemed to be pain, as if she had caught a stitch while running.

'Oh. Oh, yes, of course – retracing old steps, I see . . .'

'You've got it. Silly, but there you are.' She hesitated, then added: 'But you're here, too. *Train?* I wouldn't have thought that was you.'

Sara shrugged.

'One has to fill in time somehow.' She sighed. 'I'm on my way down to Delhi for a few days.' Again, the expansive shrug, and something in her expression that indicated there was a bitter taste on her tongue. 'Are you on your way down?'

'Yes. Just thought I'd do it this way.' Ros gestured with self-mocking ingenuousness. Don't overplay it. She doesn't think you're stupid. 'I should have booked. Second-class ordinary was all they had left!' She forced herself to laughter, waving her arms with the gesture of any memsahib confronted with India.

Sara would know about Hyde by now, know about everything. She must have been *sent* –

'God, how awful!' Then, at once: 'But you don't have to! I've got a whole four-berth to myself.' She grinned. 'Wonderful to have friends in the highest places – sometimes.' She moved her hand towards the suitcase, as if to appropriate it. 'Come on – I was just getting a last breath of fresh air before the air-conditioning!' Ros hesitated. Yet there was no alternative. No one turned down de luxe for second-class ordinary! Even if the de luxe was a carpeted, Western looed, shower-cubicled, strip-lit trap. 'God, what a piece of luck. I thought I was going to be bored out of my mind for the next fifteen or sixteen hours!'

The suitcase slid behind them, one of its wheels squeaking like a tiny, warning voice. Ros gripped the travel bag deliberately close to her side. At the corner of eyesight, she felt rather than witnessed a man detach himself from a newspaper stand and flit across the crowded platform on a parallel course. Sara's hand companionably cupped her elbow.

Don't let them get close –

– something from one of Hyde's few audible nightmares as he had struggled in sleep beside her.

Sara's manner, even if forced, began to envelop her as they moved along the crowded platform towards the carriages where bearers were deferential and luggage was boarded as gently as the first-class passengers. Sara, the slanting afternoon light, the warmth, the smells of food and pressing bodies, all a conspiracy that was narcotic in its effect. She was tired, she didn't want to feel on edge, fearful. Surely Sara was there by accident –?

No.

But there was nothing she could do, so she allowed herself to be guided towards the carriage. Her luggage was taken from her by a smiling bearer and she was assisted up the steps into the interior where she felt the air-conditioning bathe her like cool water. She glanced back in a moment of fear and Sara smiled encouragingly.

There was no sign of the man she had felt was shadowing

274

their progress like a shark whose interest had been aroused by movement in the water.

'You all right?'

Hyde brought the Land Rover to a halt. The late afternoon gloom made the Kundar River appear like a bed of flint as hard and pocked as the narrow, twisting road that climbed ahead of them towards the Babusar Pass. Behind them, the long valley descended through the massed, indeterminate darkness of pine forests towards cultivation and the activity they had abandoned. Scattered villages, hamlets and isolated, dotted houses lay on the valley floor beyond the road.

'What —?'

'Are you all right?'

Cass was quietly, continuously shivering inside his sweaters and anorak and gloves, like a very old man dragged to some inhospitable place where harm would undoubtedly be done to him. Hyde knew that if he could choose, he would ask to be returned to the bungalow in Gulmarg and the intermittent assaults of his captors. Now, all he had was the continued interrogation of the weather and the slowly fading daylight. He'd awoken only briefly from the trance that seemed to hold him to tell Hyde — after being bullied — not to join the Karakoram Highway at Mansehra but to take the narrower, slower road up the Kagan Valley to Chilas. Because of the checkpoints along the KKH and the necessary travel permits they did not possess.

'Yes,' Cass replied, wearily lying.

Dhanjal stirred in the rear of the Land Rover, but Hyde did not turn to look at the Indian, tied to a metal handhold, and gagged.

'Will we make Chilas before dark?'

'No.'

'Why not?' I got you *out*, he wanted to yell into Cass' abstracted, dumb face. *Do* something to help.

'Too far. The pass is difficult, even without snow.'

'Great.' He reached into the door pocket and withdrew a thermos he'd had filled at a stall in Muzaffarabad. 'Drink some tea,' he ordered.

With exaggerated caution Cass took the thermos cap and grudgingly sipped at it. His upper lip trembled around the plastic. The constant wind rattled the canvas hood of the vehicle and fingered through the closed windows and doors into the cab. Hyde felt his determination fading. Nanga Parbat was all but obscured by cloud, but it was still *there*, that same bloody mountain dominating his horizon. It was a huge upthrust gullet with the teeth of countless other, lower peaks in front of it. A slanted, narrow fir jutted optimistically out from the cliff face above them.

'Where are we heading?' Cass asked suddenly.

'Chilas – I told you.'

'And after?'

Hyde was aware of Dhanjal behind them, his breathing had been hoarse, but was now controlled. He was listening, but it didn't matter.

'It depends.' He leaned towards Cass, his hand gripping the man's thinned wrist hard. Cass appeared intimidated, but attentive. He whispered fiercely: 'We have to stooge around, *Phil*.' Cass' features brightened. 'We have to *wait*. Shelley's going to get us out –' Difficult that, since he didn't trust Shelley to do *anything* until he'd been shown what Ros had. 'He doesn't know *where*, yet. I have to talk to him –' He studied Cass' face, which blinked in and out of attentiveness like a revolving light in a lighthouse. 'I'll do that. But you say we won't get to Chilas tonight?'

Cass shook his head with the vehemence of denial of a child. 'The pass is so *slow*,' he enunciated angrily. Then, shockingly, he giggled like a drunk. 'The natives aren't friendly!' he burst out, subsiding at once into moroseness. 'Have to camp this side of Chilas, sleep in the vehicle . . .' The lighthouse was going out.

Dhanjal had all but stopped breathing in his effort to overhear. Hyde turned and waggled a pistol towards the dim features that hated him from the rear of the Land Rover.

It was all too oppressive, he realised. Cass· and Dhanjal crowded him into identifying with the lassitude of the one and the impotent hatred of the other. A redoubled gust of chill wind thrust against the vehicle, emphasising its smallness, its status as a tin box on wheels, liable to fail at any moment.

He rubbed his face. The action did not wake him. And there was the need to sleep. Cass couldn't drive, and he wouldn't let Dhanjal do it. Anyway, they wouldn't make Chilas and the highway tonight. Tomorrow, then. It didn't matter . . . Ros must have made Jammu by now. She'd be in Delhi tomorrow morning, Paris tomorrow night.

He had to tell Shelley to meet her there.

Another twenty-four hours, thirty-six, two days – three? There *was* one way out – but when he glanced at Cass studying the empty screw-top cup of the thermos with blank intentness, he realised that it didn't really exist. To emphasise the impossibility of it, Cass stirred half-aware in his seat and immediately winced with pain and clutched his ribcage with his wool-gloved left hand. His white face was drawn with pain. The top of the thermos rolled on the floor near his feet, unnoticed.

'The strapping too tight?' Hyde asked. Cass shook his head, his breath coming like a ragged wind in and out of a small cave; lonely and lost.

Cass had two, maybe three broken ribs. His whole left side was darkly bruised. Strapping was outdated, but Hyde had done it almost viciously tight, because somehow he had been holding the man together, or what was left of him.

It wasn't good – it wasn't *any* good. He glanced back at the straggling hamlet of Battakundi, lying like splinters from a dead log beside the cold river. Malika Parbat loomed out of the clouds, closer than Nanga Parbat. The other mountains, a wilderness of knife-sharp rock faces or snow-covered flanks, reared all around the valley. The cold they suggested reached to his marrow, freezing him.

He glanced again at Cass, who had sunk into some recollection that made his lips move quickly and fearfully, as if muttering prayers against an approaching storm.

He had to call Shelley, from somewhere.

He started the engine with cold-numbed fingers. Dhanjal growled in the rear of the Land Rover like an animal that must, sooner or later, be confronted.

'Magazines!' Ros blurted, getting up from her seat.

Sara was immediately startled, possessive.

'It's too late, Ros. The train's about to leave —!'

Ros snatched up her travel bag, empty-seeming apart from the tubs of incriminating film and the cassette tapes. She blundered into the corridor, sensing that Sara's hand reached out for her. She felt hot, desperate. It was like an attack of fever, or the bloody change, a hot flush that had been mounting irresistibly as she sat opposite that bloody woman she couldn't trust any more.

The platform was all but empty. The bookstall was fifty yards away. She glanced back, to see Sara framed in the doorway, but no one else watching her except an incurious gaggle of bearers in railway uniform. She hurried towards the bookstall, seeking the glossier, subtler covers of English language magazines scattered amid the violent colours of Indian titles.

She fumbled the magazines, perspiring freely in the smoky dusk light streaked along the platform and burning on the glass of the station roof. What was she doing? She couldn't get away —

— whistle. She started as at a gunshot. There was a man in a cream suit on the platform now, competent but undecided, glaring at Sara Mallowby, who stood beside the carriage steps. A bearer waited to remove them. A second whistle. She snatched money from her purse to pay for a month-old copy of *Vogue*. The woman who served her was smiling inanely. How could she not get on the train? Hyde had told her she had to get to Delhi, and out of India.

She whirled around, to see Sara's skirt billowing her across the platform. The man in the cream suit was speaking to the bearer, who seemed suddenly to regard the steps as immovable, something reverent. Sara's features were flushed with effort and something that could have been anger.

The travel bag was clutched against Ros' side as Sara reached her. They both seemed preeminently aware of it. The guard's whistle was continuous now.

'Ros —!'

She cowered back for an instant, surprising Sara, her eyes darting towards the train, along the platform, at the man in the cream suit, at the platform signs that arrowed the only exit. She'd *meant* to get away from Sara and the trap she represented, yet now, as Sara touched her arm, almost with solicitation, she knew it was impossible.

Sara guided her towards the train, hurrying her. The man in the cream suit had vanished and the porter was once more impatient with the steps. Ros climbed awkwardly into the carriage and, almost at once, the train jerked and began to move.

The last of the light was slipping back across Dal Lake as if it had been spread like a cloth for the duration of the day and was now being removed. Colonel Rao stood at the front of the houseboat, his chin cupped in one hand, his arm folded across his chest to support his elbow. Behind him, there was murmured activity around the big dining table and its maps and, farther away, the noise of cars and 4WDs as reports were received or despatched. Everything was being coordinated, refined, reassessed. His head was dense with detail and prolonged command. The cool air off the lake helped. The clouds had glanced aside from Srinagar, and Nanga Parbat loomed golden-flanked. The lower slopes were already dark, as if they had sprouted new forests.

There was a quiet coughing noise behind him, and he turned.

One of his aides was holding out a telephone, its lead stretching back into the houseboat's crowded lounge. Cigarette smoke moved heavily in warm lamplight. Spotlamps glared on flip-charts erected on easels towards the far end of the long room.

'Mr Sharmar,' the aide murmured. Rao reluctantly accepted the receiver.

'Yes, Mr Sharmar?' he enquired. 'What may I do for you?' However enunciated, it was the remark of a damned shop-keeper. His political master –

The line was clear, crystal as the lake. The stars were beginning to emerge from the darkening sky, large and glittering as diamonds.

'Have you news for us?' Did he use the plural because his brother, the Prime Minister, was present? 'What news is there?' There was a kind of post-coital elation in the man's voice. He had just come from the bed of his mistress, politics. Images of Mehta and V. K. Sharmar were already being erected all over Srinagar, there were loudspeaker vans on the streets in the unaccustomed lack of violence and riot.

'There is nothing definite yet, Mr Sharmar – I would have informed you had there been anything.'

'Do you need more people? Send for them if you do.'

'At present, there are sufficient.' He had effectively under his command, units of the Parachute Brigade, of a Mountain Division, the Border Security Force, air force helicopters and all the C_3I backup and input he required –

– *but you have not found them*. The thought was as clear and stinging as if it had been voiced by Prakesh Sharmar. It was almost inconceivable to admit that there was no trace of the Land Rover and its driver and two passengers. Two Englishmen and an Indian. The net had been cast, again and again, the search organised like a whirlpool's ripples spreading out from Gulmarg. But still they had not been seen. 'There are sufficient forces here,' he repeated.

'Then where are they, Colonel?' A pause, and: 'Why are they

not in custody or disposed of, if manpower is not a problem?'
The politician's insinuating threat, the stick always behind the
back.

'We have not been able to locate them. It is simply a matter
of *time* rather than men.' His teeth closed together in a bite.

The water of the lake was dark now, cold-looking, with a mist
beginning to curl off the surface like the smoke from a stubble
fire.

'How much time? It must be dark there by now.'

'It is. They will rest, they will have to. Your people – *tired* the
man Cass, and Dhanjal is not to be trusted by them. There is
only the agent to drive.'

'Presumably. You were informed of his peculiar efficiency,
Colonel. Don't underestimate him.'

'I do not.' The reply was ground out. He felt angered. Not with
Sharmar. He could deal with politicians. He and others like him
were entirely necessary to them. No, he was angry at the light
Sharmar's condescension shone on his apparent failure.

An army transport, by its navigation lights and bulk against
the stars, dropped low across the lake like a black pigeon towards
the airport. He turned. An aide, as if posted, saw his impatient
gesture and, interpreting it correctly, immediately brought him
a folded map. He shone a torch on its colours, mountains, scattered towns and hamlets. A ravined, heaved-up, jagged landscape, few roads, fewer hiding places . . . if the man Hyde had
gone north.

'Are you there, Colonel?' There was an edge of anxiety in
Sharmar's voice now, satisfyingly. Rao flicked the map over. It
dropped its folds open as if he were a fumbling conjuror who
had let slip a pack of cards. Could he have gone south, out of
the mountains and down towards the plain – Jammu? The
woman had been heading for Jammu, after all –? He shook his
head.

'Yes, I'm here. I'm checking something, Mr Sharmar.'

'What?' he heard blurted in the tone of an eager schoolboy.

'A moment, please.'

He handed the receiver to the aide and took the torch and then gathered up the dangling folds of the map. South –? No. Not in the same direction as the woman. To the east, the Zanskar Mountains were all but trackless, a few scattered villages and hamlets amid peak after peak . . . It had to be north, because to the west was Pakistan and the man Hyde would not have provided – *could* not have provided – himself with the appropriate papers to move freely on either side of the Cease Fire Line. He couldn't pretend to tourism up there –

Revelation, or merely feverish imagination? He suspected the insight that had suddenly sprung on him like a tiger from the lake. It could not be –

'Mr Sharmar,' he snapped, 'how do your irregular cargoes leave Kashmir?'

'*What?*' Sharmar was winded by the question, his subsequent breathing that of a stranded fish.

'It is not directly my business, nor has it been, Mr Sharmar. But it was Dhanjal's –?'

There was a silence, except for Prakesh's sharp inhalations, and heavy sighs. Rao pondered the notion that had come to him as if picking over rags that might conceal gems. Dhanjal was the key, if there were a key at all. Border guards would be on the Sharmar payroll.

'Mr Sharmar?' he enquired softly, firmly; cajoling a secretive child that had done wrong.

'Muzaffarabad –' followed by a throat-clearing noise, which recaptured confidence. 'At Tithwal, there are people –' Then he dismissed his confessional mood and snapped: 'Dhanjal would have *known*, Colonel –!'

'Could they have crossed the Cease Fire Line with Dhanjal's help?' The *Cease Fire Line* . . . it rankled still. It was inadmissible and yet inevitable, this *surrender* of Kashmir. And the Punjab . . . The Army had been mollified with promises of money, new weapons, greater influence, but there was still the surrender of

282

Indian territory to the Moslems. He shook his head. Old habits of thought, dying very hard.

'Depending on whoever was in command at the border posts,' Sharmar admitted. There had evidently been no expected shipment. Sharmar's voice sounded hollow.

'Then I suspect that that is what has happened to them, Mr Sharmar. They have crossed into Pakistan.'

'Damn! What do we *do*?'

'There are requests to be made, contacts to be established. I shall need your authorisation –' That, too, was difficult to admit, but necessary.

'Very well. Of course. What do you need?'

'For the moment, I must make certain. I suggest you remain near a telephone – perhaps the Prime Minister, too?'

'Yes, that can be arranged. I need to talk –'

'Yes. But not until I have made certain, Mr Sharmar.'

'Hurry, Rao! Call me as soon –'

Rao replaced the receiver, then barked at the aide:

'Get me contact with Tithwal – the border post. And get through to Islamabad. You know who to call in the ISID – quickly, man!'

The aide, like a hornet, seemed to stir the group around the table into hurried movement. Rao returned his attention to the lake, which was blank except for dotted lights and the glow from the urban sludge of Srinagar creeping along its western shore. It must be the case, he thought, clearing his head of buzzing angers. He'd *know* within ten minutes, but already he was certain. Hyde had used Dhanjal to get them into Pakistan.

But not to escape. Their escape was illusory. Islamabad would cooperate in the only area that mattered, men on the ground, machines in the air. They'd do that because of the Sharmars. Their overtures to the Pakistani army and members of the government would assist now.

He'd have them – soon.

*

The Land Rover hiccoughed over the last of the ascending track, its nose bucking down as if it sniffed Chilas in the distance. Food and warmth and lights that Hyde still could not see through eyes bleared with weariness and the obscurity of pine forest and mountainous twists in the road. They'd passed a cheerful, waving, solitary trekker climbing up towards the Babusar Pass, his raised hand diminishing in the mirror.

He rubbed his eyes again. The headlights bounced and weaved along the rutted track, whipping rock faces, drops, thin, leaning trees before his eyes. His wrists ached and his hands and fingers were numb on the steering wheel. The temperature had dropped like a stone and the wipers flicked light, flurrying snow away from the windscreen. There seemed to be snow in front of his eyes, closer than the windscreen. He knew he'd have to stop soon.

And the journey kept coming back like an ill-digested meal; the scattered villages, the narrow pines stuck like abandoned arrows in alpine pastures or bare cliffs, and the jade-green lake he had glimpsed just before the sunset lit it an unreal orange. Solitary farmers, thin sheep with muddy coats, the glimpses of sky with high eagles or hawks turning.

Cass was asleep in the passenger seat, sprawled like a drunk. Even Dhanjal dozed wearily in his awkward, trussed posture in the rear of the vehicle.

He blinked for the hundredth or thousandth time, and tried to focus, the rising of the offside wheels alerting him. The track was slushed and gleaming already, but he didn't know when the snow had begun. Time meant nothing any more, only the time of year that was already making whole villages deserted as people and their flocks drifted urgently down to lower pastures and shelter. He'd been held up for forty minutes by one flock of bemused-faced sheep and surly drovers, and the donkey-carts that had come behind, carrying the masked women and the dishevelled belongings.

He slammed on the brakes: the sheep were so real, jumbled

and bucking like snowflakes in front of his eyes. The Land Rover halted. The road ahead disappeared around a hairpin bend and the headlights strayed off into blank darkness. No, there were lights, miles away. Chilas – ?

Cass woke briefly, touched his broken and bruised ribs, rubbed his arm where the memory of pentathol lingered even now, then slid rather than fell asleep once more. Hyde listened. Dhanjal was snoring. Warily, scenting the inherent danger of his weariness, he slipped the vehicle into reverse and climbed away from the drop that lay at the side of the road. Then he eased around the hairpin, one rear wheel nibbling rather than biting at the track. Then the darkness dropped away on every side, making him begin to panic before the track gleamed in the headlights again. Nose-down, the vehicle seemed to be carrying him effortlessly into the night – he jerked awake once more.

The trees were close to the road now, like a crowd of spectators. Another hairpin, but he got round it without backing up. He saw the flash of something furred and quick, across the track and into the trees. The descent continued . . .

He awoke, terrified. One wheel was spinning. The radiator grille was against the earthen cliff at the roadside as if it nuzzled for food. The vehicle was still in gear and his foot was on the accelerator. Dhanjal shouted in panic. Cass awoke slowly. End of journey.

Rubbing his eyes, he strained to see beyond the halo of the headlights. Darkness, flowing like velvet. Chilas' lights were hidden by another twist of the road. Thin firs were stuck in the corpse of the landscape.

He opened the door and the chill struck him awake. An alpine meadow, with soft lumps like the forms of sleeping cattle, spread around them. He felt grass crunch under his feet. There was snow in the wind, but nothing settling. The nose of the Land Rover was thrust into earth, some road-repair gang's spoil, he thought as the torchlight flicked over it. The meadow and the track bumped away downwards to another twist and another hairpin that lay beyond leaning pines. The wind rushed through a clump of pines no more than twenty yards away, their branches swaying obediently, softly clashing together as if in welcome. Hyde touched the gun in his waistband, then clapped his hands against his upper arms as the wind bit. Cloud swirled seemingly only feet above him.

When he tried to speak, he sounded hoarse and rusty.

'Cass – *Cass*, you idle fucking *bastard* –!' he managed to bellow, and the echoing noise of his voice and the momentary exhalation of his weariness delighted him. 'Move your arse!' The wind and the night carried his words away, but not before they had invigorated him.

'What –?' from the Land Rover.

Hyde hurried to the passenger window, banging on it with a wind-numbed hand. Cass wound it down in surreal slow motion.

'Let's get the tent up – unless you want to go on sleeping in the vehicle? No? Right, move yourself, then – I'm bloody tired and bloody hungry –!'

His weariness came back with his next breath and he was too bone-tired to care about the tent . . . or food, even. He was cold now, very cold. *Food* –

'We'll sleep in the Land Rover,' he growled. 'But I want something hot! Understand? Something hot to eat.' He slumped against the vehicle. Cass was nodding vigorously as he looked up at him. Hyde held onto the door as Cass opened it.

He . . . remembered Cass' face, still behind the smeared window, then – later? – soup or something else, thick and hot, then someone – Cass again? – zipping him into a sleeping bag . . .

The bag that enclosed him now. There were crumbs in his teeth as his dry tongue traced across them. He remembered the biscuits now, Cass forcing him to eat them when all he wanted was to sleep.

Someone was snoring in the muffled, windy darkness. It was the tone of Cass' snores, coming from a small distance. *He* was in the rear of the Land Rover, wasn't he? Yes . . . the trees creaked like a chorus beyond the rattling canvas hood. There was a dim gleam of whiteness on the sleeping bag where snow had thrust through the canvas. *He* was in the rear of the vehicle *with* – that was the point, *with* someone . . . A bulky figure in an anorak –

Dhanjal must be the shadow that breathed hotter than the surrounding air and loomed over him. Touched him, searching for –

The sleeping bag was all around him, hampering, imprisoning. He struggled one arm free of it, and it came out rubbing against his unshaven cheek, alerting Dhanjal so that the Indian clamped a hand across his mouth. He could taste the man's palm.

Bit it, like an animal reacting.

Dhanjal cried out in a stifled way, then jerked away from Hyde's grip. He struggled away, holding something that Hyde felt dragged out of his waistband. He heard Cass cry in alarm. The canvas hood opened and the wind came in, throwing a handful of snow ahead of itself. Then the loosened flap dropped back as Hyde struggled free of the sleeping bag and lurched to his feet, his head spinning only for a moment, then clearing –

– so that he fumbled in one of the metal lockers and drew out a pistol and slid the first round into the chamber with a loud rasping noise, then ducked his head through the flapping canvas. Lighter, snowblown darkness after the interior of the Land Rover. He saw a figure shambling away across the dimly gleaming meadow, bulky in its anorak. He fired twice – to warn rather than hit, but the shapeless figure continued without pause. The gunshots echoed eerily around the meadow, deafeningly loud. Then the sighing of the trees was restored. He jumped down and collided with Cass.

'Has he gone?'

'Yes. Stay here while I –'

'I tied him up!' Cass protested.

'Yes,' Hyde replied. 'Stay inside the Land Rover – get yourself a gun, he'll want the vehicle.'

'You?'

'If he doesn't want the vehicle, he'll want to tell someone where we are. Sit *tight*.'

He knelt for a moment, catching one glimpse of Dhanjal's gorilla-like image before it disappeared into a thick stand of pines. He rose like a runner, and lumbered towards the pines. Dhanjal looked as if he was following the track, heading for Chilas to raise the alarm. Hyde did not want to kill him – Dhanjal might be as useful again as he had been at Tithwal – but knew he would probably have to. He reached the pines. They straggled away on all sides, a miniature forest moaning in the wind. Snow pattered on his upturned face. There was no sign of Dhanjal.

He waited in the darkness, listening. He heard Cass moving inside the Land Rover, the wind, the creaking of branches, the cracking of high ice . . .

. . . they were almost noiseless, but they were there, he realised. There were *others* – not Dhanjal, *others* – sifting through the pines almost as silently as the snow. *Who* – ?

THIRTEEN

strangers on a train

A flash of light – from a station? Yes, she could hear the train's noise echoing back in an enclosed space. The light gleamed at the edge of the drawn-down blind and showed her Sara's white hands hovering over the compartment's table. Ros held her breath, then began to breathe calmly, regularly . . . still asleep. The tapes and film lay on the table in a second gleam of light. Sara's hands were possessive, certain. Her blond hair hung forward, masking her face, as she bent over what she had managed to remove from Ros' travel bag. As the noise of the train died away in openness once more, she was oblivious to Ros leaning out of the upper berth.

Christ, everything's there . . . She waited, certain there would be a muffled, polite tapping at the door of the compartment, that the Indian in the cream suit would be there, to be given the tapes and film. Her breath caught and made her cough before she could suppress the strangled noise. Sara looked up, startled out of her intent distraction. Her features were bland in the moonlight that seeped around the edges of the blind, pale and staring. Ros' hand gripped the edge of the bunk, the sheet clenched into creases.

Then Sara said in a hoarse whisper: 'You did do it, then. Spied on me –' The voice and the sentiments it expressed both possessed the peculiar suggestion of a gramophone record being started, then gathering speed until it created a coherent impression. 'You – and *him*, I suppose? The man you hardly *knew*? Christ –!' She flung her hair aside from her face with a rough, dismissive gesture. The noise of the train flowed away across the emptiness of the plains of Punjab south of Jalandhar.

Ros glanced at the table, which was sheened with moonlight. As was the pistol lying beside the tapes and film. Sara had found the gun Hyde had given her. Ros' breath came and went with asthmatic difficulty, her chest tight. The pistol loomed with more menace even than Sara, or the thought of a soft knocking at the door.

'I —' Then she was angry, expelling tension rather than outrage, so that her words came breathily. 'What are you bloody doing in my luggage?' she hissed.

Sara seemed nonplussed. Just for a moment.

'What the hell are these?' she retorted, her hand gesturing towards the table where the blind flapped idly with the rolling of the train, letting in more moonlight. 'You bugged my houseboat!' The outrage was genuine. Ros rose onto her elbow and forearm. Sara's face was only a matter of inches below her own. 'What were you doing? for whom?' But she knew the answers already, that much was obvious. The pistol insisted its presence and potency.

'Look, I'm sorry it had to be you!' Ros yelled. 'At least, I was. But you're in it. That's why you're here, isn't it?' Then she added: 'You *work* for the Sharmars.' Sara flinched as if struck, her mouth stretched into a rictus of anger and admission.

'No,' she murmured, her hands pressing downwards at her sides, as if to quell nipping, importunate realisations. 'No, I don't — not as you mean it.'

'You know what it's about, don't you?'

'Do I?'

It seemed hotter in the air-conditioned compartment, but the noises from the carriages on either side seemed inexplicably loud, as if transmitted on frosty air. Ros nodded.

'You do. The poor bugger they had blamed for the wife's murder. Who *did* do it? Do you know?'

Sara shook her head in a childlike, intense way. Then she looked up.

'I – don't know.' The words seemed forced from her.

'Christ!' Ros exclaimed. 'What are we going to *do*?' She had no idea why she had included Sara, as if both of them were threatened. And yet the woman responded, even if only to ask:

'D'you want some coffee?'

'Might as well,' Ros answered in a surly, grudging tone as she swung her legs over the edge of the bunk and slid down to the floor. They were suddenly cramped in what remained of the space between the seats. Ros thrust her bunk back to its upright position. Then she collapsed onto the bench seat, her forehead slick with perspiration. Sara busied herself with the thermos of coffee the attendant had brought an hour earlier. 'We'd better talk – hadn't we?' Ros announced belligerently.

Jerkily, like a nervous trainee, Sara thrust the cup and saucer towards Ros. Then she sat hurriedly and heavily opposite her, her own cup cradled in her hands. Her eyes were angry as they glared through a sweep of blond hair.

Their breathing. Nothing else for some time except the noise of the train quickly being lost in the spaces of the Punjab night and the occasional clicking of a set of points beneath the carriage wheels. Someone coughed loudly in the next cabin, startling them both.

Sara fidgeted. She was enraged at being discovered, enraged too at Ros and the evidence of the film. There seemed to be conflicting pressures thrusting her on. The train listed as with tiredness as it followed a long curve of the track. Then Sara stood up with a robotic jerkiness and switched on the light.

'What's the point of sitting here in the dark,' she muttered, 'since we're both wide awake!'

She returned to her seat.

'While we are awake,' Ros began, swallowing her throat clear of nerves, 'we'd better decide where we go from here. Apart from Delhi. I take it you weren't planning to throw me off the train?' She was surprised at how levelly the words came out. Sara appeared deeply affronted. 'Hadn't you thought about it?'

Sara shook her head vehemently while she stared in the direction of the film and the tapes – and the pistol. Her thumb and forefinger plucked mechanically at her lower lip.

'Christ, you *hadn't*, had you?' Ros breathed. The situation was more dangerous because more unpredictable. 'I know you County Set females aren't supposed to have any minds to speak of, but what did you think you were doing here?'

Sara merely pointed at the table beside them. The blind's cord moved its small wooden acorn-like grip amid the tubs of film and the tapes. It seemed to be inspecting them like a large, inquisitive insect.

'Look, Sara – they're trying to kill Hyde and Cass, the man they had prisoner. Don't you understand that?' Ros leaned forward, the cup rattling softly on its saucer, her face intent. Sara adopted a posture more appropriate to a leisurely dinner party. 'They're not going to let *me* just bugger off, either – are they? Can't you see that?'

'What the hell were you doing interfering in my life!' Sara suddenly snapped back, her eyes glaring, cheeks high-spotted with pink. She snatched at her handbag as if reaching for a weapon, then fished inside and withdrew a packet of cigarettes. She lit one and puffed angrily. 'I'm supposed to have given these up!' she growled accusingly. 'You started this, Ros. You *intruded*.'

'All right! But while they're trying to kill Hyde, I'm not going to just stand back.'

'Are you trying to kill V.K. – kill India?' Sara asked with virulence.

'What?' Ros was bemused.

'Now it's you who understands nothing, isn't it?'

The woman was suddenly transformed. There was no languor, even if there was a regained superiority. She was calmer, certain. The look, the confidence, the intensity, were all too familiar to be misinterpreted. She'd seen it before, on charity committees,

292

from activists. Idealism . . . *the cause, my soul, the cause.* He wasn't just her lover, he was her hope.

'I'm not trying to kill anyone,' Ros offered lamely.

'Then why interfere?' She snorted, then threw up her hands in a large, dismissive gesture. 'Why did you come? You must have come to spy – *why*, for God's sake?'

Ros knew she must remain aware of her surroundings as she glanced at the door. The man in the cream suit, or maybe others, might knock at any moment; expecting Sara to hand her over to them.

'Hyde is a friend of Cass. He didn't believe he killed Sharmar's wife –' A complementary doubt appeared like pain on Sara's face for a moment, before she shook her head.

'He did it.'

'Whatever – the situation is as it is. We have to decide what can be done about it.'

'Why did you ever come here?' Sara accused bitterly, stubbing the cigarette into the ashtray beside the table with a furious, intent, grinding motion of her fingers.

Jesus –

Who? And *where* – ?

He remained with his back pressed against the bole of a narrow pine, the wind soughing through its branches above his head, listening to the human noises of the night. Where was Dhanjal? There was no sound of him blundering through the trees or crunching across the frosty pine-litter. No noises either, of the other footfalls, which had been quieter and more dangerous. *The natives aren't friendly*, Cass had said. Hyde glanced back towards the shadowed bulk of the Land Rover. He could hear, distinctly on the wind, so they could hear it too, Cass' movements. The man coughed, helpless and inviting. He slid down the tree until he was in a seated crouch.

The pistol was pressed against his cheek, both his hands gripped around it. He strained to catch movement against the faint, backcloth sheen of mountains and the lights of Chilas. A figure flitted, minutes later. His thighs and feet felt cold and stiff. Too small to be Dhanjal, a loose jacket flapping like a cloak. He waited, his eyes moving back and forth between the Land Rover, isolated amid the pallor of light snow on the meadow, and the thickening obscure perspective of the trees. Another figure, small and huddled, fled from the cover of one tree to another. Were they looking for Dhanjal?

Dhanjal, eventually. At least, he thought so. A bulky figure, moving with exaggerated and unpractised caution, perhaps fifty yards further into the trees. The wind moaned and, somewhere high and distant, ice cracked again, rumbling like an empty stomach. A harshly whispered word, then the movement of the two figures towards where he thought he had seen Dhanjal. How cautious were they, whoever they were? Afghan refugees, the local Kohistanis, bandits – troops? No, they weren't soldiers. More voices, then. Closer. They'd located him by a process of elimination. He slid upright against the tree. Then Dhanjal, unnerved, detonated the situation.

'Hyde!' he heard. 'Hyde – ?' It was querulous. Not to tempt him out of cover, just to confirm that he wasn't alone amid *their* soft noises.

One shot. Automatic rifle. The noise cracked away beneath the pines, pursued by a command in a language he did not understand. Not Afghans, he thought. Two shots in reply, towards the calling voice, the small barrel-flickers from a pistol visible beside a tree. Running footsteps. Another shot from a rifle, a big, old-fashioned noise.

Then someone blundered against Hyde in the darkness. Dark, bearded features, winded and surprised and quickly malevolent. Hyde struck out with the flat of his hand across the bridge of the hawklike nose. The Kohistani staggered against the tree, a knife's blade gleaming near his middle as he unsheathed it. Hyde struck again, plunging his fist at the opening mouth. The man's head struck the bole of the tree with a small, cracking noise and he slumped into a drunken, unconscious position at Hyde's feet. Hyde whirled round at the noise of footsteps, but they were hurrying in the direction of Dhanjal. Two more pistol shots, their gleam betraying Dhanjal's position.

'Hyde—!'

He hurried. Dhanjal was suddenly to be stolen from him, and was therefore at once valuable, indispensable.

'Patrick!' he heard from the direction of the Land Rover. He glanced back. Cass was standing forlornly beside the vehicle, a betraying torch in his hand.

'Put the bloody light out!' he roared, before sliding quickly sideways, then in another direction, zigzagging away from his betrayed position, towards which two rifle shots were fired.

Leave him, leave the bugger, his thoughts repeated. Two more pistol shots – how many's he got left?

He came up behind one of them, his outstretched hands all but colliding with the man's form before seeing him. He struck at the back of the head, that was beginning to turn, with the barrel of the pistol and jumped the body as he might have done a log. Then skidded to a halt beside a tree, scraping his hands and cheek on its icy, rough bark. Assessed, saw, aimed. One shot, and a form crumpled, only wounded but out of the game for the moment. How bloody *many* of them –?

Two shots digging into the tree above his head. Just above. Then a third, from another direction, leaving a white scar beside his hand and fragments of bark clinging to his skin. He slipped away from the tree, body crouched, moving nearer to Dhanjal, from whose direction there were no more shots. No clicking, either. Hadn't run out of bullets, not yet . . . being sensible, is he? Saving his –

He stumbled over the humped obstacle of bodies, all three of them alive. He plunged forward, off balance, and landed on gritty pine litter and sharp ice. Slid to a halt on his stomach, like a child thrown from a toboggan. Then rolled away onto his back, but only in time for one of them to throw himself down on him, his filthy sleeve across Hyde's face, the man's clouding breath noxious. A knife had hovered over Dhanjal's form as he had blundered into them. Then he saw the knife again and grabbed for the wrist holding it. Thin, wiry, strong —

He fired into the man's body, which bucked coitally, then was still. He flung it aside, rose onto his elbow, and fired again. The man kneeling over Dhanjal toppled away with a groan. Not dead. Voices, not too close. He crawled to Dhanjal and pulled at the skirt of the anorak, hoisting the man to his feet.

His head flopped. Throat wet and dark. The gun was missing. Dhanjal seemed to assault him, pressed against him by the impact of a bullet. He dropped the body and ran, skipping from tree to tree, thrust forward by the cold, reliable panic that had saved him before. Pause, run, pause. Zigzag, dodge, pause, run. For the moment, they'd be looking for the dead and wounded. He had to be sure of their numbers before they had a go at the Land Rover . . .

. . . squatting isolated and shadowy in the meadow as he emerged from the trees. Thank Christ for smaller mercies. He hesitated, then clumped towards it across the meadow, slush and frozen grass soaking his boats and trousers, restraining him like thick mud.

'Cass!' he bellowed in a hoarse whisper. 'Cass!'

His face at the flap at the rear of the vehicle. 'You all right?'

Hyde nodded. 'Dhanjal isn't — he's dead!' He shook his head, drawing in great, relieved breaths of icy air. 'Get in the front — rifle! Let's bloody get out of here.' He dragged open the driver's door and lumped into the seat, his hand at once fishing for the ignition key, turning it. The engine barked coldly. Cass clambered into the cab, the rifle as awkward as a long-handled broom in his hands. He turned the ignition again, then a third time — figures were coming out of the trees, stirred by the violence and deaths and the lack of money and valuables on Dhanjal's corpse — and the engine caught and roared. He let off the brake and skidded out of the ruts. A bullet careered off the Land Rover's side.

Cass wound down the window and poked the rifle through it with all the aggression of a meteorological instrument. The Land Rover lurched forward like a charging bull, elating Hyde.

'Keep your bloody head down!' he yelled, gripping the recalcitrant steering wheel.

The vehicle bounced over the rutted, frozen grass and skidded in slush as he struggled for the road against their tension and without the comfort of headlights. A black shape jumped aside, then another stumbled backwards out of their path. His side window shattered and the bullet spent itself against a metal upright. The trees enveloped them as he felt something collide against the flank of the Land Rover and the back wheels jump like pounding feet on what had to be a body. 'Head *down*!' Cass fired twice, probably into the air, then the road was illuminated as he switched on the headlights and followed its violent curve and drop, all four wheels leaving the ground for a moment.

Then he skidded on a bend, following the descent of the track, rutted and prickled with ice like cold sweat, down towards the distant lights of Chilas. Cass was firing blindly and uselessly out of the window, back behind them, but it didn't matter. Cass was awake, they were both alive, even if they'd lost Dhanjal. It would be minutes yet before the adrenalin evaporated and left Hyde exhausted.

'Look, look here –' Sara was saying. It was as inveigling as a remembered song. The bench seat on which she sat was littered with newspapers in English and Hindi. The one held out towards Ros was the Jammu and Kashmir regional edition of the *Indian Express*. During the early hours of their journey, Sara had done no more than leaf aimlessly through them, just as Ros had flicked the pages of *Vogue*. Now, the newspaper was thrust at her with the intensity of a copy of a religious tract on a Sunday-morning doorstep. '*Look!*' Sara commanded.

Ros looked down. A page-broad photograph of Mehta, the leader of the Hindu fundamentalists, the BJP, Sharmar's principal opponents, standing in what appeared to be a decorated chariot, waving his arms in the midst of a huge crowd. The headline proclaimed, *Star's pilgrimage from Delhi to Srinagar*. Ros looked up, to Sara's evident contempt.

'You don't understand, do you? It might as well be in Hindi, for all the sense it makes.' She gestured at the paper before flinging it back onto the seat beside her. 'He'll appear at various points on that so-called pilgrimage, that's all. If you bothered to read the article, you'd realise why he's so dangerous,' she added. 'He's calling – the BJP's calling – for an end to the secular state. This pilgrimage is to call for unity, to prevent any hiving-off of Moslem Kashmir and the Sikh Punjab – V.K.'s *plan*!' She was leaning forward now, her hands twisted together in her lap. 'He just wants more trouble in Kashmir – Hindu immigration, a stronger Hindu presence in the Punjab, the army everywhere, putting down everything that moves!' She sighed. 'I don't know why I'm bothering to explain all this. It doesn't matter to you, does it?'

Her eyes challenged. Ros eventually shook her head, a gesture confronted with another glare from Sara's pale eyes. She didn't believe in anything, she'd left nothing behind in England she didn't have contempt for . . . Sharmar offered a grail.

'It's a wonderful ideal, V.K.'s,' she added unnecessarily.

'What?'

'Letting Kashmir and the Punjab secede –'

'What happens to his bloody heroin afterwards!' Ros snapped back, angry at herself immediately.

It was as if she had introduced the subject of abattoirs at a dinner party as the guests stared down in sudden shock at their lamb or beef, disguised with herbs and sauces and the impersonal cuts of the blades. She had done that once. Hyde had laughed, but the dinner party had been ruined and though their hostess had murmured agreement they had not been invited again. Now, she might have prompted her demise rather than mere ostracism from a dinner table.

'What would you know about it?'

'Enough.' She was impelled to be angry. 'He kills people or has them killed. For his ideals!'

'He sometimes has to do it for the general good –!' She glanced towards the table and its contents, amid which the little acorn-shaped wooden insect still hovered. There was a flash of lights from some buildings the train hurried past.

'*You* can't guarantee he won't have Hyde killed.' Then, again impelled against sense: 'You can't ensure they won't kill me. But this time it won't be far away and out of sight. You'll have to watch them take me –' Sara was shaking her head.

'No –'

'Who's the guy in the cream suit?'

'What?'

'The guy in the cream suit. He's the one who'll do it, or take me to the place where they'll do it. You'll at least be able to wave me goodbye!'

'Look,' Sara countered, everything except the flicker of her eyes oblivious to Ros' words, 'you know what's going on in Kashmir. It's been happening for years. Do you want that to go on getting worse and worse? Do you? It's been happening everywhere – bloody *religion*! – ever since Partition! It will get worse, make no mistake, if you help to bring V.K. down! He's the only damned hope for this bloody marvellous country!' Ros' wrist was grabbed by a cool, fervent, long-fingered hand. 'Ros, please – you can't hand over that stuff to someone and just forget about it – please!'

The noises of the train in the ensuing silence. The clatter of points, then the resistance of a slight gradient.

Ros said, eventually: 'I can't just forget about Hyde. Walk away and not think of him.' She shrugged herself more upright in her seat. 'I can't pick up the gun and shoot you, Sara. But

I'm not giving you the film and the tapes either. Not willingly. So, you'd better decide what to do.'

There was a fleck of saliva at the corner of Sara's mouth, which her tongue, as it darted across her lips, ignored. Her eyes were troubled, filled with conflict. Ros was, now she had become silent, newly aware of the compartment, the movement of the train, the flimsy sliding door on which a knock must come, soon. She'd done it all wrong, cocked it up. The woman opposite her had been seduced by the man's dream more than by the man. She was dreaming open-eyed. She was dangerous to anyone who threatened the cubs of her ideals, which had come late in life and all the more precious for that.

Sara wouldn't let them go for Hyde's sake, not even for hers –

Prakesh Sharmar watched Singh, their Finance Minister, being interviewed on TV. One of their media analysts had had it recorded, so that Prakesh and V.K. – if V.K. could be bothered with it – could check the quality of the performance. Singh was competent, lucid, enthusiastic. It was a good broadcast and would have its effect with the educated classes . . . *In three years, the rupee will be fully convertible . . . there will be accelerated privatisation of state assets . . . a new climate of deregulation has been brought into being* . . . strictly for the cultured and business classes, Prakesh confirmed. But necessary. It gave Congress a real power; the impression that the economy, and a record that had looked bad, was beginning to look up . . . *foreign investment, our talks with the IMF* – IBM, Ford, BMW and Shell were all involved in huge joint ventures – *we will cut income and corporation taxes, and reduce interest rates . . . overhaul the banking system . . . much of this work has already been begun by the Congress government . . .*

'Yes, that's fine. Congratulate the Minister,' Prakesh murmured. He walked away from the monitor and the media analyst, to the window of the high office which looked towards Connaught Place and the government buildings.

Yes, it *was* fine. It would cut a swathe through the urban

business communities, even please the wealthier farmers, please the educated. It all sounded responsible, sane, *secular*, something for the next century ... while Mehta and his damned fundamentalists cut another swathe through the countryside with this ridiculous Pilgrimage of Unity, impressing the peasants, the poor, the Hindus! No one could win without the countryside.

The dawn was leaking into the city, outlining the India Gate at the far end of Raj Path. He could see the rows of streetlamps, Edwardian and so British, along each pavement. And the mock domes and columns, the Anglo-Indian temples of power. Everything that was at stake was there. Near India Gate – would they vote for the past or the future? He shook his head. Such speculations were more in V.K.'s cloudier line.

He turned away from the window. It would not be politic to appear to be brooding. And it was time to talk to Rao. He'd made the necessary calls to Islamabad, involved the Pakistani army units that would now be required. They would – ironically – be seeking fleeing drug smugglers, who might also be terrorists. Cooperation was another glimpse of the future ... the man Hyde could not be allowed to snatch it away with a few photographs and bugged conversations! He clenched his fist as a drying thong seemed to constrict around his temples. An aide approached carrying a sheaf of clippings from the early editions of the regional newspapers, which had been faxed to them. He waved him aside with a flick of his fingers. A few minutes, he thought, as he looked at his watch. V.K. would be on breakfast-time TV from Calcutta in ten minutes, knee-deep in the homeless and beggars. Offering *them* a future. He must be back in the room to watch it, so that his aides and the party workers could watch him for his reaction.

No one succeeds in Indian elections without carrying the countryside, the peasants. Mehta and his bloody pilgrimage! His head ached. As he closed the door behind him, he soothed his temples with the long fingers of both hands. He must talk to Rao. It had become an irresistible need for his confidence to be bolstered by conversation with the Intelligence officer. It must happen now, they must be caught and eliminated today.

Sara had inveigled the woman into her cabin on the train. That, at least, was secure, since both women were being watched. He flicked his wrist to look at his watch again. In a few hours, the Jammu express would arrive in Delhi, where his people would be waiting to whisk the woman into oblivion the moment she stepped unsuspecting onto the platform. Sara would then have repaid some of the debt she owed the Sharmar family. V.K.'s bed had never been sufficient gratitude.

'Get me Colonel Rao,' he murmured to the Intelligence officer who sat in front of the bank of communications equipment. As if to mock him, the man was, even before he spoke, fiddling with the monitors, flicking switches.

Rao would have crossed into Pakistan by now. The hunt would be underway . . . again, his confidence sagged like lead in his stomach. Damn these people – there were only *two* of them, and one of those ill and exhausted from interrogation!

Imperturbably, the dawn was making the stone of India Gate lighten, gleam brighter than the dimmed neon and the early car headlights that were closer to Connaught Place. The Rotunda and the North and South Blocks, all at the far end of Janpath from his vantage, became the most real things in the lightening city.

It had been light for more than two hours now. The Karakoram Highway had allowed them to make good time. Out of the creeping dawn, rock carvings appeared at the side of the road east of Chilas. The town had been sombre, foggy with the smoke of fires. Then the carvings. A Buddhist monk holding an incense burner, a pilgrim with a water jar – a Bodhisattva offering his body to a lioness who, along with her cubs, devoured his flesh. Later, in almost full daylight, the reassuring Buddha seated above the wheel of the law. The Indus was strong and brown beneath the Thalpan Bridge. As the road turned north towards

Gilgit, the massif of Nanga Parbat seemed closer than ever, overwhelming Hyde. There was no sense of progress or escape, that same dominant feature always there, its morning peak gleaming with ice through drifting, dark cloud.

They crossed the Rakhiot Bridge, the Indus Valley like a moonscape of barren, decayed glaciers and ice-peaks, that same mountain always persisting in the rear-view mirrors, as if pursuing them. A high desert, heaped like mine-spoil or gleaming, metallic wreckage. The wind was icy, the clouds ragged and rapid, threatening snow.

At Jaglot, Hyde halted the Land Rover, totally weary and dizzied with the encirclement of the mountains. Cass had dozed beside him after the elation of their escape had left him spent. A small remission of the exhaustion which now ate at him again. The mountains hung above them like planets – summits, snowfields, ice walls, rock, high pastures, alpine meadows and firs, dotted villages. So vast. Hyde shook his head. They were an hour from Gilgit, less than forty miles. He felt drained. He glanced at Cass, who stared unshavenly back, his eyes chilly as the landscape, his expression defeated.

An ancient donkey-pulled cart eased past them along the KKH towards the village. The driver was incurious, hardly glancing at them from within his wrappings of cloth and sheepskin, mummified against the cold. Below them, the dark ribbon of the Indus was joined by brighter, clearer water from the Gilgit River. The Indus swallowed the clear water. Hyde sighed emptily and leaned his head on the steering wheel.

'You all right?' Cass asked solicitously. 'I could drive, if you –'

'With two broken ribs?' Hyde scoffed. Some parody of a domestic quarrel seemed in the offing. Ridiculous.

He knew he had to ring Shelley from Gilgit, from a hotel lobby or the post office. It *couldn't* – he swallowed – depend on Ros, not entirely; not their lives. A bus tottered up the highway towards them, enveloped in the dust it raised. It was rendered small as an insect crawling on a brown grass-stem by the mountains behind it. Gilgit was an administrative centre. It had police and army, and an airport that linked it to Islamabad. The Sharmars would have Pakistani generals in their pockets like small change. The bus enveloped them with dust and noise, then dragged itself away and out of sight around a bend in the highway. The dust settled on the Land Rover to suggest that it was immobile, had been abandoned.

Something could happen to Ros . . . Shelley might not listen to her, at least not in time. Jesus. He felt resolve sink into the muddiness of his speculations, the silt at the pit of his stomach.

'I could try,' Cass replied sulkily.

'Sorry.'

Then his head swung up as he glimpsed something tiny as a speck on the windscreen, but moving high up against Rakaposi's flanks. A helicopter or a light aircraft, making for Gilgit. It could be anyone or no one. It could be someone like Dhanjal. Dhanjal — but his death was caused by the *natives*, not the army. Not Pakistani units — the Frontier Force Regiment, the Azad Kashmir Regiment . . . there was an airforce installation in Gilgit, wasn't there? They could easily fly in special forces, helicopters like the one on which the fugitive sun flashed for a moment. The weather wouldn't hold them up. There'd be plenty of resolve, plenty of motive.

Cass passed him a water bottle and he drank the icy liquid hesitantly, then gratefully.

'Want something to eat?'

'Only something hot.'

'What do we do after Gilgit?' Cass asked.

'What? Christ knows . . .' *I could get out, with difficulty. I could make it . . . so long as Shelley knows what I'm doing!*

But he doesn't and you couldn't . . .

His resentment of Cass remained unfocused, lacked any sharp edge.

'We'll get something in Gilgit.'

'Are you in touch with Shelley?' Cass asked pointedly, after gazing at the mountains. 'I mean – there is a plan, isn't there? You didn't just stumble across me?'

'There *was* a plan. Delhi Station was necessary to it, and you know Delhi Station. They'd all rather you were dead – Phil,' he added almost gently.

Cass nodded. 'Not surprising, in the circumstances. The Sharmars have got it sewn up then, haven't they?' His features were bleak in sudden cold sunlight.

'I'll call Shelley from Gilgit. *Make* him do something.'

'He'll probably be too busy sorting out the colour scheme of his new office for when the service moves to Vauxhall Cross!' Cass snorted.

Unconvincingly, Hyde said: 'He's not a complete tosser. He did send me –'

'Then chickened on the decision.'

'Something like that. They all want to believe the Sharmars.'

'They actually have the only sensible solutions. Pity about the drugs and the murder of Sereena –' His face crumpled into horror and genuine grief for a moment. Then he added: 'Pity I ever took a bloody interest in them really!' He slapped the dashboard with his gloved hands, shaking his head repeatedly.

'Shelley won't leave us out to dry. He daren't. Ros has got some of the evidence, I've got the rest. And *you*. If I phone him, I could call the *News of the Screws* at the same time. Or some Hindu rag that supports Mehta . . .' He grinned fiercely and clicked his fingers dully inside his gloves. 'Jesus, Mister-Bloody-Mehta the film star! That's *it*! The lever. They'll have to get us back to shut us up – won't they?'

'Bit thin, isn't it?'

'It only needs to be a cloud on the horizon. If I convince Shelley that we'll give it to the BJP, then Shelley will run round to the Foreign Office and wet himself all over the best Persian carpet!' He switched on the engine, as if he needed the warmth and noise of it and the heater to keep the idea nourished.

'What if you convince him – what then?'

Hyde stared at Cass.

'Then they'll have to get us out, won't they? *Trade* us out — or come in and get us!'

Sonipat. The Jammu express' last brief stop before Delhi. The carriage jerked slightly, just once, as the train halted. Ros stared at Sara, unable to breathe. The travel bag bulged at her feet. The tubs of film and the tapes made two separate heaps, like gamblers' chips, on the table between them. The day was already hot and the air-conditioning grumbled audibly. Beyond the window, the light hurt the eyes. Ros squinted as she looked across the tracks, beyond other platforms, towards sidings, rusted rolling stock, a steam engine shunting empty carriages. Then she turned her head. Their platform was on the corridor side.

She looked back at Sara. There were bruiselike stains under her eyes and her skin appeared to have the pallor and texture of parchment. There were tiny lines around her swollen mouth that seemed more confidently etched by time, or nerves.

'Well?' Ros managed to say.

Eventually, Sara nodded, swallowing.

'Yes. *Yes.*' Her anger was undirected. She brushed her hair aside and looked at the table. Had they been chips, she would have been the more successful. 'Oh, yes . . .' she sighed.

Ros had retained one roll of film, two of the tapes, forcing herself to remember their contents, remember beyond the numbers she had scribbled on each roll, each tape. She reached for them as for something that might bite or poison her with its sting. The numbers had been erased on the winnings close to Sara's hand. Ros shuffled the one tub and the two cassettes into the travel bag, which she then kept on her lap like a school satchel. Being sent away to school, the sense of being bereft. Through her anxiety and her mistrust of Sara, she felt the isolation of the hours ahead of her.

'I – I'll talk to him, then,' Sara said. 'The train only stops for five minutes here –' Someone passed their compartment along the corridor, easing something heavy along the wall. Sara thrust film and tapes into her handbag and zipped it shut. 'I'll keep him occupied, they won't discover you've gone for as long as I can –'

'There's not only him –!'

'He's the one in command. The others don't matter. I'll give him what he wants, then –' Her eyes narrowed. 'The rest is up to you. I can't do anything more. Wait until the train's left, then find a taxi. Then do what the hell you like!' she ended.

'Right.' It was ridiculous, but she could not avoid adding: 'You'll be all right?'

'I'm his bloody *mistress*, aren't I? What could happen to me?' Ros remembered Sereena, who had betrayed Sharmar – then shook it aside. 'You're wasting time. I'll go and see our friend –' Sara stood up violently, as if to assault her.

'Thanks,' Ros said.

'I couldn't let them kill you. That's all it is. I couldn't let his people – not him, but some of the others, even Prakesh . . .' She admitted it reluctantly, again trying to avoid the unpalatable implications. 'Look, I don't want to do this, but I don't want you on my conscience! That's all –' She hesitated, then mumbled: 'Good luck,' and slid the door open, then slammed it shut behind her.

Ros began shivering uncontrollably, gripping the bulging travel bag against her stomach and breasts as if to smother it. Her mouth filled with saliva and her eyes blurred wetly, even as she berated herself. *Pathetic, snivelling, get off your backside* . . . The hot sunlight seemed to infiltrate the window, nullifying the air-conditioning. She was hot, then chilled, hot again. The day glared outside, the tracks weed-strewn and gleaming beyond the end of the opposite platform. A bearer dozed against mailbags in the mid-morning sun. A locomotive whistled and churned steam somewhere out of sight –

She jumped to her feet and scrabbled the table into its folded position, clicking it roughly home. Fiddled clumsily with the door and then swung it open, almost over-balancing out into the hard glare of light that seemed to assail her. The tracks beside the train doubled and then redoubled, as if she was drunk. The step wavered as she felt for it with her right foot. Then she leaned her weight on the door and awkwardly clambered down to the track. It was clear except for an empty Coke can between the rails. The opposite platform was sparse with idlers. The gravel was hard and penetrating through the soles of her shoes. She stumbled to the platform end, then ascended its slope. Hurried, because that had been the plan before the panic had begun and her disorientation increased. Out of sight to the far side of the suburban platform. Found a bench because she had to, and sat down heavily. A child's huge eyes watched her from its mother's squashed, milk-supply breast. Ros' heart thudded in her chest and her head felt as if it would split open like a dropped melon.

Then the noise of a peremptory whistle which had no meaning except to startle her. The baby went on feeding from its mother's breast. A bearer passed by, bent as if chained behind a luggage trolley. An announcement over the tannoy in Hindi. The whistling ceased and a train moved.

She turned her head. The tracks slid away, polished and dazzling. The Jammu express curved into view, heading out of Sonipat towards the hazy sky above Delhi. Ros swallowed, a sense of being abandoned, as if she had unintentionally missed the train. She lifted her head to the platform roof, exhaling like a stranded fish.

What was it she was meant to do now? What was it Sara had told her?

Eventually . . .

. . . taxi. Get a taxi. She looked along the platform. The station seemed quiet, the town beyond it somnolent. A white board, the blue image of a car emblazoned. EXIT, in English and Hindi. A taxi –

*

He could see, from the bank of telephones along the wall of the lodge's dining hall, the Gilgit River and the long, delicate structure of the suspension bridge across it. In the distance, where cloud was lowering on the mountain slopes, the bigger bridge over the Hunza River. Early lunches were being eaten by trekkers and 4WD tourists – a busload of Japanese were noisy in the other window corner. The thermoplastic tiles on the floor clattered with bootsteps or squeaked with trainers. Normality enveloped him in the Riverside Tourist Lodge, easy peace and a sense of the openness of the Gilgit Valley seduced from the windows that ran the length of the noisy room. Cass was seated at one of the long tables, still eating, hunched intently over the food as if counting hoarded wealth.

There were terraced fields of rice across the river, other terraces palely-green with new grain. The ranks of apricot trees, still full-leaved, too, as if they had descended thousands of feet to another climate.

The telephone connection was risky – open and operator-placed from the local exchange. Any call from Gilgit would be, unless he asked the army if he could have a secure line to call the D-G of British Intelligence . . . or unless he tried calling from one of the plush new hotels in Gilgit, and he didn't really look the part and anyway the army and the local officials and the police hung about places like that. Nevertheless, his own nerves seeped back down the unconnected line to him like the breathing of someone stalking him. He looked at his watch. One o'clock. They'd seen more helicopters, large military transport choppers, Russian-made and Pumas, heading towards Gilgit. A couple of fly-buzzing Alouettes scouting the KKH. No military transport on the highway, yet. It looked not quite normal, not quite an operation – hovering between the two. The helicopters were parked on the military airfield by the time they reached the town.

The operator informed him, once more, that she was trying to connect him.

His stomach rumbled. Food, not nerves, he told himself, tasting the spiciness of the meal on his breath. The Land Rover was parked on the campsite: they had hired a tent to preserve a very thin cover story. They'd be expected to report to the Foreigners' Registration Office before evening, or hand their papers in to be inspected by the police. They'd be gone by then . . . smiles and enthusiasm and tourist naivety ought to last another couple of hours. He'd bought the gear they might need – were going to need, if the phone call worked –

– phone ringing out, distant and hollowly unreal as if in an empty house. Not his bloody answering machine, he pleaded silently, please . . . It was eight in the morning in London – in Surrey, to be exact, where Shelley lived in stockbroker Tudor splendour, master of all his mortgage surveyed. The phone went on ringing beyond the four of five summonses an answering machine required.

Alison's taken the kids to school and Shelley's driver's already collected him –

'Yes?' A very distant, impatient female voice.

'*Alison!*' he shouted, turning his face into the helmet of the booth. 'Can you hear me, Alison?'

'You're very faint,' he heard. 'Who is it? I was just leaving with the kids –'

'It's Patrick – Patrick *Hyde*,' he called distinctly. And that's stuffed it if the operator's been told to listen.

'Patrick –!' He could hear the catch in her voice, the shock and relief, even though her words remained distant and whispered. 'You're *alive*!' So far. 'Peter's left for the office. Do you want his car phone number?' Then: 'God, this line's awful!' Worse followed. 'Is Ros all right?'

Christ, I hope so, I really hope so.

'Yes. Fine! Don't give me any numbers. Just listen. Then tell *him*. OK? Alison – OK? You *understand*?'

After what seemed an inordinate silence: 'Yes. Got you.'

Bloody ridiculous, this – ET, phone home. He and Cass were

an alien life-form, playing the games of the 1970s in the wrong decade. No wonder he was ringing Shelley at home. Who would even want to remember how to pull off an extrication operation?

'Just listen. Ros will call you. He has to talk to Ros. Got it?'

'Yes, I'll tell him. She isn't with you?'

'No.' His forehead was damp, the helmet of the phone booth hot as an old-fashioned hair-dryer clamped over his head. 'He has to be ready to meet her.' He all but added, *Not London*, but told himself not to say where, when or how. At this end of the phone they're in a time warp, they still play the old games. 'Tell him it's *utmost* –'

'What's wrong?'

'Almost everything. Tell him –' He didn't need to threaten Shelley, especially through Alison. Just the buggers Shelley would have to convince. '– he *has* to help. If he's prevented, in any way, then I'll go to the BJP – the Hindus. If he's blocked by *anyone* then the B-J-P will get everything we have. I'll ruin the Sharmars.' Even if anyone was listening, they already knew that. They'd expect him to sell them to Mehta.

'I'm writing this down, Patrick – Sharmars. Bloody hell!' It was the comment of a housewife, half-amused, half-shocked, at the name of a local adulterer; an unexpected, unlikely neighbour. 'Have you got – *him*, Patrick?' No names, no pack drill. *She* should be the new D-G, not Shelley.

'Yes. Tell Peter that Ros will know where.' Involuntarily, he glanced at his watch once more. Her plane hadn't yet taken off, and he couldn't place her in more danger – surely? He had to tell Shelley *something*. 'It has to be –' He looked at the valley, shadowed now as the sun once more disappeared. To the north-east, Rakaposi was gloomy with snow-heavy cloud. '– twenty-four hours maximum. No more than twenty-four. He *has* to do it, Aly –' Even if only for old times' sake.

'He will, Patrick.' She understood. No fuss, no outburst, no equivocation. She wasn't even torn. No wonder Aubrey had always liked her, the old bugger! 'He will. Inside twenty-four hours. Good luck –'

'Have to go, Aly!' he burst across her wishes, and put down the phone.

Two soldiers, by their stripes a havildar and a naik, had entered the dining hall of the lodge. Their eyes slowly, methodically, scanned the clumps of diners, as if studying unfamiliar and probably dangerous terrain. They scrutinised each group, each couple, each individual face.

business class

He willed Cass not to become startled or alarmed. Willed himself, too, to remain casual, possess the slightly dazed perfunctoriness of a tourist at high altitude, dizzied with mountains and a strange language and customs. The corporal and sergeant stood close to the doors of the dining hall, their hands on their hips as if about to mimic some acrobatic circus trick. Then, as someone attempted to skirt them, they at once requested the Japanese woman's papers. Slowly, she comprehended and obeyed. Their inspection was cursory, but not necessarily without intent. The river valley beyond the window, trees and terraces climbing towards the mountains, seemed incongruous and very distant.

Hyde crossed the room slowly, hands in his pockets. Even so, the havildar's head turned to watch his progress. Was there greater interest? Yes . . . the corporal beside him was nudged into attentiveness, and both soldiers studied him as he slouched absent-mindedly to a vacated table where plates and cutlery remained littered. *His* meal, already eaten, before he made a telephone call . . . Cass was twenty feet away, puzzled and staring. Hyde glared from beneath his narrowed eyebrows and Cass seemed to understand. If they were looking, then they'd be alert for two Europeans travelling together. If they were *really* looking, then they might not be fooled. They'd have descriptions, even photographs . . . He held his breath as the havildar reached into the breast pocket of his greatcoat – the wind seemed to rattle the long window just at that moment, so that coat and noise emphasised the inhospitable landscape. He removed . . .

cigarettes. He did not offer one to the naik, merely lit one for himself. Hyde shivered, then suppressed his involuntary reaction to the immediate and to the day and night ahead. If they got out of this — the wind against the windows again, flexing the feeble glass, cutting off his thoughts.

The sergeant exhaled smoke while the naik moved towards Cass. There were elderly Americans in a small party on the other side of the dining hall but the soldiers had shown no interest in their accents, their age. They had descriptions, then. Hyde reached behind him, touching the gun in the small of his back. Cass buttered hard bread, apparently oblivious. Hyde was aware of the deep stains beneath his eyes and the dead pallor of his skin; aware of the bruises that still marked his jaw and temple. The corporal halted beside him and Cass looked up incuriously. Hyde's eyes moved between the two soldiers. The havildar was idly observing and occasionally glancing with parochial contempt at the Japanese and the Americans. Cass muttered something to the corporal — in Urdu, Hyde thought, not understanding it. Cass shrugged expressively and the corporal glanced towards the senior NCO, but only for a moment. Cass was nodding, then he pointed, looked at his watch, indicating the time — another time, the future?

The corporal nodded and moved away. Cass appeared to slump with relief in his chair, his eyes feverishly bright. Sunlight flashed blindingly into the dining hall as the sun came from behind chasing clouds. Shadow and gleam pursued each other across the landscape, then the mountains darkened as the brightness once more disappeared. Cass glared at him. The naik had moved a little away from him, hands on his hips, attracted yet reassured by Hyde's unshaven, unwashed swarthiness and small frame. Just another bloody wog.

Cass got up, nodded imperceptibly towards the doors, and left the dining hall without hurry or delay. The corporal, attracted by the laughter of the Americans and the loud voice of their courier — high-pitched, assured, dismissive of the food they were eating and of Gilgit's hotels – followed his sergeant towards the group. It was, perhaps, the volume and indecorum of the female voices rather than the disparagement of Gilgit, that provoked the two Islamic soldiers. They approached the tables around which the Americans were gathered ... *the scenery is fantastic, don't you think, but that road! And they call it a highway ...* with an enhanced swagger of authority. *You have to put up with some discomfort to see all this ... Can we help you?* The last phrase coming from the travel guide or courier or whatever she was, greying blond hair spilling from beneath a woollen hat, as Hyde rose carefully from the table and moved inconspicuously towards the doors. *Papers? Which papers?* The voice was impatient. Then Hyde was through the doors.

Cass was hovering in the foyer, close to a party of Europeans debouched from a bus parked outside the doors of the lodge. Luggage littered the foyer as did the voices of the French tourists. Cass grabbed Hyde's arm and Hyde felt the tremor of relief and weariness. It was as if the small incident had been a marathon.

'What did you tell him?'

'My papers were at the Registration Office. I was waiting for a fishing licence. I paid someone to queue at the Bureau of Fisheries – he thought I was stupid, letting my papers out of my hands.'

'Come on, let's bugger off before they get through with the Yanks.'

Hyde bullied them into the gritty, flying air outside. Cass shuddered with the bite of the cold. A military transport plane dropped towards the airfield, to join the huddle of helicopters. Troops moved away from one of the big Russian transport choppers, small as insects, numerous as ants, too, it seemed to Hyde. His gaze swung towards the mountains to the north-west. Up there, sport – up yours, more like. Cass grabbed his arm and attention before they reached the car-park and the Land Rover.

'Where are we going?' he demanded, as if Hyde had attempted to abduct him; an outrage of weariness. His eyes were feverish

315

again. 'Where the fucking *hell* are we going?' His arms waved at the enclosing mountains, the ragged, streaming rag-bundles of cloud, the airfield and the scattered trees and dwellings of the narrow valley in which Gilgit sat like a thin, twisting snake above its shadowshape river. 'What the hell were you doing while I was parked like your granny?' Cass was shouting now, expelling some of the tension of his narrow escape. He leaned over Hyde as if in threat.

Hyde shrugged.

'You won't like it –' He glanced back at the doors of the River-side Tourist Lodge. Its pennant cracked in the wind and its buildings seemed small, huddled beneath the mountains – so many bloody mountains.

'Why not?'

Hyde turned away and moved closer to the Land Rover. Cass trailed after him like a shambling idiot child.

'You won't like it because *I* don't like it!' Hyde snapped, as if challenged over some incompetence he had shown. He turned back to Cass, his hand on the door-handle of the 4WD. Cass' anger was blunted by the expression in Hyde's eyes; a flat, hard glare. 'Look down there,' Hyde said. 'They're not here for the fucking polo, Phil! They want us – *just* us. Sharmar's arranged things. Pakistan isn't safe for us.' He knew it never was, that's why they were here in Gilgit, on their way to . . . I shouldn't tell him, not just yet. 'We have to – *walk* out. Trek it.'

Cass seemed winded. His frame sagged, like wet washing dragging down a line. 'I *can't*,' he breathed at last. He leaned against the vehicle, his glazed look drawn hypnotically across the mountains to the north and west, moving as regularly as an old-fashioned typewriter carriage.

'Come on,' Hyde said, guiding him to the passenger side of the Land Rover. 'It's not *all* walking – but let's get on with it, before –' Too late.

The havildar and his corporal appeared in the hotel's doorway, the glass sliding its reflected images into place behind them.

Reflections of mountains. At once, their attention seemed to be on the Land Rover and the two Europeans standing beside it. Cass hadn't seen them . . . then he turned, before turning back to Hyde with a shocked, blank fear on his face.

'Just get in,' Hyde said.

One of them shouted in Urdu, then in English. Merely calling for their attention, almost polite. Then more peremptorily as Hyde closed the door on Cass and moved with apparent unawareness to the driver's door and began climbing in. The voice issued a command. The two soldiers had begun hurrying – not quite running, but scuttling as their hands unbuttoned their greatcoats to get at their pistols, the coats flying behind them like threatening cloaks.

The transport plane had landed and begun to taxi. One of the helicopter's rotors was whirling like a gleaming shield in sudden, brief sunlight. Gilgit glinted and retreated. The river was cold, hostile. Hyde started the engine. The naik had drawn a pistol but seemed undecided. The sergeant, too, seemed self-conscious, as if they had over-reacted. Hyde accelerated. The havildar's face, its moustache like an emphasis of surprise, loomed close to Cass' window, then the tyres screeched them out of the car park, jolted them onto the road. In the mirror, the two soldiers were still, bemused. Then the sergeant fumbled something from his greatcoat and pressed it against his cheek. Hyde swerved the Land Rover away from collision with a cart heaped with vegetables and dried fruit as strange as countless tiny lungs. He lost sight of the two soldiers who were evidently summoning assistance. But they wouldn't have been fooled a second time, not by two of them without papers. Cass lay back in his seat, his face white and thin. They were paralleling the airfield.

Two or three small private aircraft or tourist carriers dotted like boiled sweets amid the olive-drab of the military transports. Mostly Russian and French helicopters, a couple of recently arrived Hercules transports. Then the road swung into Cinema Bazaar, which stretched the length of Gilgit, and he could no

317

longer see the airfield, or the Hercules, or the troops filing out of the open cargo doors into another fugitive gleam of sunlight. The Sharmars had got their act together. They had enough Pakistani generals in their pockets to make sure that what they wanted to happen happened. And *that* was he and Cass dead.

The Land Rover raced through an endless corridor of shops and stalls, dodging between stray animals, moving carts, gaudy buses, military trucks and jeeps. Hyde swung right then left across a crowded square, easing the vehicle through the countless pedestrians, all heading along the Chitral road as if hurrying to become spectators for the pursuit he knew must occur. Cass went on staring through the windscreen as if watching a landslide, the ground opening before him. He isn't going to make it, he isn't going to make it, Hyde heard his thoughts repeat.

The restored mosque, then the crowds fell away, leaving the road ahead clear, against which the mountains pressed. The polo ground was all but full. Blurs of movement, the roaring of the crowd like an uninterrupted crashing of surf. Then, quickly, the dusty town straggled away into the tents and petrol-can lean-tos and mud shacks of the Afghan refugees, displaced, lost, listless in the wind. Huge-eyed children, one limping, his left foot vanished, a couple of thin dogs, demoralised men, patient, burdened women. It was a scene of drab clothing and habitation, as if dust had settled thickly on everything over a period of many years. The minaret of the mosque faded in the mirror. The road was empty behind them.

Ahead of them, too. The buses had already deposited spectators for the polo. They'd run on time, for once. The river ran alongside the road, the colour of cold mud. Then Cass said:

'I can't, Hyde. I *can't!*' He seemed disappointed in himself, but also accusing; as if he had been misled, deceived. It was as though he expected a prize, something almost for nothing . . . Yet he could not condemn Cass. He had two or three broken ribs, he was exhausted. Couldn't cope. Hyde had been there, he *knew*.

Hyde slowed the Land Rover, the view in the mirror obscured by dust. His hand gripped Cass' wrist as it lay idly on the man's thigh.

'There isn't any other way, Phil,' he coaxed, the effort at gentleness almost genuine. He spun the wheel as he avoided a fallen jumble of boulders that littered the side of the road, then replaced his hand on Cass' wrist. 'Believe me.'

'Where the fuck is Shelley, then?' Cass wailed like a child.

'He'll be there. It's arranged . . .' I called his wife, she promised to pass the message on! 'Ros knows where we need to be by tomorrow. I've got Shelley by the balls, he has to show up.'

'How – *where*?' Cass demanded, sniffing loudly.

'Afghanistan,' Hyde said quietly, after a pause. Cass turned his death's-head features towards him, the eyes glittering but dead.

'*Where*?'

'Across the border. They can't come in.' Or *won't*. 'We have to go out. Look, it's ten, maybe twelve miles from where we'll have to abandon the Land Rover, no more than that. We can *do* it. Up the Ishkuman Valley, the road goes as far as Chillinji – at least, it does for one of these. From there, it's just a hike, not a trek. We'll make it –'

'I just *can't*,' Cass replied at once, with utter, final certainty.

It was only one of the Sharmar family's various properties in and around Delhi, but it was the one she always chose to use. Not hers, but then no one else stayed there; no one at all *lived* there. It was, of course, a spacious Raj bungalow on the edge of the Chanakyapuri enclave, looking towards the scrubland forest of the Ridge marooned within the vast concrete sandbanks of the city. The bungalow was close enough for the noise of peacocks to be heard above the traffic on the Sardar Patel Marg, and the breezes had always seemed illusorily cool. Occasionally, from one of the long windows in the lounge or breakfast room, one could catch glimpses of a bright flash of birds or the bulk of a blue bull antelope. The seeming distance of the city, the proximity of wildness, her own and V.K.'s nudity at the windows, sipping champagne after copulation . . . the images repulsed her now.

As Prakesh did . . . The past frightened her, too, as he stood at the dusk-glowing window of the lounge, staring absently at the Ridge.

Sara swallowed, careful to avoid the slightest noise. The sigh of the air-conditioning was all but inaudible, as if absorbed into the silence; as her own noises had been during the long afternoon as she waited for V.K. – more likely Prakesh – to arrive and to begin questioning her concerning Ros . . . damn Ros! The gesture she had made, helping her to leave the train, seemed not merely futile now, but incredibly stupid, romantically naff. Prakesh remained at the window, his figure haloed by the sunset, the glasses in his hand glinting. Beyond him, she thought she caught the flick of an eagle or a large kite, scouting for prey. The image disturbed; there was a sense of a lost and self-deluding past. The place had staled on her tongue like unwanted liquor as she had stared at the Ridge through the afternoon.

Then he turned. She suppressed her nerves.

'Why didn't you come to the offices?' he asked silkily.

'Was there anything to come for?' she replied. 'V.K.'s in Calcutta. The details of the election I find boring. Sorry.'

His eyes, even in the shadow of his face, glittered. Beyond him, the Ridge ceased to exist, and she saw only office blocks and high-rise flats in the smoky, golden dusk.

'You should have come to report to *me*!' he snapped. 'You were responsible for that bloody woman!' She realised how her mind had slowed matters. He had not been in the room more than a few minutes, he had poured the drink angrily, quickly, spilling some of the whisky on the trolley's lace mat. Had stormed to the window, hovering there as if to recover his breath before he spoke. Only minutes. Her mind had been trying to avoid him, change him into a casual, diffident visitor – as Prakesh had once been, when in his brother's shadow. 'You let her get away! I had you telephoned – here – but you were *too tired*!' He crossed the room with a venom that suggested he would fling the drink into her face, and she flinched against it. If he once suspected . . . Then he paused. 'Where the devil is she?' he raged.

'How should I know? Prakesh, I have apologised already. I got you the film, the tapes. There was nothing else that I could find in any of her luggage. I assure you I searched it thoroughly. Does she matter?'

Prakesh Sharmar was indecisive, somehow adrift, at the mercy of something not of his own making. Which meant they didn't have the two men; Sereena's lover, and Ros' lover, she added. They were still loose, as was Ros. For some reason, Prakesh was afraid of that continuing freedom. They couldn't be that much of a threat, could they?

'It may very well matter. Yes, you did *part* of your job well enough, Sara. But you should have watched that woman until she left the train in *Delhi*. We were ready for –' He broke off and turned away. 'She would have been taken care of,' he added in a murmur.

'She isn't anybody. She can't hurt you, surely?'

He turned on her.

'You simply walked away from our people at the station, Sara – why?'

'I was tired! Do you think I slept on the train, knowing what you wanted me to do?' She brushed her hair aside from her face. One of the bruises he had inflicted in Srinagar seemed to prick with pain.

'I wasn't able to come here,' he growled. 'Not until now. I haven't been able to concentrate on the search for the woman. Do you understand the problems your carelessness has caused? Do you?' Again, the two small, pouncing dangerous steps towards her; again she flinched back on the sofa. The elegance of the room seemed to retreat into insignificance, as she did herself. If Prakesh ever so much as . . .

321

'I'm *sorry*,' she replied with ironic defiance. 'Your people didn't do much better. They didn't even see her get off the train.'

'They've been made to understand their failure,' he announced. 'But time has passed and the search has been in the hands of idiots!' he burst out, his arms rising and falling like those of a windmill. 'Where would she have gone?' he demanded. 'Did she say anything? Does she have friends, help here in Delhi? The British High Commission has been watched, the various offices their spies use are under surveillance. Who was she intending to see in Delhi?' It was as if his voice had hold of her and was roughly shaking her.

She shook her head. Strangely, he accepted that Ros' escape was from Srinagar, not from India. Perhaps it was merely bureaucratic of him to assume that. She must be seeking help from people here, going through channels – ? Perhaps it was because the man Hyde was still at large. They were both still in India, and he made the assumption that they would remain. What would Ros do, anyway? Run out on him? No, she wouldn't do that . . . so she must still be in Delhi, trying to obtain help.

'I don't know. If her lover is a spy, then it's to other spies she would go – surely?'

'*I* don't know.'

There'd been no travel tickets in Ros' bag, not that Sara had seen. She had plenty of money, travellers' cheques, credit cards – but nothing to indicate a plan of escape.

'Well *think*!' he bellowed.

'I *can't*!' she shouted back at him. 'I have no idea what she's likely to do – what goes on in her head. She's a stranger!'

His eyes seemed to gleam with nursed and hitherto concealed suspicion. Yet he made no further movement towards her. He *was* undecided. He couldn't imagine Ros, she didn't fit any models. He returned to the darkening window. The Ridge was a lumpy, colourless mattress now, above which a last few specks of birds soared and glided. The city's neon glow was brighter than that of the sunset.

Then there was a discreet knock at the door of the lounge which startled her. Prakesh whirled round.

'Yes?' he called.

His driver appeared in the doorway, his manner hurried, excited.

'Sir –'

'What is it, Menon? What is it?' Prakesh crossed the room as if to embrace the man or strike him.

'Sir – the airport, Indira Gandhi, sir –!' Prakesh was prompted, for a moment, to turn triumphantly towards Sara.

'What?' he yelped like an excited dog.

'There is a report, sir – the woman has been identified –'

'What flight?'

For an instant, Sara was intensely disappointed at Ros – disillusioned was a more accurate description. She was running out on . . . no. She was *getting* out, she still had film, tape, *evidence*. She was on her way back with it. A trade-off.

'She is in the Air France first-class lounge, sir.'

'What time is the plane due to –'

'Fifteen minutes, sir!'

'What –? Why haven't they –?'

'She was identified only a few minutes ago, sir, they assured me of that.'

'Get me airport security – *no!* Get me Rao's man at the party offices. Quickly, Menon, quickly!'

He moved about the room as if panicked by a fire, blinded by smoke and with no sense of the location of the doors and windows, his body desperate with energy. Then he came and stood in front of her, his face flushed.

'Sir!' the driver called, holding out the receiver.

'Sara!' he snapped. 'I hope you didn't know anything. From this morning until now, I hope you knew nothing!' Then he all but ran to the telephone, blithe as a lover.

Sara felt her stomach revolt, then weaken as if with an enteric disease. When they caught Ros, she'd tell them she had help to get off the train, that they'd *agreed* it together.

And V.K. would leave her to Prakesh . . .

She had stared at the detritus of Delhi, hazy in the distance and through tinted glass, for most of the afternoon. Now, through the thickness of the Boeing's small porthole, next to her seat in business class, there were only the pricks and flares of airport and runway lights; Delhi was an indistinct haze, like a shout muffled by an intervening wall. Ros leaned back in her seat. The safety video flickered on its screen, the artificially loud commentary meaningless. She closed her eyes, the 747 jolting and clumping along the taxiway towards the main runway, to queue patiently behind other aircraft. Her breath came raggedly, the relief evident in it startling her; as if she had breathed for the first time since she had been ushered into the Air France lounge.

Delhi had rushed against the window of the room, Indira Gandhi airport seeming small, a tussock in which she could not conceal herself with any hope of success, with the city massed against her just beyond the tinted windows.

Green lights, red, white . . . running away in diminishing lines, sliding past the porthole window as through oil. The night flared with the rush of an aircraft retreating down the runway before staggering like a dark, huge bee into the air. Her breathing calmed.

Book upendedly open on her broad lap, her feet out of her shoes, the headphones thrust beside her, the menu and the untouched glass of champagne on the armrest. The seat next to her was empty, which made her concentrate on Hyde's absence — for the first time without blaming him for the raggedness of her nerves, the wearing hours she had sat in the first-class lounge. The aircraft was on time — now time seemed normal, sliding away in whole, unnoticed minutes. A little after seven as she glanced at her watch in the dimmed lighting of the cabin.

Business class was restfully two-thirds empty. A stewardess passed, glancing mechanically at her with a mechanical smile. The inexpressive look acknowledged a rather worn-looking, middle-aged, fat woman, and Ros embraced her usual self with relief.

Even embraced the eight-hour flight, because at the end of it Shelley must be waiting, there would be activity, there would be whatever was required to pull Hyde and Cass out of Kashmir . . . she had the tiny piece of tissue paper folded in her compact. She hadn't looked at it, not once since Hyde had put it there. She knew only how to demonstrate its use, rather than convey its information, to Shelley. Who *had* to be in Paris . . . Her head ached, her temples were thong-tight. She glanced at the champagne and dismissed it before turning again to the window. The safety video ended its vain plea for attention and the screen went blank. Lights sliding past . . . more slowly −?

The 747 slowed on the taxiway, and the lights stilled, to stretch away as individual, unmoving points. Another airliner roared down the runway, suggesting that her flight had been left stranded. The heavily-accented English of the captain was badly amplified in the cabin.

Delay . . . slight . . . apologise for the inconvenience . . . only a few minutes . . . Ros felt bemused rather than alerted, already institutionalised by the cabin, the subdued lights, her vast and draining relief. Seven fifteen.

Passenger steps, climbing like a small crane from the back of what might have been a beach-buggy driven by a turbaned Sikh in a white shirt, approached the side of the Boeing like an opened jaw. There was a black limousine with blank windows behind it. Behind her, the cabin door was opened and the warmth of the darkness outside at once bullied into the air-conditioning. She turned her head, curiosity no more than an itch. Some local bigwig who'd arrived late . . . they'd hold the plane for a diplomat or some fat-cat businessman. Other business-class passengers were smiling, complacent at the delay, diverted by the prospect of who'd climb the steps and appear flurried and hot and apologetic.

Two men on the tarmac, a third ushering them to the steps with waved arms and an instructive, commanding commentary. The two men at the bottom of the steps were nodding, then they hurried – hardly baggaged, no suitcases, one small bag between them – up the steps and into the plane. A French stewardess was respectful, reassuring, though neither of them seemed apologetic to any degree, and showed them to two seats opposite Ros, on the other side of the cabin. The door closed, the steps and the limousine pulled away, vanishing almost at once behind the aircraft.

She turned away from the window and made as if to settle, closing the book on her lap, steadying the champagne flute as the aircraft jolted slightly as the brakes came off . . . until she realised she was being studied by the newcomers. Two slim, young Indians in well-cut suits, both of them all but oblivious to the casual enquiries of other travellers in the seats around them. They were looking at her as if precisely matching her face to a photograph they had been made to memorise. Identifying her.

As the aircraft swung onto the runway and the airport terminals slid distantly back into place in the frame of the porthole, they seemed satisfied. One of them removed his jacket, then rebuckled his seatbelt.

They were sure. They were on the right flight – the one she was on. They were *with* her . . .

The last gleam of light on the highest peak winked out like a bulb being switched off – sudden, complete darkness. The headlights sprang out at once, as if it was the Land Rover reacting rather than his hand, because the thin dusting of snow no longer reflected sufficient light for him to steer by. Navigation by snowfall. Hyde glanced at Cass, who dozed, drugged with painkillers because his broken ribs were now intolerable. Hyde realised it was like the aftermath of a tragic accident. The cassette player he had wired to the battery droned on, trying to get through to Cass, as if he were in a brain-damaged coma. *Don't walk away, Renée . . . What a Wonderful World . . .* Tapes of hits of the '60s and '70s, all appearing not to reach him.

Cass had retreated from the future because it had frightened him, coming at him like an unavoidable accident through the windscreen . . . but part of it was because he *couldn't* do it, anyway . . . Another part was sheer exhaustion and disorientation. *Carry no passengers*, they always said. The tape Hyde had picked up in some narrow Delhi sidestreet, while keeping Lal's house under surveillance, was pirated and poor. *Twenty-four hours from Tulsa*, coming through hiss and fog. Perhaps Cass would have preferred Brahms or ragas, but he couldn't have either –

– neither can you any longer. He switched off the tape and the quiet of the Land Rover was immediate and confining. Then the strain of the engine, the creaking of the suspension, and the grind of the wipers against the now heavier snow. By his best guess, they were half an hour away from Chatorkhand in the Ishkuman Valley. The narrow track following the river was accessible only to 4WDs and walkers and donkey carts. Trees crowded over it and the wind jolted against the vehicle like a continuing series of minor collisions.

Cass seemed to have hypnotised himself into remaining oblivious . . . your time's coming, sport, don't worry about that –

A lake spread out like black glass beside the road. The narrow, twisting river had scuttled away somewhere, as if to hide itself, leaving this dark mirror. The headlights glanced across snowy rubble and stiff sedges and the occasional bent and sullen tree. Hyde stared at the road, its surface all but vanished beneath the snow. His night vision had adjusted to the glare of the headlights, though his awareness remained just as suspicious of their betraying gleam as the moment he had switched them on. He'd seen the helicopters in the fading daylight, seen them come in close to hillsides and high meadows and riverbanks, always depositing a group of tiny figures before whirling away into the cloudy, rushing sky again. From Singal along the road to Gakuch. Then he'd turned north, more dangerously and therefore unexpectedly. The sky had been clear for almost an hour, then the first high dot, then another . . . swooping, hovering, laying the little black eggs of troops, then whisking away again. He knew with certainty there were troops ahead of them now; troops behind. There'd be roadblocks along the one road, the track that finally petered into a trekking route at Chillinji, still inside Pakistan.

The rifle was to hand on his right side, beside the seat like another brake handle. One pistol in his belt, another in a pocket of the parka he had been forced to don by the plunge of the late afternoon temperature.

A thin moon slid like a lopsided, sardonic grin above the mountains, and he switched off the headlights, halting the Land Rover as he did so. The tyres crunched, then skidded slightly – he'd changed one rear wheel that had blown east of Gakuch. The snow was thickening. He opened the door and descended from the vehicle. His boots creaked eerily. He looked down. The toecaps were whitened. His breath steamed before being snatched away by the wind. His cheeks were at once numb. Cass dozed on behind him. So far, the electrics and mechanics of the vehicle had held up. He wouldn't run out of petrol, either – just out of time and road. He rubbed his icy face with gloved hands, as if washing or distancing grief. His ears rang with the cold. There were no other sounds in the night. Round one bend or the next or the one after, there'd be a patrol of cold, bored, suspicious soldiers – and that would be that. Stop. Dead end.

He kicked the front offside wheel angrily. Sod it.

The relief from the chilly fug of the Land Rover, the imminence of Cass' presence, the depressing weight of the immediate future, were all like emotions he might have felt walking out on a quarrel in a soured marriage. The trapped helplessness he felt invested him like an ague. He continued to rub his face, but nothing was erased from the tired, continuous tape-loop his imagination had become. He banged his back against the door of the Land Rover, as if to irritate a disliked neighbour. The wind soughed through firs and the cold black surface of the lake was wrinkled like ancient skin. The sedges crackled.

Up ahead somewhere, within the next few hours, it would come to an end. *He*, not just it. This time was different, too different to survive. Even Afghanistan had not been like this; at least, not in recollection. Here, there was no *warrant*, he wasn't official. He had slipped through a crack in the Whitehall pavement, to become casually employed, without importance, without backup. And there was no one, not even Ros, who knew where he was. And he was carrying a passenger he would have to abandon, when not to do so had been the whole point.

He opened the door of the Land Rover dispiritedly. Cass stirred from his doze and his white, empty, drawn features stared at Hyde, the bruises like the atlas of an ancient world, the eyes black gleaming holes.

'You all right?' he asked. Hyde tossed his head, clearing his throat in a growl.

'What do you think?'

Cass' gloved hands were pressed against his sides, as if he were suffering acute indigestion. His head hung forward, his breath in the now-colder vehicle smoking against the windscreen. The snow melted on Hyde's hair, running in icy trickles against his neck and ears. The windscreen was opaque with it, the lake lost to view. He suddenly realised how much snow had fallen on him during the few minutes he had been standing outside.

'I – I'll try,' Cass offered, his voice filled with foreboding.

'You're right you will,' Hyde began, then added more softly: 'Yes, sure. Just take it easy.'

He switched on the engine and reached for the headlight switch.

Headlights glared against the snowblind windscreen, bouncing wildly in a ghostly parody of lamplight inside the Land Rover. A vehicle approached them down the narrow track.

'Shit.' Cass' features were in wild disorder, the muscles slow to deflect the fear. Hyde felt his forearms quiver as his grip on the steering wheel tightened.

'What —?' Cass began.

Hyde turned irresolutely in his seat as if seeking a bolthole. The headlights closed, tossing up and down as if mounted on a wild horse. He could make out nothing behind their glare. The lights washed the sedge. As the Land Rover's wipers cleared the windscreen, the snow flew across the challenge of their headlights and those approaching them.

Hyde tossed the rifle into the rear of the Land Rover and covered it with a heavy backpack. Then he pressed the air in front of him with his hands, staring at Cass as he did so.

'Just play along,' he announced. 'And be ready.'

Cass fumbled at his parka, as if to locate the pistol Hyde had given him, seeming inordinately pleased as he did so. God —

Hyde opened the door and stepped out of the vehicle, slamming the door behind him. The approaching vehicle's headlights swept across him like a gleaming arm. Then it drew to a halt at the edge of the lake, almost beside the Land Rover, pressing Hyde vulnerably between the metal flanks of the two vehicles. It was Russian-made, a UAZ-469, looking like a cheap imitation of their own vehicle. The Russian Federation, the Ukrainians, every bugger and his mother were selling off anything they could turn into cash. The family gun room rather than the family silver. Hyde waved, his mind as cold and contracted as his face. There could be up to six men behind the driver. The canvas flap at the rear of the Russian 4WD crackled with frozen snow. Hyde stamped his feet and flapped his arms in protracted innocence as a greatcoated shape detached itself from the darkness of the vehicle and the night. Two other shadows clambered without complaint from the interior of the UAZ. The snow's gleam displayed their upright black sticks of automatic rifles. The driver grinned from behind his half-opaque window, his lips pressed around a cigarette.

'Good evening,' Hyde called, extending his right hand. His left hand was behind his back, waiting to snatch at the pistol. The extended hand was aware of the other pistol, a pocket away. 'Does anyone speak English?'

The first figure, tall, hawk-nosed and gleaming-eyed beneath the Russian-style fur hat, wore the epaulettes of a major. The snow poured into and through the splash of the UAZ's headlights. The origin of the vehicle was somehow comforting, less empty and unknown than the landscape and the immediate future. It was a vestige of the old game.

'Yes.' There was a medal ribbon on the greatcoat, the *Hilal-i-Juraat*. *For Valour*. 'I do. Who are you? Where are your papers?'

The wind was hollow, as if a cloak of sound had been dragged aside to reveal the vast emptiness of the place.

'Geomorphologists – yes?' Hyde replied with an edge of insult, his head cocked to one side in the arrogance of all experts. 'Taking seismic readings, checking our stations, instruments –' He laughed. 'People round here keep pinching them!'

Again, the slight insult. He had heard Cass' window creak down against the silted snow. Good, he was listening to the sudden cover story there hadn't been time to inoculate him with.

'Seismology? The Karakoram Project was many years ago,' the major replied. 'There has been no new expedition.'

Hyde shrugged. 'Ah – some funding that came along. We're just scouting the old sites, preparing for new work.' His voice had already become bored with his explanation.

'There is to be another project, of the same kind?'

The two soldiers, a corporal and a private, stamped rhythmically behind the major, rifles held across their chests. Snow thrust itself between Hyde and the major; the Pakistani officer, assured and even amused, loomed over Hyde. The water of the lake rustled like paper being screwed into a ball.

331

'Might be. We're checking it out. Costing, you might say. University of Sussex, England –' Again, he thrust out his gloved right hand, which the major ignored. It retreated again to the warmth of the parka pocket and the location of the second pistol. 'Mean anything to you – er, Major?' *Blow the bugger away*, something prompted in a hectic, unexpected whisper in his thoughts. He knew he didn't have himself under much control.

'Perhaps. Your papers would mean a great deal more. Sir.' The irony was palpable, like a metallic taste at the back of Hyde's throat.

'Pete!' he called, turning to the blind windscreen of the Land Rover. 'Papers, mate! The major doesn't believe we're who we say we are!'

'Your assistant?'

'Senior lecturer, actually. Almost my boss,' Hyde demurred. 'Hurry up, Pete – it's cold out here!' *Start inventing now.*

'I thought you had them,' Cass said. Hyde could not make out any more than a dull and shapeless shadow behind the windscreen. He prayed he'd got his gun at the ready. 'They're not in the dash or the side pockets, I've looked. Christ, *Bill*, you had them last in Gupis – or was it Pingal?' Travelling from the other direction, west to east, the fiction established. *Well done, Cass.*

'Are you sure?' Hyde persisted, moving to the driver's window. He opened the door and winked at Cass. 'I thought *you* showed the papers last time? I remember you putting them in *your* door pocket, I'm sure I do –'

'That was the map!'

Hyde patted his parka in bemusement, shutting the door behind him. He grinned apologetically.

'Look, I know this is stupid, but we can't find our papers!' He laughed. 'Christ! Oh, sorry – look, I know how important it is to show our papers whenever, but we really are engaged in scientific work, we are who we say we are . . . why *else* would

332

we be up here? With all due respect, it's almost the most God-forsaken place on the entire planet!' He laughed once more, with forced and embarrassed jollity.

'Really?' the major replied. He hesitated for a moment, then moved to the passenger side of the Land Rover and opened Cass' door, flicking on a small torch at the same moment. The interior of the vehicle glowed with an artificial, ghostly light. 'Would you step down – sir?' Then, as Cass did so, the major added, 'You seem to be in some discomfort –?'

'Nothing. Just a few bruises. Slipped and fell.' Then Cass all but shrieked. The two soldiers appeared electrocuted into jerky movement. Cass' breathing was audible, as was the slump of his body against the Land Rover. The metal quivered under Hyde's hand. Cass was doubled up, nursing his ribs. The major had jabbed him just where he expected a pained response. Identity confirmed.

He was luxuriating. Confident of his own perspicacity. Smilingly superior.

'A very bad *fall*, Mr Cass –?' Then he began to realise that cleverness was sharply two-edged and at once turned towards Hyde –

– who fired twice, three times because the corporal failed to fly back and fall at once.

'Kill that bastard!' Hyde roared at Cass, then he turned and fired across the small distance of the Land Rover's bonnet.

The major decorated for valour flinched away and dropped out of sight behind the vehicle. Two shots at once, together like a sonar's instantaneous echo. Hyde turned and fired into the cab of the UAZ, at the driver's alarmed face. It disappeared from the side window. Another shot from beyond the bulk of the Land Rover – *Christ, no* – then Hyde was shielded by the vehicle from the rear of the UAZ. Noises of alarm from inside the 4WD, almost of panic rather than response. He didn't look around the Land Rover, preferring not to know. Instead, he fished beneath the backpack and hauled out the rifle, switched to automatic fire and squeezed the magazine empty in an elongated, terrifying cry.

The silence came back, wrapped in the wind, hollow and suggesting great distances. Swallowing, Hyde rounded the bulk of the Land Rover, his boots creaking on the hard snow. The two bodies lay together, all but entwined, greatcoated and parkaed, two shapeless and unmoving lumps.

Quiet inside the wind, the blowing snow, the rippled blackness of the lake, the creak of wind-bent firs. And the two bodies lying in the slushy, disturbed snow beside the Land Rover.

Christ, *no* –

V.K. sat across the coffee table from her, the settee and floor near his feet littered with press cuttings, faxes curling like cheap parchment, digests, estimates, open-mouthed folders. While Prakesh spoke, he merely studied Sara; as if he were attempting, after a long absence or a sexual betrayal, to accommodate himself once more to a domestic charade. There were no emotions on his features. His sole change of expression lay in the slow disappearance of the glow he had worn on entering the room, and which had been sustained and even heightened by the reports from his aides and senior party workers – all of whom had now been dismissed, leaving just the three of them in the smoky, lamplit lounge. Delhi bellowed with lights beyond the long window and the Ridge lay in darkness, except for the occasional flash of headlights. Almost Central Park.

And the bungalow almost like an hotel, and herself certainly like a houri, registering the minutiae of a man's moods towards her. She was frightened, self-contemptuous, unanchored between the immediate past and immediate future.

'Then they are on that flight?' V.K. asked suddenly, himself uncertain. Prakesh nodded.

'Two of them. The woman boarded the flight – we managed to get them aboard.'

'Paris, Prakesh?'

'To throw us off the scent. She's simply fleeing, V.K. There is no alarm on her behalf, there are no suspicions in London.'

'The man?'

'Will be found, V.K.'

'You're certain?' Sara responded, like the sensitive insect she had become, antennae waving for every disturbance of the smoky atmosphere. Regretting what she had done ... that bloody, *bloody* woman –! It was as if she had been mesmerised or infected with something. 'You are *certain*, Prakesh?'

It was all up in the air, falling in slow-motion, the priceless porcelain of his dreams and ambitions ... which she shared, for God's sake, had done for years, unlike that sexually-motivated cow he had married.

And she had stuck out a foot to trip the smooth progress of the porcelain in safe hands. What had she done?

And what would they do if they knew?

'I'm sure. It's a matter of time, nothing more. Be certain of it, V.K. The news is good!' He gripped his brother's forearm as it lay on the arm of the settee and shook it encouragingly.

'What of the woman, now?' A pause, then: 'When?' he all but whispered, his eyes still on Sara but secretive; perhaps embarrassed that she should witness his ruthlessness.

'Any moment that offers itself. During the flight, even afterwards ... No violence. A heart-attack –'

V.K. was nodding quickly, accepting and at the same moment dismissing the detail. Prakesh looked at her then with hard interrogation. She blanched inwardly, but remained outwardly calm. Even sipped at her whisky. Prakesh's suspicion seemed deflected.

Ros was to be executed. Not brought back – not questioned, just killed –

– then good luck to them, whoever they were. Ros *had* to be killed. There was no other way *she* would be safe ...

*

'You OK?' Hyde asked at last.

His shoulder ached as he gripped the steering wheel. They were between Bohrt and Chillinji and the track was worse. Narrow, climbing, twisting like something alive always trying to shrug them off, obscured by still-falling snow. Almost a blizzard now. He had bruised his left shoulder heaving the bodies of the major and the two soldiers into the back of the UAZ. There'd been two others inside, and the driver. All dead. Ribboned by the automatic fire. A lot of blood, smelling sick-sweet even in the icy cold. He'd bruised the shoulder then, or minutes later when, after searching the vehicle, he'd jumped from the UAZ after sending it roaring down the slight slope to the water's edge. He had the food and thermoses of hot tea and coffee and the ammunition they could adapt. He'd watched it, lying prone, the pain of impact shuddering through him, as the vehicle had sunk with a drowning flurry of bubbles beneath the thin ice and dark water at the edge of the lake. The black water had closed like a mouth on the last stream of noisy bubbles.

'What?' Cass replied, groaning as he roused himself. 'Sure.'

He looked like someone staring into a high wind, enduring its force. No longer expecting change, diminution or relief. Less than twenty miles from the border, it was the best that Hyde could hope for . . . and the bleeding seemed to have stopped. The major's bullet had passed through the muscle and fat just below the ribs, on Cass' left side. Powder burns on his parka, his shirt reddened as Hyde had pulled open his coat to expose the wound. The UAZ's emergency medical kit was better than theirs, he'd used that to patch Cass up. The major's face was a mess. Cass' second bullet must have caught the Pakistani as he turned, and entered the base of the skull, exiting at the front.

'Good,' Hyde muttered.

They were skirting the vast bulk of Koz Sar, nearly twenty-two thousand feet, beyond which was the Chillinji Pass across the border into Afghanistan. Maybe no more than eighteen miles away . . . fifteen of which they'd have to *walk*. The pass was seventeen thousand feet up. They'd been climbing steadily up the narrow river valley ever since Chatorkhand. The weather had worsened, like some animal sure of its prey and prepared to wait for the kill. A snowstorm a day keeps the choppers away . . . The headlights betrayed them, but darkness would tip them into the river within a hundred yards. Snow flew across his eyesight, even seemingly behind his eyes.

How far could Cass possibly walk? His thoughts quarrelled and debated the inevitable.

The Land Rover's rear wheels squeaked and slid, then the four-wheel drive righted the vehicle and it turned slow as a tortoise around a sharp-edged cliff and climbed again. The blackness where the river valley dropped away beside the road seemed to run like dark water at the edge of the headlights. The occasional stunted tree, then clumps of firs as if gathered for mutual safety. The wall of Koz Sar's western flank heavier and more threatening than the cloud, glimpsed through wind-gaps torn in the curtains of snow.

They'd seen nothing, no one, after Chatorkhand. Imit had been silent, the occasional glimpsed light, the tiny gleam of a fire. Low, squat houses huddled against the weather. Bohrt had been the same. No soldiers, even though by now they'd know the major's patrol was missing or in trouble because they wouldn't have answered their radio or called in their position. They'd be looked for, and there was only the one road, going north to the border. The Chillinji Pass, unless they supposed them to have branched north-west, to Ishkuman. No, they'd know a 4WD was better heading directly north.

Have you prayed tonight, Desdemona? . . . Too bloody right, sport. He glanced aside at Cass, once more slumped in his seat, his body moving painfully in the troughs and peaks of each lurch of the Land Rover. Bugger that. *Othello* reminded him of Ros and her cultural outings, his programme of improvement – and Ros now, wherever she was, and the frail cord he and Cass were holding –

337

– blinked it away, but the snow-rush remained, speckling his vision. In half an hour they'd have to abandon the Land Rover and go out there, in that weather. The interior of the vehicle was already colder, the inefficient heating coughing small puffs of warm air that had no effect. And how the hell could Shelley get anyone to them, anyway, along the thin finger of Afghanistan that stretched between Tadjikistan and Pakistan, pointing towards China? There wasn't *any* way – was there? You've really buggered it this time, really *fucked* it up!

A frozen waterfall beside the track glittered behind the snow as the headlights slid across it – then wobbled, then slid. The lights were wiping a smear of light across the waterfall which they were not passing but turning to confront even as the Land Rover backed away from it like an animal startled yet attempting to defend itself. He juggled his foot on brake and accelerator, used the handbrake. Its rasp awoke Cass.

'What –?'

Goodnight, Vienna ... The vehicle was sliding across a sheet of ice beneath the snow and he couldn't prevent its gradual, inexorable retreat towards the edge of the track and the drop to the river. Not a long drop, quite shallow really, we might even survive it ...

'Fuck off out of it!' he screamed at Cass. *'Jump!'*

Whitefaced, clownlike incomprehension, then the survival mechanism. A blast of icy air as the door was opened, then a gap where Cass had been, then his body rolling in the headlights as they swept lazily across the waterfall, Cass, their tracks in the snow, the black and white snowladen arms of the trees, then the blackness of the gap of air above the river. The vehicle pirouetted delicately on the unmasked ice, then the front wheels roared over nothing. The headlights dived over the edge of the track, illuminating the black river, narrow and far down, it seemed. Then the lights gobbled at the slope as the Land Rover left the track and leaned out into air.

the undiscovered country

It was midnight in Delhi – and wherever *he* was now. She looked at her watch, perhaps for the hundredth time. The inflight movie flickered with grinning, vacuous, soundless images on the tiny screen set into the back of the seat in front of her. She didn't dare use the headphones, cut herself off from the murmur of the engines or the noises of the cabin – or from any movement either or both of them might make towards her. Didn't dare sleep. Ate in snatched nibbles from the tray she hadn't allowed them to clear away, like a harvest mouse anticipating the rush of the white wings of a hunting owl. In Paris it was seven in the evening, just getting dark. She had to endure another two and a half hours of this –!

At times, the tray opened across her lap seemed to suggest safety, like a child's high chair, at others it trapped her. The stewards and stewardesses were now casual, patrolling occasionally and perfunctorily, like warders not expecting a disturbance. They could cross the cabin at any time they chose. It would be a needle, a pill, something silent and not even discovered until the autopsy. Fat woman dies of heart-attack during flight. *We found her when we removed her tray . . . just as we were about to land – how awful . . . she seemed to be sleeping.* End of story. Her travel bag might be missing, but who'd ever connect its disappearance with those two Indian diplomats who boarded the aircraft while it was on the taxiway?

No one.

Two and a half hours.

She was not even certain that Shelley would be at Charles de Gaulle to meet her. She'd rung from the Air France lounge, but Shelley was unavailable. Alison had relayed a message from Hyde, that much she knew. But – *I can't reach Peter again, he told me not to. Don't call here, he said. Nor you*, Alison had added.

So, what the hell did he intend? Anything, or nothing? It had to be nothing. His little unofficial operation had disgraced itself at the dinner table. He'd pinch his nostrils, and hope the smell would go away. He'd ignore it –

Then how do I get away from them? In the tunnels of Charles de Gaulle airport, in the baggage hall, Customs –!

If you get that far!

She looked across at them. One of them seemed to be asleep, the other, in the aisle seat, intent upon the film. Some feminist buddy movie – oh, *buddy*, do I need one now. Occasionally, the one watching the movie, headphones masking his profile, glanced across at her. He seemed to be content to wait while she remained alert. *He* was assured of her future. Certain.

Ros swallowed drily. She'd ring for a glass of mineral water, display she was awake, parade the stewardess like a bodyguard.

She reached beside her and pressed the button, her hand shaking.

'Are you all right?'

The constant need for reassurance seemed to be the only communication between them. Cass' words lost their impetus against the force of the wind, reaching Hyde at the bottom of the slope as dissipated as the snowflakes that numbed his face. He stared up through the rushing whiteness towards the top of the slope down which the Land Rover had plunged, to end nose-down in the river.

Two, three times he might have jumped before the impact. Instead, he had controlled it. There were skewed and violent wheel tracks and a disturbance of pebbles and rocks on the riverbank. The vehicle was finished, but it hadn't caught fire and hadn't spilt their supplies into the black water. Now, having clambered the slope and staunched Cass' renewed bleeding, then descended again by means of the rope rescued from the back of the vehicle, he was ransacking it like any local bandit. The two backpacks – one too bulky for Cass but he'd *have* to carry it – the tight bundle of the tent, a second rope, ice axe, crampons, compass, torches . . .

'Yes!' he yelled back at Cass.

Set fire to the bloody thing or leave it? Leave it. Get going.

He struggled the two backpacks across the narrow fringe of pebbles to the end of the rope he had let down, anchored to a thin, strong tree that whined with foreboding as the wind distressed its branches. He'd got everything. He looked up as he struggled his sodden parka into one of the backpacks and adjusted the weight on his hips. Right –

Finger of light, tiptoeing at the edge of vision. His head turned stiffly. A crawling white finger of light moving along the surface of the black water, a finger whose hand was black, a bulk against Koz Sar, all but obscured by the snow. Helicopter. Searchlight stabbing down, flicking in and out of the snow and dark wind, following the course of the river. It was seventy, eighty feet up, slipping as elegantly as a slow-motion dancer along the valley, parallel with the track. It must have some kind of terrain-following radar or be flying by computer map. There was a square of light, a welcoming window, on one side of the dark bulk. IR binoculars would be scanning the road through the open cargo door.

He felt leaden with the weight of the two backpacks, the rifle across his chest and the ammunition. Handicapped, tethered like a goat. Then he began to clamber up the rope, his boots scraping and slipping, yelling to Cass:

'Keep your bloody *head* down!'

The second backpack trailed from his bruised shoulder, seeming to drag him backwards. The rifle jolted against his stomach. The finger of light had become a thicker, more discernible walking leg now, stamping martially towards the Land Rover half-drowned in the Ishkuman. His arms ached with the strain of hauling himself up the slope with frantic running motions against the loose scree and jutting rocks. Then he tumbled wearily over the lip of the slope onto the edge of the track. Cass' hand reached him at once, seeking reassurance. Hyde shrugged it away, turning onto his stomach to watch the light walking, walking . . . hesitating, stepping backwards, scrabbling as if to squash a cigarette-end, then locating the Land Rover. The light caressed it, nose-down in the river, as if stroking a dog, the noise of the rotors and engines of the big Russian helicopter banging back off the rocks of the narrow slit of the river valley. *Déjà vu* all over again, he thought, chilled and panting for breath. The cargo door was open, he could see two outlined figures squatting in the window of light. The motionless beam now telescoped as the helicopter dropped down towards the Land Rover.

'Will they land?' Cass bellowed in his ear; a whispered noise.

'I don't think so –' he began.

The eruption of flame from the open door of the MiL startled him. The Land Rover was engulfed as the missile detonated. Almost at once, the flame was itself swallowed by the wind and snow, dying down to aftermath. He thought he heard what might have been a cheer from the MiL. Then there was a second explosion as the debris from the first rattled against the slope below them and he smelt petrol, metal on the wind. The glare blinded Hyde for a moment, then, out of the glare, the MiL dropped lower, hovering beside the flickering bonfire, its landing wheels down but not choosing to settle on the pebbly margin of the river. Two men descended on a rope ladder that trailed across the bank, then cautiously approached the wreckage. The fuel had already burned, but they were nervous. He heard shouts, saw waving arms. A loudhailered reply.

The two men climbed back up the rope and into the lighted opening in the side of the helicopter. Then, after a minute or so, the rotor noise changed pitch and the walking leg of light extended once more, then proceeded as if tiptoeing away from the wreckage, north along the river, its foot splashing on the black water, its noise retreating.

Eventually, he heard the wind again, unadulterated and icy and filled with thousands of miles of emptiness. He shivered, the reaction seeming to displace organs, make his heart quail. He looked at Cass, who was staring after the retreating light, which had become a finger, then a smear, then an illusion.

'Jesus,' Cass exhaled, 'you were down there!'

'I wasn't. I was up here, *watching*.' He glared at Cass, who nodded, then swallowed. 'Want a drink?'

'I think I'd better, don't you?'

The coffee was still warm in the thermos. The major's thick, sweet coffee. Missing patrol, all hell let loose. 'Here.'

Cass grasped the cap of the thermos gratefully, swallowing at the coffee as if he had found an oasis. Hyde felt exhausted, squatting in the slushed snow, his lower body and legs numbed by the cold. He swallowed the thin trickle of warm liquid, tracing its reluctant progress and lack of effect down to his stomach. He threw the remainder of the coffee away. Cass, almost guiltily, handed back his emptied cap. Hyde screwed it onto the flask and thrust its shell-case back into the pack. Two packs, two rifles, the tent, the rest of their equipment littering the zipped pockets of their parkas. Map? US Army Map Service U502 Series . . . Like Hillary and Tensing. He wondered if Cass had got the flag for when they reached the summit!

He rose to his knees, them clambered upright like a very old man. Cass looked up pleadingly, then, childlike, licked snow from his lips. Hyde tossed his head.

'Let's begin.'

He pulled Cass to his feet. The pain in his side and ribs doubled him up, making him cough and groan. Hyde rested his weight on his knees, gloved hands gripping them, feeling their quivering weakness and reluctance.

Eventually, he inserted Cass into the embrace of the backpack, handling the equipment and the flesh as gently as he could. Cass' continual groans of protest and pain unnerved him. He was relieved when they became a torrent of expletives. They rested again. Time was slipping away, it was after midnight – tomorrow morning –

He stood up. The wind howled angrily.

'Fifteen miles – maybe twelve. Maybe less!' he shouted, knowing it was all uphill. 'Let's *begin*.'

He walked away from Cass, following the track, suddenly struck that he had been driving along it half an hour earlier . . . along this narrow, treacherous snake of a thing. The snow crunched under his boots. He paused, but did not look round.

After what seemed like minutes, he heard, through the wind, the crunch of Cass' boots behind him; slow, reluctant, but coming on. He nodded fiercely, then bent his face aside from the flying snow and continued walking; knowing there were other, unheard footsteps, close behind Cass and getting closer.

At first, it wasn't Paris, just somewhere laid out in light like a vast circuit board. Then, as the 747 settled lower over the city, she could make out the black snake of the Seine and the garishly illuminated specks of the Arc de Triomphe and the Eiffel Tower. Other landmarks she left unidentified, her glance flicking again and again across the cabin to the two Indians, apparently absorbed like her in the city. Roads rushed with processions of glow-worm lights, then the countryside was present for a moment as scattered suburbs and clumps of darkness, before the glow of the airport.

Oh, Hyde –

The ground was somehow his element – she needed him especially after the plane landed. She glowered at the two oblivious Indians, who were trying to lull her, their silence assumed.

Her travel bag was zipped, her coat returned to her and lying across her lap. The click of a seatbelt as the sign came on startled her. Neither of the Indians had moved. A businessman drifted past her, refreshed with expensive, cloying aftershave. His shirt was creased across the small of his back. The stewardesses had reassumed their smiles with their makeup, and she felt crumpled and jet-lagged. She dismissed the sensation; she'd managed to stay awake so far – she would now.

Should she dash for the door? Be first or last out? She mustn't get stuck in a crush in the disembarkation tunnel. The fear of needles, one slight, quick nudge with something and she wouldn't fall over until they were thirty yards away, innocently separated from her. First out of the door, then.

The airport was suddenly near, looming up underneath the aircraft as if climbing to meet it. Lights and traffic on the road, then the runway lights – she tensed, her palms wet – and the jolt of touchdown. Roar of deceleration. The lights coming out of their oily blur, separating, slowing. The irritating jingle of muzak and the landing announcements in French, English, Hindi – *en Paris, l'heure est* . . . nine thirty by her watch. On time. Wherever Hyde was, it was two thirty tomorrow morning.

The Boeing turned off the runway onto the taxiway, and the terminal wobbled ahead of her, glimpsed through the porthole which streamed with condensation. She tried to remember the complex hub-and-spoke layout of Charles de Gaulle, but memory came from a Paris weekend with Hyde and that merely confused and unnerved. Baggage claim lay at the end of the spoke, down one floor, she thought.

The 747 slowed. She watched the two Indians, one of them struggling into his jacket, the other adjusting his tie then putting on his shoes. Just like the other businessmen and the few women in business class. All normal, nothing awful could happen now, they'd landed. Relief all round.

She saw the tunnel's mouth extending to meet them, closing like a gourmand's against the door. French kiss, she thought, but there was no giggle inside the image, it was a husk drained by her growing, quick fear. She got to her feet, hefted her bag, and moved down the aisle to the door. The stewardess reproved, then became absorbed in opening the cabin door. Paris was cooler than the cabin, just for a moment, then her own temperature overtook her again. She looked behind her. The two Indians had their bags in their hands, almost standing to attention – faces frustrated as a couple pushed colonially past them. She thrust past the stewardess the moment the door opened, hurrying at once up the carpeted slope of the tunnel, listening for the first hurried footfall behind her. The murmur of passengers pursued her. Her bag was heavy. She looked round. The couple, she fur-coated, he polo-necked and cashmere-sweatered, remained ahead of the two Indians as if determined to reach some sale bargain first. But the Indians were still confident. They saw her only as a fleeing, lone female, their contempt casual and assured. She turned into the long, bright tunnel with its whispering moving walkway. The plane lay beached beyond the windows, a catering truck already nuzzled against it.

She stepped onto the walkway and hurried herself along it, her footsteps spongy on the moving rubber. Then they were on the walkway, too, having elbowed the couple aside or dodged around them. They were hurrying, but not running. They'd needle her, do something, spray something in her nostrils and mouth as they passed her. Were there others to meet them? She looked ahead, into the diminishing perspective of the walkway. Just a blur of lights, people, shops. She passed a lone French policeman, small and armed beneath his Foreign Legion cap. How could she explain? They were twenty yards behind her and catching up quickly. Her legs felt weak, her body heated and trembling. Oh, *bugger*! she wailed inwardly. Christ, Shelley, where are you?

Ten yards behind now, the taller of the two slightly ahead of his accomplice. The walkway was more spongy under her heavy, stumbling tread, the policeman now fifty yards or more behind them. Seven yards, six strides. The taller one increased his pace. Would anyone remember that they weren't met like diplomats, would anyone connect them with her anyway? Five strides, four . . .

There were people at the end of the walkway. A luggage trolley with flashing lights and a wailing horn passed her. An invalid woman sat on the back of it in her wheelchair. Too potent. A hand reached for her sleeve, grasped it. She swung the travel bag and missed the Indian, who side-stepped without losing his balance, and smiled. The man behind him pressed forward, too, so that they blocked the walkway. Ros' hand gripped the moving rail. A poster of the Eiffel Tower, another of the Place de la Concorde, one of a tiger's face through greenery – *Magical Kashmir*.

The tall couple in their elegant clothes were strolling twenty yards behind, a gaggle of first- and business-class passengers trailing behind them. The policeman was invisible far down the perspective of the tunnel. The Indian darted his briefcase forward, as if to spar with her travel bag. Something gleamed at its edge, she was certain. A needle. She backed away, losing balance, everything happening with frightening speed except her reaction. She stumbled. There *was* a glitter at the corner of the briefcase as it darted at her again. She fell away from it with terrible slowness, her heel caught by something, her body accelerated as she tripped against the end of the walkway. The Indian was immediately above her and bending towards her with mock solicitousness. All she could see was the briefcase, filling her vision. Blood rushed in her ears like people shouting –

Hyde rose above the rock and fired twice. The shadow disappeared behind the blown snow; random gusts now. Stars pricked out in a ragged, clearing sky. His breath smoked and he dropped into cover again. A bullet whistled away, puffing snow from the rock behind which he was hidden. The thin, lopsided smile of the narrow moon was high in the sky. The stars watched like surprised, inert eyes.

There were four of them, perhaps six. Not knowing was bad

enough. Almost tripping over them was worse. The wind swept snow off the rocks around him, and ice cracked somewhere with a groan. Where was Cass?

He sat, the Kalashnikov pressed against his chest. Where? Cass had tumbled to the right, unhit he was certain, and he had scrabbled away to their left, at the first shot. Ten minutes ago. The straps of the peak ground into his shoulders, the harness pressed into the small of his back.

Moon, diminishing snow, a clearing sky, and they were a thousand feet above the timberline, close to the pass. The wind howled, asthmatically angry. The peak of Koz Sar gleamed out whitely through a pause in the snow. Ice shone on its flanks; everywhere, it seemed. Another planet.

He heard someone moving, after a muffled order. He raised himself above the parapet of rock, the lichen scarred into exposure by ricochets, and fired. The greatcoat lost form and volition, becoming merely a lump of rags on the snow. Ducked down again. The returned fire whistled away wildly off the rocks.

'Cass?' he called. 'Phil?'

'Yes!' he heard, all but lost in the fire directed at himself and the location he and they guessed was that of Cass. Away over there, across the narrow track, closer to the grumbling little tarn locked into the embrace of the mountains. They'd been resting, looking down at it, or just staring at nothing, when the first shot had been fired. 'Yes!' Cass bellowed again after the gunfire, in ragged defiance. He was holding up – just.

Until they call in a chopper . . . The moonlight cast shadows now and there were great, torn gaps in the cloud. The river was a dark-silver ribbon away to the west. The wind was still fistlike in its repeated buffets, but it wasn't too strong for a gunship, just difficult.

He listened, head cocked. Nothing inside the wind. Then a muffled groan and a shuffling noise. Cass moving. Two shots, which whined away. The mountains stretched everywhere beyond Hyde, the Hindu Kush to the west, the Karakoram to the east. There was nothing other than endless mountains. The thought crushed. He looked for navigation lights against the glaciers and snowfields, but saw nothing. The wind made his eyes water. Around him the land fell away in a delusion of space, except up ahead. It was nothing more than a scratch in the mountains, this track and the slight gap of the Chillinji Pass.

Three in the morning. They'd made reasonable time, trekking up towards the border. They'd managed to skirt Chillinji – there'd been a patrol there, gathered around a truck, the glow of cigarettes visible. The tiny hamlet of scattered, snow-gripped huts was silent, except for one invisible dog barking at imaginary disturbance. The place might have been long deserted, except for the patrol. Three in the morning. They'd eaten once – soup, tinned meat, rice, coffee. Chocolate and biscuits. Cass had seemed a little refreshed, though that might have been illusory.

Again, he listened, and thought he caught the crackle of a radio, the whisper of voices and ether and the tiny clicks of switches or buttons.

'We have to move!' he called out – in Russian. What else did he speak they wouldn't understand? He couldn't remember whether Cass spoke Russian or not. 'We have to move!' A desultory shot whined away above his head, not even striking the rocks behind which he was hidden.

That made it certain.

'OK, comrade!' Cass called back. More shots towards his position, but again, without enmity or aim. Just restraint. Hyde gritted his teeth.

'They must have called up choppers – gunships!'

'I understand,' Cass called back in English. It seemed to provoke more intense fire. He heard someone scrabbling – not Cass – leaned to one side and fired off three quick shots. The noise was louder, possessing an echo. The wind was dropping. The clouds moved more slowly. The anoraked figure – Frontier Force – ducked out of sight thirty yards away. They weren't closing in, just closing the gaps. There were at least two of them up ahead, farther along the track, the others would be half-encircling them. They just wanted to keep them where they were.

'Wait till I move!' again in Russian.

'Two – up there!' Cass called back in Russian.

'*Kak pozhivayete?*' Hyde called. What state are you in, tourist version.

'OK!'

Good. But they must know Cass is in difficulty, know the background? He *sounds* bad. He heard the crackling of the radio, but they'd retreated with it, so that he couldn't hear what was being said. The cavalry's on its way, they want reassuring that we're still pinned down. Easy targets, precise references. They might even send this lot down the toilet with us, for the sake of surprise. He listened again, as intently as he could. The night was calmer, almost silent, the sky bright with hard stars. He couldn't hear the sound of engines, just the scrape of metal on rock as someone moved.

Five, ten minutes – an hour? The border region was littered with temporary and permanent army bases. All of them were supplied by helicopter. It wouldn't take long to put up a couple.

He had to move up the track, keeping to the shelter of the rocks as best he could, try to take out the two men up ahead of them.

Someone snapped out an order in Urdu. At once, Cass shouted:

'They're dropping back!'

'Out of range!' Hyde called back, his voice high with an onset of nerves.

He moved on his haunches, like a Cossack dancer skittering across the ground. Then he saw the flicker of a darkened knife-blade as the man leapt from the rocks at him. He raised the blunt Kalashnikov and the knife clashed on the barrel between Hyde's hands. Then the barrel was under the man's arm and Hyde

350

heaved upwards with it. The Pakistani's assault knocked him off balance, but carried the man's bulky, anoraked form over the top of him. He turned onto his stomach and fired two shots. Immediately, shots from the left, and from up ahead. The Pakistani got to his feet and fumbled his own rifle from behind his back. Hyde squeezed the trigger again. Nothing.

Empty or jammed.

The noise of engines, the chilling mutter of rotor blades, very close, masked until that moment by the –

– it sprang up like a huge spider, over the lip of the scree slope. The Pakistani soldier was startled by it, his attention distracted. Hyde, lungeing from his haunches, struck the man across the cheek with the butt of the rifle. The rock ten yards away roared with flame, and the concussion of the explosion threw him off his feet, struck him with sharp shards of rock. He was deafened by the noise.

He was right, he realised, they hadn't waited. Surprise was everything. They didn't care who they killed, so long as they got them.

His mouth was filled with snow, it was difficult to breathe. He realised it slowly. The explosion still roared in his ears. Then there was a second flash of light and a rain of debris on his back and head. The rotor noises were distorted and distant and yet filling his head. He thought someone was screaming, but it might even have been himself. He couldn't think, there was only the noise.

Two more explosions in swift succession. He could hardly hear them, his hands pressed too late over his ears. The continual bellow of noise was already inside his head. Someone was screaming. He could see only the faint glimmer of the snow in front of his face through the retinal dazzle. Something heavy landed on his leg.

He looked up. The MiL was hovering in a mist of updraughted snow just where the slope fell away to the grumbling tarn. Its insect-eyed cabin was blind. The updraught wobbled it like a spider at the end of a long, invisible thread. Retinal spots danced around it like small flares. He dropped his head, exhausted. Then the noise in his head subsided and he began to hear the rotors.

Something dragged at him, something that screamed. A shadow above him, leant over him, a shadow that screamed.

'Get up, *get up!*' it kept bellowing, like a child discovering a dead parent. 'Get moving – *move!*' Panic, desperation.

Hyde turned his head sideways and looked up. It was Cass, his hand gripping Hyde's backpack, pulling vainly at it. Behind him, the gunship loomed like a dark moon through the mist of snow. Then the helicopter danced away.

Hyde struggled to his feet. Cramp in his calf. He looked down. His trousers were torn, flapping wetly. The pack weighed like a great stone. Cass was still screaming at him, his voice hoarse and high-pitched.

Then they were stumbling up the track, hauling themselves along the fringe of boulders and rocks, slipping on hidden ice, their breaths clouding round them. There was someone, a shape no more, ahead of them, waving a gun, confused as to their identity. Cass shot it from a distance of five or six yards and stumbled over the body as it fell. There was no sign of anyone else, no shooting. Hyde turned. Cass fell rather than leaned against him, almost unbalancing him. The snow-mist was settling now and the MiL was moving back towards it, its dark snout thrust forward, the rocket pods visible beneath its stubby wings.

Come on, Hyde waved, when no sound would emerge from his throat. He half-pulled, half-jostled Cass ahead of him. The taller man was bent double as if by age, his legs struggling through his total exhaustion. Twice, Hyde hauled him to his feet, looking back each time. The snow was being drawn up again by the rotors. Then someone must have moved and there were two more bright explosions, followed by a concussive wind that reached them like a hot breeze, then the noise of tearing rock.

The third time Cass fell, Hyde fell with him, stumbling into a

snowdrift that was suddenly shoulder high around him, sparkling with frost, numbing his body and his cheek. Cass lay on the
hidden track, his chest heaving. Hyde struggled out of the drift.
They had rounded a bend. There was nothing behind them now.

Hyde crossed to Cass.

'Come on,' he said hoarsely. Ominously, Cass was pressing his
hand to his side. 'It isn't over. It's just begun. Act Five. Come
on – on your bloody feet!'

They were above fifteen thousand feet. The air's cold hurt his
lungs. Cass' chest seemed on the point of eruption as he fought
in the thin air. There were four, perhaps five miles to the
border –

– and to what? Nothing, probably.

The needle, bright-tipped, was jutting through the corner of the
briefcase – rich brown leather, gold clasped. People shouting as
if encouraging the swing of the needle towards her. The legs
of the taller Indian, the bent-down face of the other. She was
entangled with her travel bag, couldn't get her legs to move –
one shoe'd come off, one leg was twisted under her. Oh, *Christ* –!

No police whistles, no one near enough. But someone kept
shouting and shouting in French, then English, the voice distorted through effort and panic. Surely it was a yell of alarm, a
warning –?

Then arms were pulling her along tiles that were still wet. She
collided with the notice that declared such to be the case and it
collapsed on her. Someone swore in French. The smaller Indian
raised his gun at her and she cowered away from it against
blue-serge trousers, striped like a uniform down the outside leg.
Then there was a noise, a sharp twig-crack of sound, and the
Indian fell down, as if he, too, had tripped. Then there were
people screaming, panicking to run backwards on the moving
walkway, yet being propelled towards the fallen body.

The Indian with the briefcase bent slowly, carefully, and
placed it upright on the gleaming tiles. A policeman removed it,

another inspected the Indian lying down and shook his head. Took the pistol from a dead hand. The passengers on the walkway were being channelled to one side with brutally shouted orders and the occasional thrust or gesture of a sub-machinegun. They streamed away in a gabbling, semi-hysterical troupe, staring back like excited schoolchildren.

Then Shelley was kneeling beside her, holding her upper arms, looking into her face with genuine concern and relief.

'Christ, Shelley – where have you *been*?' she screamed at him. Then pulled him against her, holding onto him, feeling her whole body shudder against his. There were suited legs standing behind him, the drape of long overcoats. Police uniform trousers, too. Eventually, she pushed him away, shook his hand free of her hair. 'That's enough of that,' she announced with a mock brusqueness that came out with a peculiar inflection, as if she were losing her voice.

Shelley was openly grinning. His eyes were still moist with relief.

'Thank God!' he sighed. 'Thank God . . .' Then: 'I got in an hour ago, I thought I'd have more time, but something blew up. It's taken me until now to put the squeeze on Claude – ' He glanced behind him, as at someone he expected Ros to recognise. The Frenchman, elegant to the point of provoking irritation in a long camel-coloured overcoat and a Burberry scarf, nodded as if they had been formally introduced. Ros sat up, legs splayed unselfconsciously, and brushed her hair from her face and eyes.

'Who's Claude when he's at home, Shelley?' It seemed the only thing that might reasonably be asked. It was, at least, prompted by a desire for normality. Her hands were shaking violently.

'DST – their MI5. I couldn't do anything here without their supervision.' Then his eyes clouded, his brow creasing. 'You're all right? You're sure? I couldn't really take it in for a moment – luckily, Claude realised . . .' His voice trailed away and he shrugged.

Claude Whoever was bending over the dead Indian, then murmuring to his companion, who at once appeared to protest some form of diplomatic immunity. The Frenchman smiled thinly, shaking his long dark hair. He was taller than the Indian who had tried to murder her –

– hands shaking again, stomach turning over. Jesus.

Then the DST officer gestured to two uniformed policemen and they placed themselves at either side of the Indian. Then Claude Whoever walked swiftly towards her and Shelley. He all but clicked his heels as he nodded to her.

'I am Claude Rousseau, DST. Welcome to Paris, M'selle Woode.' He reached out his hand and she shook it. He helped her gently to her feet. She brushed her clothing into some kind of tidiness and modesty, then her hair into a semblance of order. Then she was bent double by stomach cramps, having to catch at her breath and swallow the sweet nausea that threatened.

Rousseau held her arms as she straightened up, wiping the moisture from her lips. Thank Christ she hadn't thrown up! Then someone pressed a bottle of Evian water into her hand and she sipped at it.

'Something stronger?' She shook her head. The water was dizzyingly strong, invigorating. Rousseau nodded in satisfaction.

Immediately, she sensed the fictitious paint of the situation begin to peel and fall away. Shelley stripped the remainder of it as he said, low and urgently:

'Where is he, Ros? Is he still alive?' Adding almost at once: 'You don't know, do you – you can't tell us?'

As if exposed in some humiliating failure, she shook her head. Then blurted: 'I know where he was aiming for, that's all.'

Shelley glanced at Rousseau, who nodded, then snapped out a stream of orders to those around him. Then he said:

'Come with me, both of you. Somewhere more private, I think.'

Shelley took her arm.

'Do you know if he's alive?' she asked, turning on him.

355

Shelley looked lugubriously at his watch. 'He was, twelve hours ago – a little more.'

'I know *that*!' she snapped.

'Sorry. That's the last news of him.'

Then they were hurrying through the clotted passengers, then down a narrow flight of iron stairs to a corridor that echoed with their footsteps, to an unmarked door. Rousseau closed the door behind them. The room was cramped, sparsely furnished. Rousseau locked the door. The place seemed designed to intimidate and disorientate. Rousseau indicated a stiff-looking armchair.

'Some coffee?' he asked solicitously. She shook her head.

'Patrick said you'd know where he was heading. Right – where?' Shelley asked. He appeared uncomfortable.

'I just have something . . . you need a map. The US Army Service map . . . ?' Rousseau was nodding. Shelley opened his slim briefcase on a low coffee table and riffled through its contents.

'Which one, Ros?'

She fished in her handbag and found her powder compact. Her urgency made her fumble and the powder spilt onto the stained cord carpet and over her skirt.

'Oh, *shit* –!' she bellowed, ridiculous tears clouding her eyesight. Then she shook the folded piece of tissue paper and held it out to him. 'There's a reference written on that,' she said, sniffing. Shelley unfolded it with delicate movements of his fingertips. 'You place that over the right map.'

He continued searching in his case, then unfolded a map with unnaturally loud cracking noises. He spread it out on the floor. Rousseau knelt beside him. Shelley shuffled the powdery sheet of paper across the map. The landscape was nothing but mountains, she realised. He made finer adjustments, as if finishing a jigsaw. There was perspiration on his brow.

'There,' he sighed. 'The – er, Chillinji Pass.' He looked up, shocked. 'He's crossing into *Afghanistan*.' Then, to Rousseau, he murmured something like: 'Tomorrow, he said,' and glanced at his watch. 'It's almost four over there – *tomorrow*.'

'What are you going to do?' Ros asked as she saw Rousseau shake his head, then shrug.

'I – I'm not sure –' Shelley began.

'Get him out!' she heard herself growling, leaning forward on the narrow, uncomfortable chair, her hands clenched into fists.

'Where's your evidence?' Shelley asked urgently.

She clutched the travel bag. 'In here. I've got it – so has he. Get him out.'

'You're *sure*?'

'I'm sure. It would ruin them. The Sharmars.'

Shelley nodded, and turned solemnly to Rousseau. 'Claude, there's one way. Medicins Sans Frontières. They'll have a helicopter, more than one, closer than anyone else –'

'I can't arrange that, Peter. Not even for you.'

'You have to, Claude. The lady insists. I *know* SDECE people fly with or even *fly* some of those medical helicopters. They have to, Claude, just to protect the doctors! *Please* speak to someone senior in Intelligence. I'll regard it as being in the Big Favour class. *Grand obligation.* I will reciprocate in kind and degree.'

The room was hot now, with the tension of all three, and with her impatience. Hyde's situation had drowned her own and her only fear was for him. Shelley seemed pained by her demands and those of what might have been his conscience. Rousseau weighed advantage against the risk to valuable pawns, but seemed drawn to study her.

Eventually, he nodded, his dark hair falling across his forehead. He flicked it away from his broad, pale brow. He smiled at Ros.

'Very well, Peter.' He wagged his long index finger. 'I want to know – everything.' He pointed at the travel bag, which Ros at once clutched against her as if he intended a mugging. Shelley made to protest, then he, too, succumbed to the delicate adjustment of scales.

357

'Agreed.'

Satisfied, Rousseau crossed to the telephone in a corner of the room and snatched it up from the grubby carpet. Ros sighed as he began, without hesitation, to dial.

'I'm sorry, Ros,' Shelley murmured, watching the travel bag as if it were a small animal that might, at any moment, jump from her arms and flee. 'We'll do everything, of course . . .' He shook his head. 'We'll do everything we can.' He already seemed to partly regret his bargain with the Frenchman. His tone was bereft of optimism, and his attention remained on the bag – its contents. They were forfeit to Rousseau – for *nothing*.

'You think he's dead already, don't you?' she challenged.

Shelley nodded. He had, evidently, made a bad bargain and regretted it. Wanted to breach the contract. Then he said:

'He put the phone down in a panic, Aly said. They were on to him twelve hours ago and more! Look what a risk they took in trying to stop *you*, Ros.' He spread his arms. Genuine regret flickered like a flame of exotic colour, burning differently amid the calculation and negotiation. He had wanted to do good, the proper thing, but the mood was dissipated by a chill breeze of pessimism. He murmured: 'I don't know if even he can make it this time, Ros.'

She shook in the force of her own brush with death, which now raged like a gale.

And neither do I, she admitted. Neither do I . . .

Cold, now. Snow had become ice crystals, needles in his skin. The weight of Cass' laboured progress dragged on the nylon rope that bound them together. The rifle slung across his chest was frozen to the parka. The weather had surged into the pass, thrusting them back towards their pursuers. The wind howled as it circled and buffeted them.

Hyde could see little. The path was treacherous with ice beneath the newest snow, and he stumbled often, bringing Cass down – Cass bringing him down or at least to a grudging halt each time he fell. The flesh wound in his leg was now no more than a numb ache.

The Chillinji Pass wound unseen ahead of them, clambering its way towards the border. He had begun to sense they wouldn't reach it, simply because his perception of what was beyond that border had diminished into a single faith. There'd be no one, nothing on the other side, just the same appalling weather and the slow process of freezing to death. Or survival until morning and a clearing sky brought anyone following them at the run to finish their task. A few rounds of automatic fire into two already-stilled bodies.

His internal temperature had dropped. He was certain of that. Beneath the layers of thermal clothing and the icy skin there was a sluggishness about his blood that was echoed by his thoughts. *You're not going to get out of here* . . . The thought repeated itself, as on a tape-loop, and he no longer had the energy, the *warmth*, to fight it. It was the bloody-fucking weather that had caused that. Landscapes he could deal with; desert, mountain, forest, scrub, tundra. In *good* weather, so that men were still the only real danger . . . but not here. The bulky, armed shapes would rush in only to find the job already done.

Cass stumbled again.

His mind reached back like frozen fingers along the nylon rope to realise the reason for his having been dragged off-balance. In a moment between driving snow, he saw vast glaciers and frozen sheets of water gleam like crumpled tinfoil. He turned awkwardly, his feet lacking purchase, and saw Cass lying in the hard snow, a whitening lump. He'd have started to bleed again, if the temperature allowed bleeding. He stumbled back towards the prone form, collapsing onto his knees, shaking Cass at once because he dared not believe this was something final. He screamed at him, the curses all but soundless, as the air required to expel them burnt in his chest.

Cass, turned onto his back, stared up at Hyde's ice-lidded eyes through a bushy, frozen rime on his own lashes and eyebrows.

His stubble was frozen, his lips cracked and approximate as he attempted to reassure. His mittened claw gripped Hyde's sleeve, tugging at it. Hyde hefted him into a sitting position, growling against the frozen collar of his parka:

'Ready?' He had to bellow. *'Ready?'* Against both the wind and the cold burn of his throat – and against the black heaviness that had begun the moment he halted. To impel Cass was as burdensome as to carry him – it might come to that. He seemed content to lie staring up into the blowing snow. *'Come on!'* Hyde yelled, dragging him once more into a sitting position, then roughly turning him onto his stomach, hoisting him then onto all-fours, as if arranging a dog for inspection at a show.

He bullied him upright. Cass pressed his hand against his side, then bent double as if to vomit. Hyde wanted to leave him, let the rope slacken from around his waist, as if Cass would drift off on black water to drown out of sight. He couldn't. It would make it purposeless, it would be admitting that he couldn't win. Cass was the necessary luggage that suggested there was a destination to his appalling journey. He leaned Cass' weight against his body, in a loose embrace. The howling wind rocked them, his parka was thickly whitened, seeming to crackle into ruts and folds as he moved. There must be a patrol close behind, had to be. He pulled Cass forward, felt his freezing breath against his cheek as he leaned their faces together.

'Come on, sport! All in a bloody day's work!' he shouted. Cass nodded dumbly. 'They can't catch up with us as long as we keep moving!' Two steps, the third, fourth, fifth and sixth; stumbling upwards to where Hyde's own footprints were busily being covered by the falling snow. 'Moving, moving, *moving . . .*' he grunted, as much for his own encouragement as for Cass.

'Where are they?' he heard.

'Back there. Behind us. Must be!' Cass paused in new snow – up to their ankles now – dizzily righted himself and flapped his arms like a drowning man. His face was grizzled, weak. Then he turned and bellowed coughingly:

'*Bugger* off! Bugger *off*!'

Hyde grinned. His lower lip split. He dragged Cass after him as he prodded ahead. The river was somewhere out of sight beside them, like something dangerous tracking their progress, its icy grumblings heard in the small gaps between the gusts of the storm. The cliff face alongside them loomed and danced closer then farther, like an assailant always threatening to hurl them into the river. It was insane to be there, insane to continue their futile movement. He looked back. Slowly, woodenly, Cass came up with him and at once slumped against him. Yet within the icy fringes of his lashes, his eyes seemed more determined. Hyde nodded, and turned to continue.

The shot was almost silent, no more than a flat, hoarse whisper. As were the two shots that quickly followed. Hyde fell to one side, dragging Cass with him – who groaned on impact with the snow-covered ice.

Hyde could see nothing. Nothing at all. Snow raced across the track behind them, obliterating whoever had fired at them. He listened, but the wind swallowed all sounds other than its own. Except where ice cracked and thundered distantly.

'Where?' he heard from Cass. Hyde merely shook his head. Back there, somewhere. They'd been glimpsed through a ragged hole in the curtains of snow. Lost again now, though.

He staggered to his feet, climbing against the steep staircase of the wind. Dragged Cass upright, too, and bullied them both on. He shuddered with more than the cold. They were too close, maybe only a hundred yards or so. Hours yet to daylight. It wouldn't take that long, not anywhere near. There were a couple of shots, which made him crouch, but he heard no ricochet or whine of a bullet anywhere near them. They turned a snake-twist of the track and Hyde pulled them into the inadequate lee of a jutting shoulder of rock. He could hear their breathing like a revelation. Cass was still aware enough to be gripping the rifle with frozen hands.

You're not going to get out of here . . . It came back, then, into

361

the relative lull of the rock's shelter. *You're not . . .* Eventually, the hypnotic whisper of defeat would shut out everything else from his thoughts. Freeze his mind.

'Let's go!' he growled against Cass' ear. He nodded in exhausted reply.

A shadow on the track, a bulk that struggled through the snow. Hyde fired without thought, feeling a wild exhilaration. The bulk slipped, stumbled, flung itself outwards and disappeared, as if the snow and wind had digested it. Something clattered down towards the river. He heard no splash.

'Come on!'

There seemed no one else, only perhaps a faint shouting, a sheeplike and inconsequential noise amid the storm. He couldn't be certain. He might be imagining it. They lumbered together up the track – twenty yards, thirty even, before they stopped to drag in freezing air, bent double with effort. The track dropped away, and they slithered after it. Clumsy, shifting pebbles suddenly under the snow. The noise of the river, water threading between the plates and banks of ice that grumbled together, quarrelling with the river's momentum.

'Where's the track?' Cass wailed.

'Christ knows!' Hyde yelled back.

The river, narrow and black except where fringed with ice, lay across their progress. Hyde, on one knee, traced it to either side of them. To the right, it rushed away, swelling and lessening in gradient. To the left – upwards – it vanished into a narrow crack in the rocks, followed by no discernible track. They were stranded on the bank of the river. The route up the pass had disappeared.

'Where is it?'

It had to be on the other side of the narrow river. He strained to see through the flying snow and ice crystals. No larger perspective, no sky or mountain peaks. Just the black, narrow defile from which the source of the river emerged.

The rustle of moved pebbles, grating icily together.

Dark figures within the storm.

'Get down!' he yelled at Cass, dragging at his sleeve. The first shots went wide. The approaching figures — two of them — became smaller, closer to the ground. Prone. 'Get across the river, Cass!' he whispered urgently against the man's ear. 'Get moving — get across the river! Cover me!'

Cass shrugged away, slithering across the pebbles like a wounded animal. Two more shots. IR nightsights. Cass' movements would have made him light up just enough in this weather. He raised his own rifle. The nightsight was old-fashioned, ineffective . . . except that the two of them lay in prone firing positions close together. He heard Cass stumble into the shock of the icy water. He squeezed the trigger of the Kalashnikov, three times. The blurred, partial IR image did not fade, but he heard a groan of pain. The returned fire was sporadic, disorderly. He slid away on his stomach, across the snow-covered pebbles of the riverbank towards the water.

'You all right?' he heard from somewhere ahead of him.

'Keep your head down!'

'The track's here! I'm sheltered —'

The river was a couple of feet deep, the rocks and pebbles slippery, the close farther bank obscured, then there, then obscured again. He couldn't feel his feet or ankles or calves. His knees and thighs worked by memory rather than volition. No more shooting, just the noise of raised voices.

Hyde collided with the bank of snow-covered rock. He clambered thankfully out of the freezing water, ice jolting against him with the malice of knives. He lay on the bank, shuddering with intensified cold.

There must be a bloody rope bridge across the river, probably no more than thirty feet away! He crawled like the first amphibian towards Cass' voice, into an alien element.

'Over here — *here*!'

Then his mittened hand was gripped by another hand, his arm pulled unmercifully. He rolled awkwardly behind the rock litter

363

where Cass crouched, the backpack skewing sideways as if to separate from him.

Their voices echoed immediately. The wind was quieter. There was rock all around them, hemming in the river at this point. But the track continued on this side of the river, Cass said it did. He needed to believe him. He listened to the soldiers' voices again, then raised himself behind the rock and rested the rifle on it. The nightsight gathered what light it primitively could. He fired again, three times, but believed he hit nothing.

He stood up, stamping his sodden boots. They couldn't halt long enough to change socks, never mind light a fire. There'd be others, soon, close behind them. They had to keep moving.

He shrugged Cass ahead of him and they located the track. Narrower now, winding away from the river between high, sheer cliffs, a litter of snow-covered rocks and gravel. The storm whisked aside, as if to encourage and then disabuse them. Peaks reared like the great heads of wild horses around them as the track climbed more steeply. A vast ice sheet glimmered. The track seemed to slip furtively beside it – or perhaps had been swallowed by it, he thought, before the snow obscured the scene once more. If the track had disappeared beneath the glacier or whatever it was –

– it hasn't. You can't afford to believe that.

It was after four thirty. The border was somewhere less than a mile ahead now. A last mile.

He was jolted into a shiver of admission. He had no idea what kind of border post or fence there might be, none whatsoever. But there had to be something, some barrier to the smugglers and separatists and bandits and refugees. Some paranoid outpost in this vast nowhere that claimed that *here* Pakistan ended, *there* Afghanistan began, however much the high peaks and the snow-fields and the glaciers mocked the idea. Soldiers.

They were clambering exhaustedly towards soldiers, not away from them.

*

'Peter, they say it's impossible –'

She caught the whisper, shook her head at it as at maddening flies. *'No –!'*

Shelley seemed afraid; genuinely concerned. 'Claude, they *must*,' he insisted. 'They must *try*.'

Rousseau was lugubrious. 'The weather is impossible. They have *one* helicopter, an old Chinook. They need it for *everything*. They can't risk it.'

'They have to.'

But, Ros realised, Shelley's eyes were already back on her travel bag. Some of the gold was inside it. Enough of the precious metal, even it wasn't to be used as a ransom for Hyde.

'No! Do something – *do* something!' she protested out of deep anguish, the tears blinding her, scalding her cheeks. 'You *must do* something!'

Colder now. Frozen. Hands and feet totally numb, even in the shelter of rocks and the storm blown out as suddenly as it had begun. So cold . . .

The noises of the soldiers thirty feet below them. The occasional, distant noises of their pursuers, coming up quickly, knowing where the border post lay and certain they were trapped between the border and pursuit.

They were. Hyde knew they wouldn't hurry, knew they were confident that this would be their last border with anything, that only death lay ahead.

The sky was filled with high, icy stars, scraps of glinting glass. The moon had gone down, having mocked them enough; satisfied it was over. He rubbed a frozen mitten over his face. Its shock failed to wake him. Cass dozed, roused, dozed beside him. His determination had fatally weakened him. Even if he got him moving, just once more, then the next time they halted, he'd roll over and die. Hyde had seen it in his eyes. And he was too exhausted to carry him. It was a vast effort even to keep nudging him awake when all he wanted was to sleep himself. The storm had retreated into Afghanistan like an apparition they couldn't follow. It obscured the more distant peaks. Beyond the border post, the track fell sharply away down a snow-covered slope towards the timberline. Seventeen thousand feet. The air was thin, debilitating. The chocolate was almost too hard to break in clumsy fingers, too cold to chew and swallow. He could smell harsh coffee being brewed below them.

The border was marked by obligatory, casual barbed wire, rolled out at either side of the track, across which lay a barrier. A hut stood beside the ridiculous painted pole. A larger barracks hut – from which most of the occasional noises emanated – lay immediately below them, smoke curling from its single tin chimney. Its roof was thickened with snow. Two guards sat in the smaller hut. There might be another half-dozen or more in the barracks hut.

He studied the scene again and again, concussed by it as he might have been by collision with the rocks around him. Dead end.

You're not going to get out of here . . .

He sat with his back against a rock, the Russian rifle cradled in his stiff arms and numb fingers, Cass nodding again into icy unconsciousness beside him – he nudged him awake once more – staring down at the smoking chimney of the hut, smelling the woodsmoke. In the other hut, the two guards were playing cards, or hunching over something else that lay interestingly between them. The snow on the roof was a faint sheen in the starlight, the chimney's skein of smoke only slightly less dark than the night.

He looked down at his hand. It was shivering, either because his eyesight was affected or his numb hand retained the capacity to register cold. It was gripped like a claw around something larger than a cricket ball and not quite round that it had found in one of his pockets. Very slowly, he relearned its nature. Weight, two-fifty grammes, the ring was a safety clip, there was the lever, the plug . . . weight of explosive, sixty grammes . . . nine hundred tenth-of-a-gramme fragments around the explosive. Lethal radius, nine metres. Four-second fuse. It was a fragmentation grenade. Now, he knew all about it . . .

The chimney smoked above the glimmer of the snow-covered roof. The barracks hut was perhaps forty feet long, but the cots or bunks would be as close to the fire as possible. Lethal radius, just about twenty-eight feet. The hut was narrower than that.

There were subdued noises from the guard hut, a startling, clear mutter from the barracks hut with its iceblind windows. Nothing from the track behind them, no sign or sound of pursuit. Not yet –

He nudged Cass awake once more. The man groaned softly, hardly protesting. It had to be now, before they both fell asleep for the last time. The roof sloped shallowly. The chimney was less tall from the peak of the roof than a standing man.

He leaned against Cass' dull face.

'*This* – ' He held up the grenade. ' – is going down the fucking chimney – understand? *Understand?*' Eventually, Cass nodded. 'When it blows, there'll be casualties *and* survivors. Mostly, there'll be panic – understand?' Again, the robotic, concentrated nodding. '*You* have to be down *there* –' He pointed at the guard hut. ' – to take care of those two.' Cass looked at the smaller hut as if for the first time. Nodded slowly, deliberately. 'Don't fucking fall asleep on me.'

'I won't.' He shifted his bulk. Ice crackled as the landscape of the parka changed. 'I won't,' he promised earnestly.

'OK.'

Cass would be awake as long as he was moving. If he stopped and fell asleep immediately, Hyde could kill the two in the guard hut from the roof of the barracks. He brought the coil of nylon rope that had bound them together out from beside him, then looped it about a sharp thrust of rock. He lashed it tight, tested it, then moved away from the cliff to lean out against the rope's tautness. The roof was directly below him. He scrabbled gently over the edge of the narrow ledge and began walking carefully backwards. His body was heavy against the air beneath him, dragging at his arms and shoulders.

Then, almost at once, he was squatting on the roof, close to the chimney. He heard gruff laughter from the guard hut. He loosened his hold on the rope and left it dangling. Dug into the snow like a small, crouching bear. Maybe two or three inches of snow, then a layer of ice – shit. Cautiously, he began moving up the slope of the roof, his frozen fingers curled into claws, his dulled feet pushing gently inside the ice-stiffened, unyielding boots. He slid forward softly, mechanically. Weight thrown forward, not looking up. There were quiet noises from beneath the roof. He glanced once towards the guard hut. Two faces in warm light glimpsed through the window's closing pupil of ice. He leaned his weight further forward as the angle of the roof increased, a frozen wave repelling him. With relief, he heard Cass moving, the scrape of his boots on frozen rock. Bugger hadn't fallen asleep, then –

He began sliding, his feet losing purchase, hands unable to grip, everything happening slowly. He dropped flat, spread-eagling himself on the snow, toes digging in, hands searching for the edges of wooden tiles, finding, finding – *one*. His body skewed to a halt, then, scrabbling with his right hand, he found a second tile that wasn't flush. He stopped. Incredibly, his body was hot.

He listened. Began again, easing himself on his stomach, sloughing himself through the snow, making more noise. At first it would be snow falling from the roof, then the noises would be too regular and suspicious to those awake. He wriggled up the angle of the roof, finally slapping one hand over the ridge, then the other hand. Shimmied sideways towards the chimney. Someone muttered from inside now, drawing attention to the noises he had made. He gripped the blackened tin chimney. The smoke leaked out of it, reluctant to leave the barrack hut's warmth. He eased himself upright, one foot planted uncertainly on either side of the apex of the roof. More murmuring below now, and an angry response from someone newly disturbed. He reached into his pocket and brought out the grenade. Pulled the pin, released the lever with a relaxation of the clawed right hand, and dropped the grenade down the chimney. It rattled like a stone.

Three – four.

Smoke and soot erupted over him as he slid away from the chimney. Snow grumbled down the roof. Windows shattered. Screams. The glare of the scattered fire blazing on the snow – no, the place was catching alight. The chimney belched smoke and screaming. The door of the barracks hut opened – door of the guard hut was banging open, too. Something fell on the snow beside the track, burning and torn. The screaming was louder, tormented. Nine hundred fragments. A spirally bound steel wire, pre-notched, which the explosive charge metamorphosed into splinters. Lethal radius, nine metres. Eyes, face, arms, legs, organs.

He slid down the roof, reached its edge and dropped onto the blind side of the hut, his boots crunching on fragments of glass buried in the snow. The screaming just went on, helplessly. Firing from the guard hut. He raised himself and looked into the burning interior of the barracks hut. Two bodies still in their bunks, bedclothing ripped as if by savage beaks or claws. A torn body, lying on the floor. Something that had once been human must have been crouched near the fire, for warmth. It had been shredded by the steel splinters from the grenade. Then he moved, clumping heavily through the snow that had drifted on that side of the hut, towards the guard hut, where fire was being returned through the broken pupil of the window. *And* from the door.

There'd been four in the barracks hut –

– *officer?* Separate quarters. He whirled round, but the figure with a heavy greatcoat flung over a nightshirt was already fumbling with the safety of the rifle. Hyde dropped to one knee and fired. The Kalashnikov, on automatic, emptied itself in a fraction of a second. The greatcoat fell leadenly into the snow beside the track, lit by flames as the wooden barracks hut really caught and flames gouted above the roof and through the windows like desperate, pleading arms. He dimly felt the warmth of the fire on his face.

Jammed a new magazine into the rifle, turning on his knee. He couldn't see Cass. Saw one figure at the window and fired two shots. Hit nothing, was almost glad. Except that they had to pass the hut. Fired again as a shadow moved.

'Where are you?' he called in the silence that crackled with unreal flames. Warmth on his neck, seeping into him.

'Other side!' he heard.

'All right?'

'– not much more help!' he heard, fainter. Cass was blown out, shuddering down into silence like a rackety machine.

He looked up at the night sky. Grey was leaking into it somewhere over China, beyond the closer peaks. No navigation lights, but it wouldn't be long, and they wouldn't be friendly either –

He could hear nothing from the pass beyond the barracks hut, just its cold, crackling fire. He raised himself into a crouch, as if carrying a huge rock. His legs were quivering as weariness buffeted him. Then he lurched towards the guard hut, watching it joggle in his vision, watching the window, the window, watching –

– *one.* Fired. Window empty. Watching, watching –

– blundered against the wood of the hut, making the structure quiver. Glanced through the shattered window. Nothing at first, then a leg stuck out from beyond the crude table. A shadow slumped over its edge. Moaning softly. Wounded. The scene blurred and then was gone as he left the window. He ducked heavily beneath the pole – the *border*, welcome to Afghanistan. It didn't work because he had no good memories the country's name could dredge up.

He found Cass beside the road, kneeling on the ground as if praying. Slumped beside him, heavily on one knee. Weariness was at once paralysis.

'All right? *Phil* – all right? Bugger you, all *right*?'

Cass looked up blankly.

'There's no fucking more of this, is there?' he growled.

Hyde shook his head.

'Let's get moving . . . come on, Phil,' he coaxed. 'There's no one alive, no one following –' For the moment anyway. Hyde got to his feet, one stiff, weak arm around Cass, hoisting him. They leaned together like saplings in a gale. The grey was staining the eastern sky with cautious optimism. The barracks hut was diminishing into a smaller fire. 'Come on.'

The track remained narrow, but sloped downwards. They stumbled along its twists until they were out of sight of the border post's ruins.

Cass stumbled, fell spreadeagled as if staked out on the snowy track. Didn't move. Hyde knew he wouldn't get up again. They were both finished.

Then he heard the rotor noise. Saw the navigation lights blinking against the stars, coming on fast from inside Pakistan. Pakistan . . . Cass was right, just lying there. He was making the right choice. There were two sets of lights, two helicopters. They emerged around their lights as black, bulbous-headed shapes, hovering like great insects over the dying flames of the barracks hut. Hyde sat in the snow, dumbly fascinated by the instruments of his defeat. He couldn't see the fire, but it flickered on the bellies of the two helicopters. Snow drifted in the updraught, the rotor racket banged back off the walls of the pass. Then they dropped out of sight, and their noise nosed ahead of them as they began following the track. Only moments now. Two Alouette IIIs. The dying firelight had flickered on wire-guided missiles slung at each flank of both helicopters. Eight missiles, two cannon – minimum armament. *You won't feel a thing* . . .

The rotor noise boomed ahead of the invisible Alouettes,

becoming louder, deafening him. Snow began to pucker and lift at the last twist of the track, then become a tiny blizzard blowing ahead of the two helicopters. The noise and power of the engines throbbed in the rutted, gravelly track. The finger of a searchlight moved into view. It was hypnotic, mesmerising, so that he wished to bring it to an immediate conclusion by running back up the track towards them. The light splashed on the beard of a frozen stream.

'Oh – *shit*!' Cass yelled, his voice tiny and hoarse. He glared wildly as the first of the Alouettes drifted into view, shadowy behind the smoke of snow its rotors threw up. Nose down like a hound.

Cass struggled to his knees, grimacing with pain and exhaustion. Pushed himself, but couldn't stand, then began scrabbling on all fours away from the helicopter. Hyde watched him, motionless. The blunt, blind nose of the Alouette stared at him as he sat in the snow, cross-legged like a Buddha. It paused. The second chopper lifted out of the snow and swept up and over them, then dropped into position farther down the track, nose up in the hover. Cass was blindly crawling towards it.

Hundreds of feet below them, the pass opened out into a narrow valley. Now that the sky was almost half stained with the pre-dawn, he could make out the distant timberline, even the faint spot of a frozen lake. And the mountains stretching away. You weren't – ever – going to get out of this . . . not ever.

Cass had stopped crawling. He remained on his knees, staring at the Alouette that had blocked the track below them. Hyde stared at the other helicopter as it studied him.

Snow drifted down on his shoulders and head. On his arms, hands, the rifle. The snow crept forward from the updraught. The helicopter was diminishing inside its own created snow-storm, like the miniature scene in a glass ball turned upside down. It lost feature – *he* lost feature. From shape to shadow to indeterminate something –

– he crawled to Cass, nudged him, shivering with anticipation. Gestured upwards, behind them. A gleam of frozen water. A slit in the rocks, big enough for two of them?

He braced himself against the rock, half-thrusting Cass into the crevice behind the narrow, frozen dribble of the waterfall. The Alouette lifted out of its own snow-fog, disconcerted. Hyde watched it. The other one did the same. They buzzed together like pedagogues discovering disobedience to their authority.

Then, a third set of navigation lights.

All remaining resolve collapsed.

The lights dropped lower as the two Alouettes stared at each other, then turned, looking in different directions, bemused but still ultimately assured. A big troop carrier, by the look of it. Chinook?

At once, the Alouettes flipped upwards like fleas towards the bigger, two-rotored helicopter. They entered the hover on either side of it. A light splashed down from the Chinook, spraying the frozen track with droplets of silver. The light raked back and forth like a finger locating a word amid a page of text.

Red cross on the belly of the Chinook, illuminated by the light from one of the Alouettes.

Swallowing icy air, he stepped out onto the track, arms raised above his head, waving feebly. The light moved towards him, then beyond, then flicked back, surrounding him. The two Alouettes remained peremptorily in the hover. Then the Chinook dropped towards him.

'Phil!' he bellowed hysterically. 'Phil – *get out here, for Christ's sake –!'*

Cass was heavily beside him, blundering into him, to be contained in the blinding, magic aura from the Chinook's searchlight. The Alouettes remained stationary – they needed orders.

Medicins sans Frontières. He could read it blazoned along the flank of the Chinook. An arm waving, near the open cargo door. The Chinook fitted itself into the narrowness of the pass like a matron settling into a small chair. The arm beckoned.

Cass and he stumbled forward together. French helicopters, French doctors, *French* . . . untouchable, never know when you might want arms or aid from the Frogs. God *bless* the bloody Frogs —!

Hands and arms lifted them gently into the interior of the Chinook. Into safety.

POSTLUDE

'Change is not made without inconvenience,
even from worse to better.'
Richard Hooker: *Ecclesiastical Polity*

Hyde looked out across Bennelong Point, where the Opera House glittered almost as fiercely as the wrinkled, yacht-carved water. Then he looked towards the Harbour Bridge and then the ferries waddling like the pigeons in and out of Circular Quay. The sun was high and hot. Almost Christmas, in Sydney. He chewed on a burger and sipped at the frosted can of Foster's. Tourists and office-workers drifted past him, luxuriating in another almost endless day of sunshine and heat. He wriggled his feet in his trainers.

The burger bun was tasteless and dry and he put down the remainder of his lunch on the bench beside him. The light on the water hurt. Ros was with her lawyers. Her uncle's estate was becoming like Jarndyce versus Jarndyce. She'd get through it though, and be wealthy, he had no doubt. He turned on the bench and looked, as if with irritation, at the massed soldiery of the business high-rises, over-shadowing Government House and the Botanical Gardens. The sun heated his back now. He smiled when he remembered that he thought he might shatter like a cartoon cat when Ros had first grabbed hold of him and almost squeezed the breath from him. He tossed his head, amused.

The Chinook hadn't bothered to argue with the two Alouettes, merely challenged them to follow it into Afghanistan. All the *élan* the Frogs could muster, and they were home free, wrapped in crackling foil like oven-ready turkeys ... drugged, chafed, debriefed. Rubbing them back to life in the Chinook had been more significant than Shelley's endless, patient questions.

He looked down at the copy of *The Australian* he had bought to read while he hung about for Ros – in her best suit, like a uniform with braid and buttons. She'd soon have plenty of cash, own a sheep station, property in King's Cross and Paddington – *Sydney* not London, and that struck him like indigestion. Good old Uncle Bruce.

Third headline, front page. *Congress Party squeezes home in Indian election.* The Sharmars had done it – just. Mehta, the film star and fundamentalist, had been edged out after six weeks of neck-and-neck.

And Shelley and the Foreign Office – and the French, he suspected – knew all about the drug-smuggling. They had a *lever*. Already, Sharmar had had *very* nice things to say about European investment in India. The Foreign Secretary himself had appeared briefly in Hyde's life. His bespectacled features and quiff of white hair had been sufficient warning, even without the reminder of Hyde's obligations towards the Official Secrets Act. Don't tell the *Sun* was what it amounted to. Or *Private Eye*.

He finished his beer and spread his fingers on his thighs. A happy ending. He'd survived, he'd got Cass out, saved his life. Cass had been patched up but had taken longer to recover than he had. He was now on extended leave, Florida or somewhere warm, and Tony Godwin had promised him a job on his return. He hadn't got Ros killed by dragging her into it – thank God. He was a wealthy woman's lover . . . a woman who, he was certain, wanted to stay in Oz. Didn't want either of them to go back . . .

Hyde sighed, frowning. A tiny sense of betrayal in his chest.

He attempted to ignore everything except the flexing of warm muscles in the sun, entertain nothing but the darts and glides of small sailing boats. Every detail would disappear into that glitter of light if he so much as squinted.

Everything except the letter he'd had from Aubrey. The one he'd crumpled into his pocket, unopened, suspecting Ros' reaction. The letter he'd read after leaving her at the lawyers'. The letter he'd just finished re-reading.

Aubrey needed his help. Unofficially, since the old man was as retired as he was himself. He was offering him a job, *work*. He'd ring him, soon . . .

CRAIG THOMAS

SEA LEOPARD

For Mike, agent and friend
and in memoriam Anthea Joseph,
a kind courageous lady

Acknowledgements

I wish to thank particularly my wife, Jill, for her strict and expert editing of the book, and for her initial suggestion that I attempt this story.

My thanks, also, to GH who acted as captain of the submarine HMS *Proteus*, and to the Royal Navy, without whose assistance, given so freely and willingly, I could not have completed the book. Gratitude, too, to TRJ for coming to my assistance in developing the 'Leopard' anti-sonar equipment on which the story hinges.

As usual, I am indebted to various publications, particularly to Breyer & Polmar's *Guide to the Soviet Navy*, Labayle & Couhat's *Combat Fleets of the World*, and *The Soviet War Machine*, edited by Ray Bonds.

Any errors, distortion or licence for dramatic purposes is my responsibility, not that of any of the above.

Craig Thomas,
Lichfield 1980

Principal Characters

Kenneth de Vere AUBREY	: Deputy Director, British Intelligence (SIS)
Patrick HYDE	: a field agent of SIS
Ethan CLARK, USN	: on liaison to the Admiralty
QUIN	: an eminent electronic engineer
Tricia QUIN	: his daughter
Col. Giles PYOTT, RA	: a member of the NATO StratAn Committee
Comm. Richard LLOYD, RN	: captain of the submarine HMS *Proteus*
Lt. Comm. John THURSTON, RN	: first lieutenant, HMS *Proteus*
Sir Richard CUNNINGHAM	: Director of British Intelligence ('C')
Peter SHELLEY	: assistant to the Deputy Director, SIS
Sqn. Ldr. Alan EASTOE, RAF	: Nimrod pilot
Valery ARDENYEV, Red Navy	: O/C Underwater Special Ops. Unit
DOLOHOV	: admiral of the Red Banner Northern Fleet
Tamas PETRUNIN	: KGB Resident, Soviet embassy in London
Viktor TEPLOV	: petty officer to Ardenyev's unit

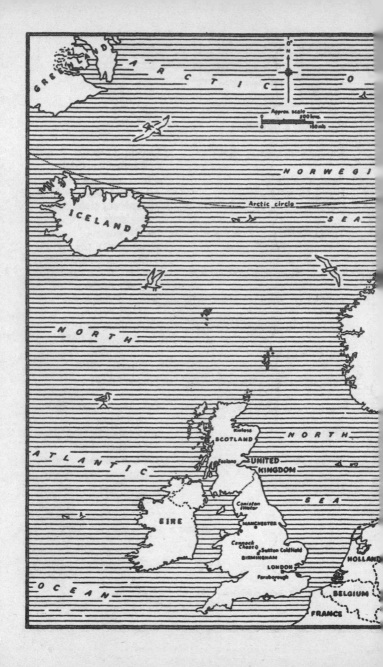

PLESSEY The Plessey Company Limited
Millbank Tower, 21-24, Millbank, London SW1 4QP
Telephone: 01-834 8641 Telex: 917830

Commodore D. N. Blackshaw, R.N.,
Senior Projects Officer,
Royal Navy (Projects),
Old Admiralty Building,
Whitehall,
LONDON.

Dear Commodore,

In considering your urgent request to the company
to accelerate the final stages of development of
the field prototype of our 'Leopard' project, I
am advised by the project head, Dr. A. J. Quin,
that it is possible to shorten the time prior to
full sea trials, only by a matter of a few days.
I respect the urgency of the matter, and understand
the kind of mission on which 'Leopard' would be
of inestimable value, but I am afraid that is the
best we can do.

Yours sincerely,

R. M. Bennett,
<u>Deputy Chairman</u>.

Registered in England and W₂ les at Vicarage Lane, Ilford, Essex IG1 4AQ Number 203848

PLESSEY The Plessey Company Limited
Millbank Tower, 21-24, Millbank, London SW1 4~
Telephone: 01-834 9841 Telex 917530

INTER OFFICE MEMO

<u>from</u>:   Head of Project L

<u>to</u>:   Head of Research

<u>ref</u>:   LEOPARD'

I quite realise the pressure you must be under
from the Board to achieve results.   You may,
when you report to them, inform them of the
following:-

The broad effect of 'Leopard' is already working.
We have progressed to the point where we can
prevent an enemy sonar signal registering the
presence of a vessel using 'Leopard', and we
can also, after nullifying that signal with the
equipment, return to the enemy a false echo as
if from the sea bed below the submarine.

The remaining problems are related to the
variable quality of the false signal.   I am
confident the improvements can be made.

Registered in England and Wales at Vicarage Lane, Ilford, Essex IG1 4AQ Number 292048

SIS
F. TTR 1a
TAPE TRANSCRIPTIONS

FILE REF   SIS/26554/3A - PH/Aubrey

TAPE No   B/163487/68/4/23

DATE

REFERS   QUIN - DISAPPEARANCE

Tape
Mark

.......continued

furthermore, none of his personal effects appear
to have been removed from the flat.   There is
still mail behind the door, dating back more than
three weeks.   There have been no subsequent
sightings.

In conclusion, I think the bird has flown.   On
the other hand, I don't believe it was his decision.
There was no pre-planning.   Coupled with the
information regarding the 'Trade Mission' arrivals
and departures at the Soviet embassy during the
relevant period, I am certain that Quin was snatched
and is now in Moscow.

I am inclined to believe that his daughter is with
him, since Birmingham Special Branch haven't had a
peep from her since the time of Quin's disappearance.

I have ordered the continuance of 24-hour
surveillance on the flat Qu'- occupied in Bracknell
and on his estranged wife's home in Sutton Coldfield.

P4

Patrick Hyde

LEOPARD 42
MOST SECRET

You requested a copy of the accompanying report on the
sea trials of the LEOPARD anti-detection equipment as
soon as possible, together with a summary in layman's
terms.

As you know, a specially equipped Nimrod and a Sea King
helicopter were used in the sea trials with HMS _Proteus_.
They could not effectively detect or pinpoint the submarine
on any single occasion.

The full report is complex and highly technical, as well
as being liberally sprinkled with service jargon!
However, I have discussed it with the Director of
Technical Services Section, and he has summarised the
sea trials in the following terms:-

   i.   No problems were encountered with the hull sensors;

  ii.   The 'noise generator' unit effectively cancelled
        all external acoustic emissions, and dealt
        successfully with all attempts to detect the
        submarine using sonar;

 iii.   In shallower waters, the unit's delayed response
        system effectively transmitted a sonar echo
        which accurately simulated a 'seabed' response -
        in other words, the vessels seeking out HMS _Proteus_
        only registered the seabed and not the submarine.
        She was effectively 'invisible', as expected.

DEFENCE DEPARTMENT (NAVY)
UNITED STATES NAVAL INTELLIGENCE

USN (Intelligence) Form TAL 1

Our Ref	Deputy Director
Your Ref	Capt. E. V. Clark, USN
Date	

page 2 of 2

so I don't have to tell you how much of a threat
to the British, to ourselves and to the whole of
NATO the new Soviet sonar buoy carpet in the
Barents Sea represents. Unless it is fully
mapped, and therefore neutralised as a threat,
the Soviet Navy can close the Barents Sea at any
time, and that would mean the loss of NATO's
northern flank without a shot being fired.

For the reasons I have outlined, it was decided
that the Navy Department ask the British Royal
Navy to investigate and chart this new sonar
carpet, codenamed CHESSBOARD, using the submarine
<u>Proteus</u>, with the new LEOPARD equipment. The
submarine, if your reports on her sea trials are
accurate, should remain undetected throughout
the time she is in the area of the Barents Sea.

Your brief is liaison and observation, both for
the Navy Department and for NATO. Don't overstep
your mission orders, but get back to this office
immediate and direct through the embassy if
anything happens you don't like. Neither the
Director nor myself are really happy about risking
this LEOPARD equipment, if it's as good as they
say. But, we don't have much choice.

Adml. J. K. Vandenburg, USN,
Deputy Director,
US Navy Intelligence.

Part One

A Game At Chess

One: BAIT

The office of Tamas Petrunin, Trade Attaché at the Soviet embassy in London, looked out upon Kensington Palace Gardens, across the lawns of the embassy grounds. The straight lines of bare plane trees marked the boundary between himself and the western city he both despised and coveted. A fierce early spring wind searched for, and found, the remains of last autumn's leaves, and hurried them along the road and beneath the wrought-iron gates into the drive of the embassy, finally scattering them like burnt secret messages and papers over the gravel and the grass. The sky was unrelievedly grey, and had been threatening rain all morning. Tamas Petrunin had leisure to reflect, as he listened angrily to the tape cassette from the duty room and its recorded conversation, that London irritated him particularly at that time of year. *There was no snow.* Wind, and rain – an umbrella threatening to turn inside out carried by an old man passing the gate, unceremoniously jostled by the wind – wind and rain, but little snow. Only sleet in the evening air sometimes, turning instantly to slush in the gutters, like a promise broken. In Moscow, there would be inches of snow, and everyone rotund and animalised in fur coats and hats.

The Scotsman's recorded voice enraged him. Almost always it did. Now nasality and meaning combined to grip his stomach with an indigestion of rage.

'We have been trying to contact you for two days,' the authoritative Russian voice insisted. Ruban, the Naval Attaché who worked under the auspices of Petrunin and the KGB at the embassy. 'You fully understand how difficult movement outside London is for our people here. Why have you not contacted us on schedule? Now you say the submarine has sailed.'

There was an additional nasality, and a promoted, cultivated cough in the Scot's voice when he replied. 'I've been in bed with the flu. It's no' my fault. I havena been to

3

work all week. I've been in my bed, y'understand?' The whine was almost rebellious.

'We do not pay you to be ill, MacFarlane.'

'I couldna help it. I still feel lousy. I got up to come to the phone. There's fog, too.' A small, projected bout of coughing followed the weather bulletin. Petrunin, in spite of his anger, could not suppress a smile.

'When did the submarine sail from Faslane?'

'Three nights ago, early hours.'

'What? *Three* nights? What else did you learn?'

'I couldna ask, could I? Just that she sailed three nights ago.'

'You are useless to us!' stormed Ruban on the tape behind Petrunin. One of the embassy chauffeurs was walking, leaning against the wind, towards a parked black Mercedes saloon. His black uniform trousers were flapping around his legs, and he was holding his peaked cap firmly on his head.

'I couldna help it – it was no' my fault if I caught the damn flu, was it?'

'Was the equipment on board? Do you know that much for certain?'

'I heard it was.'

'You don't *know*?'

'Yes, dammit, it was on board!' The Scot sniffled on the tape. Petrunin pictured him. Pale, rat-faced, unshaven, untrustworthy. Trash. He was poor material with which to start a blaze. Ruban thought so too, by the sound of his voice. Ruban would have to report to Murmansk, via himself, and they would have to decide, on MacFarlane's word alone, whether the British submarine *Proteus* was carrying the 'Leopard' equipment or not when she slipped out of Faslane into the Atlantic three nights before.

'You're guessing,' Ruban said after a pause. 'You can't know for certain.'

'I'm sure, dammit! Nothing was taken off the ship after she returned from sea trials with this "Leopard" stuff!' MacFarlane had forgotten his habitual ingratiating manner. 'I found out that much. Nothing came off the ship.'

'And where is she now?'

4

'I dinna know.' MacFarlane retreated from anger into surliness.

'And that ends your report?'

In the silence that followed, Petrunin moved to his desk and switched off the cassette player. Then he returned to the window of his office, rubbing his chin. In no more than thirty minutes, he would have to summon Ruban, and they would have to make a decision before five or five-thirty as to the nature of the signal they would send to Moscow Centre and to Red Banner Northern Fleet HQ, Murmansk, EYES ONLY Admiral Dolohov. Damn MacFarlane and his attack of influenza.

'Leopard'. Was it on board? If so, then the likelihood that *Proteus* was on her way to map the location and extent of the newest Soviet sonar-grid across the Barents Sea from North Cape to Murmansk was transmuted into a virtual certainty. The only way to do that was by means of a submarine indetectable by sonar; which would mean *Proteus* using the 'Leopard' equipment. Ethan Clark, the American expert, was in London on liaison work, *Proteus* had sailed on secret orders to an unknown destination as soon as her sea trials were complete. It was a likelihood – was it a certainty?

Petrunin paced the room carefully, keeping to the border of the patterned Turkish carpet, studying his footsteps with apparent intentness, rubbing his chin lightly with thumb and forefinger in a ceaseless motion of his hand. *Proteus* had to reach North Cape in order for the Red Banner Fleet's cock-eyed plan to be put into operation. If she were sailing elsewhere, all the preparations would have been a waste of time and effort.

Petrunin found himself before the window again. The newly-imprisoned leaves seemed to be scurrying aimlessly across the embassy lawns, seeking escape. He shook his head. *Proteus*'s target had to be 'Chessboard'. The development of 'Leopard' had been violently accelerated during the past six months, the sea trials had been conducted with maximum haste; both facts implied an urgent task for the equipment. After all, there were no other 'Leopard' units as yet, none fitted to any submarine or surface ship in the Royal Navy. Just this one priceless

5

example of anti-sonar equipment, being used for one special task –

Yes. He nodded vigorously. He would go over it again with Ruban in fifteen minutes or so, but he had decided. They would signal Moscow and Murmansk that *Proteus* was on her way north, making for North Cape. Then it was up to the Red Banner Fleet.

And, he reminded himself, not for the first time that afternoon, there then devolved upon himself the task of finding Quin. Quin, the inventor and developer of 'Leopard'. Disappeared without trace. Not under protective custody, because British Intelligence, the Directorate of Security and Special Branch were all looking for him. Quin. More important – at least in Petrunin's estimation – than 'Leopard' itself. Where was he?

He realised, with a mounting disappointment, that his decision with regard to *Proteus* was no decision at all. Merely a side-issue , a piece of self-indulgence, a war-game for sailors. Quin was what mattered. And Quin could not be found.

It had become routine, watching the house in Sutton Coldfield, in a quiet, residential street between the roads to Lichfield and Brownhills. A pre-war detached house, standing a little back from the road and elevated above its level, partially screened by a stone wall and a dark hedge. Leaded windows, trained ivy like an artificial ageing process climbing wooden trelliswork around the front door, and cherry blossom trees waiting for the spring. The street was still stained from the recent rain, and the slim boles of the trees gleamed green. Routine, boring routine. The young officer of the Special Branch unit attached to the West Midlands constabulary knew the façade of the house in which Quin's divorced wife lived with a familiarity that had become sour and stultifying. She worked part-time in the elegantly refurbished premises of an antique shop a hundred yards away. She was there now. The Special Branch Officer had parked his unmarked Ford Escort so that he had a clear view of the house and the entrance of the shop. He had observed well-dressed women, the occasional couple, a small delivery van, but no

6

sign, none whatsoever, of Quin or of his daughter who had disappeared from her teacher training college in Birmingham at the same time that he had vanished. And there had been no visitors to the house except the milkman, the grocery delivery on a Thursday, the fish van on Wednesdays –

Sugden found himself idly flicking through the leaves of his notebook, rehearsing the boredom of two weeks' surveillance of the quiet street in a quiet suburb, shook his head, and snapped the notebook shut on the seat beside him. He put another cigarette to his lips, lit it, looked at his watch – Mrs Quin would be coming home for a salad lunch in another half-an-hour – and slid lower in the driving seat, attempting to stretch his legs. He yawned. He and Lane, day and night for two weeks, just in case the missing man contacted the wife he'd left four years before, or in case the daughter turned up.

No chance, he told himself with a spiteful satisfaction that seemed to revenge him on the London superiors who had placed him in his present limbo, no chance at all. It was even duller work than preparing for the visit of the Queen to a Lichfield school a couple of years before, or Princess Margaret's opening of another Lichfield school before that, just after he had joined the Branch in Birmingham. Dull, deadly, dead. Quin and the girl had gone over. Not voluntarily, of course. Kidnapped. Snatched. Sugden yawned again. Quin was building 'Leopard' for the Soviet Union by now, watched by his friendly neighbourhood KGB man. Despite wishing to maintain a frosty contempt for his present task and for those who had given him his orders, Sugden smiled to himself. Once Mrs Quin was inside the house, a quick sandwich and a pint for him in the pub opposite the antique showroom. In the window seat, he could just about see the path up to the Quin house. Well enough, anyway. Certainly he could observe any car that parked near the house, or a pedestrian on the pavement.

He wondered why Quin had left his wife. Perhaps she had left him. They'd moved down to London when he began working for Plessey, and she'd come back to the Midlands after the separation because both of them were from the area and because the girl, Tricia, was enrolled at a

7

training college in Birmingham. She'd repeated her first year twice, the file said, then failed her second year after the decree nisi, and only someone's pull high-up had prevented her from being expelled from the college. Now she'd disappeared along with her father. Another lever for the KGB to use on him, Sugden presumed. Mrs Quin looked pleasant and capable. Greying blonde hair, smartly turned out, could be taken for early forties. Quin, from the look of his picture – on the dash of the Escort – wasn't much of a catch, at least not in looks. The girl was pretty, but student-scruffy rather than making the most of herself. Almost drab, like the female of some brightly-plumaged species of bird.

She came down the path as Sugden rubbed his face and stifled another yawn. Tricia Quin, coming out of her mother's house. The closing of the door alerted him. She took no notice of the car, turned left, and began walking briskly down the hill towards the Lichfield Road. Frayed denims, a long cardigan in some sludgy colour beneath a *cagoule*, untidy fair hair. Tricia Quin.

She was almost fifty or sixty yards down the hill before his hand jerked at the door handle, and he got out of the Escort. He could not believe it, though the confirmatory photograph was in his hand. He opened his mouth, fish-slow and silently, and then slammed the door behind him with an angry curse. He appeared stupid, would appear stupid, even when he took the girl in . . .

A rush of thoughts then. Quin might be in the country after all – the girl, how had she got in last night, how had Lane missed her? – comfortable thought, that. Lane's fault – where was Quin? Door opening and closing in the empty house with its For Sale notice, the one he'd suggested using but permission had been denied, too much paperwork to take it over – door closing, the girl further away down the hill, oblivious of him.

Or of the squat-featured, heavy-looking man in the grey double-breasted suit coming down the path of the empty house, a taller, thinner man running behind him. Both of them running, no more than twenty yards away from him now, and perhaps a hundred or so from the girl. KGB, so obvious he wanted to laugh, so sudden their appearance he could not move and was aware only of their numerical superiority.

'Wait a minute –' he managed to say, stepping round the Escort on to the pavement. The one in the grey suit ran with his thick arm extended; palm outwards, to fend him off like a rugby player; the thinner man dodged round the offside of Sugden's car. They were going to get past him, no doubt of it. 'Wait!'

He ducked outside the extended hand, felt it heave at his shoulder, then got a hold on the arm behind it, ripping the grey sleeve of the suit immediately. A heavy fist swung at the edge of his vision and caught him on the temple. He was immediately dizzy.

The heavy man said something in Russian. Mrs Quin was coming out of the shop. Sugden could see her over the roof of the car as the heavy man lurched him against it. The thinner man was galloping down the middle of the road, no athlete but certain to overtake the still unaware girl.

Sugden opened his mouth and bellowed her name. The heavy man struck upwards into Sugden's groin with his knee. Sugden doubled up, retching and groaning, his head turned sideways. The girl had become instantly alert, then had begun to run. The heavy man cursed, and moved away after aiming a foot at Sugden's head and connecting with his shoulder. Both men were running off. Sugden, groaning, his eyes wet with the latest wave of pain, knew he had to concentrate. They would want everything in his report.

Three hundred yards away, still just identifiable, Tricia Quin boarded a cream and blue bus as it pulled away, heading into the centre of Sutton Coldfield. The two Russians were just short of her, and the traffic lights were in the bus's favour. She was gone; they'd lost her, just as he had.

He rolled on to his back, still clutching his genitals, and listened to the tattoo of Mrs Quin's high heels on the pavement as she ran towards him.

Patrick Hyde hurried through the rooms of the empty house, as if their last, impermanent occupants might yet be overtaken and restrained, just so long as he displayed sufficient haste. Two camp beds in one of the bedrooms, spare linen in the airing cupboard on the landing, food still in cardboard boxes, mostly tinned stuff, the refrigerator half-full, six-packs of lager, bottles of vodka. The two KGB men must have arrived before Birmingham Special Branch began its surveillance. The almost full dustbins at the side of the house suggested they had moved in almost as soon as Quin first disappeared.

Hyde snorted with self-derision and with an anger that included himself, Kenneth Aubrey, the DS, Special Branch, everyone. Quin had simply panicked, hidden himself. Or had he – ? He could even be dead, and they might want the girl for some other reason . . .

Quin is alive, and well, and living somewhere in England, he reminded himself.

He turned to the police inspector who had followed at his heels through the house. 'No sign of them now, sport?' He dropped immediately into a strengthened accent, one he had never himself possessed but which he used always to remind others of his Australian origins – because he knew it irritated them, and it served in some way to dissociate him from their incompetence. The only person secure from its mockery was Kenneth Aubrey. 'A right bloody cock-up, mate. Wouldn't you say?'

The police inspector controlled his features. He disliked having to deal with someone from Intelligence rather than from what he would have considered the 'proper channels', counter-intelligence. He could see no reason why Hyde, as SIS operative, should be officially functioning inside the United Kingdom, and displaying his superiority so evidently. A bloody Aussie . . .

'You'd like to speak with Sugden now, I suppose, Mr Hyde?' he said through thinned lips, hardly opening his teeth to emit the sounds.

Hyde scowled. 'Too bloody right, Blue. Where is he?'

The inspector pointed to the lounge window, across at the Quin house. 'Mrs Quin looked after him, then he radioed in. He's still there. The doctor's taken a look at him.'

'Bruised balls. He's lucky they were only playing with him, okay let's have a word with him.' The inspector made

10

as if to precede Hyde from the room. He was taller, thicker set, in uniform. Hyde's voice and manner seemed to dismiss all of it. Hyde wagged a finger at him, bringing two points of colour to the policeman's cheekbones. 'And *you* called the Branch?'

'Sugden is their man.'

'You were instructed to call me – not the Branch, or the DS, or the Home Secretary or Her Majesty the Queen Mum – me. Next time, call me direct. Reverse the charges if you have to, but call me. Quin is mine.' Hyde made Quin sound like part of his diet. The inspector seethed in silence, allowing Hyde to leave the room in front of him, just in case the Australian saw his eyes and their clear message. 'It's a bloody cock-up!' Hyde called back over his shoulder. 'Too much bloody *time* has gone by!'

Hyde banged open the front door and went down the path, the same urgency possessing his slight frame. His denims and pale windcheater over a check shirt did nothing to endear or recommend him to the inspector, who nevertheless dutifully followed him across the road and up the path to Mrs Quin's door. Hyde rang the bell repeatedly.

'The woman's had a shock, you know,' the inspector cautioned.

Hyde turned on him. 'She bloody well knew we wanted her husband and her daughter. Did she ring? No bloody fear. She almost got her precious daughter nobbled by the KGB – '

Mrs Quin opened the door on its safety-chain. Her hair had freed itself from the restraint of lacquer, and two separate locks fell across her left eye. She brushed at them. Hyde showed her no identification, but she studied the uniformed inspector behind him, then released the chain on the door. Hyde walked past her into the cool, dim hall. Mrs Quin caught up with him. Her mouth trembling. The inspector closed the door softly.

'Where is he, Mrs Quin?'

'In the lounge, lying down.' Her tone was apologetic. She offered Sugden's comfort as a token of her good intentions. 'Poor man.'

'I'll talk to him. Then I'll want to have a word with you, Mrs Quin.'

11

'Mr Hyde – ' the inspector began.

Hyde turned to look at him. 'Too late for that.'

Hyde went into the lounge and closed the door behind him. Sugden was lying on a chaise longue, his face still pale, his tie askew, jacket draped over the arm of an easy-chair. His face arranged itself into a memory of pain, through which guilt thrust itself like the outbreak of some malady.

'Mr Hyde – ' he began.

'Don't apologise, sonny, it's too late for that,' Hyde pulled an armchair in front of the chaise.

'But I am sorry, Mr Hyde. I just didn't know they were there.'

'You cocked it up, son. You didn't expect the girl, you didn't expect the heavy mob – what did you expect?'

Sugden tried to sit up, to make himself feel at less of a disadvantage. Hyde waved him back, and he slumped on the chaise, his hand gently seeking his genitals. He winced. Hyde grinned mirthlessly.

'I don't know.'

Hyde took out a notebook and passed it to Sugden. 'These are your descriptions of the two men?' Sugden nodded. 'They don't ring any bells with me. They could have been brought in for this. The KGB has trouble travelling. They didn't get the girl?' Sugden shook his head vehemently. 'Neither did we. When did she arrive?'

'Mrs Quin didn't say.'

'She will. You know what it means, mm?'

'They haven't got Quin?'

'Too true they haven't. Shit, we should have guessed they didn't have him!' Hyde slapped his hands on his thighs. 'Why the bloody hell did we assume they did? Too many post-Imperial hang-ups in Whitehall, sport – that's the bloody answer. Quin's gone, we're so incompetent and wet, they must have him. It's what we British deserve.' He saw Sugden staring at him, and grinned. The expression seemed to open his face, smooth its hard edges. It surprised Sugden as much as his words had done. 'My hobby-horse. I race it around the track once in a while. Trouble is, I fell for it this time.'

'You don't think much of us, do you?'

12

'Too right. Not a lot. You're all a lot more sophisticated than us Aussies, but it doesn't get you anywhere, especially with the KGB. Bloody Russians wouldn't last five minutes in Brisbane.' Hyde stood up 'OK, sport, interrogation's over for now. I'm going to have a word with Mum. She has a lot of explaining to do.'

He found Mrs Quin and the inspector sitting in the breakfast kitchen, sipping tea from dark blue and gold cups.

'Mr Hyde – '

'Very cosy,' Hyde sneered, and the inspector coloured. Mrs Quin looked guilty, and defiant, and Hyde was brought to admire the manner in which she stared into his eyes. She was afraid, but more for her daughter than herself.

'Tea, Mr Hyde?' she offered.

Hyde felt pressed, even ridiculed, by the scene; by the pine furniture, the split-level cooker, the pale green kitchen units. Only he expressed urgency, was in haste.

'No time.' He stood over the woman. The inspector played with his gloves on the table. 'Will you check with the bulletin on Miss Quin, Inspector?' The policeman seemed reluctant to leave, but only momentarily. Hyde remained standing after he had left. 'You weren't going to tell us, were you, Mrs Quin?' She shook her head, still holding his gaze. 'Why not, for Christ's sake?'

'Tricia asked me not to.'

'We'd have looked after her.'

'She said you couldn't, I don't know why not. She didn't explain.' Her hand shook slightly as she lifted the cup to her lips. They quivered, smudging pink lipstick on to the gold rim of the cup.

'She knows where her father is, doesn't she?' Mrs Quin nodded, minimising the betrayal. There was nothing in her eyes but concern. She cared for her daughter, it was evident, but regarding her husband she was composed, perhaps indifferent. 'Did she say where?'

'No.'

'Has she gone back to him now?'

'I don't know.' The exchanges had achieved a more satisfying momentum which disguised the emptiness

13

behind the answers. The woman knew little, perhaps nothing.

'Where has she gone?'

'She wasn't supposed to be going out.' Mrs Quin waved her hands limply. They were as inanimate as gloves at the ends of her plump arms. 'I don't know where she is.' The voice cracked, the mouth quivered.

'She came to put your mind at rest, is that it?' Mrs Quin nodded. 'And she said nothing about your husband – her father?' Mrs Quin shook her head. Her face was averted from Hyde's eyes now. But she was concealing nothing, except perhaps inadequacies that belonged to her past. She was keeping only herself from him, not information. 'She gave you no clue?'

'No, Mr Hyde. Except that he's well, and is in hiding. I think she hoped I would be pleased at the news. I tried to show I was.' The confession stuck into their conversation like a fracture through skin.

'She's been with him?'

'Yes.'

'Since his disappearance? She disappeared *with* him?'

'Yes, Mr Hyde. And then she came back here. She's always bounced between us, ever since the divorce.' Mrs Quin tried to smile. 'She is a trier, even if she's a failure.' Assumed cynicism was an attempt to shut him out, he realised.

'Where might she be now, Mrs Quin?'

'I have no idea whatsoever. Back with him, I suppose. But I have no idea where that might be.'

Hyde breathed out noisily. He looked at the ceiling, his hands on his hips. The texture of their conversation had become thickened, clogged with personalities. There might be clues there as to the girl's character, behaviour, whereabouts, but such enquiries possessed no volition, no urgency. Hyde was impatient for action. The girl was vital now, and he and the KGB both understood that. She'd been shown to them like some tempting prize which would be awarded to the swiftest, the strongest, the most ruthless.

'Thank you, Mrs Quin. I may be back. I just have to use your telephone – '

Mrs Quin dismissed him with a slight motion of one

hand. The other rubbed at the edge of the pine table, erasing memories. Hyde went out into the hall.

Aubrey had to know. The Deputy Director of SIS had been with the Foreign Secretary when the call from Birmingham had finally been routed through to Queen Anne's Gate. Hyde had left a message, but now Aubrey had to know the extent of their problem, and their hope – or lack of it.

He was dialling the number when the front door opened, and the inspector re-appeared. Hyde ignored him and went on dialling.

'Whoever you're reporting to,' the policeman remarked with evident, hostile sarcasm, 'you'd better mention the car that just drove past. I'd say it contained the two men who worked Sugden over.'

'What – ?' The telephone was already ringing in Aubrey's offic even as Hyde examined a residual sense that he had once more blundered into, and through, a private world. Mrs Quin hadn't deserved the way he had treated her. Yet, had he altered his manner, even though he might not have bludgeoned there would have been little gentleness, almost no sensitivity. He took the receiver from his cheek. 'You've got them?'

The inspector shook his head. 'Foot down and away, as soon as they saw my lads. The registration number won't be of any use either, I shouldn't wonder – '

'Shit!'

'I beg your pardon!' Aubrey's secretary demanded frostily at the other end of the line.

Ethan Clark, of the US Naval Intelligence Command (ASW/Ocean Surveillance), had been made to feel, throughout the week since he had joined the 'Chessboard Counter' team in the Admiralty, very much like an executive of some parent company visiting a recently taken over small firm. He was present in both his USN and NATO capacities, but these men of the Royal Navy – of, more precisely, the Office of Naval Intelligence (Submarine Warfare) – exuded a silent, undemonstrative resentment of him. Which, he well knew, made any doubts and hesitations he had concerning the mission of HMS *Proteus* seem no more to them than American carping. The commodore and his team in this long, low room in the basement of the Old Admiralty Building in Whitehall were dry-land sailors playing a war-game, and thoroughly and blithely enjoying themselves.

Clark supposed it had its basis in a buried sense of inferiority. For years, the contracting Royal Navy had belied its great history, and now, quite suddenly, they had developed 'Leopard' and installed it in a nuclear-powered fleet submarine and were engaged in mapping the 'Chessboard' sonar grid in the Barents Sea. Their high summer had returned. NATO needed them as never before, and the USN wanted greedily to get its hands, and its development budgets, on the British anti-sonar system.

Nevertheless, he told himself again as he sipped coffee from a plastic cup and observed the British officers waiting for the ritual serving of afternoon tea, 'Chessboard' should have waited. NATO and the Navy Department had required of the Royal Navy that they install the only operationally-functioning 'Leopard' unit in a submarine, rush their sea trials, then send it racing north to the Arctic Circle. The British had responded like a child doing everything at top speed to show its willingness and its virtue. Even before they had paid Plessey the bill for what they had, and before they had ordered any more 'Leopard' units. With that kind of haste, things often got smashed, plates got dropped. Boats had been lost before. It would be a great pity if 'Leopard' was lost; a tragedy if anyone else found it.

The long room, with its officers seated at computer terminals in front of their screens, its maps, wires, cables, fold-away tables, was dominated by a huge edge-lit perspex screen which stood upright in the middle of the room. The perspex secreted a multitude of optic fibres which registered the input of the computers that controlled the screen. The lighting at the edges of the perspex allowed the team to use chinagraph for temporary handwork additions to the computer-fed information. At that moment, much as it had done for the last week, the screen displayed a projection of the fjordal north coast of Norway, from North Cape to Murmansk. The coast was green and brown, the sea a deepening shade of blue as it reached northward. A fine grid of red lights, no larger than dots, was shown off the coast, as if some current in the screen were knitting, or marking a school register. Other lights moved slowly or remained stationary, units of the Red Banner Northern Fleet, ships and submarines. One or two NATO units. The Commodore's team seemed to scuttle round the base of the perspex screen as if propitiating some idol.

The room was now quiet, orderly. An hour before, *Proteus* had come up to periscope depth for one of her periodic, random but pre-determined transmissions. The transmission, using RABFITS (Random Bit Frequency Intelligence Transmission System) and via a satellite link, had contained every detail of the mapping work of the submarine since the previous message. This had been fed into the map-board's computers, updating the network of red spots which marked the 'Chessboard' sonar grid.

Clark could not but admire, and envy, the 'Leopard' equipment. He had been aboard *Proteus* as an observer during some of the sea trials, and he had also been aloft in the RAF Nimrod as the specially equipped plane tried to find the submarine. The Nimrod had been unable to locate, fix or identify the submarine, not even once, either in the Channel, the North Sea, or the north Atlantic. Not even in conjunction with the US-laid sonar carpet in the north Atlantic. No sonar trace, little and poor infra-red, nothing. It worked. Even pitted against surveillance satellites, it worked.

Perhaps, he told himself, his concern arose – like smoke, unformed but dense and obscuring – solely from the fact that when he had lunched with Kenneth Aubrey at his club at the beginning of the week, he'd learned that the man who had developed 'Leopard' at Plessey had gone missing, presumed lost to the Russians. 'Leopard' was both useless and unique, if that were so.

'It's going splendidly, Captain Clark, don't you agree?' Clark snapped awake from his unseeing contemplation of the dregs in the plastic cup. Lt.-Commander Copeland, the anti-submarine warfare expert on the 'Chessboard Counter' team, was standing in front of him, six inches shorter and exhibiting a grin that shaded into smug mockery. The lights of the perspex map were bright behind him. 'You don't seem to be too pleased,' Copeland suggested with a more pronounced mockery. He waved an arm towards the glowing map. 'Everyone else is feeling on top of the world.'

'You're really pleased, aren't you, Copeland.'

'Your people will be delighted, too, and NATO will be over the moon.'

'Sure.' Clark shifted his weight on the edge of the desk where he had perched.

'Really, Clark!' Copeland's exasperation was genuine. 'Neither the United States nor ourselves have been able to send a ballistic missile boat, or any other sort of submarine for that matter, east of North Cape for two months, ever since the *Ohio* was first traced, shadowed, and escorted from the area.' Copeland turned to study the huge map-board. 'We're helpless up there until we know how big, how good, and of what kind "Chessboard" is.' He turned back to Clark. 'Your Chief of Naval Operations saw that quite clearly, so did Supreme Allied Command, Atlantic. *Proteus* has the most distinguished sponsors.' Again, the silent, mocking smile.

'What if we lose her? Then we've lost "Leopard" for good.'

'Lose? Lost? What do you mean? Oh, Quin, I suppose.' Copeland shrugged. 'If Quin is over on the other side, then "Leopard" will be useless in a matter of months, don't you agree?' Clark nodded. 'Well, then? We must neutralise "Chessboard" now, while we have the means.'

Clark looked up at the board again. A trelliswork of red dots. The carpet of active and passive sonar buoys, and other detection devices, began inside Norwegian territorial waters, less than four miles out, and extended, at present indication, perhaps fifty or more miles north into the Barents Sea. It could be a hundred miles. *Proteus* was moving between North Cape and Kirkenes like a tractor ploughing a field. The work could take weeks. Copeland was right, of course. The northern flank of NATO was imperilled by 'Chessboard'. The Norwegian coast was prohibited to British or American submarines, the coast of the Soviet Union rendered inaccessible to short-range attack; the Barents Sea finally transformed into a Russian lake.

'Sure. Yes, you're right, Copeland. You're right.'

Copeland smiled with evident relief, and looked very young and enthusiastic. 'I'm so glad you agree,' he said without irony.

'Just one thing,' Clark added maliciously, pointing towards the map. 'Don't you think there's just too *little* Soviet naval activity up there?' The board's computer was feeding into the map display whatever the North Cape monitoring stations, the surveillance satellites, and air patrols were supplying via SACLANT's huge central computers. 'Two "Kotlin"-class destroyers, one "Sverdlov"-class cruiser, two "Romeo" submarines and one "Quebec". They're usually crawling all over the Barents Sea. Where are they?'

'Our information is Murmansk, old man. Perhaps they're taking things easy now they've got "Chessboard" to do their work for them.' The suggestion was in earnest.

'Maybe.'

Copeland was about to reply when the door opened and a Wren wheeling a tea-trolley appeared. 'Ah, tea,' he exclaimed. 'Excellent!'

Richard Lloyd, captain of HMS *Proteus*, was suddenly aware, on entering the cramped computer room aft of the main control room and its almost cathedral-like spaciousness, of the claustrophobia that most people imagined was the inevitable lot of the submariner. He did not experience it, merely understood what it must be like for people who never inhabited submarines; or who had served in them forty years before. The computer room was more cramped than ever, since at least half of its available space was now taken up by the 'Leopard' equipment.

'Don,' he said, nodding. His senior electronic countermeasures officer, Lt.-Commander Hayter, had been nominated as trials officer for 'Leopard' because of his existing special navigation and electronic warfare qualifications. Lt.-Commander Hayter's comprehension of the equipment had relieved Lloyd from all but superficial knowledge of the effects and benefits of 'Leopard'. Hayter

19

was seated in front of a computer screen, watching the pinpricks of light that emerged from its bland grey surface blankness, then slowly faded. As Lloyd watched, one pinprick brightened while two others were fading. They formed a vague triangle on the screen. Then one was gone while another emerged, glowing brighter. To the left of the screen was another, an acoustical holograph screen which displayed the buoys seemingly in three dimensions, giving them an identity, a shape. Neither Lloyd nor Hayter regarded the holograph display. There was something more obsessive about the silent, brief lights.

'Sir,' Hayter acknowledged. 'Welcome to the broom cupboard.'

'They had submarines smaller than this room in the last war,' Lloyd observed dismissively. He glanced from the screen to the holograph display, then at the accompanying print-out.

'Weird,' Hayter said, as if to himself. 'Really weird.'

'What?'

'This feeling I have that we don't exist. Not for any practical purpose, that is. Sonar buoys, temperature transducers, hydrophones – ' He pointed at the holograph as the shape of a sonar buoy formed in light. 'Mile after mile of them, but we just don't exist as far as they're concerned. Like limbo. Yet I ought to feel excited, sailing east.' He turned to Lloyd, grinning. 'Oughtn't I, skipper?'

'Something's missing from your diet, obviously.'

'Much activity?'

'Very little.'

'You sound puzzled?'

'Maybe. No, not really. I suppose they're relying on this stuff – ' He indicated the two screens. 'They must be relying on "Chessboard". One or two surface vessels, a few submarines. Something moving well to the north, one of their "Echo-II" missile boats off to take up station on the eastern seaboard of the States, no doubt. It wouldn't be much interested in us, even if it could spot us. Apart from those few items, nothing in the shop today.'

'I can't say I'm sorry.'

'You're not running down your pride and joy, are you?'

20

Lloyd nodded in the direction of the main cabinet of the 'Leopard' equipment.

'No. But utter reliance on an incredibly complicated system of matching sonar signals, and emission dampers and the like – it's not the same as having a big stick in your hands or a suit of armour on, is it? "Chessboard" is the most advanced, extensive and thorough submarine detection system ever laid down. We both know that. Like tip-toeing through a minefield, or burgling the Chubb factory – ' He smiled. 'And here we are, same old faces and same old submarine, but now we're invisible. Mm, I think I feel excited, after all.'

'How much of it have we mapped – just a guess? I won't hold you to it.'

'My computers don't make rough guesses – just mistakes.' Hayter typed on the computer keyboard below the screen. He waited for a few seconds before a message appeared, superimposed on the pin-pricks of light, making them more ghostly and unreal than before. 'See. Twelve days and a few hours more.'

'That means this sonar carpet must extend at least a hundred and fifty to two hundred miles out into the Barents Sea.' Lloyd's tone was one of surprise, even though he had half-expected 'Chessboard' to be as impressive as he had now learned.

'It could be bigger. There's an assumed twelve to fourteen per cent error built-in at the moment. That'll get less the more we chart.' Hayter turned to Lloyd again. 'I'm willing to bet that there's a similar sonar-buoy carpet being laid to stretch south and west from Novaya Zemlya. The Russians, I think, are going to close the Barents completely as far as we're concerned.'

Lloyd rubbed his chin, 'Could be. Not our worry, old son. Even if we end up doing trips round the Isle of Wight because there's nowhere else we can go. Okay, twelve days it is. Don't let the men find out, will you?'

The intercom crackled above Lloyd's head.

'Captain to control room, please.' It was the voice of his first-lieutenant. Calm and urgent. Lloyd recognised the puzzled imperative in the guarded tone.

'So you think,' he said, 'that if ever "Leopard" conked

out or was developed by the other side, we'd see the end of NATO's submarine strike power?'

'I wouldn't be at all surprised,' Hayter replied without looking at him, and not entirely without seriousness.

'Captain to control room.'

Lloyd shook his head at Hayter's back, and left the computer room, passing through the open watertight door into the control room of the *Proteus*. He straightened, stretching the unaccustomed stoop from his shoulders. Artificial light was almost his natural visual medium. The control room – *his* control room – was light, almost airy after the cupboard-under-the-stairs in which Hayter spent much of his time.

Lloyd's first-lieutenant, Lt.-Commander John Thurston, was standing near the main bank of communications monitors, leaning over one of the operators, a headphone pressed to one ear. He looked up with something akin to relief when he saw Lloyd at his side.

'What is it, John?'

'Listen to this, sir.' Thurston pressed the headphone set into Lloyd's hand. The communications petty officer twisted in his chair, watching for his captain's reactions. A brief splash of code, repeated again and again. Lloyd looked questioningly at Thurston.

'One of ours – distress code isn't it?'

'Not one of ours. The computer identified it as a quite low-priority Soviet submarine code, one we broke three months ago. Distress, yes.'

'When did you start picking it up?'

'About fifteen minutes ago, sir,' the petty officer replied. 'It's being transmitted regularly. I fed it into the signals computer, and it came out as a distress call.'

'Any ident?'

'Yes, sir,' Thurston replied, acclaiming the drama he perceived in the situation by a lengthening of his saturnine face.

'Well?'

'It's a "Delta"-class ballistic missile submarine. The full works.'

'You're sure?'

'Yes, sir.'

22

'What the hell is the matter with her, using a low-grade code? What's her trouble?'

'Massive explosion in the computer room. Most of their ECM systems have gone, and there's gas in the air-purification system. They've shut down almost everything. They're sitting on the bottom.'

Lloyd screwed his face up. 'They're very descriptive.'

'Panic, sir. Sheer bloody panic.'

'Any idea where?'

'Yes, sir.'

Again, Lloyd looked puzzled. 'How did we get a fix?'

'We didn't. They told us where to find them. They're screaming for help. They could begin transmitting in clear any minute now, they're so scared.'

'Where are they?'

Thurston, who had evidently prepared the little scene between himself and Lloyd in minute detail, nodded towards the chart table against the aft bulkhead of the control room. Lloyd followed him across.

'Here,' Thurston said. 'Right here.' His finger tapped the chart. He had drawn a livid red cross, dramatic and oversized, on its surface. 'Tanafjord.'

'What? You must have got it wrong – '

Thurston shook his head. 'No, sir. They're wrong to be there, and to be using a broken code to transmit their position. But they're inside Tanafjord. They're in Norwegian waters in a ballistic missile submarine, and they're scared they're going to die!'

'My God,' Lloyd breathed. He was silent for a moment, and then he said, 'We'll break radio silence for this one. Run up a transmission buoy. We'd better tell the Admiralty – and the sooner the better!'

Admiral of the Red Banner Northern Fleet Dolohov paced the gantry, his footsteps and those of his aides ringing on the metal catwalk. Continually, he stared down into the well of the fleet's central Operations Room beneath Red Banner headquarters in Murmansk. Below him, the huge map table glowed with light. He had just arrived, and the warm lighting of the room, and the pin-point glows in fairy-light colours from the computer-projected map seemed to celebrate and promise. It was a welcome. He paused, placed his hands on the rail of the catwalk, and turned to his aide. He might have been on the bridge of a ship.

'Sergei – status report, if you please.'

The younger man smirked with pleasure, real and anticipated. 'Sir. The British submarine is in this area – ' He clicked his fingers, and a chart was passed to him. It was attached to a clipboard, and over the exposed fold was fixed a transparent plastic sheet. There were faint, reddish smudges on the plastic, one or two firmer images. 'The infra-red satellite picked these up, sir. Very, very faint, but there. It must be the *Proteus*.' He pointed out one of the brighter images. 'This is the cruiser in the area. A clear image, even with the cloud cover. The faint smudges – '

'It works, then? This anti-detection equipment, it really works as well as we have been led to believe?'

The aide considered the possible implications of the question, then said, 'The weather satellites promise the break-up of the cloud cover. It will improve our chances of getting a good infra-red trace.'

'I didn't mean that, boy!' Dolohov snapped, his pale eyes fierce and alert. 'I *understand* that it is a hit-and-miss, even with our new geostationary satellite and every unit of the fleet looking for this submarine. I am *delighted* that it works, that the prize will be worth the game.'

'I see, sir – ' the aide said shamefacedly. 'When the submarine moves closer to the Norwegian shelf, into shallower water, we may have a better trace. Not much better, but enough, sir,' he added with solemn candour. Dolohov laughed.

'It is a *gamble*, Sergei, a great game!' he explained. 'As long as the prize is sufficient, then one accepts the chances of losing the game.' He transferred his intent gaze to the map table below. The plotters moved about it busily, yet expectant, knowing that they were as yet simply filling in time, rehearsing.

'Oh, the prize is a good one, sir. It works, only too well. We have had nothing from our sonar carpet, nothing, even though the British have been in the area for two days now.'

Dolohov turned his back to him, his eyes vacant, his gaze inward. The smile still hovered around his mouth. He nodded, like a very old, semi-senile man. Sergei would not have been surprised had an unregarded spittle appeared on his lips.

Then Dolohov was alert again. 'Yes. Satisfactory.' He looked down into the well of the huge room, at the map table. The different coloured lights. Cruisers, destroyers, the carrier *Kiev*, submarines, the special salvage vessel *Dioklas* and the submarine rescue ship *Karpaty*, all ready to sail from Pechenga and Poliarnyi, as soon as the word was given. Hours – mere hours – away from the Tanafjord and the distress signal. The thought spoiled his almost complete satisfaction. He turned to Sergei again. 'If only we knew the precise moment when the *Proteus* picked up the distress call and her computers broke the code – eh, Sergei? Yes, I know when they transmitted to London, I know that. I would have liked to have known when they picked it up, though. The precise moment. What they thought, and felt, and said. Everything.' He laughed. Then he spoke more softly, looking down on the map table once more. 'Come, let us begin. Set course for Tanafjord, and sail into our elaborate trap. Come.'

Two: CONTACT

The commodore was still closeted with a hastily assembled committee of staff officers, arguing for an investigation by *Proteus* of the distress signals from Tanafjord. In the 'Chessboard Counter' room, Clark found himself a lone voice, disregarded and even derided, as he argued against any diversion of the submarine from her mission.

He could not have explained to himself the reasons for his reluctance. The cleanly-shaven, smartly-uniformed young men who surrounded him beneath the huge perspex map-board enraged him with their confidence, their boyish enthusiasm. It was their cheerful dismissal of any doubts on his part that had stung him to contempt and counter argument. He repeated himself again and again, and the baffled, kindly smiles and the frowns of dismissal greeted every statement he made. He knew it was the commodore he needed to convince, yet he once more reiterated the central thrust of his argument in a snapping, irritated tone. He justified his own stubbornness by reminding himself that he was the Navy Department's – America's – only and solely responsible representative.

'Look, you guys – ' Lips twisted in derision or disdain. 'You already know her type, you might even verify which boat she is. Only ten per cent of their ballistic subs are out of Murmansk at any one time. If she's screaming for help, then there may be nothing left to investigate by the time *Proteus* reaches the fjord.' He could see the disbelief opening on their faces, livid as blushes. It angered him. 'Hell, why should she be in a fjord in shallow water with limited sea room if she was going to play rough? Use a nuke depth bomb on her – it might work out cheaper than sending in "Leopard".'

'Really, Clark, you're quite the hysterical virgin this morning,' Copeland remarked waspishly.

Clark was about to answer when the door opened. He recognised Giles Pyott as soon as he entered the room. Pyott was in army uniform, and the commodore, who entered behind Pyott, was also in uniform. A glassy, urbane, impenetrable officialdom had suddenly settled on the room, the kind of formality that the Pentagon or the Navy Department could never muster or imitate. Thank God, Clark added to his observation. Pyott, grey hair immaculate, part of his pressed, polished uniform, looked pleased and elated. Clark was again reminded of children and their haste to please or to upstage.

'Shall I tell them, Commodore, or will you?'

'Carry on, Colonel Pyott,' the commodore demurred, a smile leaking into his face and warping the firm line of his lips.

'Very well.' The two men had approached the group beneath the map. Pyott studied it theatrically, glanced at Clark and nodded to him, then spoke to the group of Royal Navy officers. His manner implied that Clark had left the room. 'Gentlemen, it has been decided that *Proteus* be ordered to proceed, with the utmost caution and all practicable speed, to the area of Tanafjord.' A sigh of communal satisfaction, one or two murmurs of congratulation and pleasure; the empty compliments of sycophancy, they appeared to Clark. He was a man in a grey suit with a pocketful of unfamiliar and rather despised credit cards. Not a gentleman, they might have said of him. Worry twisted in his stomach again, and he knew he could not keep silent. 'Yes, gentlemen,' Pyott – who was from some faceless and important MoD/NATO committee called StratAn – continued, 'the first Sea Lord and the Chiefs of Staff assign the gravest import to this intrusion into NATO territorial waters – ' Again, the murmur of support. 'The government of Norway, when informed, officially requested our assistance. *Proteus* will be instructed by yourselves to carry out a monitoring and surveillance action at the mouth of the Tanafjord.' He smiled, at once the headmaster with his junior staff. 'I leave the form of the task orders and encoding to you.'

'We'll get on with it, Colonel,' Pearson, the communications officer, offered, wiping his spectacles. Without them for the moment, he seemed more to suit the dark uniform and the gold cuffs. Returning them to his aquiline nose, he became clerkish again.

'Are you certain of all this, Pyott?'

It was as if Clark had cheered for an opposing team. Pyott turned a lordly glance to the American, who was as tall as he was and more muscular but who did not pose his figure in quite the same seignorial manner.

'I beg your pardon, Captain Clark?' The mention of rank was a reminder of good manners and the proper forms of address. 'I don't quite catch the drift of your question.' Outsider, the tone cried. Buccaneer. Pyott took in, with a raking glance that went from face to feet and back again, the civilian clothes, the muscular chest and shoulders, the tanned, square features. Clark was evidently a pretender engaged in some dubious masquerade.

'I asked if you were certain? Are their Lordships certain? Are the Chiefs of Staff certain? Is NATO certain?'

'The proper channels, the protocol, all have been observed, Captain Clark,' Pyott replied frostily.

'What in hell do they think the Russians are up to in Tanafjord, with a ballistic missile boat?' Clark almost bellowed, goaded by the imperturbable arrogance and self-assurance of the army officer. Like a line of automatons, the operators in front of their screens and terminals snapped to attention in their seats. The group beneath the map seemed to move slightly away from him, as if he had begun to exude a powerful, offensive body odour. 'You think they're invading Norway, starting the next war?'

'I do not know,' Pyott said icily, his face chalk white. 'I do not make assumptions, especially ones that might be dismissive and therefore comforting. That is why *Proteus* must do our investigating for us. Your own Navy Department has been consulted, and has agreed. Brussels is in agreement. *You* are out of step, Clark.'

'*Proteus* has "Leopard" on board. Doesn't that worry you?'

'That fact weighed heavily with everyone at the meeting, and with everyone consulted. It is to our inestimable advantage that *Proteus* is the submarine on station, so to speak – '

'Bullshit! Crap and bullshit, Pyott! You people – you want to play games, you want to *really* try out your shiny new toy. You want to walk close to the cliff. Now I understand – '

'Perhaps we could continue this conversation outside,' Pyott remarked through pressed, almost unmoving lips. His face was now livid with anger. The naval officers, including the commodore, had moved away from them, sensitive of the embarrassment they knew Pyott must be experiencing.

'I wouldn't want the time of day from you, Pyott. You're an asshole. A pompous asshole, at that.'

Clark brushed past Pyott, who avoided him like an experienced matador. Clark had allowed the situation to escape him. He was angry with himself, angry that it was Pyott he resented more than Pyott's suggestion concerning *Proteus*. As he prepared to slam the door of the 'Chessboard Counter' room behind him, he could hear Pyott already reiterating StratAn and NATO's orders concerning *Proteus* to the assembled company. His voice was laconic, controlled, smooth as glass.

It enraged Clark, and he knew he had to talk to Kenneth Aubrey. Something in him, deep as a lust as yet unfocused, knew that he had to stop this *adventure* with 'Leopard' and *Proteus*.

He slammed the door loudly behind him.

Aubrey studied Hyde's face. It was evident the man's challenge with regard to the fact of Quin's disappearance was intended to irritate, and intended also to disguise the Australian's own new doubts.

Aubrey smoothed the last, vestigial wings of grey hair above his ears, and leaned back in his chair. Shelley, his aide, watched Hyde from the tall windows of the office in Queen Anne's Gate.

'You're not sure now, are you?' Hyde repeated.

'Don't jump to conclusions,' Aubrey remarked severely. 'What you saw was the girl. We know that she is unreliable, something of a failure, a drop-out. Is there any reason to suppose that she knows where her father is? She wasn't just trying to keep her mother calm?'

'The KGB chased her to the bus stop. Those two blokes were like rape on legs.'

'Perhaps Quin won't play ball with them in Moscow without having his daughter with him?' Hyde shook his head vehemently. 'Your own source at the Russian embassy gave you quite clear – almost categorical – indications that a snatch squad had stayed overnight, and left again on Aeroflot the day after Quin disappeared. You believed your man then. Why not now?'

'Wait till I see him again. I was led up the garden, taken walkabout if you like. I admit that. But don't *you* go on believing there's nothing we can do. Quin dropped out of sight for his own reasons – he could have had a breakdown, for all we know – and the girl's gone back to him now, or she's on her way back. I *know* the Russians haven't got him yet, but they will have as soon as they get their hands on the girl.' Hyde was patting Aubrey's desk, gently and continuously, to underline his words. He looked at Shelley when he had finished speaking, then asked, 'You think they've got him?'

Shelley shrugged. Hyde, understanding his influence with Aubrey, wanted him on his side. Shelley plucked at his bottom lip with thumb and forefinger, then said, 'I don't know. There's some room for doubt, I think. It seems too good to be true, after the last few weeks – '

'I will make the assumption – because it is preferable to do so – that the appearance of the girl means that the KGB have not taken Quin to Moscow, Patrick,' Aubrey said slowly. Hyde exhaled noisily and relaxed in his leather chair. 'I still believe that Quin has gone east – ' He held up a liver-spotted, wrinkled hand. 'Until there is stronger evidence to the contrary. Therefore – ' he smiled slightly, 'your first task is to contact your helpful but possibly misleading friend at the Soviet embassy.'

Hyde nodded. 'Today's pick-up day. He's not likely to stay away after yesterday, whether he's straight or crooked.'

'I suppose we might have to consider him planted, or at least re-turned?' Aubrey mused.

'The abortion was a long time ago. Perhaps he's back in favour with his bosses,' Hyde suggested.

'Ask him. Then find the girl. Simply that. What about her college, for instance?'

'CID talked to some of her friends last night. Nothing.'

'You will go back over the ground. And you will be careful, Patrick, if you are going to begin crossing the path of the gentlemen who were in Sutton Coldfield yesterday. You'd better draw a gun.' He waited for Hyde's reaction. The Australian nodded after a lengthy pause. 'Good. Don't draw attention to yourself. If your theory is correct, then they might soon begin following you as their best lead to Miss Quin.'

'Anything else?'

Aubrey shook his head. 'Not for the moment.' Then he added, 'This girl – ' He tapped a file near his right hand. 'Unreliable. Unconventional. Is that your impression?'

'Her Mum loves her. If she isn't just a nut-case, then she might be more difficult to find.'

'I think we'd better find her, don't you? She's in danger, whether Quin is in the country or not. They want her, apparently.'

'How much time is there?'

'I don't know. We have "Leopard". It can be manufactured in large numbers, eventually, without Quin. From that point of view, there is a great deal of time. But we are no longer alone. The girl's time, at least, would seem to be running out.'

'I'll get on with it, then,' Hyde said, getting up. The leather of the chair squeaked as his frame released it. 'Pardon,' he said with a grin. 'You can talk about me when I'm gone. I'll let you know this afternoon what Comrade Vassiliev has to say.' He smiled, and left the room.

Aubrey's returned smile vanished as soon as the door closed behind Hyde.

'What do you think, Peter?' he asked.

Shelley rounded Aubrey's desk to face him. Aubrey indicated the Chesterfield, and Shelley sat down, hitching his trousers to preserve their creases as he crossed his long legs. Shelley lit a cigarette, which Aubrey watched with a dry, eager concentration. He had obeyed his physician for more than a year in the matter of smoking. The occasion when the service lift at his flat had not been working for a week, and he had had to walk up three flights of stairs every evening – shortness of breath, body's fragility indicated to him like a sound blow on his shoulder. No more cigarettes, not even the occasional cigar.

'I'm afraid Patrick's right, however irritating that may be.' Shelley smiled.

'We have been misled – and principally by his source of information at the Soviet embassy.'

'Agreed, sir. But we all accepted Vassiliev after Hyde cleared up the matter of the abortion and the girl in the case was paid off. Vassiliev had walked into our honey-trap, we let Hyde go with him as chief contact. If Vassiliev is forged, then he's an expert job. Of course, he may just have been trying to please Hyde. The swagman's not often fooled. That's why he's so angry now. I can't say that I blame him.'

Shelley exhaled, and Aubrey ostentatiously wafted the smoke away from himself by waving his hand. Shelley appeared not to notice the inconvenience to his superior.

'This incident in Sutton wasn't an elaborate charade, for our benefit?'

'I doubt that, sir.'

'So do I. The problem is, this "Leopard" business is so damned important. It really is one of those pieces of military technology the Russians haven't even begun to develop. Or so they tell me at MoD and Plessey. It would put us perhaps years ahead in the anti-submarine warfare game. I really would like to believe that they haven't got Quin. It just seems too good to be true.'

'Agreed. But there is such a thing as not looking a gift horse, et cetera, sir –'

'Perhaps. Another thing that worries me – what price the safety of Comrade Vassiliev? If he fed us duff gen at their orders, then they know Hyde will be coming back now with more questions.' Aubrey shook his head. 'I don't like that idea.'

'Bruce the Lifeguard can take care of himself.'

'I hope so. Peter, get some Branch people to check around Bracknell again – the avenues we haven't explored or didn't give much credence to. Holiday rentings, cottages, that syndrome. People usually run for the hills not the city if they want to hide. I don't know why that should be.'

'Very well, sir.'

'And this file –' He tapped Tricia Quin's folder. 'Get all

the material out of it for Hyde. A list of people and leads. I have the distinct feeling that very little time is available to us, don't you?' Aubrey looked up at Shelley as the young man got to his feet.

'No comment, sir.'

'Well?' Lloyd, slumped in his chair, seemed to embrace the small, neat captain's cabin of the *Proteus* as he opened his hands for an answer. Then, as if drawn by some new and sudden gravity, his hands rested on the chart on his desk. Thurston had brought the chart with him from the control room. He and Carr, the navigator, had marked the course of the *Proteus* as far as Tanafjord. Thurston sat opposite Lloyd, Carr standing stockily and red-haired behind the first-lieutenant, Hayter leaning against the closed door of the cabin. The air conditioning hummed like a sustained note of expectancy. 'Well, John? You two? Any comment?'

Thurston cleared his throat, and in the sidelong movements of his eyes Lloyd saw that these three senior officers had conferred. They were some kind of delegation.

'No,' Thurston said at last, 'not now we know its position.'

'Why not?' Lloyd looked up. 'You two are in on this, I presume?'

Carr said, abruptly, 'It makes the whole thing messy, sir. I can't understand what MoD thinks it's playing at, ordering us to the mouth of Tanafjord. It smells, sir.'

'It does, sir,' Hayter confirmed. 'A "Delta"-class sub in a fjord. Why? What good can it do there? It could loose any missile it wanted to from its berth in Murmansk as well as from that fjord. Why was it there in the first place? Shallow water, no sea room. Sir, we both know it's a very unlikely beginning to the next war.' Hayter smiled, ingratiating his nerves with his captain.

Lloyd rubbed his face, drawing his features into a rubber mask, then releasing the flesh. It assumed a kind of challenged look. Thurston observed Lloyd's expression with a mild dismay.

'You're suggesting we disobey a highest priority instruction from the Admiralty?'

'No. Let's request confirmation. We could do that – '

33

'We could.' Lloyd looked down at the chart again. 'How many hours' sailing, rigged for silent running, taking *all* precautions?'

'A little over thirty-seven,' Carr replied. Hayter looked at him in reproach, as if he had changed allegiance or betrayed a secret. 'But I think we should request confirmation, skipper.'

'Thirty-seven.' Lloyd tapped the chart with his forefinger. 'Our course alteration is minimal for the first six hours or more. We're to continue our work on "Chessboard". For six hours, at least, nothing's changed.' He smiled. 'In that time, we'll send one signal to MoD, asking for confirmation, and for a fuller definition of our mission status. Does that satisfy you trio of doubting Thomases?'

'I still don't like it,' Thurston volunteered.

'You were as excited as hell when we picked up the signal from our Russian friend, John. What's changed?'

'I used to like watching boxing – it never tempted me to take it up as a hobby.'

'Don, I want a full tape test and computer check run on "Leopard" as soon as we alter course.'

'You'll get it.'

'Are we still getting signals from the Russian boat?'

Thurston nodded. 'Sandy's been monitoring them since we got a reply from MoD.'

Carr said, 'She's broadcasting in clear now. Being careful, of course. But the power's down on the transmission. I think they're using a low-power emergency backup set, and they're altering the frequency with preprogrammed cards. It's a bloody mess.'

'Any more details?'

'No. Code-names, damage indications in some Cyrillic alphabet sequence. Can't decipher that. The letters and numerals could refer to anything.'

'What other traffic?'

'Murmansk's been pouring out coded stuff – ' Carr shook his head at the light in Lloyd's eyes. 'We don't have it broken. Code of the day only, frequency-agile transmissions, the lot. But there's a lot of it. They're panicking all right.'

'Okay. Sandy, time to fetch Lt.-Commander Hackett.'

Lloyd nodded at the cabin door, and Hayter moved out of his way as the navigator went in search of the engineering officer. When Hayter closed the door again, Lloyd said, 'You don't really think MoD are wrong on this one, do you?'

Thurston pulled a melancholy face. 'They aren't infallible. I think they like the idea of the game, that's all.'

'We're risking this ship, and ourselves, and "Leopard" on this wild goose chase,' Hayter added with a quiet vehemence. 'That doesn't seem to have struck their lordships. I think the intelligence yield from this "monitoring action" won't be worth a candle, anyway.'

'I agree with Don.'

Lloyd was silent for a time, his hands over his face, the fingers slightly parted as if he were peeping child-like at them or at the chart on his desk. Then he rubbed his eyes, and shrugged himself upright in his chair.

'I'll ask for confirmation from MoD. Meanwhile, we'll rig for silent running – and I *mean* silent from now on.' A grin, unexpected and gleaming, cracked the seriousness of his expression. 'It isn't for real, you two. We won't be responsible for starting the next war. Nothing is going to happen to us. It's *Norwegian*, the Tanafjord. Cheer up. Just look on it as another sea trial.'

Thurston was about to reply, but fell silent as they heard a knock on the cabin door. Lloyd indicated to Hayter that he should open it. The grin was still on Lloyd's face when Carr ushered Hackett into the cabin.

The wind seemed to follow Hyde into the entrance of Lancaster Gate underground station, hurrying pages of a copy of the *New Evening Standard* ahead of him, with chocolate bar wrappers. He hunched against the wind's dusty, grubby touch at his neck. He went through the barrier, and descended past the framed advertisements to the Central Line eastbound platform. A woman's legs, gigantic and advertising tights, invited him from the opposite wall. Lunchtime had swelled the numbers of passengers. Hyde lounged against the wall and observed Vassiliev further down the platform. Even here the wind moved the dust in little eddies or thin, gauzy scarves along the platform. Vassiliev wore a dark overcoat across his shoulders, over a pinstriped suit. He looked English enough despite the high Slavic cheekbones and narrow nose, yet he appeared nervous beneath the clothes and the residential veneer England had given him. Hyde was still unsure of him; whether his crime was one of omission or commission.

The train slid into the arched bunker of the platform. Hyde watched Vassiliev board it, then waited until he was the last still person on the platform, then he got into another carriage as the doors shunted together behind him. He stood watching the retreating platform as the train pulled out. Nothing. There was nothing to be learned from nothing.

He and Vassiliev left the train at Tottenham Court Road, Hyde staying twenty yards behind the Russian, closing with him as they transferred to the Northern Line and then getting into the same carriage of the first northbound train. He studied the carriage and its passengers until they pulled into Euston, then took a seat next to Vassiliev. The Russian embassy official, in making a pronounced movement away from him, squeezing himself against the window, suggested either dislike or nerves. Hyde placed his hand on Vassiliev's arm in a gesture which he knew the man – superficially confident of his heterosexuality but with sexual doubts nagging at him like toothache spoiling good looks and appetite – loathed. The arm jumped beneath his touch.

'Now, sport, you and me have some talking to do, don't we?'

Vassiliev looked out of the window. Mornington Crescent. The name slowed and materialised, like oil adopting a mould. 'I – I knew you would question me,' he offered.

'Too bloody right, mate! You sold me the wrong stuff, Dmitri – told me Quin was over on your side. Taken away by the bogeymen.'

Vassiliev turned at the pressure on his arm and stared at Hyde. Sitting, he was slightly taller than the Australian. His face was thinly imperious for a moment – Hyde, seeing the expression, was strangely chilled – then it subsided quickly into nervousness and apology.

'I am not a member of the KGB, you know that. I am not privy to the things they do. What I told you was a fact. I also heard rumours of who their objective was, I passed these on to you. I can do no more.'

Vassiliev glanced away from Hyde, into the lightless tunnel.

'I don't pay you for crap, Dmitri. I don't blackmail you for rubbish. Now, what do you know?'

Vassiliev shook his arm impatiently, and Hyde released it, thrusting his hand into his pocket and slumping more theatrically in his seat, feet on the seat opposite, to the irritation – silent and frightened – of an elderly man.

'I – it is difficult to ask, I can only listen. In the staff restaurant, there is talk of what happened yesterday. I – I am, well, yes, I am almost certain that they are still looking for this Quin – ' Hyde listened, every sense aware of the man in the seat next to him. Body temperature coming through the thin sleeve of his windcheater, thigh trembling slightly against Hyde's own, the faint body odour noticeable above the dusty, greasy smells of the carriage and the mothball scent from the old man. The voice, grabbing at sincerity, the breathing somehow artificially fast. The words broken by intelligence rather than emotion; thought-out hesitations. 'I have not seen the two men – they were low-grade sleepers, I understand, without accreditation to the embassy – ' The officialese flowing now like a broad, uninterrupted stream, but not quite because of habit. Learned, Hyde thought; but he remained silent. Quiver gone from Vassiliev's body. He believed he had acted sufficiently well. 'However, there was talk about them, and about the girl – and I'm sure now it is their way of getting to the father – '

'You picked up a lot yesterday and this morning,' Hyde remarked laconically.

'I am *trying*,' Vassiliev pleaded, turning his face to Hyde. Mirror of helpfulness, of urgent sincerity. The eyes expressionless. 'I knew what you would want. I was as surprised – shocked – as you must have been. What else can I tell you?'

Camden Town, slowing down outside the window. Hyde swiftly surveyed the passengers on the platform, those who entered their carriage. He could not believe that they would have let Vassiliev out by himself, without a minder, with such an important role to play. But he could not find his companion. What role was he playing, anyway? Why admit that Quin was still at large?

'I want more detail, more information, Dmitri. That's what you can tell me, and I want it tonight.'

'I can't do that!'

Hyde stared into the Russian's face. 'Yes, you can. Oh yes, you can. After all, you're my creature, I've got the arm on you. It's not the other way round, is it?' Hyde watched the face. Mouth sloping downwards in admission, cheekbones colouring slightly with a sense of shame, brow perspiring in tiny silver beads – ignore, the temperature in the carriage and the overcoat explained it – the eyes quizzical, blank, then striving for the hunted look Hyde expected. Finding, losing, catching and holding it. Vassiliev was playing with him, at the orders of the London Resident or one of his senior staff. Again, he felt momentarily chilled.

'Yes, I will try,' Vassiliev said mournfully.

Highgate. A moment of silence, no one getting on or off the train. Stillness. Then the doors breathing noisily as they closed again. The lights elongating, the words smudged, the darkness of the tunnel, the walls pressing close to the window. Hyde shook off the awareness of himself, the pressing vulnerability. He was being led by the nose, being set up to do their work for them.

'You're sure?' he asked, staring at his feet.

'Of what?' Vassiliev asked, momentarily confused.

'He hasn't been taken over?'

'The man Quin?'

'Yes.'

'No. No, they do not have him.' East Finchley. Vassiliev began to look uncomfortable, as if he had entered unexplored territory. 'They think the girl will lead them to him. I am sure that is what they think.' He looked pleadingly at Hyde.

'You were sure they had him three weeks ago.'

'I am sure now. Then, I was wrong. There was no *talk*, then. This time, there is gossip.' He was looking over

Hyde's shoulder as the lighted platform slipped away behind them, then he glanced at his watch. 'I must get off – I am sure. Mr Hyde, I am sure this time!'

'Okay, okay.'

'Gossip, that is all I bring. You know that. You knew that when you – *found* me.'

'Saved your bloody neck, sport – don't forget that.'

Vassiliev blushed with dislike. 'I do not forget.' The train was slowing into Finchley Central. Vassiliev was eager to get up. 'Where do we meet tonight, what time?'

Hyde hesitated, then: 'The club. Eleven.'

'Good – good. Yes, yes, I will be there – ' The train had stopped, the doors had slid back. Hyde, shifting his weight, moved his feet and Vassiliev brushed past him, hopping out of the carriage. He immediately lit a cigarette, but Hyde, looking quickly up and down the carriage and the platform, did not consider it a signal. Then Vassiliev hurried into a patch of windy sunlight towards the southbound platform.

Hyde watched him disappear, then settled back in his seat, putting his feet up again. The old man still smelt of mothballs. He closed his eyes. The smell of relatives from England coming out to Wollongong, bringing clothes they hadn't worn for a long time, uncertain of the Australian climate. Big bosoms – Aunti Vi, Auntie Maud, Auntie Ethel – covered by cardigans that smelt of mothballs. He with bare feet and shorts, like an urchin or a school-boy marooned in Australia. Mothballs. And the voices through his bedroom wall, conveying the magic of England, the rain and snow, the television.

Woodside Park. He bolted upright, eyes wide. His spine was cold. The childhood memories, evoked like a cloud of masking ink, faltered and retreated. He was being played. They would be one step behind, or alongside, every moment of the journey.

Aubrey had not enjoyed Ethan Clark's narrative. It was too easy, and perhaps correct, to regard it as tales out of school. He had lunched with the American, as a protégé of various senior CIA officers of long acquaintance, when Clark had first arrived in London the previous week. At numerous points, he had wanted to protest, request Clark to desist, even to leave. Gradually, however, he had become intrigued, then alarmed.

Clark described the 'Delta'-class submarine in the Tanafjord, then his voice faltered and he fell silent. Aubrey, his face gilded by weak sunshine from his office window, sat with his eyes closed and in silence. On an inward screen, he could see Quin's face, and knew that his mind had forged some obscure yet inescapable link between the man and his invention. A link of mutual danger?

'What did Giles Pyott say?' he asked at last.

'He didn't listen – '

'What did he *say*?'

Clark choked back his anger. 'He said,' he began slowly, 'that it was none of my damn business and that everyone, including my own Navy Department, agreed with sending *Proteus* in.'

'I can hear him saying it, though not quite in those words,' Aubrey remarked acidly. 'Everyone agrees, through to Brussels?'

'Yes,'

Aubrey sat bolt upright. He appeared unconvinced, even unconcerned, then he said, 'You've told me about the Russian submarine. Tell me about "Chessboard". That *is* important?'

'It is. "Chessboard" could close the Barents to us unless we map it.'

'And "Leopard". That is of inestimable value, you assess?'

'While it's unique and while the Russians don't have it, yes.'

'I agree. But, what if, as we discussed the other day, Quin, its developer, is with the Russians?'

'Then the sooner we map "Chessboard", and use "Leopard" for whatever else we want to know before the Russians develop it themselves, the better.'

'Then I must tell you, Ethan, that it appears that Quin may not be with the Russians after all. How would that affect your thinking?'

Clark was silent with surprise at first, then with concentration. Clouds played shadow-games across

Aubrey's carpet, across the man's head. Then he said. 'It makes all the difference.'

'You do believe this distress signal is genuine?'

'It – seems to be.'

'I see. We know the Russians know about "Leopard". They must have had someone inside Plessey at some time. They were interested in acquiring Quin's services on a permanent basis. They still are. Perhaps they would like "Leopard" instead?'

'You can't be serious?'

'I am merely speculating. Would you say that *Proteus* might be endangered by her new orders?'

'It's closer to the Soviet Union.'

'Is that why you are so disturbed by all of this?' Aubrey snapped. 'Or is it because you don't like Giles Pyott or the people at the Admiralty?' Aubrey's face was fierce, even contemptuous.

'Look, I came to you in good faith – '

'You came to me to moan about your lot!'

'The hell with you, Mr Aubrey!' Clark made as if to rise.

'Sit down, Ethan!' Aubrey had turned to his desk again. His hands were calm and unmoving as they rested on its edge. 'Sit down.'

'Sorry – '

'Not at all. You came to me because you do feel *Proteus* might be endangered by her new mission. I did not like her sailing orders in the first place. I wanted her kept at sea undergoing trials, or in safe harbour, until the matter of Quin was resolved. I wished "Leopard" removed from *Proteus* until such time as Quin was either recovered or known to be lost to us. I was ignored – overruled. It really isn't my field, you know.' Aubrey smiled. 'The trouble is, MoD is occasionally – and this is one of those occasions – filled with a few too many clots for my liking or reassurance. Giles Pyott is a clever, experienced soldier. He is also a Cavalier rather than a Roundhead. I have always seen myself in the New Model Army rather than Prince Rupert's cavalry. It always seemed much more sensibly organised, and much safer – ' Clark, invited to return Aubrey's dazzling, self-deprecatory smile, did so. Apparently, he had been tested, and passed. He bore Aubrey no

41

resentment. 'My problem is that I find it hard to distinguish between death rays emitting purple light and anti-sonar systems and sonar carpets laid in the Barents Sea. However, we must turn our hand to the work that presents itself.' He studied Clark. 'We have one extant "Leopard" system, in one British submarine, engaged upon a task of singular importance. We have one missing scientist. Until the one stray lamb is returned to the fold, I suggest we don't let the other one loose. Don't you?'

'What can you do?'

'I wonder. I would like to stop *Proteus* – I would like to find Quin. Ethan, I trust your judgement. I trust those intuitions that a man like Pyott would not countenance. You have worked in intelligence, he has not. We are all chronically suspicious, perhaps paranoid. However, you and I and the others like us are all we have. Perhaps all "Leopard" has. Hm. Go back to the Admiralty, apologise to Giles Pyott – yes, please – and then keep your eyes and ears open. Ring me tonight – '.

The intercom's buzz interrupted him. His secretary announced the arrival of some sandwiches and the imminence of a pot of coffee. Aubrey ordered her in. Before the door opened, Clark said swiftly. 'What can you do?'

'I don't know, Ethan. Unfortunately, I shall have to do something, or else I shall begin sleeping badly at night. Ah, coffee and sandwiches – splendid!'

'We've got her.'

'When?' Dolohov asked as Sergei closed the door of the Ops. Room behind him.

'Only minutes ago. The satellite's had terrible trouble with the cloud cover – '

'Show me. Admiral – ' Dolohov nodded to the Ops. Room commander, then almost snatched the folded chart overlain with its sheet of developed infra-red film. Poor, pale smudges, like smeared rust or very old blood.

'The pattern's changed, as you can see.' Sergei was leaning over Dolohov's shoulder. His finger tapped the sheet over the chart. 'This was her three hours ago – same intermittent smudges, her mapping course, enough for us to tell she was still following the same search pattern. Then here we think there was another trace – ' The smear was almost invisible. Dolohov did not move the chart closer to his face. 'Then nothing for two hours, then this – then another fifty-four minutes before we got this.' It was like the last ember of a dying fire. It was out of the random yet sequential pattern, and it had moved south and east of the other smears.

'You're certain?' Dolohov was looking at the rear-admiral.

'We've used sonar in that area, and we got nothing. If it is a submarine, then it is the British ship.'

'Excellent! It works, how well it works, mm?'

'Too well.'

'Come, Admiral – no sour grapes. You have a computer prediction on speed and course?'

'We have one, based on the last three traces. We need at least two more to be at all accurate.'

'Show me, man, show me!'

One of the rear-admiral's aides scuttled into the control room, Dolohov leaned over the rail of the gantry. As he watched, the rear-admiral joined him. Then a curving line appeared on the projection below, from a position far out in the Barents Sea, making south and east towards the Tanafjord. It rendezvoused with the imaginary Soviet submarine trapped in the fjord.

'In excess of thirty hours,' the rear-admiral murmured, 'and no longer than thirty-six. That's the best we can do without another infra-red fix from the satellite. For the moment, she's disappeared again. Possibly cloud again.'

'Good man,' Dolohov said incongruously. He gripped the rear-admiral's shoulder. The man was considerably younger than himself, bespectacled and clerkish. A computer expert, perhaps, an academic; scientist rather than sailor. Nevertheless, at that moment Dolohov felt an unaccustomed affinity with the man. 'Good man.' He turned to Sergei. 'Call Leningrad. Whether they're at the Grechko Academy or the Frunze Naval School, I want Ardenyev and his team informed at once. They will depart for Murmansk immediately.'

'Yes, sir.'

Dolohov turned back to the rear-admiral. 'Keep up the

good work. If the Red Banner Special Underwater Operations Unit does its job as well as you are doing yours, then nothing can go wrong!' He laughed throatily. 'Excellent, excellent! I don't care what success the KGB has now in finding the man Quin – we will be able to present Moscow with Quin's toy. The man himself will have no value, and *we* shall enjoy the sunshine. Excellent, excellent!' His continued laughter caused one of the map table operators to look up.

The strip club was a short walk from Oxford Street, hunched in a narrow side street on the edge of Soho, as if aspiring to membership of that district, or recently expelled from it. Hyde had used it as a meeting place with Vassiliev because clubs of its type attracted the diplomats and officials of East European embassies, especially early on in their tours of duty, and even if Vassiliev had been under surveillance by his own people, such visits would have been regarded as misdemeanours rather than as suspicious or dangerous.

Hyde glanced at the membership ledger, having bribed the doorman. One or two new members that evening, but it told him nothing. They might be Vassiliev's friends, or football fans or businessmen staying overnight in London. Vassiliev's friends would have ensured their membership some time earlier, if this was an entrapment exercise. Hyde did not consider it was. They wanted him running, moving with apparent freedom. He went down the steps beneath a dim green under-sea light, the mingled odour of sweat, smoke and tawdriness coming up to meet him. The door opened to admit him – he had heard the buzzer sound from the doorman's cubicle as he began his descent.

Disco music thumped against his ears, flat, enervating, unmemorable. Strobe lights played over the heads of the audience. The tiny stage was empty, but there was a narrow bed lit by a silvery, ghostly light at the back of it. Hyde remained by the door. The large man with cropped hair wearing an out-of-style dinner jacket loomed at his shoulder. Hyde suspected he knew his profession and did not confuse him with the Vice Squad or CID. At worst, he would assume him to be Security rather than Intelligence.

It did not matter. Rather, it legitimised the club, provided a governmental patron.

There were only a small number of people waiting for the next bout on the stage. Vassiliev – he saw as his eyes accustomed themselves to the peculiar, winking gloom – was in a corner, near the stage, mournfully staring into a glass. There seemed no one who had noticed, or become concerned at, his entrance. He threaded his way between the tables with their grubby cloths and expensive drinks towards Vassiliev. The Russian seemed relieved to see him. If there were other emotions, conflicting ones, then the strobe flicker hid them. Hyde settled in a chair which faced the door, and immediately a waiter appeared at his side. No girls on the floor of the club, no hostesses. A curious puritanism pervaded the place. Untouchable, flaunting, indescribably crude, silicon-enhanced, the women came and went on the stage, separate and inviolable.

Near them, the pianist resumed his seat. The drummer rolled softly, as if communicating with his drums. A bass player leaned tiredly over the neck and shoulders of his instrument. All of them appeared to be awaiting some summons to Ronnie's in Frith Street, two blocks away. Most of the girls stripped to records, anyway. Hyde ordered a beer. It came in a half-pint glass, and there was no change from his pound note. He clicked his tongue and winked at the waiter.

Hyde sipped at his drink. The trio drew attention to the stage with a peremptory call to attention that echoed Oscar Peterson, then slipped into the strait-jacket of 'I'm forever blowing bubbles' as a bath was wheeled on.

'Oh, Christ – bath night again,' Hyde murmured. 'Ivy the Terrible.' The subdued chatter of the audience tailed off into a silence that was weary rather than expectant. 'Well, Dmitri?'

Vassiliev leaned towards him, eyes flicking over Hyde's shoulder towards the stage, as the pianist imitated a fanfare. Hyde could never decide whether Vassiliev's interest in the girls was genuinely naïve and crude, or merely a badge of his manhood, designed to be noticed by those in his company. The KGB regarded homosexuals in only one light – as victims; malleable, male prostitutes. If

Vassiliev had any hidden proclivities towards men, then he was wise to hide them.

'You were wrong,' he said.

It was the one statement Hyde had not expected to hear. It generated a mass of complex doubts, questions and fears in an instant. The woman on stage was young, breasts extended to unnatural size by injection and implant, face expressionless beneath the make-up. See-through negligée, towel and loofah, bar of soap. The trio vamped the only expectancy in the now darkened room. Hyde watched the stage, picking his way towards the appropriate degree of innocent surprise. 'Dmitri, what do you mean I was wrong?'

'They *have* got Quin. They have him, but they want the girl.' Vassiliev's sweat gave off the pungency of the body rub he used. It clashed with his after shave, with the girl's scent, the omnipresent cigarette smoke.

'I'm not wrong,' Hyde began, but Vassiliev was already nodding eagerly. Hyde felt cold.

'Yes. Look, I risked everything this afternoon. There was no more gossip. I looked in the travel ledger. I went back and checked on the people who came in. They left with a third man – the next day. They flew to Paris in a light aircraft. I have the address, the booking. Three passengers – ' He reached into his pocket, but Hyde grabbed his hand – it quivered in his grip, which was slippery against Vassiliev's skin, informing Hyde that his nerves were taking him over. The girl was testing the supposed temperature of the water in the bath, letting the negligée fall open almost to the crutch. None of the audience was watching their corner of the room.

'Three? Three? What proof's that? I don't believe you, Dmitri. I don't think you know,' Hyde hissed at the Russian, still gripping the man's hand near his chest. The girl had stepped – with something less than elegance – over the side of the bath. Her negligée was drooping from one shoulder, tented by one enormous breast.

'You must believe me, you must!'

'I don't, Dmitri. Now, what bloody game are you playing?' The girl was obviously going to bath with tassels on her nipples. She slid down into the supposed water.

Then Vassiliev's eyes began moving, darting round the room. Hyde forced himself not to turn round. It did not mean there was someone in the room, only that there were others, either nearby or simply giving orders. Hyde gripped his thigh with his free hand, forcing the calm of angered puzzlement into his frame and face and voice. 'What bloody game are you playing, mate?' The girl had divested herself of the negligée, but not the tassels. She was stroking herself with the loofah.

'No game, Mr Hyde, no game!' Vassiliev was leaning towards him like a lover in the hot darkness, but he could not keep his eyes on Hyde's face. Escape, help, answers. He repeated the formula they had taught him. 'Three men left in that plane for Paris. Yes, they want the girl, but they have Quin in Moscow – I'm certain of it.'

'You don't know who the third man was. It couldn't have been Quin – ' Hyde found himself engaged in an attempt to justify the suspicions he had voiced to Aubrey; as if he believed Vassiliev. The girl was on the point of engaging in intercourse with the loofah. Soon she would be dropping the soap. 'No,' he said, 'you're lying, Dmitri. Why should they want you to lie?'

'They? What do you mean?' Too innocent.

'You weren't lying or mistaken at lunchtime. You *knew*, then. Now, you're working for them. Did they ask you how much you told me? Did they?' Hyde's face was close to Vassiliev. He could smell the man's last meal on his breath, and the brandy after dinner. Too much brandy – no, they wouldn't have allowed him more than one or two. 'They knew about you all the time, but they didn't let on. Not until they realised you must have told me more than was good for me.' He was shaking Vassiliev's hand, in anger and in community. The girl had dropped the soap, which did not slide across the stage. Her enormous breasts were hung over the side of the bath as she attempted to retrieve it. The trio was playing palm court music. The prissy, virginal sweetness of it assailed Hyde. 'You were doing all right until you told me you thought they didn't have Quin. And you *know* it!'

'I – must go,' Vassiliev said. Now the soap was back in the bath, but lost again. The girl was looking for it on her hands and knees. Snake-charmer music, and she rose to her feet, backside to the audience, buttocks proffered, swaying.

'You're going nowhere. Where are they?'

'Not here, not here!'

'You're coming in, Dmitri.'

'No!'

'You have to. We'll take care of you. I can't behave as if I believe you. You're the one in danger now.' Vassiliev had thought of it, but had ignored it. He shook his head, as if the idea was only a pain that would move, dissipate. The girl had the loofah again, standing up now, in profile to the room. The loofah was being energetically applied. 'Come on,' Hyde added.

'No! I can't leave with you, I can't!'

'Why not?'

'I can't!' He was pleading now. They were outside. If he emerged with Hyde, they would know Hyde had not swallowed the tale. The almost religious silence of the room was broken by hoarse cries of encouragement, underscored with what seemed like a communal giggle. The girl's body acknowledged the response to her performance.

'You can!' The gun, the gun – he'd left it at his flat, held it in his hand, almost amused, for a moment before stuffing it under a pile of shirts in a drawer. The gun –

'No, no, no – ' Vassiliev was shaking his head vehemently.

'It's your only chance. Come on, the back way.' Hyde got up, stood over the Russian, willing him to his feet. Vassiliev rose, and they shuffled through the tables towards the toilets. The door into the concrete, ill-lit corridor sighed shut behind them.

Vassiliev immediately turned to him. 'No,' he said.

'They concocted this story, right?' Vassiliev nodded, nerveless, directionless now. 'Why?'

'I don't know. They told me they had known, that they had fed you the information about Quin through me, deliberately. Then yesterday happened, and while they were deciding what to do about me, we talked. I – I told them everything.' A sense of shame, as sharp as a physical pain, crossed his features.

'It's all right, it's all right – was there anyone in the club?'

48

Vassiliev shook his head. There was applause on the other side of the door. 'Come on.'

Hyde half-pushed Vassiliev towards the emergency exit beyond the toilet. He heaved at the bar, remembered letting in friends by similar doors in Wollongong cinemas just before the start of the main feature, then the door swung open. The windy night cried in the lightless alley. He paused momentarily, and looked at Vassiliev. Then he nodded.

They went through the door almost together, but even so the man with the gun must have been able to distinguish between them. Vassiliev cried out – Hyde hardly heard the brief plopping sound of the silenced gun before the Russian's murmured cry – then he slumped against Hyde, dragging at his clothes, smearing the front of the Australian's shirt with something dark and sticky. Then he fell back, for a moment his face green from the exit sign's light, then all of him was simply a barely distinguishable bundle of clothes on the other side of the alley. Hyde waited for the noise of footsteps above the wind's dry call, or the sound of another stone-into-water plop that would be the last sound he would ever hear.

Three: INTRUDER

The gilded French clock on the marble mantelpiece chimed twelve, a bright, pinging, musical sound. Aubrey paused in his narrative, and he and Sir Richard Cunningham, Director of the Secret Intelligence Service, listened to the sound, watching the blue-numeralled face of the clock. When the chimes had ended, Aubrey stared into his brandy balloon, aware of how out of place his employment of technological and military jargon seemed here, in the study of Cunningham's flat in Eaton Place. Books and paintings – Cunningham had a small Braque and two Picasso etchings in that room – heavy furniture, civilisation. A conspiracy to belie the reality of detection systems, anti-sonar, satellites and distress signals in broken codes. Aubrey, for a moment, wished devoutly for a double agent, for the intimacies of a debriefing or an interrogation, for the clear boundary between SIS and MoD. Clark had pushed him across that border.

Cunningham had hardly spoken throughout Aubrey's recital of events, suspicions, fears. He had assiduously filled and refilled Aubrey's glass and his own, refrained from smoking a cigar, and listened, his half-closed eyes regarding his slippered feet crossed at the ankles. The book he had been reading when Lady Cunningham had shown in Aubrey lay on the occasional table at the side of his chair, the Bach to which he had been listening lay still on the turntable. his half-glasses rested on the end of his patrician nose, and his lips were set in a firm, expressionless line. Aubrey felt extremely reluctant to continue.

Then Cunningham spoke. 'What, exactly, do you wish to do, Kenneth?'

'Go in there – assess the situation for myself.'

'I see. You know how MoD regards us. You know how the navy regards itself. It's tricky. You've no just cause or impediment, after all.'

'I realise that, Richard. However, there is a mutuality of interest that might be stressed. Quin – '

'Ah, yes. MoD will tell us that he is our proper concern, one of Her Majesty's submarines more properly their sphere of authority. They will not take kindly to you suggesting they should reverse their decision. Nor will Brussels, nor will Washington. Sure you're not simply acting the old warhorse smelling the battle afar off?'

Aubrey smiled. 'I don't think so.'

'Mm. Neither do I. Devilish tricky, though. I can quite well see the importance of this anti-sonar system, and of Quin, and of keeping both out of Soviet hands. But we are not the experts, we are not the military. *They* don't seem to believe there is any risk – this man Clark, the American. Trust him?'

'And his judgement.'

'Mm. Knew you did.' Cunningham spread his hands, wafting them in the air. 'I just don't know – '

The telephone rang. Cunningham got up heavily and crossed to it. He listened, then gestured with the receiver towards Aubrey. His face was impassive.

'Yes?' It was Hyde. Aubrey listened to the voice at the other end of the line, his eyes watching Cunningham, deep in thought in his chair.

' . . . they obviously didn't want the hassle of killing me – just Vassiliev out of the way. They must have known I would try to take him in if I got suspicious . . .'

'You're all right?' Cunningham looked up at the note of concern in Aubrey's voice.

'Unhurt, I said. What now?'

'You'll see Mrs Quin tomorrow, and take a trip to the girl's college. Someone must be able at least to *guess* where she might be.'

'If you say so – '

'Tomorrow, you will go armed. Good night to you, Hyde.'

As Aubrey put down the receiver, Cunningham stared at him. 'What is it?'

'Hyde. His contact at the Soviet embassy has just been expertly dispatched in a dark alley. Before he was eliminated, Hyde had discovered that the news of Quin's removal had been deliberately leaked, and yesterday's events in Sutton Coldfield were being hidden behind a smokescreen. The KGB were on to the poor blighter, tried to turn him, realised they'd failed, and shot him.'

'Our man is all right?' Aubrey nodded. 'They don't have Quin, then. I think we can be certain of it now. There is still no connection between these events and the submarine.'

'I agree. Could we not argue a suspension of operations employing "Leopard" until the Quin matter is settled?'

'We might. The first thing, I suppose, is to get you inside this "Chessboard" matter. Once there, it will be up to you. *You* will have to find the means to persuade the minister to ask Cabinet to postpone this little adventure. I suggest you go in there for a briefing on this "Leopard" business, sniff around, and weigh the worth of what's being done. If you can convince me, then we'll go to the minister together, and he can take it from there, if he agrees with us. Satisfied?'

Aubrey pursed his lips, studied his glass, and then nodded. 'Yes, Richard. That will do nicely. I'll make an appointment for tomorrow – perhaps with Giles Pyott.' His face darkened. 'I'm too old for hunches and intuitions. But Clark is a clear-sighted, intelligent individual with a genuine talent for our work. I'm sorry to say it, but I think there is cause for concern, and I'm *sure* we should recall *Proteus* until we find Quin.'

'Make certain, Kenneth. There are a great many sensitive corns in MoD. Tread softly.'

'Mrs Quin, you must have some idea where we can find him! I just don't believe you can't help me.'

'Have you ever been divorced, or separated?'

'No.'

'Your parents?'

'No.'

'What happened to some of the girls you've known? Where are they now – just one of them? Tell me what she did yesterday.'

'It isn't the same.'

'It is, Mr Hyde, believe me, it is. Tricia's coming here was one of her impulses. She spent her childhood making believe that my husband and I were happy when we weren't, and the last three years trying to put Humpty-Dumpty back together again.' Mrs Quin sighed, and her brow knitted into deep, thread-like lines. 'I'm sorry for her – sorry for myself, too.'

Hyde sat back in the chair she had shown him to when she allowed him into the lounge. Occasional traffic outside, her day off from the antique shop, the Panda car conspicuous across the street. Trees still leafless, bending and moving with the wind. The gin-hour for lonely or bored suburban housewives. She had given him tea, and seemed not to resent his behaviour of two days before.

'Jesus, Mrs Quin, it's a bloody mess,' he sighed, rubbing his hands through his hair. 'Your daughter is in real danger – all right, you already know that, I'm sorry to remind you. Nevertheless, she is. So's your husband. She's with him, or still on her way back to him. The – the other people interested in your husband know that. They know we're interested – '

'Why did he have to involve her?' the woman suddenly cried, her voice and expression full of blame, even contempt. 'No, that's not fair, I suppose. She involved herself. I know Tricia.'

'I don't. Tell me about her.'

'You mean you don't already know?' There was an arch, mocking sharp little smile, a glimpse of white teeth. Today, the hair was firmly lacquered in place, the clothes well chosen, the whole being groomed. 'About the pop groups, the drugs – '

'Drugs? Soft or hard?'

'The sort you can smoke, I believe.'

'Soft. Occasionally?' Mrs Quin nodded. 'OK – rock bands?'

'Not in your files?' The easy contempt. She had forgotten her alliance with the uniformed inspector, her concern for young Sugden. Neighbours had talked, asked questions, and the police were an embarrassment, a minor disgrace.

'Yes – some references. Some time ago, though?'

'She – the phrase is *slept around*, I believe. With them.'

'A groupie?'

'I believe so. Am I entirely stupid to blame her college, and the kind of people they allow into them, and to teach in them, these days?' She evidently had little interest in his opinion.

'Probably,' he said. 'It's your privilege.'

'It ended, anyway. But she never seemed to settle afterwards.'

'Who – which group?'

'I don't know any of their names. I believe they were famous.'

'Did she travel with them?' A nod. 'When?'

'Two summers ago – all over the country, even to the Continent. And an open air festival.'

'But you don't know their names?'

'Had I ever known them, I would have forced myself to forget.'

'I see. Would her friends in college know anything about all this?'

'I'm sure they would have been regaled with the sordid details.'

'Perhaps I should talk to them?'

'It's past now – can't you leave it?' A naked plea, the face smoothed young by concern, softened.

Hyde stood up. 'If there's anything, anything at all, ring this number. A man called Aubrey. You'd like him.' Hyde grinned humourlessly.

'Why didn't he come himself?' The tone knife-like.

'He's too important. Thank you, Mrs Quin.' As they reached the door, he turned to her and added, 'I'll get to her first, if I can. You just pray a little, mm?'

'Stop engines!'

The Soviet submarine was back. It had crossed their bows an hour earlier, fifty fathoms above them, moving away to starboard. Lloyd had ordered silent running, the engines moving them very slowly ahead, because the computer identification had been of a 'Victor-II'-class attack submarine, nuclear-powered and a hunter-killer. A shark had met another shark. Then the 'Victor-II' had altered course again, possibly picking up faint traces of heat emission or prop noise. And she had begun looking, knowing that there was something to find.

The *Proteus* hummed with tension in the new, complete silence. Electronics murmured, those aft sonars required to keep track of the Soviet submarine, someone cleared his throat softly; Lloyd even heard the movement of Carr's sleeve across his chart as he updated the Contact Evaluation Plot at his chart table. The whisper of the hydroplane control wheels as the planesmen worked continuously to keep *Proteus* level and unmoving, constantly balancing the submarine's own attempts to alter position and depth. A juggling act. Easier on the bottom, but they weren't on the bottom.

Lloyd crossed to Thurston, who was standing behind the sonar operator monitoring the approach of the 'Victor-II' and whose screen displayed the snail-trail of light that revealed the position of the Russian vessel. Below the screen, red numerals supplied the read-out of bearing and distance. The 'Victor-II' was closing.

Submarines had been lost before, Lloyd reminded himself involuntarily. There was no fear and no courage, either. Vessels encountering each other in the dark, crowded sea. Collision or avoidance, attack or retreat. The 'Victor-II' was following their scent – heat, prop-wash, hull noise, the tiny skin-flakings of their passage which 'Leopard' could not completely neutralise. The twin hulls that enclosed them like plasterboard walls waited to transmit any sound they might make. Closer. Bearing unaltered. Speed a cautious, stalking twelve-point-seven knots. Time to contact, five minutes.

Lloyd mouthed silently at Thurston, who nodded. The first-lieutenant framed his lips to reply in the slightest whisper, after swallowing hard.

"If she doesn't find us, she might just miss us.'

'By much?'

'Not much,' Lloyd's hand was on the back of the sonar operator's chair. Some transmitted electricity from his captain made the rating twitch. Lloyd moved his hand. He turned to watch the two planesmen, juggling the control wheels like nervous car drivers. As if not in control of the vehicle. *Proteus* remained still, lying in the dark, waiting. Other trails of light – not new, but suddenly noticed and rendered significant by heightened nerves – on the sonar screen. Four other submarines, two destroyers and what might be the carrier *Kiev*, flagship of the Northern Fleet. She was too distant for a positive identification, and Lloyd had tended to discount her appearance in the Barents Sea. This early in the season, she was normally still refitting in Murmansk. And the 'Victor-II', brighter than all of them. Contact time, four minutes fifty. Lloyd felt, despite himself, that his hands were beginning to perspire. He opened them. The control room seemed hotter. Illusion.

Bearing unaltered. Speed constant. Cancel. New red numerals appeared in the read-out panel. Speed ten knots. The 'Victor-II' was slowing. Contact time three minutes twenty-eight, seven, six –

The sonar operator turned to Lloyd, his face puzzled. The 'Victor-II' was stopping, contact time and distance read-outs slowing down, then settling. Stopped. Contact time two minutes thirty-one frozen. The small, cramped space of the control room hot. Thurston was perspiring, a line of beads along his hairline. Lloyd felt the sweat dampening his shirt, running chilly down his sides. The sonar operator's hair cream, a sickly smell of which he was suddenly aware. Stomach light, disturbed.

Stopped. A third of a mile away. Six hundred yards. Close enough for temperature sensors. The movement of bare forearms in the corner of his vision as the planesmen juggled the *Proteus* to stillness. The auto-suggested hum of electronics, like the buzzing of an insect seemed very difficult to discount. The 'Victor-II' digesting the scraps of information, her captain waiting for an answer from his computer. *Is there an enemy submarine close to us?*

Red numerals flicking off. A bare, dark green panel beneath the sonar screen with its bright blip of light. Then new numbers. Speed four knots, five, six. Contact time two minutes nineteen, eighteen, seventeen, fifteen, twelve, seven – one minute fifty-nine. Bearing unchanged.

Lloyd waited. He could hardly bear to see the 'Victor-II' as it moved through the darkness towards them. One minute twenty. Speed ten knots. Distance two hundred yards, a little more, the little more eaten up even as he thought it. Eleven knots, bearing unchanged; as if they knew where *Proteus* was.

Then they listened. Two steam turbines driven by a pressurised water reactor. They would hear them, even though they were little more than idling at eleven knots.

Faces turned to the ceiling. Always that, Lloyd observed. A familiarity of orientation brought with them on to the submarine. It could be below, alongside, anywhere.

The churn of the screws. A slight, almost inaudible thrumming in their own hull. Faces tightening, the sense of fragility obvious. Louder. The illusion of a rising tremor in the eggshell of the hull. Hands sensing it where they rested damply against any part of the hull, any instrument – the planesmen juggling more violently now as the distressed water outside the hull assaulted the *Proteus* – feet feeling it, muscle-spasms in the calves. Louder.

Loudest, going on for what seemed like minutes, the planesmen failing to stop the submarine's bow from dropping, the whole vessel slipping forward into the beginnings of a dive, then arresting the movement, bringing the vessel back to stillness. Retreating noise and vibration. All around them the noise and motion had been, but Lloyd was certain the Soviet submarine had passed below them, slightly to port.

Then it was gone. Thurston mopped his brow enthusiastically, and grinned shakily at Lloyd.

'Close,' he murmured.

'Too close.' Then the idea came to him, and he voiced it before he considered its effect. 'I think she was expecting us – I mean us, this boat and its anti-sonar.'

'What?'

Lloyd looked down at the sonar operator, then at the others in the control room. He did not want to explain, not now. The idea, half-formed, frightened him, and he wanted to ignore it.

Thurston waited for his explanation, and Lloyd said, lamely, 'That Russian has been following a very poor trail for an hour. As if he knew we were here.'

'You're imagining it, skipper.'

'As if he knew he was looking for a submarine that wouldn't show up on his sonar,' Lloyd added.

'The evidence is in front of you, man. It may not be conclusive, but there is evidence there to suggest *Grishka* encountered the British submarine with its anti-sonar system working. Surely?'

57

'I will admit that not every trace of heat emission can be explained by temperature differences in the sea – perhaps there are identifiable traces of prop-wash and turbine activity, perhaps the faint gas traces help us – ' The rear-admiral looked round at his subordinates, then shrugged. 'We will pinpoint the British submarine at the position signalled by the *Grishka* and await any satellite confirmation there might be.'

'Excellent. She is on course. ETA?'

'On the basis of our supposition, no more than eighteen hours.'

Dolohov was about to reply when the door to the control room opened, and a man in civilian clothes – very Western, Dolohov noticed, a sweater, windcheater and corduroy trousers – stood in the doorway. The man came forward into the light, and Dolohov saw that he was grinning. His hair was blown awry. Dolohov returned the smile, and waved away the junior officer accompanying the man.

'Valery – Valery, my boy!' he announced, ignoring the others in the room, embracing the newcomer, kissing him on both cheeks, a greeting that was returned by the younger man.

'Admiral – sir,' the younger man acknowledged when held at arm's length by Dolohov. The rear-admiral seemed surprised to discover that the civilian, in addition to having a permit of entry to his operations room, was some species of naval officer. The haircut, the acknowledgement of rank. Yet almost like a son to the admiral. A little spurt of envy flared in the rear-admiral. This man was not to be treated like a schoolboy slow at his sums, apparently.

'You've come straight here?' Dolohov, even as he asked, was already drawing the younger man towards the window of the control room, already extending his free arm to direct the other's gaze. He was revealing a prized object of desire. The rear-admiral bowed frostily as he was casually introduced, resenting the intimacy that had invaded his clinical, sterile control room. 'Captain Valery Ardenyev, commanding the Red Banner Special Underwater Operations Unit,' Dolohov explained with evident pride, almost with a proprietorial, parental tone, then ignored the rear-

58

admiral. 'Down there,' he said to Ardenyev. 'We've marked her with a green light. A colour all to herself.'

'You're sure, sir?'

'We think so. She's on course, eighteen hours away from the fjord.'

Ardenyev stood looking down at the map table for some time. Dolohov, like a senior priest, allowed him silence and lack of interruption to his meditations, even though there was an impatience about his flinty features that made him appear both older, and much younger.

'The weather's worsening, sir,' Ardenyev said finally. 'But of course you know that.' Ardenyev grinned as he brushed his hair back into place.

'It isn't that bad, Valery,' Dolohov replied with a touch of acid.

'Not yet. I'll have to study the reports, and the predictions.'

'You have doubts?'

'Not yet, sir. Not yet.'

'We've eighteen hours, Valery.'

'We have to transfer to the salvage vessel long before that, sir. By helicopter.'

Dolohov gripped his arm. 'Valery – it will be all right,' He was instructing Ardenyev, even the weather. Commanding them both. 'It will be. We'll have her.' He turned to Sergei, his aide, whose position within the small group of the rear-admiral's team seemed an obscure insubordination to Dolohov. 'Sergei, get me an up-to-the-minute weather report for our area of interest. And get me *all* the met. predictions for the next twenty-four hours – *now*, Sergei.' Then Dolohov turned back to Ardenyev as to a child he had indulged, and who now must become obedient. 'It must be done, Valery. It must be done.'

'If it's possible, sir, it will be. I promise you that.'

The rear-admiral, observing the dialogue, conceived the idea that Ardenyev was not without calculation and guile. Dolohov responded by grabbing the younger man's arm, and pressing it with gratitude and what appeared to be affection. The rear-admiral recalled gossip concerning the way in which Ardenyev's career had been jealously promoted by the admiral. Some connection with

Ardenyev's father, even grandfather, he had heard. For his own part, the rear-admiral had risen by loyalty to the Party, and distrusted this Soviet version of what the British called the 'old boy network'. And he distrusted young naval officers in civilian dress with easy manners and obvious self-confidence. Elitist adventurers.

The rear-admiral withdrew to the other side of the control room, to await the updated satellite surveillance information. A small hope that Dolohov was precipitate, even mistaken, he nourished in his stomach like the warmth of a drink.

The college of education was a new one, built in the grounds of a Victorian magnate's former residence in the suburb of Edgbaston. The original house, having fallen into disrepair both before and after the compulsory purchase of the grounds, had disappeared. A tower block hall of residence stood on the site, bearing the same name as the grandiose house that one of Birmingham's Ozymandiases of trade or industry had erected to his own glorification. Two or three small, supposedly exclusive housing developments encroached on the perimeters of the college campus.

Hyde parked his car outside the tower block and sat for a moment considering his forthcoming interview with Tricia Quin's flatmate, Sara Morrison. Birmingham CID had talked to her the day the Quin girl appeared and disappeared, and had described her as unhelpful. Hyde had checked with the interviewing DC, who had amplified his observation by referring to the Morrison girl as a 'Lefty cow, anti-police, good background – isn't it usually the case', and wished Hyde the best of luck with her. A moment of futility as dispiriting as weariness overcame Hyde, then he got out of the car and slammed the door.

The sky was overcast, sombre with rain. The downpour that it threatened was postponed only by the strong, gusty wind that swept paper and dust and old leaves across the grass and the concrete walks around the hall of residence; hurried and chafed the few figures he could see. An overriding impression of concrete and glass and greyness, a modern factory complex. He hurried up the steps into the foyer of the tower block.

A porter, uniformed and officious, emerged from a cubicle, wiping his lips. Hyde showed him the CID warrant card which avoided explanations, and asked for Tricia Quin's flat. The porter, evidently unimpressed by the length of Hyde's hair and his casual dress, begrudgingly supplied the number, and the information that Sara Morrison was in the flat at that moment. He had seen her return from a lecture half-an-hour before. Hyde went up in the lift, unamused by the mock-intellectual graffiti that decorated its walls. He gathered, however, that punk rock had achieved the status both of an art form and a political weapon.

A long corridor, blank, veneered doors. The carpet was marked and already worn, the plaster on the walls evincing settlement cracks. He knocked on the door of 405.

The girl who opened the door wore her hair in tight curls. Her face was instantly suspicious rather than intrigued or helpful. A mouth that pulled down into a scowl almost naturally, it seemed. Sallow skin, no make-up, a creased blouse and uniform denims. Her feet were bare.

'Yes?' A middle-class, south-east accent, overlain with the drawl of the fashionable urban. 'What d'you want?'

'Sara Morrison?' She nodded. 'Could we have a word about Tricia Quin. I believe – ' the warrant card was in his hand, his shoulder against the door as she tried to shut it. 'I believe she shares this flat with you.'

The girl resigned herself to not being able to close the door on him.

'Past tense,' she said, her eyes bright with calculation.

'Really?'

'You're Australian.'

'Too right.' He grinned disarmingly, but the girl did not respond.

'In Birmingham?' she mocked. 'An Australian pig, in Birmingham?'

'Could be. It's not only politics that travel distances. May I come in?'

The girl shrugged and released the door. He opened it on an untidy, cramped room with two single beds against opposite walls. A window in the end wall overlooked the campus car-park. Clothes draped over a functional chair,

61

books spread across a small, cheap desk. Posters on the wall – Mao, Lenin, Sex Pistols, a *Playboy* centrefold with a crudely drawn moustache and glasses and even white teeth blacked out, Castro, Margaret Thatcher used as a dartboard, a Two-Tone band.

'What do you want?' the girl demanded belligerently as he observed the door leading off, bathroom and toilet. 'She isn't here, you know.' Her accent wavered between the glassy superiority of her background and undoubted money, and the urban snarl she felt he deserved.

'I suppose not. Someone would have seen her. The porter for instance?'

'Beria, you mean?'

Hyde laughed. 'May I sit down?' The girl swept her clothes off the single chair, and squatted on the edge of her bed, feet drawn up beneath her, signalling indifference. Hyde sat down. The girl studied him.

'A trendy pig.'

'We try, darling – we try.'

'You fail – or should I have said, try and condemn?' She parted her lips in a mirthless grin, flashing her cleverness in that precise visual signal.

'A hit, I do confess. Can we talk about your erstwhile girlfriend?'

'What is there to say? She isn't here. End of story.'

'Not her story. You know she's been seen. Have you seen her?' The girl shook her head, her face betraying nothing. 'Sure?'

'I told your thick mate from CID that I hadn't seen her. Don't you believe me?'

'Not if I asked you for the right time. What would I get – the time in Moscow, or Peking?'

'Cuba,' Sara Morrison replied without expression.

Hyde looked up at the ennobled poster of Fidel Castro. 'He's a bit out of style, isn't he? Even Arthur Scargill's heard of him.'

The girl applauded ironically. 'Very funny – oh, too witty for words.'

'Blimey, thanks, darling,' he replied in his broadest accent. 'Now we've both tried on backgrounds we never came from.' He leaned forward in his chair. Unexpectedly, the girl flinched. He said, 'This isn't France or South America, darling. Or Nazi Germany or Kampuchea or the Soviet Union. I could have you down the station, true, but your daddy would get you out by tea-time, I should think,' The girl's face wrinkled into contempt, then smoothed to indifference again, as if she had revealed too much of herself. 'Always too busy at the office, was he? Chased other women? Self-made man?'

'Fuck off.' The obscenity came almost primly from her lips.

'In a minute. Look, Tricia Quin is in trouble – not with us, before you harangue me again, with some people who you might think you like, but wouldn't if you met them.'

After a silence, the girl said, 'National security bullshit, I presume.'

'Sorry darling, it's the only excuse I have.'

'Why can't you fucking well leave her alone!' the girl suddenly yelled at him, her face bright red with rage. The mood was sudden, manic in its swing.

'I *want* to. She has to be protected.'

'Crap.'

'Not crap. Listen to me.' The girl's hands were bunched into fists in her lap, or twitched open, as if gripping some imagined weapon. There was a violence of rage and guilt and outrage in her that found the body inadequate to express such depths of feeling. 'I can't help the situation in which she finds herself. Blame her father, blame national security, blame the bloody arms race if you want to – but I'm the only chance she's got. People want her because they can get to her father through her. They won't mind what they do to her to discover her father's hiding place. And before you say it – yes, I want her father, too. But I don't want to harm him, and I want to help her.'

His dismissal passed like a flicker caused by dust in her eyes. Politics in place, attitudes firmly fixed, cemented. She would not tell him. Hyde saw the weapon of threat present itself, and wanted to reject it.

'I don't know where she is – and I wouldn't tell you if I did.'

'For Christ's sake, girlie!' Hyde exploded. 'Some of the two hundred or so Soviet diplomats with the ill-fitting suits

63

and the poor-diet boils are looking for your girlfriend right now! When they find her, it will be a little bit of slapping about, then the closed fist, then the bucket over the head and the baseball bats, then the cigarette ends for all I know – they won't have time to talk to her politely, some bigger bastard will be breathing down their necks for results. Even if they wanted to be nice. Your friend could tell them she was a card-carrying member of the Party and they'd pull her fingernails out until she told them what they wanted to know.' He was speaking quite calmly during the last sentence, but the girl's face was white with anger and with surprised fear. There was something unselfish as well as disbelieving about her.

'You really believe all that?' she said at last. Her composure, her closed-minded prejudices, had reasserted themselves. 'Christ, the perfect functionary!'

'My God, but you're stupid – '

'Tricia's been frightened out of her mind – don't you realise that?' the girl shouted at him. 'Before her father disappeared, she was depressed, moody, frightened. Then she left – just like that. She hadn't slept a wink the night before. Doesn't that make *any* impression on you?'

'Was she frightened when you saw her two days ago?'

'Fuck off, clever sod.'

Both of them were breathing hard. Only the wind, moaning more loudly round the building, offered a larger perspective than the cramped hothouse of the small room. The girl's face was implacable.

Hyde stood up, then crossed swiftly to her, clamping his hand over her mouth, holding her wrists in his other hand. He pushed her flat on the bed, kneeling beside her.

'You know what's coming now, darling. You've imagined it, talked about it, often enough. You're Blair Peach, love – you're a Black in Detroit, you're Steve Biko. I'm untouchable, darling. It'll be an accident.' He could feel spittle on his palm, and sweat, and her eyes were wide with terror. 'Everything you've ever thought about the pigs is true. Now you're going to find out.'

Then he released her, moved away, sat down. The girl wiped at her mouth, rubbed her wrists. When she found her voice, she coughed out his eternal damnation.

'Sorry,' he said. 'You would have told me. Your eyes were already regretting your earlier bravado.' His voice was calm, casual, unemotional. 'We both know that. Tricia would tell them even quicker, even though it was her father.'

'For God's sake – ' the girl began, but there seemed nothing she could add.

'Yes. You're right again. She came here, didn't she?'

'She bloody didn't!' He knew, with an empty feeling, that it was true. The girl appeared hurt and useless. She'd have helped – lied, hidden Tricia, given her money, taken on the pigs, anything. But Tricia Quin hadn't even asked. Hyde felt sorry. Useless energy and emotion slopped around in Sara Morrison, mere ballast for a pointless journey.

'I'm sorry about that. Tell me where she might be, then?' On an impulse, he added: 'Her mother mentioned she hung out with a rock band a couple of summers ago – pot, groupie-ing, the whole naughty bag. Any news on that?'

'Those dinosaurs,' the girl remarked, glancing up at the Two-Tone group posturing down at her.

'Them?' he asked, looking up. The girl laughed.

'You remember a band called Heat of the Day?'

'Yes. I liked them.'

'You're old enough.' The girl had slipped into another skin, represented by half of the posters on the wall, and by the cassette tapes on one of the shelves, next to a huge radio with twin speakers. Something an astronaut might have used to contact the earth from deep space. The girl was now a pop music aficionado, and he someone with parental tastes. Hyde had wondered which way the retreat into shock would take her. It looked more promising than other possible routes, but it would not last long. Eventually, she would be unable to disguise from herself the threat he represented.

'I thought they disbanded.'

'They did. You don't read *Melody Maker* any more, obviously.'

'Nor *Rolling Stone*. My age.' He invited her to smile, but she did not respond. She did not look at him now, merely at her hands in her lap. She might have been drugged, or meditating.

'They're back together – on tour. I remember Tricia was interested.'

'How did she get in with them, originally?'

'The lead singer, Jon Alletson, was in school with her brother – the one who emigrated to Canada.'

'Would she have gone to them by any chance, would she still be in touch with them?'

Sara's face closed into a shrunken, cunning mask. 'I wouldn't know,' she said, and Hyde knew the conversation was at an end. In another minute, it would be police brutality, threats of legal action. He stood up. The girl flinched.

'Thanks,' he said. 'Take care.'

He closed the door quietly behind him, hunger nibbling at his stomach, a vague excitement sharp in his chest. Rock supergroup? Friend of her brother? Perhaps the girl knew she was being chased round and round the garden, and had gone to earth where she would be welcomed and wouldn't be looked for, amid the electronic keyboards and yelling guitars and pounding drums, the hysteria and the noise and the cannabis and the young. In that thicket, she would recognise her enemies, from either side, with ease.

It might just be –

Tedium, anger, even anxiety, were all now conspiring to overpower caution. Aubrey felt within himself a surprising violence of reaction to his hour-long tour of the 'Chessboard Counter' room and operation. The broaching of *Proteus*'s diversion to the Tanafjord proved the sticking point, broke the camel's back of his discretion. Perhaps, he reasoned with himself, it was the blasé, confident, aloof manner in which the monitoring action on the stricken Russian submarine was explained that so infuriated him. But images of Quin, with their attendant fears, and the pervasive odour of a possible trap, conspired to assist the wearing of his patience. Clark, too, seemed to be waiting for his cue; expecting Aubrey to make some decisive move, influence events.

And the smoothly running, almost mechanical individuals in the room; the obtrusive freemasonry of serving officers. The sterile hangar of the room; his own sense of himself regarded, at best, as the man from the Pru. He could no longer keep silence, or content himself with brief, accommodating smiles and innocuous questions. The excuse that he merely sought enlightenment regarding Quin's project became transparent in its flimsiness, insupportable. Even so, the vehemence evident to himself, and to Pyott and the others, in his voice when his temper finally broke through, surprised him.

'Giles, what do you hope to gain from this monitoring action?' he snapped. He waved his hand dismissively at the huge map-board.

'Our northern security is in question here, Kenneth,' Pyott replied in surprise, his nostrils narrowed to slits, the tip of his nose whitened with supressed anger at Aubrey's tone. 'Surely you can see that?'

'It is a point of view.'

'Kenneth, you are not an expert – '

'No, this distress call, now. You don't suspect its genuineness?'

'Good Lord, no.'

'What about you, Captain Clark?'

'Not really. I just don't think the matter's important enough to risk "Leopard".' He looked up at the cluster of lights on the board. They seemed to have one centre, where the wavering arrow of the light indicator being operated by Pyott demonstrated *Proteus*'s position.

'Ah. Now, my immediate reaction, employing my own peculiar expertise, would be to suspect the distress call. I would need proof that it was genuine.'

'We've identified the submarine concerned,' the commodore explained brusquely. 'We have triple checked. I don't think the matter is in doubt.' He looked to Pyott for support, and received it in an emphatic shake of the head.

Aubrey was intensely aware of the opposition of the two officers. They represented an opposite pole of interests. Also, they were in some way legitimised by their uniforms. Third Murderer again, he observed to himself.

'I see. It would still be my starting point.'

'What would be the object of an elaborate deception, in this case?' Pyott drawled.

'"Leopard."'

'Good Lord, you're surely not serious – ?'

'How would you react to the recall of *Proteus* until this chap Quin is found?'

'Utter nonsense!'

'The two matters haven't the slightest connection with one another Kenneth.'

'Great idea.'

'Ah. You would support such a move, Captain Clark?'

'I would.' Pyott looked pained by a spasm of indigestion, the commodore appeared betrayed.

'I do really think it's dangerous, risking "Leopard" in this way without having Quin safe and sound.'

'You made that point weeks ago, Kenneth. Try another record.'

'Giles, the KGB have started killing, such is their interest in Quin. Am *I* to rate his importance any lower – or that of his project?' Aubrey pointed up at the map, then indicated the rest of the room and its occupants. 'Who else is looking into this distress call?'

'It's our show.'

'Your work here is important, even if I consider it precipitate. But this present adventure – Giles, what can you possibly gain?'

Aubrey saw the answer in Pyott's eyes before the man spoke.

'Kenneth, I am at liberty to inform you – you, too, Clark – that this present adventure, as you term it, has a highest category security tag on it.'

'For a distress call?'

'For *Proteus*'s mission,' Pyott explained quietly and fiercely. Aubrey guessed at the nature of the mission, and was appalled. It was what he had suspected he might hear, if he needled Pyott sufficiently, and what he had wished devoutly not to hear. 'The mission has been code-named –'

'You mean it's another, and extreme, *sea trial* for the "Leopard" system, Giles?'

'Why, yes,' Pyott admitted, somewhat deflated.

'What in hell – ?'

'Excuse me, Captain Clark. Giles, you mean that

approval has been given to sail *Proteus* almost into Soviet home waters, merely to prove the efficacy of the anti-sonar system?'

'That's it precisely.'

'My God, Giles, it's lunacy. Playing games. You have put the system, the submarine, her crew, at risk, just to score extra marks in the examination. It is nonsense, and furthermore, dangerous nonsense!' He studied Pyott's face, which was colouring with anger, and then the commodore. An identical, undented confidence.

'What is *Proteus*'s ETA in the Tanafjord?'

Pyott smiled thinly. 'I see no harm in telling you, Kenneth. Disregarding changes of course and speed, we estimate sixteen to eighteen hours. Some time early tomorrow morning, GMT.'

'Giles, what intelligence do you have from the Norwegians?'

'They've backed off, fortunately.'

'Aerial surveillance?'

'We have some confirmation – infra-red, naturally. We've more or less pinpointed the Russian boat.'

'It *is* just an excuse, isn't it, Giles?'

Pyott shrugged, expansively; self-deprecation and dismissal featured jointly in the gesture of his shoulders and hands.

'It is an important – crucial – NATO exercise. A sea trial, as I explained. It cannot be described as an *excuse*.'

Aubrey paused for a moment, then he said quietly and distinctly: 'Giles – Giles, I am deeply sorry about this, but I must act.' His throat seemed tight, and he coughed to clear it before adding, 'Everything I have seen today, every instinct in my body, tells me to act.' In his turn, he shrugged; a smaller, more apologetic movement. 'There is no justifiable reason for this mission which outweighs its inherent risks to men, boat, or security. I have no other choice.'

'You'll never obtain authority to override StratAn, MoD *and* NATO.'

'I do not need to. This intelligence mission is on the point of going critical. I shall, therefore, invoke an ETNA order. I shall apply to the foreign secretary to make *Proteus*'s mission an SIS operation, and then I shall cancel it and recall the submarine.'

Pyott was almost visibly shaking with fury. When Aubrey finished speaking, the silence of the huge room pressed in upon the tight group beneath the map; silence lapping against them like waves.

'Be damned to you, Aubrey,' Pyott said at last. 'I'll oppose you every inch of the way.'

Aubrey regarded him for a moment. There was nothing conciliatory he could say, no palliative he even wished to offer. He said, 'It should not take long. I expect to return later this afternoon with the appropriate authority – authority to stop this foolish school prefects' prank!'

Four: CLOSING

'Kenneth – I'm with the minister now.'

'Yes, Richard.' Cunningham had called him on a scrambled line direct from the Foreign Office.

'Your request for special status – the ETNA order – '

Aubrey grasped at Cunningham's hesitation. 'C' would have talked to one of the ministers of state, and undoubtedly to the Foreign Secretary directly after lunch. As a Permanent Under-Secretary, the director of the intelligence service could command such immediate access, as might Aubrey himself, whose civil service rank was Deputy Under-Secretary. However, Cunningham had chosen to represent Aubrey's case himself, and alone. It appeared he had failed to convince the politicans.

'Yes, Richard?' Aubrey repeated, prompting his superior.

'The Secretary of State has agreed to your request. The Admiralty has been informed of the decision. "Chessboard Counter" is, as of three-fifteen this afternoon, an SIS intelligence operation.'

Aubrey's sigh of relief must have been audible to Cunningham. 'Thank you, Richard,' he said. He wanted to know more, disliked having been kept waiting upon events. 'I'm sure you were most persuasive.'

'I think we might say that the moment was opportune,' Cunningham drawled. Aubrey understood. The Secretary of State, for his own reasons, had perceived and employed a means of impressing his authority upon another ministry. 'Your authorisation will be waiting for you here. I suggest you come over right away.'

They knew, and they resented him. Each and every one of the 'Chessboard Counter' team, with the exception of Ethan Clark, met his entry to the underground room with silence and a carved hostility of expression. One tight group stood beneath the map-board, Pyott and the commodore

71

were at the latter's desk, standing as if posed for some official portrait which recaptured the aloofness and distance of ancestral oils; the communications and computer operators had their backs to him not so much in gainful employment, more in some communal snub.

Aubrey went immediately to the desk, shedding his dark overcoat, taking off his hat. Man from the Pru, he reminded himself, and the image amused rather than belittled him.

'Gentlemen – I'm sorry.'

'We're not simply going to lie down under this – ' Pyott began, waving Aubrey's written authorisation, but Aubrey raised his hand. At the edge of his vision, Clark was moving towards them, triumphantly.

'I'm sorry gentlemen, the time for discussion is past. I regret having usurped your authority, but "Chessboard Counter" is now my responsibility. And I expect your co-operation.' His voice was heavy with interrogation. The commodore appeared, strangely, more reluctant than Pyott. It was the soldier who finally spoke. Clark hovered a few yards away.

'Very well, Aubrey, you shall have our co-operation. The damage you have done today to NATO's security, and to the good relations between the various intelligence branches, is something that will only emerge with time.' He paused, his lips smirking. 'I shall make every effort to see that this matter is fully and properly investigated.'

'I expect nothing less, Giles. When the time is right.' Aubrey smiled; challenge and sadness in the expression. Then he turned to Clark. 'Captain Clark, our first priority – ' His voice invited the American into conference with himself and the two senior officers, 'is to recall the *Proteus*.'

'That, I'm afraid, is impossible,' the commodore remarked bluntly. Aubrey realised he had been mistaken. The posed and still expressions had not expressed resentment, not in Pyott and the commodore. Rather, the closed, secret blankness of card players. They did not consider themselves beaten.

'Why, pray?' Aubrey asked frostily.

'*Proteus* is observing the strictest radio silence until the mission is completed and she has returned to a position off North Cape. Only then will she transmit, and be able to receive.'

'Sorry, Kenneth,' Pyott added. 'I omitted to tell you before. It's quite true what the commodore says — no communications facility exists between ourselves and *Proteus*.'

Inwardly, Aubrey was furious, but his face retained an icy control. 'I see,' he said. 'Impossible?'

'Not quite,' Clark remarked quietly at Aubrey's shoulder. The old man looked round and up into the American's face. It was gleaming with satisfaction, with the sense of outwitting the two senior British officers. Clark was working out his private grudge.

'Go on,' Aubrey prompted.

'*Proteus* has pre-determined listening out times. She could be reached then. With a hydrophonic buoy.'

'Dropped from an aircraft, you mean?'

'Yes. One of your Nimrods. Highest priority code, continuous frequency-agile transmission. An unbroken, one-time code. Just tell *Proteus* to get the hell out.'

The commodore appeared deflated. Pyott was merely angry, but he kept silent.

'I want to look at the state of play,' Aubrey said with gusto, as if he had come into an inheritance and was about to be shown over the property. 'Ethan, come along. Giles – ?'

Pyott shrugged, and followed. The group of young officers beneath the huge map-board dispersed a little. They sensed that Aubrey had won. They had been betrayed by the American who had opened the judas-gate into the castle. The enemy was amongst them; they had been routed.

Aubrey looked up, then turned to Clark and Pyott: 'Well? Where is she?'

'About here.' Clark flashed on the light-indicator's arrow. A cluster of lights surrounded it, very bright like falling meteors.

'Those lights are all Soviet vessels, I take it?' Aubrey asked in a quiet voice.

'Right.'

73

'Explain them to me.'

Now the arrow dabbed at each of the lights, as Clark talked.

'These positions haven't been updated for three hours – we have another hour before the satellite comes over the horizon and we can pick up transmission of the current picture. This is the carrier *Kiev*, the pride of the fleet. She's changed course three times, the last one took her from here to here – ' Southwards. 'She *was* heading west. These two are "Kashin"-class destroyers, they left Pechenga yesterday. These three are ELINT vessels, probably spy-ships rigged as trawlers, but they're not with fishing fleets – they've change course, here to here – ' Southwards and eastwards. 'This, according to some very bad satellite photography yesterday is a rescue ship, the *Karpaty*. She left Murmansk a couple of days ago. Why she's in the area, I wouldn't know. It may not even be her, could be another ELINT vessel, but a big one. And there are the submarines – ' The arrow dabbed now at spot after spot of light. 'Hunter-killers, every one.'

'Thank you, Captain Clark.' Aubrey turned to Pyott and the commodore, who had now joined them. Behind them, the junior officers formed a knot of silent supporters. 'Is it because I am a mere layman that these Soviet naval dispositions frighten me, make me leap to one conclusion, and only one?' He paused, but there was no murmur of reply. He continued: 'Gentlemen, it would seem obvious to me that the Soviets have at least surmised that *Proteus* is in the area and making for Tanafjord. This activity is not directed towards the rescue of the crippled submarine. What is intended I do not propose to guess. If anything happens to *Proteus*, I am now required to accept responsibility. If I can prevent it, nothing untoward will happen. Clark, come with me. We apparently require the co-operation of the Chief of Air staff. Commodore, a secure line, if you please.'

'Thank God for sanity,' Clark whispered. Aubrey turned on him.

'Ethan, it may already be too late. It is simply a matter of deciding tenses, from what you have shown me. *Proteus* is walking into – *has* walked into – a trap. Pray that the present tense still applies!'

A bright yellow TR7. It was an easy car in which to be tailed, and the two men in the Ford Granada had stuck to him from Edgbaston through the centre of Birmingham – even in the afternoon traffic – and out on to the M6 motorway. Standing in the doorway of the café near the college, the *Melody Maker* tucked under his arm, one hand disguising the burping indigestion that the sausage and chips had given him, he had seen the car parked across the street from his own. It had U-turned and followed him. He had never lost sight of it in his mirror, and they had never lost sight of him.

Thus he passed his turn-off eight miles further back towards Birmingham, and now the signs indicated the next service area. He signalled, and pulled off the M6, up the slope into the car park. He got out of the car without glancing at the Granada sliding into an empty place twenty yards from him, and went into the foyer of the building. He slipped into the toilet, walked the length of it, and exited through the second door, leading out again to the car park from the side of the building. He approached the corner slowly, peering round it. One of the two men was standing by the Granada, the other was nowhere to be seen. Presumably, he had followed Hyde into the service station.

Hyde waited impatiently. If the second man didn't move almost at once, he would have to go back into the toilet and attempt to shake them later. And now impatience was a nagging toothache. The man by the Granada was smoking, and picking at his teeth with the hand that held the cigarette. Come on, come on –

The man patted his stomach, which was ample, resting over the lip of his waistband. He hesitated, then he drifted towards the shop at the front of the building, moving with angering slowness out of Hyde's line of vision.

Hyde began running then. He reached the TR7, jerked open the door, and slid into the low seat. He had left the keys in the ignition. He started the engine, and squealed in reverse out of his parking space, swinging the car towards the car-park's exit. In the wing mirror, for a moment, the running figure of the fatter man, then the other emerging from the building behind him, yelling. Then he was down the slope and into the entry lane. He pulled out in front of a heavy lorry, and stamped on the accelerator. The next exit from the M6 was two miles away. He would lose them there, then double back to his intended destination. The speedometer registered ninety. He was still breathing hard, but he was grinning.

Hyde turned the TR7 into the most convenient car-park for Hall 5 of the National Exhibition Centre. The fountain in the middle of the artificial lake in front of the huge hotel complex looked cold and stiff, like dead, blowing grass. It had taken him almost an hour to backtrack the twelve miles or so to the NEC site. He had not been followed through the suburbs of Coventry, back towards the airport. They might – just might – have assumed that he was heading east, towards the M1.

Streamers bearing slogans. A queue had formed already, sleeping bags were in evidence, denim like a uniform or prison garb, combat jackets blazoned with insignia, out-of-style long hair worn by many . The audience, or part of it at least, for Heat of the Day's concert at the NEC, kick-off at eight o'clock. It was now almost five. Edwin Shirley's trucks were already unloading the sound and light equipment. Policemen.

Hyde showed his CID warrant card, and was allowed through the cordon. He immediately picked out Fat Mary, one of the formerly much-publicised road crew. Many of the faces seemed half-familiar from television documentaries when Heat of the Day were on their pinnacle. They had come back like lost disciples.

'Excuse me –'

'Piss off,' the fat girl replied.

'Police, darling.' He tiredly waved the warrant card.

'Nobody's carrying.'

'I'm not interested. Are the band here?'

'Two hours yet. Want some autographs?' She watched two of the road crew carrying a huge mirror, and bellowed, 'For Christ's sake, haven't you got all the mirrors up yet?'

'No autographs. Tell me – is Tricia Quin with them?'

A flicker, like a wasp sting, at the corner of her mouth, then the sullen look returned. 'Who?'

'Tricia Quin. She was with you on the Europe tour two years ago. Her brother knew Jon.'

'Oh, yes. I remember. No, haven't seen her. It's not *all* the same as before, you know.'

'I don't suppose it is. She's not with them, then?' The fat girl shook her head. Her pendulous breasts distorted the claim on her T-shirt that she had attended the University of California. 'Perhaps I'll stick around. Collect a few autographs.'

'Or a few smokers.'

'Who knows, Fat Mary.' The girl seemed pleased at the use of her name, the recollection of a former, half-celebrity status. 'Keep it in your pocket, not in your mouth. See you.' The girl scowled after him.

Tricia Quin, unless he was mistaken – no, he wasn't – was with the band. Two hours seemed an intolerable length of time.

The one-time code message was lengthy, and even the computer's rendering of it into plain seemed to occupy far more time than was usually the case. Even so, when the KGB Resident Petrunin possessed the plain-language text, irritation immediately replaced impatience. He felt hampered by his instructions from Moscow Centre at the same time that he wished, fervently, to comply with those orders.

He left the code room in the embassy basement and took the lift to his office. *At any cost – immediately. The girl.* It was almost demeaning that an unavoidable test of competence and loyalty should have as its object an immature girl unable to cope with growing up. And it was infuriating that superior officers as eminent as the Deputy Chairman responsible for the KGB's 2nd Chief Directorate should indulge in some vulgar, glory-seeking race against the Red Banner Northern Fleet to see who could first acquire 'Leopard' for the Soviet Union. All those old men belonged to the same class, the same era. *Dolohov appears confident the submarine is sailing into his trap. You have little time.* The girl, the girl –

He locked the door of his office behind him, and flung

the high-security document case on to one of the armchairs. He thrust his hands into his pockets, and stood at the window. Lowering clouds, pulled across the sky by a fierce wind. Trees bending.

Damn those clowns in Birmingham, losing Hyde. Correction. Letting Hyde lose them. Hyde was the key, even more so than the girl. And he was at one further move from Quin, and that was another cause of anger at the unfairness of the task set him. Hyde must know something, must have discovered some clue as to the girl's whereabouts, otherwise he would not have bothered to shake the tail.

What did he know?

The girl student , the mother? Either of them? Something popping into his head as he was driving out of Birmingham? Tamas Petrunin grinned. It was impossible to know. Interesting to speculate. It was what he enjoyed. Guesswork. He rubbed his hands together, and turned his back to the window where the wind rustled tinnily outside the double glazing. Birmingham. He couldn't send anyone to see the girl Morrison, nor the mother. Not so soon after Hyde. And it might not be necessary.

Birmingham. When did he spot the tail car? Petrunin opened the wad of newspapers on his desk. Normally, they would be sent down to junior staff for analysis, but Petrunin often liked to glance through the provincial newspapers for evidence of KGB activity, actual or potential. The *Birmingham Post*. A rather stuffy, empty paper. He flicked through the pages. Nothing. The *Evening Mail*. Nothing. Hyde would not expect to find the girl at a football match.

Then where? Where would he expect to find the girl? Be Hyde, he instructed himself. Talking to the mother and the friend, then suddenly there is something to cling to, some chance of finding the girl. And the need to shake the surveillance he had discovered – *clowns*.

Where?

He returned to the newspapers. The girl now. What did he know about her? He crossed with rapid, bustling steps to a large filing cabinet against the far wall of the office, wood-veneered so that its function did not obtrude upon the room. He opened one drawer and removed the file on

Quin's daughter. A narrow, shadowy file. He carried it back to his desk, dumping most of the newspapers on the carpet, leaving open the two Birmingham dailies. Where would Hyde expect to meet the girl?

Movements in Birmingham: he scanned the digest in the file. Clubs, pubs, cinemas, one or two exhibitions, concerts, visits to her mother. Dull stuff.

Social habits: clubs, pubs, cinemas. *Sexual behaviour*: Petrunin scanned the itemised digest. For the last two years, one or two casual, short-lived relationships within the college, a very brief affair with one of her lecturers, then a teacher she met while on teaching practice. Hyde had had Birmingham detectives question all these people. No one had seen her recently. When she ended an affair, she never revisited the scene of the crime. Petrunin savoured the epithet, then grew angry at the truism it contained. It was true that the girl never went back.

Alletson? Oh, the pop singer. The big affair, travelling with the pop group from place to place. Her parents had been worried by that, from all acounts. Soft drugs, promiscuity. A nightmare in Sutton Coldfield. Again, Petrunin grinned. Even Alletson had failed to make any lasting impression upon the girl. A pity.

Psychological Profile: a fine example to us all, he told himself. He skimmed through it. He already knew the girl, as well as she could be known at second hand, and even though her background and past history prompted him to indulge in stereotypes to account for her – she so easily fitted Western and Soviet myths about modern youth and permissive societies – he was certain that there was nothing in the Profile to explain why Hyde had charged off in his little yellow car.

He slapped the file back on his desk. He knew it almost by heart, it had been the merest illusion to assume that the answer would spring from its flimsy sheets. Had she been his own daughter – as he supposed she could have been, in age at least – he would have no real clue to her whereabouts. As KGB Resident, he could not walk around in her head with ease or certainty. Hyde's head bore more similarity to his own.

Where?

The newspapers. He put the file to one side. Football, cinemas, factories on strike, a Royal visit proposed for later in the year – the appropriateness of the blank crossword – share prices . . .

He folded the morning paper to one side, and returned to the tabloid evening newspaper from the previous day. Grinning beauty queen, footballer with arms raised gladiatorially. Cinemas, clubs, discos, concerts.

The print began to blur. He knew he was not going to find it. Picture of a queue of people, sleeping bags, combat jackets, long hair. He wasn't going to find it. Pop concert at the National Exhibition Centre. Headline to the picture caption, 'Who are we waiting for?'

He flicked over the page, then the next page, before what he thought he had not bothered to read entered his consciousness and immediately caused his heart to thud and his hand to tremble. He creased the pages of the paper turning back to the picture and its caption. Other, smaller pictures underneath, of course. The heroes of yesterday. Heat of the Day. Alletson, the girl's lover. Long hair and soft, almost feminine features. The NEC, Birmingham, concert tonight.

He laughed aloud, congratulating himself. Accident, luck, good fortune, chance never disturbed him. He had placed himself in the way of it. Hyde had stumbled across this in the same kind of way. Something the Morrison girl said, or the mother, or two years ago merely popping into his head.

Whether the girl would be there or not, Hyde would. That was a certainty, and perhaps the only one. In which case, Tamas Petrunin would also be there. He looked at his watch. After five-thirty. He calculated. Just time, if they could get out of the centre of London without delay, to the M1. Just time –

'Is that extra signals traffic co-ordinated?'

'Sir,' Sergei answered. The young aide swallowed a mouthful of bread before he answered Dolohov. Then, finding it stuck in his throat, he washed it down with tea. One corner of the Ops. Room control centre had become a preserve, marked off by invisible fences – authority, nerves, tension – from the normal staff. Around a metal chart table, Dolohov, Sergei and Ardenyev sat drinking tea and eating bread and cheese. There was something spartan and disregarded about the food and drink with which Dolohov kept them supplied, as if the three of them were engaged in the field, kept going by survival rations. Sergei began slowly to understand the feverish, self-indulgent manner in which the admiral regarded the operation. The admiral was an old man. He had selected this capture of the British submarine as some kind of suitable valediction to his long and distinguished career. Hence he attended to every detail of it himself, however small and insignificant.

'Just in case,' Dolohov explained to Ardenyev, the young man nodding in a half-impatient, half-attentive manner, 'in case she receives any signals, or monitors our signals, we'll appear to be making every covert effort to reach, and rescue, our own submarine.' He smiled, the mouth opening like a slack pouch in the leathery skin.

'I understand, sir,' Ardenyev supplied.

'You're impressed by the British equipment, Valery?'

Ardenyev paused. Sergei felt he was calculating the degree of flattery his answer should contain. 'Very. We must have it, sir.'

'Yes, yes – but, its effectiveness? It exceeds our expectations, mm?'

'Yes, sir.'

'She'll keep on course?' Dolohov asked suddenly.

'I – think so, sir.' Ardenyev seemed struck by the idea, as if he had not considered it before. 'I think so. She's committed, now, under orders.'

'Our activity won't discourage her?'

'I doubt that. The captain of the *Proteus* would have the authority to abort – I just don't think he will. As long as "Leopard" functions, he'll enjoy the cat-and-mouse of it.'

'Exactly my reading of the man – of the situation.' Dolohov looked at his watch. 'She appears to be maintaining course and speed. We have five hours, or less. Success or failure.' Sergei could hear the admiral's breathing. Hoarse gulps of air, as if the sterile atmosphere of the control room offered something more necessary than oxygen. 'You'd better get off to Pechenga to join your men, Valery.'

Ardenyev immediately stood up, an automaton galvanised by the order. Sergei felt the man was simply supplying an impression of instant action such as Dolohov would expect, had waited for.

'Wish me luck, sir.'

Dolohov stood up and embraced the young man. 'I do, Valery – I wish you luck. Bring me back the British submarine, eh?' He clamped Ardenyev's forearms again with his liver-spotted hands. Ardenyev felt the strength of desperation in the embrace. And of old age refusing to admit the growing dark. He felt sorry, and irritated. He felt himself no more than Dolohov's creature. Later, it would be different, but now it was unpleasant. He would be glad to be aboard the chopper, being flown to the port of Pechenga. 'The weather won't prevent you?' It was a command, and a doubt.

Ardenyev shook his head, smiling. 'Not if I can help it.'

'Report in when you arrive – then wait for my order to transfer to the *Karpaty*.'

'Of course, sir.'

When he had left the room, Dolohov went on staring at the door which had closed behind him. From the concentration on his face, Sergei understood that the old man was attempting to ignore the voice of one of the rear-admiral's team who was reading off the updated weather report from a met. satellite for the Tanafjord area. To Sergei, it sounded bad.

Almost as soon as it lifted clear of the main runway at RAF Kinloss on the Moray Firth in Scotland, the Nimrod surveillance aircraft turned north-eastwards, out over the Firth, and was lost in the low cloud. A blue flare beneath the wings, the flashing red light on her belly, the two faint stars at wingtips, and then nothing except the scudding cloud across the cold grey water, and the driving, slanting rain.

It had taken less than two hours to authorise a Nimrod to pursue the *Proteus*, carrying, in addition to her anti-submarine electronics, the encoded instruction to the submarine to return to base with all possible speed. The time was two minutes after six in the evening.

*

It was almost dark when they arrived. A luxury coach pulled up at one of the rear entrances to Hall 5, and Hyde, standing with the uniformed superintendent responsible for security and order at the rock concert, watched as Heat of the Day descended from it and slipped into the open door to their dressing rooms. Arrogance, self-assurance, denim-masked wealth. Hyde absorbed these impressions even as he studied the figures he did not recognise; managers, road managers, publicity, secretaries. The girl had not been with Alletson, and Hyde's immediate uncontrollable reaction was one of intense disappointment. After the hours in the car park and on the platforms of Birmingham International station and inside and outside Hall 5 – all with no sign of the KGB or the Ford Granada, but the more intensely wearing for that – there was an immediate impression of wasted time, of time run out. Of stupidity, too.

But she was there. Denims and a dark donkey jacket too big for her – was it her, certainly the jacket was too big for the present wearer? – slipping out of the coach without pause, walking with and then ahead of the two other women. The white globe of a face for a moment as she looked round, then she was through the lighted door and gone.

'Was she there?' the superintendent asked. His manner was not unfriendly, not unhelpful. Hyde had been scrupulously deferential and polite.

'I don't know.' He felt a tightness in his chest. Was it her? Furtive, certainly furtive. Alletson had paused, allowed himself to be recognised, taken the limelight. Declaring he was alone, there was no girl. 'I think so.'

'The one with the too-big coat?'

'I think so.'

'Okay. You'd better go and find out. Want one of my chaps to go with you?'

'No. I'll be enough to panic her by myself.'

'Suit yourself.'

'Thanks for your help.'

Hyde crossed the tarmac, rounded the coach, and showed his warrant card to the PC on duty at the door. The superintendent was apprised of Hyde's real capacity, but it was unnecessary for anyone else to know. 'Where are the dressing rooms?'

'Down the corridor, turn left. You'll see another bloke dressed just like me. And the press, and the bouncers and the hangers-on. Can't miss it.'

'Not your scene, this?'

'I'd rather be at the Villa, yobs and all.'

'They playing at home tonight?'

'Too bloody true.'

'Shame.'

Hyde followed the corridor, and turned the corner into a crowd of pressmen and cameramen, carefully orchestrated outside the closed dressing room doors. Heat of the Day were back in business. Interest had to be stoked, and kept alight. Hyde pushed through the crowd towards the policeman on the door of one of the rooms. He waved his warrant card.

'Which one is Alletson in?'

'Who?'

'The short bloke with the wavy hair.'

'Uh – that one,' the PC supplied, indicating the other door, outside which two bulky men in denims and leather jackets stood, arms folded. Hyde wondered who, precisely, they were guarding. A press or publicity secretary was informing the cameramen that they would be allowed to take their pictures just before the band went onstage. Her announcement was greeted with a chorus of groans. Hyde showed his warrant card to one of the band's security men, who seemed to loom over him.

'Who do you want?' The question was wrong, and revealing. Again, Hyde felt his chest tighten with anticipation. The girl was in there.

'I'm not after his autograph.'

'So, what do you want?' Both of them seemed uncertain what to do.

'Just a security check. And I want to talk to Jon about after the concert. Getting away.'

'I'll ask him.'

'Don't bother. I'll talk to him.' He made to reach for the door handle. A large hand closed over his own, and he looked up into a face adopting aggression reluctantly, uncertainly. 'Don't be stupid,' Hyde said. 'It might be big trouble – *will* be big trouble.' The two men glanced at one another, then his hand was released.

'Easy, eh?'

'I'll take it easy – don't upset the artiste, right?' Hyde opened the door without knocking. The girl turned in her chair, alert, nervous, instantly aware of what he was and why he was there. Alletson was lying on a camp bed, and the keyboard player, Whiteman, was scribbling with a pencil on stave paper.

'Who the hell are you?' he asked. Alletson's voice provided a more nervous, knowing undertone.

'Trish – what is it?'

The girl simply stared at Hyde as he shut the door behind him. Whiteman, oblivious to the other two and their anxiety, added, 'Piss off, we're busy.' He glanced contemptuously at the warrant card. 'Autographs later,' he sneered.

'Miss Patricia Quin, I presume?' Hyde asked. The girl said nothing. Her face, however, was voluble with confession. Alletson got up lithely and stood in front of her.

'What do you want?' he asked.

'The lady in the case.'

Alletson took the warrant card, inspected it, then thrust it back into Hyde's hand. 'Harassment?' he asked.

'This isn't about smokes or shots, Jon-boy,' Hyde drawled. 'It isn't really any of your business. You get on rehearsing or composing or something.' Whiteman was standing now, just behind Alletson. Long blond hair, his frame bulkier with good living than two years before. He looked healthier.

'Why don't you piss off?'

'Why did they let you in?' Alletson demanded.

'They'd have been silly not to.'

'What sort of copper are you?' Whiteman was a Londoner. 'You're a bloody Aussie by the sound of it.'

'Too true, Blue. I'm the sort that wants to help her. Can I talk to her?'

'Not unless she wants to.'

'Stop it, Jon. It won't do any good.' Tricia Quin pushed to Alletson's side, and held his arm. 'Who are you?'

85

'My name's Hyde.'

'I didn't think it would be Jekyll – he was the goody, wasn't he?' Whiteman sneered.

'He was. Look, Miss Quin, I'll talk to you with your friends here, if you wish, as long as they can keep their mouths shut.' He looked steadily at Alletson and Whiteman, then continued. 'You are in danger, Miss Quin. It's stopped being a game. You know there are people after you?'

'You are.'

'No, not me. Not even my side.'

'What's he talking about, Trish?'

'What do you mean?'

'The men in Sutton, at your mother's house?' She nodded, fear flickering in her pale eyes. Cleverness, too. 'That wasn't us. Our bloke got kicked in the balls trying to look after you. You need protection – mine. Will you come back with me?'

She shook her head. 'No, I won't. I'm safe here.'

'I can't risk that, Miss Quin. We want you and your father safe. You could lead the KGB right to him.' She was shaking her head violently now. Her fair hair flopped about her pale, small face. She looked vulnerable, afraid but determined.

As if her shaking head was some signal, Alletson stepped up to him and aimed his knee at Hyde's groin. Hyde bucked backwards and the blow struck his thigh. Off-balance as he was, Alletson pushed him against a tall metal locker. Hyde, watching Tricia Quin move towards the door, jarred his head and shoulder against the locker, then slumped into the corner of the dressing room.

'Trish!' Alletson called, but the girl was already out of the door. Two hopeful flash-bulbs exploded. Hyde got shakily to his feet.

'You stupid buggers!' Hyde snapped, rubbing his shoulder. 'She's a menace to herself at the moment, as well as to her father. Christ – you stupid buggers!' He opened the door, and yelled to the PC on duty. 'Which way did the girl go?' Someone laughed.

'Towards the hall.'

'Who is she?' someone asked.

'It'll be pot,' someone else answered. 'Poor bitch.'

Hyde forced his way through the press, jabbed uncomfortably more than once by the lens of a camera, then he was running. At the far end of the corridor, the door into the hall was open. He rubbed his thigh as he ran, his resentment against Alletson growing not because of the pain but because of the girl. Stupid bugger, silly bitch, he chanted to himself, grinding his teeth at the opportunity that had been spoiled. He had had the girl safe, for a moment. It was only a matter of getting her to his car, getting her to Aubrey – *shit*!

In the hall, lighting gantries were being pulleyed up to the ceiling, mirrors were being positioned for the light-show that the band used, and the roadies were still working furiously to rig and test the amplification equipment. Two grubby girls passed him without a glance, pushing one of Whiteman's electronic keyboards. Up the ramp and on to the stage. He was standing just below the stage. Lights, mirrors, amplifiers, instruments – and Tricia Quin picking her way delicately like a cat through the maze of boxes and wires. She must have taken the other turn in the corridor to enter on to the stage itself.

She saw him. Part of her slow and delicate passage across the stage was due to her continual backward glances. She began to move more quickly, upstage towards the far side. Even as he moved, she disappeared into the wings. He pushed past the girls with the keyboard, and ran as quickly as he was able through the maze of cables and boxes – someone yelled at him – and then he was in the semidarkness of the wings. He paused, listening. Above his heartbeat and breathing, footsteps. Running. He blundered forward again, sensing rationality disappearing and panic encroaching. He suddenly knew that the KGB were out there, and that she was running towards them. He shook his head, cannoning off a wall as he rounded a bend in the corridor.

Lights again. The foyer and main corridor connecting Hall 5 with its companions and with the railway station. A handful of people moving slowly, and one slight figure running. He did not call after her, merely pursued her, his feet pounding, his blood beating in his ears. He felt a sickness of self-recrimination, an anticipation of disaster.

A tunnel of lights down which she fled, a small dark shape. The scene wobbled in his vision. He seemed no nearer to her. The station concourse was at the end of the wide tunnel. She was almost there, sixty or seventy yards away.

Someone turning, moving with her, after her. She was oblivious to whoever it was, didn't even look round for him as she reached the concourse. He began running, impelled by the certainty of disaster now. Someone had recognised her – other men, two of them in overcoats, just come in from the cold of the car park outside the station, moving to intercept her.

He reached the concourse. The girl had disappeared. Two men had pushed into the small queue for tickets, one of them arguing. He hadn't imagined it. They were stereotypes. The girl must have gone down on to the platform. Two of them, three – where was the other one, the one who had turned in the tunnel, recognised her?

Petrunin. Hyde could not believe it. Standing beneath the announcement board, impatiently watching his men create the wrong kind of disturbance, then turning to the platform ticket machine and banging it because it appeared jammed or empty. No, girl, no girl –

Petrunin, London Resident. KG-bloody-B. Where the hell was the girl? Petrunin. The clever bugger must have worked it out. Tickets being issued, the small queue silenced by embarrassment. Petrunin almost hopping from foot to foot. Train announcement, the next train arriving, Petrunin turning his head from side to side as if regretting something or because he had lost something – and seeing him. Knowing him not so much by his face as by his colour and heaving chest and wary, tense posture.

Hyde ran at the barrier, Petrunin moved to cut him off, slowly drifting, so it seemed, on a collision course. The next train arriving, for Birmingham – special train? He saw the dark, frightened face of the ticket collector, then he vaulted the turnstile, almost stumbling on the far side, hearing the noise of the train. He ran headlong down the flight of steps to the platform, round the corner, skidded, righted himself, flung open the glass doors.

She was almost alone on the platform. He saw her immediately. And she saw him. Policemen, too. Clattering footsteps behind him, but it was all right. Policemen. All round them, policemen. He hadn't lost her. He called to her as she stood looking at him. The noise of the train covered his words as it slowed, then came to a stop.

One of Petrunin's men grabbed him from behind. He turned, lashed out to try to prevent a second man passing him, heading towards the girl. Then they seemed to be drowning in bodies as the special train from Euston debouched hundreds of rock fans on to the platform, every one of them intent on reaching the exit first. Noise assailed Hyde, and perfume. He was brushed aside, the only certainty the hand holding his collar. He raised his fist, but the crowd trapped it against his chest, pinning it there as in a sling. Petrunin's man had his arm above the heads of the crowd. He was waving a rubber cosh. He struck slowly down. The movement was awkward because he was being relentlessly pushed back towards the exit. Hyde lost sight of the girl, of Petrunin who seemed to have retreated back up the steps, and of the cosh which struck him across the neck and shoulder, numbing him after the spurt of fire through his head. Then the Russian's hand was gone from his collar and he stumbled forward, flung sideways to his knees. Then on to his chest. Feet pressed on his back, compressing his lungs. People began surging over him. He was drowning for a moment, then he could not breathe, and then it was dark.

Five: CRIPPLE

'Sir, why the hell is the *Kiev* in the area? There's no major Soviet exercise on, and she couldn't possibly be any help in rescuing those poor dead buggers in the crippled boat – so why do they need an aircraft carrier? What's her game?'

'I don't know, John.'

'And the course changes – sir, we remained rigged for silent running for too long. If we'd had the magnetic and acoustic sensors working, and gone to active sonar, we'd have known sooner she was closing on us.'

'I know that, John. I know we're the quarry.'

'Sir, what in hell are we doing here?'

'Playing MoD's games for them, John. Undergoing our final examination.'

'What?'

'I mean it. In this sea trial, the danger's all the better for MoD for being real.'

'Bastards. Sir, we're being gathered into a net. The net is in the Tanafjord, and we're being driven towards it.'

'Agreed.'

'What do they want?'

'I should have thought that was obvious. What they want is called "Leopard". As to what they'll do, you guess.'

'What do *we* do?'

'ETA Norwegian territorial waters?'

'Two hours plus some minutes.'

'Then we'll run for shelter. We might just get away with it, inside Norwegian waters. We'll hide, John. Hide.'

'Ethan, has the Nimrod's position been updated?'

'She's here, Mr Aubrey, as of five minutes ago.'

Aubrey stared up at the huge map-board. The cluster of lights glowed with what he could easily imagine was malevolence. A single white light had been introduced to the board to represent the *Proteus*. Aubrey periodically wished it had not been done. The white dot was in a ring of

90

coloured lights representing the Soviet naval vessels in the immediate area. Far to the south and west of that cluster, a second white light shone like a misplaced or falling star over the fjordal coastline of western Norway, perhaps a hundred miles south of the Arctic Circle.

'Not enough, not far enough,' Aubrey murmured. The dot seemed hardly to have moved since the aircraft's previous signal.

'You can't know that, Mr Aubrey.'

'Don't offer me morsels of comfort, Ethan!' Aubrey snapped, turning to the American. Heads turned, and then returned to screens and read-outs. Aubrey had subdued the 'Chessboard Counter' team by cajolement and command, and by exploiting their sense of failure. The map-board had completed their change in function as it increasingly betrayed *Proteus*'s danger. They were now a rescue team, busy and helpless.

'Sorry.'

Pyott and the commodore had sought another place of residence. Vanquished, they had left the field to Aubrey. Rather, he saw them as children running away from the broken window, the smashed greenhouse.

'My apologies. What's the Nimrod's ETA?'

'A little more than an hour to Hammerfest, then maybe another twenty minutes to the Tanafjord.'

Aubrey looked at his watch. 'Eight-fifteen. Can we do it, Ethan?'

Clark rubbed his chin. To Aubrey, he looked absurdly young, and much too unworried to be a repository of authoritative answers. And he was tall enough to make Aubrey physically uncomfortable.

'Maybe. Then *Proteus* has to get the hell out.'

'Why hasn't Lloyd aborted on his own initiative?'

'Maybe he wants to. Maybe he's running for the coast and keeping his fingers crossed. Who knows?'

'My *God*, what an impossible situation!' Aubrey's face darkened after the quick rage had passed. He leaned confidentially towards the American. 'Ethan, I'm worried about Quin. I haven't heard from Hyde. He was at the NEC in Birmingham, some sort of pop concert. He thought – no, he was certain – the girl was with this group. She

91

knows them, once travelled with them.' Aubrey's face was drained of colour and expression now. 'It is very hard to contemplate, Ethan, but I feel myself staring at the loss of the *Proteus* and of the man responsible for the development of "Leopard". It is not a comfortable prospect.'

Clark recognised, and admitted to himself, Aubrey's age. Yet he respected the man's intellect and his expertise. Aubrey might, appallingly, be correct in his diagnosis.

'Maybe,' was all he could find to say.

'I think we have to consider the possibility that what is happening up there – ' he waved a hand at the top of the map-board – 'is deliberate.' He paused, but Clark said nothing. 'We have no proof that there is a Soviet submarine in distress. It has stopped transmitting, and still no Russian vessel has gone in after it. But a great many Russian ships are concentrating in the area we know contains *Proteus*. If they *find* her – and they may be attempting to do just that – then we will have surrendered an almost priceless military advantage to them. If we lose Quin, too, then we will place ourselves in an abject position indeed.'

Aubrey tapped at the surface of the commodore's desk, which he had had moved to a position beneath the map-board. As if the gesture was a summons, the telephone rang.

'Shelley, sir.'

'Yes, Peter?'

'I've just been informed of a routine surveillance report from the DS team at the Russian embassy – '

'Yes, Peter?' Aubrey found it difficult to catch his breath.

'They think Petrunin left the embassy unofficially around five-thirty this evening.'

'Where was he going?'

'I've checked that, sir. His numberplate was spotted heading north, I'm afraid, on the M1.'

'Damn!' Aubrey's lips quivered with anger. 'Thank you, Peter. You'd better inform Birmingham Special Branch. Get them over to that concert at the NEC – quickly!'

Aubrey put down the telephone.

'I guess I see what you mean,' Clark said slowly. 'Without even really noticing, we're down to the wire.'

'I think we are. The KGB Resident wouldn't charge off

unofficially without good cause or strong suspicion. Hyde couldn't have lost his trail. Damn that girl and her father!' He returned his attention to the map. The dot of the Nimrod was crossing the Arctic Circle. *Proteus* was surrounded. The *Kiev* was steaming at full speed to the Tanafjord, and the rescue ship *Karpaty* was on station. There really was no escaping the conclusion, and little chance of avoiding disaster. Aubrey felt very tired, entirely incompetent. 'I think we have already lost, Ethan. This may be the view from the canvas, from the loser's corner.'

'I hope to God you're wrong about that.'

'I don't think I am.'

The interference crackled in front of Ardenyev's voice, masking it and giving it, to Dolohov's ears, a peculiarly unreal quality, as if the man were fading, becoming ethereal. Then Dolohov raised his voice, not to be heard but to remove the strange, uninvited perception; the whisper of failure.

'Get aboard the helicopters, Valery! you must transfer to the *Karpaty* now!'

'Sir, I'd really like you to have a word with one of the pilots – ' Ardenyev's voice seemed more distant still, the storm smearing his words mockingly.

'No! It is too late for words! The traces are piling up. We're almost there.' Dolohov looked round at Sergei, who stood obediently and silently at his elbow as he hunched over the table in front of the telephone amplifier. To Sergei, it seemed that the admiral was losing control, was dangerously elated by events, by the slipping, chasing minutes that passed and the sightings or partial and unconfirmable reports of the British submarine that kept coming in. The old man was racking them up like a score, mere multiplication stimulating his confidence and his arrogance. 'We have them, Valery, in the palm of our hand. They're *ours!*'

'Sir, you don't seem to understand. It's a question of whether they can put us down on the deck of the rescue ship – '

'Don't argue with me, boy!' Dolohov thundered, his fist beating a counterpoint to his words on the surface of the table. 'You have your orders – the pilots have their orders. You will board the helicopters at once and set course for the rescue ship. Understand?' There was a gap, then, of space and silence in which the storm hissed. 'Do you hear me?'

'Yes, sir. Very good, sir. Your orders will be carried out, to the best of my abilities.'

Dolohov was suddenly, manically expansive and generous. 'Good boy, good boy. Good luck and good hunting. Over and out.' The old man flicked off the telephone amplifier and stood up. He moved with some of the robotic jerkiness of arthritis battled and temporarily overcome; or the driven, muscular awkwardness of someone possessed of an unquenchable desire. He slapped his hand on Sergei's shoulder and the young man hoped that his smile did not appear too artificial. Dolohov looked at him, however, with eyes that had little perception in them. Not glazed or dulled, rather fierce and inward-looking. 'The end-game, Sergei – the end-game,' he murmured in a strange, ugly, caressing voice.

The rear-admiral was punctilious, almost smirking, full of a bustle that had previously been absent. 'Final positions, Admiral,' he offered, indicating the computer print-out sheets in his hand.

'Good, good – come, let me see.' He took the rear-admiral's arm, ushering him to the window, clutching the sheets with his other hand. Sergei realised that the rear-admiral had cast aside all doubts and reservations; whether from self-interest or because he had contracted the admiral's current illness, Sergei could not decide. Probably both. 'Where?' They were at the window.

'There,' the rear-admiral proclaimed, histrionically waving his hand down towards the map-table. '*Kiev*, *Karpaty* on station waiting for Ardenyev, *Grishka* and the other submarines – see? There, there, there, there, there – ' The finger jabbed out at each of the lights below. 'The other units of the fleet in back-up positions, or sailing on deception courses.' He looked at Dolohov. 'It's up to them now. They have their orders. All they need is a positive ident on the British submarine.'

Dolohov's face possessed a beatific expression. His eyes

were almost closed. Sergei, embarrassed and disturbed, realised that it was a moment of love. The cold, stern, paternal admiral was unrecognisable. Sergei did not know, however, what it was that Dolohov embraced – this challenge, the drama of the moment, the prize, or the winning of the game. Perhaps even the game itself?

'Good, good,' the old man murmured again. Then, suddenly, his eyes opened and all his attention was concentrated on the voice of one of the officers behind him in the control room.

'Submarine unit *Frunze* reports a magnetic contact – '

Dolohov was across the room and at the officer's shoulder with the speed and physical grace of a younger man. 'Where?' he demanded. 'What range?' Then, before the man could answer: 'Can they lock on to her course?'

The communications officer listened to his headphones after repeating Dolohov's questions, and the old man could see his head begin to shake. 'No, sir – they've lost it. Could have been sea temperature – '

'Rubbish. It was a *magnetic* contact, not infra-red! It was *them*, you idiot!' He turned to the rear-admiral. 'Order all submarine units to converge on the *Frunze* at once!'

'Admiral, is that – ?'

'Do it.'

'Very well, Admiral.'

Dolohov walked aimlessly yet intently back to the window. He appeared to have little interest in the glowing map below him. The situation had been ingested in its entirety or – here Sergei corrected himself – perhaps it had always been in his head. Sergei half-listened to the rear-admiral issuing a stream of orders, half-watched Dolohov, principally being aware of himself as an unimportant cipher, something like a parcel left in one corner of the room.

Then: 'Submarine unit *Grishka* reports another magnetic trace – '

'Magnetic trace fading, Captain.'

'Thermal trace fading, Captain.'

'Planesman – ten degrees down, level at eight hundred feet.'

'Sir.'

'Steer twelve degrees to starboard.'

'Sir.'

There was silence in the control room of the *Grishka*. The bow sonars were blank and silent, their sensors absorbed or deflected by the British anti-sonar equipment. The infra-red trace was decaying, was already almost non-existent, illusory. The magnetic anomaly detection equipment was already inducing a frustrated hunching of the shoulders in its operator. The advanced, delicate, heat-sensitive 'nose' was sniffing cold ocean water without trace of the British submarine. Every trail was cold, or growing cold.

'Steer fifteen degrees to port.'

'Sir.'

Guesswork, the captain of the *Grishka* admitted. A blind dog with a cold in its nose seeking an elusive scent. No prop wash even, not a trace of the trail she ought to be leaving in the sea from her movement and her turning propeller. They had picked that up once before, then lost it again.

'Nine knots.'

'Sir.'

Silence.

'Weak magnetic trace, sir. Bearing green four-oh, range six thousand.'

'We're almost on top of her – don't lose it. Steer starboard thirty.'

'Starboard thirty, sir.'

'No thermal trace, sir.'

'Magnetic trace fading again, sir.'

'Stand by, torpedo room. Any sign of prop wash?'

'Negative, sir.'

'Steer starboard five, speed ten knots.'

'Magnetic trace lost, sir.'

'Damn!'

'Steer port four-five.'

'Port four-five it is, sir.'

There was silence then in the control room of the *Proteus*. Whispered orders, like the rustling voices of old men, lacking authority. The sonars which, in their passive mode, were difficult for any enemy to detect with his electronic sensors, registered the movements of the Russian submarine; demonstrating the proximity of the hunter.

'Computer ident, Number One?'

'A "Victor-II"-class submarine, sir. Our friend is back.'

'Range and bearing?'

'Moving away, sir. Speed approximately nine knots, range eight thousand, bearing green one-seven-oh. She's passing behind us.'

'Other activity, John?'

'"Kashin"-class destroyer, range eleven thousand. "Alpha"-class attack submarine, range fourteen thousand, bearing red six-five, and closing. *Kiev* at range sixteen thousand, and increasing. The submarine rescue ship is holding station, sir.'

'Coffee, sir?'

'What – oh, thanks, Chief. ETA Norwegian waters, John?'

'At present course and speed, eleven minutes, sir.'

'Speed fourteen knots.'

'Prop wash, sir?'

'Correction – twelve knots.'

'Twelve knots it is, sir.'

'Steer port ten.'

The transmissions from the *Grishka* and the other Red Banner units were being received via the aircraft carrier *Kiev*. Dolohov had ordered the abandonment of coded signals in favour of high-speed, frequency-agile transmissions in plain language. Transferred to tape and slowed down, Dolohov then heard them broadcast in the control room. The voices, and the silences between the words, seemed equally to agitate and excite him. Sergei observed his admiral closely, worriedly. He felt like a youthful relative watching a grandparent growing senile before his eyes.

Dolohov's shoulders were hunched as he stared down into the well of the operations room, watching the moving, dancing lights and the flickering, single light that represented the British submarine. It flickered on and off as if there were an electrical fault in the board.

Sergei guessed that Dolohov had begun to entertain

doubts; or rather, the doubts he had formerly crushed beneath the heel of certainty had now sprung up again like weeds. It was more than an hour since the first contact signal had been received from the submarine *Frunze*. Since then, the *Grishka* and two other units had reported traces on more than one occasion – *Grishka* three times – but the British submarine still eluded them. Dolohov had been able to ignore his doubts for hours, even days; but now, watching the cat-and-invisible-mouse game of the board below him, he had begun to disbelieve in success. Or so Sergei suspected.

The old man was talking to himself. His voice, in the silence from the loudspeaker, was audible throughout the room.

'Can it be done, can it be done?' He repeated it again and again, a murmured plea or a voiced fear. 'Can it? Can it?' The shorter phrase became more final, more full of doubt. 'Can it? Can it?' The old man was entirely unaware that he was speaking audibly, and Sergei felt a hot flush of shame invade his features. To be associated with this old man, muttering to himself in this moment of crisis like a geriatric in a hospital, was embarrassing, insulting. Others were listening, everyone in the room –

Then the voice of the monitoring officer on the *Kiev* silenced Dolohov, smearing across his words, erasing them. The admiral's shoulders picked up, his head inclined like a bird's as he listened.

'Submarine unit *Grishka* reports lost contact – '

Dolohov's shoulders slumped again. It was evident he thought he had lost the game.

'The "Victor-II" is turning to starboard, sir.'

'Damn. John, insert our track and that of the "Victor-II" on to the display screen.'

'Track memory is on, sir. Submarine bearing red one-six-eight, range nineteen thousand.'

'Do we still have that layer of warmer water below us?'

'Yes, sir.'

'Right. Let's make it much more difficult for them. Take us down through it.'

'Aye, aye, sir.'

Lloyd sensed the dipping of the *Proteus*'s bow. The Russian submarine was on their tail again. They were still three minutes out into international waters, and the 'Victor-II' was closing rapidly. Even though he doubted now that an imagined political line on a chart would have any beneficial effect on their circumstances, Lloyd knew of no other move he could make. The display screen traced their track over the seabed, and that of the Russian. A swifter-moving, hazy line of light was dead astern of them now that the Russian captain had altered course.

'Information on the "Victor-II" becoming unreliable, sir.'

'I can see that. The warmer layer's causing ghosting and refracting. Are we through it yet?'

'Yes, sir.'

'Level at eighty fathoms, cox'n.'

'Eighty fathoms, sir.'

'Is that the coast at the edge of the screen John?'

'No, sir.' Thurston was at his side, staring down at the screen. The image of the Russian submarine was faint. The warmer layer of sea water through which they had descended would be confusing the Russian's sensors, hiding the *Proteus*. 'It's a small plateau. Our depth makes it look like a mountain.'

'"Victor-II" now bearing green one-seven-oh, range fourteen thousand, and she's in a shallow dive, sir.'

Thurston looked into Lloyd's face. 'We didn't fool her. She's back with us,' he whispered.

'The computer confirms course and bearing, sir.'

Lloyd hesitated for only a moment. Then a tight determination clamped on his features. He had accepted the evidence of his sonars and his computers.

'John,' he said in a steady voice audible to everyone in the control room, 'call the crew to Alert Readiness. The time for playing games with this Russian is over. He's after us, all right.'

'Aye, aye, sir.'

'Negative contact on magnetic, Captain.'

'Maintain present course for one minute, then hard starboard – mark.'

'Marked, Captain. One minute.'

'Negative contact, sir.'

Always the negative. The Russian captain sensed the *Grishka* around him, slipping through the blind darkness of the sea. He sensed the crew closed up to Action Stations, as they had been for more than half an hour on this occasion alone; and three other times he had spoken to the torpedo room, readying them, and calling his men to Action Stations. It could not go on for much longer, he would have to relax them. He was wearing them down. He sensed, especially, the torpedo crew room and the wire-guided, wake-homing torpedoes, one with reduced warhead and the second with the special MIRV warhead, the 'Catherine Wheel'. Once he ordered their launch, one expert crewman would guide them to their target, relying solely on his own skills. His man was good enough, and the torpedoes would do their job. Yet everything – *everything* – depended on tiny, delicate sensors in the bow of the boat; magnetic sensors, thermal sensors. Somewhere ahead – or below or beside or above or behind – there was a magnetic lump of metal which was emitting heat and which could not be entirely damped and rendered invisible. The British submarine was leaving faint traces, flakings of her skin, faint noises of her breathing. Somewhere in the ocean, those traces lay waiting for him to discover them.

'Coming hard round, Captain.'

'Planesman – hold her steady.'

'Sir.'

Somewhere, out there in the dark, lay the *Proteus*.

'Sir, the "Victor-II" is coming hard round – '

'I have her. Engine room – plus fifty revolutions.'

'Plus fifty, sir.'

'Heat trace confirmed and growing stronger, Captain.'

'Ten degree quarter – sixty second rate.'

The captain of the *Grishka* leaned against the periscope housing. The range of the British submarine was still too great, and though the trace was strengthening it was still elusive. The game might continue for hours yet. He sensed the pressure on him not to fail, but more importantly he was aware of the growing, slightly desperate need for action in himself and his crew. His loyalty was, therefore, to the stifled, tense atmosphere of his control room.

'Torpedo room,' he said distinctly, pausing until everyone was alert with attention to his voice, despite their own tasks. 'Torpedo room, load manual guidance torpedo, set it for a screw-pattern search. Set maximum range and wait for my order.'

There was relief, palpable as cold, fresh air, in the set of every man's shoulders and on every face that he could see. He kept a sudden assault of doubt from his own features.

'Heat trace strengthening, Captain.'

'Magnetic trace positive, Captain.'

'Sonars negative, Captain.'

'Range and bearing?'

'Bearing unchanged, sir. Range thirteen thousand, and decreasing. We're overhauling her, sir.'

'Very well.' He paused. The low-warhead torpedo was in the tube. He had four of them, and four multiple-warhead 'Catherine Wheel' torpedoes. Could he risk the first one at that range? 'Torpedo room – fire One! Keep calling.'

'Tube One away, sir, and running. Sensor on, lights green. Negative readout.'

The Russian captain looked at his first lieutenant standing at the depth indicator panel. He shrugged expressively.

'Torpedo sensors have made contact, Captain.'

The wake-homing torpedo began its search immediately it was launched. The wire that connected it with the *Grishka* transmitted to its tiny computer the instructions of the experienced operator in the torpedo room. Its guidance control was tested, and responded, then the speed of the torpedo was altered a number of times in quick succession. On each occasion, the torpedo responded immediately and precisely.

The torpedo crossed the traces of the *Proteus*'s wake one thousand metres from the *Grishka*. Its corkscrewing movement through the sea, which enabled it to search in three rather than in two dimensions, took it across the wake well astern of the British submarine's position. There was, however, sufficient trace of the wake remaining for the torpedo to register it.

The torpedo nosed on through the dark water until it reached the conclusion of its next one thousand metre run, then it began retracing its course, back towards the wake. Once it crossed the wake for the second time, and its sensors registered either a stronger or a weaker trace, then it would be instructed to turn to port or starboard, and to run down the submarine's track until it made contact. Once its path was chosen, and the wake's direction established, contact was unavoidable.

The torpedo crossed the wake and turned to port almost immediately with a flick as lithe as that of some hunting sea creature. Its corkscrewing track evened out as it began tracing its way down the wake of the British submarine.

'Contact continuous, Captain.'

'Excellent – keep calling.' The captain of the *Grishka* grinned at his first-lieutenant.

'Lock on indicated . . . three thousand five hundred metres of run completed, sir . . . four thousand metres completed . . . heat sensor responding and locked on . . . command override on, sir . . . proximity fuse armed and *on*, sir . . . seven thousand metres of run completed . . . TV camera on, light on – '

'Come on, come on,' the Russian captain murmured. Too long, too long, he told himself. Should have waited, she's out of range.

'Seven and one half thousand metres of run completed, sir . . . eight thousand metres of run completed.'

'Positive contact, sir!'

'Cox'n hard astern!'

'Hard astern, sir.'

'Contact identified as a torpedo, sir!'

On the tiny television monitor in the *Grishka*, receiving pictures from the camera in the nose of the torpedo, there was nothing more than a weakly illuminated rush of grey water, almost like a heavy, dull curtain being continually whisked aside. Then there was a blur of darker water, then the grey, whale-like shape of the *Proteus* as the British submarine began her turn. The torpedo seemed to dip towards the submarine, strangely hesitant, and the proximity fuse detonated the reduced warhead. The television screen at which the captain of the *Grishka* stared went blank, making him wince as if the flash of the explosion had been visible and had startled, even blinded him.

'Target acquired, Captain! Hit, hit, hit!'

'We've got her?'

'Direct hit, Captain!'

There was cheering, which he immediately silenced.

'Torpedo room, load Two. Multiple warhead torpedo, set range at nine thousand. Manual guidance, direct search track.'

'Tube Two ready, Captain.'

'Fire Two!'

'Planesman, check that roll!'

' – can't hold the turn – '

'Emergency lights – cancel – '

'Can't hold the trim, sir!'

'Trim responding, sir.'

'Engines down one-fifty revolutions.'

'The dampers aren't controlling the oscillation, sir.'

'All stations – immediate damage report.' Lloyd wiped a hand across his forehead, his eyes riveted on the forearms of the two planesmen as they struggled to right the trim of the *Proteus*. The muscles flexed and strained, veins standing out, the tattoo of an anchor and chain livid on one of the arms. The whole submarine was oscillating wildly, like a bicycle out of control. A child in the saddle, feet unable to reach the pedals. The lights had come back on. His arms felt nerveless and weak as his thoughts churned like his stomach, over and over, and fused into a circuit. The Russians had fired on them, fired on them ... Thurston crossed the vibrating control room towards him and lurched against the periscope housing, where he clung unsteadily. 'Christ, John – they fired on us!'

Thurston's face confirmed the inadmissible. Enemy action.

'Chief engineer, sir,' Lloyd heard over the control room speaker.

'Yes, Chief?'

'Initial damage report suggests external impact, sir. Pressure hull okay, outer plates and aft ballast tanks ruptured. Planes and rudders misaligned, but responding, sir. The vibration we're experiencing is linked to our revs, so there must be prop damage. Or maybe it's the shaft. Or both. The main shaft bearings are heating up.'

'Can we still remain under way, Chief?'

'I think so, sir. We'll have to try various rev settings to find an optimum for remaining under way with least vibration and some degree of control. We may be lucky, if the bearings don't get too hot. They're in the orange now, sir.'

'Very well, Chief. In your hands.'

'Aye, aye, sir.'

The multiple-warhead torpedo tracked down the wake of the *Proteus*, following the range and bearing instructions fed into its tiny computer. It, too, was armed with a proximity fuse. The Red Navy's experts had concluded that a reduced warhead, although capable of damaging the *Proteus*, might not have sufficient stopping-power to render the British nuclear submarine immobile, which condition was essential to the success of the operation. Therefore, an experimental multiple-warhead, code-named 'Catherine Wheel', had been hurried through its last stages of development and its laboratory and sea trials, to fulfil the preliminary work of the reduced-warhead torpedo that would cripple, but not ensnare, the *Proteus*.

The TV camera switched on at an instruction from the torpedo room operator, and the light came on at the same moment. On the tiny screen, the Russian captain watched the swirling rush of water, and thought he detected the bubbles and general disturbance of the *Proteus*'s wake. He tensed himself, almost as if he had been riding the torpedo like a horse, then the grey-black, whale-backed shape of the submarine emerged from the darkness of the sea. He imagined – saw? – the damage to the rudder and the hydroplanes, and bent his head and cocked it to one side in order to perceive the outline of the stern more easily. Then the warhead detonated, and to his intense disappointment the TV screen went blank. Memory continued the succession of images.

He had seen the 'Catherine Wheel' in operation on an old sub during trials. The film had been poor, grainy and cut-about, but the images had been stark, vivid, deadly. When the separate warheads split from the body of the torpedo, they would whirl and spin and weave outwards in a net-like circle. Some of them carried small explosive charges, some barbed hooks of super-strengthened steel, some suction caps or magnets. Twelve in all, each of them trailed a length of toughened steel cable, whipped into a frenzy of whirling movement by the spinning-top effect of the small warheads. Two, three, four or more of these would make contact with the hull and rudder and hydroplanes of the *Proteus* and, as the submarine moved forward under power, the trailing, whipping steel cables would slash at the hull, be dragged with it, and would fasten and entangle the propellers, twisting tighter and tighter like strangling cords.

It would take no more than seconds, and little more than a minute to halt the submarine, her propeller bound and made immovable by the entangled steel cables.

He closed his eyes, seeing the drama on an inward screen, himself seated in the darkness of the briefing room as the film was shown. He did not hear, did not need to hear the exultant cry from the torpedo room, nor the cheering in his control room. He awoke when his first-lieutenant shook his elbow, startling him. The young man was grinning.

'Direct hit, sir. Another direct hit!' he bubbled.

'Good,' the captain said slowly. 'Well done, everyone.' He stood upright. Already, the British submarine would be slowing, her crew terrified by the vibration as the cables tightened against the revolutions of the propeller, strangling it. 'Very well. Send up an aerial buoy. Transmit the following message, Lieutenant. Message begins TOLSTOY, followed by target impact co-ordinates. Message ends. Direct to Murmansk, code priority nine.'

'Yes, sir!'

'Retrieve the aerial buoy as soon as the transmission ends.'

'It's no good, sir,' Lloyd heard the voice of the chief engineer saying, 'that second impact has either damaged the prop even further, or we're entangled in something.' Lloyd was shuddering with the vibration, and the noise of the protesting propeller and shaft was threatening to burst his skull. It was impossible to stand it for much longer. The submarine was slowing , the prop grinding more and more slowly. The Russians had done something, caught them in a net or some similar trap, choking them.

'Very well, Chief.' He could not utter the words clearly, only in an old man's quaver because of the shudder in the hull which was worsening with every passing second. He shouted his orders above the noises. They were in a biscuit tin, and someone was beating on the lid with an iron bar. 'First-Lieutenant.' Thurston nodded, holding on to the depth indicator panel, his legs as unreliable as those of a drunk. 'John. I want a reading of the bottom as soon as we're over the plateau. If we find a flat bit, set her down!'

'Aye, aye, sir!'

The tension in the control room, even though it remained filled and shaken by the increasing vibration, dispelled for a moment. He'd done what they expected of him, demanded of him. The two planesmen struggled with the increasing difficulty, veins proud like small blue snakes on their skin, muscles tight and cramped with the strain. They had to slow down, stop.

'Captain to all crew!' he yelled into his microphone, which jiggled in his hand. 'Prepare for bottoming and maintain for silent running!' Silence. A bad joke. The protest of the propeller, the shaft, the bearings drummed in his head.

'Lieutenant, come about and set up another sweep pattern two thousand metres to the east. Sensor control – no relaxation. We *can't* have lost her! She's here somewhere. Keep looking.'

'Well done, John.' Lloyd tried to lighten the sudden,

sombre silence. 'Light as a feather.' No one smiled. The tension in the control room tightened again like a thong around his temples. The din had ceased, the torture of the prop and shaft was over. Yet the silence itself pressed down on them like a great noise. 'All non-essential services off. Stand down non-operational crew and safety men. Get the galley to lay on some food.'

'Hayter to Captain.'

'Yes, Don?'

'The "Victor-II" is still sniffing around, but I think she's lost us for the moment.'

'Good news, Don.'

The lights blinked off, to be replaced by the emergency lighting. The submarine seemed to become quieter, less alive, around him. They were more than twenty fathoms down on a ledge jutting out from the Norwegian coast, and the Russians would now be looking for them, more determined than ever.

Part Two

Search and Rescue

Six: LOST

Part of him, immediately he left the warmth of the headquarters building, wanted to respond to the driving sleet and the howling wind and the lights of the port of Pechenga gleaming fitfully like small, brave candles in the white-curtained darkness. He wanted the weather not to be critical, merely something to be endured, even enjoyed. Instead, there was the immediate sense of danger, as if a palpable, armed enemy was closing at his back. He turned up the collar of his heavy jacket, and crossed the gleaming concrete, slippery already, to the waiting car.

His driver was a *michman* – petty officer – from Pechenga base security, and he saluted despite the fact that Ardenyev was not in uniform. His face was cold and washed-out and expressionless in the purpling light of the lamps. Ardenyev had the strange and unsettling impression of death. Then the driver opened the rear door of the Zil staff car, and the momentary feeling evaporated.

The car wound swiftly down from the hump of higher ground on which the Red Banner Fleet's headquarters in Pechenga stood, towards the port and the naval helicopter base. Lights out in the roads, the glare of the arc-lamps from the repair yards, the few commercial and pleasure streets sodium-lit and neon-garish, like the stilled arms of light from a lighthouse.

Ardenyev was disturbed by Dolohov's manic desire for success. The admiral had never been careless of risks before. This adventure with the British submarine obsessed him. He knew the details of the met. reports as well as anyone, and yet he ignored them. Ardenyev had, on his own authority, delayed his departure for the rescue ship out in the darkness of the Barents because of the worsening conditions. Delayed, that is, until further postponement would have meant running behind the schedule of the operation; and that he was not prepared to do. Instead, he nursed his conviction that Dolohov was unjustified in ordering them out.

It was cold in the back of the staff car despite the powerful, dusty-smelling heater. Ardenyev rubbed his hands together to warm them. Then the staff car slid under the canopy of white light of the helicopter base and the driver wound down the window to present his pass to the naval guard at the gate. The guard took one swift look at Ardenyev, the cold air blanching his face from the open window, more out of curiosity than to identify him. Then the heavy wire-mesh gates swung open, and the driver wound up the window as they pulled forward. The car turned left, and they were passing hangars and repair shops where warmer light gleamed through open doors. Then a patch of darkness, then the sleet rushing at the windscreen again. Through it, Ardenyev could see the two helicopters, red lights winking at tail and belly. Two MiL-2 light transport helicopters, the only naval helicopters in current service small enough to land on the seemingly fragile, circular helicopter pad of the rescue ship *Karpaty*.

The car stopped almost in the shadow of one of the small helicopters. Snub-nosed, insect-like, frail. Ardenyev thanked the driver abstractedly, and got out of the car. The sudden wind and cold sleet did not drive out the unwelcome, crowding impressions that seemed to have taken possession of his imagination, leading into the rational part of his mind, polluting clear thought. The Zil staff car pulled away behind him.

'You changed your mind then, skipper – decided to come?' came a voice from the door of the MiL. A grinning, cold-pinched face, blown fair hair above a dark naval jersey. Senior-Lieutenant Andrei Orlov, Ardenyev's second-in-command and leader of Blue section of the special operations unit. Ardenyev summoned a wave he hoped was optimistic, then looked up at the sky, wrinkling his face.

'The pilot's moaning about the weather, skipper,' Orlov added. 'It's just having to turn out in this muck, I reckon.'

Orlov took Ardenyev's arm, and he swung up into the hollow, ribbed interior of the helicopter. The door slammed shut behind him. Someone groaned with the cold. Young faces, five others besides Orlov. Blue section. Ardenyev nodded at them, business-like. Then he clambered through into the helicopter's cabin. The pilot nodded to him. His face was disgruntled.

'Get your clearance – we're on our way,' Ardenyev told him, 'just as soon as I get aboard your pal's chopper. Take care.' Already, the inertia of the mission had affected him, sweeping him along like a current growing stronger each moment. An easy and familiar adrenalin invested his body. His mind was clear now. He clambered back into the passenger compartment. 'OK, you lot?' Each man nodded. Most of them grinned, nerves flickering like small electric shocks in their faces and arms. 'Good. See you on the *Karpaty*. Open the door, Andrei.'

The door slid back, and Ardenyev dropped lightly to the ground. He crossed the patch of wet, slippery concrete to the next pad, and the door to the second MiL opened with a screech. The senior *michman* who was his deputy leader in Red section hauled him aboard, wiping sleet from his jacket even as he slammed the door shut behind Ardenyev.

'Thought you weren't coming, sir,' he offered. His face was bony and angular beneath the cropped hair. Viktor Teplov.

'Thanks Viktor. Lieutenant Orlov thought just the same.' He looked round at the other five men, grinning. One or two older faces. Red section was the senior team in the unit. The faces were as they should be. A couple of good youngsters, too. 'Everyone keeping warm?'

'With difficulty, sir,' Teplov answered.

'Let's get going, then.' He clambered through to the passenger seat beside the pilot. 'Very well, Lieutenant, shall we proceed?' he said as he strapped himself into the seat.

'You're going to be very lucky, Captain, to get down on to the *Karpaty*. The weather out there is worse than this.'

'I have implicit faith in your skills, Lieutenant.' He gestured towards the windscreen of the helicopter where two huge wiper blades and the de-icing equipment struggled with the sleet. 'Shall we go? I take it you're cleared for take-off?'

'We are. We've been waiting an hour, fully cleared.'

'What's the matter, Lieutenant?'

'I've told my superiors – I've told anyone who will listen.'

'Told them what?'

'The wind is force four plus. What if we can't get down, just can't make it?'

'The *Kiev*, I suppose. Why?'

'Let's hope it's not too bad for the *Kiev*, then. The range of this chopper means that once we get out there, we haven't enough fuel to get back. You should be in a MiL-8, one of the big boys, all of you. They shouldn't have assigned this –'

'Shouldn't have assigned you, you mean? Two small, light helicopters were requested. The rescue ship contains all our equipment. The *Kiev*'s no good to us. MiL-8s can't land on the *Karpaty*. Now, we can go?'

'All right. Just wanted you to know.'

'I'm grateful.'

The pilot lieutenant cleared with the tower. Ardenyev settled himself more comfortably in his narrow seat. The two Isotov turbo-shafts began to whine, and above his head the rotor blades quickened, cutting through the sleet, swirling until they were transformed into a shimmering dish. The lieutenant altered the angle of the rotor blades, the engine pitch changed to a higher note, and the helicopter moved off its chocks. The pilot paused, checking his instruments, the wheels of the MiL were just in contact with the ground. The pilot's knuckle was white on the stick.

'The wind,' the pilot observed gloomily.

'Yes.'

The MiL lifted, with seeming reluctance, from the patch of concrete. The sleet whirled round them in the downdraught. A fist of wind swung at them, made contact, knocked them sideways. The pilot shuffled his feet on the rudder bar, juggled the stick and they steadied, drifted, steadied again, and rose above the lights of the helicopter base. A white dish beneath them, darkness above.

'See what I mean?' the pilot offered. 'We're right on the edge of possible flying conditions.' The wind buffeted them. It seemed a physical strain on the pilot to maintain course. It had seemed a struggle to alter the stick and head the MiL out to sea, as if the helicopter was some reluctant, untamed animal.

'Yes, I see,' Ardenyev replied thoughtfully. 'Is our fellow traveller with us?'

The pilot looked in his mirror, then spoke into his throat-mike. The other pilot's voice was a pinched, unreal sound.

'He's there.'

A shudder ran through the fuselage, as if it had received a powerful blow, some direct hit with a weapon.

Hyde opened his eyes. For a moment, Shelley's features were unfamiliar. Then he recognised Aubrey's aide, and attempted to sit up. Pain shot through his ribs, and his back, and he groaned. Hands pushed him back down on the hard bed. He could feel the thin, hard, uncomfortable blanket beneath his fingers, and he wiggled his toes, eyes very tightly shut for a moment until he opened them in relief.

'You're all right,' Shelley said. 'God knows how, but you're just bruised pretty badly.'

His neck and shoulder ached more than his back and ribs. 'One of them hit me,' he complained.

'We assumed that was the case. It's why you've been out so long.'

'How long?'

'Almost four hours.'

'Christ.' He covered his face with his hands, as if the light hurt him or he was ashamed. 'Jesus, my head.'

'I caught the end of the concert. Mine feels much the same.'

'Very funny.'

'Who was it – Petrunin?'

Hyde's eyes snapped open. 'How did you know?'

'Routine surveillance report on the embassy. Unauthorised trip north by the Resident. It had to be you and the girl.'

'I saw him.' Hyde saw Shelley motioning towards another part of the narrow, cream-painted room. A door closed. Shelley's face appeared above his own again, and then he was being helped to sit up. Shelley proffered a mug of tea. Hyde sipped the sweet, scalding liquid, hands clasped round the mug as if to warm them. 'I almost had her.' They were alone in the room now. 'I'm all right?'

Shelley nodded. 'You're all right – just a bit crook.'

'I feel it. The girl panicked. She's like something high on

115

LSD. Seems to think they're coming out of the woodwork for her.'

'She's right.'

'That bloody rock band. They got in the way.'

'Where do you think she is? Do you think they've got her?'

'I don't know. She could be anywhere.' Hyde concentrated. 'I got the impression Petrunin had gone back off the platform – the bloke who clobbered me was being pushed towards the steps – the girl was down the other end of the platform. One of them went after her. He might have made it.'

'By the time I got here, they'd all disappeared. No one saw the girl.'

'Shit.'

'I know.'

'What does Aubrey want us to do?'

'He's otherwise occupied. He's taken control of the submarine business. He seems to think it's in a hell of a mess.'

'He's got the set now, then. It's all a bloody mess.'

'Where is she, Patrick? If she isn't at the embassy or one of their safe houses? I've got everything I can screened. They won't be able to get her out – I hope. If they want to, that is. But if she's free, where is she?'

'Why not Heat of the Day? It's where she ran for help and cover in the first place? She might have nowhere else to go.'

'The group?'

'Yes.'

'Where are they?'

Hyde groaned as he swung his legs off the bed and sat up. He touched his ribs gingerly. 'Are they sure nothing's broken?'

'Quite sure.'

'Free Trade Hall, Manchester, is their next venue. Where they're staying tonight, I've no idea. Maybe here?'

Shelley shook his head. 'Not here. Some country hotel in Cheshire. I'm having it checked out.'

'You won't find the girl. She won't stick her neck out again. They could even have hidden her somewhere. She'll go to ground for the duration if the Branch trample all over the garden in their big boots.'

'You can't do it yourself.'

Hyde rubbed his neck and shoulder, groaning softly. Then he looked into Shelley's face. 'I'll accept discreet cover, but nothing more. The girl doesn't believe me as it is. If I go in mob-handed, she'll never tell us where Dad is. You can see that, can't you?'

'Aubrey wouldn't like it.'

'He might. The girl is frightened. She knows one mob is after her, one mob and me on my own. Give me until tomorrow night, and if I can find her and talk to her, she might come in. I won't lose her again.'

'Petrunin won't let go of you.'

'All right. But the girl's more important. It won't be any good arresting a rock band and sweating the lot of them. She has to be coaxed. She's near panic. Her father must be a mistrusting bastard. She's neurotic about us.'

Shelley paced the room, one hand rubbing his chin, the other thrust into the pocket of his overcoat. He glanced at Hyde from time to time. Indecision blossomed on his face. Eventually, he said: 'I don't know – I just don't know.'

'Look, you work on the assumption that Petrunin has her, and I'll work on the assumption he hasn't. Get back to London and mobilise the troops. I'll go up to Manchester, and sit on my arse and wait. Get me cover, *discreet* cover, from the Branch up there, and then let me try to get to the girl. If she isn't in Manchester, and they won't tell me where she is, then you can take over. Okay?'

'All right,' Shelley said after another lengthy pause. 'All right. We'll do it your way, for the moment.'

'At least I'm a familiar face.'

'You won't be if you get knocked about any more.' He glanced at the telephone on a folding table, next to a black medical bag. 'I'll try to talk to Aubrey, though. I want him to be fully informed.'

It was a tableau of activity, a frozen still-life of tension, fear close to panic, routine and emergency procedures. In other parts of the submarine, men lay in their bunks or sat on the floor. No one moved unless movement was unavoidable and essential to the survival of the *Proteus*. In the control room, men stood or sat as their functions dictated, and when they moved – which was rarely, and with Lloyd's express permission – it was with an exaggerated, burglar-like stealth. All unnecessary electrics had been switched off, and the control room was made eerie by the emergency lighting. Only Lloyd stalked the control room like a hunter, like an escapee.

The sonars, in passive mode, their screens illuminating the faces of their operators from beneath, making arms and chins and cheeks blue or green or red, a ghastly imitation of disco strobe-lights, revealed the *Proteus*'s danger. Under the cloak of 'Leopard' the submarine lay on the ledge almost fifty fathoms down, while Soviet submarines moved back and forth around, below and above them like prowling sharks outside a diver's cage. As Lloyd watched over the shoulder of one of the sonar operators, a bright trail on the screen slid slowly to the port like the hand of a clock, mere hundreds of yards from their position. Noise – any noise – would be like blood to that shark, and bring others.

Lloyd left the screen and stood beneath one of the emergency lights. Once more, he scanned the damage report that his chief engineer had compiled in silence and semi-darkness. They had not dared send a diver outside the hull, outside the cloak of the anti-sonar. Much of it was guesswork, or deduced from the instruments and the computer. The damage was relatively slight, but almost totally disabling. Thurston and the chief engineer had guessed at a low-charge torpedo – wake-homing, as they had known in those last seconds before it struck – which had damaged the propeller blades and the port aft hydroplane. It left the *Proteus* with no effective propulsion, and little ability to maintain course and depth. She needed repairs before she could go anywhere. And in that conclusion, Lloyd perceived the Russian objective.

He was calm. It was partly an act for the benefit of the crew, and yet it was genuine too. He had not known he would react in this way, in harm's way. It had little to do with the fact that the pressure hull remained undamaged, or with the invisibility bestowed by 'Leopard'. It was, simply, him. He had no inclination to curse MoD or to blame himself for not aborting the mission hours earlier. The past, even as recently as two hours before, was dead to him. The Russians did not know where they were and, eventually, help must come – diplomatic, military, civilian, mechanical, political.

Thurston left the navigator and Hayter, who was taking a much needed break from monitoring the functioning of 'Leopard', and crossed the control room. In his hand he had a notebook and pen. He held it up to Lloyd.

Thurston had written: *What do we do?* Lloyd merely shook his head. Thurston was puzzled, then scribbled furiously on a fresh sheet of the notebook: *We have to tell someone.* Lloyd took a pen from his breast pocket, and borrowed Thurston's notebook. He scribbled: *And tell them where we are?* Thurston – Lloyd could not help being amused by the pantomime they were enacting – wrote: *Must be Nimrod in area by now.*

We can't transmit. Too risky. Lloyd scribbled.

They want 'Leopard' – but how? Thurston wrote. *Salvage?*

They couldn't, Thurston began writing, then his hand trailed off to the edge of the sheet. Savagely, he crossed out what he had written. Defiantly, he wrote: *Have to find us first.* Lloyd patted his shoulder, then wrote: *Only a few days.*

The sudden noise was deafening, literally terrifying to every man in the control room. It was more than two seconds before the rating at the code-signals console cut the amplification with a hand that dabbed out, as if electrified, at the switch. He stared at Lloyd guiltily, afraid, his youthful face behind his ginger beard blushing. Lloyd tiptoed across to him, his whole body shaking with reaction. The chatter of a high-speed coded signal, incoming. The rating removed his headphones, offering them like a propitiation to Lloyd, something to avert his wrath. Lloyd pressed him, firmly but not unkindly, on the shoulder, and held the headphones to one ear. He nodded, as if deciphering the signal for himself, or hearing an instruction in plain language. The rating flicked switches, and waited. His screen remained blank. Lloyd watched it, looking into a mirror, a crystal ball. Thurston arrived behind him, his breath ragged and only now slowing down. Lloyd felt the tension in the control room of the shrilling chatter of the signal, and the awareness of the Russians beyond the hull, and the knowledge that the signal was continuing. It crawled on his skin like St Elmo's Fire, or a disturbed nest of ants.

The screen displayed a line of white print. A message buoy. Thurston nudged Lloyd, and mouthed *Nimrod*, and Lloyd nodded. The code indentification then appeared, deciphered. *MoD*, then the placing of the security level of the instructions. *ETNA*. Lloyd looked startled. A civilian override by the intelligence service. The comprehension of their danger by some outside authority made him feel weak. They had known, had tried –

The message unreeled on the screen, line by line, then began to repeat itself. *Abort the mission, return to home waters immediate. ETNA. ETNA. Acknowledge, code 6F, soonest. Compliance immediate –*

Compliance impossible. Someone had known, someone in SIS or the Directorate of Security or the CIA, or the Norwegians, the Germans, the Dutch – someone somewhere had known, or suspected, and had tried to warn them, recall them. The knowledge was like a debilitating illness.

There was a Nimrod in the area, on-station. It would, perhaps, wait for an acknowledgement. It would, doubtless remain on-station to monitor Soviet naval activity. Such would be its orders. It was up there, somewhere.

Signal, Lloyd wrote on Thurston's pad. The rating watched the screen. The message began repeating for the third time. Lloyd reached out, flicked a switch angrily, and the screen darkened. The rating's shoulders hunched as if against a blow from behind.

You can't, Thurston had written by the time Lloyd looked back at the pad. The two men stared at one another, their faces seeming agonised in the dimness of the emergency lights.

Lloyd crossed the control room. Four trails of light, not one of them more than a mile-and-a-half from the ledge on which they lay. Four hunter-killer submarines, waiting for the blood that would spur them, fix the position of *Proteus*. That blood might be any noise, even the sonar shadow of the aerial buoy they would have to send to the surface to contact the Nimrod.

You can't.

Lloyd realised he still had Thurston's pad in his hand. He dare not, in his anger, tear out the sheet or throw down the pad. It would not make a detectable noise. Yet he did not dare.

In how many rooms had he waited, on how many occasions? Clocks. How many clocks? So many of them with large, plain faces and a red sweeping second hand. Arms that clicked on to the next minute. Clocks. The persistence of memory. Even now, there was no clarity to his thoughts, no cleanness. Only the many other occasions on which he had endured the same, endless waiting.

Aubrey sighed. He had not been aware of the number of clocks in the underground room until all the protocol had been observed and Brussels and Washington and MoD had agreed to his assumption of complete authority over the safe return of the *Proteus*. Furious telephone and signal activity, followed by a post-coital lassitude, restlessness. Waiting for the Nimrod's report, waiting then for the first safe occasion when the submarine could send an aerial buoy to the surface and answer their peremptory summons home. Until a certain time had passed – the remainder of that night, perhaps the next day, too – they could make no assumptions. Nor would they be able to prevent dread from flourishing like a noxious weed in each of their minds.

Aubrey knew it, understood the Soviet scheme in its entirety. Daring, almost foolhardy, reckless, extreme. But impossible of fulfilment. 'Leopard' as the prize. Clark, too, he knew agreed with his insight. He had not asked the American; he had asked no one. He stared at the cup of coffee in his hand, and found its surface grey. His watch peeped like a rising, ominous sun over the curve of his wrist, from beneath his shirt-cuff. He ignored it.

He had never been interested in seconds, in the sweep of the quick hand. Blister or burn operations that relied on that kind of exactitude had never been his forte. Yet he had waited longer, and more often. Back rooms of empty buildings near the Wall, with the rats scampering behind the skirting-board and the peeling wallpaper; or beneath the slowly revolving ceiling-fans, in hotel rooms with geckos chasing insects up the walls or places where, with the fan less effective against even hotter nights, crickets chorused outside; or with windows fugged by the warmth of wood-burning stoves, and wooden walls; and so many embassy basements and signals rooms, and so many rooms like this, in London and a dozen other cities. Memory's persistence, its retained vivacity, wearied and oppressed him.

Shelley's telephone call was, perhaps, the worst moment; the small, personal act of spite or neglect amid a more general ruin. Of course Hyde was correct – he must reach the girl himself, if they were not only to possess her, but to possess her confidence also. Manchester. Aubrey was doubtful that the girl had returned to the pop group; and at the same moment wondered whether his disdain towards their kind of music made him think that. He could not, he found, identify in any way with a modern girl of twenty-plus. An alien species. And Shelley's background was probably wrong. Hyde might know more than either of them.

With great reluctance, Aubrey looked at the clock on the wall opposite his chair. Another minute clicked away. Twelve twenty-four. Another six minutes, with good fortune and communications, before the Nimrod transmitted a status report on Soviet activity in the area of the Tanafjord.

And, despite the weariness of the waiting, he felt no desire to receive that report.

'No trace of them? After almost three hours, no trace of them?' Dolohov raged at the rear-admiral, who blanched with a suppressed indignation of his own, and the sense of humiliation at once more being berated in front of junior officers, his own and those who had come with Dolohov. 'It is not good enough, Admiral. It is very bad. We *knew* it would come to this, we knew it! They found her, crippled her so they say, and now they have lost her. It is not good enough!'

'I – can only repeat, sir, that everyone, every unit on station, is using every means to locate the submarine. We have reduced the search area to a matter of fifty or so square miles of the seabed. The British submarine is inside that square. It is only a matter of time.'

Dolohov stared through the window of the control room, down at the map table. A cluster of glowing lights, now merely the decoration for the fir-tree. He dismissed the childhood image, but he could no longer believe in the symbolic importance of those lights. They were strung together for no reason. The rear-admiral's voice seemed to whine in his ear, and his own breath whistled in and out of the spaces under his ribcage.

'They could stay down there for weeks, unless the hull has been damaged, which evidently it has not.' As he spoke, his exhalations clouded a little circle of glass in front of his face, as if he were attempting to obscure the signals of temporary failure that glowed below him. 'It will be wearying for them, but not uncomfortable or dangerous, while we listen for the whispers of their breathing, the sound of their feet.' He turned on the rear-admiral. 'We should not have lost contact when the submarine was hit. *Grishka*'s captain should not have lost contact.'

'Admiral, he had poor target acquisition, just a trace of the submarine's wake. The torpedo had to be launched, or held, and he made his decision. I – I happen to think he made the right decision.'

'You do?' Dolohov's face was bleak with contempt and affront. Then it altered; not softened, but it became more introspective. His voice was softer when he continued. 'Perhaps. Perhaps. If they don't find her soon, then we shall pass from the realm of action into that of diplomacy, achieve an international situation. She is in Norwegian waters, and they will attempt to rescue her. Already, they have made contact. You have no idea what that message contained?'

The rear-admiral shook his head. 'A one-time code. We would need all their computer cards, and then know which one.'

123

'Very well. It was probably a recall signal. What of the aircraft?'

'A British Nimrod. It will be watching us.'

'You see my point, Admiral? Once they understand what we are doing, they will attempt to intervene. There will be evidence, photographs, computer print-outs. It will all serve to complicate matters.'

'Yes, sir.'

'Temperature sensors, sonar, infra-red – all useless.' Dolohov rubbed his chin, staring at the ceiling above his head. In a quiet voice, he said, 'Likelihood. Likelihood. If there was some element of *choice* open to the British captain – eh?' He turned to the rear-admiral. 'If he was able to decide, at least to some extent, his final location, where would it be ? A ledge, a cleft, a depression? Feed into the computers every detail of every chart and every sounding we have of your fifty square miles. If necessary, we can send down divers – *before* Ardenyev's team are let loose. Or we can use submersibles with searchlights – ' Dolohov was elated again. He controlled, he contributed, he conceived. 'Yes, yes. We must be prepared.' Then, seeing that the rear-admiral had not moved, he motioned him away. 'Get on with it, get on with it!'

Twelve twenty-nine. Clark had joined him, together with Copeland, one of the less reluctant members of the 'Chessboard Counter' team. He had requested a conversation with Eastoe, the pilot and captain of the Nimrod. The high-speed, frequency-agile transmissions would delay question and answer but not prevent it. When Eastoe spoke, his words would be recorded on the Nimrod, speeded up to a spitting blur of sound transmitted on frequencies that changed more than a hundred times a second, re-recorded in MoD, slowed and amplified for Aubrey. Then his words would take the same few seconds to reach Eastoe in comprehensible form.

'What's she doing now, Ethan?' he asked suddenly. '*Proteus*, I mean?'

'Getting the hell out, if her captain's got any sense,' Clark replied gloomily.

'You really think they're on to her, don't you?' Copeland

124

challenged Clark. Clark nodded, his face saturnine with experience, even prescience. 'I can't believe that – ' Copeland turned to Aubrey and added: 'Nor should you, sir. "Leopard" is undetectable, and they'll have taken no action against her.'

'Ah,' Aubrey said. 'Would they not?' Copeland shook his head vigorously. 'I wish I shared your faith, young man.'

The communications officer approached them. 'Transmission time, Mr Aubrey.' He was punctiliously polite, but here was little respect. As if Aubrey had somehow, by some underhand trick, succeeded to the commodore's job and salary and pension.

'Thank you – we'll come over.'

Aubrey ushered Clark and Copeland towards the communications console with its banks of switches and reels of tape. Almost as they arrived, a red light blinked on, and a tape began to whirl at near impossible speed. A spit of noise like static.

'The Nimrod's transmitting,' Copeland explained off-handedly.

'Thank you.'

The communications console operator typed on the bank of switches like a competent secretary. Another tape began to turn, slowly. After more than a minute-and-a-half it stopped and the operator rewound it. Aubrey was aware of the other people gathered behind him, much as men might have gathered around a radio for the cricket scoreboard.

Eastoe's voice, a man Aubrey did not know. Nevertheless, informed of the ETNA order and aware of its significance, Eastoe addressed his words to Aubrey. Call sign. Identification. Then: 'We have concluded a square search of the area, dropping patterns of sonar buoys while surveying the area by means of infra-red and radar. There is a great deal of Soviet naval activity, surface and sub-surface – ' Clark scribbled the co-ordinates, even though they were already being fed into the map's computer. 'We have identified by sonar at least four hunter-killer submarines in the immediate area, and the VTOL carrier *Kiev* and the rescue ship ident is confirmed.

There are other surface units of the Northern Fleet engaged in what appear to be sonar searches of the area. Infra-red and radar is also being extensively and intensively used by all surface and sub-surface vessels – '

'They're looking for her,' Clark remarked unnecessarily.

'We conclude an intensive search of a very small area of the seabed, especially inshore. Two Tupolev "Bear"-Cs function exactly similar to our own, are also on station in the immediate area. All units are aware of us, we conclude. Over.'

Aubrey glanced around at Clark, then at Copeland.

'You can speak to Squadron Leader Eastoe now,' Copeland informed him.

'I realise that, young man. I am merely considering my reply.' Aubrey remarked frostily. He paused. The open channel hummed in the silence.

'Squadron Leader,' he began without introduction, 'you evidently have no trace of the *Proteus*. Is it your opinion, your considered opinion, that the submarine has received your message and is acting upon it? Over.'

The fast tape whirled, and again there was the little asthmatic cough of sound. Then the humming silence again, into which Pyott's drawl dropped theatrically, startling Aubrey.

'Not quite as easy as you thought, Kenneth?'

Aubrey did not turn round. Pyott had entered the room without his noticing. Aubrey sensed a lofty acquiescence in his tone.

'Ah, Giles,' he said, 'I'm afraid things don't look awfully sunny, just at the moment.' Aubrey's own voice was similarly affected, announcing the draw, the honourable compromise. Pyott pushed past Clark and arrived at his shoulder.

'Have they got her?' he asked. Genuine guilt, concern.

'We don't know. I've asked the captain of the Nimrod to make a guess.'

Tape whirl, then the slow tape, then Eastoe's un-emotional voice.

'My guess is she's on the bottom, not moving.' A pause, then, as Eastoe realised that Aubrey could not comment immediately, he continued: 'The submarines and surface ships are concentrating in a very, very small area. Either they've lost contact altogether, or they have a pretty good idea where they'll find her. Over.'

Immediately, Aubrey said, 'In your estimation, is the *Proteus* damaged?'

'You're not serious, Kenneth?' Pyott asked while they waited for Eastoe's reply.

Aubrey looked at him. 'The possibility has to be considered. If they are searching a very small area, it may be because they suspect, even know, she can't move out of that area.'

'God,' Pyott breathed, and his face was slack and grey, much older. His mouth was slightly open, and he looked very unintelligent.

'I don't think we could raise Him on this set,' Clark observed, having overheard Pyott's admission of negligence, culpability. Pyott glanced at the American malevolently. Clark raised his hands, palms outwards. 'OK, I'm not crowing, Pyott.' Giles Pyott nodded.

Then Eastoe's voice, as naturally, it seemed, as if he was in the room with them. 'It's possible, sir.' Aubrey's astuteness had won Eastoe's respect, at least for the moment. 'The search appears to be concentrated well inshore, but it isn't being extended outside a certain radius. They're refining the search all the time, they're not widening it. I think she's in there somewhere. Over.'

Aubrey looked at Clark. 'Could they have damaged her, Ethan?'

'It's possible.'

'How?'

Clark considered the problem. 'Wire-guided torpedo, maybe. If they got a temperature trace – ' Hidden fear now made itself apparent on his face. 'Wake-homing – yes.' He shook his head. Copeland's face was lengthened with realisation, complicity in fear. Clark cleared his throat. 'If they got some kind of heat trace, and then used a wake-homing torpedo, maybe with a proximity fuse, then the torpedo would follow the *Proteus*'s wake like a hound. Yes, it could be done.'

'Do we accept that it has been done, and act accordingly?'

127

'I – guess so,' Clark replied.

'No,' Copeland said softly.

'What action, Kenneth?' Pyott asked.

'Diplomatic, of course, through the Norwegians. And practica!. What other vessels do we have in the area?'

'Not much – and far away. Maybe the closest is a day's sailing from the Tanafjord.'

'I see. I wouldn't like to escalate NATO activity in the area, anyway, with the present Soviet concentration of vessels.' He paused. 'I shall instruct Eastoe to monitor and report continuously. It would seem that, at the moment, the Red Banner Fleet cannot find our elusive submarine. That situation may not exist for much longer. There is a rescue ship in the area – Eastoe must monitor its activities with particular care. Meanwhile, gentlemen, we must consider all possible scenarios for the prevention of the loss of the "Leopard" equipment to the Russians. Even at the expense of the *Proteus* herself.'

Aubrey turned back to the communications console. It was a few seconds before his audience realised the implications of his statement and the uproar prevented him from completing his instructions to Eastoe and the Nimrod.

The sand dunes on the northern side of the airfield at Kinloss appeared momentarily through the lashing rain, and then vanished again. Tendrils of low cloud were pulled and dragged like bundles of worn grey cloth across the higher ground. Glimpses of hills and mountains were just discernible between the heavier squalls. Three RAF Nimrods gleamed in the rain, their nose sections shielded under protective covers, and the only colour in the scene was the brilliant red of a lone Hawk trainer. All four aircraft were lifeless, abandoned like exhibits in some open-air museum.

The controller watched, from the fuggy warmth of the control tower, a khaki-coloured crew bus returning across the concrete, its lights fuzzily globed by the rain, its whole appearance hunched, its roof shining like a snail's shell. Beyond it, two red anti-collision lights winked rhythmically, and a fourth Nimrod was just discernible. A fuel bowser edged cautiously away from it. Because of his headset, the scene had no sound for the controller, not even that of the incessant rain beating on the control tower roof and windows.

'Kinloss tower – Kestrel One-six requesting taxi clearance.'

'Roger, Kestrel One-six. You're cleared to the holding point, runway Zero Eight.'

Take-off conditions were bordering on the critical. A decision taken on the station would have resulted in the Nimrod's flight being cancelled. The controller disliked the interference of civilians with all the habitual ferocity of the long-serving officer. Eastoe was over the Barents Sea, waiting for his relief Nimrod. This crew were going to take off in distinctly risky conditions at the order of the same civilian, a little old man from the intelligence service. The controller had not been present at the crew's briefing, and the station commander had not seen fit to inform him either of Eastoe's mission or of the origin of their orders from Whitehall. That small resentment flickered through the controller's mind like one of the anti-collision lights out there in the murk.

If he kept quite still, he could line up the nearest Nimrod's fin with a joint in the concrete. He could see the shudders through the airframe as the wind buffeted it. Someone in a nice warm Whitehall office – *ah, tea Miss Smithers, excellent, is it still raining outside?* – giving easy orders with his mouth full of digestive biscuit and risking other people's lives –

The Nimrod Kestrel One-six was almost invisible now, tail-on to him, its winking red lights accompanied by white strobe lights. They alone announced its presence and movement.

'Kestrel One-six – Kinloss tower. You have your clearance.'

'Affirmative.'

'Roger. One-six. You are cleared for a left-hand turn out above five hundred feet.'

The lighting board showed all the lights on the taxiway and the runway to be on. A telephone near him blinked its light, and the duty corporal picked it up, interrupting his

129

making out of the movements slip. The controller lifted one headphone, and caught the information that Flying Officer Harris was sick and would not be reporting for the first shift the next day. He replaced the headphone.

'Kestrel One-six ready to line up.'

'Kestrel One-six, you are cleared to line up, runway Zero Eight, for immediate take off. Wind zero-two-zero, gusting thirty-two.'

'Roger, Kinloss tower. Kestrel One-six rolling.'

The controller picked up his binoculars, and stared into the gloom. At first, there were only the pinpricks of the lights, then a slate-grey and white moving shape began sliding down the corridor of high-intensity lights, the shape resolving itself into the familiar outline of the Nimrod. He imagined the pilot's struggle to hold the aircraft steady against the fierce cross-wind.

The nose wheel began to lift from the runway. The four huge Spey engines began acting like hoses, blasting sheets of water up from the runway beneath them. Fog flickered across the wings as the change in pressure condensed the water vapour. The Nimrod began to disappear almost immediately.

'Kestrel One-six, I'm aborting.'

'Roger – '

Too late, he thought, too late.

'I can't hold her – I'm off the left of the runway – '

The controller could see only one indication of the whereabouts and the danger of the Nimrod. The spray of water thrown up had changed colour, dyed with brown earth as the aircraft ploughed across the field alongside the runway.

'The port leg's giving way!'

'No.'

Then there was a silence that seemed interminable, he and the corporal staring frozenly at one another, until he managed to clear his throat and speak.

'Kestrel One-six, do you read, Kestrel One-six.'

No flame, no explosion, nothing. The corporal's finger touched the emergency button. He could hear the alarm through his headphones.

'Kestrel One-six – '

A bloom of orange through the rain and murk, like a distant bonfire or a beacon. The windows rattled with the explosion, which he heard dully. Irrelevantly, yet with intense hostility, he heard the voice he had earlier imagined. *Sorry to hear that, Miss Smithers. All dead, I suppose. Is there any more tea?*

It had been so easy, and so pointless. The dull orange glow enlarged and brightened.

Seven: FOUND

The helicopter dropped through the murk, and there were no longer rags of cloud and a sensation of unreality. The night was empty, blacker than the cloud and the wind squalled around the cramped cabin with a demented shrieking that Ardenyev simply could not accustom himself to accept or ignore. Only the momentary absence of the snow and sleet reduced the unnerving reality of the wind's strength and velocity, because he could no longer see the wind as a visible, flying whiteness against the dark.

Then he spotted the *Karpaty*, below and to port of them. Blazing with light like a North Sea oil platform, yet tiny and insubstantial, her lights revealing the pinprick flecks of wave-crests against the black sea. Beyond *Karpaty*, outlined like an incomplete puzzle-drawing by her navigation lights, was the bulk of the *Kiev*. Even at her greater distance, she seemed more secure, more a haven than the rescue ship.

The second MiL emerged beside them, dropping into view, an eggshell of faint light.

'Express One to *Karpaty* – Express One to *Karpaty*, over.'

The pilot's voice in his headphones startled Ardenyev with the immediacy of their attempt to land on the rescue ship's helipad. He strained his eyes forward, but could not even see the illuminated, circular platform. The *Karpaty* was a blur of lights seen through the still-running tears that streamed across the cockpit canopy and the windscreen of the MiL. The rescue ship was tiny, and they seemed to be making no visible progress towards it.

'*Karpaty* to Express One. We read you, and have you on radar. Range eight point five kilometres. Over.'

'Weather conditions, *Karpaty*?'

'Winds oh-five-oh, thirty-five knots, gusting to forty-five. Sea state five to six, waves varying ten to twenty feet. What are your intentions? Over.'

The pilot looked across at Ardenyev. He seemed satisfied by the glum, strained silence he observed. Ardenyev considered the shadow of the *Kiev* beyond the lights of the rescue ship. And rejected them.

'Well?' the pilot asked.

'Can you get down?'

'It's on the edge. I don't recommend trying – '

'Express Two to Express One, over.'

'Go ahead, Express Two.'

'Are we going down?'

'I don't like it.'

'We can make it. I'll go in first, if you like. Over.'

'You haven't got all night,' Ardenyev remarked, looking at his watch. They were running perhaps thirty minutes behind schedule already. A diversion to the *Kiev*, and then a sea transfer back to the *Karpaty* would delay them perhaps as much as two hours. Dolohov would find that delay unacceptable. The *Proteus* might be located at any moment, and Ardenyev had no wish to be still airborne when that happened. 'We're late.'

'I fly this crate, not you, Captain. My judgement is all that counts, and my judgement tells me to divert to the carrier.' The pilot was calm, irritated with his passenger but unafraid. He assumed his authority would carry the day.

'Hold on, Express One – I'll set down first. When *Karpaty* has filled my tanks, I'll get out of your way.' The other pilot sounded to Ardenyev to be less afraid, yet he wondered whether his own pilot might not be right.

'Express Two – I suggest we divert to *Kiev*.'

'I'm not putting my bollocks on the chopping-block with Dolohov, Andrei, even if you're prepared to. Just watch my technique!'

Ardenyev's pilot's face was tight with anger, resentment, and something deeper which might have been self-contempt. Ardenyev watched, in a new mood of satisfaction, as the second MiL surged ahead and below them, towards the *Karpaty*. His pilot was playing safe, they would get down now. It meant only that Orlov and Blue Section would be kitting out by the time they arrived, and amused at their superiority.

The second MiL banked, looking uncertain for a

moment below them, as if turning towards the surface of the black ocean itself rather than to the Christmas tree of the ship. Then it appeared to steady and level, and began to nervously, cautiously approach the stern of the rescue ship. The helipad was now a white-lit dish, no bigger than a dinner plate from their altitude. The radio chatter between the pilot and the ship flicked back and forth in his headset, suggesting routine, orderliness, expertise.

Ardenyev's pilot brought his MiL almost to the hover, as if they were drifting with the wind's assistance, feather-like. Yet when Ardenyev glanced across at him, the man's knuckles were white. It did not indicate mental or emotional strain, merely made Ardenyev aware of the turbulence outside; its heaving against the fragile canopy of the helicopter. The pressure to move them, overturn them, crush them, was like a great depth of seawater. Once the image made contact with reality, a circuit was formed that alarmed him. The slow-motion below was fraught, dangerous now.

The fly-like MiL drifted towards the helipad. Ardenyev could see tiny figures on the deck, and their bent shapes, their clinging to rails and surfaces, indicated the force of the wind. Its volume seemed to increase outside.

The deck of the rescue ship heaved, and the light seemed to spill like liquid over the ship's side on to the surface of the water. The whitecaps opened like teeth in a huge black jaw. The sight of the water's distress and power was sudden, making the rescue ship fragile and the helicopter approaching it more insect-like than ever. It was a fly hovering above a motorway, awaiting an encounter with a windscreen.

The helicopter flicked away, much like a gull caught by a gust of wind, and the pilot's voice was high-pitched, his relieved laughter unreal and forced.

'Mishka, get away from there! We'll divert to the *Kiev* and winch them down. You'll never be able to use auto-hover, the deck's pitching too much.'

'Don't worry, Grandad,' the voice of Orlov's pilot came back. 'Just a temporary hitch. Watch this.'

The words now seemed to Ardenyev to have an empty bravado which he despised and which frightened him. Yet the rescue ship seemed to have settled again, the whitecapped waves to have subsided, slipping back into the shadows beneath the deck of the *Karpaty*. The MiL began to sidle towards the helipad again. Tiny figures crouched, as if at its approach, ready to secure the helicopter the moment its wheels touched.

The pilot instructed the *Karpaty*'s captain that he would switch to auto-hover just above the deck, which would allow the helicopter to automatically move with the pitching of the ship, so that the deck would always remain at the same level beneath the MiL. Ardenyev saw his own pilot shaking his head.

'What's wrong?'

'What?'

'I said, what's wrong? You're shaking your head.'

'The deck's pitching and rolling too much, and I think he's out of the limits for auto-hover and height hold.' The pilot shrugged. 'Perhaps it isn't from where he is. I don't know.' He glanced at Ardenyev as if daring him to comment, or inviting personal insult.

'If there's any real danger, order him to divert – or I will.'

Creeping whiteness appeared at the edges of their canopy, like some cataract or a detached retina beginning to float. The sleet had returned. Ardenyev's pilot increased the beat of the wipers, and they watched, oblivious of everything else, even of attempting to interfere, as the MiL below them banked, levelled, sidled forward, moved above the white dish of the helipad. There was a long moment of stillness, accompanied by the breathy whispering of Ardenyev's pilot: 'Go on, go on, my son, go on, go on – '

The noise irritated and disturbed Ardenyev. The MiL was above the deck now, and lowering towards it. Stillness. A white-knuckled hand at the corner of his eye, whiteness creeping around the canopy, flying between them and the garishly-lit scene below. The navigation lights of the carrier, outlining a huge, safe bulk, in the distance. Ardenyev held his breath. They were going to make it. When they, too, had landed, Orlov would study his face; there'd better be no trace left of anxiety or doubt, or the young man would burst out laughing –

Dropping slowly like a spider coming down its thread;

very slowly. Ardenyev could see himself, years before, watching such a spider in his bedroom, coming slowly down its thread, confident, small, agile, an acrobat. And slowly he had begun to blow upwards, making the spider swing, making it uncertain, vulnerable, that tiny creature who had abseiled from the ceiling with such arrogance. It had crawled, scuttling upside-down, back up its rope of thread, then dropped again with slightly more caution. Blow again. He had blown again.

The MiL hopped away from the deck as if electrocuted. Then it began to drop slowly, more slowly than before, towards the deck as it once more became level. The glimpse of the whitecaps vanished into the night.

The spider had scuttled away, dropped again, but its weight now could not deaden or steady the swing of the thread to which it clung. It had been descending from the lampshade, like a small black god climbing out of the sun. Swinging, unable to control the motion.

Ardenyev's hand touched his throat, feeling for the transmitter switch of his microphone. The spider was swinging across the ceiling above his bed, interestingly, helplessly. The helicopter shifted in a grumble of the wind, and the deck of the *Karpaty* shifted, too. Pitching towards the MiL, which hopped out of its way, then moved back down, drawn by magnetism, it seemed. The deck steadied. The spider swung across the ceiling, flying the landscape of cracks and damp patches, swinging to almost touch the shadows in the corners of the room. And nearing his face all the time as fear or instinct or helplessness made it pay out more of the rope of thread.

Six feet. Stillness now. White knuckles, his own fingers dead as he fumbled with the microphone, tried to think what to say, why he was going to speak. Appalled and fascinated. Five feet, four –

The spider just above his face. Cheeks puffed out, he waited to catch it at the optimum moment, blow it across the bedroom, perhaps at his younger brother's bed and his sleeping form. Cupping his hands round his mouth to direct the breath when he expelled it.

Three feet, two –

'Auto-hover – come on, come on – '

A foot, then two feet, three, four – the deck of the *Karpaty* pitched again, the lights spilling across the angry sea. Five feet – spin, flick, twist upside-down, turning like a top. The MiL staggered with the blow of the helipad, and then the repeated punching of the wind. The spider flew through the air, into shadow, its rope of thread loose, wafting in the air's current he had disturbed.

The MiL hung upside-down for a second or more, then drove back towards the port side of the ship, breaking its rotors then its back on the side of the *Karpaty*, just forward of the helipad. A billow of flame, incandescent and paling the ship's lights, a tiny figure struck like a match falling into the sea, the MiL's wreckage pursuing him into the whitecaps. Flame flickered over the wild water for a second, then the MiL was doused like a torch – and gone.

Ardenyev came to himself, yelling into his microphone that the pilot should abandon his attempt and divert to the carrier. His words were clipped, orderly, syntactically correct, but he was hoarsely yelling them at the top of his voice. He must have begun shouting even before the MiL crashed.

'Shut up, shut up – !'

Ardenyev's mouth remained open, his throat dry and raw. There was nothing. On the pitching deck of the rescue ship, fire-extinguishers were playing over spilled fuel that travelled like lava along the deck and down the side of the ship. Slowly, the flames flickered and disappeared.

'My God,' Ardenyev breathed finally. Teplov was at his shoulder.

'All right, sir?'

'No, Viktor, it is not all right,' he said in a small voice. 'Tell the team that Blue Section have crashed and that we are diverting to the *Kiev*.'

'Sir.' Teplov offered nothing more in reply. Ardenyev was aware of his departure to the passage compartment. Ardenyev looked at the pilot.

There was a silence in which each man registered the other's pain, and guilt, then the pilot cleared his throat and spoke into his microphone.

'Express One to *Kiev* – permission to land.'

'Permission granted.' An older voice, senior. A commiseration of rank. The same voice went on to supply velocity and the effect of the sea and wind on the pitch of the *Kiev*'s deck. As he acknowledged, the pilot continually shook his head. Then he looked at Ardenyev.

'I was right – for fuck's sake, I was right!'

'We can get down?' The pilot nodded. 'Christ – '

'Express One to *Kiev* – message received. We're on our way.'

Ardenyev sat in a misery of grief as the MiL increased speed and the *Karpaty* slipped beneath its belly. He was appalled at the deaths of Orlov and the others, *his* men, *his* people, *his* responsibility. And he was shaken and anguished at the ease with which it had happened and with which he had allowed it to happen. Distance, slowness, lights – it had all become innocuous, something for spectators, cardboard danger. He had meant to issue the order to divert, but he had not. He had not believed it would happen. A child stepping from a pavement, behind a milk-float, crushed like an eggshell by the car it had not seen. But the distance between the front gate and the road is so small, it cannot signify danger –

He wiped savagely at his eyes. Through the blur as he blinked, the shadowy bulk of the *Kiev* drew closer, then lights sprang out on her starboard after-deck. The superstructure bulked beyond these lights. Tiny pinprick men moved on the deck, bent and huddled to display the ominous force of the wind. Ardenyev wiped his eyes again. The pilot and the carrier were in constant contact, as if instruction and counter-instruction, speed, distance, altitude, pitch, wind velocity would all render the collision of the two objects safe.

Ardenyev felt Orlov and the others in the burning MiL go away and his own fear for himself emerge, invading his stomach and chest and consciousness. The floor of the cabin under his feet was thin, so thin he could sense the buffeting air streaming beneath it, and anticipate the deck of the *Kiev* rushing up to meet them.

The MiL drifted towards the *Kiev*, so like Express Two just before it collided with the *Karpaty*. The deck did not, to Ardenyev's comprehension, enlarge with proximity. It was a grey strip, angled across the substance of the carrier, all the lower decks between them and the sea.

The pilot turned to him. 'You'll winch down while the chopper's on auto-hover.'

'Can't you land?' There was a strange relief amid the surprise.

"Yes – but I'm not risking it with you lot on board. You'll winch down. OK?'

Ardenyev nodded. 'We haven't got a winchman on board.'

'Can you do it?'

'Yes.'

'Get back there and get on with it. I'll clear it with the bridge.'

Ardenyev paused for a moment, and then forced himself out of his seat and climbed over it into the passenger compartment. The imperatives of Dolohov's orders were insinuating themselves again, until he saw the blank, automaton faces of his team. Stunned into emptiness of mind, except where their own fears peered over their shoulders or crawled like indigestion in their stomachs. A sharp pain of fear, a bilious taste in their throats.

'Viktor, we're winching down. Get the door open.' Teplov looked up at him, acknowledging the necessity of the snapped order, resenting it, too. The offices for the dead, their mates, their importance to the operation; all clear in Teplov's eyes. Then he got up and went aft, unlocking the door and sliding it open. The wind howled amongst them as if Teplov had admitted an enemy already triumphing. 'Get ready – one at a time.' The helicopter lurched, one man getting to his feet was flung back against the fuselage, and his face revealed no pain, only a concentration of fear.

Ardenyev lifted him to his feet and shuffled him to the door. They clung to the straps, watching the lighted deck beneath them edge closer, shifting as the sea willed. The young man looked into Ardenyev's face, and seemed to discover something he could trust there. A habit of obedience, it might have been. He allowed Ardenyev to slip the winch harness beneath his arms, and to guide him to the open door. His hair was blown back from his white forehead, and his hands gripped the edges of the doorway Ardenyev placed his hand against his back, and nodded to Teplov. The motor of the winch started up, and the man sat down, dangling his legs over the deck. He looked up as it swung away from the chopper, and then suddenly the MiL was moving with the deck, perhaps thirty or forty feet above it, swaying as in a breeze by virtue of the auto-hover matching its movements to the pitch of the carrier's deck.

'Right, off you go.' Ardenyev held the man's shoulders for a moment, and then propelled him through the doorway. He spun on the wire for a moment, then straightened and dropped slowly and smoothly towards the deck. Uniformed and oilskinned men waited in the downdraught, arms reaching up to him. His legs were held, he was lowered like a child or cat from a tree, then Teplov was recalling the winch harness. Ardenyev looked at him, and nodded. 'Next.'

Shadrin, the explosives expert, was at his shoulder in a moment, grinning. 'Let's get out of this bloody tin box, skipper,' he said. There was a shadow in his eyes, but Ardenyev was thankful for the man's attempt at normality. A small re-establishment of cameraderie, teamwork. Sinkingly, Ardenyev realised that when he got them safely aboard the carrier, he had to rebuild them in his own image; an image in which he felt uncomfortable, even treacherous, at that moment.

He strapped the harness around Shadrin, and slapped him on the shoulder. As Shadrin sat down, then dropped out of the MiL, Ardenyev recollected broiling flames and ignited, spilled fuel and a spider, and prayed that they would locate the British submarine soon. Very soon.

Aerial buoy, Lloyd scribbled on his pad. It rested on the chart table, beneath a dim emergency light. The temperature of the control room seemed higher, and could not be entirely discounted as illusion, which he knew it to be. Silence was humming in his ears.

We can't, Thurston scrawled in ugly, misshapen capitals, and added two exclamation marks for additional emphasis.

You were right – we must.

Lloyd and his first-lieutenant stared at one another. The

pads between them on the chart table were like scraps of food each of them envied the other. Thurston was now confirmed in Lloyd's original opinion that they must do nothing more that sit and wait out the vessels that searched for them. Lloyd – his calm eroded by the dead, limping passage of time, the slowness of clocks, and the sense that the forces mobilised against them could not indefinitely go on seeking and not finding – had now succumbed to the desire for action.

There was an RAF Nimrod above them – twenty, thirty, forty thousand feet it did not matter – on station, not knowing where they were, what condition they were in. MoD had to be told they needed rescuing, otherwise the Russians would inevitably get to them first. Lloyd was utterly convinced that the Russians wanted 'Leopard'. He could not envisage how they intended obtaining it, or conceive the recklessness that must have led them to this course of action, but he understood their objective. MoD had to be told; there was no time to be lost.

He scribbled again on a fresh sheet of the pad. *It's an order*. A helpless, obedient malevolence crossed Thurston's features for a moment, then it was gone. His face was blank of all expression as he nodded his acquiescence.

They crossed silently to the bank of sonar screens. Two only in closest proximity, the other submarines further off, nudging their sensors into other corners of the box in which they had contained the *Proteus*. Lloyd read off distance and bearing. Both of the nearest submarines were, for the moment, moving away from the ledge on which they rested. Lloyd glanced at Thurston, and whispered: 'Now.'

Thurston moved away, and Lloyd found the control room crew, almost every one of them, and Carr the navigator, looking in his direction. He nodded meaningfully, miming the sending up of the aerial buoy. Thurston, at the encoding console, gave the thumbs up – temperature of the control room suddenly jumping – and his hands played over the bank of switches which would release and direct the aerial buoy to the surface. Its journey would take it perhaps a whole minute. Depth figures unreeled on a tiny display unit near Thurston's hand.

Breathing. Ragged, stifled, louder. The control room

was full of nervous men trying to control their breathing Lloyd, his arm draped around the periscope in the centre of the control room, felt hotter, less sure, supremely aware of the aerial buoy bobbing up through the layers of water to the surface.

A small object, a tiny pinprick. Capable of receiving and bouncing back a sonar signal. Something solid that betrayed their location. A flare they had sent up – we're over here, can't you see us?

Lloyd clamped down on the thought, and crossed to Thurston. He gestured for the first-lieutenant's pad and then wrote quickly, in block letters, the message he wished encoded and transmitted to the Nimrod. Thurston nodded reluctantly when he read it, and turned in his chair. The console operator beside him began typing at the keyboard, and the code-of-the-day card was automatically fed in. The operator added the transmission instructions – high-speed, frequency-agile. Lloyd watched the depth figures unreeling near Thurston's elbow. The aerial buoy was still twenty fathoms from the surface, almost twenty seconds still to run until it bobbed up into the waves.

Sweating, now. Cold sweat, surprising in the heat of the control room. Lloyd tried to control it, to calm his body. Ten fathoms. Nine –

Someone clearing his throat, the noise of someone else scratching the cotton of his shirt. Six fathoms, five, four. Almost a minute since they had released the aerial buoy. Three fathoms.

Lloyd broke away from the encoding console and crossed to the passive sonars. Pinpricks, distances, bearings. Still moving away. One moving back, one moving back –

Bearing green nine-five, almost amidships, range two thousand yards. Speed eleven point two five knots. Lloyd looked over his shoulder. Thurston saw him, raised his thumb. The aerial buoy was transmitting the message, a split-second blurt of sound, repeated and repeated. They would have to repeat at least fifty times to be anywhere near certain their message had been picked up by the Nimrod. Ten seconds, no more.

Speed twelve point three knots, bearing unchanged,

range closing. Lloyd stared in disbelief. Twelve point seven knots and rising. Dead amidships, a Russian submarine. The buoy, or the message, untranslatable but audible to the Russians, had pinpointed them. Lloyd waggled his hand at Thurston, and the first lieutenant ceased the transmission and began recalling the aerial buoy.

Thirteen point six knots. Closing.

Lloyd crossed to Thurston, and indicated in savage mime that he must release the buoy, a chopping motion of his hand, again and again. Thurston paused for a moment, then his hands flickered over the console's keyboard. The figures near his knuckles on the digital read-out slowed, then stopped. The buoy was gone, up to the surface again where it would be swept away from their position by the current. Lloyd wiped his forehead with his handkerchief in undisguised relief, not even beginning to think that they had now only the back-up aerial buoy.

He hurried back to the sonars. Speed fifteen point nine knots, bearing unchanged, closing amidships. Range little more than a thousand yards. He realised he had been standing mopping his brow for almost a minute after they released the buoy. Speed fifteen point seven, fifteen point five.

He sighed audibly, a ragged sound from an old man's asthmatic chest. Speed fourteen knots and dropping, bearing green eight-four. Change of course, uncertainty setting in, scent lost.

Scent lost.

The Russian navy had sea-bed maps they could feed into their computers, superimposing them on their sonars and infra-red. It couldn't last for much longer. 'Leopard' would be defeated by likelihood and by the concentration of vessels in their immediate area.

It couldn't last long. Lloyd felt weary, and depressed. It was hard to believe that the Nimrod had heard them, knew where they were and what had happened. No one knew. No one at all.

The decoded message from the *Proteus* unrolled on the screen of the Nimrod's display unit with the kind of stutter given to the pages of a book when they are riffled quickly. Squadron Leader Eastoe bent over the shoulder of his communications officer, and sensed the man's shoulder adopt the quiver of excitement that was evident in his own body. Like an audience of two, they were experiencing the same emotions, the gamut of surprise, shock, satisfaction, hope, and anxiety that the words had little apparent power to evoke.

When the message began repeating on the screen, Eastoe straightened and rubbed his cheeks with his hands. He yawned, surprising himself, then realised it was a ploy of the mind to gain time; time for consideration. *Proteus* on the seabed, position unknown, immobilised by a reduced warhead torpedo, surrounded by Russian vessels, surface and sub-surface. It did not bear consideration.

'Inform MoD immediately – Flash, code of the day. Poor sods.'

'Skipper – ' A voice behind him, the Nav/Attack officer in his niche in the fuselage of the Nimrod.

Eastoe crossed to him. Beyond the man's head the porthole-type window revealed the late slow grey dawn beginning outside; only at their altitude, and above the cloud cover. Below them, the *Kiev* and other surface vessels would be moving through darkness still, and beneath them *Proteus* lay in the permanent darkness of the seabed, where hunter-killers attempted to sniff her out.

'What is it, Bob?'

'Something's happening down there, on the rescue ship.'

'You mean in connection with last night's little party?'

'*Karpaty* is changing course, moving closer to the *Kiev*.'

'I wonder why. You think one of those two choppers crashed on landing, mm?'

'Yes, skipper, surface wind would have made a landing very dicey. There was that quick infra-red reading, and I'm almost sure only one chopper eventually moved off in the direction of the carrier.'

'Then what did they deliver, or try to deliver, to the rescue ship?' Eastoe considered, staring out of the tiny window, down at the roof of the cloud cover, lightening in its greyness, but thick and solid as the roof of a forest. Eastoe felt a detachment he did not enjoy, and which somehow interfered with his thinking. Being on-station, just watching, for so many hours had deadened the reality of what they could only see by means of radar and sonar and infra-red. Detachment; making thought and decision unimportant, without urgency. 'Some sort of team? Experts? People important enough to be ferried out in this weather, anyway. Now you think they're going to transfer to the rescue ship?'

'I do.'

'Okay, Bob, I'll tell Aubrey. Leave it up to him. We'll be off duty in a couple of hours, anyway. Someone else's problem, then.'

Eastoe went forward again, into the cockpit of the Nimrod.

'Anything, skipper?'

'Signal from *Proteus*,' Eastoe replied glumly.

'Bad?'

'She's been hit, Terry.'

'Christ – they're all right?'

'At the moment. But she can't move.'

'He was taking a chance, sending up a buoy.'

'Wouldn't you want someone to know?' Eastoe paused. 'Now who the hell was in those two Russian choppers, and why do they need to get aboard the *Karpaty* so desperately?'

'Skipper – ?'

'Doesn't matter. It's Aubrey's problem, not ours.' Eastoe got out of his seat again. 'Call up Bardufoss – tell them we're off-watch in an hour, and we'll need to refuel. Meanwhile, I'll tell Mr Aubrey straight away. He might need time to think.'

'You saw what happened last night, Captain Ardenyev. I can't guarantee any greater degree of success this morning.' The captain of the carrier *Kiev* studied his hands, folded together on the table in his cabin. To Ardenyev he appeared carved, unyielding, even unsympathetic. Yet he was right. A helicopter transfer to the *Karpaty* could not be risked. He even wondered whether his team, Red Section, would board another helicopter. When they reached the *Karpaty* by whatever means, Ardenyev was uncertain of their

145

reaction. The scorched plates, the damaged, twisted rail –
he'd seen them through binoculars from the bridge as the
grey, pallid light filtered through the heavy cloud – would
be too potent, too evident a reminder of their mates, their
rivals.

'Then it will have to be by launch, sir.'

The captain of the carrier looked up. 'I'm not unsympathetic, Captain. I am as concerned for the success of this
operation as you are. Which is why I must minimise the
risks with regard to your – depleted forces.'

Dolohov had signalled the carrier during the night, when
he had been informed of the MiL's crash and the loss of
Blue Section. His message had been terse, steely, anxious. It
had not been humane. He had asked, principally, whether
the mission could now be completed. He had not expected a
reply in the negative, and Ardenyev had not given him such
an answer. Instead, he had assured the admiral that the
Proteus could still be boarded by Red Section working
alone, as soon as they found her.

For Ardenyev, it seemed the only answer he could give,
the only possible outcome of his mission. His team wasn't
ready, perhaps it never would be. He could only attempt to
purge them of fear and shock and grief through action.
Desperation might prove effective.

'I understand, sir. I'll assemble my men on the boat deck
immediately.'

'Very good, Captain. And good luck.'

'Sir.'

Ten minutes later, Ardenyev was forced to admit that
Teplov had done his best with them, and the older men –
Shadrin, Petrov and Nikitin – would do, but the two
younger members of the team, Vanilov and Kuzin, were
unnaturally pale; cold so that they shivered beneath their
immersion suits. It was really their mates who had died, all
the younger ones. They seemed hunched and aged,
standing amid the others in the companion-way to the aft
starboard boatdeck. The movement of the carrier in the
waves, slow and sliding and almost rhythmical, seemed to
unsettle them even though they were experienced sailors.

'Very well,' Ardenyev said, 'as soon as we've transferred
to *Karpaty*, I'll want a very thorough equipment check. It

could take hours, I'll want it done in one. If a signal is picked up from that sub again, we'll be going straight down to her. Okay?'

He scrutinised them in turn, not especially selecting the two younger men, but with his eyes upon each face until there was a nod of acquiescence. In one or two gestures, there seemed almost to be a quiet enthusiasm. Not from Vanilov or Kuzin, perhaps, but from Teplov and Shadrin certainly. It would have to do.

He turned to the watertight door, and swung the handle. The wind seemed to howl through the slight gap he had opened. He pushed against a resistance as heavy as a human body, and they were assailed by flying spray. They were below the flight deck, on a narrow, railed ledge on the starboard side of the carrier where two of the ship's four big launches were positioned on their davits. A sailor waved them forward, towards the launch allocated to them and which had been manned in readiness. White-faced, white-handed sailors fussed around the davits, ready to swing the launch out over the water and lower it into the waves.

'Come on, come on,' Ardenyev said, hurrying them aboard, clapping each of them on the shoulder as they passed him, climbing the ladder into the launch. Ardenyev followed them, then leapt down again on to the boatdeck as one sailor lost his footing as the deck pitched. He grabbed the man's arm and hoisted him to his feet. He grinned at the sailor, who nodded his thanks. Ardenyev understood how everything except the activities of the moment had gone a long distance from him, and prayed that their mission would begin soon and would have the same numbing, enclosing effect on Red Section. He climbed the ladder again, ducked through the doorway, and joined the officer in charge of the launch, a junior lieutenant, in the wheelhouse.

Karpaty lay a matter of a few hundred yards to starboard of the carrier. In daylight, however gloomy and unreal, the sea raged. Ardenyev was chilled already through his suit from the wash of icy water on to the boatdeck.

'Captain,' the young officer acknowledged.

'Lieutenant. We're ready?'

'As we'll ever be. I don't think we ought to make the attempt, Captain – to put it bluntly.'

'Forget your thoughts, Lieutenant. We're going. Give the orders.'

The junior lieutenant appeared reluctant, disliking his own junior status and the obedience it required him to express. He nodded, stiff-lipped, and spoke into his microphone, adjusting the headphones and the speaker to comfort, or as an expression of disagreement. The launch shifted on its blocks, then began to swing free, moving out over the boatdeck as the davits swung it away from the hull of the carrier. The launch oscillated alarmingly on its davit wires, demonstrating its frailty. Then they began to slide down the side of the *Kiev* the fifty feet or more to the water. The hull of the carrier moved in Ardenyev's vision. It was almost easier to imagine that they were the still point, and that the carrier moved with the wind and swell.

Rivets, rust, sea-life, spillage marking the plates of the hull. Then a grey sheen acquired by distance, then rivets and rust again. A constant chatter of instruction and comment from the lieutenant into his headset, then a shudder as the sea leapt up to meet them. The windscreen of the launch obscured by water for a moment, the hull of the *Kiev* splashed white and grey before the swell let them hang over a trough. The lieutenant spoke rapidly, and the rate of descent increased. Then they were wallowing, and the davit wires came free, and the engine of the launch coughed into life, just as the next peak of the swell broke over the bow and side of the craft, obscuring everything. The screw whined as it was lifted out of the water for an instant, then a trough released them, and the lieutenant ordered full speed and a change of course, towards the rescue ship *Karpaty*.

They butted and rose and dipped their passage across the few hundred yards of sea towards the *Karpaty*. Movement, however violent and uncertain, deadened thought, promised action. The coxswain's hands were white like those of the helicopter pilot the previous night, holding the vessel to her course. Everything was immediate, physical or sensuous.

It took fifteen minutes to make the crossing. Then *Karpaty* was above them, rusty-plated, grey, grubby with use, expressing a kind of toughness that comforted. Less than half the height above them of the carrier, nevertheless the rescue ship was one of the biggest of its type in the fleet. The scorched, blackened plates came into view, the sea working at them as if to scour off the evidence of disaster. The twisted rail, buckled plates at the stern, the damaged helipad, one edge broken as cleanly away as the snapped edge of a biscuit or a dinner plate. Simply missing.

The launch bucked and rode in the swell. The lieutenant was chattering into his microphone. Ardenyev heard the voice of the tiny, black-clothed, gleaming figure on the port side amidships, beneath the archway of the rescue ship's central gantry, where the cargo deck was located. The boom swung across, and a specially rigged harness was slowly lowered towards them. Teplov appeared, as if by some instinct, at Ardenyev's elbow.

'You first this time, sir,' he said. 'Just in case.'

Ardenyev was about to reply when the lieutenant broke in.

'I have the captain of *Karpaty*, sir. He'd like you aboard without delay. Apparently, one of the submarines has picked up a trace and he's been ordered to alter position.'

Teplov grinned. 'Come on, sir – get moving.'

Patrick Hyde studied the façade of the Free Trade Hall in Manchester. He was sheltering from the rain in a shop doorway in Peter Street, almost directly opposite the home of the Hallé Orchestra, which now displayed, like some unbecomingly young dress on an ageing aunt, the banners and streamers and posters that bellowed the appearance that evening of Heat of the Day. The KGB man on the opposite pavement appeared uninterested in the announcement as he walked down the serpentine, bunching queue of people that stretched almost as far as the Midland Hotel. Hyde did not know whether the man had been detailed to look for the girl or for himself, but he kept the collar of his raincoat turned up and his cap pulled down over his eyes. If one of them was in the immediate vicinity, then he would not be alone.

Two. The other one was coming along the pavement on Hyde's side of Peter Street, walking slowly, conspicuous because he carried no umbrella. Umbrellas handicapped surveillance. There were a couple of young, denimed Special Branch officers in the queue for the rock concert, and plain-clothes police in cars parked at the junction with Watson Street and in the square at the other end of Peter Street. A presence inside the Free Trade Hall, too.

Hyde had spoken to Aubrey – the second KGB man he recognised was drawing level with the doorway in which he sheltered – at the Admiralty and persuaded him that Petrunin and the others should not be approached. Most of them were 'unofficials', agents not attached to the Soviet embassy or to trade missions or cultural organisations. They could not be certain how many there were. Removing Petrunin would be a false security. Free, Petrunin was a focal point. Hyde turned to the window. Transistor radios, stereo equipment, TV sets. The KGB man paused, but his inspection of Hyde was cursory, and he moved on. Petrunin running free would never be far from the action, and those under his control would gather round him, magnetised by his rank. They needed Petrunin and the few they knew from the files in order to identify the others.

Hyde moved out of the doorway. The KGB man inspecting the queue was returning to the main entrance of the Free Trade Hall, the second man was crossing Peter Street to meet him. Hyde nor the police had seen any sign of Petrunin during the morning.

Aubrey had been very clear about the risks, and the responsibility. It rested with Hyde. The girl must be found that day, that night, otherwise alternative methods would have to be employed. The girl would be taken in, regardless, and persuaded to co-operate. Hyde had one chance. Shelley's enquiries at the country hotel where Heat of the Day had stayed the night had proved fruitless. The girl had gone to earth. Shelley was inclined to the opinion that she had abandoned Alletson and the band. Hyde disagreed. There was nowhere else for her to run. Evidently, she was staying clear of her father, desperate not to lead anyone to him.

The two KGB men strolled together towards Watson Street. An Austin Allegro drew level with them, and they bent to the window as it opened, becoming instantly engaged in a voluble conversation with the driver of the car. Then the lights changed, and the green Austin turned into Peter Street. As it passed him, Hyde saw that the driver was Petrunin. There was no one else in the car, which drew in and parked in the square. Petrunin did not get out.

Hyde felt hunger expand as a sharp, griping pain in his stomach. Nerves were making him hungry. He had probably another seven or eight hours to wait. This time, he would not go in until the band was on stage.

He crossed Peter Street to speak to the Special Branch men in the queue. If he was going to wait that long, no one was going in before him.

Aubrey, Clark and Pyott had become, with the passage of the night and morning, an uneasy, indecisive cabal inside the organisation of the underground room and the parameters of the rescue operation.

'Kinloss have another Nimrod standing by, with a fresh crew,' Pyott argued. 'They can be on-station in two or three hours. They won't resent the job, they won't be tired.'

Aubrey shook his head. 'Get them to contact Eastoe at Bardufoss. He and his crew must go back on-station immediately. I cannot afford to have that area unsighted for that long – no, not even with satellite surveillance. The cloud cover is making things difficult. Eastoe will have to go down to sea level if necessary. I must have *eyes* there, Giles.'

'They'll be dog-weary, Mr Aubrey,' Clark offered.

'I have slept for three hours in the last twenty-four, Ethan. We must all make sacrifices.' Clark grinned at the waspish remark. 'Very well, when the relief Nimrod is on-station, Eastoe and his crew will be recalled – for the moment. Let us discuss ways and means to preserve the security of "Leopard". That is our real priority.'

'We're to take it you have abandoned any notion of destroying the *Proteus*?' Pyott asked with a mocking lightness.

'That was never my intention – you misconstrued. We may have to expose *Proteus*, however, by ordering Lloyd to destroy the "Leopard" equipment.'

Pyott nodded. 'We may have to. We can, however, run it

extremely fine. No need as yet. I'm not sure you'd get Lloyd to do it, anyway.'

'He would disobey a direct order?' Aubrey asked in surprise.

'For the sake of his vessel and his crew, he would be entitled to do so.'

'Very well, Giles. What can we do – before *tomorrow*, when the first NATO vessel arrives in the area? We must do something.'

'Diplomacy?'

Aubrey snorted in derision. 'I'm afraid the Foreign Office is running its head against a brick wall of denials. The Soviet ambassador has denied all knowledge of the matter. Soviet vessels are engaged in bad-weather exercises in the Barents Sea. He confirmed that, apparently with Red Banner headquarters in Murmansk. It will take too long, I'm afraid, to unstick this matter through the proper channels.' Aubrey looked drawn, thinner, older. He had slept in a cramped cupboard-like room off the main operations room, on a thin, hard bed that seemed to imprison him. It had not improved his temper, or his patience. He wondered at his frenetic desire for action, and at the inertia of events which seemed to be bearing him with them like a great tide. Yet he could not retreat into the dim, cool, shadowed walks of military sang-froid as Pyott did. 'It will take too long,' he repeated. 'Far too long.'

'And tomorrow never comes,' Clark remarked. 'by tomorrow, they may have a fix on *Proteus*, and then you'll find – what'll you find?' He looked at Aubrey. Clark in shirtsleeves and without his tie seemed more American; less sophisticated, stronger. Perhaps a hard-boiled newspaper editor, or a policeman. Yes, without the formality imposed by his suit, he looked more like Patrick Hyde; of the same type or species.

'What will we find, Ethan?'

'My guess is a salvage operation – if they can pinpoint the sub.'

'You're serious, aren't you?' Clark nodded. 'Why so certain?'

'There's no other way. They have to salvage *Proteus* if they're to save "Leopard". At least, I think so.'

'And Lloyd may not destroy "Leopard" now, if we order him to do so – I agree with Giles there. Then we are on the horns of a dilemma, gentlemen.'

'Kenneth, we're left relying on "Leopard" itself. At the moment it protects *Proteus* and itself. It must continue to do so for at least another twenty-four hours.'

'The rescue ship from Tromsø will take longer than that,' Aubrey remarked gloomily, staring at his liver-spotted hand caressing the edge of the commodore's desk. 'All we will have in the area tomorrow is one American submarine and a Norwegian "Oslo"-class frigate. The day after, more, I agree. But, too late. We have to have surface ships engaged in any rescue operation, a counter to the Soviet concentration. They will, hopefully, go away when we arrive. I did no want to escalate our presence, but there is no alternative. We have nothing there *now*, that is our problem.' His hand slapped the wood of the desk.

'Sorry to be the bad-news boy,' Clark said, 'but you're ignoring the latest movements of the rescue ship the Soviets have on-station, and those helicopters that arrived last night.'

'Yes?' Aubrey snapped impatiently. Then: 'Sorry – go on.'

'The boarding party?' Pyott queried, and Clark nodded.

'Damnation! What do we *do*? Tell me that. What do we do?'

'Send Eastoe down on the deck to look over the rescue ship and the immediate area – and continue our orisons, I should think,' Pyott drawled. Aubrey looked venomously at him, and Pyott blushed slightly with the memory of his culpability. 'Sorry,' he said softly.

'It's escaping from us,' Aubrey sighed. 'I feel it. It is too far ahead of us to be overtaken.'

Lloyd paused for a moment at the door of the computer room, aft of the control room. Don Hayter's summons – a rating tapping his captain on the arm, beckoning him theatrically – had been peremptory and urgent, and Lloyd's sense of bodily temperature had leapt. Yet he could not bring himself to move through the door, not for a moment. The rating's face had been worried, pale and disturbed in the red lighting. It had seemed, immediately and without embroidery by Lloyd's jumpy imagination, to indicate disaster. Then Hayter saw him, and urgently waved him in. Hayter was bent over one of the "Leopard" screens. The noise he was making tapping a pencil against his teeth shocked Lloyd.

Hayter grabbed Lloyd's arm as he reached the panel, and tapped at the screen with the pencil, underlining the computer-print words the screen displayed. He tapped again and again at one phrase.

FAULT NOT IDENTIFIED.

Then he looked up at Lloyd, who concentrated on reading the rest of the computer's assessment of the situation.

'Leopard' had developed a fault.

'What is it?' Lloyd asked, then repeated his question in a whisper that was not clogged with phlegm. 'What is it?'

Hayter shrugged. 'It's been happening for four minutes now. We've checked— ' he nodded at the rating who had brought Lloyd to the computer room, and the sub-lieutenant who was Hayter's second-in-command, '— everything, so has the computer.'

'What— what is the fault doing? What effect is it having?' Lloyd almost wanted to smile at the exaggerated serious-ness of Hayter's expression. Lugubrious.

'It's blinking. On, off, on, off. Sometimes, they can see us, sometimes they can't.'

'*What?*'

'Whatever the malfunction is, it's intermittent.'

'And now— at this moment?'

'Invisible. A moment before you came in, it came back on, full strength, fully operational. Before that, for eleven seconds, nothing, nothing at all.'

'Christ.'

The sub-lieutenant, Lloyd now perceived, was removing the front panel of the main container housing the 'Leopard' equipment, a metal box little bigger or taller than a large filing cabinet.

'We're going to have to do a manual, if the computer can't tell us.'

'How long?'

'No idea.'

'Could it have happened when we were attacked – the damage to the prop and hydroplanes?'

'Possible. The sensors and dampers at the stern could have been damaged. If they have been – and the fault's outside – then we can't do a bloody thing down here without divers.'

'Complete failure?' Hayter nodded. 'What about the back-up system?'

Hayter's face became more lugubrious than ever; not a painted clown's downturned mouth but a human expression of concern and fear. His fingers played over the keyboard beneath the display screen, and the message vanished. Then he typed in a new set of instructions, and the response from the computer was almost instantaneous.

MALFUNCTION

Hayter opened his palms in a gesture of helplessness.

'The back-up system won't cut in.'

'It doesn't work at all?'

'At the last check, it worked. Now, it doesn't. I don't understand it. Immediately after the attack, we checked everything through on the computer. It registered no malfunction in either the main or back-up systems. Then we start winking at the Russians, and the computer doesn't know why. At the same moment, the back-up system is u/s. We'll do our best – that's all I can tell you.'

The message vanished from the screen before Lloyd had finished reading it. More words came spilling across the screen, line after line in block letters.

MALFUNCTION IN MAIN SYSTEM.　　　　UNIDENTIFIED

'Is it – ?'

Hayter nodded. 'It's gone again. "Leopard" isn't working. Anyone who cares to look in our direction can see a British submarine lying on her belly.'

Lloyd looked at his watch. The second hand crept across the face like a red spider's leg, ugly, jerking, uncoordinated. Eight, nine, ten, eleven –

'Longer this time,' Hayter murmured.

Twelve, thirteen, fourteen –

'Come on, come on, –' Lloyd heard himself saying a long way below his mind. 'Come on –'

Sixteen, seventeen –

There were four submarines within a radius of six miles of the *Proteus*. He had been studying the sonars just before he was summoned by Hayter.

Twenty-one, two, three, twenty-four, almost half a minute –

'I think she's gone,' Hayter whispered, flicking switches on the console in an almost demented fashion. The movements of his hands appeared all the more frenzied because of the expressionless lines and planes in which his face seemed to have coalesced. The message on the screen blinked out, then returned with a status report on the back-up system.

MALFUNCTION.

Thirty-two, three, four –

Lloyd could not remove his gaze from the second hand of his watch. Hayter's hands still played across the banks of switches as he attempted to coax life back into 'Leopard' or to rouse its back-up system. Complete failure.

MALFUNCTION.

The word seemed to wink on and off the screen at a touch of a key or switch; as if the whole system had failed in each of its thousands of parts and circuits and microprocessors and transistors and coils.

Forty-two. Lloyd knew he ought to be in the control room, knew that they would be picking up changes of course and bearing, changes of speed. Forty-four.

The word vanished from the screen. A status report replaced it. Hayter sighed, perspiration standing out on his forehead, which he wiped with the back of his hand. He grinned shakily.

'We're back in business – for the time being,' he said.

'Everything's working?'

'As normal. The main system. Back-up's still dead.'

'Get working on the back-up system.' Then Lloyd almost ran from the room, down the companion-way to the control room, anticipating what he would see on the sonar screens.

'Skipper, I'm getting a reading from one of our sonar buoys – it's *Proteus*.'

'What? Bob, are you certain?'

'Skipper – I picked up a trace. It disappeared after about ten seconds, so I assumed it was a shoal of fish or something of the sort, or a false reading. Then a couple of minutes later, the same reading on the same bearing, for almost a minute. Now it's gone again.'

'What's happening?'

'Could be a malfunction in their equipment?'

'I don't know. Have you got a fix on her position?'

'Not the first time. The second time she came in on two of the buoys. Yes, I've got her.'

'Well done. Where is she?'

'What looks like a ledge. Shall I bring the chart through?'

'No. Not until I've decided what message to send to MoD. Have the Russians picked her up?'

'I don't know. Perhaps not –'

'You hope. Keep looking. The moment anything moves closer to *Proteus*'s position, let me know. You're *sure* it's her?'

'What else could it be? I don't understand "Leopard", even after the briefing, but I know what it's supposed to do. We couldn't see her, now we can. Correction, we *did* see her.'

'Okay, Okay, I believe you. Pass her position to John and tell him to stand by to transmit a Flash signal to Aubrey.'

'I'm already standing by, skipper.'

'Good. We'll take her down for a look-see first.'

Eastoe turned to his co-pilot, and nodded. The cloud cover beneath the nose and the wings of the Nimrod gleamed with sunlight, innocent; yet it extended downwards almost to sea level and it was moved by gale-force winds. Their calm was illusory, achieved only by altitude.

'Give me a bearing on the carrier,' Eastoe requested into his microphone. Almost immediately, the navigator supplied the coordinates and the course change that would take them over the *Kiev*.

Eastoe dipped the Nimrod's nose towards the clouds. Sunlight, the dense, smoothed roof of the cloud-forest, then a creeping greyness, the first rags and twigs of mist, the darkening of the flightdeck, then the cloud rushing past, swallowing them as they moved into it. The co-pilot switched on the wipers, and water streamed away from their furious beat. Eastoe felt the tremor of the winds through the control column as he watched the altimeter unwind. Down through twenty thousand feet, nineteen, eighteen.

Turbulence buffeted the Nimrod as the aircraft dropped towards the sea. Eastoe sensed for a brief moment the fragility of the airframe around him, imagined the last moments of the Nimrod that had crashed on take-off, remembered the pilot and the crew who had died, and then they broke through the lowest fringes of the cloud, into squalling rain and a headwind. He levelled the Nimrod no more than a hundred and fifty feet above the whitecapped water. The carrier was a fuzzy, bulky shape through the rain, less than a mile ahead of them.

In his headphones, the senior Nav/Attack officer began calling out the readings from his screens and sensors, describing the movements of the surface and sub-surface vessels during the time they were descending. The carrier seemed to leap towards them like a huge stone across the stormy water.

The subs were altering, or had altered, course, and all were closing on the same bearing. The carrier appeared to be lumbering on to a new course. All units closing on the fixed position of the *Proteus*. They'd found her. Maybe foxed for the moment, but they had her now.

Eastoe throttled back the four Rolls-Royce engines, and the Nimrod appeared merely to float above the deck of the *Kiev*. No activity, launches stowed on both the port and starboard boat-decks – the co-pilot calling out confirmation of what Eastoe had seen for himself – and then the rescue ship was ahead as the *Kiev* passed out of sight beneath them. The *Karpaty* was making slow headway and, as Bob called out her course, Eastoe realised that the rescue ship was on a heading that would take her over the *Proteus*.

He realised, too, the significance of the rescue ship. He

throttled back once more, and they drifted towards the *Karpaty*.

'See it?' he said.

'Yes, skipper. They're trying to launch a boat from the starboard side, looks like.'

The Nimrod crept towards the rescue ship. Tiny figures, moving with what seemed hopeless and defeated slowness around the starboard launch on its davits. Eastoe strained forward in his seat. The co-pilot increased the beat of the wipers. Shiny, oil-skinned crewmen – no, not all of them, surely?

'What in hell – ?'

'Divers.'

'*Divers*! Shit and hell!'

The Nimrod floated over the dipping bow of the *Karpaty*. A chaos of water flung up over her deck, the surge of an animal as the wave released her into the next trough. Men in shiny, tight-fitting suits, face-masked, oxygen cylinders on their backs. They were pinpricks, tiny matchstick men, but they were divers, climbing into the launch.

'How far is she from the *Proteus*?'

'Less than a mile,' he heard the navigator reply as the nose of the aircraft blotted out the scene directly below them.

'I'm going round for another look and some more pictures,' Eastoe said, 'and then we'd better send Aubrey the bad news – they're going down to the *Proteus*, for God's sake!'

Eight: SEIZURE

Aubrey stared at the note he had scribbled, the small, neat handwriting suddenly expressive of powerlessness, and realised that they had lost. 'Leopard' had malfunctioned, betraying the position of the *Proteus* to the Russian submarines in the immediate area. The rescue ship *Karpaty* was preparing to launch a small boat on which were a team of divers. They had received photographic proof of that over the wireprint. Opposite his note, Clark had scrawled in his strangely confident, large hand *RB Spec Ops Unit – Ardenyev*. Aubrey presumed it was no more than an informed guess, and it had no significance. The identity of the divers did not matter, only that they existed and were less than a mile from the reported position of the British submarine.

It was dark outside now. Perhaps not quite. A drizzling, gusty dusk. Aubrey had taken a short afternoon walk in St James's Park, but he had been unable to shake off the claustrophobic, tense gravity of the underground room beneath the Admiralty, and had soon returned to it.

Lost. Found by others. The Russians evidently intended that *Proteus* should be salvaged, perhaps even boarded, and the 'Leopard' equipment inspected before it was presumably returned, together with the submarine and her crew. An accident, not quite an international incident, no real cause for alarm, no ultimate harm done. He could hear the platitudes unroll in the days ahead, perceive the diplomatic games that would be played. He knew the Russians would take *Proteus* to one of their closest ports – Pechenga, Poliarnyi, even Murmansk – and there they would effect apologetic repairs, even allowing the American consul from Leningrad or a nominated member of the British embassy staff from Moscow to talk to the crew, make the noises of protest, send their London ambassador to call on the foreign secretary and the PM, heap assurance upon assurance that it was an accident, that all would be well, that this indicated the willingness for

160

peace of the Soviet Union – *look, we are even repairing your submarine, send experts to inspect our work, why are you so suspicious, so belligerent, you will have your submarine back as good as new –*

The diplomatic support for the operation sprang fully-envisaged into Aubrey's awareness, like a childhood or youthful moment of extreme humiliation that haunted him still in old age. It did not matter that it was all a blatant lie; it would work. It would give them enough time to photograph, X-ray, dismantle 'Leopard', and learn its secrets.

And, at the same time, they might obtain its designer, Quin, who would help them to build more. In the moment of the loss of 'Leopard', Aubrey feared Hyde's failure and the girl's capture.

'What do we do, Kenneth?' Pyott asked at his shoulder. The channel to Eastoe in the Nimrod was still open, the tapes waiting for his orders. Aubrey waved a hand feebly, and the operator cut the communications link.

Aubrey looked up into Pyott's face, turning slightly in his chair. 'I do not know, Giles – I really do not know.'

'You have to order Lloyd to destroy "Leopard" – I mean literally smash it and grind the pieces into powder,' Ethan Clark remarked, his face pale and determined. 'It's the only way. The guy must know by now that's what they're after, and how close they are to getting it. He has to get rid of "Leopard".'

'Just like that? I seem to remember the *Pueblo* made a monumuntal cock-up of a similar procedure some years ago,' Pyott observed haughtily. 'It won't be easy. "Leopard" isn't in a throwaway wrapper, Clark.'

'You British,' Clark sneered. 'Man, you're so good at inertia, you make me sick.'

'There has to be something else we can do – besides which, "Leopard" is working again.'

'For the moment.'

'Gentlemen,' Aubrey said heavily, wearily, 'let's not squabble amongst ourselves. Ethan, is there anything else we can do?'

'You're not able to rescue *Proteus*, Mr Aubrey.'

'Then perhaps we should warn her what to expect.'

Aubrey got up from the chair at the communications console, and crossed the room to the map-board. He seemed, even to himself, to be shrunken and purposeless beneath it. *Proteus* – white light – had been repositioned, closer inshore, and the updated courses and positions of the carrier, the rescue ship, the destroyers and the submarines created a dense mass of light around one thin neck of the Norwegian coast. The sight depressed Aubrey, even as it galvanised him to an action of desperation. He had lost the game, therefore he must damage and make worthless the prize.

'Encode the following,' he called across the room, 'and transmit it to Eastoe at once, for relay to *Proteus*. Mission aborted, destroy, repeat destroy "Leopard". Priority most absolute. Append my signature.'

Every man in the room listened to him in silence, and the silence continued after he had finished speaking. A heavy, final silence punctuated only by the clicking of the keys of the encoding machine.

Ardenyev watched Vanilov's feet begin to slip, saw the white face surmounted by the facemask and half-obscured by the bobbing mouthpiece of his breathing apparatus, and felt the wave surge round his own ankles and calves. His hands gripped the rail of the launch, but Vanilov's grabbed for a handhold like clumsy artificial claws he had not learned to operate. Ardenyev reached out and gripped the younger man's elbow, almost as if he were about to twist Vanilov's arm painfully behind his back. He pulled the frightened, off-balanced man to him, hugged him upright, then pushed at his back and buttocks until Vanilov was over the rail of the launch and into it, a look of fearful gratitude on his face. They were all in.

The sea flung itself against the *Karpaty* more ferociously than had been apparent on the carrier, as if encouraged by its success in making the rescue ship bob and duck and sway in the water. Amidships, where they were boarding the launch that would then be swung out on its davits, the sea boiled across the deck as each succeeding wave caught them in the trough behind its predecessor. Ardenyev watched a grey, white-fringed, boiling wall of water rise

162

level with and above the deck, and tightened his grip on the launch's rail and widened his stance. Teplov offered his hand, and Ardenyev shook his head.

'Get below!' he yelled.

The wave smashed against the side of the hull, then flung its broken peak across the deck, drenching Ardenyev. He was deafened and blinded by the water, and he thought the thin, inhuman noise he heard distantly was merely illusion. When he opened his eyes again, there was one yellow-oilskinned figure less than before, gathered around the boat station— and other men were looking blankly and fixedly towards the boat's side. Ardenyev realised, as he shivered and tried to control his chattering teeth, the fragility of their enterprise, even its lunacy; resented to the point of hatred an old man ensconced in the non-climatic, antiseptic surroundings of the Red Banner headquarters in Murmansk. He wanted to open his mouth and yell his anger as the *Karpaty* wallowed her way into the trough behind the wave that had killed one of her crew.

He swung himself up and over the rail, and hurried into the shelter of the launch's cabin, seeking the determination to order the officer in command of the frail little boat to issue his own orders for the launching of the vessel. A tiny yellow blob for a second, out there in the water— ?

Ardenyev shook his head, clearing the last of the water from his face and eyes with his hands. The air tanks were heavy on his back. He'd insisted— despite the discomfort and the loss of agility— that they don their full equipment, everything except flippers, in the comparative calm of the *Karpaty*, while the ratings of the rescue ship struggled to load their special equipment into the launch.

The lieutenant in command of the launch watched him, immediately he entered the cabin, with a thin-lipped, colourless expression. His face reflected Ardenyev's thoughts, with its sense of the threadbare rationality of Dolohov's scheme that now made the old man seem mad. Dolohov appeared to have cobbled this operation together in a fit of lunacy.

'Gone again, sir,' the *michman* on the launch's sonar called out, and the lieutenant appeared to take this as a final condemnation of what they were doing, the last bitter irony of forces he could hardly comprehend but which controlled him.

Ardenyev crossed the cabin to the sonar. 'Show me,' he said.

The *michman* indicated a line across the screen with his finger, as if slicing the perspex surface of the sonar. 'That bearing,' he said. 'Range six hundred.'

Six hundred metres from them, the British submarine lay on a ledge, less than fifty fathoms down. The invisible Norwegian coast had thrust out a hand, a fingertip, to aid her. Her anti-sonar was flicking on and off like a signalling torch.

'That's it – let's go.'

Teplov's head appeared at the door at the rear of the cabin.

'It's all in good shape, sir.'

'What about the men?' Teplov paused for a moment, then he nodded slowly. 'Good,' Ardenyev added. 'Make sure everything's secure. Tell them to hang on tight, and be ready to move fast when I give the order.' Teplov nodded again, and his head then disappeared as the door closed.

The launch lurched off its blocks, swung fragilely outwards above the deck and then the grey water – they were in another trough between great waves – and the winches with their tiny, yellow-garbed figures working furiously at them, trundled them downwards towards the water. Speed seemed to lend stability and cancel the force of the wind, even still the water as it rushed up towards them. The rusty plates again of the hull, the thin wires above them, then the launch's keel smacking into the water, screw churning, its whine in air disappearing and its power failing to move the launch. Ardenyev grabbed a handhold and braced himself as the launch was lifted towards the grey-white peak of the next wave. It teetered there for a moment, deck awash, windows blind and running with water, the coxswain spinning the wheel feverishly and without apparent effect, then it began falling.

Ardenyev heard someone cry out just after he registered a metallic, screeching slither from beyond the closed door at his back, then he was aware only of the ugly frightening sensation of being swallowed by a huge grey-fleshed, open mouth. Then they were in a trough and the rudder and the screw began taking effect and the boat moved with some of its own volition rather than that of the sea. A sense of stability returned to his legs and feet, the illusion of a firm surface, a level world.

The warble of the sonar again, then, as if hearing were just returning.

'She's there again, sir!' the *michman* called out.

'Has she changed position?' Ardenyev asked.

The *michman* calculated swiftly. 'No, sir. Bearing now red one-five, range five-seven-eight.'

'Helmsman – port one-five.'

'Port one-five, sir.'

Teplov's face, white and drained and old, appeared at the door again.

'Sir, it's Petrov – his leg. The hose broke loose, sir, wrapped itself around his leg – think it's broken, sir.'

'God,' Ardenyev breathed, closing his eyes. Six of them now. Dolohov was a fucking lunatic –

'Will you come, sir?'

'It should have been stowed properly!' Ardenyev yelled in his enraged frustration.

The launch teetered, then the bow fell drunkenly down and forward, the noise of the screw disappearing, sinking into the throb of the labouring engine. Six of them had to get themselves, their sleds, hoses and canisters, welding equipment and communications over the side of the launch, below the surface, down to the *Proteus*. There should have been thirteen of them. Impossible now.

'I'll come,' he said, suddenly weary and cold.

'One minute ten seconds, eleven, twelve, thirteen – ' Lloyd whispered the lowering of his voice an act of mockery, pointless. 'Sixteen, seventeen – twenty.'

Hayter and the sub-lieutenant were examining the mass of wiring and circuitry and microprocessors inside the main metal cabinet housing 'Leopard'. Hayter and the sub-lieutenant were checking the efficiency of each component manually, with multi-meters. The rating was removing the panelling of the second box, kneeling like a safecracker against the metal.

Hayter looked up desperately, shaking his head. 'It's no good, sir. We could be doing this for hours yet. Unless it switches itself back on, we're finished. It's no good pretending we're not. Everything here appears to be working, dammit!'

'Get to work on the back-up system, will you?' One minute forty-two seconds. It wasn't going to come on again.

'You know where that's housed. We can't work in there with the space and freedom we've got here. It'll take even longer – '

'Christ, Don – what are you going to do, then?'

'I don't *know*, sir!'

One minute forty-nine, two minutes of visibility on any and every sonar screen in the area. On the *Kiev*, the rescue ship, the subs, the destroyer, the aircraft overhead. Everyone could see them.

The subs were holding off, not coming in for the kill. But then, they wanted 'Leopard', not blood. And they were jamming every radio frequency they could. *Proteus* couldn't talk or receive. In a corner, beaten, defenceless –

Two minutes ten. Hayter was back at his orisons in front of the exposed innards of 'Leopard', kneeling in what might have been a prayer of desperation. If he could get it functioning again, if it would only switch itself back on, then he would risk the ship by moving her, limping off into another dark corner. At least he'd try to play hide-and-seek with them as long as he could, if only 'Leopard' would work.

Hayter looked at him again, shaking his head. Two minutes twenty-four. It wasn't going to work.

Carr, the navigator, appeared at the door of the cabin. 'Sir, sonar's picked up a very small vessel moving away from the rescue ship.' As if there had been a public admission of failure, Carr spoke in his normal tone, normal volume. 'Ship's launch, we think.'

'What does the First-Lieutenant think?'

'Divers, sir. Some attempt to inspect our damage.'

'Very well.' Two minutes fifty. It wasn't going to come on, now. Now it was too late. The rescue ship was less than half-a-mile away. They'd fixed her position by now. Lloyd looked with helpless vehemence at the exposed, purpose-less interior of the 'Leopard' cabinets. 'Tell the First-Lieutenant I'm on my way.' Carr disappeared. There was no attempt to modify the noise of his footsteps now. It was an admission of defeat, a surrender. 'Keep me informed, Don— for Christ's sake keep on trying!'

As he headed for the control room, the image of the opened useless cabinets remained with him, like a sudden, shocking glimpse of a body undergoing surgery. Hideously expensive, sophisticated almost beyond comprehension, impossible to repair. So much junk—

A team of divers. A threat that somehow diminished even as it presented itself. Perhaps a dozen men, outside the twin hulls of the *Proteus*. His own crew numbered one hundred.

The control room reasserted Lloyd's sense of authority, supplying also a fugitive sense of security. They were almost fifty fathoms down. He must consider moving *Proteus*, when the critical moment arrived. Thurston looked up from one of the sonar screens, and Lloyd unexpectedly grinned at him.

'Sorry, skipper— nothing. Just the howl of the jamming.'

'Make a guess— did *Proteus* pick up Aubrey's order?' Eastoe demanded.

'Doubtful. Almost impossible.'

'So Lloyd doesn't know he must destroy the equipment?'

'Don't you think he's done so, skipper? She's been on sonar for over four minutes now.'

'That could be the malfunction. Can we contact MoD?'

'No.'

'Okay everybody. I'm taking her down again, for a look-see. It's almost dark down there. Keep your eyes wide open. Cameras ready. We might as well get any gen we can.'

Hyde looked at his watch. A minute before eight. He got out of the unmarked police car parked in Watson Street, then looked back in at the Special Branch inspector before closing the door.

'Half an hour. Just keep clear of the place for half an hour, okay?'

'You're taking an unnecessary risk, Mr Hyde,' the policeman offered without inflection. 'Yours is a face they know. They'll pick you up on your way in, and bingo – '

'Maybe. And if your lot go in, the girl will panic and either run off or refuse to talk when we've got her. Sorry, sport, we have to take the risk. He looked at his watch again. 'Thirty minutes from now, you can come running blowing whistles, anything you like. But not till I've talked to the girl.'

'Have it your own way '

'I will. Look – ' Hyde felt a sudden need for reassurance, a desire to ameliorate the police resentment of him. 'The girl's almost paranoid about us. *We're* the enemy, not the Russians. Christ knows how she came by that idea, but it's what she believes. I have to *talk* her out.'

Okay. You've got thirty minutes.'

yae shut the car door softly. It was almost dark, and the shadows were black pools between the street lamps. Shop windows lighted, and a few pedestrians scuttling ahead of the wind. According to reports, there was one man at the back of the Free Trade Hall – but only one. Hyde thrust his hands into his pockets, and began slouching up tne narrow street leading to the rear of the concert hall.

The cars were parked and empty, the street lamps betrayeo no pedestrians or loiterers. The weak strains of a country-and-western song came from a slightly open upstairs window of a flat above a shop. The pervasive odour of fish and chips fluttered on the wind, then gone. It made Hyde feel hungry. He felt small, and aione.

Dim, unlit shop windows. Dust in his eyes. Bookshop, sex shop, barber's. Then Hyde saw him, on the other side of the street, no more than a shadow that moved, perhaps a bored man shifting his weight on tired, aching feet. Hyde stopped, starmg into the unlit window of a tiny record shop. Garish LP covers, posters, price cuts daubed in white. The language English but the place no longer Manchester. Some foreign place where he was outnumbered, known, sought. He shivered. If he passed the man, presumably his presence ould be noted and reported. They would conclude it was hım, even if he hadn't been recognized. On the other hand, if he removed the man from the board, his failure to contact .

Petrunin – still reported to be sitting in his car in the square – might similarly prove Hyde's presence in the area.

The man had emerged from the doorway of a baker's shop, and was standing on the pavement. As Hyde turned slowly to face him, it was evident that the man was staring directly at him, aware of who he was. Hyde, hands still in his pockets of his corduroy trousers, shoulders hunched, feet apart, was helpless. A Volvo was awkwardly parked, pulled right up bumber-to-bumper against the rear of a Ford Escort directly in front of him. Between him and the man across the street.

One hand of the bulky figure in a raincoat and a hat was moving towards his face, as if to feed himself the tiny R/T set. They hadn't picked up any transmissions all afternoon, Hyde thought, and had discounted R/T. In a moment, two or three paces of time, Petrunin would know that Hyde was about to enter the Free Trade Hall. The hand was moving, Hyde's foot was on the Volvo's bumper, his left foot on the bonnet of the car, the man's hand stopped moving – Hyde could not see the finger press the tranceiver button – one step on the bonnet, then down half-way across the street. The man was surprised, the hand moved away from his face, his other hand fumbled in his raincoat, two strides, one more, collision –

The man staggered back into the darkened doorway of the shop. Old mosaiced threshold, the man's mouth opening in a groan as the ornate, polished brass door-knocker thrust into his back. Hyde, one hand scrabbling at his side, reached for the transceiver in the Russian's hand, and punched at the face that had opened in pain. The Russian's head ducked to one side as if he had avoided the blow, but the knees were going, and the body sagged. Hyde felt the hand surrender the transceiver, and hit the Russian again, behind the ear. Then he lowered him in his arms on to the mosaic of the threshold. The Russian was breathing as if asleep, on the verge of snoring

Hyde dropped the transceiver, and was about to grind it beneath his shoe. Then he picked it up and put it into the pocket of his windcheater. If Petrunin tried to contact the man in the doorway, then at least he would know; know, too, that he would have only minutes after that

He hurried now, shaking from the brief violence, the surge of adrenalin.

There were double gates at the rear of the hall. A uniformed constable opened a small judas-door to him, and closed it behind him. Hyde debated for a moment whether to tell the young policeman of the Russian in the doorway, or the others that might come looking for him, then decided against so doing.

The Edwin Shirley trucks were drawn up in convoy, as if the Free Trade Hall were some cargo terminal. Hyde skirted them, searching in the almost complete darkness for the rear entrance that the Special Branch inspector had pointed out on a plan of the building. He climbed three steps, his hand resting for a moment on a cold metal railing, then tried the door. It had been left unlocked by one of the plainclothes detectives who had been inside the building all day. Hyde went in and closed the door behind him. A lighted passage in need of a fresh coat of cream paint. Dark brown doors. Cramped, uncomfortable, draughty, strip-lighting the only modernism. There was no one in the corridor.

Heat of the Day – Hyde paused to listen, Alletson's high, clear voice riding over the keyboards and guitar, part of the suite of pieces 'No Way Back' – could be heard mutedly but plainly. He would have to hurry. Normally the band followed the suite with a keyboard display by Whiteman, the other four leaving the stage to him. He had only a few minutes, he realised, becoming aware at the same moment of the small transceiver in his pocket. He opened a dressing-room door. The room was empty and in darkness.

The second room was locked and he saw, looking down, that there was a light on, gleaming beneath the door. Then it went out. He fished for the stiff little rectangle of mica in his pocket, and inserted it in the door jamb. He paused, listening. The noise of an opening window?

Alletson's voice silent, the slow keyboard section of the suite, building to the ensemble climax. Three, four minutes. A window opening?

He sprang the Yale lock and opened the door. In the light that entered the room from the corridor, he could see a small, slim figure at the dressing-room window, balanced on the sill. He crossed the room in three strides, knocking over a chair, hearing the slight, rustling twang of a guitar he had disturbed, then he had his arms around the figure, keeping his head back from the fingernails that instantly sought his face. He pulled Tricia Quin back into the room, clamping one hand over her mouth, pressing her against him with his other arm. Her body wriggled in his embrace, small, slippery. She backheeled his shins, and he winced with pain but did not let go. He felt the door behind him, raised his elbow, found the light switch, and held her against him after the light came on, but more gently. Eventually, he turned her head so that she could see his face. She stopped wriggling and struggling for a moment, then tried to tear away from him.

'Listen to me,' he whispered, 'just listen to me without struggling, will you?' His voice was almost petulant rather than threatening, and it's tone struck her. Her eyes widened, and he took his hand from her mouth carefully. 'Okay, will you listen? You'd have broken your bloody neck if you'd jumped from that window.'

'We're on the ground floor,' she remarked in a superior tone. 'What do you want?' she pulled down her T-shirt – a pointing hand in white, black background, the legend *Keep your eyes on the face, sonny* – and then tugged her cardigan straight on her narrow shoulders. She looked vulnerable, intelligent, arrogant, and somehow old-fashioned, out of date. A flower-child who had wandered into the wrong decade. 'Well, what do you want? Or was it all for a quick feel in the dark?'

Hyde studied his hands, then looked up. Slowly, slowly, he instructed himself. In his broadest Strine he drawled, 'I like 'em with bigger tits, girlie.'

Her face narrowed in anger, then she seemed more puzzled than anything else. 'You're very persistent, aren't you?'

'And you're very elusive.' He stepped forward, hands raised in a signal of harmlessness, and righted the chair he had knocked over. He sat down. 'Give me five minutes of your time – just listen to me. I'll try to make you an offer you can't refuse.'

'You don't have anything with which to trade, do you?'

'Maybe not. Sit down, anyway.'

Tricia Quin slumped untidily, sullenly into a sagging armchair. 'All right. Talk.'

'I know your mates will be back in a couple of minutes – they're almost finished with "No Way Back" – ' The girl's eyes narrowed with cunning. 'So, I'll be brief. There are Russian agents – no don't sneer and don't laugh and don't get clever – outside. The real McCoy. They're interested in contacting your father, and they're sure you know where he is.'

'They're just like you.'

'No.' Hyde bit down on his rising temper. The band murmured beyond the door, close to the climax of the suite. Perhaps no more than a minute. 'At this moment, there are a hundred lives at risk under the Barents Sea because of your dad.'

'What?'

'The submarine, girlie. Shit, the little old submarine with your old man's wonderful piece of machinery on board, the one everyone wants to know all about.' Hyde's voice was scornful, carefully modulated. The band sounded louder, closer to the finish. 'Only it isn't working so bloody well at the moment. The Russians have damaged our side's submarine, and your father's bloody expensive equipment isn't working properly. Keeps going on and off like Radio Caroline in the old days.'

'I – what am I supposed to do about it?' She was attempting to regain her composure, and she was listening to the sounds from beyond the door.

'Let me talk to your dad – tell him what's what.' The girl was already shaking her head. 'A telephone number – *you* ring him, I won't watch.' Tricia Quin examined the offer for its concealed booby-trap. 'No trick,' Hyde added.

Alletson walked into their intent silence. Whiteman's tumultuous keyboard playing could be heard through the open door. Alletson's tight-curled hair was wet with perspiration, his damp shirt open to the waist.

'What the hell do you want?' he asked.

'What's up, Jon?' Hyde heard someone in the corridor ask. The lead guitarist, Howarth, pushed into the room carrying two cans of lager. 'Who's he?'

'The *secret agent* I told you about.' Tricia Quin explained with laden sarcasm. 'The *spy*.'

'What's he want – you?'

'If you're coming in, close the bloody door,' Hyde said lightly, 'there's a bloody draught.'

Howarth closed the door, and leant against it, still holding the cans of lager. He studied the guitar lying near Hyde's feet with a silent malevolence. Hyde turned on his chair and looked up at Alletson.

'Jon-boy,' he said, 'tell her to piss off, tell her you don't love her any more, tell her she's a bloody nuisance who could ruin the tour – tell her anything, but persuade her to come with me.'

'Why should I do that? She's afraid of you.'

'You should see the other side, mate. They frighten me.' Alletson grinned despite himself. 'See, I'm not such a bad bloke after all.' He stopped smiling. 'I've told her why I have to find her father – '

'You're probably lying,' she remarked.

Hyde turned back to her. 'I'm not as it happens. Your father's bloody marvellous invention has dropped a hundred blokes in the shit! Now, will you call him and let me tell *him*?'

It was evident the girl was on the point of shaking her head, when Alletson said quietly, 'Why not, Trish?' She stared at him, at first in disbelief then with a narrow, bright vehemence, sharp as a knife. 'Look, Trish,' Alletson persisted, 'go and call him; we'll keep James Bond I – ' Hyde laughed aloud – 'here while you do it. *Ask* your father if he wants to talk to Don Bradman.'

The girl screwed up her face in concentration. She looked very young, indecisive; an air of failure, inability, lack of capacity emanated from her. She irritated Hyde as he watched her.

'All right,' she said finally, resenting Alletson for making the suggestion, the capitulation, in the first place. Hyde also noticed that in a more obscure way she accepted the role forced upon her. Perhaps she was tired of running, tired of keeping her father's secrets. Alletson had made a decision for her that she could not entirely resent. 'Make sure he stays here,' she added. Hyde controlled his sudden fear, and made no effort to follow her. She pushed past Howarth, and closed the door behind her.

Hyde studied Alletson. The man was nervous of him now, had accepted that he could do no more to protect Tricia Quin.

'Sorry – about last night,' Alletson said eventually.

Hyde shrugged. 'I don't blame you, mate,' he said, raised palms facing outwards. 'Pax. I will help her,' he added.

'I told you, Jon, we ought to dump her – ' Howarth began but Alletson turned on him.

'Piss off. For old times' sake. It was for old times' sake.'

'How's the tour going so far?' Hyde asked pleasantly, wondering whether Tricia Quin had taken the opportunity to bolt again. He did not think she had, but the closed door at Howarth's back troubled him.

'You're interested?' Howarth asked in disbelief.

'I'm old enough to remember your first album.'

'Thanks.'

'Why is she running?' Alletson asked, looking almost guilty.

'Her father's paranoid about security. She's caught the infection.'

'It is all real, then?'

Hyde nodded. 'Oh, yes. Silly, but real. The Russians want her dad, or her, or both, because he's invented a purple deathray which will give world domination to whoever possesses its deadly secret. I'm Flash Gordon, no less.'

'That's about what we thought,' Alletson admitted, grinning in a puzzled way. Then he looked at his watch. 'We're back on. You – you'll take care of her?' Hyde nodded.

Alletson and Howarth left the room, Howarth picking up the acoustic guitar lying on the floor at Hyde's feet before he went. Then Tricia Quin was standing in the open doorway as Whiteman's final keyboard crescendo echoed down the corridor. Her face was white. She looked guilty and afraid.

'Okay?'

She nodded. 'Yes. Yes, he's very tired. He'll talk to you, but only to you. I think he's got a gun.' He words were a warning, and an attempt to excuse her own and her father's capitulation. 'He's been worried about me.'

174

'He's still safe?'

'Yes.'

'Where?'

'I'll tell you when we've left here.'

'Luggage?' She shook her head 'Let's go, then.' She looked up sharply at the tone of his voice. Hyde had remembered the KGB irregular lying unconscious in a windy shop doorway on mosaic tiles. He hadn't reported in –

His hand patted the pocket of his windcheater in which he had placed the tiny transceiver. As if he had triggered it, it began bleeping. Tricia Quin's face blanched, her hand flew to her mouth. Hyde cursed.

'It's one of their radios,' he explained, getting up quickly. His chair clattered over, and she began to back into the corner of the room, as if he had threatened her with violence. The transceiver continued to bleep, its volume seeming to increase. Her eyes darted between Hyde's face and the door she had left defencelessly open. 'Come on, let's get moving!' She was opening her mouth, all capitulation forgotten, betrayal seeping into her features. Hyde bellowed at her. 'It's no time to change your mind, you stupid, mixed-up cow! Shift your bloody arse!' She reached for her jacket.

He grabbed her arm and propelled her towards the door. The corridor was empty. At the back of his mind, Hyde could see the Russians fitfully on a dim screen; wondering, worrying, beginning to move, guessing, *knowing* –

He could hand her over now to the police, to the Branch, and she would be safe. If he did, they'd spend days trying to find out where Quin was hiding. She'd be in a catatonic suspicion, comatosed with her secret. If he went with her, alone –

'You're hurting – ' she said meekly as he bundled her down the corridor through the door. He released her arm, and paused to listen, holding his hand in front of her face, indicating silence. He could hear her ragged breathing, like the last ineffectual plucking of his mother's lungs at the hot Sydney air in the darkened room. The day she died.

'Shut up!' he whispered fiercely.

'Sorry – '

175

He strained to hear. Nothing. The dim music from inside, the murmur of a radio in one of the trucks, traffic muted in the distance.

'Come on.' He propelled her down the steps, reached for her hand – she allowed him to hold it, it was inanimate and cold in his grip – and they moved swiftly across the yard. The transceiver in his pocket became silent. Moving; fearful, angry, *quick*, closing in –

The same police constable was on the gate, and he acknowledged their appearance with a nod. He did not seem surprised to see the girl.

'Everything all right, sir?'

Tricia Quin seemed reassured by the manner of his addressing Hyde.

'I think so, constable.' Nothing in the narrow, dimly-lit street, but he could not see the baker's shop from the gate. They could be there already. Petrunin might already be out of his car, his minions much closer than that. There was little point in the constable being involved. 'Nip inside, constable. Now I've got her, we can start sniffing them out.'

'Very good, sir. I'll just report in.'

'When you get inside.' He realised he was still holding the girl's hand, and he squeezed it. 'Come on. My car's only round the corner.' Probably with someone very unfriendly in it, he added to himself.

A curious but unfamiliar elation seized him. His chest seemed expanded with some lighter-than-air gas like helium, and his head was very clear. One of his Vick moments, as he had once described them. Everything clear, cold, sharp. The TR7 was behind the Midland Hotel, in the old railway station that had become, without redecoration or conversion, a huge car park. He jiggled her arm, and they began running up the narrow street, away from the rear of the Free Trade Hall and the baker's doorway. Sensuous information flooded in, his brain sifting it swiftly, unerringly.

Light from around the corner – Peter Street. Their footsteps, the girl's padding lighter in flat, crêpe-soled shoes, the rubbing of her arm against her borrowed, too-big jacket, the spillage of music – Brahms – from an upstairs window, the splash of one foot in a puddle, the gun

176

cold and noticeable in the small of his back, thrust into his waistband. The emptiness of the end of the street, no shadow against the lights of Peter Street. He was grateful.

The Midland Hotel was across the bright, traffic-filled street. It was a moment before Hyde remembered that Petrunin's car was parked in the square in front of the hotel.

'Okay?' he asked the girl. She was gulping air, but she nodded and tried to smile shakily. 'Keep going, then, shall we?'

Pavement. Pedestrians crossing. Normality. Red man, traffic swooping past them and round into the square or into Oxford Street or Moseley Street. Central Library, Midland Hotel. Forget it, don't turn your head, stop searching for them. You either fully pretend or not at all –

Red man. Green man, traffic stopping. Walk. He tugged at her hand. One pace, two, you can hurry a little here, people always do on zebra crossings.

They were almost across the street before he heard the first shout, the answering call, and sensed the acceleration of the pursuit. On the pavement, he turned. A man waved to him, as if to call him back over a matter of a dropped book or wallet, or an unpaid bill. He stepped off the opposite pavement. Petrunin himself. He'd been the closest, most experienced, sharpest mind. He'd guessed and just strolled round the square from his car, and seen them emerge. Petrunin, who knew him, knew the girl's face, no mistake –

'Is that one of them?' the girl asked, as if facing some extremely difficult task of recollection or recognition.

'That's him.' Petrunin was almost smiling. Green man still. Two others, running out into Peter Street from the rear of the Free Trade Hall. Not the man in the doorway, two others who had found him and come running. 'Ready?' Hyde asked.

'Yes.' Her hand trembled in his.

Red man. Petrunin, three paces on to the zebra crossing, paused so that the others could catch up with him. The sound of an impatient horn, then the blare of another and revving engines. Petrunin skipped back on to the opposite pavement.

'Now!'

They raced down the shadowy side-street alongside the bulk of the Midland Hotel. The illuminated façade of the old railway station was ahead of them, the car park barrier like a border to be crossed into a safe country. Hyde pulled at the girl's arm, urging her on, sensing that she was flagging.

The squeal of brakes behind them, the bellow of a car horn. Petrunin wasn't waiting for the green light. They ran together across the road, up the slope to the barrier. A black face was behind the glass of the booth. Hyde looked behind him. All three men were across Peter Street and running towards them. Hyde inwardly cursed the bravado of his isolation with the girl. There were police in the square, in Peter Street, Watson Street, in the Free Trade Hall, and he had chosen to run with the girl, making Manchester as alien and dangerous as Prague or Warsaw or Moscow. He slapped notes and change on to the counter of the booth, together with his ticket.

He swallowed saliva, said 'I'm in a hurry. Keep the change. Open the barrier when I drive out – yellow TR7. got it?' Then his hand was in his pocket and he was waving the shorthand of the CID warrant card. The Indian nodded.

Hyde ran on, the girl ahead of him now, but slowing because there seemed no safety amid the cars under the cracked, glassless station roof.

'Where?' she said.

'Over there,' he said, pointing.

One or two weak lights revealed the massed, hunched, beetle-like shells of car bonnets and roofs. The girl stared around her wildly. Hyde glanced back. Petrunin and the other two had slowed their pace, almost strolling past the barrier, confident but wary, imitating legitimacy. Seconds between them. Hyde ran out on to the platform with the girl. Dully gleaming, crustaceous cars; silence. The wind soughing thinly in the shell of the station. The three Russians were past the barrier and had paused on the threshold of the station itself. Hyde ducked down, pulling the girl into a crouch, and began weaving awkwardly between parked cars.

He paused, listened, then moved on. They came to the edge of the platform, and he dropped down. He reached up and the girl surrendered to his grasp on her waist. He lifted her down. A row of cars, one of them yellow.

'Mr Hyde?'

He thought for the moment it was the girl speaking, because of the light, interrogative tone. But it was Petrunin – accent and authority seeping into Hyde's awareness just behind the words. He gestured to the girl to remain silent, and they moved, crouching, along the rear bumpers of cars until they were leaning against the TR7. He heard the girl's ragged breathing again, but not like his mother's now; too alive for that, too much wanting to live. Hyde fished the car keys from his pocket and reached up to unlock the door.

'Mr Hyde?' Then whispered instructions above the girl's breathing, the shuffle of footsteps as the three men spread out. Petrunin was confident. He hadn't left anyone at the barrier. 'Mr Hyde.' A sharper tone, impatient.

Hyde eased open the door of the TR7, and indicated that the girl should climb in. They'd be looking for the yellow car. He crept round to the driver's door, unlocked it, clambered into the low hard seat. He eased the door shut on the footsteps that were coming closer. Steel-tipped heels to the heavy shoes. He slipped the key into the ignition, and pulled out the choke. He looked at Tricia Quin. Hair damp on her forehead, face pale, cheeks quivering.

'Which way?'

'North,' she said, hugging herself as if to keep warm; trying to retreat from her danger.

Hyde breathed in deeply, then turned the key. Cough, chatter of the ignition, cough, firing of the engine, drowning a surprised and delighted cry from up on the platform. He thrust the gears into reverse, screeched out of his parking place, heaving on the wheel. The TR7 skidded, almost stalled, and then the car was bucking over the uneven ground.

He reached the end of the platform, and swung the car left, across the hard-packed earth where the tracks had once been, until he mounted the platform ramp at the other side of the station. He had heard no gunfire, nothing after

that shout of discovery. The engine whined, the tyres
screeched as he roared along the platform, then turned
again on to what had been the concourse, heading for the
entrance.

One man, stepping out from behind a car, gun levelled.
Hesitation, a slight turning of his head – a cry of protest
from Petrunin? Then the TR7 was almost on top of him, a
spit of flame from the shadowy bulk of the man before he
flicked aside like a matador, between two cars. The bullet's
path was a groove in the thin metal of the roof, directly
above Hyde's head. He screeched the car round and
through the entrance to the station, and the barrier was
going up, very slowly. Another man was entering the booth
alongside the barrier – barrier going up, making a chopping
motion as it reached the peak of its swing, beginning to
descend almost immediately. The TR7 raced beneath it,
bounced over cobbles, and squealed into the road behind
the Midland Hotel.

'North,' Hyde said loudly when his breath returned and
the hotel's bulk was between them and the station. His
palms were damp on the steering wheel, and he was
perspiring freely. 'North.'

'Come on, come on!' Ardenyev yelled, his voice already
hoarse from its combat with the wind and the sea, his
gloved hands seemingly frozen and incapable as he
attempted, with Teplov and Nikitin, to drag the largest of
the sleds across the deck of the launch to its side.

The trough made them wallow as the helmsman steadied
the launch. The young lieutenant watched them through
the cabin window, his head flickering back and forth like a
tennis spectator, towards them then towards the next peak,
looming ahead of them.

'One more, sir!' Teplov bellowed back at him, even
though they were not more than three or four feet apart on
either side of the sled and its mound of cylinders. Shadrin
and Vanilov and Kuzin were already submerged, safe
under the water, with the second sled and the welding and
cutting gear. Their ten minutes already begun. There
should have been four sleds, more communications
equipment, more everything. Petrov was lying on a bunk,

his leg broken and splinted in an inflatable plastic bag. Groaning and useless.

The sled tilted on the side of the launch as the next wave reared up in the darkness and opened its jaws. Teplov glanced over his shoulder. Regret was useless, too. Ardenyev strained like someone demented or terrified as Nikitin, attached by a line, flipped over the side of the launch into the water, mask and mouth-piece in place, his ten minutes already beginning. One thought re-emerged from the panic of Ardenyev's mind. Unless they could get on to the *Proteus* within ten minutes, then they would have to spend hours coming back to the surface to avoid the bends, and no launch would be able to pick them up with ease – perhaps not at all – in this sea and at night. It was a one-way journey.

Nikitin's barely discernible bobbing head was accompanied by a raised hand, and then he swam close to the side of the launch. Ardenyev felt the dead weight of the sled pull towards Nikitin, and saw Teplov's face grey with strain. He yelled at the senior *michman*, who nodded, and went over the side. The wave loomed over the launch, flecked, old, immense. Two black-capped heads bobbed in the water. Slowly, almost out of his control, the sled dipped into the water and sank immediately. Teplov and Nikitin struck down after it.

Then the water, even as he turned his head to look and thought of time once more, lifted him and threw him across the deck of the launch. He glimpsed the lieutenant's appalled face, the rearing nose of the launch, then he was headfirst into the water, spun and tumbled like a leaf or twig in a stream's torrent, whirled down as he fitted his mouthpiece by instinct. His legs were above his head, just discernible; then blackness, and orientation returning. There were lights below him, two pale blobs like the eyes of a deep-ocean fish. He breathed as calmly as he could, then struck down towards the lights.

He tapped Teplov on the shoulder, and signalled with upraised thumb. Teplov's relief sounded withdrawn and almost mechanical through his throat-mike. Teplov slid further back against Nikitin on the seat of the sled, and Ardenyev swung himself into the saddle, holding on to the steering column. Directly in front of him, the tiny sonar screen was switched on, and the bright spot of the British submarine lay below and thirty degrees to port.

'Shadrin?' Ardenyev enquired into his microphone. All formality, all wasted words and energy and air disappeared beneath the surface.

'Skipper?'

'Got her fixed?'

'Yes, skipper.'

'Let's go.'

Ardenyev dipped the nose of the sled – a light, frail craft now that it was in its own element, not being manhandled across a sloping, slippery deck – towards the ledge on which the *Proteus* lay, not two hundred yards from them. The headlights of the sled picked out the winking, vanishing shoals of fish before they glanced across the silted ledge. Blackness beyond the ledge, but the lights turning the ledge itself almost sand-coloured, almost alive and three-dimensional. The cold seeped through the immersion suit, began to ring in his head like the absence of oxygen. Teplov clung to him, and Nikitin to Teplov. Without Petrov, Ardenyev had decided that two main sleds would suffice. He hadn't been thinking clearly on the launch, only swiftly, rapping out orders and decisions as if keeping a mounting, insidious sense of failure, of utter futility, at bay with the sound of his voice and the fence of quick thought.

Grey, white numerals, then the blackness of the sea behind. Ardenyev, feeling Teplov's tap on his shoulder in response to what they both had seen, turned the sled slowly in a sweeping curve. He circled slightly above the British submarine like a gull in the wind, and watched as the headlights of Shadrin's sled slipped like a caress across the midships section of the submarine, then up and around her sail.

They'd found her. He looked at his watch. Seven minutes remaining. He pushed the nose of the sled down towards the *Proteus*.

'There she is skipper!'

'Infra-red cameras?'

'Cameras running, skipper.'

'Can you see them, Terry?'

'No – wait – *there*?'

'What the hell is that?'

'Looks like a sled. It's going, going over the side. They'll get caught by the wave, no, one of them has – he's going over!'

'All fall down. Can we communicate with MoD yet?'

'No, skipper.'

'Then you'd better send the pictures over the wire straight away. Even Aubrey ought to be able to work this one out!'

'I'm sorry, Mr Aubrey, it could take hours to analyse these pictures.' Clark was holding irritation in check, his apology an exercise in calming his breathing and no more.

'There's no way we can communicate with the Nimrod?'

'I'm sorry, sir,' Copeland replied lugubriously, shaking his head, folding down his lower lip to complete the mask of apology. 'The jamming makes that impossible. Eastoe must have sent these by way of a substitute – and without sub-titles.'

'I am in no mood for cheap remarks, young man!' Aubrey snapped wearily.

'Sorry, sir.'

Aubrey turned back to Clark. 'How many men, would you say?'

They were still clustered round the wireprint machine, and the grainy reproductions of the infra-red photographs that the Nimrod had transmitted, torn off the machine as each frame appeared, were in every hand, or lay scattered on the bench near the machine. The whole room seemed crowded, like boys urging on two unwilling combatants, around Aubrey and Clark.

'This sled?'

'What do you mean *this* sled?' Aubrey wanted, demanded information, answers to his question upon which he could base a decision. The desire to make a decision, to act, pressed upon him like a manhole-cover which would mask a trap. Failure, complete and abject and humiliating, stared up at him like a nightmare into which he was falling.

'I mean there may be more than one sled. It looks like two, it's a two-man sled all right. Could be three – ?' Clark was examining the photograph with a magnifying-glass. It seemed old-fashioned, inappropriate to the advanced technology that was their pressing concern. 'Leopard' lying like junk on the floor of the Barents Sea.

'That equipment, then?' Aubrey asked snappily, using his own magnifying-glass, making nothing of the shapes and bulky outlines of the underwater equipment that was strapped and secured on the back of the sled. Yes, he could see it was a two-man sled, there were two men, perhaps one of the grainy dots was another head bobbing in the water – ? 'You say this man Ardenyev would be in command here?'

'That equipment – welding or cutting gear, oxygen, who knows? And yes, I guess it would be Valery Ardenyev.'

Clark was grinning.

'You've met him, then.'

'We've been – *observers*, at the same oceanographic conferences, sure.'

'What is his field of expertise?'

'Red Banner Special Operations – rescue, salvage, demolition, offence, defence, – you name it, they can do it.'

'The launch, Ethan – how many of these sleds could it hold?'

'No more than two, three – why?'

'The numbers involved, my dear fellow.' Aubrey was expansive again, confident. Clark was amazed at the brittle, transitory nature of the old man's emotions, whether optimistic or pessimistic. When he encountered the next obstacle, he would fall back into a trough of doubt and anxiety. 'Can I assume that they would not attempt salvage – or anything more *intrusive* – with so few people?'

'You might do. Inspection? Maybe.'

'Come, Ethan. Give me a best guess. Is this likely to be an inspection?'

'They'll have little time down there, at that depth. Just enough time, maybe.'

'Then we have some little time available ourselves?'

'To do what?' Clark turned on Aubrey angrily as it seemed self-satisfaction was the object, the sole purpose, of his questions. Feel good, put your mind to rest – and then you don't need to do any more. He almost voiced his thought.

'I don't know. We are prevented from making any moves other than diplomatic and political, until tomorrow or the following day. Have we that much time?'

'I don't know. Let's hope Eastoe goes down for another set of pictures when these divers return to the surface. Then we'll know it was only an inspection.'

Aubrey's face darkened. He wondered what madcap idea had sprung into Clark's mind, and whether, because he was younger and of the same experience and background, he might not have perceived something of what was in the man Ardenyev's mind. He did not, however, ask Clark his meaning.

'Norway must make another protest about this incursion into her territorial waters,' he said, and even to himself it sounded both too little and too late. He avoided looking at Clark as he pushed his way out of the circle of people around them, towards the telephones.

The *Proteus*'s stern lay bathed in the headlights of the two sleds, parked side by side on the ledge. The silt which they and the submarine had disturbed had settled. There was a wide ugly furrow the *Proteus* had gouged before she finally stopped. Beyond it, the damaged stern was grey, twisted, scorched metal, flayed by the coils of steel the MIRV torpedo had released. Ardenyev saw, as he picked his way fly-like in the illumination of the lights, that the fifteen-blade propeller had been thrown out of alignment, or dragged so it became embroiled with the whipping tendrils of steel cable, and that three of the phosphor-bronze, boot-shaped blades had been sheared off. One or two of the others were distorted, but intact. Without the MIRV torpedo, the damage wreaked by the low-warhead hit would not have been sufficient to stop the submarine.

Teplov's shoulder nudged against his as they clung to the port aft hydroplane. A steel cable twisted away from them like a great grey snake slithering towards the silt beneath the submarine. The hydroplane was buckled and torn beneath their hands and flippers, and its skin of metal had begun to unpeel like layers of an onion, having been damaged and then subjected to the pressure of the water before the *Proteus* slowed and halted. In front of them, the bulk of the submarine retreated into the darkness. Buckled plates, damaged ballast tanks, but there was no evidence that the pressure hull had been ruptured.

'They made a bloody good job of it,' Teplov's voice croaked in his earpiece. Ardenyev nodded.

The rudders were misaligned, too, but not badly.

'We can patch it – she'll have to be towed. We don't have time to repair the prop.'

It was Teplov's turn to nod. His eyes seemed to be grinning behind his facemask.

'What next?'

'Let's move amidships. Signal the others to start making a din in – ' He looked at his watch, 'one minute.' Ardenyev pushed away from the damaged hydroplane. His watch informed him that four minutes had already passed for himself, and perhaps five for Shadrin, Vanilov and Kuzin. No time to waste. He had six minutes to get aboard. Teplov behind him instructed the others, his voice tinny in the earpiece as Ardenyev glided like a black fish along the whale-like back of the *Proteus*. Each man knew his job; they had performed a hundred time trials in the deep tanks at the Frunze Naval School, and off-shore in the same depth and sea conditions as now pertained. Ardenyev's hands touched the two canisters strapped to his chest, smaller imitations of the two air tanks on his back.

They'd rehearsed it on submerged mock-ups, on the old 'Whiskey'-class boat they'd commissioned for practice. After the first month's training the ten minutes had always been sufficient even with the adrenalin running lower than now. But Ardenyev could not help remembering one severe case of the bends he had suffered by going through the mock-up's escape chamber too quickly, which had incapacitated him and he could not forget the first full sea trial which had included the use of the MIRV torpedo. The steel cables had ripped open the hull of the old submarine they were using, killing its crew. He and his two teams had been in the launch, waiting to go down, when the wreckage and the released air and the oil had come to the surface.

The great fin-like sail of the *Proteus* loomed out of the darkness. His lamp played on it. Below it, the officers and control room of the submarine. And 'Leopard', his target. He hovered, and Teplov joined him. Ardenyev gave him the thumbs-up signal, and the senior *michman* swam down to the base of the sail, his shape becoming indistinct, the light of his lamp feeble, winking on and off, it seemed, as he moved away and sought his own objective. Teplov would begin communicating in morse on the hull of the *Proteus*, offering apology and assistance and reassurance in the name of the Red Banner Fleet, distracting the officers of the submarine and retarding suspicion and activity.

Ardenyev kicked on, moving more swiftly now, dipping down to touch the hull once with his fingertips, then moving off again as soon as he sensed the vibration. The other four were using cutting gear and making as much noise as they could at the stern, a further distraction. Now, everything – the whole operation and its success – depended upon himself. The knowledge satisfied him as he urged his body through the water. He could just make out the forward hydroplanes. A shoal of fish, brief as a torch-signal, were caught in the light of his lamp. He glanced again at his watch. Four minutes fifty since he had reached bottom. Three-and-a-half minutes to decompress slowly enough not to be incapacitated. He kicked on more urgently gliding over the hull, his lamp playing upon it now with an almost frenzied movement, sweeping back and forth like a small searchlight. The diagram of the submarine was vivid in his mind, as if he possessed vision that allowed him to see beneath the skin of the double hull. He was passing over the officers' wardroom and the crew's quarters beneath them, towards the torpedo room. He reminded himself that the submarine would be silent, alert. He would be making noises almost next door to the wardroom, which would contain the off-duty officers, sitting in silence, nervous of moving. Would they be sufficiently distracted by the tapping, by the noises from the stern thrumming through the hull?

His lamp washed across the hull, then swung back. He had found his objective, the forward escape hatch above the torpedo room. Even here, the British had made it easier for him. A Royal Navy fleet submarine had gone down in the North Sea two years before. The crew had died because the air purification system had suddenly failed, and the rescuers had taken too long to cut their way into the hull. Since that disaster, it had been specified that all nuclear submarines, as well as all the older diesel subs in the Royal Navy, be fitted with two-way hatches that could be opened without difficulty from the outside. The Red Navy had known that when it began to plan the abduction o 'Leopard'.

He gripped the wheel of the flood control valve and began to twist it, wrenching at it violently, then turning it more easily. He looked at his watch. He had been under for six minutes, some of the others for seven. He had already lost them half a minute. It increased decompression time by the same amount. He began turning the wheel more rapidly. He could not account for the strange loss of time. How much time had he wasted looking at the damage, almost enjoying it, satisfied at the helplessness of the huge submarine? That must have been when he lost the forty seconds he was now behind schedule.

'Viktor?' he whispered into his mouthpiece.

'Sir?'

'How is it?'

'They're demanding to know what we're doing, and how their submarine was damaged?'

'Have you asked to come aboard?'

'Yes, sir. They've refused a liaison officer. I'm giving them the fictitious damage report now.'

'I'm going in.'

'Good luck, sir.'

Ardenyev lifted the hatch slowly, sensing its great weight even under the water. A rush of bubbles enveloped him. He would have made a noise already that might have been heard. They'd rehearsed that, too. The other distracting noises had been sufficient to mask his entry – but were they now, when it mattered? He dropped slowly into the chamber, and pulled the hatch down on himself. Then the submarine lurched forward, and his head banged in surreal slow-motion against the side of the compartment. His lamp's light wobbled on the walls around him. He was in a cylinder like the inside of an artillery shell which felt as if it was being slid into the breech of a gun.

The *Proteus* was moving, wriggling like an animal trying to rid itself of fleas. He pressed feet and back against the walls of the cylinder, simply hanging on because the buoyancy within the flooded chamber allowed him no weight, no steadiness. He could imagine, vividly, the control room where the decision has been taken; imagine, also, the hull of the submarine. Teplov might have been flung off – what about the others, the flail of cutting gear, the roll of tanks, the whip of the steel cables around the prop. He could sense the grinding as the submarine's prop struggled to turn against the restraint of the cables, his teeth grinding in his head, his whole head aching with the vibration. They must stop, must –

A glimpse of his watch. Seven minutes and ten, eleven seconds. Then the lamp banged against his arm painfully. He squeezed himself flatter, taller, bigger, holding himself still. Welding gear, cutting torches, tanks, the whip of cables. He sensed like a medium that one of them, perhaps more, would be dead or injured. All of them were running out of time. Time. That was the calculation; they knew it in the *Proteus*. Twenty fathoms equalled ten minutes' working time, then the excess nitrogen in the blood slowed the body, hampered the mind, began to kill. He was killing them now –

The scraping, the cries of metal as the crippled submarine dipped time and again to the bottom of the ledge, dragging her belly across silt and mud and rock, the grating, thrumming noise and vibration of the captive prop as it tried to turn, the smaller vibration – almost normality – of the small docking propeller being used. It seemed endless, unbearable.

He turned in the chamber, banged against the wall of the cylinder, gripped the lower hatch venting wheel, turned again, banged, was thrown off, his lamp flickering wildly against the flooded metal of his prison, gripped again, braced himself – the vibration and movement slowing now? – and turned a third time. The water began to seep slowly from the hatch into the torpedo room. Three-and-a-half minutes. He had practised the number of turns to allow the pressure to alter at the necessary rate, the precise amount of water to release per second, perhaps two hundred times. But not when it really mattered. He remained gripping the wheel of the lower hatch, the light of his lamp playing on his watch.

Ten, eleven, twelve seconds. Almost eight minutes of time gone, and another three minutes fifteen before the water had drained away and he had safely depressurised. A total of more than eleven minutes. And where were they? Had they hung on? Were they alive?

Slowing, vibration bearable. Scraping on its belly, lurching to starboard, a cry of rent metal, the main prop not being used, docking prop dying away. The *Proteus* was stopping again. He had waited too long. He should have acted earlier, when the noise and vibration were at their height. Now the water dripped on to the empty torpedo room floor in the sudden silence as men's hearing returned. Thirty-seven seconds, thirty-eight, nine, forty –

Silence. He stood upright in the chamber. The water was at shoulder-height. He ducked back beneath its surface. Fifty-five seconds. He couldn't wait, *had* to wait. Perhaps the great bulk of the submarine had rolled on one or more of them? Teplov? Nikitin? The others? If they were alive, could they find the *Proteus* again in time in the forest of silt that must now obscure her? They would swim through an unending, almost solid grey curtain of silt, looking for the submarine that was their only hope. It was already too late to begin slowly ascending to the surface. Now he was safely decompressing, no one could enter the torpedo room escape chamber until he had left it. If any of them were still alive. He thought of the whip of a loosened steel cable across an immersion-suited body –

One minute twenty seconds. He was crouching against the floor of the chamber as the water drained slowly into the torpedo room below. Not a trickle, not a drip, but a slow, steady fall, noisy. The wardroom next door, normality returning, things being righted again, objects picked up from the floor, bruises rubbed, hearing returning, awareness of surroundings increasing. *What's that noise? Sprung a leak? Better go and take a look –*

Ardenyev was on his own. He remembered the helicopter going down in flames, then Petrov's broken leg, then the hellish noise and vibration of the *Proteus*. Dolohov, he was able to consider distinctly, might have killed every member of the special Underwater Operations Unit, *his* unit. For a box of tricks to make a submarine invisible.

Two minutes five. The compartment was less then half full of water. He was squatting in a retreating tide, as he might have done at Tallinn or Odessa as a child, watching the mysterious, fascinating water rush away from him, leaving the froth of foam around him and the stretch of newly exposed wet sand in which shells sat up in little hollows. Two minutes twenty.

Noise, they must hear the noise, no they won't, they're too disorientated, they'll be listening for water, the dangerous water of a leak, a buckled or damaged plate, they'll hear it –

Two minutes thirty-two. Fifty-eight seconds remaining. He pulled at the hatch, and it swung up, emptying the chamber in an instant. His hands had been locked on the wheel, turning it slowly though the forebrain had decided to wait. The pressure of imagination as to what might have happened outside the submarine was greater than any other, pressing down and in on him like the ocean. He dropped through the hatch into the torpedo room, the water already draining away, leaving the cold, clinical place merely damp. Instantly, he felt dizzy, and sick. Too soon, too soon, he told himself. He had never tried to get through decompression at this depth in less than two minutes fifty. He'd been prepared to cope with the dizziness and sickness, the blood pounding in his head, that would have assailed him only half-a-minute early. This was worse, much worse. He staggered against the bulkhead, his vision unable to focus, his surroundings wobbling like a room in a nightmare. The noise in his ears was a hard pounding, beneath which he could almost hear the accelerating blood rushing with a dry whisper. His heart ached. Pain in his head, making thought impossible. His hands were clutched round the two canisters on his chest as if holding some talisman or icon of profound significance and efficacy. His legs were weak, and when he tried to move he lurched forward, almost spilling on to his face like a baby trying to walk for the first time.

He leaned against the bulkhead then, dragging in great lungfuls of the mixture in his air tanks, trying desperately to right his vision, and to focus on the door into the torpedo room. It was closed, but its outline shimmered, and threatened to dissolve. It was no barrier. Around him lay the sleek shapes of the torpedoes. Cold, clinical place, the floor already almost dry, except for the puddle that still lingered at his feet from his immersion suit. He tried to look at his watch, could not focus, strained and blinked and stretched his eyes, pressing the face of the watch almost against his facemask. Three minutes fifty, almost four minutes. He could have – should have – waited. He was further behind now. He snapped the lock on the weighted belt around his waist. It thudded to the floor.

He looked up. Close the hatch, close the hatch. Moving as if still under water, with the diver's weighted feet and restraining suit, he reached up and closed the hatch, turning the handle with aching, frosty, weak limbs. If they were alive – he felt tears which were no longer simply another symptom of decompression prick helplessly behind his eyes – then now they could open the outer hatch.

Door opening. Refocus. Slowly refocus. He had been about to focus on the port and starboard air purifiers on either side of the torpedo room when the door began opening. But it still ran like a rain-filled window-pane, the image distorted. A figure that might have been reflected in a fairground mirror came through the door, stopped, yelled something indistinct above the rush and ache in his ears, then came towards him.

Quick, quick, useless instincts prompted. He pushed away from the bulkhead. He could make out the port purifier clearly, then it dissolved behind rain again for a moment, then his vision cleared. He could hear the words, the question and challenge shouted. Another figure came through the open bulkhead door. Two of them. Ardenyev moved through a thicker element than air, and hands grabbed him from behind, causing him to stagger near one of the torpedoes. Slowly, aquatically, he tried to turn and lash out. His other hand cradled one of the two canisters on

192

his chest, and the young face seemed riveted by his hand and what it held. Ardenyev could distinguish expression on the face now – knowledge, realisation. The young man enclosed him in a bear-hug, but Ardenyev heaved at the thin, light arms, pushing the man away by his very bulk.

He bent, opening the inspection plate; then his hand was pulled away, and another, larger hand clamped on his own as it held the first canister. The second canister was torn from its strap and rolled across the floor, beneath one of the torpedo trestles. All three of them watched it roll. The two British officers feared it might be a bomb after all.

Ardenyev chopped out with the lamp attached still to his wrist, catching the smaller officer on the side of the head, knocking him aside. He flipped over one of the torpedoes, and subsided to the floor, a vague redness staining the side of his face. Then Ardenyev was hit in the stomach and he doubled up. Another blow against the side of his facemask, then he lunged upwards with his upper torso, catching his attacker in the chest with his head. A soft exhalation of air, the man staggering backwards –

He turned, twisted the canister in both hands, releasing the incapacitating gas, then jammed the canister into the air purifier, closing the inspection plate immediately. Then he was punched in the small of the back, just below his air tanks, then hands were round his shoulders and face, and his mask was coming off. He felt the mouthpiece ripped out of his mouth, and he inhaled the warm, sterile air of the submarine. He staggered across the torpedo room, still held by the second man, lurching against the trestles, his eyes searching the floor for the second canister, oblivious even of the need to re-insert his mouthpiece before the gas passed the length of the submarine down the air ducts and returned to them in the torpedo room.

He dropped to one knee in a feint, then heaved with his shoulders. The second man, the heavier, bearded officer, rolled up and over his neck and shoulders, falling in front of him, winded by the metal floor of the room. Ardenyev scrabbled under a torpedo trestle, his fingers closing over its damp coldness, gripping it. He got to his feet, clutched the canister to his chest, which was heaving with effort, and staggered clumsily across the torpedo room in his flippers, to the starboard air purifier.

Other men were coming in now. He opened the inspection plate, twisted the canister, and jammed it into the purifier, closing the plate after it. He was grabbed, then. The room was full of noise, an alarm sounded somewhere, while he tried to jam his mouthpiece back into his mouth. They wanted to stop him. It was as if the hands that reached for him had only that one minor object, to prevent him regaining the safety of the air mixture in his tanks while the gas moved swiftly through the submarine. He felt himself hit, but his attention could not be spared for his torso, arms and legs, kidneys, stomach, chest. He went on trying to force the mouthpiece back into place.

One breath, two, three, doubling over on the floor, not resisting now, hoping they would assume he was beaten, even unconscious. Someone turned him over; he saw through slitted lids a hand reach for the mouthpiece and mask again – the mask askew, obscuring much of the scene – then the hand lunged past him, a body toppled down beside him, subsiding with a peculiar, slow-motion grace, mimicking death. He opened his eyes now, knowing he had nothing to fear. Others fell like skittles, ninepins, but in the same seeming slow-motion.

Ardenyev closed his eyes. He alone was conscious on board the British submarine. There was no hurry, no hurry at all. They would be out for an hour, perhaps longer. There were no noises from the escape chamber, and therefore there was no hurry whatsoever. He had captured the *Proteus* and 'Leopard', and he was entirely alone. A sad, even vile heroism. He surrendered to the exhaustion that assailed him, as if he, too, had inhaled the incapacitating gas.

Nine: RETRIEVAL

From their identification papers, Ardenyev knew them to be Thurston, the first-lieutenant of the submarine, and Hayter, the officer responsible for 'Leopard'. Because of their importance, he had allowed them to remain with Lloyd in the control room of the *Proteus* after the remaining officers and ratings had been confined to the wardroom and crew quarters 'for security reasons'.

Ardenyev had watched Lloyd come round, come to an almost instant wakefulness, and he had immediately warmed to the man and granted him his respect and his wariness. Lloyd would now sabotage 'Leopard' in a moment, if he could. Ardenyev stood before the captain of the submarine and his two senior officers at attention, like a junior officer presenting his compliments. It was part of the charade he was now required to play.

'As I was saying, Captain,' he began again, having been interrupted by an expletive from Thurston, 'we very much apologise for the manner in which we were required to board your vessel. However, it is lucky that we did. Your purification system had developed a fault that would almost certainly have proved fatal had we not arrived.' He said it without a flicker of amusement or self-mockery. The truth did not matter.

His men, his team were missing, presumed dead. Vanilov, brokenly, had told him he had seen Kuzin catch a whipping, freed tendril of steel cable across his back, and he had seen him flung away into the dark, his body tumbled and twisted in a way that would have been impossible had it been unbroken. Nikitin had fallen beneath the weight of the *Proteus*, forgetting in surprise to loosen his hold on the cutting gear. Stabs of blue flame had come from the cutting-pipes as the silt had boiled round, and swallowed, Nikitin. Shadrin he had not seen at all. Teplov and Vanilov alone had clung to the submarine, been dragged through the water and the boiling mist of silt and mud, rested dazed and exhausted and were slowly being poisoned by nitrogen in the blood until Teplov had crawled back to the stern and found Vanilov and boarded the *Proteus* through the aft escape hatch, into the electic motor room. They had waited in the slowly-draining compartment for five minutes, until it was safe to emerge into the submarine. Dizziness and exhaustion, yes, but not the bends. Teplov had put the neutralising agent through the aft purifiers, and then come seeking his commanding officer.

Ardenyev felt his left cheek adopt a tic, the last, fading tremors of weariness and shock. These men in front of him had killed three of his men, indirectly killed Blue Section. The knowledge that he would have done precisely the same, threatened as they had felt they were, intruded upon his anger, dimming it. Lloyd, the captain, was watching him carefully, weighing him, the expression on his face like a suspicion that they had met before, or always been intended to meet.

'Fucking piracy, that's what it is,' Thurston offered into the silence, and Hayter rumbled his agreement. 'How do you explain the guns if you're here to help us?'

Ardenyev smiled innocently. 'We understand your concern with security. We would not wish to be blamed for any – *mistakes* you might make, any damage you might cause to sensitive equipment. It is merely a precaution.'

'Locking up my crew is just another precaution, I presume?' Lloyd asked sardonically, sitting in a relaxed manner in one of the sonar operators' chairs, which he swung to and fro slowly, almost as if he intended mesmerising the Russian. A relaxed, diffident, confident child. Ardenyev was pricked by his seeming indifference to the fate of Nikitin and the others.

'Captain, I would understand, even expect, some reaction such as that of Commander Thurston translated into action, either from one of your officers, or some of your men. That would only complicate an already complicated situation. We are here to *help* you – ' Here, sincerity seeped into his voice in a measured, precise dose – 'because it is our fault that you are in this situation.'

'You admit it, then?'

'What else can we do? The captain and officers of the

submarine *Grishka* will be severely disciplined for their provocative action.'

'This is unreal – !' Thurston exploded.

'Not at all – is it, Captain?' Ardenyev said with a smirk. 'It will be the agreed version of events.'

'How do you explain the cuts and bruises on two of my officers?' Lloyd enquired. 'The air purifiers struck them, I suppose?'

'Falling to the deck, I suppose,' Ardenyev replied, 'overcome by the lack of oxygen. I came aboard when your signals from inside stopped – you.tapped out one word, HELP, before that happened. You don't remember?'

Lloyd shook his head. 'No, I don't. Oxygen starvation plays tricks with memory, obviously.'

Ardenyev sighed with pleasure. 'I see we understand each other, Captain.'

'What happens now?'

'From the damage report, there will be some repairs, to your buoyancy and to your hydroplanes. Then you will be towed back to Pechenga, our nearest naval base, for sufficient repairs to allow you to return to Faslane under your own power.' He spread his hands innocently in front of him. 'It is the least we can do, apart from the sincerest diplomatic apologies, of course. It will take little more than a day or two before you are on your way home.' He beamed.

'If your mission is so humanitarian, why is your petty-officer carrying a Kalashnikov with the safety-catch in the "Off" position?' Thurston remarked sourly.

'Security.' Ardenyev sighed again. He was tiring of the charade. It was not important. Everyone knew the truth. 'Now, I will have to contact the rescue ship *Karpaty* and arrange for divers and equipment to be sent down to us.'

'I'm sure you're reasonably familiar with our communications?' Lloyd remarked with forced lightness, as if his situation had come home to him in a more bitter, starker way.

'Thank you, yes.' Ardenyev's hand released the butt of the Makarov pistol thrust into the belt of his immersion suit. He tousled his hair in an attempt to retain the mocking, false lightness of his conversation with the British officers. He wanted to clamber back into the fiction of a terrible accident, a life-saving boarding-party, apologetic repairs in Pachenga, as into a child's tree-house. But he could not. Whipping steel cables, boiling flame from a crashed helicopter, accompanied him vividly to the communications console.

As if admitting that the fiction could not be sustained, he drew the Makarov and motioned the three British officers to the far side of the control room before he seated himself in front of the console.

'These pictures were taken forty minutes after the previous set,' Aubrey remarked. 'You are telling me, Captain Clark – ' the excessive politeness seemed designed to stave off any admission of disaster – 'that since no divers have resurfaced, they must be on board *Proteus*?'

'Right.'

'Why?'

'They couldn't stay down more than ten minutes at that depth. Then they'd come back up slowly, but by now they'd be back on board the launch. Sure, the launch has returned to take station on the port beam of *Karpaty* – ' Here Clark nodded in Copeland's direction – 'but as far as I can make out, they're loading heavy cutting gear from the rescue ship. And these men on deck. More divers. In full rig, not scuba gear. They're going down. Therefore, you can bet Ardenyev's men are on board.'

'But why and how would Lloyd have allowed him on board?' Aubrey asked in exasperation. He was baffled and plagued by the murky high-resolution and light-intensified photographs transmitted from the Nimrod. Clark seemed to be reading tea leaves. The whole matter seemed like a fairy tale.

'He wouldn't need to – '

'The escape hatches,' Copeland blurted out. 'After *Phaeton* went down a couple of years ago, all the hatches had to open two-way. They'd know that, dammit!'

'Exactly,' Clark said drily. 'Ardenyev would have let himself in.'

'Eastoe reports a change in position of *Proteus*.'

'Lloyd trying to get rid of his guests,' Clark commented acidly. 'Someone's in there, you can bet on it.'

'Then none of our messages got through?' Aubrey asked forlornly. ''Leopard'' will not have been destroyed.'

'I'm afraid not.'

'Clark – what will they do now, for heaven's sake?' Aubrey's eye rested on Giles Pyott's expressionless face with a glance of pure malevolence. Pyott's implacability refuted the accusation of the gaze. Clark cleared his throat, breaking the tension between the soldier and the intelligence agent. Aubrey shrugged.

'Raise her – depending on the damage, or simply take what they want down there. The situation's complicated by the fact that ''Leopard'' isn't operational at present. I guess they'll raise her and tow her into port.'

'What?' Pyott asked in disbelief. 'That would be piracy. The international repercussions would be – enormous.'

'You'd declare war?' Clark asked ironically.

'Don't be stupid.'

'Then the shit hitting the fan will have been worth it. What will you do? All of you. You won't go to war, *we* won't go to war on your ·behalf, you won't tell anyone because it's all too embarrassing – so nothing will happen. ''Leopard'' will belong to both sides or to none. That'll be the only outcome.'

'What can we *do*, Clark?' Aubrey demanded with the impatient emphasis of a frustrated child on a wet day. He was almost shaking with rage and frustration.

'You've been outboxed, Mr. Aubrey.'

'Don't be so damned American,' Pyott drawled. 'So insufferably smug and patronising.'

'Sorry, Colonel Pyott,' Clark apologised. He could not mask his grin completely, even though he sensed the gravity of the situation as completely as anyone else in the room beneath the Admiralty. It was so – so *caricatured*, this panic in the dovecote. The new shiny toy was missing. There was an absence of concern for the crew of the *Proteus* that Clark resented on their behalf, even in Aubrey. He also felt, and admitted, a sneaking admiration for the man he felt must have masterminded the boarding of the submarine, Valery Ardenyev. He could remember the man's face and build now, and he could entirely believe in the Russian's ability to successfully surprise and overcome a crew of over one hundred.

Everything depended upon the degree to which *Proteus* was damaged. The nearest NATO units were twenty hours' sailing from the present position of the submarine, except for certain small Norwegian units which the government in Oslo would not deploy in the Barents Sea. They could watch, by radar, sonar and aircraft, but they could not intervene. If it took more than twenty hours to raise and tow the *Proteus*, then the full five acts of the disaster might not be performed. Unless Ardenyev and his men simply unplugged 'Leopard' and took it away with them. Clark was inclined to doubt this. The Russians would preserve, at some effort, the bland, apologetic face they had begun to present via the Soviet Ambassador in London.

'Can we rescue it – them?' Aubrey asked. 'Can we get out of the elephant trap that has been dug for us?' he insisted, worrying at the insuperable problem as at a bone. There had to be some hope within the situation, surely?

'Rescue?' Copeland blurted in disbelief.

'I can't see how,' Clark said more carefully as Aubrey glared at the young Royal Navy officer. The map-board loomed over them all, all its lights gleaming and unmoving, except for the plotted course of the Nimrod on-station as it was updated every few minutes. A fly buzzing above the scene, a carrion bird over a kill.

'I don't see why they need to raise the sub,' Pyott said. 'They're interested in only one thing, surely?'

'Ardenyev's done maybe a half-dozen of these rescues on Russian boats in his career. Board and raise operations. He's an expert at it. They needed him to get on board, sure – but they maybe want his expertise at raising boats, too.'

'I must talk to "C" at once,' Aubrey remarked. 'Our talking is pointless at the moment. We must establish what the Soviet authorities intend.'

Clark shrugged, unoffended that Aubrey doubted his prognosis. His respect for Aubrey had seemed to waver during the past twenty-four hours, like a light revealed and obscured by the movement of clouds. Yet the American, despite the clarity of his own mind, realised he still expected a solution to occur to Aubrey; even a successful solution.

Aubrey made no distinction of security between himself and the 'Chessboard Counter' team, and used one of the battery of telephones in the underground room. Cunningham, he knew, was with the Foreign Secretary, having been summoned to a second meeting with the Soviet Ambassador. He heard Cunningham at the other end of the line within half a minute of placing the call to the Foreign Office.

'Yes, Kenneth? What news?' Cunningham sounded breathless. Aubrey supposed it stemmed from events rather than exertion.

'Expert opinion – ' Aubrey could not suppress an involuntary glance towards Clark and the tight-knit group around and beneath the map-board – 'has it here that the Russians may have boarded *Proteus*.'

'Good God, that's outrageous!'

'The Ambassador hasn't confirmed as much?'

'He's talking of rescue, of course – but not of boarding. Not directly. Not as yet, that is.'

'How does he explain the incident?'

There was a chilly chuckle in Cunningham's voice, the laugh of a man succeeding, just, in appreciating a joke against himself. 'The captain of the Russian submarine suffered a nervous breakdown. He ordered the firing of the torpedo in question before he could be relieved of his command by the usual heroic young officer, loyal to the Party and the cause of world peace.'

'That is perhaps the unkindest cut of all, that they can get away with such a ridiculous tale, knowing we can do nothing to refute it. And nothing to rescue our submarine.'

'The Foreign Secretary has informed the PM, Kenneth. She's monitoring the situation. Every effort is being made to pressurise the Soviet Union into leaving the area and leaving *Proteus* to us.'

'And – ?'

'Very little. They insist, *absolutely insist*, on making amends. For the lunacy of one of their naval officers, as the Ambassador put it.'

'Washington?'

'The President is gravely concerned – '

'And will do nothing?'

'Is prepared to accept the Russian story at face value, for the sake of international tension, despite what his military advisers tell him. I don't think he quite grasps the importance of "Leopard".'

'I see. We are getting nowhere?'

'Nowhere. What of this man Quin?'

'Nothing. The girl is the key. I'm waiting for a report from Hyde.'

'Would it help if we recovered him, at least?'

'We might then destroy "Leopard", I suppose.'

'The PM will not risk the lives of the crew,' Cunningham warned sternly. 'The Foreign Secretary and I were informed of that in the most unequivocal manner.'

'I meant only that we could attempt sabotage, or Lloyd could if Quin was in our hands again.'

'Quite. You don't think "Leopard" had been damaged by Lloyd or his crew?'

'It is possible, but I think unlikely. None of our signals reached the *Proteus*.'

'Very well. Kenneth, I think you'd better come over here at once. You may have to brief the Foreign Secretary before he sees the PM again. Leave Pyott in command there.'

'Very well. In fifteen minutes.'

Aubrey replaced the receiver.. The room was quiet with failure. Clark watched him steadily, some of the younger men regarded him with hope. Pyott appeared resigned. It was, he admitted, a complete and utter intelligence disaster – precisely the kind he could not tolerate or accept.

'Giles,' he called, and then thought: where the devil is Hyde?

Quin beckoned like a light at the end of a dark tunnel. A false, beguiling gleam, perhaps, but he had no other point of reference or hope.

Hyde wished he could call Aubrey from the row of telephones with their huge plastic hair-dryer hoods that he could see through the glass doors of the cafeteria. He was afraid, however, of leaving the girl for a moment. He was afraid of letting her out of his sight for any length of time, however short, and afraid, too, that she was beginning to regret her earlier decision. And he was also wary, treading delicately on the fragile, thin-ice crust of the trust she meagrely afforded him, of reminding her that there were other, more faceless, more powerful people behind him. The kind of people her father had fled from originally.

The telephones remained at the edge of his eyesight, in the centre of cognition, as he sipped his coffee and watched her eagerly devouring a plate of thin, overcooked steak and mushrooms and chips. For himself, beans on toast had been as much as he could eat. Tension wore at him, devouring appetite as well as energy. Quin was somewhere in the north of England – the girl had said nothing more than that, and he refrained from pumping her further for fear of recreating the drama of obsessive suspicion in her mind. He behaved, as far as he was able, as a driver who was giving her a lift north. The adrenalin refused to slow in his veins. He was nervous of pursuit – though he had seen no evidence of it – and he was suffering the stimulant effects of their escape from Petrunin.

'How's the tour going?' he asked conversationally.

She looked at him, a forkful of chips poised at her lips, which were shiny with eating. Her face was amused, and somehow obscurely contemptuous.

'I didn't have time to notice.'

Hyde shrugged. 'I thought you might have heard. I hope they do well.'

'You expect me to believe that's all that's on your mind – the profits of an over-thirties rock band?' she sneered, chewing on the mouthful of chips, already slicing again at the thin steak. The cafeteria of the motorway service station was early-hours quiet around them. One or two lorry drivers wading through mountainous plates of food, a carload of caravanners avoiding the traffic of the day by travelling by night, smuggling their way to their holiday destination, the two waitresses leaning at the cash register, grumbling. Just south of Lancaster. Hyde hoped that Quin was somewhere in the Lake District. The sooner he got to him, the better.

He shrugged. 'No, I don't think you're that stupid. Just filling in time, trying to lull you into a false sense of security.' He grinned in what he hoped was an unsuspicious, engaging manner.

She studied him narrowly. Her plate was empty. 'You're odd,' she said eventually. 'And too bloody clever by half. Don't pull the dumb ocker stunt with me.'

She was still in control of their situation, leading him by the hand to her father, only because her father had agreed. She would tell him nothing until the last minute, to retain control.

'Thank you. Tell me, why did your father up and away like that? He wasn't really frightened of us, was he?'

She screwed her face up in thought, then released the skin into clear, youthful planes and curves again. With a bit of make-up, Hyde thought, she wouldn't look bad. They all wear a sneer these days.

'He was frightened of them – people like the ones tonight,' she said. 'And he didn't believe people like *you* –' An old and easy emphasis lay on the words like a mist. *Pigs, Fascists, cops, the fuzz*. The necessary vocabulary of her age and her education. The silence after the emphatic last word was strained, and she looked down, suddenly younger, more easily embarrassed.

'I see,' he said. 'We would have looked after him, you know.'

'No you wouldn't!' she snapped, looking up again. 'They watched him all the time. *Your* people took time off for meals, and the pub, and to go for a piss – *they* didn't! They were there all the time. Dad said there were a *hundred* times he could have been kidnapped while your lot weren't there or weren't looking!' She was leaning forward, whispering intently, a breathy shout. 'You wouldn't have taken care of him – he took care of himself.'

'I agree we're not as efficient as the KGB,' Hyde said evenly. 'But he wasn't in any real danger.' Immediately, he was sorry he had uttered the words. The girl's features were rich in contempt, and he had no business defending the DS. Quin had been right, in a way. The KGB might have lifted him, any time. 'Sorry,' he added. 'No doubt he was right. Sloppy buggers, some of them.' Her face relaxed. 'But he's safe now?' Her eyes narrowed, and he added: 'Do you want coffee?' She shook her head.

'You?'

'No.' He hesitated, then said, 'Look, you have to trust me. No, I don't mean because you realise I'm trying to save you and your old man from the baddies – you have to believe I can do it. I'm not tooling around Britain waiting for you to make up your mind.'

She thought for a moment, then said, 'You'll have to turn off the motorway at the exit for Kendal.' She watched his face, and he suppressed any sign of satisfaction.

It was the importance of it, he decided. That explained her almost fanatical care for her father. She was the key, even to herself. Importantly useful for the first time in her parents' lives. Crucial to her father's safety. She clung to her role as much as she clung to her father. 'Ready? Let's go, then.'

The man near the telephone booth in the car park watched them approach the yellow TR7, get in, and drive off down the slip-road to the M6. There was just time for the brief telephone call to Petrunin before they set off in pursuit. Once clear of Manchester and on to the motorway, Hyde had not driven at more than sixty or sixty-five. If he kept to that speed, there would be enough time to catch him before the next exit. He dialled the number, then pressed the coin into the box. Petrunin's voice sounded hollow and distant.

'I may have some trouble getting away. A slight delay. Keep me informed.'

'Trouble?'

'No. I must, however, be careful leaving Manchester. I am known by sight. Don't lose them.'

The man left the booth, and ran across the car park to the hired Rover and its two occupants. They were less than a minute behind the yellow TR7.

Lloyd was still angry. The effort to keep his appearance calm, to portray acquiescence to the inevitable, seemed only to make the hidden anger grow, like a damped fire. His father, encouraging the first fire of the autumn by holding the opened copy of *The Times* across the fireplace in the

205

morning room. He smiled inwardly, and the memory calmed him. His stomach and chest felt less tight and hot. It was worse, of course, when the Russian was there – even when Thurston with his impotent raging and coarse vocabulary was in the same room.

There was nothing he could do. With his crew confined to their quarters and one guard on the bulkhead door, and his officers similarly confined to the wardroom, three men had held them captive until a relief, augmented guard had arrived from the rescue ship and the damage repair team with their heavy equipment had begun their work on the stern of the *Proteus*. Ardenyev forced one to admire him, and that rankled like a raging, worsening toothache. The effort of three weary, strained men to drag unconscious bodies through the submarine to monitor the essential, life-supporting systems, to inspect 'Leopard', and only then to call for help, surprised him. Enraged him afresh, also.

There was a knock at his cabin door. Presumably the guard.

'Yes?'

Ardenyev was looking tired, yet there was some artificial brightness about his eyes. He was obviously keeping going on stimulants. Lloyd tried to adopt a lofty expression, feeling himself at a disadvantage just because he was lying on his bunk. Yet he could not get up without some admission of subordination. He remained where he lay, hands clasped round his head, eyes on the ceiling.

'Ah, Captain. I am about to make an inspection of repairs. I am informed that they are proceeding satisfactorily.'

'Very well, Captain Ardenyev. So kind of you to inform me.'

'Yes, that is irony. I detect it,' Ardenyev replied pleasantly. 'I learned much of my English in America, as a student. Their use of irony is much broader, of course, than the English – I beg your pardon, the British.'

'You cocky bastard. What the hell are you doing with my ship?'

'Repairing her, Captain.' Ardenyev seemed disappointed that Lloyd had descended to mere insult. 'I am sorry for much of what has happened. I am also sorry that you killed

206

three members of my team. I think that your score is higher than mine at the moment, don't you?'

Lloyd was about to reply angrily, and then he simply shrugged. 'Yes. You haven't – ?'

'One body, yes. The youngest man. But that is usually the way, is it not? The others? No doubt they will be awarded posthumous medals. If I deliver your submarine to Pechenga.'

'What happened to the fraternal greetings bullshit?'

'For public consumption, Captain. That is what our ambassador will be telling your foreign secretary, over and over again. I'm sorry, but your inconvenience will be short-lived and as comfortable as possible. My interest in the affair ends when we dock. Now, if you will excuse me – '

Lloyd returned his gaze to the ceiling, and Ardenyev went out, closing the door behind him. The guard outside Lloyd's door was stony-faced, and his Kalashnikov was held across his chest, stubby metal butt resting lightly against one hip. Ardenyev nodded to him, and passed into the control room, His own team should have been there, he reminded himself, then wished to quash the reminder immediately. The pills, damned pills, juicing up the emotions, making pain easy and evident and tears prick while they kept you awake –

They would have a steering crew brought down from the rescue ship once the repairs were complete. Under his command, they would raise the submarine in preparation for towing to Pechenga. Teplov looked up from monitoring the life-support systems, and merely nodded to him. Vanilov was slumped in a chair, his head on his arms next to a passive sonar screen. Teplov was evidently letting him rest.

Ardenyev went out of the control room and into the tunnel which passed through the reactor housing to the aft section of the *Proteus*. He ignored the windows into the reactor chamber, and passed into the manoeuvring room above the huge diesel generators. Empty. Then the turbine room, similarly empty. The silence of the submarine was evident in the huge aft section, despite the banging and scraping, setting his teeth on edge, that thrummed in the hull; the noises of the repairs under way. Empty, silent, to the imagination beginning to smell musty with disuse. He passed through the bulkhead door into the room housing the electric motors, where the aft escape hatch was located. His replenished tanks waited for him on the floor by the ladder up to the hatch.

He checked the air supply, then strapped the tanks on to his back. He adjusted his facemask, and fitted the mouthpiece. He breathed rapidly, re-checking the air supply. Then he climbed the ladder and opened the hatch. He closed it behind him, and turned the sea-cock to flood the chamber. Water rushed down the walls, covering his feet in a moment, mounting to his ankles and knees swiftly.

When the chamber was flooded and the pressure equalised with the depth and weight of water outside, he reached up and turned the wheel of the outside hatch. He pushed it open, and kicked upwards, drifting out into the sudden blind darkness of the sea, his eyes drawn by pinpricks of white light and the flashes of blue light at the stern of the submarine. He turned, swimming down the grey back of the submarine where streaks of turning, swirling small fish glided and winked in the passing light of his lamp. Slowly, he made out the tiny figures working on the damaged stern, outlined and silhouetted by the flare of their cutting and welding gear and by the arc lamps clamped to the hull.

He crouched on the hull of the *Proteus*, next to the underwater salvage chief from the *Karpaty*, a man he had trained with for the past three months, Lev Balan. Beyond them, the hydroplanes and the rudder were being patched. The force of the seawater against their damaged, thin steel skins as the *Proteus* moved on after being hit by both torpedoes had begun stripping the metal away from the ribbed skeleton of steel beneath. The effect, Ardenyev thought, was like exposing the struts and skeleton of an old biplane, where canvas had been stretched over a wooden frame, and doped. Or one of his old model aeroplanes, the ones that worked on a tightened elastic band. The repairs were crude, but sufficient to prevent further damage, and to make the minimal necessary use of rudder and hydroplanes now possible. The propeller would not be needed, but the evidence of the MIRV torpedo's steel serpents was being removed twenty fathoms down rather than in the submarine pen at Pechenga. The hull around the propeller and even forward of the rudder and hydroplanes was scarred and pocked and buckled by the effect of the whiplash action of the flailing steel cables as they were tightened and enmeshed by the turning of the propeller.

As Ardenyev watched, one length of cable, freed from the prop, drifted down through the light from the arc lamps in slow motion, sliding into the murk beneath the submarine. A slow cloud of silt boiled up, then settled.

'How much longer, Lev?'

'Two, three hours. In another hour we should be able to start attaching the tow lines.' Lev Balan was facing him. Within the helmet of the diving suit, his face was vivid with enjoyment and satisfaction. Airlines snaked away behind him, down to the huge portable tanks of air mixture that rested on the ledge near the submarine. 'We'll have to come in for a rest before that. Temperature's not comfortable, and my men are tired.'

'Okay – you make the decision. Is the docking prop damaged?' Balan shook his head. 'What about the ballast tanks?'

'When we get her up to towing depth, we might have to adjust the bags. We've repaired one of the tanks, but the others can't be done down here – not if we're sticking to your timetable!' Despite the distortion of the throat-mike, Balan's voice was strong, full of inflection and expression, as if he had learned to adapt his vocal chords to the limitations of underwater communication.

'Okay. Keep up the good work.'

'Sorry about your boys.'

Ardenyev shrugged helplessly. 'Don't they call it operational necessity?'

'Some shits do.'

'I'll get the galley operating ready for your men.'

Ardenyev registered the drama around him once more. Now that his eyes had adapted completely, the arc lamps threw a glow around the scene, so that figures appeared caught in shafting sunlight, the minute sea life like moths and insects in summer air. He patted Balan on the shoulder, and kicked away back towards the hatch. As he travelled just above the hull with an easy motion of his legs and flippers, a curious sensation of ownership made itself apparent. As if the submarine were, in some part, his own, his prize; and some kind of repayment for the deaths of Kuzin, Nikitin and Shadrin.

When he dropped through the inner hatch again, he passed through the compartments of the huge submarine as a prospective purchaser might have strolled through the rooms of a house that had taken his fancy.

Teplov was waiting for him in the control room. Vanilov was sheepishly awake, and seated at the communications console.

'Message from Murmansk. The admiral wants to talk to you, sir,' Teplov informed him. Obscure anger crossed Ardenyev's features.

'Weather and sea state up top?'

'It's no better,' Teplov answered, 'and then again, it's no worse. Forecast is for a slight increase in wind speed and a consequent slight worsening of sea state. The skipper of the *Karpaty* is still in favour of waiting the storm out.'

'He doesn't have the choice, Viktor. In three hours' time, we'll be on our way home. Very well, let's talk to Murmansk, and endure the admiral's congratulations.'

The feeling of possession and ownership had dissipated. The congratulations of the old man in Murmansk would be empty, meaningless. It wasn't about that, not at all. Not praise, not medals, not promotion. Just about the art of the possible, the art of making possible. And he'd done it, and Dolohov's words would make no difference, and would not bring back the dead.

'I see. Thank you, Giles. I'll tell the minister.'

Aubrey put down the telephone, nodded to the Foreign Secretary's Private Secretary, and was ushered into the minister's high ceilinged office. Long gold curtains were drawn against the late night, and lamps glowed in the corners of the room and on the Secretary of State's huge mahogany desk. It was a room familiar, yet still evocative, to Aubrey. The Private Secretary, who had been annoyed that Aubrey had paused to take the call from

Pyott, and who had also informed him that His Excellency the Soviet Ambassador was waiting in another room – protocol first, last and all the time, Aubrey had remarked to himself, hiding his smile – closed the double doors behind him.

Her Majesty's Secretary of State for Foreign and Commonwealth Affairs rose and came forward to take Aubrey's hand. In his features, almost hidden by his tiredness and the strain imposed by events which brought him unpleasantly into collision with the covert realities of the intelligence service, was the omnipresent memory that he had been a junior boy at Aubrey's public school and, though titled and wealthy, had had to fag for the son of a verger who had come from a cathedral preparatory school on a music scholarship. It was as if the politician expected Aubrey, at any moment and with the full effect of surprise, to remind him of the distant past, in company and with the object of humiliation.

'Kenneth. You were delayed?'

'I'm sorry, Minister. I had to take a telephone call from Colonel Pyott. The Nimrod has been picking up signals from the *Proteus*, as have North Cape Monitoring.' The minister looked immediately relieved, and Aubrey was sorry he had chosen an optimistic syntax for what he wished to convey. 'Russian signals, I'm afraid,' he hurried on. 'We can't break the code, but it is evident that the Soviets are in command of the submarine.'

'Damnation!' Cunningham offered from the depth of the Chesterfield on which he was sitting. The Foreign Secretary's face dropped into lines of misery.

'The PM must be informed at once,' he said, returning to his desk. 'Find yourself a seat, Kenneth.' He waved a hand loosely, and Aubrey perched himself on a Louis Quinze armchair, intricately carved, hideously patterned. Cunningham looked at Aubrey, and shook his head. The Foreign Secretary picked up one of the battery of telephones on his desk, then hesitated before dialling the number. 'Is there anything you can suggest, Kenneth? Anything at all?' He put down the receiver, as if to display optimism.

'Minister – I'm sorry that this incident has had to spill over into legitimate diplomacy. I can only recommend that

211

all diplomatic efforts be maintained. There is nothing else we can do. We must press for details, of course, and demand that one of our people in Moscow is in Pechenga when the *Proteus* docks. He must be allowed immediate access, and there must be every attempt to preserve – by complaint, fuss, bother, noise, whatever you will – to preserve the security of "Leopard".' Aubrey spread his hands on his knees.

'Pechenga?'

'The nearest naval base. Murmansk if you prefer – or wherever?'

'One of your people?'

Cunningham did not reply, but looked towards Aubrey.

'If you wish, Minister,' Aubrey answered. 'But I would prefer someone rather senior on the embassy staff, and someone *legitimate*.'

'Very well. I'll put that in motion.'

'I think, however,' Aubrey pursued, 'that the Russians will delay the travel permits, and that sort of thing, so that by the time our people are on the scene, they will have done whatever they wish and be waving *Proteus* goodbye from the quayside.'

'I'm inclined to agree,' Cunningham murmured.

'Then there is absolutely nothing we can do!' the Foreign Secretary fumed, slapping his hand repeatedly on the surface of his desk. He looked towards Aubrey as if he were to blame for the situation. Aubrey's features were impassive. 'This really is not the way to play the game. The Russians have disobeyed every rule of international behaviour. It really is not good enough.' There was a peculiarly old-fashioned inflection to the voice, to accompany the outdated sentiments.

'They are inclined to do that,' Aubrey observed mockingly and received a warning glance from Cunningham. 'I agree, Minister. Obviously, the Kremlin has fully involved itself with, and sanctioned, this covert operation. Because they have done so, they place us at a considerable disadvantage. It is, indeed, a mixing of the legitimate and the covert which is both improper and very difficult to counter. And it has worked. This sort of mixed marriage usually flops badly – like the Bay of Pigs. The Russians seem to have more success than we do.'

212

'You imply that any remedy is strictly the concern of the intelligence service?'

'I have no answer.'

'The PM will give her blessing to *any* counter-operation, I'm quite sure of that. Our hands are tied, as you say. We do not even wish to become involved. Our people are in no danger, they will be released within the next couple of days. Our submarine will be repaired. Only "Leopard" will no longer be our property. Therefore, if you can prevent the loss of "Leopard", do so. But it must be— and the PM would wish me to stress this, even at the same time as she gives you her blessing— *it must be* an intelligence operation. It will be disowned, it must not endanger the crew of the submarine or any non-intelligence personnel, and it must be done immediately.' The Foreign Secretary smiled glumly, though there was a snuff-pinch of pleasure in his gloom because he considered he must have discomforted Aubrey. 'Is there anything, anything at all?'

Aubrey cleared his throat. 'NATO naval units are too far from the area to intercept. The Soviet government wish to apologise to us by repairing the damage they have inflicted. I have one agent-in-place in the Pechenga district. He is a grocer. I do not have a satellite-mounted laser beam whereby I can secretly and silently destroy half of the Red Banner Fleet— therefore, Minister, I am inclined to conclude that there is very little I can effectively do to secure the secrecy of "Leopard" and the remainder of the sensitive equipment aboard HMS *Proteus*.'

'Very well,' the Secretary of State said tightly, 'I will inform the PM of the state of play, and recommend that we have only the diplomatic alternative.' Again, he picked up the receiver and placed it to his ear.

'Unless,' Aubrey began, amazed at his empty temerity and observing his own words as if spoken by another; and that other a pompous ass without sincerity or resolution. 'Unless we can get one man into the naval dockyard at Pechenga or wherever, with a brief to destroy the "Leopard" equipment before the Soviets have time to inspect it.'

Aubrey was intensely aware of the eager, then disbelieving gazes of Cunningham and the Foreign Secretary. But, he told himself, attempting to justify what some obscure part of his mind or imagination had prompted him to utter, the whole capture of *Proteus* was the work of little more than one man, in the final analysis. Why not the reverse, then? The question echoed in his mind, but no answer appeared. Not so much as the first whisper of an answer. He asked himself a second, perhaps more pressing question.

Where the blazes was Hyde, and where the devil was Quin?

Kendal was asleep and windy. At one set of traffic lights, a board advertising ice cream outside a newsagent's shop, where the lights were on within as the proprietor marked up the morning editions for delivery, blew over in a gust, noisily startling the girl who was dozing in the passenger seat. Hyde had watched her face in repose from time to time since they left the M6. Her lips pouted, still greasy from her meal, and her features were pale, small and colourless. Obscurely, he felt responsible for her. She had passed from being the object of a search, the key to a security problem, into a chrysalis stage where she was almost a person, with human rights and human demands upon his time and energies. She hovered, waiting to be born into his emotional world. He did not welcome the change. It complicated matters. It was a pity he seemed to understand her. It would have been easier had she been a replica of her Left-wing, feminist friend Sara, whom he could have comfortably disliked.

He paused on the outskirts of Kendal and waited, but no cars approached in his mirror or passed him. He relaxed until they passed through Staveley and turned west on the main Windermere road. Headlights followed him out of the village, keeping behind him for almost two miles before turning off down a narrow track. He discovered himself sweating with relief the instant the headlights disappeared. Like a cat being woken by a tension in its owner, the girl stirred and sat up.

'Anything wrong?'

'Nothing. Go back to sleep.'

'I'm not tired any more.'

'Great. Pity you can't drive.'

The girl subsided into a sullen silence. There were people on the streets of Windermere, standing at bus stops, walking with bent heads beneath black hoods of umbrellas in the misty drizzle that clung to the town. The roof of a train gleamed darkly in the lights of the station, which lay below the main road.

By the time they were on the outskirts of Windermere again, the dog-leg of the long ribbon of the lake lay to their left, its further shore tree-clad, wreathed with a chill mist, its steep sides buttressing the low cloud that was just turning from black to grey. It was a slow, wintry, unwelcome dawn as they crossed Trout Beck, heading for Ambleside.

'I reckon Wordsworth lived in Croydon and made it all up,' he remarked. 'He never said it was always pissing with rain while he was having his visions of nature.'

'You have no soul,' the girl replied lightly. She seemed to warm herself at humour as at a small fire. He looked at her. She glanced away.

'It's all right,' he offered, 'I'm not about to pull the car into the side and take advantage of you.'

The girl did not reply. A tinge of colour in her cheeks, but no other reaction. He glanced at her from time to time, but she continued to gaze out of the side window, watching the far shore of Windermere slide past, the cramped, heavy firs crowding down to the water like a herd or an army, then giving way to damp, grassy outcrops, almost colourless under the low cloud cover. The land climbed away on his side of the car above the tree-line to bare-sided, long-backed hills, scalily wet and monstrously slumbering. Ambleside was shiny in its hollow between the hills and the grey water.

He pulled into a lay-by overlooking the northern end of the lake, just south of the town, and turned to the girl.

'Where to now, sweetheart? I've driven as far as Ambleside on trust, now where?'

She got out of the car without replying, and walked to the edge of the lay-by. Hyde followed her. She turned and looked up at him. She appeared to be entertaining another bout of distrust, even fear of him. She shook her head, and looked away towards the perspective of the long lake stretching away south. Water and sky merged no more than a couple of miles from them into a non-existence. Hyde found the scene extraordinarily depressing. He touched her shoulder, but she shook his hand away.

'You *have* to trust me,' he said.

'I know!' she almost wailed, so that he wondered whether she might not be psychologically disturbed. She certainly seemed neurotically suspicious. 'I – can't . . .'

Anger welled up in him. Stupid little bitch. He bellowed at her: 'You're wasting my bloody time, girlie! I don't know what's the bloody matter with you, or what the hell the world could have done to make you act like this – but I'm interested in what happens to a hundred blokes at the bottom of the sea relying on your old man's invention!'

In the silence that followed, he heard the water lapping gently out of sight below the verge of the lay-by, some water bird calling, the hum of a generator from somewhere behind them, the noise of the chain-saw from the trees on the far shore, and her quiet sobbing. Then she spoke without turning to him.

'You're a bloody shit, you are.' Then, as if intending to be both more precise and younger, she added, 'A bully.'

'Sorry.' He began to consider that Mrs Quin was the strongest member of the family, and felt a preconceived anxiety about the girl's father, and his similarity to his daughter. He found her, at that moment at least, too helpless to be a sympathetic figure.

'It's a cottage, off the road between Ambleside and Coniston. Less than half an hour in the car. I'm ready to take you there now.'

The noise of the car startled him, appearing round a bend in the road that had masked its noise until it was almost upon them. His reaction was instinctive, but it revealed also the stretched state of his nerves. Before he assimilated the Renault and its trailing white-and-brown caravan and the two mild faces behind the windscreen, the pistol was in his hand, and beginning to move up and out into a straight-arm firing position. A moment later, it was behind his back again, being thrust back into the waistband of his corduroy trousers. But not before the girl, at least, had witnessed the tiny incident. She appeared terrified, hands picking around her face like pale bats.

'Don't be bloody stupid,' he told her, his hands shaking as he thrust them into his pockets, an inward voice cursing his jumpiness. 'What do you think it is, a bloody game?'

She hurried past him towards the car.

'What's the time?'

'Eight-thirty.'

'The blip's stopped moving and the signal strength is growing. Listen.'

'All right, turn it down. That means the car's stopped somewhere, less than a couple of miles up the road.'

'Great. Stop at the next phone box, and we can call Petrunin.'

'And sit around all day waiting for him to get out of Manchester, I suppose? Marvellous!'

'Don't grumble. With a bit of luck we've got Hyde, the girl, and her father. Ah, there's a phone box. Pull off the road.'

'Yes?' Ardenyev prevented an anticipatory grin from appearing on his lips, until Lev Balan nodded and rubbed his hand through his thick dark hair with tiredness and relief. 'Great!' Ardenyev hugged Balan, laughing, feeling the man's helmet digging painfully into his ribs as Balan held it under his arm. 'Great! We can go?'

'Any time you like. My boys are knackered, by the way – not that it'll worry you.' Balan's answering grin was like a weather crack opening in seamed grey rock. Only then did Ardenyev really look at him, and fully perceive the man's weariness.

'Sorry. Tell them – tell them when we get back to Pechenga, we'll have the biggest piss-up they've ever seen. On me!'

'You've done it now. You're on.'

'Tow lines, too?' Ardenyev asked eagerly, surprised at his own child-like enthusiasm. Again, Balan nodded, his cigarette now pressed between his lips, in the corner of

217

his mouth. He looked dishevelled, unkempt, and rather disreputable. Insubordinate, too. 'Great. What about buoyancy?'

'We've got the bags on. Just sufficient to keep you at snorkel depth for towing. Any fine adjustments we'll make when you take her up. Then we'll do some more fine-tuning in the outer basin at Pechenga, before you dock. Assuming you can drive this bloody thing, of course!'

Ardenyev indicated the skeleton crew of Soviet ratings in the control room. 'All volunteers,' he said wryly. 'They can drive it, I'm quite sure.'

'Just in case, I'm on my way back outside – to watch the disaster from there. Good luck.'

'And you. See you in Pechenga. Take care.'

Balan walked wearily back through the aft section of the *Proteus* to the stern escape chamber. He strapped his auxiliary air tank to his back, requiring it until he could be recoupled to the hoses outside, and climbed through the lower hatch. He flooded the chamber, and opened the upper hatch, climbed the ladder and floated out into the darkness. His legs felt heavy, not merely because of his boots but because of the surpassing weariness that had invested itself in every part of his body. He waddled slowly and clumsily down the whale's back of the submarine, arms waving like some celluloid ghoul, or as if in imitation of one of the cosmonauts space-walking. He was bone-weary, he decided. Another half-hour's working and one of them might have made some small, fatal mistake. Any one of the cables, the jagged edges, the cutters could have injured or killed any of them.

Another underwater cosmonaut, looking ridiculous in a way that never failed to amuse Balan, came towards him from the upright, aircraft's tailplane of the rudder, almost staggering with the resistance of the heavy air hoses. The two men patted each other and clung together like the automatons on a musical box, then Balan turned his back and the hoses were fitted. A moment of breath-holding, then the rush of the air mixture, putting pressure on his ears and face, then the auxiliary tank was in his hands. He looked at it, grinned, and heaved it over the side of the submarine. It floated away down into the darkness.

Balan inspected his work once more. The stern of the *Proteus*, in the hard light of the lamps, was a mess, but it was a mess of which he felt justifiably proud. The rudder and the hydroplanes had been patched with a skin of metal, or their plates twisted back into shape and form by use of the hammer, the rivet-gun, the welding and cutting torches. Scarred, twisted, cracked metal, blackened and buckled. The propeller had not been repaired, merely cleared of the entangling, choking seaweed of the steel cables from the MIRV torpedo. Balan thought the shaft might be out of true, but that was Pechenga's worry not his. Then, masking the operation scars along the side of the hull, where the ballast tanks had been ruptured and the outer hull of the *Proteus* damaged, a lazily flapping, transparent growth idled in the currents moving across the ledge, like the attachment of a giant, translucent jellyfish to the submarine. Buoyancy bags, ready to be inflated when Ardenyev gave the order to blow tanks, they would serve in place of the unrepaired ballast tanks at the stern of the submarine, giving it a workable approximation to its normal buoyancy control.

Balan was proud of what amounted to almost ten hours' work on the British submarine. The work had been as dispassionately carried out as always by himself and his team. Unlike Ardenyev, there was no pleasure at the meaning of the task and its completion. It was merely a job well done, a task completed successfully. The nature of the submarine, its nationality, had no meaning for Balan.

He spoke into his headset. 'Right, you lot, clear away. Our gallant, heroic captain is going to take this tub to the top, and I don't want anyone hurt in the process!'

'I heard that,' Ardenyev said in his ear, slightly more distant than the laughter that soughed in his helmet from some of his team. 'I've been in contact with *Kiev* and *Karpaty*. Ready when you are.'

'Okay. I'm clearing the slaves from the hull now. I'll get back to you.'

Balan took hold of his air hoses in one hand, checking that they did not snag anywhere and trailed away across the ledge to the pumps and the generator. Then he turned clumsily but surely, and began climbing down the light steel ladder that leant against the port hydroplane, attached by small magnets. He lowered his air lines gingerly to one side of him as he climbed tiredly down to the surface of the ledge. The crewman who had attached his lines came after him. They were the last to descend, and when they stood together at the bottom of the ladder, Balan and the other diver hefted the ladder between them, and they trudged through the restless, distressed silt to where the arc lamps had been re-sited near the generators and the sleds on which they had brought down their equipment. The small group of diving-suited figures who composed his team was gathered like nervous spectators beneath the bloom of the lights. Balan joined them, dropping the ladder on to one of the sleds and securing it before he spoke again to Ardenyev.

'Okay, chief – you can make your attempt on the world rate of ascent record now. We're safely out of the way!'

'Thanks, Lev. Don't forget our piss-up in Pechenga – if you're not all too tired, that is!'

There was a murmur of protest and abuse at the remark. Balan was almost prepared to admit his tiredness, but there were certain fictions that had to be preserved, whatever the cost; one of them being the indestructibility, the immortality of salvage men.

'We won't forget. You just bring your wallet.' The banter was required, expected, all of them were recruiting-poster figures, without separate identity, without reality. Living their own fictions; heroes. Silly, silly –

'I will. Okay, here we go.'

Balan studied the submarine, partly in shadow now, the light of the arc lamps casting deep gloomy patches over their repair work, rendering it somehow shabby and inadequate. The *Proteus* looked half-built, half-destroyed. He did not attend to Ardenyev's orders, still coming through the headset, presumably for his benefit, until he heard 'Blow tanks!' and the submarine – after a moment in which nothing seemed to happen – shifted under the discharge of sea water from her ballast tanks, and then the jellyfish bags began to bloom and roll and fold and inflate. Balan felt the new currents of the submarine's movement and the discharged water. They could feel the hull grinding

220

against the ledge through their boots; the stern of the submarine seemed to be lifting slightly higher than the bow. It would need adjustment. The bow itself was in darkness, where the tow-lines were attached. They'd have to be inspected, too.

Someone cheered in his headset, making him wince. One of the younger men, he supposed. There were sighs of pleasure and relief, though, like a persistent breeze; noises that were their right.

The *Proteus*, still a little bow-heavy, drifted up and away from them, out of the boiling cloud of silt, becoming a great shadow overhead, just beyond the arc lamps, then a dimmer shape, then almost nothing as it ascended the twenty fathoms to the surface. The bags round its stern like nappies, he thought. Around its bum.

'Come on, you lot. The volume on those bags is going to have to be changed for a starter! Don't waste time, get organised!'

Theatrically, the arc lamps began flicking off, leaving them in a sudden darkness, where their helmet lamps and hand-lamps glowed like aquatic fireflies. Above them, as they began climbing on to their sleds, the *Proteus* stopped at snorkel depth and waited for them.

'Well done, Hyde— excellent work, excellent!' Aubrey effusive, his tiredness gone in a moment, if only briefly. Hyde had Quin, beyond all reasonable expectation, and at this critical moment. Their first real piece of luck— a change of luck? They needed it. 'Well done. Bring him directly to London. You'd better let me arrange for a helicopter from the Cumbria force to pick you up. I want Quin here as soon as possible— What? What do you mean?'

Hyde's voice had dropped to barely more than a whisper, something conspiratorial. Aubrey swivelled in his seat as if in response to its tone, turning his back on the underground room and its occupants. Pyott and Clark, attentive to his enthusiasm at the call that had been put through, now remained some yards away. Clark was making some point about the *Proteus*, his finger tracing across a large-scale cutaway plan of the submarine which Aubrey had had brought down from the second floor of the Admiralty.

'Back-up's here,' he heard Clark saying. 'Right out of the way – ' Then he was attending to Hyde's quiet voice.

'He's in a bad way, Mr Aubrey. Out in the garden now, blowing his nose a lot and upsetting his daughter. Can you hear me all right?'

'Yes, Hyde, yes,' Aubrey replied impatiently. 'What do you mean, *a bad way*?'

'One of those who can't take isolation, even if he is a loner,' Hyde replied flatly, without sympathy. 'He's been up here for weeks, almost a week on his own. And when the two of them were here together, I reckon they just wore each other down with mutual nerves. Quin's a neurotic bloke, anyway.'

'Spare me the psychology, Hyde.'

'You have to understand him,' Hyde said in exasperation. 'He doesn't want to come back, he's scared stiff of his own shadow, he doesn't seem to care about the *Proteus* – all our fault, apparently.'

'That, at least, is true.'

'I've spent hours talking to him. I can't get through to him. He'll come back because he's scared not to, and because he thinks the opposition may have followed us here – '

'Have they?'

'No. But now we've found him, he thinks it'll all start up again, and he wants to hide. I don't want him scared off by a helicopter. He'll come back with me, or not at all.'

'What about the girl?'

'She's the one who's just about persuaded him to trust me. *I* have to deliver him somewhere safe.'

'I didn't mean that. What will you do with her?'

'She'll stay here. Either that, or I'll put her on a train.'

'I haven't time to waste, Hyde. Is he fit to work?'

'No.'

'Then he'll have to work in an unfit state. Very well. Drive back to Manchester. You and he can fly down from there. I'll arrange it. *You* can hold his hand.'

'Yes, Mr Aubrey.'

'And– once again, well done. Keep him happy, promise him anything – but he must be here this evening, and ready to work!'

222

Aubrey put down the receiver, and stood up, the purposefulness of his movements keeping doubt at bay. He had dozed lightly and fitfully on the narrow camp bed in the adjoining cupboard-like room without windows. The darkness had seemed close and foetid, and the light and noise under the door had drawn him back into the underground operations room. Cold water had restored a semblance of wakefulness, and Hyde's message had completed the work of reinvigoration.

'Well?' Giles Pyott asked, turning from the chart pinned to a board, resting on an easel. 'What news?'

'Hyde has found Quin.'

'Thank God! Where is he?'

'Lake District – near Coniston Water, I gather.'

'He's been there all the time?'

'Apparently. Rented a cottage through an agency.'

'Can he get here today?' Clark asked more purposefully.

'He can. Hyde says that the man is in a state close to nervous exhaustion.' Aubrey shrugged his shoulders. 'I don't know how that complicates matters. Better have a doctor to look at him, I suppose. It really is too bad – '

'Hell, can he *work*?'

'Whether or not, he will work.' He indicated the drawing of the *Proteus*. 'He has to do something about this, after all. Doesn't he?'

It was almost three before Quin was finally ready to depart. His luggage, which consisted of one small suitcase and an overcoat, had been a means of delaying his departure. He had driven Hyde to the edge of rage again and again, and then capitulated, afraid of the Australian in a more immediate way than of the other figures and dangers that crowded his imagination. Aubrey had telephoned the cottage at noon, and had been frustrated and angered at the further delay. After that, Hyde had handled Quin like unstable explosive; cajolement and masked threat had eventually subdued him.

He stood now at the door of the whitewashed cottage, hesitant while Hyde carried the suitcase to the TR7. Tricia Quin was at his side like a crutch, touching his arm, trying to smile him into complacency. In some obscure and

223

unexpected way, she had strengthened during the day, adopting much of Hyde's attitude and many of his arguments. It was as if she had adopted the plight of the *Proteus* as a charitable cause worthy of contribution; or perhaps she sensed her father needed help, that the greatest danger to his health lay in his present solitary surroundings. Hyde wondered what Quin would have made of the Outback, even the dead centre of Australia. The unnerving silence *was* audible there. The Lake District hummed and buzzed with life, by comparison.

He looked away from Quin and his daughter, towards the stretch of water that was The Tarns, and then at the road and the land falling away, down from Black Fell behind him through the firs towards Coniston Water two miles away. The land pressed in upon the cottage, and Hyde admitted a claustrophobic isolation so different from the Australian hinterland. Perhaps it wasn't surprising Quin couldn't take it after all, staying in that cottage and its garden for a week without seeing another soul after his daughter left. They'd quarrelled about her going to see her mother, apparently. That might have set him off, created his sense of abandonment amid danger.

Hyde shrugged, and opened the boot. The weather was windier now, moving the low cloud but breaking it up, too. Gleams, fitful and unoptimistic, of blue sky; a hazy light through the clouds. It had, at least, stopped drizzling.

The bullet whined away off the yellow boot before the noise of the gunshot reached him. He stared at his hand. The bullet had furrowed across the back of it, exposing the flesh. An open-lipped graze which still had not begun to hurt, matching the furrowed scar on the boot lid. He looked stupidly around him.

A second shot then, chipping pebble-dash from the wall of the cottage two feet or so from Quin's head. His frightened, agape features, the girl's quicker, more alert panic, her hands dragging at her father's arm, the shrouded hills, the distant dark trees – he took in each distinct impression in the moment that he heard the heavy report of the rifle, and then the pain in his hand began, prompting him like a signal. He began running for the door of the cottage.

Part Three

Plumber

Ten: RESCUE?

'What are they waiting for? Why don't they *do* something?' Quin's voice was plaintive, fearful; yet the words sounded strangely irritated, as if the men outside had disappointed him.

'You've seen the bloody cowboy films, haven't you?' Hyde replied, almost snarling, weary of Quin's unabated nerves. 'The lynch-mob always waits for dark.' The man seemed to possess an infinite capacity to remain on edge, and his emotions rubbed against Hyde's attempts to evolve a solution to their situation like sandpaper against skin.

'Why *are* they waiting?' Tricia Quin asked in studiedly calm tone , sitting near him on the floor beneath the cottage window.

Hyde turned to her. 'Petrunin can't be here yet.'

'Who?'

'The bloke who chased us – the big cheese. He's got a face everyone will have a copy of. Must be hard to get out of Manchester. They'll be waiting for orders.'

'How many of them do you think there are?'

Hyde watched Quin as he listened to the girl. The man was sitting in a slumped, self-pitying posture with his back against the wall, near the settee with its stained stretch covers. Hyde disliked Quin intensely. The man got on his nerves. He was a pain in the backside. He was going to be useless to Aubrey, even if he delivered him.

'Two, maybe three.'

'You don't think they might try something before dark?'

'Why? They'll assume I'm armed, they know I'm a professional, just like them. They're not going to volunteer to get their balls blown off. Your dad's here, and he isn't going anywhere.'

She studied her father, then looked away from him.

'What about your people? This man Aubrey?'

'When we don't turn up in Manchester, he'll worry. He knows where we are.'

227

'Will he worry in time?'

'That's what I'm worrying about.' He smiled, and studied her face. 'How are you?'

'I'm all right.' She avoided looking at her father.

'What are you going to do?' Quin asked.

'For Christ's sake, stop moaning!'

'It's your fault – you brought them here! This is just what I tried to avoid – what I came here to get away from,' Quin persisted. Hyde perceived deep and genuine and abiding fears, disguising themselves in self-pity. He could almost feel sorry for Quin; might have done so, had their situation at that moment been less acute. And had Quin's voice been less insistent, less whining. 'I knew I couldn't be adequately protected, that no one took my fears seriously. and now look what's happened – they're out there, the very people I tried to avoid. And *you* – you brought them here. You've as good as handed me to them on a plate!'

'All right. So they stuck a bleeper under the car. Sorry.'

'That won't do us any good.'

'Shut up! It's *your* bloody fault we're all stuck here.'

'Leave him alone,' Tricia Quin pleaded softly.

'All right. Look, once it's dark, I can try to get to a telephone that hasn't had its wires cut. But I'm not walking out there just at the moment. He'll have to sit it out, just like us.'

'As long as nothing happens to him.'

'It won't. Petrunin's in a corner himself. It's a stalemate. Nothing's going to happen to Dad – unless I break his bloody neck for him!'

Quin scowled like a child sulking. Hyde looked at his watch. Just after three. Patience, patience, he instructed himself. Aubrey has got to catch on soon.

He wondered, without letting the thought tinge the bland expression on his features, whether Petrunin's orders might not have changed because of the capture of the submarine by the Russians. The death of Quin, rather than his capture, might be a satisfactory conclusion to the operation.

It was hard to discard the thought, once he had admitted it. It was unlikely, but possible. Of his own death, he did not think. That, he had considered almost as he closed the cottage door behind him after he had run from the car, would be inevitable whether Petrunin wanted Quin alive or dead. He looked at his hand, wrapped in his handkerchief. His gun made an uncomfortable, pressing lump against the small of his back. It was not entirely a stalemate, it merely gave that impression. Petrunin wanted Quin badly. Petrunin was finished in the UK anyway, after this. When he went, he'd want Quin with him. As soon as it was dark, he'd come for him.

'Ethan, it is not an old man's vanity, or sense of hurt pride – or even senility. I am asking a serious question. Could someone get into Pechenga and destroy "Leopard" before the Russians can examine or dismantle it?'

'You're crazy, Mr Aubrey. In twenty-four hours the Russians will have that submarine turned around and on her way. There's no time to do anything.'

'I'm not sure about that.' Aubrey looked up from the narrow camp bed where he sat perched like a tired, dishevelled prisoner under the hard strip-lighting of the cupboard-like room. Clark leaned against the door, dressed like a golfer in sweater and slacks. Clark's increasing informality of dress during the past days had been a badge of defeat and of defeatism. Aubrey felt tired, directionless; yet at the same time he was possessed by the quick seductive glamour of a counter-operation. 'I'm not sure about that,' he repeated.

'You don't even know it's Pechenga,' Clark persisted.

'Satellite and Nimrod suggest it might be. There are signs of what might be preparations for *Proteus*'s arrival at Pechenga, but not at Murmansk.' Aubrey rubbed his hands together in a washing motion. To Clark the activity suggested a pretended, mocking humility. The room was coffin-like, stale and dead, and pressed in on him uncomfortably.

'Maybe. Look, these quick-burn operations always look good on paper. Our intelligence is *nil*, Mr. Aubrey, and there's no time or capacity for back-up. Face facts – the Russians have *Proteus* on their ground, on their terms. They'll give her back.'

'I realise that,' Aubrey snapped, 'but I am not prepared

229

simply to wait until she is handed back like a toy that no longer works.'

'Listen, Mr Aubrey,' Clark began angrily, turning from the door which he had been facing as Aubrey spoke, as if to hide the expression on his face, 'I can't give you what you want. I don't know enough about "Leopard" to be able to tell you how to destroy it effectively without blowing up the damn boat, too! The Russians may have their superman in Ardenyev, but don't put the rôle on to me. I can't help you.'

'Someone at Plessey, then,' Aubrey murmured disparagingly.

'You need Quin.'

'I realise that. If I get you Quin, can you do the job?'

'What?'

'I said – if I get you Quin, will you do the job? *Can* you do the job?'

'Job?'

'Don't be dense, dear boy. You would have to do it. You are familiar with the whole operation, you are familiar with the equipment, you are in naval intelligence, you have a great deal of field experience. Who else would I consider sending?'

'One man?'

'One particular man, yes.'

'And all I have to do is get into Pechenga, board the *Proteus*, destroy the equipment, and get out again with no one any the wiser?' Clark raised his hands in the air. 'You've really flipped, Mr Aubrey. It can't be done.'

'It must be attempted.'

'I'm not on your staff.'

'I'm sure I can arrange your temporary assignment.'

'There's no time.'

'We must *try*!'

'So where's Quin? Your house of cards falls down without him.'

Aubrey's face became saturnine. 'I don't know. Hyde should have arrived at Manchester airport by now. He has not done so.'

'Then he's in trouble.'

'You think so?'

Clark paced the tiny cubicle. 'You've spent all your time

dreaming up this crazy scheme instead of worrying about realities. Your guy has to be in trouble, and you haven't even given him a thought!'

Aubrey's face registered an expression of rage, directed at Clark. Then, in admission, his look turned inwards. He had been taking an afternoon nap of the intellect. Clark was perfectly correct. He had ignored Hyde, and Hyde must now be in trouble. He clenched his fists in his lap, then got up and opened the door.

'OS map of the Coniston Water area!' he shouted into the underground room, directing the order at every one of its occupants. Pyott looked up, startled, and then reached for a telephone. 'Quickly!' He slammed the door and looked steadily at Clark. 'You are right. I have been foolishly, dangerously remiss. But if we get Quin here, we shall talk again. You are not off the hook, Ethan!'

'Neither are your guy and Quin.'

The *Proteus* reached a moment of equilibrium after her seeming rush from snorkel depth to the surface, and then the motion of the waves began to affect her. Ardenyev watched as the hatch above them slid back. Water dripped on him and Lloyd and the armed guard, and then the platform of the bridge was raised electronically until their heads rose above the fin of the submarine. The *Proteus* rolled gently in the swell of the outer harbour of Pechenga, the adjusted buoyancy bags at the stern maintaining her at the correct depth but impairing her stability.

Ardenyev smiled, and waved an arm towards the low shoreline.

'Welcome to the Soviet Union, Commander Lloyd.'

Rain whipped into their faces, and fuzzy lights glowed through the dark late afternoon. Low submarine pens lay ahead of them, beyond the harbour wall with its guard towers and its anti-submarine net. The rain was chilly, mingled with sleet which numbed the side of Lloyd's face as he studied the scene with the hunched shoulders of a prisoner. The rescue ship *Karpaty* made cautious headway, still towing the *Proteus*. He turned to look back aft of the sail. Huge jellyfish bags surrounded the stern of the submarine like splints on a damaged limb. He could make out, through the white-edged spray and the driving rain, the scars and the rough repairs that had been affected beneath the surface by the rescue team. The bow of the *Proteus* was still angled slightly below the horizontal because of the crudity of measurement employed in inflating the bags. A bow-wave surged along the forward deck as Lloyd turned his gaze back towards Pechenga. The *Karpaty* had passed through the gap in the harbour wall where the net had been swung electronically away to allow her access, and *Proteus* was slipping, in an almost lurching, ungainly fashion between the towers on the wall. Lloyd could see faces looking from the towers; they all seemed to be grinning, and an arm waved. The sight created a sense of humiliation in him.

Ardenyev was speaking.

'I'm sorry – you were saying?' he said, indulging his sense of defeat and self-blame. He had made mistakes, fatal ones for 'Leopard'. Because the situation was so unreal, and its consequences dangerous only for a lump of inoperable equipment in the bowels of his vessel, his mind was more keenly aware of errors of judgement and tactics. He should not have been so slow in realising their danger, he should not have settled on the bottom. There seemed no limit to the catalogue of blame.

'I intrude upon your self-examination?' Ardenyev asked lightly. 'But there is no danger. No cause for alarm.'

'That's the most unreal thing of all, isn't it?' Lloyd replied.

Ardenyev ignored the reply. 'As I was saying, we will have the submarine docked in two or three hours. Of course, we will not delay you more than is necessary. Your reactor will not be run down, you will be docked in a wet dock – we can manage the repairs quite adequately without a dry dock – and you will be ready to sail in no more than forty-eight hours. That I promise you.'

'You would be able to make such a promise, of course,' Lloyd replied acidly, 'since the damage to my ship was quite precisely calculated, no doubt.'

'I'm sorry – ?'

'Forget it. It was all an accident, a most unfortunate accident.'

'Of course.'

The swell was hardly discernible inside the harbour wall. Lloyd was uncomfortably aware, however, of the forward motion of the submarine and of the other vessels in the harbour basin. Pechenga was unsubstantial still, masked by the murk and the flying rain and sleet and remained as unreal as the satellite pictures he had seen of it and of dozens of other Soviet naval ports, but the big ships were real, uncomfortably so. Two 'Kara'-class cruisers at anchor, one half-repainted. Three or four destroyers, like a display of toys, small and grey and bristling with aerials and radar dishes and guns. Frigates, a big helicopter cruiser, two intelligence ships festooned with electronic detection and surveillance equipment. A submarine support ship, minesweepers, ocean tugs, tankers. The sight, the numbers, overawed him, ridiculing Portsmouth, Plymouth, Faslane, every naval port and dockyard in the UK. It was like going back into the past, except for the threatening, evident modernity of these vessels, to some great review of the fleet at Spithead between the two world wars, or before the Great War. The harbour at Pechenga, a satellite port for Murmansk, daunted Lloyd. He felt completely and utterly entrapped.

The submarine pens, mere nest-holes in the concrete at this distance, winked with lights ahead of the *Karpaty*. One of those small black holes would swallow his vessel, contain it until people like this Russian on his bridge said they could leave, gave them permission. He shrugged hopelessly.

'You're impressed?' Ardenyev asked.

'As long as they're not all cardboard mock-ups, yes.'

'They're not.' Lloyd looked at Ardenyev. The man seemed unenthusiastic about the conversation he had begun.

'So familiar as to be boring?' he asked.

'What? Oh, this. I was just thinking what a dull town Pechenga is.'

'I see.'

'I doubt it.' They slid beneath the lee of a cruiser. Crewmen leaned over the rails, looking down at the British submarine, waving their caps, yelling indistinguishable words and greetings. Ardenyev watched them as he might have observed the behaviour of monkeys at a zoo. 'The brothels are quite dreadful,' he continued. 'All right for conscripts, but not for the likes of you and me. A good job you will not be allowed ashore. The casualty rate would be staggering. Quite unacceptable to the Admiralty.'

'You seem to have run out of steam,' Lloyd remarked.

'What? Oh, perhaps.' Ardenyev brushed a hand through his wet hair, and assayed a tired grin. His waving arms indicated the whole bulk of the *Proteus*. 'It's over for me. The dull time after excitement. I am feeling sorry for myself. Forgive my bad manners.'

They were slowing now. *Karpaty* seemed to lag, and they began to overtake her in a snail-like pursuit, until the *Proteus* herself came to a stop. Tiny figures emerged from the forward hatch and scuttled along the slippery, gleaming deck, casting off the tow-lines swiftly and expertly. A hard-lit submarine pen gaped before them. *Proteus* began to edge towards the open gates of the pen on her intact docking propeller, the 'egg-beater' located forward of the main propeller and retracted when not in use. Lloyd shuddered.

'As soon as we dock, I must leave you to make my report,' Ardenyev murmured. Lloyd ignored him, watching his vessel slide forward into the maw of the submarine pen. Down the line of pens, men had stopped work to watch. The sterns of Soviet submarines were visible through the open gates of other pens, but Lloyd, after one quick, self-concious glance, returned his gaze to the bow of the *Proteus*. She stopped again, and men scrambled over the deck, attaching the hawsers whereby she could be winched into the pen, An order was given, the deck was cleared again, and then the winches picked up the slack, measured the bulk of the submarine and began to pull her forward.

Each moment was marked by a further surrender to circumstances. Lloyd felt an emotional pain that was as acute as a physical injury. The hull of the *Proteus* seemed marked like a ruler, measuring off her entry into the pen. Hard lights gleamed in the roof. The pen contained the torpedo tubes, the forward hatch, the forward hydroplanes, then the fin itself. *Proteus* was half-swallowed.

There was cheering from the dockyard workers lining the concrete walks on either side of the water, which sickened and enraged him. Lloyd could see the first teams of men with the props that would support the hull, eager to begin berthing the *Proteus*.

Then Ardenyev's hand was on his shoulder, and he was shouting above the echo of the cheering bouncing back from steel and concrete.

'I'm sorry, my friend! You have lost!'

Lloyd shook his head, not to deny but to admit defeat. *Proteus* was slowing as orders were passed from the officer in charge of the docking procedure to the winch operators. Even the motion of his vessel was out of his control. He felt utterly humiliated. Strangely, there was an air of dejection about Ardenyev, too, amid the coarse cheers and their magnified, inhuman echoes.

A mist was beginning to rise in the dusk. The wind had dropped to an occasional breeze which stirred the tendrils and shrouds of grey. The landscape was subsiding into darkness, the hills already no more than smudges, the trees merely dark, crayon shadings. Hyde saw the mist as a final irony. It cloaked Petrunin now, not any attempt on his part to reach a telephone. Petrunin had arrived too early, just before six, announcing his presence with a deadline for Hyde's surrender. Yet in another sense he was belated. Hyde had already, slowly and reluctantly and with an inward fury, decided he could not leave the girl and her father exposed to capture, and there was no way the three of them could get safely away from the cottage. He had to make the difficult, even repellent assumption that they would be safer, if only because they would be alive and unharmed, in surrender than resistance. Hope springs eternal was a difficult, and unavoidable, consolation. He had admitted to himself that they were successfully trapped even before Petrunin reiterated that simple message through a loud-hailer.

Quin had rendered himself useless, like some piece of electrical equipment that possessed a safety curcuit. He had switched himself off like a kettle boiling too long. He was slumped where he had sat for hours, staring at his lap, sulking in silence. Even his danger no longer pricked him to complaint. The girl, moving only occasionally to check on her father's condition, had remained near Hyde. Their conversation had been desultory. Hyde had hardly bothered to alleviate the girl's fears, possessed by his own self-recriminations. The bug on the car, the bloody bug –

Then Petrunin was talking again. 'Why not attempt to reach a telephone, Mr Hyde?' his magnified, mechanical voice queried from behind a knoll a hundred yards or more from the cottage. Hyde was certain he could hear soft laughter from one of the others. 'This mist should hide your movements quite successfully.' Again the accompanying, sycophantic laughter, coarser now? Hyde could not be certain he was not mocking himself, imagining the amusement. Petrunin was enjoying himself. Was he covering an approach, distracting them? 'The problem is, your friends would not be safe while you were away. Can the girl use a gun? Can her father?'

'Fuck off,' Hyde replied with a whispered intensity. The girl touched his arm, making him start.

'Give me the gun. Why don't you try to get out?'

'I gave that idea up hours ago, girlie. We're right in the shit, and bloody Lenin out there knows it.'

'Won't your people be looking for us?'

'I bloody hope so! But, he knows that, too. He won't wait much longer now.'

'Your time is up,' Petrunin announced, as if on cue. Hyde grinned mirthlessly. 'Please show yourselves at the door. Throw your gun out first, please. We have night-sights. No movements you make will be missed, I assure you.'

'The trouble with bloody desk men when they get in the field is they're so bloody gabby.' He looked at the shadowy outline of Quin across the room, then at the girl. His hand was clenched around the butt of the Heckler & Koch pistol, and it would take one movement to smash the window and open fire. Useless to try; but in another, more febrile way, satisfying to do so. Bang, bang, he recited to himself, pointing the gun into the room as if taking aim. Bloody bang, bang, and these two would be dead, or wounded. 'Nowhere to go, nothing to do,' he announced aloud.

'You can't – ' the girl began.

'I'm bored with sitting on my bum,' he said. 'Besides, when the shooting starts, someone else always gets hurt. It's in the rules. Petrunin knows I won't risk your father or you, and *I* know I won't. Shitty, but true. Now, we have no chance. Later, who knows?' He stood up to one side of the window. It was open at the top, and he raised his voice to a shout. 'All right, Trotsky – we're coming out. We've both seen this bloody film before!'

'No cavalry, I'm afraid. Only Apaches,' Petrunin called back through the loud-hailer. Hyde tossed his head.

'I'll open the door and chuck my gun out. Then Mr Quin will come out first.'

'Very well. Please do not delay '

Quin was sitting upright now, and seemed to have sidled towards one corner of the room. His white, featureless face seemed to accuse Hyde in the room's dusk. Hyde bumped the edge of the table as he moved towards him.

'No – ' Quin said feebly, putting his hands up in front of him, warding off Hyde like an evil presence.

'Sorry, mate. We don't have any choice. They're not going to do *you* any harm now, are they?' He reached down and pulled Quin roughly to his feet, embracing him as the man struggled halfheartedly. There was a mutuality of hatred and blame between them. Hyde sensed it in the tremble of Quin's arms.

He studied Quin's face. The man appeared as if he had been confined in some prison, with no hope of release or escape, for a long time. The prison had been his own mind, of his own making. No, Hyde corrected himself. The KGB had done that, created the stifling sense of the trap closing on him. And perhaps the DS, and even SIS and himself, should have been quicker, smarter, more thorough.

'We may have a chance if we go out now,' he said in a soothing, allaying voice. 'In here, we have none. You get hurt, Tricia gets hurt. I'm sorry, mate, but it's our only chance.'

'I don't *want* to – !' Quin almost wailed. 'They'll take me with them. It's not you they want, it's me!'

'I know that. For God's sake, I'm trying to help you!'

'I can't spend the rest of my life in Russia, heaven help me!'

'Better Red than dead,' Hyde offered, his shallow sympathy exhausted. Quin's fear and reluctance were now no more than irritants, slowing reaction, muddying thought. Quin would just have to accept his situation. Hyde no longer had time or energy to expend on his psychological condition.

'Now, as the patient said to the dentist as he grabbed his balls, "we're not going to hurt each other, are we?" Just wait until I give you the word, then walk slowly out of the door. Okay?' Quin slumped in resignation against Hyde. Hyde's mockery was expressed, incongruously, in a comforting tone of voice. 'A nice little plane ride across the Channel, then another ride to Moscow. You might even like it there. They'll like *you*, anyway.' He gripped Quin's arms as the man's body protested at his envisaged future. 'Nothing bad's going to happen. Just do as they say.'

He took Quin by one arm to the door, and opened it, keeping the scientist out of sight. He threw his gun in a high arc towards the knoll, away from his car so that it was easily visible.

'Excellent!' Petrunin confirmed. 'No other little toys?'

'I left my bloody death-ray in the car!'

'Very well. Come out, one at a time. Mr Quin to lead.'

'Right, off you go. Just walk straight towards the knoll. don't deviate, and don't run.'

Quin moaned. Immediately, the girl was at his side, holding his other arm. She shouted through the door.

'My father's not well. We're coming out together.' Without hesitation, she guided Quin through the open door. Hyde stood framed in the doorway for a moment, then he moved out into the dusk, his feet crunching on the gravel in front of the cottage. He raised his arms in the air, studying the knoll, waiting for the first head to appear. Unreality seized him, and he wanted to laugh. Captured by the KGB, in England! It was laughable, a joke for Queen Anne's Gate for years to come. Perhaps they'd use his urn on Aubrey's mantelpiece to knock their pipes out while

238

they giggled at the story of his demise. As Aubrey would have said, *It really was too bad* –

Petrunin came down the slope of the grassy knoll towards them, a second man following him, carrying a rifle. Quin and Tricia stopped, awaiting him. A third man moved out of the shadow beneath a stand of firs towards Hyde, his rifle bearing on its target. Hyde felt weak, and sick. Petrunin stopped to examine Quin as carefully and as unemotionally as he might have done a consignment that had been delivered to his door. He ignored the girl. The third man had reached Hyde, studied him warily, and then moved in to touch-search him. When he had finished, he spoke to Petrunin.

'He's clean.'

'Good.' Petrunin approached Hyde. He was smiling with confidence and success. He was a bigger, taller man than the Australian, and this increased his confidence almost to a swagger. He paused before Hyde, hands on hips, appraising him.

'I know I don't look like much,' Hyde offered, 'but it's the public spending cuts. They're going in for smaller spies.'

'Aubrey's man, of course? Mm, I don't think you are the cheerful colonial idiot you pretend. Not that it matters. Thank you for leading us to Mr Quin.'

'Not my pleasure.'

'Quite. Very well,' he said, addressing his two companions, 'let us not waste time.' He looked at Hyde. 'Just a wound, I think,' he said with surgical precision and lack of concern. 'This incident is already too – significant. We mustn't create an international event from it.' He stepped aside. 'We don't want him going anywhere. Both legs, I think.'

'No – !' the girl shouted, but one of the riflemen knocked her down, swiping the barrel of his gun sideways into her ribs. Hyde remained quite still, tensing himself to accept the pain. He lowered his hands to his sides. The marksman stepped forward – the third man had moved away, Petrunin was still appraising him with an intent curiosity – and raised the gun to his shoulder. Hyde felt the tremble begin in his left leg, and could not control it. Knee, shin, thigh, calf, foot, ankle –

His imagination made the skin on his legs crawl. Hyde tried to concentrate on only one of his legs, letting awareness of the other one become numb. The blood rushed in his ears like a howl of protest.

Then the helicopter. Loud enough at once in the silence to be apparent even to Hyde. Petrunin glanced up at the cool evening sky, then his head whipped round as he located the source of the noise. Red lights beneath a shadowy belly, the racket of the rotors yelling down into the hollow in which the cottage lay.

Hyde's thoughts came out of shock, out of their mesmerised concentration on his still quivering left leg, and prompted him towards Quin and the girl, who were huddled together. The girl was on her feet but almost doubled over with pain and fright. Then a pain wracked him, and he fell to his knees, groaning as if he had been shot. His whole body was trembling, and he could not move, merely grip his stomach and retch drily again and again.

The noise of the helicopter beat down on him, and he heard a voice through a loud-hailer, yelling the same kind of authoritative noises over and over. The helicopter's down-draught distressed his hair, inflated his windcheater, but he could not straighten up. He waited for the sound of firing, but there was none.

Eventually, he rolled over on to his side. He saw scattering figures running, and Quin and his daughter clinging together. Then he heard shots. One of the marksmen – he saw with a fierce delight that it was the one who had been ordered to maim him – crumpled near Quin and Tricia. Other figures moved into, merged with, the trees, and were gone. The police helicopter settled heavily on to the grass below the knoll, comfortingly large, noisily business-like. It was over.

The girl was kneeling over him, one hand pressed against her ribs.

'All right?'

He nodded. 'Just scared stiff. You?'

'Bruised.'

'How's your father?'

'Mr Hyde?' A shadow loomed over them. A policeman in denims and a combat jacket.

'Yes.'

'Are you hurt?'

'Only my manly pride.' Hyde stretched and sat up. He rubbed his hand almost without thinking through the girl's hair. She did not seem to resent his touch.

'We're to get you on a plane at Manchester as soon as we can,' the police officer informed him.

'Right. What about my car?'

'One of my men will drive it down.'

'I want to see my mother,' Tricia Quin announced.

'Your father's to go straight to London, Miss. Mr Aubrey's instructions,' he added by way of explanation to Hyde. 'He'll want to see you, no doubt, at the same time.'

'Get us to Manchester,' Hyde replied. 'We'll see, then.'

'I'm not going to London.'

'Okay, okay,' Hyde conceded. 'I'll take you to see Mummy as soon as we've got your dear old dad on the plane. All right?' The girl nodded firmly. 'Christ, why you spend your time worrying so much about them, I don't know!' He looked up at the police officer. 'Caught 'em?'

'I doubt it. We haven't the time to waste. Leave that up to the Cumbria constabulary. Come on – let's get moving.'

Hyde stood up. The girl immediately held his arm to steady him, unnecessarily.

'You're all bloody solicitation, Tricia,' Hyde observed. 'No wonder you get hurt all the time. People aren't worth it.' She saw that he was looking at her father as he spoke, and a wince of pain crossed her face. Misinterpreting the expression, he added: 'Your ribs okay?'

'Yes!' she snapped, and walked away from him. Hyde watched her go, and shrugged. Relief returned in a rush of emotions, and he exhaled noisily. It was over. The cavalry had arrived, with a loudhailer instead of a bugle. But they had arrived –

They allowed Quin five hours' sleep, under light sedation, before Aubrey had him woken. The doctor had examined him as soon as he had arrived at the Admiralty, and had pronounced him unfit for strain or effort, mental or

241

physical. Aubrey had thanked the doctor and dismissed him. He pondered whether Quin should be prescribed stimulants, and then reluctantly decided against this course. Aubrey suspected drugs, except in their interrogational usefulness. He wanted Quin completely and reliably rational. Quin was the lynchpin of the scheme that was increasingly obsessing him, it had prevented him from taking any sleep himself, it had made him impatient of Quin's rest and impatient during his first conversation with the man, so much so that Ethan Clark had intruded upon their conversation and eventually commandeered it. Aubrey, seething at Quin's weariness, his retreat from reality, his reluctance to consider the plight of his own invention, had left the Admiralty to walk for half an hour on Horse Guards, but the military statues and the mobility of the buildings had made him flee to the more agreeable atmosphere of St James's Park.

The park, across which people hurried at the beginning of a bright, windy day, offered him little solace. From the bridge, he could see, in an almost gilded white clarity, Buckingham Palace in one direction, Whitehall in the other. If he followed the path from the bridge, it would bring him to Birdcage Walk and Queen Anne's Gate and his own office. Shelley would bring him coffee and soothing information of other parts of the world; not Pechenga, not the place on that blown-up aerial photograph propped on an easel. The parade of government officials and office workers passing him composed a race to which he did not belong. His office was barred to him until this business was resolved.

He skirted the lake, back towards Whitehall. The sun was gilding the roofs, providing an unremarked beauty. Aubrey was profoundly doubtful whether Quin would be of the least use to them. He seemed a poor specimen, physically, emotionally. He certainly seemed inadequate to the role in which Aubrey wished to cast him.

One man, who is a grocer. A Harrier jet. The AWACS Nimrod at Farnborough which was used to give *Proteus* her sea trials with the 'Leopard' equipment. Eastoe and his crew, returned by now to RAF Kinloss, no more than two hours away by aircraft from Farnborough. And Clark.

And Quin. Miserable, whining, ungrateful, uncaring Quin. Aubrey clenched his hat more firmly, savagely in his hand, mis-shaping its brim with the rage he felt against Quin. It could work, but only with Quin. With Quin as he was, it was doomed.

Pyott and Clark were alone in what had once been the 'Chessboard Counter' operations room. Aubrey had stood-down all RN personnel, who would be briefed to run what had become, in his mind, a rescue rather than a destruction operation. He intended that 'Leopard' should be repaired and that *Proteus* make her escape, under cover of its anti-sonar, from Pechenga. The scheme seemed utterly unworkable to Clark and Pyott, and it had seemed so to him in the windy light of the park, between the gilded buildings. In this underground room, precisely because Quin had obviously been allowed to rest by Clark, it seemed only a little less ridiculous. An old man's fancy. He had code-named it 'Plumber'.

Clark's face expressed disappointment, beneath the surface of superiority. He had been proven right; Quin was a broken reed. Yet Clark evidently wished it had been otherwise. There was an undisguised disappointment on Pyott's handsome face as he stood with Clark in what had the appearance of a protective hedge of easels supporting mounted photographs and charts. The bric-à-brac of an operation that would never be allowed to run. The board would never be set up for it, the timetable never decided, the communications and the back-up never arranged. It was already dead.

The knowledge made Aubrey furious.

'I'm sorry, Mr Aubrey,' Clark began, 'but that guy's in no condition to cross the street. He's in bad shape, psychologically.'

Pyott fiddled with his moustache, as if caricaturing his uniform and rank. 'I'm afraid so, Kenneth. Nerves shot to bits, willingness to help nil. Bloody little man – '

'What are these?' Aubrey asked, pointing at the easels in turn. 'Did we order these?'

'I did,' Pyott admitted, 'before we had a good chat with our friend Quin.'

'Is this *Proteus*?' Aubrey had stopped in front of one of

the grainy, enlarged monochrome pictures. A harbour, the slim, knife-like shape of vessels seen from the air.

'Yes.' Clark sounded suddenly revived. He joined Aubrey, Pyott coming to the old man's other shoulder. Aubrey felt hemmed in by younger bone and muscle. 'The quality's poor. Satellite picture in poor conditions. Getting dark down there, and the cloud cover obscured most of the shots. This is the inner harbour at Pechenga. That's her.' His long, thick finger dabbed towards the top edge of the picture.

'What damage has she sustained?'

'Hard to tell. Look through this.' Clark handed Aubrey a magnifying glass, and the old man bent to the photograph, moving the lens slowly over the scene, which threatened at any moment to dissolve into a collection of grey, black and white dots. 'Those look like buoyancy bags at the stern. Must have been a low-warhead torpedo, maybe two. She's not under power, she's being towed by the rescue ship ahead of her.'

Aubrey surrendered the magnifying glass. 'How long?' he asked.

Clark shook his head. 'Impossible to guess. One day, two. I don't know. No one could tell you from this shot, not even with computer enhancement.'

'Show me where on the chart of Pechenga.'

The three of them moved, in a tight little wedge, to another easel. Their voices were echoing drily in the empty room. There was a marble, sepulchral atmosphere about it. The huge map-board in the middle of the floor registered, frozen like something unfinished but preserved in ice, the conditions and dispositions at the time the *Proteus* was boarded. Even the dot of the relief Nimrod was frozen on station above the coast of Norway. The board had not been allowed to continue revealing the extent of their defeat.

'Here,' Clark said. 'These are the submarine pens.'

'Well? Well? Is it only Quin we are worried about? *I* will take responsibility for him. We have discussed this operation for most of the night. Is there more than Quin to hold us back?'

'You never give up, do you?' Clark said.

'Would *you* drop out?'

'No.'

'Giles?'

'Too risky – no, I'm not sounding like a granny just for the sake of it. Quin is crucial. If Clark can't get the right information, at the *precise* split-second he requires it, then everything could be lost – including Clark.' Pyott shook his head, held his features in a gloomy, saturnine cast, to emphasise his words.

Aubrey was exasperated. He had *seen* the *Proteus* now. He had to act.

'You've talked to MoD air?'

'There's no problem there. A Harrier could get Clark across Finland and into the Pechenga area – yes. You have the authority to send it. The AWACS Nimrod that was rigged up especially for sea trials with *Proteus* is on stand-by at Farnborough. They could accommodate yourself and Quin. Eastoe and his crew are on stand-by to be flown down from Kinloss to Farnborough.' Pyott's face now changed to an expression of exasperation; he was angry with Quin for wasting his time and his organisational talents.

'Communications?'

'Yes, we can do that. Between the Nimrod and Clark, with a range of a hundred miles, speaking in a whisper.'

Aubrey had passed to the cutaway chart of the submarine. A multitude of hand-written labels had been appended, explaining and exposing each minute section and piece of equipment and function of the *Proteus*. Aubrey, by studying it, would know as much about the most secret of the Royal Navy's submarines in an hour as the Russians would know by the time *Proteus* sailed again from Pechenga.

'Damn,' he said softly as the realisation sprung itself upon him like a bad dream. 'Jamming or interception? Location?'

'Can be overcome,' Pyott admitted reluctantly. His enthusiasm had dimmed again, with his own realisation. His eyes had strayed towards the door of the room where Aubrey had slept and which now contained a sedated Quin.

'Your equipment, Clark?'

'Portable – just. I could make it, with an infinite amount of luck, without drowning under the weight of what I need – *would need*, Mr Aubrey. It can't be done without Quin. I can't learn enough in time. He has to be there – in range of my transmitter – all the time, and able to talk me through whatever I find.' He jabbed a finger at one section of the hull of the *Proteus*. 'Hell, the back-up system's *here*! Not to mention that this stern section, where some of the sensors are, has been damaged by one, maybe two, torpedoes. I can't go climbing over the hull spot-welding alongside Russian dockyard workers! It's crazy.'

'If it can't be done, you will abort "Plumber" and destroy the "Leopard" equipment with the maximum efficiency,' Aubrey said in a tight, controlled voice. 'But perhaps it can be done.'

'What will you do with Quin? Twist his arm, Kenneth? Threaten to fling him out of the Nimrod if he doesn't answer Clark's questions correctly and without hesitation? I'm afraid that Clark and I agree on this occasion. It would be a complex, expensive, dangerous and ultimately wasteful operation. If Clark must go in, let him go in simply to destroy "Leopard". Someone other than Quin could point him in the right direction there.'

Aubrey was plucking at his bottom lip, staring at the chart of the submarine, its workings and innards exposed like a biological specimen or drawing. The ringing of the telephone was loud and startling in the room, and Pyott rushed to answer it as if he were afraid that its noise would waken Quin. Immediately he answered, he glanced at Aubrey, and beckoned him to the desk. It was Cunningham.

'"C",' Pyott whispered as he handed him the receiver.

'Richard?'

'Kenneth – how is our patient?'

'Not good. Uncooperative, unreliable, withdrawn. chronically suspicious and afraid.'

'I see. No use to you, then?'

'Why? Has the operation been cleared?'

'Yes, it has. The Secretary of State has cleared it with the PM. She's enthusiastic, I gather.'

'The Prime Minister obviously wasn't made aware of the

difficulties,' Aubrey said sarcastically. Cunningham had had to clear the proposed operation with the cabinet minister responsible for the SIS, the Foreign Secretary who, in his turn, had consulted the Prime Minister. The recruitment of another national, Clark being American, the incursion into Soviet territory, and the special circumstances pertaining to the submarine, had removed the operation beyond the sphere of the intelligence service acting alone and covertly.

'She has cleared the operation with the President, if it proves feasible in your judgement. NATO ministers will be informed under a Priority Two order. I have been successful on your behalf, but you now seem to imply that I've been wasting my time?'

'I hope not. I *hoped* not. It does seem rather hopeless, Richard.'

'A great pity. Then Clark will have to go in just to get rid of "Leopard"?'

Aubrey listened to the silence at the other end of the line. Behind Cunningham, there was the enthusiasm, the permission, of the politicians. A chance to give the Russian Bear a black eye, a bloody nose, without risking more than one life. Turning the tables on the Kremlin. He did not despise or disregard the almost naïve way in which his operation had been greeted with enthusiasm in Downing Street and the White House. It was a pity that the seriousness of the operation's parameters and its possible repercussions had required the political sanction of the two leaders. The NATO ministers, with the exception of Norway, would be informed after the event. They did not matter. The naïvety, however, gave him cause to doubt the rationale of his scheme. To be praised by laymen is not the expert's desire. Aubrey now suspected his operation's feasibility.

Cunningham seemed to have no desire to add to what he had said, or to repeat his question. Whatever Aubrey now said, he would, with enthusiasm or reluctance, pass on to the Foreign Office and Downing Street.

'No, he will not,' Aubrey heard himself say. The expression created an instant sense of lightness, of relief. It was a kind of self-affirmation, and he no longer cared for pros and cons, doubts and likelihoods. It *would* be attempted. 'Captain Clark will be briefed to examine and, if possible, repair "Leopard", and to instruct the commanding officer and crew of the *Proteus* to attempt to escape from the Soviet naval base at Pechenga.'

Cunningham merely said, 'I'll pass your message on. Good luck, Kenneth.'

Aubrey put down the receiver quickly, as if Clark or Pyott might make some attempt to snatch it from him and reverse his instructions. He had spoken clearly, precisely, and with sufficient volume for them to hear him. When he looked at them, Pyott was fiddling with his moustache again, while Clark was perched on the edge of a foldaway table, arms folded across his chest. He was shaking his head. Then, unexpectedly, he grinned.

Pyott said, as Aubrey approached them, 'You're taking a grave risk with this young man's life, Kenneth. And perhaps with Quin. Do you think it's worth it?'

'Of course he does,' Clark interposed. He was still smiling. 'He knows I won't refuse, on any count. Uh, Mr Aubrey?'

'Perhaps, Ethan, perhaps. I'm sorry you have to enact my romantic escapade, but your President is relying on you, too, I gather.'

'That's the last time I vote for the guy.'

Aubrey looked at his watch. Nine-fifteen.

'Giles, get Eastoe and his crew moved down to Farnborough immediately. Ethan, get Quin in here again. We have less than three hours. I want to be at Farnborough, and you must be on your way by this afternoon.' Pyott was already on the telephone. 'Get that Harrier put on immediate stand-by, and get Ethan's equipment details over to MoD Air.'

'Very well, Kenneth.'

There was no longer a sepulchral atmosphere in the room. Instead, a febrile, nervous excitement seemed to charge the air like static electricity forerunning a storm.

The grocer, Aubrey thought. My immediate task is the grocer. He must meet Clark tonight as near Pechenga as we can get him.

*

Unexpectedly, it had snowed lightly in the Midlands during the night, and Cannock Chase, where they had stopped at Tricia Quin's request, was still dusted with it. The sky was bright, dabs of white cloud pushed and buffeted across the blue expanse by a gusty, chill wind. Small puddles, some of them in hoofprints, were filmed with ice, like cataracted eyes. They walked slowly, Hyde with his hands in his pockets, relaxed even though he was cold. The girl huddled in her donkey jacket, the one in which she had tried to slip into the NEC unnoticed. She seemed concerned to explain why she had asked him to stop, to have requested him to leave the motorway at Stafford and drive across the Chase until they had passed through a sprawling housing estate on the outskirts of Rugeley and found themselves, suddenly and welcomely, amid firs and grazing land. It was early afternoon, and they were no more than fifteen miles from the girl's mother.

An occasional passing lorry, back on the road across that part of Cannock Chase, caused the girl to raise her voice as she spoke.

'I don't know why I always made their problems mine. They even used to argue whenever we came up here, when I was quite young, and I used to hate that especially.'

'Rough,' was Hyde's only comment, because he could not think of a suitable reply. He could not join the girl's post-mortem on her parents. His memories of Quin were too recent and too acerbic for him to consider the man either sympathetic or important. He allowed the girl, however, to analyse herself in a careful, half-aware manner. She, at least, had his sympathy.

'I suppose it always sprang from the fact that Dad was much brighter than Mum – much brighter than me, too,' she added, smiling slightly, cracking the film of ice over one sunken hoofprint, hearing its sharp little report with evident pleasure, with a weight of association. 'He *was* intolerant,' she conceded, 'and I don't think Mum appreciated what he was doing, after the firm got a bit bigger and she no longer did the bookwork or helped him out. I think they were happy in the early days.' She looked at him suddenly, as if he had demurred. 'Mum needs to feel useful. I'm like her, I suppose.'

'You're a good girl, and you're wasting your time. It's *their* business, not yours. You can't do anything except be a football. Is that what you want?'

Her face was blanched, and not merely by the cold. He had intruded upon her version of reality, casting doubt upon its veracity.

'You're very hard,' she said.

'I suppose so.' He had enjoyed the drive down the crowded M6 in the borrowed car, after a night's stop which had refreshed him and which the girl had seemed to desperately require the moment her father's plane had left Manchester. Sutton Coldfield for dinner was an amusing prospect. He considered Mrs Quin's reaction to him as a guest. 'Sorry. I'll shut up.'

'You don't have to –'

'It's better. It isn't my business.'

She paused and looked back. The fern was still brown and stiffly cramped into awkward, broken shapes and lumps by the frost. Birdsong. She wanted to see a deer, the quick flicker of grey, white hindquarters disappearing into the trees. In some unaccountable way, she believed that if she saw deer, things would be improved, would augur well. It would fuse the circuits that existed between present and past. She looked down the perspective of the bridle path, back towards the car park, unaware, while Hyde shivered at her side.

He heard the approach of the small, red and white helicopter first. Its noise intruded, and then it seemed to become a natural and expected part of the pale sky. Tricia Quin knew it would startle the deer, make them more difficult to find, over beyond the line of numbered targets against the high earth bank that composed the rifle range. She looked up, following Hyde's gaze. He was shielding his eyes with one hand. The tiny helicopter in its bright, hire-firm colours swung in the sky as if suspended from an invisible cable, a brightly daubed spider, and then it flicked down towards them.

Hyde's nerves came slowly awake. His other hand came out of his pocket, his body hunched slightly in expectation. The helicopter – a Bell Jetranger he perceived with one detached part of his awareness – was still moving towards them, skimming now just above the line of trees, down the track of the bridle path. The helicopter had hesitated above the car park, then seemed more certain of purpose, as if it had found what it sought. Hyde watched it accelerate towards them, the noise of its single turbo-shaft bellowing down into the track between the trees. Lower, and the trees were distressed by the down-draught and even the stiff, rimy ferns began buckling, attempting and imitating movement they might have possessed before death.

'Run!' he said. The girl's face crumpled into defeat, even agony, as he pushed her off the path towards the nearest trees. 'Run!'

She stumbled through frozen grass, through the thin film of snow, through the creaking, dead ferns. Deliberately, he let her widen the distance between them – they wouldn't shoot at her, but he didn't want her killed when they tried to take him out – before he, too, began running.

The first shots were hardly audible above the noise of the rotors. The downdraught plucked at his clothing, his hair and body, as if restraining him. The girl ran without looking back, in utter panic.

Eleven: FLIGHTS

The jellyfish bags were gone, except on the port side of the *Proteus*. The starboard ballast tanks had been repaired, and the rudder fin had begun to look like the result of a half-completed, complex grafting operation; spars and struts of metal bone, much now covered with a sheen of new plates. One part of Lloyd, at least, welcomed the surgery. He paced the concrete wharf of the submarine pen, under the hard lights, his guard behind him, taking his midday exercise. The Red Navy had extended the farce even to giving each member of his crew a thorough medical check-up; routine exercise, as much as was permitted by the confines and security necessary to Pechenga as a military installation, had been prescribed. Also permission to use the crew cinema had been granted, alcohol had arrived, in limited and permissible amounts; and fresh food.

Lloyd held his hands behind his back, walking in unconscious imitation of a member of the Royal Family. The diplomat he had requested from Moscow had not arrived, unsurprisingly. Lloyd had made the required formal protests without enthusiasm realising their pointlessness. Better news lay in the gossip he and some of the crew had picked up from their guards. Everyone was waiting on the arrival of a Soviet expert, delayed in Novosibirsk by bad weather. He it was who would supervise the examination of 'Leopard'. It was the one element of optimism in Lloyd's situation.

The fitters and welders were having their lunch, sitting against the thick, slabbed concrete walls of the pen. They looked a species of prisoner themselves, wearing blue fatigue overalls, lounging in desultory conversation, eating hunks of thick dark bread and pickles and cold meat – in one instance, a cold potato. They watched him with an evident curiosity, but only as something belonging to the foreign submarine on which they were working and which was the real focus of their interest.

Lloyd stopped to gaze back down the two hundred and fifty feet of the *Proteus*'s length. Nuclear-powered Fleet submarines possessed a menace not unlike that of the shark. They were long, shiny-sleek, but portly, massive. Three and a half thousand tons of vessel, well over twice the size of a Second World War ancestor. Backed like a whale, but a killer whale. It hurt Lloyd's pride as her captain to have watched, before the hooter sounded deafeningly in the pen to announce the lunch break, Russian fitters clambering and crawling over her; Lilliputians performing surgery on a helpless Gulliver. He turned away, looking over the gates of the pen, into the tunnel which led to the harbour. One o'clock. In the circle of light he could discern a Soviet destroyer moving almost primly across his field of vision. The view was like that through a periscope, and he wished, with clenched fists and an impotent rage, that it had been.

Pechenga harbour lowered under heavy grey cloud, and he resented the weather as an additional camouflage that aided the Red Navy.

He turned to look back at his submarine once more, and Ardenyev was standing in front of him, hands on his hips, a smile on his face. The smile, Lloyd saw, was calculated to encourage, to repel dislike rather than to sneer or mock. With a gesture, Ardenyev waved the guard away. The man retired. The stubby Kalashnikov still thrust against his hip, barrel outwards. The guard swaggered. A Soviet marine, entirely satisfied with the guard-prisoner relationship between them. Young, conscripted, dim. Ardenyev's amused eyes seemed to make the comment. Yet the wave of Ardenyev's hand had been that of the conjurer, the illusionist. *There is nothing to fear, there are no guards, we are friends, abracadabra –*

Lloyd suddenly both liked the man and resented him.

'Come to gloat?' he asked. For a moment, Ardenyev absorbed the word, then shook his head.

'No.' There was a small satchel over his shoulder, which he now swung forward, and opened. 'I have food, and wine,' he said. 'I hoped you would share lunch with me. I am sorry that I cannot invite you to the officers' mess, or to the only decent restaurant in Pechenga. It is not possible.

Shall we sit down?' Ardenyev indicated two bollards, and immediately sat down himself. Reluctantly, Lloyd joined him, hitching his dark trousers to preserve their creases, brushing at the material as if removing a persistent spot. Then he looked up.

'What's for lunch?'

'Caviar, of course. Smoked fish. Georgian wine. Pancakes.' He opened the plastic containers one by one, laying them like offerings at Lloyd's feet. He cut slices of bread from a narrow loaf. 'Help yourself,' he said. 'No butter, I'm afraid. Even Red Navy officers' messes sometimes go without butter.'

Lloyd ate hungrily, oblivious of the greedy eyes of the nearest fitters. He drank mouthfuls of the rough wine to unstick the bread from his palate, swigging it from the bottle Ardenyev uncorked for him.

Finally, he said, 'Your people seem to be taking their time.'

'Our workers are the best in the world,' Ardenyev answered with a grin.

'I mean on the inside of the hull.'

'Oh.' Ardenyev studied for a moment, then shrugged. 'You have heard rumours, it is obvious. Even Red Navy marines cannot keep anything to themselves.' He chewed on a slice of loaf liberally smothered with black caviar. 'Unfortunately, our leading expert in naval electronic counter-measures – the man designated to, shall we say, have a little peep at your pet – is delayed, in Siberia.' He laughed. 'No, not by his politics, merely by the weather. He was supposed to fly from his laboratory in Novosibirsk three days ago. He is snowed in.'

'You're being very frank.'

'Can you see the point of being otherwise?' Ardenyev asked pleasantly.

'It was a clever plan,' Lloyd offered.

'Ah, you are trying to debrief me. Well, I don't mind what you collect on this operation. It has worked. We're not likely to use it again, are we?' His eyes were amused, bright. Lloyd could not help but respond to the man's charm. 'It was clever, yes. It needed a great deal of luck, of course – but it worked.'

'If your Siberian snowman arrives.'

'Ah, yes, Comrade Professor Academician Panov. I have no doubt you will also be meeting Admiral of the Red Banner Fleet Dolohov at the same time. He is bound to come and see his prize.'

'You sound disrespectful.'

'Do I? Ah, perhaps I only feel annoyance at the fact that an old man with delusions of grandeur could dream up such a clever scheme in his dotage.' He laughed, recovering his good humour. 'Drink up. I have another bottle.'

'They intend removing it, then?'

'What?'

'I'm obliged not to mention sensitive equipment. May I preserve protocol? Their Lordships will be most anxious to know – on my return – that I gave nothing away.' Lloyd, too, was smiling by the time he finished his statement.

'Ah, of course.' Ardenyev rubbed his nose. There were tiny raisins of caviar at one corner of his mouth. His tongue flicked out and removed them. 'No. I doubt it will be necessary. I am not certain, of course. I have done my bit, the balls and bootstraps part of the operation.'

'I'm sorry about your men.'

Ardenyev looked at Lloyd. 'I see that you are. It was not your fault. I would have done the same, in your place. Let us blame our separate masters, and leave it at that.'

'When will they let us go?'

Ardenyev looked swiftly down the length of the *Proteus*, taking in the repairs, the fitters slowly getting up – the hooter had blasted across Lloyd's question, so that he had had to shout it, making it seem a desperate plea rather than a cool enquiry – the new plates, the buckled hull plates, the stripped rudder, the skeletal hydroplane below them in the water.

'Twenty-four hours, assuming it stops snowing in Novosibirsk,' Ardenyev said, turning back to Lloyd.

Four days, Aubrey thought. It is four days – less than one hundred hours – since I became involved in this business. I have slept for perhaps fifteen of those hours. I have been out of that damned room beneath the Admiralty for even fewer hours. And now I am consigning myself to another box, something even more uncomfortable, something much more evidently tomb-like.

He took the crewman's hand, and allowed himself to be helped up the last steps of the passenger ladder into the fuselage of the AWACS Nimrod. He did not feel, despite his reflections on age, mortality, sleep and habitat, either tired or weary. True, the adrenalin was sufficient only to forestall such things rather than to invigorate him, but he was grateful, as he ducked his head through the crew door near the tail fin and directly adjacent to the huge RAF roundel on the fuselage. Then the bright, quick-clouding windy day was exchanged for a hollow, metallic interior. And Eastoe was waiting for Quin and himself.

'Here you are, Mr Aubrey. You and Mr Quin here, if you please.' He indicated two seats, facing one another across a communications console from which thick wires and cables trailed away down the fuselage floor, in a channel that might have been a gutter in an abattoir, the way in which it riveted Quin's fearful gaze. Other swivel chairs, bolted to the floor and the curving sides of the fuselage, stretched away down the untidy, crowded interior of the Nimrod towards the flight deck. For Quin's benefit, Eastoe added as Aubrey seated himself, 'You're wired into *all* our communications equipment, sir, and the principal sensors. We'll do a full test with Clark when we're airborne. Your equipment operates through this central console – '

'Yes, yes,' Quin said impatiently, like someone interested only in the toilet facilities provided. Eastoe's face darkened. His patience was evidently running out. The door swung shut on a gleam of sunlight, and a hand clamped home the locks. Quin appeared physically startled, as if suddenly awoken, and he protested, 'I can be of no use to you!' His voice was high-pitched. He held his hands out in front of him, demonstrating their incontrollable quiver. 'I am no use to you!'

'Quin!' Aubrey barked. 'Quin, sit down! Now! None of us is here to be self-indulgent, especially you. We all have a task to perform. Kindly see to it that you do yours, when the time comes.'

Eastoe studied both civilians like a strange, newly-encountered species. There was an easy, adopted contempt around his mouth which Aubrey had met before in military officers. Pyott was an expert at it, when he chose. No doubt even Lloyd in his confinement was employing the sneer *militaire*. Aubrey almost smiled. The French, of course, had always been world champions. He remembered the young de Gaulle of London-exile days, when Aubrey had been at SOE. The nose had helped, of course.

Aubrey thrust aside the memory, almost with reluctance, and confronted Quin and the RAF Squadron Leader who, he well knew, considered his scheme to rescue *Proteus* wildly incapable of success. Quin slumped into his seat, swivelling in it instantly like a sulking child; there was a moment of debated defiance which only reached his hands as he clenched them into weak fists. He rubbed a nervy hand through his wiry, thinning hair which stood more comically on end as a result of the gesture. The inventor of 'Leopard'; the machinery made of silicons, plastics, metal, the man constructed of straw. It was easy to feel contempt, hard to dismiss that emotion. For Eastoe, it was evidently impossible to remove that attitude from his calculations. Aubrey spent no time in conjecture as to Eastoe's more personal feelings towards him because of the crashed Nimrod and its dead aircrew.

'Squadron Leader Eastoe,' Aubrey said levelly, 'how long before we are ready to take off?'

Eastoe looked at his watch. 'Fifteen minutes.'

'You will make that ten, if you please,' Aubrey said, treading with a delicate but grinding motion of his heel on all forms of civilian-military protocol. Eastoe's eyes widened in surprise. 'As I said, Squadron Leader. Ten minutes. Please see to it.'

'Mr Aubrey, I'm the skipper of this – '

'No, you are not. You are its pilot. In matters of flying, I shall consult you, even defer to you. But I am in command here. Please be certain you understand that fact.'

Eastoe bit his lip, and choked back a retort. Instead, he nodded his head like a marionette, and went forward to the flight deck. Aubrey, controlling the tremor of weakness he felt in his frame, sat down again opposite Quin, who was looking at him with a new kind of fearful respect.

Aubrey calculated his next remarks, then observed: 'It

was MoD who originally cocked-up this operation,' he said casually, confidentially. 'I do not intend to let them do so again. Damn fools, playing war-games with "Leopard". It simply showed little or no respect for – or *understanding* of – your development.'

Aubrey watched Quin's ego inflate. He had suspected a balloon of self-admiration in the man, and was not disappointed; except in the arcane sense that Quin was so readily comprehensible, so transparent in his inner self. Whether the ego would keep him going, make him sufficiently malleable and for long enough, remained to be seen. Quin had talked to no one except his daughter for weeks. He required the conversation and the admiration of intelligent men; of men rather than women, Aubrey suspected. A deal of chauvinism there, too; Mrs Quin would have been useful in the early days, but not a sufficient audience for the man's intellect and achievements. It cast a new light on why Quin had allowed the take-over of his small firm by the Plessey giant. It had enlarged his audience of admirers.

'You understand?' Quin asked, almost in surprise.

'Of course. Don't you think I get tired of dealing with these people, too?' Aubrey relaxed, offering Quin a cigarette. The man's right forefinger was stained brown. Quin reached for the cigarette case, taking one of the untipped cigarettes. He used his own lighter, and inhaled deeply, exhaled loudly. Confidence was altering his posture in his seat. He did not slump now, he relaxed.

'I see,' Quin said. 'I advised them against using "Leopard" so early, and relying on it so totally. They wouldn't listen.' There was self-pity there, just below the surface of the words.

'Arrogant,' Aubrey murmured. 'They're all so arrogant. This time, however, they do as *we* say, Quin, my dear fellow. They do exactly as we instruct them.'

It was six minutes later – Quin had just stubbed out his second cigarette – when the Nimrod reached the end of the taxiway, turned, then roared down the main Farnborough runway, lifting into the patchily cloudy sky, the ground shrinking away from them at a surprising speed. As the buildings and aircraft had sped past his porthole-like

258

window, Aubrey had reminded himself of the delicacy, the weakness of his control over Quin. Leaving him with the oil of flattery; no grounds for confidence there, he remarked to himself, watching the man as his hands gripped the arms of his seat and he sat with closed eyes. No grounds for confidence at all.

The Harrier was a T.4 two-seater trainer, and it was unarmed because of the load it would have to carry and the extra fuel tanks, each of one hundred gallons, beneath its wings. There were no circumstances in which it would require cannon, bombs or missiles, for its mission would be aborted unless it could avoid all contact with Soviet aircraft or ground defences. Despite being a training aircraft, however, it was fitted with the latest type of laser range-finding equipment in the nose.

Ethan Clark was able to move only with difficulty in the pressure suit with which he had been supplied, because of the immersion suit he already wore beneath it. It made him waddle awkwardly, flying helmet under his arm, giving him the appearance of a circus clown imitating a pilot. The pilot of the Harrier, an experienced Squadron Leader whose response to his mission was shading to the cautious side of excitement, walked in front of him across the tarmac of Wittering RAF base, in Lincolnshire. Clark's packs of communications equipment, explosives, sensors, meters, spares and tools had been stowed beneath the wings in two pods where bombs might normally have hung.

Clark had been transported by helicopter to Wittering, and he had briefed the pilot, in the presence of the station commandant and Giles Pyott, who had provided the MoD authority appropriate to the commandeering of an aircraft and a pilot. Now Pyott strode alongside him, the wind plucking at his thick grey hair, his bearing upright, his form cloaked in the camel-coloured British warm.

The pilot clambered up the ladder, and swung himself into the cockpit, looking down immediately from behind the face panel of his helmet as Clark paused before his ascent. Pyott extended his hand at once, and Clark took his cool, tough grip.

'Good luck, Clark,' Pyott said stiffly, as if avoiding the

real subject of a conversation that was both necessary and important.

'Thanks, Colonel.' Clark grinned, despite the gravity of the moment. 'Here goes nothing, as they say.'

'If you can't make it – if you can't *repair*, you *must* abort,' Pyott warned solemnly. 'Remember that. No heroics over and above the required minimum.'

'I appreciate your concern, Colonel.'

'Right. Get on with you. I think we're keeping your pilot waiting.'

Clark glanced up. 'Sure.'

He released Pyott's grip, and began clambering awkwardly up the ladder. It was difficult to swing his unaccustomed weight and bulk over the lip of the cockpit, and hot and strenuous work to ease himself into the narrow rear seat. Eventually, he achieved a degree of comfort, strapped himself in and adjusted his flying helmet. The pilot reached up, and closed the cockpit cover. Instantly, nerves raised his temperature, and he felt a film of perspiration on his forehead. He looked down, and the ladder was being carried away by a member of the ground crew. Pyott was striding after it like a schoolmaster harrying someone for a breach of school rules, his walking-stick accompanying his strides like a younger limb. Clark had never noticed Pyott's limp before.

When he reached the grass margin of the taxiway, Giles Pyott turned, almost posing with the little knot of the ground crew.

'Fingers in your ears, sir,' a flight-sergeant informed him.

'What? Oh, yes.'

Pyott did as instructed. The Harrier was using the runway in a standard take off, instead of its unique vertical lift, because of the extra weight of fuel that it carried. Lights winked at wingtips and belly, suddenly brighter as a heavy cloud was pulled across the early afternoon sun by the wind. Then the aircraft was rolling, slowly for a moment, then with an accelerating rush, passing them – Pyott could see the helmeted blob that was Clark's head, turned towards him – and racing on down the runway. The heat of its single twenty-one and a half thousand pound thrust Pegasus 103 turbofan engine distorted its outline like a heat haze might have done, so that the aircraft appeared to have passed behind a veil, become removed from them. It sat back almost like an animal for an instant, then sprang at the sky and its low, scudding cloud and patches of gleaming brightness. The runway was still gauzy, but the Harrier was a sharply outlined silhouette as it rose then banked to the east.

Pyott took his hands from his ears, realising that the ground crew had already begun making their way towards the hangar area, leaving him a somewhat foolishly isolated figure in an overcoat, a retired officer out for a constitutional who had strolled by mistake into a military installation. He turned on his heel, and followed the others, his imperative now to return to the room beneath the Admiralty.

The Harrier had already climbed into the lowest of the cloud and was lost from sight.

The safety offered by the trees had come to seem a kind of privileged imprisonment, the further they ran. Hyde had seen figures, three of them, drop out of the helicopter into the buffet of the rotors' down-draught in the moment he had paused at the first trees, and knew they were cut off from the car. By now, someone would have driven it out of the car park and hidden it and removed the distributor. The trees masked them – they heard the helicopter roaming in search of them every few minutes – but they bordered a long, higher stretch of barren heathland where summer fires of a drought year had exposed the land even further. Dull, patchy with snow and fern, treeless, exposed. A minefield as far as they were concerned.

When they first stopped, he had held the frightened, shivering girl against him, but even before her breathing calmed and she had drawn any comfort from the embrace, he was asking her urgently, 'How well do you know the area? Can you see it in your mind's eye? Where's the nearest road? How far? Can you run? What's the shape of this plantation? What *do* you know? *Anything?*'

Roads? No, she didn't know, she couldn't explain the shape of Cannock Chase, she'd never seen a map of it –

A childhood place, he understood even as he fumed

silently. She remembered it as a series of snapshots, the sight of deer, high blue skies above whitened landscapes, the fall and rise of the land only as a viewer who wished the ability to paint would perceive and remember. Useless to them now.

They followed the edge of the plantation north for almost two miles, further and further from the road and the car park and the town of Rugeley. Then the girl announced that she did not know that part of the Chase. They were north-east of the rifle range, but it was hidden from them by the trees.

'The road from Stafford to Lichfield,' the girl said, her face screwed up in thought, her chest still heaving with the effort of their last run.

'What?' he said.

'It runs through the Chase.' She looked up into the dark trees, as if for inspiration. She was painfully trying to remember turns in the road, bearings from her childhood, signposts. 'Past Shugborough Hall – Wolseley Bridge, turn right . . .' She shook her head while he slapped his hands against his thighs in exasperation. Then she was looking at him, a sense of failure evident in her eyes. She added, hesitantly, 'I think if we continue north, we'll hit the main road.'

'Trees all the way?' he snapped, unable to restrain the sense of entrapment that glided out of the dark trees and accompanied them at every step. They were like her precious deer, confined to the trees.

She shrugged hopelessly. 'I don't know.'

'Oh, Christ!' She looked as if he had struck her. He added, in a tone that aspired to more gentleness, 'Any wardens', gamekeepers' houses around here?' Again, she shook her head.

Beyond the trees, the afternoon was bright, dazzling off the last paper-thin sheet of snow on the higher, open ground. The chilly wind soughed through the upper branches of the firs. To the north and west, the direction of the weather, there was heavier cloud. It was a weekday afternoon, and they had seen no other people since they left the car park, which had contained just one other car. Once, they had heard a dog bark, but they had seen neither it nor its owner. A distant vehicle's engine had sawn into the silence at another point, but again they had not seen it. Hyde had never realised before how isolated he could feel in a part of the cramped island that had become his home.

'I'm ready,' Tricia Quin offered.

'Okay, let's go.'

Their feet crackled on fallen twigs, or crunched through the long winter's frosty humus and leaf litter. An eerie, dark green, underwater light filtered through the firs, slanting on the grey and damp-green trunks. Hyde had time to think that he could not imagine how it had ever been a magic place for the girl, before he dragged her without sound off the narrow, foot-pressed, deer-run track they were following, behind the mossy trunk of a fir. Deep ravines in the bark, its hardness against his cheek, his hand over the girl's mouth, his breath hushing her before he released her; the movement of an insect over the terrain of the bark, almost so close as to be out of focus. He held the girl against him, pulled into his body. She was shivering, and her head was cocked listening. Her breath came and went, plucking at the air lightly yet fervently; an old lady dying. He dismissed the inappropriate image.

She reached her face up to him in a parody of intimacy, and whispered in his ear, 'What is it? I can't even hear the helicopter.'

He tossed his head, to indicate the track and the trees in the direction they had come.

'I heard something. I don't know what. Let's hope it's an old lady out for a brisk stroll.' The girl tried to smile, nudging herself closer against him. He felt her body still. He listened.

Footstep. Crack, dry and flat as snapping a seaweed pod. Then silence, then another crack. Twigs. Footstep. The timing was wrong for an old lady, a young man, even a child. Wrong for anyone simply out for a walk, taking exercise. Sounds too careful, too slow, too spaced to be anything else than cautious, careful, alert. Stalking.

His heart began to interfere with his hearing as he stifled his breathing and the adrenalin began to surge. He should have moved further off the track. It was *their* tracks that were being followed, easy to do for a trained man, too much leaf-mould underfoot not to imprison the evidence of their passage, along with the deer prints, the hoof prints, the dogs' pawmarks, the ridged patterns of stout walking shoes.

Crack, then a soft cursing breath. Close, close. He pushed the girl slightly away and reached behind him, feeling the butt of the gun against his palm. She watched him, uninitiated into that kind of adulthood, looking very childlike and inadequate and requiring him to be responsible for her.

She pressed against the fir's trunk beside him. The tree was old enough, wide enough in the trunk, to mask them both. He nudged her when he could not bear the waiting any longer and substituted nerves for knowledge, and she shuffled two small paces around the trunk. He remained where he was, his hand still twisted, as if held by a bully, behind his back.

Breathing, heavier than the girl's, the sense of the weight of a heavy male body transferring from one foot to another, the glimmer of a hand holding something dark, the beginnings of a profile. Then they were staring at one another, each holding a gun, no more than seven yards apart, each knowing the stalemate for what it was, each understanding the other's marksmanship in the extended arms, the crouch of the body into a smaller target. Understanding completely and quickly, so that neither fired.

A heavy man in an anorak and dark slacks. Walking boots, the slacks tucked into heavy woollen socks. A Makarov pistol, because a rifle couldn't be hidden.

The man's eyes flickered, but did not look up, as the noise of the helicopter became apparent to both of them. A slow, confident smile spread on the man's face. Not long now. The stalemate would be broken. Hyde concentrated on watching the man's eyes and his hands. Perspiration trickled from beneath his arms, and his mouth was dry. His hand was beginning to quiver with the tension, beginning to make the gun unsteady. The noise of the helicopter grew louder, and the trees began to rustle in the down-draught. He could not kill without being killed, there was no advantage, not a micro-second of it –

A noise in the undergrowth, a small, sharp stamping

pattern. The brushing aside of whippy low branches and twigs. High, springing steps. Then the deer was on them.

Hyde it was who fired, because it had to be another pursuer, even though the subconscious was already rejecting the idea. The Russian fired too, because he had been startled out of the confidence that it was a friend, another gun against Hyde. Tricia Quin screamed long before reaction-time should have allowed her to do so, as if she had foreseen the animal's death. The small, grey deer tumbled and skidded with cartoon-like, unsteady legs, its coat badged with dark new markings, then it was between them, veering off, then falling slowly, wobbling as when new-born, on to the crisp, rotting humus, where it kicked once, twice –

Reaction-time, reaction-time, Hyde screamed at himself, even as a wrench of pain and guilt hurt his chest. He swung his pistol, the Russian doing the same, a mirror-image. Reaction-time, reaction-time; he hadn't totally ignored the deer, kicking for a third, fourth time, then shuddering behind the Russian –

Hyde's gun roared, the split-second before that of the Russian. The man was knocked off balance, and his bullet whined past Hyde's left shoulder, buzzing insect-like into the trees. The man lay still instantly, unlike the deer which went on thrashing and twitching and seemed to be making the noise that in reality was coming from the girl, a high, helpless, violated scream.

He ran to the deer, placed the gun against its temple – the dark helpless eye watching him for a moment, the red tongue lolling – and pulled the trigger to shut out the girl's screams which went on even after the report of his gun died away.

'Shut up,' he yelled at her, waving the gun as if in threat. 'Shut up! Run, you stupid bitch – run!' He ran towards her, the noise of the helicopter deafening just above the treetops, and she fled from him.

Thirty thousand feet below them, through breaks in the carpet of white cloud, Aubrey could make out the chain of rocks that were the Lofoten islands off the north-west coast of Norway. Clark was perhaps a hundred miles away from them at that point, to the south and east, near Bodø, linking up with the RAF Victor in order to perform a mid-air refuelling of the Harrier. Until that point, both the Nimrod and the Harrier had maintained strict radio silence. Now, however, Aubrey could no longer delay the testing of the communications equipment that would link Clark and Quin together when the American reached the *Proteus*.

Quin was sweating nervously again, and a swift despisal of the man passed through Aubrey's mind, leaving him satisfied. The emotion removed doubt, even as it pandered to Aubrey's sense of authority in the situation he had created. The man was also chain-smoking and Aubrey, with the righteousness of someone forced by health to give up the habit, disliked Quin all the more intensely for the clouds of bluish smoke that hung perpetually around their heads, despite the air-conditioning of the Nimrod.

'Very well, Flight-Lieutenant,' Aubrey instructed the radio operator assigned to monitor the communications console Quin would be using, 'call up our friend for us, would you?' Aubrey could sense the dislike and irritation he created in the RAF officers who were crewing the Nimrod. However, having begun with Eastoe in a testy, authoritarian manner, he could not now relax into more congenial behaviour.

'Sir,' the young officer murmured. He flicked a bank of switches, opening the channel. There was no call-sign. Clark's receiver would be alive with static in his earpiece. He would need no other signal. The maximum range of the transceivers was a little over one hundred miles, their range curtailed by the need to encode the conversation in high-speed transmission form. A tiny cassette tape in Clark's more portable equipment recorded his words, speeded them up, then they were transmitted to this console between Aubrey and Quin. As with the larger equipment in the room beneath the Admiralty, tapes in Quin's receiver slowed down the message, then replayed it as it had been spoken – whispered, Aubrey thought – by the American. And the reverse procedure would occur when Quin, or himself, spoke to Clark. Clumsy, with an unavoidable, built-in delay, but the only way the signals could not be

266

intercepted, understood, and Clark's precise location thereby exposed.

'Yes?' Clark replied through a whistle of static, his voice distant and tired, almost foreboding in its disembodiment. Clark was a long way away, and alone.

'Testing,' Aubrey said, leaning forward. He spoke very quietly.

'Can't hear you,' Clark replied. There had been a delay, as if old habits of call-sign and acknowledgement waited to pop into Clark's mind.

'This is a test,' the flight-lieutenant said in a louder voice.

'That's too loud. Clark, I want you to speak quietly.' The RAF radio operator evidently found the whole business amateurish and quite unacceptable. Even Aubrey found the conversation amusing, yet fraught with weaknesses. He would have liked to have taken refuge in established routines of communication, in batteries of call-signs and their endless repetition, in jargon and technicalities. Except that his communications network was simply about being able to communicate in a whisper over a distance of one hundred miles, Clark lying on his back or his stomach in a dark, cramped space, out of breath and perspiring inside an immersion suit, working on a piece of incredibly complex equipment he did not understand, trying to locate a fault and repair it. Call-signs would not help him, even though they seemed, by their absence at that moment, to possess the power of spells and charms. 'What?' Aubrey said, craning forward towards the console. 'I didn't catch that.' There was an open sneer on the flight-lieutenant's face. 'Yes, I heard you clearly. Now, I'll hand you over to Mister Quin, and you can run through that technical vocabulary you worked out with him. Random order, please, groups of six.'

Aubrey sat back, a deal of smugness of manner directed at the radio operator. Quin looked like a nervous, first-time broadcaster or interviewee. He cleared his throat and shuffled in his seat, a clipboard covered with his strange, minuscule, spidery writing in front of him. Then he swiftly wiped his spectacles and began reading – Aubrey motioned him to lower his voice.

For five minutes, as the Nimrod continued northwards

267

towards North Cape and her eventual station inside Norwegian airspace off the coast near Kirkenes, Clark and Quin exchanged a complex vocabulary of technical terminology. Aubrey remembered occasions of impending French or Latin tests, and the last minute, feverish recital of vocab by himself and other boys, before the master walked in and all text books had to be put away. The dialogue had a comforting, lulling quality. When Quin indicated they had finished, he opened his eyes. Quin appeared drained, and Aubrey quailed at the prospect of keeping him up to the mark.

'Thank you, Clark. That will do. Maximum communication, minimum noise. Good luck. Out.'

Aubrey cut the channel, and nodded his satisfaction to Quin and the flight-lieutenant. Out of the tiny round window, he could see the herringbone pattern of a ship sailing north through the Andfjord, inshore of one of the Vesteralen islands. The Nimrod was perhaps little more than half an hour from North Cape, and the same time again from their taking up station on the Soviet border. In an hour, they would be committed. 'Plumber' would really be running, then.

Clark flicked off the transceiver, and shook his head as if he doubted the reality of the voices he had heard. The Harrier was seemingly about to settle on to the carpet of white cloud beneath them, and the tanker, the old Victor bomber, was a dot ahead and to starboard of them. Below the cloud, where the weather had let in small, almost circular viewing ports, the grey water and the slabbed, cut, knife-carved coastline were already retreating into evening, north of the Arctic Circle. Half an hour before, he had looked down between clouds and seen the vast sheet of the Svartisen glacier, looking like a huge, intact slab of marble fallen on the land, tinged by the sun into pinks and greens and blues.

The Harrier moved forward, overtaking the Victor tanker. The pilot changed his position until the tanker was slightly to port, then the probe that had needed to be specially fitted aligned with the long trailing fuel line from the wing of the Victor and its trumpet-bell mouth into which the pilot had to juggle the Harrier's probe. Bee and flower. Clark considered another, more human image, and smiled. Not like that. This was all too mechanical, and without passion.

The Victor's fuselage glowed silver in the sunlight from the west. The RAF roundel was evident on her side as the Harrier slid across the cloud carpet, and there seemed no motion except the slow, dance-like movements of possible combatants as the two aircraft matched speeds and height. The probe nudged forward towards the cone, the fuel-line lying on the air in a gentle, graceful curve. The probe nudged the cone, making it wobble, and then the Harrier dropped back slightly. Too high, too much to the left. Again, the probe slid forward towards the flower-mouth of the cone. Clark watched its insertion, felt the small, sharp jerk as it locked, then saw the glimmer of the three green locking lights on the instrument panel. The fuel began to surge down the fuel line.

Six and a half minutes later – it had become noticeably more evening-like, even at that altitude – the refuelling was complete, and the probe withdrew, the cone slipping forward and away as the speed of the two aircraft no longer matched. The gleaming, part-shadowed fuselage of the tanker slid up and away from them, the fuel-line retreating like a garden hose being reeled in. In a few more moments, the Victor had lost its silhouetted identity and was little more than a gleaming dot. The cloud brushed against the belly of the Harrier.

'Ready?' the pilot asked in his headset.

'Yes.'

'Hang on, then. This is where it gets hairy. Don't look if you've got a weak stomach.' The pilot chuckled.

'I can stand it.'

Even before he finished speaking, the nose of the Harrier dipped into the cloud, and white turned grey and featureless and dark immediately. Clark felt the altitude of the Harrier alter steeply as she dived through the clouds, descending from thirty-five thousand feet.

They emerged into a twilit world, and the pilot levelled the Harrier and switched on the terrain-following radar and the auto-pilot which would together flick and twist them through the mountainous Norwegian hinterland.

Clark watched as the dark water of the Skerstadfjord rose to meet them, then flashed beneath the belly of the aircraft. The pilot was flying the Harrier at five hundred miles an hour. The tiny lights of fishing hamlets flickered along the shore, and then were gone. Small boats returning from the day's fishing, the main north-south highway, then the dark, high, sharp peaks of the mountain range engulfed them. Clark winced, despite his experience, as the tiny insect of the Harrier flicked between two peaks, then followed the snail-like track of a narrow fjord, a smear of lighter grey in the gloom.

The aircraft lifted over the back of a line of hills, then dipped down to follow the terrain again. A huge glacier seemed to emerge suddenly from the darkness, gleaming with a ghostly, threatening light. The Harrier banked, and slipped as buoyantly and easily along its face as a helicopter might have done. Clark had never flown in one of the US Marine Harriers, built under licence by McDonnell Douglas, and it was the only means of comparison he could apply; a demented, speeded-up helicopter. Then the glacier was behind them, one eastern tip of it falling into a small, crater-like lake.

'Sweden,' the pilot announced.

'Nice view,' Clark replied drily.

'Want to go back for your stomach?'

'I'm okay.' Clark noticed the change in his own voice, the subconscious attempt to discourage conversation. He had moved into another phase of 'Plumber'. Already, he was alone, already it was another, different border they had crossed.

There were lakes as the terrain slowly became less mountainous, the peaks less sharp against the still lighter clouds and the few patches of stars. Grey, almost black water, the jagged lillies of ice floes everywhere. A rounded space of mirror-like water, a few dotted lights, then two companion stretches which the Harrier skimmed across like a stone. Then a long ribbon of lake, almost like a river because he could not perceive, at that altitude, either end of it, which the Harrier followed as it thrust into the centre of Swedish Lapland.

A village, like one dim street lamp at their speed, even the momentary flicker of headlights, then the Harrier banked to port, and altered course, following the single road north through that part of Sweden, the Norbotten, towards the Finnish border. The sheer rock faces closed in again, and the darkness seemed complete, except where the swift glow-worms of hamlets and isolated farms and the occasional gleams of car or lorry headlights exposed the whiteness of snow in the narrow valleys through which the road wound. Then, lower country, and a gleaming, humped plain of whiteness stretched before and beneath the aircraft.

'Finland,' the pilot announced, but added nothing else.

Clark attempted repose, sensing like a man with a severely limited water supply, the waste of adrenalin his tension betokened. The shadow of the aircraft raced over the snow less then a hundred feet below them as the Harrier skimmed under the radar net. Bodø radar would have reported a loss of contact immediately they had finished refuelling, and the matter would not have been taken further. Neither neutral country, Sweden nor Finland, had been required to know of the passage of the Harrier, nor would they have sanctioned its incursion into their airspace.

A herd of reindeer, startled by the roar of the engine, scattered at the gallop beneath them. Then the darkness of trees, then whiteness again. The cloud cover above the cockpit was broken, mere rags now, and the moon gleamed. They were so close to the ground, it was like impossibly fast skiing rather than flying. It was a mere seventy minutes since they had ended their refuelling, and their flight was more than half completed. Clark glanced to port and starboard, and considered the packs in the two underwing pods. Right hand good, left hand bad, he told himself with a smile that did not come easily. Right-hand pack, repair equipment, meters, spares. Left-hand pack, explosives, detonators, the end of 'Leopard'. He believed that it was the left-hand pack that he would be forced to use. He did not consider his own fate. He would be arrested as a spy, naturally. Prison, interrogation, exchange for a Russian agent. It was a pattern of events that was predictable and not to be considered. The trick was, not to get caught, even when walking – swimming – into a Russian naval base; don't get caught.

The quick, easy toughness amused and comforted him. There was always a persistent sense of unreality about field operations, until the clock started ticking and the adrenelin became uncontrollable, and he knew, from experience and from training, that there was no alternative but to exist within that spacious immortality. It was the state of mind the CIA called 'concussive readiness'. It was the state of mind of the successful field agent.

Lake Inari, the sacred lake of Finnish Lapland, began to flow beneath them, illuminated by moonlight, the town of Ivalo a smear of light, then a mild haze, then nothing. The occasional lights of boats, the carpet of ice-dotted water persisting for mile after mile, an unrelieved, gleaming expanse where only the few black humps and spots of islands relieved its unreflecting mirror.

Before they reached the north-eastern shore of Inari, the Harrier banked to starboard, altering course to the east and crossing the border into Norway, a tongue of NATO thrusting southwards from Kirkenes and the coast between Finland and the Soviet Union. A tidier, smoother landscape – though he wondered whether that was not simply illusion – well-dotted with lights, then within a mile they were skimming the treetops of well-forested country, and there was a sullen, hazy glow to starboard.

The pilot throttled back, and the blur of the landscape became a dark flowing movement. Clark could not see the trees themselves, not even small clearings in the forest, but the landscape now possessed a life of its own. It was no longer a relief map over which they passed, or a three-dimensional papier-mâché model.

The lights to starboard were from the watch-towers and the rows of lights along the wire of the border fence separating Norway from the Soviet Union. Clark swallowed, then breathed consciously at a relaxed pace, spacing the intervals between each inhalation and exhalation exactly and precisely. Right hand good, left hand bad, his mind recited again.

He saw the lights of a string of hamlets along the one good road north to Kirkenes. Kirkenes itself was a dim glow on the horizon ahead of them. Then the Harrier flicked to starboard, altering course eastwards to run along the Norwegian border. Pechenga was eight miles beyond the border. Eight miles, and they were perhaps now twelve miles from the border as it swung north to the coast. The Harrier was at little more than one third speed and well below the radar net. Four miles per minute. Three minutes. No, already two minutes fifty. The landscape seemed to take on more vivacity, as if he were studying it in order to remember it. The ribbon of a road, dark patches of trees, vague lights, sheets of white snow. Lumpy, softened white hills. Then the sullen, ribbon-like glow, enlarging to a string of lights, decorating the dárkness beyond. A gap in the trees, after a narrow strip of water no more than a pool at that speed, where the two fences and the lights marched north and south, and then the glow was behind them, fading.

He was inside the Soviet Union.

The pilot flicked off the auto-pilot and the terrain-following radar, and assumed manual control of the Harrier. The plane's airspeed dropped. Pechenga was a bright, hazy globe of light ahead. The Soviet Union. Fortress Russia. Clark had never taken part in a penetration operation before.

'Ready? It's coming up to port.'

He saw the water of a lake and an uninhabited landscape of woods and open stretches of snow. The Harrier slowed even further, almost to a hover, above a tiny white space between the trees. The image of a helicopter came to Clark again. The sound of the Pegasus engine faded, and the pilot modulated the air brake. Then he increased the engine's thrust once more, directing it downwards through the four nozzles beneath the fuselage, putting the Harrier into a hover.

Snow blew up round the canopy, and the dark seemed to grow above them by some freak of fertilisation. More snow, obscuring the canopy, then the final wobble, the dying-away of the engine, and the heaviness of the aircraft settling into the snow and slush.

'Right. You're on your own. Don't waste time.'

'See anything?'

'No.'

Clark opened the canopy. Snow powdered his upturned face. He hefted himself upright, and then swung his body awkwardly over the high sill of the fuselage, beginning his burglary of the Soviet Union. He looked around him, the sudden chill of the early night and the wind making his teeth chatter. He scanned the area of trees around the clearing three times, then he saw the pale, easily missed wink of a torch signalling.

'Right. He's there,' he said to the pilot.

'Good luck.'

'Thanks.' He placed his feet firmly in the foot-holds on the side of the fuselage, and climbed down. He moved beneath the port wing and snapped open the clips on the underwing pod. He lifted out the pack – left hand bad – and laid it on the snow. Then he unloaded the starboard pack.

He picked up the two packs and moved away from the Harrier, dragging the heavy packs through the snow, which was deeper outside the half-melted circle caused by the downthrust of the Pegasus engine. When he looked up, a small, bulky figure was hurrying towards him. There was the inevitable, electric moment of doubt, was it the right man, was it the KGB, almost bound to be the KGB? Then the man spoke.

'Welcome, my friend –'

The remainder of what he said, Clark could see his lips moving, was drowned by the increasing whine of the engine. Clark, still gripping the man's hand tightly, turned to watch as the Harrier rose above the level of the trees, lurched forward, then smoothly accelerated. He was inside the Soviet Union, a couple of miles from the naval base of Pechenga, and on his own, except for the help of a grocer. It was difficult not to feel a sense of hopelessness nibbling at the feeling of concussion which he required if he was to succeed.

The grocer picked up one of the packs, and hefted it on to his back.

'Come,' he said. 'Come.'

Leper. The girl wanted to get up, talk to the two people passing twenty yards away below them, but he held her down, his hand now almost out of habit over her mouth. Fortunately, they didn't have a dog with them. The man wore an anorak and carried a camera, swinging by its strap, and the woman was wearing a fur coat that looked almost like camouflage, white with dark patches. Hyde listened to them talking, watched the man put his arm around the woman because she remarked on the cold of the evening, watched them, too, look up at the fading light and the gathering clouds; finally recognised that they were heading back towards the car park.

Two reasons. He didn't know them and therefore he distrusted them, and also he could not risk enlisting anyone on their behalf. He'd killed now. Anyone who came into contact with him was thereby endangered. Leper.

He released the girl, and she shuffled away from him, rubbing her arms, touching her mouth where his hand had been clamped.

'Why?' she almost wailed. 'Why not?'

'Because you could get them killed, or us killed. Take your pick.' The wetness of the ferns was soaking into him. He was hungry, his stomach hollow and rumbling. He was thirsty. He scooped up a thin film of half-melted snow, and pressed it into his mouth. Then he rubbed his wet hand over his face in an attempt to revive himself. The girl looked no fresher than he felt.

'They were out for a walk,' she said sullenly.

'Maybe. Look, just let it rest, will you? We're on our own, and that's all there is to it.'

'Why – why are they chasing us?' the girl asked, her face recovering earlier anxieties, past terrors.

Hyde studied her in disbelief. 'What?'

'My father's safe – why do they want us?'

'Oh, Christ – don't you understand the simplest moves in the game?' Hyde shook his head. 'Perhaps you don't. Obviously, Petrunin has had new orders. You're as valuable to them now as you were before. If they have you, they can trade you off for your dad. See?'

'How? You've got him, for Christ's sake!'

'He's not in prison. If he knew they had you, he'd take the first chance of walking out to join you. On a plane to Moscow.'

The girl appeared about to ask another question, then she fell silent, watching her hands as if they belonged to someone else while they picked at the stiff, rimed grass.

275

'You ready?'

She looked helplessly, tiredly at him, then got slowly to her feet. 'Yes.'

'Come on, then.'

After the death of the deer and the Russian, they had worked their way east across the Chase, assuming that other men on foot, and the helicopter, would pursue them north, towards the Stafford road. The helicopter, blinded by the shroud of firs through which they ran, drifted away northwards, its noise following it like a declining wall. They saw no other Russians.

Hyde waited until this moment, when it was almost dark and the thin, half-melted sheen of snow had begun to gleam like silver, before attempting to make the car park and the road where they had first stopped. The rifle range was behind them now, to the north.

They trod carefully down the slope of dead ferns, then began to ascend slowly along a tiny deer-track through the tightly growing, restraining heather. Almost dark. Perhaps they could risk this open slope –

The shout was alarming, but almost as unnoticed, except by Hyde's subconscious, as the bark of a dog. The girl looked round slowly, but only because he had stopped. A second shout brought him out of his lassitude. A figure on a rise, perhaps two hundred yards away, waving what might have been a stick. Rifles now. No easy-to-hide handguns. They had put them less than equal with him. His body protested at the effort required of it. The girl bumped into him, staggering as though ill or blind. He took her hand. A second figure rose over the edge of the rise, outlined against the pale last gleam of the day. Cloud pressed down on the open bowl of dead heather in which he had allowed them to be trapped.

The helicopter. Almost too dark to see them, too dark for them to make it out until it blurted over the rise and bore down on them, its noise deafening by its suddenness. He did not have to tell the girl to run. The deer track was not wide enough for both of them and he floundered through wet, calf-high heather keeping pace with her.

Shots, deadened by the noise of the rotors and the racing

of his blood. Wild shooting. The helicopter overshot them, and began to bank round.

'Over there!'

The land folded into a deeper hollow. Deer scattered out of it as they approached it, startled by the helicopter. A hallucinatory moment as the grey, small, lithe, panicking forms were all around them, and Hyde remembered the pain-clouded eye into which he had looked that afternoon before he squeezed the trigger; then the deer were gone and the hollow was dark and wound away in a narrow trench which they followed. It led northwards, back towards the higher ground and the rifle range, but he had no alternative but to follow it. They ducked down, keeping below the level of the ground, then the trench petered out and they were left almost at the top of the rise.

Hyde threw himself flat and looked over the lip of the ground. Nothing. The light had gone. In no more than a few minutes, there was nothing. The noise of the helicopter was a furious, enraged buzzing on the edge of hearing, as if already miles away.

Couldn't be – ? He turned on to his back, and groaned. Worse then he thought. He had imagined a flesh wound, a scratch, but it was throbbing. His whole arm was throbbing. He tried to sit up, and then lay back, another groan escaping him.

'What is it?'

'Nothing – '

'What's the matter?'

She touched his shoulder, and immediately the pain was intense, almost unbearable, and then he could not decipher her expression or even see the white blob of her face any longer. It rushed away from him at great speed, down a dark tunnel.

Twelve: ACCESS

'On station.' Eastoe's communications with Aubrey were now of a single, close-lipped, unhelpful kind, the RAF officer providing only a grudging assistance. Aubrey, knowing it would not interfere with the pilot's efficiency, was prepared to allow the man his mood.

The Nimrod had begun flying a box pattern over an inshore area of the Barents Sea which would take her to within a few miles of the Soviet border at the end of each eastward leg of the pattern. Travelling westwards, the Nimrod would pass up the Varangerfjord, then turn north across the block of land jutting into the Barents Sea known as Varangerhalvöya, then turn on to her eastward leg which would again take her out over the Barents. A rigid rectangle of airspace, at any point of which the Nimrod was no more than seventy miles from Clark's transceiver in Pechenga.

Aubrey glanced once more through the window in the fuselage. A red, winking light to port of the Nimrod, a little behind and below. A Northrop F-5 of the Royal Norwegian Air Force, one of three somewhat outdated fighter aircraft that provided their screen. The arrangement had been considered necessary by MoD Air, and by the Norwegians, but Aubrey considered it mere window-dressing. He did not anticipate problems with Soviet aircraft, and if there were any such problems, the F-5s would be immediately recalled to the military airfield at Kirkenes.

'Thank you, Squadron Leader,' Aubrey replied to Eastoe. 'Would you come forward to the flight deck, Mr Aubrey?' Eastoe added, and Aubrey was immediately struck by the conspiratorial edge to the voice. He removed his headphones and stood up, not looking at Quin.

He moved down the aircraft gingerly, an old man moving down a bus or a train, hands ready to grab or fumble for support. He paused between the two pilots' chairs, and Eastoe turned to him. His face was grave, that of a messenger with bad news to impart; some battle lost.

'What is it, Squadron Leader?'

'This.' He handed Aubrey a sheet torn from a message pad. 'It's for you, Eyes Only. No good letting Quin hear the bad news.'

The message was from Shelley, and it informed Aubrey – who felt his heart clutched by a cold, inescapable hand – that Hyde and the girl had disappeared somewhere between Manchester and Birmingham, without trace. Shelley had organised the search which was now proceeding. Aubrey looked up from the sheet, and found Eastoe's gaze intently fastened on him, as if demanding some human frailty from him by way of reaction.

'Thank you, Squadron Leader,' Aubrey said stiffly. 'You were quite right to keep this from Mr Quin. You will continue to do so.'

'Makes things a bit awkward, mm?' Eastoe sneered. 'Any reply?'

'Nothing I could say would make the slightest difference,' Aubrey snapped, and turned on his heel, retracing his steps down the tunnel of the aircraft, composing his features and silencing the flurry of thoughts and images in his mind. Now all that mattered was that Quin functioned like a machine, when the time came.

He regained his seat. Quin seemed uninterested in his reappearance. Aubrey studied him.

Quin, under scrutiny, became quickly and cunningly alert. His posture was totally self-defensive. Then he attempted to achieve the academic trick of distracting attention by vigorously polishing his spectacles. Aubrey's features wrinkled in impatience, and this seemed to further embolden Quin.

'Your man hasn't called in, not since he left the aircraft,' he said.

Aubrey was incensed. 'His name is Clark,' he remarked icily.

'But, the time factor?' Quin persisted. Aubrey realised that the man's silence for the last hour had led to a consolidation of truculent fear. He had, as it were, husbanded his bloody-mindedness until they arrived on station. Every minute that Clark had not reported in satisfied Quin that there would be a premature, and not long delayed, end to his confinement aboard the Nimrod. Clark, in fact, because of the short range of his transceiver, had not signalled them since the test. The Harrier pilot, making for Bardufoss to refuel had sent one brief, coded signal to inform Aubrey that Clark had landed safely and without trouble. That had been forty minutes before.

Aubrey looked at his watch. Eight-thirty. He knew that in two, at most three, hours, he would cancel the operation. 'Plumber' would be over unless they heard from Clark within that time. He would have been caught, or killed. Aubrey composed himself to wait, wishing that he could do it somewhere where he did not have to confront Quin across a silent communications console in the skeletal, untidy fuselage of a Nimrod. It was, he considered, rather too much like sitting inside a television set. At least, its screens and wiring and circuitry and sensors gave much the same impression as did the innards of his set, whenever the engineer from the rental company had to come to his flat to effect a repair.

But it was Quin, more than anyone, who angered and threw him into doubt. Clark had to depend upon this pompous, cowardly, indifferent man, and it seemed unfair.

Abandon that line of thought, Aubrey instructed himself. You will have to make the man helpful, when the time comes. He felt the Nimrod, at twenty thousand feet, make its turn on to the eastward leg of its flight pattern, out over the Barents and towards the Soviet border. Somewhere to the north of them, perhaps no more than twenty or thirty miles away, was the location of the attack on the *Proteus* and the ledge where she had rested until the Russians had raised her to the surface.

He found his fingers had adopted a drumming, impatient pattern of movement against one side of the console. Guiltily, he stopped the noise immediately. Quin seemed wreathed in self-satisfaction. He had evidently decided that Clark would fail, even had failed, to penetrate Pechenga. He was like a man sheltering from the rain. The shower would stop, soon, and he could make his way home.

'What about the air tanks?'

'Those I have stored for you with a friend. No, not one of

us, but he can be trusted. It is lucky I had them still. I have not been asked to make a – what do you say, reconnaissance – ?' Clark nodded, smiling. 'Yes, a reconnaissance of the harbour for a long time. My old wetsuit – perished, alas. But the tanks are good, my friend, I assure you.'

'And I believe you.'

They were seated in the small, cramped room above the grocer's shop. The Pechenga agent-in-place for SIS was a short, rotund man with a stubble on his jaw. His eyes were small and black, like raisins folded into the sallow dough of his flesh. When he smiled, he showed remarkably white dentures. Clark trusted his ordinariness as much as his thoroughness. His name was Pasvik. Once, generations before, his family had been Norwegian. Whether that had been before the war, before the first war, before the Revolution, even Pasvik did not know.

Pasvik owned the grocery shop himself. His father had acquired the contract for supplying eggs and flour to the naval base, for use in preparing officers' meals. It was his patronage, his 'By Appointment' that had enabled him to retain control of his shop, collect the naval intelligence London required and used, and which gave him freedom of movement and access. Also, it provided him with what Clark suspected was a thriving black-market business involving smuggling from Scandinavia and supplying to the naval base and Pechenga's Party officials modest but lucrative luxury goods. Pasvik had made only passing mention of these activities, as if he felt they qualified his status as an accredited agent of London, but for the American it only increased his awareness of the man's intelligence and nerve.

Clark studied the large-scale map that Pasvik had laid on the wooden table between them. A large brandy glass stood near Clark's right hand. The odour of the liquor mingled with the smell of bacon and flour and washing powder – one of the modest luxuries, Clark supposed, since he had seen the brand-name Persil on one shelf of the store-room behind the shop.

Much of the map was originally blank, but the censored, sensitive areas of the town and the naval base had been pencilled in, and labelled, by Pasvik. Pechenga lay at the neck of a narrow inlet in the coast where the river Pechenga reached the Barents Sea. It was a thriving northern fishing port as well as an important subsidiary base to Murmansk, headquarters of the Soviet Union's most important fleet. The fishing harbour lay on the northern outskirts of the town – Clark had smelt it on the wind, even locked in the back of Pasvik's delivery van – while the naval base, as if hiding behind the civilian port, seemed from the map to be entrenched across the neck of the inlet, behind its massive harbour wall. The submarine pens, his mission target, were arrayed and dug in along the southern flank of the base, furthest from the fishing harbour.

It was evident to Clark that Pasvik regarded himself with some reluctance but without evasion as expendable in the cause of 'Plumber'. Clark, however, realised that he could not efficiently exploit the man to the degree of endangering his life, and was pleased at that fact. Pasvik making a late, night-time delivery to the base would be a transparent pretext, and the man would undoubtedly be searched. Clark would have to go in by water, not with the groceries.

'We could easily do it,' Pasvik said hesitantly, as if he had read Clark's thoughts. Clark shook his head.

'Uh-uh. That's the obvious way to get caught. The water is the only way.'

Only then did Pasvik display his full fear and pleasure, in the same instant that exposed his dentures, creased up the dough around his eyes, and brought beads of perspiration to his forehead. These he wiped away with a red handkerchief.

'Thank you.' he said.

'No problem. This,' he added, dabbing his finger on the map, 'the net?' Pasvik nodded. 'Here, too?'

'Yes. You will need to go over, or beneath, two nets.'

'Mines?'

Pasvik pulled a leather-bound, slim notebook from his pocket. It seemed misplaced about his person. It required an executive's breast-pocket, in a grey suit. Pasvik laughed at the expression on Clark's face.

'One of a consignment that I kept for myself,' he

282

explained. 'They are very popular with junior officers.' He opened the book. 'This, you understand, is a digest of gossip and observation collected over some years.' He fished in the breast pocket of his shirt, and hitched a pair of wire-framed spectacles over his ears. Then he cleared his throat. 'The mines are of different types – proximity detonated, trip-wired, acoustic, magnetic. They are set at various depths, and the pattern is very complicated. I do not have any details. Indiscretion in Red Navy officers goes only so far, you understand?'

'The mines I don't worry too much about. Except the contact stuff. Are they marked? Do you have any idea of their shape and size?'

'Ah, there I can help you, I think.' He showed a page of the notebook to Clark. The sleeve of the old dressing-gown that he had borrowed from Pasvik brushed the brandy glass, spilling what remained of the drink across the map in a tobacco-coloured stain.

'Damn!' Clark exclaimed, soaking up the liquid with the sleeve of his dressing-gown. 'Sorry.' Some of the neatly written labelling on the map had smudged.

'No matter.'

Clark studied the drawing. A small mine, probably, activated by direct contact with the horns. To deter and destroy small vessels venturing into the restricted waters of the inner harbour, even to kill a swimmer. He handed the notebook back to Pasvik. The stained map absorbed his attention like an omen.

'Okay. Where's the *Proteus*?'

'Here are the submarine pens. This one, as far as I can make out. Gossip, as you will imagine, has been rife.' He tapped at one of the numbered pens. There were two dozen of them and *Proteus* was supposedly in the fifth one, measuring from the eastern end of the pens. 'Many of them are empty, of course.'

'Where will you be?' Clark asked.

'Ah – here,' Pasvik replied, 'you see, in a direct line. It is, or was, a favourite picnic spot in summer.' He sighed.

Clark looked at his watch. 'Nine-forty. Time to get going?'

'Yes.'

'Will you be stopped on the road?'

'Yes, but it's not likely I will be searched. Not going in the direction of the fishing harbour. Anyone who knows me will assume I am making a pick-up of some smuggled goods from a freighter. On the way back, they may be more nosey. So I will have some of the old favourites – stockings, perfume, chocolate, cigarettes, even sex books from Sweden – in the back of the van. I make a habit of free gifts, once in a while. You are ready?'

Clark found Pasvik studying him. The raisin eyes were deep in their folds, but bright with assessment and observation. Eventually, Pasvik nodded and stood up. 'You will make it,' he announced, 'of that I am reasonably sure.'

'Thanks.'

Clark took off the dressing-gown and laid it on Pasvik's narrow, uncomfortable-looking bed. Then he donned the immersion suit again, heaving it up and around his body, finally pulling on the headcap.

'Another brandy?'

'No thanks.'

As they went down the bare wooden stairs to the store-room and the small, noisome yard where Pasvik had parked his van, the grocer said, 'So, Mr Aubrey is not very far away at this moment, up in the sky, mm?'

'He is. At least, he ought to be. I'll signal him before I take to the water.'

'I can do that.'

'Better me than you.' In the darkness, Clark patted the side of his head, then the tiny throat-mike beneath his chin. 'This stuff has got to work. I don't want to find out it doesn't after I get aboard the *Proteus*.'

Pasvik unbolted the door and they went out into a wind that skulked and whipped around the yard. Clark looked up at the sky. A few light grey clouds, huge patches of stars. The clouds seemed hardly to be moving. Almost a full moon, which he regretted. However, the improvement in the weather would mean a less choppy surface in the harbour, and he might need to conserve the air in Pasvik's tanks. Pasvik, he noticed as the man crossed to the van and opened the rear doors, moved with a leg-swinging shuffle.

Presumably the limp explained why he no longer carried out immersion-suited surveillance of the harbour.

Clark climbed into the rear of the van, and the doors slammed shut on him. He squatted in a tight, low crouch behind stacked wooden crates, near the partition separating the rear of the van from the driver. He watched as Pasvik clambered into the driving seat, slammed his door, and then turned to him.

'Okay?'

'Okay.'

Pasvik started the engine, and ground the car into gear. A moment later, they were turning out of the narrow lane behind the row of shops into a poorly lit street on which a few cars and one or two lorries were the only traffic. Clark felt tension jump like sickness into his throat, and he swallowed hard. He squeezed his arms around his knees, which were drawn up under his chin. His two packs – right hand good, left hand bad – were near his feet. Without conscious thought, he reached out and unsealed one of the packs. He reached into one of the small side pockets and withdrew a polythene-wrapped package, undid the elastic bands, and removed the gun. A small, light .22 Heckler & Koch pistol with a ten-round magazine, effective stopping range less than thirty metres. He unzipped the neck of his immersion suit and placed the re-wrapped pistol inside. If he ever needed the gun, he was close to being finished.

The grocery van trailed a tarpaulin-shrouded lorry along the northbound road, through a dingy, industrialised suburb of Pechenga. Pasvik seemed to have no desire for conversation. Perhaps, Clark admitted, he thought talk would make his passenger more edgy. Pechenga was little more than a ghost town after dark. There were few pedestrians, fewer vehicles. The town seemed subdued, even oppressed, by the security that surrounded the naval installation. The place had a wartime look, a besieged, blacked-out, curfewed feeling and appearance which depressed and yet aggravated his awareness.

There was a haze of light to be seen over the low factory roofs from the naval base, a glow like that from the border lights as he had seen them from the Harrier. Then he felt the van slowing. The brake lights of the lorry in front of them were bright red. There was a squeal of air brakes.

'A checkpoint – outside the civilian harbour. Get down,' Pasvik instructed him. 'Cover yourself with the tarpaulin.'

White light haloed the bulk of the lorry. Clark could hear voices, and the noise of heavy military boots, though he could see no one. He slid into a prone position, and tugged the tarpaulin over him, which smelt of cabbage and meal. Once underneath, he unzipped the neck of his immersion suit once more, though he was able consciously to prevent himself from unwrapping the gun. Nevertheless, through the polythene his finger half-curled around the trigger. His thumb rested against the safety catch. He could not prevent finger and thumb taking what seemed a necessary hold upon the pistol.

A voice, very close. Clark's Russian was good, but he reacted more to the interrogative tone. A guard leaning his head into the driver's window. Pasvik's voice seemed jocular, confiding in reply.

'Hello, Pasvik. Out and about again?'

Pasvik smiled, showing his dentures, opening his hands on the wheel in a shrugging gesture.

'You know how business is, Grigory.'

'Keep your voice down, Pasvik – the officer'll hear you.'

'Then you'll be in trouble, eh, my friend?'

'You want me to search your van, have everything out on the road, now and on the way back – eh, Pasvik?'

'Don't be irritable, my friend.'

'Look, I've told you – I'm not your friend. Just keep your voice down.'

'You want to see my papers?'

'Yes – quick, here's my officer. Bastard.' Grigory uttered the last word almost under his breath.

'What's going on here?' the officer enquired above the noise of the lorry moving off and pulling into the docks. Beyond his short dapper figure Pasvik could see the outlines of cranes, the silhouettes of cargo and fishing vessels. 'Are this man's papers in order?'

'Yes, sir.'

The officer took them from Grigory, perused them in a showy, self-satisfied, cursory manner, then handed them back. He turned on his heel and strutted away. Grigory pulled a scowling face behind his back, then thrust the papers back at Pasvik. He bent near to the window again.

'I want some more,' he whispered.

'More what?'

'Those books.'

'You sell them off again, eh, Grigory?'

'No!' Grigory's face changed colour.

'I'll see what I can do. Stop me on the way back, get in the back of the van then. I'll leave some for you, under the tarpaulin. Okay?'

'Okay. I'm off duty at midnight, though.'

'I'll be back before then.'

Grigory stepped back, and waved Pasvik on. The red and white pole between the two guard huts swung up, and Pasvik drove the van into the civilian harbour. In his mirror, Pasvik could see the officer speaking to Grigory. The posture of his body and the bend of his head indicated a reprimand rather than an enquiry as to Pasvik's business. He would have to be careful when Grigory collected his sex books from the back of the van on the return journey. Perhaps he needed something for the officer, too?

He drove out of the string of white lights along the main thoroughfare of the docks, turning into a narrow, unlit alley between two long, low warehouses. Then he turned out on to a poorly illuminated wharf, driving slowly past the bulk of a Swedish freighter. Music from the ship, a drunk singing. A head peering over the side. Two armed guards patrolling, leaning towards each other in conversation, stultified by routine and uneventfulness. Pasvik stopped the car in the shadow of a warehouse, beneath the dark skeleton of a dockside crane.

'Very well, my friend. You can get out now.'

Pasvik slipped out of the van, and opened the rear doors. The two guards, unconcerned at the noise of his engine, were walking away from him, into and then out of a pool of light. Clark sat on the edge of the van, stretching. Then he hefted the two packs on to the concrete of the wharf.

'Thanks,' he said.

'You have everything in your mind?'

Clark nodded. 'Yes. What about the tanks?'

'One moment.' Pasvik limped off swiftly, towards the door of the warehouse. He appeared to possess a key, for Clark heard the door squeak open, then the intervening moments before the door squeaked again were filled with the singing of the Swedish drunk, who had become utterly maudlin. Clark heard, as the door closed again, the reassuring metallic bump as the tanks struck the concrete. Then Pasvik came scuttling out of the shadows, hefting the two air tanks over his shoulder. He placed them, like game retrieved, at Clark's feet. The American inspected and tested them. The hiss of air satisfied him. Both gauges registered full.

'Good.'

'The patrol will be back in five minutes. By that time, I must be aboard the freighter and you must be in the water. Come.'

Pasvik helped Clark strap the tanks to his back, lifting the mouthpiece and its twin hoses gently over his head like a ceremonial garland. Then they carried the packs across the wharf, slipping quickly through the one dim patch of light into the shadow of the freighter. Pasvik make a lugubrious face at the singing, still audible from above. The water was still and oily below them, against the side of the ship. Clark could smell fish on the windy air. He unwound short lengths of nylon rope from each pack, and clipped them on to his weighted belt. As he did so, he felt he was imprisoning himself. An anticipation of utter weariness overcame him for a moment, and then he shrugged it off. He would make it, even with that weight being towed or pushed, since the packs would become buoyant in the water.

'Okay,' he said, about to slip the mouthpiece of his air supply between his lips. 'Thanks.'

'Don't forget the landmarks I described – don't forget the patrol boats – don't forget the contact mines, some of them are small enough, sensitive enough . . . ' Pasvik halted his litany when Clark held up his hand.

'Okay, okay.' Clark grinned. 'I'll take care, Mom.'

Pasvik stifled a delighted laugh. 'Goodbye, my friend. Good luck.'

He lifted one of the packs as Clark moved to the iron

ladder set in the side of the wharf, leading down to the water. Clark, holding the other pack, began to climb down, his back to the freighter's hull. Then he paused, his head just above the level of the concrete, and Pasvik handed him the second pack. Clark appeared almost to overbalance, then he stumbled the last few steps and slid into the water. Pasvik peered down at him. Clark waved, adjusted his mouthpiece and facemask, then began swimming out and around the bow of the freighter, pushing the two packs ahead of him, slowly and awkwardly.

Pasvik watched until the swimming man was hidden by the hull of the Swedish ship, then softly whistled and shook his head. Then he slapped his hands together, shrugging Clark away, and headed for the boarding ladder up to the deck of the freighter.

Clark swam easily, using his legs and fins, his arms around the two packs, guiding them through the water. Their buoyancy made them lighter, easier to handle in the water. After a few minutes, he trod water, and opened the channel of his transceiver. The ether hummed in his ear.

'All is well,' he said.

Aubrey's voice, slowed down from the spit of sound on his earpiece, replied a few moments later. 'Good luck.'

Clark switched off, and began swimming again. Ahead of him, there was a rippling necklace of lights along the harbour wall, with one dark gap like a missing stone in the middle. The water was still calm, its surface only riffled like pages quickly turned by the wind. He headed for the dark gap in the lights, keeping the flash of the small lighthouse to his left, and the steering lights of a small cargo ship to his right. It was a matter of some seven or eight hundred yards – or so he had estimated from the map – to the harbour wall. He moved with an almost lazy stroke of his legs, using the buoyant packs like a child might use water wings. The mouthpiece of the air supply rested on the packs just in front of his face.

It was twenty minutes before he reached the choppier water of the inlet beyond the fish and cargo harbour. Suddenly, as he passed between the lights, the water confronted him instead of allowing him easy passage. The packs began to bob and move as if attempting to escape him. He checked his compass, took a sighting on the lights above the twin guard towers at the entrance to the naval installation, and rested for a few moments, accustoming his body and his breathing to the choppy sea. Then he swam on.

The wall of the harbour curved away from him, as if enclosing him, then it rose in height and the lights along it were brighter and closer together. He was paralleling the wall of the Pechenga naval base.

His awareness, despite his experience and his desire that it should not be so, began to retreat into the confines of his immediate surroundings and experience – the packs behind him like brakes moving sluggishly through the water, the choppy little wavelets dashing against his facemask, his arms moving out in front and then behind, even the tight cap of his suit seemed to contain his senses as well as his mind. Thus the patrol boat was a light before it was a noise, and a light he could not explain for a moment. And it was close, far too close.

A searchlight swept across the surface of the water. The boat, little larger than a motor yacht, was a hydro-foil. Clark, catching the high-bowed outline behind the searchlight as he was startled out of his dreamlike state, saw its forward and aft gun turrets, its depth charge racks. It was paralleling his course, moving along the harbour wall. Even though startled, he continued to observe the patrol boat move lazily across his vision. The searchlight swept back and forth, moved closer to the wall, swept back and forth again, moved closer . . .

Clark panicked into acute consciousness. He fumbled with the two packs, hauling them into his embrace. He ripped clumsily at the valve on the first one – the light moved towards him again – and failed to turn it at the first attempt, and his hand hovered towards the valve on the second pack – the light swung away, then began to swing back, the patrol boat was sliding past him sixty metres away – then he turned feverishly at the first valve, hearing above the panic of his breathing and blood in his ears, the hiss of air. The bag sank lower in the water, and he grabbed at the second valve, telling himself ineffectually to slow down – the light moved forward, closer, like lava flowing over the wrinkled water, almost illuminating the pack that remained afloat – he twisted the valve, heard the air, watched the light swing away, then back, then begin its arc that would reach his head. The pack slipped beneath the water, and he flicked himself into a dive – the light slid across the distressed water where he had been, hesitated, then moved on.

Clark thrust the mouthpiece between his teeth, bit on it as he inhaled, and drove downwards against the restraint of the two packs from which he had not released sufficient air. They pulled like parachute brakes against his movement. The twin diesel engines of the patrol boat thrummed through the black water. He looked up. Yes, he could see the light dancing across the surface, as if it still searched for him. Slowly, it faded. The vibration and hollow noise of the boat's engines moved away. He allowed the buoyancy of the two packs to slowly pull him back to the surface. When his head came out of the water, he saw the patrol boat some hundreds of yards away, its searchlight playing at the foot of the harbour wall.

He lay in the water, the packs bobbing just beneath the surface on either side of him, until his breathing and his heart rate had returned to normal. Then he embraced each of the packs in turn, pressing the button on each small cylinder of oxygen, refloating the packs on the surface. Having to drag them through the water would have exhausted him long before he reached the *Proteus*.

He swam on, still resting his frame on the packs as he clutched them to him. Ten minutes later, he reached the entrance to the harbour. The guard towers on either wall, apart from beacon lights, carried powerful searchlights which swept back and forth across the dark opening between them and swept, too, the water of the harbour and the basin beyond it. He trod water, absorbing the pattern of movement of the searchlights. He saw the silhouettes of armed guards, the barrels of anti-aircraft cannon pointing to the night sky. He felt cold, the chill of water seeping through his immersion suit. Thought seemed to come slowly, but not because of the cold; rather, because he already knew the dangers and the risks. There was no necessity to discover or analyse them. The submarine net stretched across the entrance to the harbour, perhaps fifteen feet above the water. He would have to climb it.

He edged with furtive strokes of his fins around the base of the harbour wall, touching its barnacled sliminess with his hand, reaching the steel net directly beneath one of the guard towers. The packs had begun to resist him, he imagined, as if they had lost their buoyancy. He let them drift behind him as he clung to the mesh, watching the lights. Thirty seconds. He lowered his arm as his watch confirmed the gap of darkness between the passage of each light across the harbour entrance for the second time. He had thirty seconds in which to climb the net, mount it like a rider, drag his packs after him, and climb down again to the water. He could not wait for the chance of the net being opened on its boom to admit a vessel.

The light of the searchlight on the opposite wall slid down the concrete and swung away into the harbour. His fins hung round his neck, and his mouthpiece dangled between their strange necklace. He felt clumsy, burdened. He reached up, and began climbing. The heavy steel cords of the submarine net did not even vibrate with his effort.

Seven, eight, nine, ten, eleven –

The seconds began racing away from him. His mind was blind and indifferent to the progress of the light, hearing only the moving numbers in his head. The numbers ran ahead of him, as his breathing did. *Thirteen, fourteen.* He felt the weight of the packs thrum lightly through the steel net.

Top. One leg, *sixteen*, other leg, packs holding him back, *seventeen*, swing the other leg over against the restraint of the two packs, *eighteen*, his stomach was stretched and pressed painfully along the steel boom, *nineteen*, stand up, *twenty*, five seconds behind already, lift the packs, lift the first one over, drop it, *twenty-three*, hold on, hold on, as the inertia of the pack tried to pull him from the net, arms full of pain as he resisted the pack's weight, *twenty-five*, other pack now, easier, drop it, hang on, pain again, *twenty-seven*, go now, go –

He scuttled down the net, feeling it vibrate now, his breath ragged, his body as tense as a spring, as vulnerable as an insect's. He was aware of the light on the opposite side of the entrance swinging back now, a hazy blur at the corner of his vision. *Thirty-one*. The light slid down the net, opening the shadow beneath the harbour wall, slipping across the small blur of bubbles his entrance into the water had made.

Clark clung to the net, forcing the mouthpiece back between his teeth, trying to calm his breathing, feeling the packs tugging him lazily back towards the surface. He held on to the net with one hand, and reduced their buoyancy with the other, his hand completing the task robotically. They bobbed beside him in the darkness, nudging him as if to remind him of their presence, or to ingratiate themselves because they had almost betrayed him.

He clung to the net until the searchlight's wavering globe of light had passed over his head another four times. Then he further adjusted the buoyancy of the packs so that they began to pull at him, drag him down. He fitted his fins, and let go of the net, moving smoothly down into the darkness.

The mines, now. Magnetic, electronic contact. Pasvik had been unable to provide the pattern. MoD had had some detail, but not enough. There did not seem to be channels through the minefield, since the mines would all be armed or disarmed by remote signal. If a Soviet vessel entered the harbour, the mines would be switched off. Simple. Effective. Clark reasoned that he must dive deep, almost to the bottom, to avoid the contact mines which would be set off by a touch, and which would have been laid at varying depths. He swam down, levelling off when his depth gauge registered a hundred feet. Time closed in on him immediately as decompression became a determining factor. He flicked on his lamp. The packs idled alongside him as he trod water. Compass direction checked, together with the time and the depth, he began swimming, moving rapidly now, ignoring the sense of isolation in his system like an antidote to adrenalin, and which assailed him for the first time since he had left the cockpit of the Harrier. The weak glow of the lamp illuminated the dull silver of fish and the strange forest of cables growing up from the harbour bed below. Above him, invisible, the mines sat at their determined depths. He jogged one cable, then another, and occasionally the packs snagged against them, operating like brakes. He had guessed correctly. He was too deep for the mines themselves.

He swung the lamp from side to side, however, in a precautionary swathe. The mine that came suddenly out of the darkness still surprised him. He flicked aside, remembering the two packs only as he did so. He stopped himself. The chill disappeared from his body. He flicked the light of his lamp behind him. One of the packs rubbed against the cable. It seemed to be sliding upwards towards the mine's old-fashioned, deadly horns. A small contact mine, almost too small to do any damage, but enough to pull a human frame into shreds. He moved slowly. The mine seemed to bob and weave like a fighting animal watching him. The water distressed it and wafted around the pack, moving it upwards. It was only inches from the mine.

He reached forward, trying to keep the light of the lamp steady. The mine bobbed, the pack imitated it. Inches. He reached forward, hardly moving his fins, feeling his body sinking away from the mine and the pack. He could not tread water any more violently. He reached forward along the short line which attached him to the pack. Touch. The buoyant pack crumpled then reshaped as he touched it. Inches. He swept at it, banging his hand down past the horns of the mine on to the pack. It bobbed away like a struck ball, and he reeled it in on its line, clutching it to him like a child who had avoided a road accident, feeling weakness envelope his body.

Eventually, he moved on, holding the packs closer to him by their lines, making slower progress but gradually sensing some kind of courage return. He ran up against the inner net, separating the outer basin of the harbour from the submarine pens, almost before he saw it in the light of his lamp. He clung to it with a kind of desperate relief which surprised him. He realised how much his nerves had been strained already. He released the net eventually, dropping down towards the bottom, dragging the unwilling packs with him. His lamp searched ahead of him. The mud and silt, its lightest elements disturbed and lifted by his movement, drifted up to meet him and almost obscured what he sought. The net ended some four or five feet from

294

the bottom. He gripped it and slid under, pulling the packs after him.

He swam on immediately he had checked his bearings and the time. The mine cables were fewer, as if he had moved above the tree-line for these growths. Soon, they straggled out. The water became slightly warmer, and it appeared lighter. He checked his watch, then ascended twenty feet. Here, he waited, them climbed another twenty feet, waited again. Nerves began to plague him now, the need for action, for arrival, nudging at him, irritating him.

His head bobbed above the surface. The packs lay below him at the end of their lines. The row of concrete pens was in front of him. He counted. Fifth along. Lights, noise – no, no noise, just plenty of light. The gates of the pen were closed.

Proteus was in there. He had got to within fifty yards of his destination.

Pasvik the grocer studied the harbour through his night-glasses. He squatted on a blanket which protected his buttocks from the cold of the damp ground. Beneath the blanket he had spread a ground sheet. He had a hamper of food beside him, and he had his back to a tall, old tree.

He moved the glasses up, and the dim, night images blurred and smeared until they were lit with the glow of the submarine pens. He refocused, and he could see, with some degree of clarity, the lights in the fifth pen and a shadowy bulk beyond them that must be the British submarine behind the high gates. Good.

He lowered the glasses. No one would come up here in this weather, but he had a spare blanket to throw over the small dish aerials he had set up alongside him. Clark would be unable to communicate with the Nimrod from within the concrete pen without his messages, and those of the Nimrod, being relayed through the two aerials situated on a small knoll overlooking the harbour of Pechenga, the one with narrow beam facility directed towards Clark, the other, capable of handling broad-beam signals, directed towards the Nimrod.

Pasvik had no fear as he sat there, waiting for the first transmission. He was patient, warmly dressed, and he was engaged in a flatteringly important piece of espionage. However, a dim and long-past regret seemed to move sluggishly in his awareness like a tide coming slowly in. He realised it would be his companion while he remained on the knoll, hidden by the trees. He voiced it.

'Ah, Ivan, Ivan,' he murmured, 'remember the times we used to come here, eh? Remember?'

A chill, gusty wind plucked his sighs away and scattered them over the darkness of the harbour.

Clark bobbed in the water beneath the repaired propeller of the *Proteus*. He was exhausted after climbing the gate into the pen, exhausted in a subtler, more insidious way by the tension of waiting of absorbing the routine of the guards patrolling the pen, of choosing his moment to slip over the gate and down into the water. The good fortune that no one appeared to be working on the submarine did little to erase his weariness.

Despite their buoyancy, the packs were like leaden weights beneath the surface. His arms ached from them and from the deadweight of his own body. Now he had to climb the stern of the *Proteus*, to the aft escape hatch. He did not even want to try, could not entertain the idea of beginning. His air tanks and weighted belt he had left on the bottom of the pen. Yet it was the weight of the packs that unnerved him.

The repairs appeared almost complete. There were a number of scarred and buckled hull plates, but the propeller possessed new blades, the rudder fin and the hydroplanes gleamed with new metal. He looked up. The hull of the *Proteus* loomed above him. He groaned inwardly. His feet, flipperless again, rested on a rung beneath the surface, his hands had hold of another rung of the inspection track up the rudder. Tiny, separate *pitons* in the rock-face of the hull. He looked around him. A guard, bored and dulled by routine, turned at the end of his patrol, and walked back out of sight along the pen. Clark heaved his body out of the water and into the irregular rhythm of his ascent. His wet feet slipped, his hands wanted to let go, but he climbed up the rudder, level with the huge fifteen-bladed propeller, until he could clamber on to the hull, dragging the two packs behind him. There, he paused. Along the smoothness of the hull, on the whale's back, was the impression of the escape hatch, a circle cut in grey, shiny dough with a shaping knife. It was sixty feet from where he crouched.

He raised himself, pressing back against the high fin of the rudder, in its shadow to escape the white lights glaring down from the roof of the pen. The guard he had seen, on the starboard side of the *Proteus*, was half-way along its length, back to him. The other guard, on the port side, had almost reached the extent of his patrol, in the dimness of the other end of the pen. He would not make it to the hatch, open and close it after him, before that guard turned and was able to see him. He waited, the tension wearing at him immediately and violently. He felt inadequate to the demands made upon his physical strength, his nervous system.

A voice called out, and he believed for a long moment that a third guard, one he had not spotted, had seen him and was addressing him. But the voice was distant. He watched, heart pounding, as the port guard moved out of sight behind the bulk of the *Proteus*, presumably having been hailed by his companion on the starboard side. It was his chance, perhaps his only one. He weighed the two packs, one in either hand. An obstacle race. He remembered basic training from long ago; fatigues and punishment and discipline like a thin crust of ice over sadism. He gritted his teeth. He'd run up sand dunes carrying two packs then.

Then he began running, hunched up with fear and the weight of the packs, his feet threatening to slide on the smooth metal of the hull. Fifty feet, forty, thirty –

The packs began to slither on the hull, restraining him. His breath began to be difficult to draw, his heart made a hideous noise. Then he slid like a baseball player for the plate, legs extended and reached the hatch. Feverishly, he turned the wheel, unlocking it. Two turns, three, four. His head bobbed up and down like that of a feeding bird. No one. He raised the hatch, and slid into a sitting position on its edge. His feet fumbled the ladder, and he climbed into the hatch, packs pushed in first and almost dragging him with them; then he closed the hatch behind him, allowing his breath to roar and wheeze in the sudden and complete darkness. He slipped from the ladder and landed on the lower hatch of the chamber. He rubbed his arms, and his body remained doubled over as if in supplication. It was another five minutes before he could bring himself to move again. He unsealed one of the packs – right hand good – and rummaged in one of its pockets. He removed a bundle, and flicked on his lamp to inspect it. Blue, faded blue overalls. He stood up, unrolling the bundle, taking out the socks and boots and putting them on. Then he donned the overalls. His immersion suit was still damp, but the effect might look like sweat, with luck. He patted the breast pocket, feeling the ID there. If the repair and maintenance crew had a specially issued ID for this pen and this job, he still would not be blown as soon as he was challenged. Not with that ID.

He stowed the two packs in the chamber, deflating the second one, securing them to the ladder in the wall. If someone used the hatch, they would be found. He, however, dared not be seen carrying them inside the submarine. His watch showed twelve-fifty. He switched out the lamp, and stowed it with the packs. He would be back within an hour. They should be safe.

Cautiously, he turned the wheel of the lower hatch, then lifted it a couple of inches. He peered into the room housing the electric motors. It appeared empty. He pulled back the hatch and stepped on to the ladder – imagining for a moment Ardenyev or someone like him making his entry in the same manner – closing the hatch behind him and locking it.

He looked around the engine room, rubbing his hands tiredly through his short hair, untidying his appearance. He looked at his hands. They possessed that wrinkled, white, underwater deadness. He thrust them into his pockets as he stared down at the main turbine shaft running across the length of the room. There appeared to be little or no sign of damage. *Proteus* was almost ready to go. She could be taken out of Pechenga and into the Barents Sea on her turbines, even on the electric motors whose bulk surrounded him now. If 'Leopard' worked –

He cautiously opened the bulkhead door into the turbine

room. Empty. The submarine was silent around him, huge, cathedral-like, unmanned. Clark presumed the ratings were being kept in their accommodation under guard, and the officers in the wardroom. Lloyd would be in the control room, more likely in his cabin, also guarded. He looked down at his creased overalls. A uniform would have been an impossible disguise to have transported in one of the packs. A pity.

He entered the manoeuvring room, aft of the nuclear reactor. For a moment he thought it, too, was empty. Then a figure appeared from behind one section of the computer housing. He was short, almost bald, and dressed in a white laboratory coat. He carried a clipboard, and when he saw Clark, adjusted his glasses and studied him.

'What do you want?'

'Who are you?' Clark replied in Russian. There was an instant, well-learned wariness behind the thick spectacles. Clark continued, 'What are you doing here?'

The man was already proffering the clipboard, but then resisted the craven instinct. He did not recognise Clark, and would, presumably, have known which ones to be wary of. Clark appeared officer-like, perhaps, but he did not suggest KGB. He lacked swagger, the birth-right.

'Who are you?' the man in the white coat insisted.

Clark reached into his breast pocket. Aubrey had insisted, pressing it upon him like a talisman. A red ID card. Clark tried to remove it insolently, and waved it briefly at the other man.

'Okay?' he said. 'Or do you want my birth certificate as well?' He laughed as coarsely as he could. 'Don't say you don't think I have one.'

'I wasn't going to – ' the man said. Clark took the clipboard. He understood enough to realise that the technician was from a naval laboratory or testing centre. He riffled the sheets of graph paper. He was checking to make certain that none of the machinery in the manoeuvring room was essential to, or part of, 'Leopard'. Perhaps – Clark suppressed a grin here – he was even trying to locate the back-up system. He handed the clipboard back to the technician.

'I don't understand all that bullshit, Comrade Doctor,'

he said in a belligerently unintelligent voice. The technician succeeded in quashing the sneer that tried to appear on his face. 'See you.'

Clark, hands in pockets, tried a swaggering, lazy, confident slouch out of the manoeuvring room into the tunnel through the reactor. Pausing only for a moment to register that the reactor had not been shut down, he opened the door into the control room. As he had expected, it was not empty. There was no sign of Lloyd or any of the British officers, but white-coated men and a handful of armed guards had occupied the control room, like terrorists in a foreign embassy. Undoubtedly, every piece of machinery and equipment was being tested and examined during the hours when the crew were confined to their quarters. *Proteus* would be a known, familiar thing by the time they had finished. A dog-eared book, a faded woman lacking all mystery. They would possess every secret, half-secret and secure piece of design, knowledge and equipment she had to yield. The computers would be drained, the sonars analysed, the inertial navigation system studied, the communications systems and codes learned by rote.

Clark did not believe that Aubrey had envisaged how much and how valuable would be the information gained from the temporary imprisonment of the *Proteus*. However, Aubrey was right to believe that 'Leopard' was the cherry on the cake. This was the present, 'Leopard' was the future. He slouched his way across the control room. No one paid him more attention then to look up, and glance down once more. He had acquired the swagger. *Exaggerate it*, Aubrey had said, fingering the red ID card. *However ridiculous and opera buffa you think it is, it will work. You are an immortal.* And then Aubrey had smiled, cat-like and with venom. The red ID card claimed he was a KGB officer.

Clark stepped out of the control room into the corridor. There was a single guard opposite a door, no more than a few yards from him. The guard turned to him. Clark waved the red ID and the guard relaxed at once. He was a young, conscripted marine.

'I want a word with our gallant British captain,' Clark drawled. 'See we're not disturbed, okay?' The marine nodded. He had probably never met a KGB man of any rank in his life. He had an entire and trusting awe of the red card. Aubrey had been right. Clark opened the door without knocking, and closed it behind him.

Lloyd had been reading, and had dropped off to sleep with the light above his bunk left on. He awoke, startled, fuzzy-eyed.

'Who are you – ?' The book resting on his chest slipped to the floor as he stood up. Clark bolted the door, then leaned against it. 'Who are you?' Lloyd repeated, more irate than disturbed.

'The Seventh Cavalry,' Clark said softly, then put his finger to his lips.

'What? You're an American – ' Lloyd studied Clark, his manner, features and dress. His face went from shock to hope to suspicion. 'What is this?' he asked with surprising bitterness. To Clark, the man looked tired, dull, captive.

'No trick.' Clark sat on the end of Lloyd's bunk. The captain of the *Proteus* hunched away from him. Clark said, in a louder voice and in very accented English, 'Just a few simple question about your sailing orders.' Lloyd looked as if Clark had proved something to his satisfaction. 'I'm here – ' Clark grinned, despite himself, – 'to repair "Leopard" and help you get out of here.'

Lloyd appeared dumbfounded. 'Rubbish – ' he began.

'No kidding. Look, I can spend hours trying to convince you who I am. How about one simple thing, to prove my credentials?' He paused, but Lloyd remained blank-faced. 'Your daughter has a pet tortoiseshell cat called Penelope and a white rabbit called Dylan.'

Lloyd's mouth dropped open, then he smiled and tears prompted by relief and remembered domesticity welled in his eyes. He took Clark's hand. 'Who are you?' he asked.

'Ethan Clark, Navy Intelligence.'

'Assigned to "Chessboard Counter"?'

'Right.'

'We didn't meet.'

'I don't think it matters – uh?'

'No. How the devil can you repair "Leopard"? Alone? In these surroundings?'

'First, I talk and you listen. Then you tell me everything

301

that happened and everything your people think might have gone wrong. Okay?'

'Okay. You begin, then.'

'Just a moment.' Clark raised his voice, and again produced the heavy accent. 'Your sailing orders. We already know a great deal. Just fill in a few details, okay?' He smiled and tossed his head in the direction of the locked door. 'Now listen,' he said.

'We will be with you before first light, Valery. I want *you* to conduct me around your prize.' Dolohov was in a mood that Ardenyev could not match and which did not interest him. Behind him, through the glass doors into the mess, Balan and Teplov and the others were raucously into a round of obscene songs and another crate of vodka. The drink and the noise whirled in his head, separating him as surely as static would have done from the admiral's voice.

'Yes, sir,' he said as enthusiastically as he could.

'Panov's weather has improved. He's reached Moscow. He'll be here in a few hours' time. Then we'll fly up to you by chopper.' The old man might have been a relative reciting his holiday travel arrangements. Ardenyev almost giggled at the thought, and the image it evoked. Old thin legs wrapped in a travelling-blanket, back bent under the weight of a suitcase, and the admiral's mind full of worries about the toilets, obtaining food in transit and would he be there to meet him with the car. 'What's all that noise?'

'A— small party, sir.'

'Excellent, excellent. Polish vodka, I presume.'

'Yes, sir.' The old man's voice sounded boringly full of reminiscence. Ardenyev hoped it was not so.

'Good, good.' Dolohov sounded offended. Ardenyev cursed the casualness of his tone of voice, his lack of control. Even when half drunk, he should be able to pretend respect. 'Make sure you're sober by the time I arrive, Valery. Understand?' The question was a slap across the face.

'Yes, sir.'

'See you in, say, seven hours' time? Enjoy your party.'

The receiver purred in Ardenyev's ear. His mood was suddenly, inexplicably deflated. He felt sober and dry-mouthed. He looked at his watch. One o'clock. Dolohov and his scientist from Novosibirsk would be here by eight. Shrugging, he pushed open the door to the officers' mess, to be greeted by a roar of welcome and insult.

The two packs were still in the aft escape chamber. He removed his overalls, rolled them into a bundle, and stowed them in the pack containing the explosives. This he took with him as he climbed back through the hatch into the room below. He hid the pack in a steel cupboard containing repair equipment. Then, he once more closed himself into the darkness of the chamber. He flicked on his lamp, and checked the second pack. He removed a tool-kit already clipped to a belt, and two bulky packages which he strapped to his thighs. He had an image, for a moment, of his ridiculous appearance if he were seen and caught on top of the hull of the *Proteus*, and then it vanished in a rush of nerves and tension. He had trembled, and the pool of light cast on the floor of the chamber wobbled.

He turned the wheel of the hatch, and lifted it. The hard light of the pen poured in and he felt exposed and vulnerable. His legs felt weak, despite the reviving swallow of rum Lloyd had given him, and the coffee he had ordered from the galley in his KGB persona. He waited, but the nerves did not seem to abate. He cursed them silently. He wanted to drop from the ladder to the floor of the chamber. He held on, grinding his teeth audibly, his eyes squeezed tight shut. It was like a malarial illness. His whole body was shaking, revolting against the idea of leaving the dark in order to climb into the spotlit brightness of the submarine pen.

Then the mood passed. The illness retreated, and he was able to swallow the phlegm in his throat, and to feel strength returning to his legs. He lifted the hatch once more, and raised his head above it. The curve of the *Proteus*'s hull prevented him from being able to see either of the guards, and he waited. Two minutes later, the port guard appeared, his head bobbing along the horizon of the hull. He was smoking a cigarette. Clark waited until he had turned in his patrol, with hardly a glance at the submarine, and the starboard guard had come into view, making for the seaward end of the pen. Still only two of them. He was able to diminish what opposed and endangered him to these two men. Two against one, that's all it was. He felt calmed.

He waited, but without the bout of nerves returning, until the two men had passed out of sight, and returned. Each patrol, from the point opposite the escape hatch back towards the bow of the submarine and returning to the escape hatch, took three minutes and a few seconds. The time, however, when they both had their backs to him was less, since they were not on identical courses. Two and a half minutes of running or working time.

He watched them, heads down, one of them whistling tunelessly and the other slouching with both hands in his pockets, Kalashnikov slung over his shoulder, until they passed out of his vision towards the bow of the *Proteus*. Then he climbed out of the hatch on to the smooth curve of the hull, crouching like a sprinter on his blocks for a moment as he looked over his shoulder. Neither man had turned, and he straightened and ran for the rudder fin sixty feet away.

He hid in its shadow, hardly breathing more rapidly than normal, then climbed swiftly down the *pitons* in its smoothed, repaired surface to the water. He held one of the propeller blades and trod water gently.

Lloyd had given him Hayter's assessment of the damage to 'Leopard'. The submarine officer had said, in simpler and clearer terms, what had sprung instantly to Quin's mind when he heard the estimate of damage the submarine must have sustained. Clark, by seeing for himself the repairs and hearing Lloyd's account of his experiences and his conversations with Ardenyev, agreed with Hayter and Quin. At least one, and possibly as many as three or four, of the hull sensors must have been damaged. In themselves, Clark knew with a heavy sensation in his stomach, they would not account for the manner and degree of 'Leopard's malfunction, but without their being repaired the equipment would never work effectively. Before investigating the back-up system which had never cut in, Clark had to inspect and repair the sensors on the outer hull.

When Lloyd had described his conversations with Valery Ardenyev, Clark had sat listening with a faint smile on his lips. He had known it, all along. It had to be Ardenyev. Even the wine and the caviar would have been in character, just as would killing Lloyd if it had proven necessary.

Clark watched the two guards approach the seaward end of the pen once more. The whistler was now being echoed by his companion, who provided a shrill descant or counter-melody as the fit took him. They laughed at their musical antics frequently, the noise having a hollow quality under the bright roof. Lloyd had confirmed that work on *Proteus* had stopped early the previous evening, as a delaying tactic. The repair crew might return at any moment, just as the man from Novosibirsk might also arrive in minutes or hours. Clark felt the weakness pass through him once more, like the debilitation of a stomach infection, and he realised that it was Lloyd's report of Panov's expected arrival, learned from Ardenyev, that had struck him more forcibly than anything else. It all hinged on the weather in Siberia; everything. It was that random, uncontrollable element that had thrown him.

One guard began telling a joke. The two men loitered at the seaward end of the pen, giggling at each other across the stretch of imprisoned water. Clark ducked further into the shadow of the propeller, only his head out of the water. Clark's impatience began to mount. Then some vestigial fear of a *michman* or even an officer arriving seemed to prompt the storyteller, and they began to move again, the storyteller's voice rising in volume as the bulk of the *Proteus* interposed itself between himself and his audience of one.

Clark ducked beneath the surface of the water, and switched on his lamp. Its weak beam would probably not be noticed, reflecting through the water, unless someone looked very hard. The two guards wouldn't. He swam along the hull, only a few feet below the surface, holding in his mind as clearly as a slide projected upon a screen a diagram of the hull showing the locations of the numerous sensor-plates. His left hand smoothed its way along the hull, and his lamp flickered and wavered over the metal. Eventually, as his breath began to sing in his head and his eardrums seemed to be swelling to fill his head and mouth, he touched against one of them. A shallow tear-drop dome of thin metal protected the sensor beneath. It was intact, undamaged.

He rose to the surface, breathed in deeply three times, then ducked beneath the surface again. He began to locate the sensors more quickly now, as if he had found the thread that would lead him through the maze. Surprisingly, and to his relief, the wafer-thin titanium domes over the sensors seemed to have withstood damage from both the torpedoes. Beneath each dome lay either sonar or magnetic or thermal signal detectors and, within the domes, baffles like those in a stereo loudspeaker guided and channelled any signals, whether from enemy sonar or other detection equipment, into a transducer. The signals were then fed via fibre optics into 'Leopard', where they were analysed, reverse phased and then returned to the transducer. The process was virtually instantaneous. The effect of this was to nullify or deflect any enemy's detection transmissions. The signals returned to the enemy vessel unaltered, thereby confirming that they had not registered or been deflected off another vessel. In addition, some of the hull sensors worked to damp the noise emissions from the *Proteus*'s propellers and hydroplanes, rendering the submarine ninety-eight per cent immune to detection. Clark had to assume that some sensors, at least, would be damaged.

Four of them undamaged, then five. It had taken him almost thirty minutes, working on the starboard side of the hull and avoiding the patrol of the guard, who now had a tiny transistor radio clasped to his ear. Clark had heard a sliver of pop music once as he ducked beneath the surface. When the man had gone again, Clark dived and swam down, following the curve of the hull until he surfaced on the port side. Checking the sensors on that side took him twenty minutes. He worked with greater and greater confidence and speed. He moved towards the stern of the submarine, where the damage was more evident to the lamp and to his fingertips. Then he found the first damaged sensor-cowl. The titanium skin had been torn away, whether during the attack or the subsequent repairs he could not guess, and beneath it the delicate transducer had been torn, smashed, rendered useless. In the light of his lamp, he saw the tangled mess of wiring within; it looked like a ruined eye. He cursed, bobbed to the surface, exhaled and drew a new breath, then flipped down towards the bottom, his lamp flickering over the rust-stained, oil-smeared concrete until he saw, to his left, the huddled bulk of his air tanks.

He strapped on the weighted belt, then the tanks, and began swimming back towards the surface. As soon as the short helical antenna clamped to the side of his head broke surface, he spoke into the throat microphone. He described the damage to the hull sensor and its location, and only moments later Quin began speaking excitedly in his ear, sounding very distant and obscured by static.

'You'll have to replace the transducer unit, of course – that will be quickest. You have three of those units with you. As to the cowl, you'll have to do without that. It should be okay. The domes are normally water filled.'

Clark acknowledged the instructions, and swam down again to the damaged sensor. Immediately, he began to clear the mass of loose wiring and circuitry and fragmented glass and metal out of the hole, which was no more than a foot in diameter at its widest point. A small shell-hole.

The cleared depression in the hull looked merely empty, of no purpose. He released the locking ring and prised the transducer from its seat. Once he had to surface and request Quin to repeat part of the procedure, but he worked swiftly and with a keen and sharp satisfaction. The new unit plugged directly into the box of the signal converter. It took him no more than ten minutes to complete the task. He swam back to the stern of the *Proteus* and rose slowly and cautiously to the surface, once more in the shadow of the propeller.

The guard was looking at him, looking directly at him. He had to be able to see him.

Clark waited, his hand holding the zipper of his immersion suit, ready to reach for the Heckler & Koch .22. Then the guard blew out his cheeks and spat into the water. The noise was sufficient for Clark to grip the handle of the small pistol tightly, and almost draw it from his suit. The guard seemed to watch the small blob of spittle intently, then he began his desultory walk back to the other end of the pen. He had been staring absently at some point on the hull, some part of the stern, and had not seen Clark's head bob to the surface. Clark zipped up his suit once more, as quickly as his nerveless hands would allow, then he removed the air tanks from his back. They clanged softly, like a sounding bell, against one of the propeller blades, and he held his breath. There was no sound from the guards, and he hooked the webbing of the tanks over one of the propeller blades so that they hung below the surface.

He looked up, then at his watch. Two-fifty-seven. Shaking away the tiredness that seemed to have insinuated itself behind his eyes while he studied his watch – an intent, staring moment which seemed hypnotic, sleep-inducing – he began climbing the hull again, ascending the rudder fin until he could see both guards, backs to him. He had perhaps a minute before the port side guard reached the limit of his patrol. He scuttled out along the hull, unreeling a fine nylon line from around his waist. He had to check every sensor on the stern of the hull in full view. One head had only to turn, one figure emerge from the sail of the *Proteus*, one officer or *michman* come into the pen to check on the guards, Panov to arrive, eager to inspect 'Leopard' –

He placed the magnetic pad at the end of the nylon line against the hull, jerked hard on the line, then abseiled down the curving hull, watching the port side guard continually. The sensor was beneath one of his feet, then level with his eyes. He ran one hand over the titanium tear-drop. Undamaged. He looked at the guard, almost out of sight behind the swelling midships section of the submarine, then clambered back up the line to the top of the hull. One.

He saw the starboard guard little more than half-way up the pen, his feet jigging unconsciously to the noise coming from the tiny radio. He swung down on the starboard side until he was level with the tear-drop dome. It was loose, and he cursed silently. He pulled a screwdriver from his kit, and prised at the thin titanium. Beneath it, the sensor appeared undamaged. He juggled his lamp in his hand, and switched it on. He checked, feeling the arm that gripped the line begin to quiver with nerves – guards nearly at the end of the pen, moving into the shadows beyond the hard lights – and his body heating with the tension. Undamaged – yes, undamaged. He loosened his grip on the lamp, and it dangled from his wrist again on its thick strap. He made to replace the screwdriver in his belt, and it slipped from his fingers – the guard was out of sight behind the swell of the midships, and in the shadow – and slid down the hull with a rattling noise that sounded deafening in the intense silence. It plopped like a large fish into the water. They must have heard it. He clambered, feet slipping, then able to grip, body hunched, almost jerking upwards on the line as if he were a fish and was hooked, waiting for the challenge, the shout of recognition at any moment.

He flattened himself on the hull, bunching the nylon line beneath his body, feeling his whole frame quivering. Another malarial attack. He could not stop himself shaking.

'Progress report,' he heard in his earpiece. The port guard was in sight again, meandering down the pen towards him. Then the starboard guard came into sight, chewing and cocking his head into the tinny noises of the transistor radio at his ear. 'Progress report', Aubrey requested again in his ear, this time with more asperity. Clark wanted to howl into his throat mike for the crazy old man to shut up.

The guard passed beneath him on the port side, then the starboard guard was level with him again. The radio made tinny, scratchy noises. A Western pop station, beamed in from Norway or Sweden.

'Lend us your fucking radio,' the port guard called across to his companion in a not unamiable manner. 'Bored stiff.'

'I'm not,' his companion replied, facing him. 'You bloody Ukrainians are all the same – scroungers.'

'Clark – progress report.' *Shut up, shut up –*

'Fuck off.' Clark craned his neck. The port guard, the taller of the two with the cropped haircut and the stooping shoulders, had unslung his rifle, and was pointing it at the man on the starboard side. 'Hand over your radio, or I'll fire,' he demanded.

The man on the starboard side laughed. He wore spectacles and a thin, weak moustache and looked no more than fifteen. He, too, unslung his rifle, and pointed it across the water with one hand, the other still pressing the radio to his ear. 'Bang, bang,' he said, hooting with laughter when he had done so.

'Piss off.'

'Progress report, Clark. Clark?' *Shut up, shut up* –

Clark knew what would happen next, and knew it would be audible. Sharp, painful bleeps of sound, like morse dashes, to attract his attention, then a continous tone like that of a telephone that has been disconnected because the subscriber has moved. Both guards looked up. Clark squeezed himself flatter against the top of the hull, praying for the curvature to be sufficient, to hide him like high ground or a horizon.

'What's that?'

'Dunno. Fucking radio. Our lot trying to jam it.' The starboard guard laughed again, a thin high cackle as if his voice had not yet broken.

'Race you to the other end, you skinny, underfed Ukrainian!'

'What about – ?'

'Ready, set – *go*!'

The noise of their boots echoed off the concrete walls and roof of the pen. The tone stopped, and then began again in his head. Clark whispered intently into his throat-mike.

'For Chrissake, get off my back, Aubrey!' He went on quivering, his body seeming to jump with the detonations of their footsteps bouncing off the roof, until Aubrey replied.

'Clark – what is wrong?'

'I'm lying on the fucking hull, man, with two goons training for the Olympics right below me. I can't *talk* to you!'

A few seconds later – he could hear a thin, breathless cheer from the far end of the pen as the taller guard won the race – Aubrey replied stiffly and formally, 'Very well. Report as soon as you can.'

'Okay, okay.'

'And again?' the shorter guard called angrily.

'You're on. Ten roubles on this one?'

'Twenty, you Ukrainian bullshitter!'

'Ready, set – *go*! Hey, you jumped the gun, you cheating sod!'

Then the bootsteps rained down from the roof again as they charged towards the seaward end of the pen. Clark lay icily still now, his tension expended with his anger, his sense of time oblivious to anything but the slow passage of seconds on the watch-face he held in front of his eyes.

The starboard guard won, by virtue of a flying start, and crowed and pranced. His companion, now his deadly rival, challenged him to a return. They regained their breath, watched each other like combatants for a fortune in prize money, crouched into sprinting starts, and then began running on the call of the taller man. Clark got to his knees. Their row would bring someone, soon. He scuttled along the hull, careless of the noise he made, fixed the pad, and lowered himself feverishly down the nylon rope, checked the undamaged sensor, climbed the rope again, imagined the ragged breathing of the two runners, waited until he could hear them arguing with out-of-breath shouts, and swung down the port side of the hull. He was elated by the clownish behaviour and the stupidity of the two young guards; almost reckless with confidence. Undamaged. He climbed the line again.

They were still arguing, their voices coming from the far end of the pen. He could dimly discern them, shadows in shadow. He moved back along the hull, lowered himself on the port side again – the two men had moved slightly to starboard of the bow of the submarine – and checked another sensor. The titanium blister was dented, but undisturbed. Then the starboard side, his luck beginning to extend beyond the point at which it was simply acceptable and becoming instead a source of anxiety, where he checked two more sensors. He was almost level with rudder fin again, almost finished –

Another voice, a snarling petty-officer voice, and silence from the two guards. Berating, angry, loud. Their parentage was stripped from them, then their maturity, then their manhood. Layers of the onion, until they would be left with nothing but total humiliation and punishment duties. They would be replaced, the new guards would be fearfully alert, punctilious in their patrols. The crushing reprimand went on and on.

Clark lowered himself down the port side of the hull

again. The plates were scarred, as if the metal had been lashed with a giant whip. He knew what he would find. A weal like a furrow lay along one hull plate, and whatever had caused it had crushed the wafer-thin titanium in upon the sensor beneath it. He reached into his belt, moving with feverish haste now as the *michman*'s voice rose again, perhaps towards a peroration. He drew a smaller, stubbier screwdriver and jabbed it into the slot on the locking ring and heaved. It moved, and then turned. He lifted it clear and snapped it into a hook on his belt. As he prised out the transducer he could see the damage clearly. Shattered fragments fell from the transducer and rattled and slid down the hull to the water.

Bare wires. The sheathing was cut through, and half the wiring was severed. Dangling from the end was an ABS multipin plug. Half of it. Half a smashed multi-pin plug. He registered it with helpless fury. Silence. The *michman* had finished. Christ—

A door slammed, and then there was silence again, a heavy, ringing silence. He was alone in the pen for perhaps a few minutes at most. Perspiration drenched him. He wiped the back of one hand over his face.

'I got problems,' he announced. 'Stern sensor fourteen—one of the sonar signal nullifiers. The wiring behind the transducer's a hell of a mess.'

He continued to lever at the wiring with the screwdriver while he waited for Quin to reply.

'What extent is the damage?'

The rest of the transducer slid away with a noise like the claws of a crab on metal. Then it plopped into the water. Clark hefted his lamp and shone it into the hole.

'Bad. Most of the wiring has been sheared; but there's worse. The connector's smashed.'

'Can you check beyond the breaks?'

'Maybe.'

'Can you see the socket and the box?'

'Yes.'

Clark peered into the hole. He tidied the sheared and twisted wiring to one side and looked again. The wires reached the fibre optics converter box on the underside of the outer hull.

'Remove it complete,' Quin instructed. 'Fit a new one. And Clark – '

'Yes?'

'There is a second plug, for the fibre optics. A bayonet fitting. Be careful. The first has forty pins, and it fits only one way.'

'Right.'

Clark looked at his watch. One minute since the door had slammed. He reached in, pressing his cheek against the hull, feeling the activity within the submarine as a slight vibration. His fingers flexed in the narrow space, snagged and cut on the exposed, shorn wires, and then his fingertips had hold of the upper section of the box. He pulled. Nothing happened. He pulled again, surprise on his face. The converter box would not budge.

'It's jammed,' he said. 'Jammed.'

The door slammed. Marching boots, double time, the voice of the *michman* savagely drilling the two replacement guards. Clark clung to the nylon line and the converter box and prayed for the fifty-fifty chance to work in his favour.

The boots clattered down the starboard side of the *Proteus*. He had a moment or two yet –

'Have you got it? Can you see what's wrong?' Quin was frightened.

Clark heaved at it, curling his fingers round the edge of the converter box. Nothing moved. One finger touched the clip – *clips, strap*, he'd forgotten the clips and the strap securing the box – he flipped open the catch with his thumb, felt it loosen, and then gripped the box again. He gritted his teeth and strained. His arm shot out of the hole and he wriggled on the nylon line, holding on to the dangling wires and the box as the velocity with which he had jerked them free threatened to make him drop them. The *michman*'s voice snapped out orders to the new guards. In a moment, they would appear on the port side –

He ripped open one of the two thick packs and drew out a replacement converter box already wired to the transducer. He fed the complete unit into the hole as carefully as he could. He pushed it forward. Then he let go of the rope, dangling by its tight, cutting hold on his armpits, and shone

313

his lamp. The *michman* had stopped shouting. He was watching the two guards doubling on the spot. Push – no, slight adjustment – push, get it into the clips – push home, feel for the strap ends, yes – hook them over, clamp the catch. He fitted the fibre optics plug, then fastened the transducer into place, and fitted the locking ring to holding it. The *michman* had ordered them to stop doubling.

Clark's arms felt lifeless and weak. He heaved at the nylon line, but his body hardly moved. His feet scrabbled on the smooth hull. The *michman* ordered the second new guard to follow him. It was like a yelled order to Clark. He clambered back up the line. Fifty feet to the hatch. Seconds only.

He ran. He heaved open the hatch, not caring any longer whether or not he had been seen, and tumbled into darkness, the hatch thudding softly shut on its rubber seals behind him. He lay breathless and aching and uncaring in the safe, warm darkness of the escape chamber, every part of his body exhausted.

'Well done, Quin,' Aubrey offered, and watched the slow bloom of self-satisfaction on the man's face. He was difficult to like, but Aubrey had ceased to despise him. Quin was back in the land of the living, as it were. Flattery, cajolement, even threat had all played a part in his rehabilitation. Finally, however, Aubrey had seen the danger to his invention, his project, overcome and prompt Quin. The man would not surrender 'Leopard' without some effort on his part.

'Thank you,' Quin returned. Then his face darkened, and he shook his head. 'It's almost impossible,' he added. 'I don't know whether Clark has the necessary concentration to keep this up –'

'I understand the strain he must be under,' Aubrey said, 'but there's no other way.'

'I'm – I'm sorry – stupid behaviour earlier – apologies – ' Each word seemed wrenched from Quin, under duress. Aubrey respected the effort it was costing the cold, egotistical man to offer an explanation of himself.

'Quite all right.'

'It's just that, well, now I don't want them to get their hands on it, you see – '

'Quite.'

'It is the only thing of importance to me, you see.' He looked down at his hands. 'Shouldn't say that, but I'm afraid it's true.' He looked up again, his eyes fierce. 'Damn them, they mustn't have it!'

'Mr Aubrey?' There was something trying to force itself like a broken bone through Eastoe's frosty reserve.

'Yes, Squadron Leader?'

'We have some blips on the radar. Four of them.'

'Yes?'

'Coming up rapidly from one of the airfields on the Kola Peninsula. Not missiles, the trace is wrong for that. Four aircraft.'

'I see. Range?'

'Not more than thirty miles. They'll be with us in three minutes or even less.'

'With us? I don't understand.'

'They've already crossed into Norwegian airspace, Mr Aubrey. They didn't even hesitate.'

Thirteen: CONCEALMENT

They were MiG-23s, code-named Flogger-B, single-seat, all-weather interceptors. Four of them. Even Aubrey could recognise them, in a moment of silhouette that removed him more than forty years to basic aircraft recognition tests at the beginning of the war. A vivid streak of lightning to the north, and the brassy light illuminating the night sky, outlined the nearest of the MiGs. Slim, grey, red-starred on its flank. One wing-tip rose as the aircraft banked slightly, and Aubrey could see the air-to-air missiles beneath the swing wing in its swept-back position.

Immediately, Eastoe was talking to him. 'Mr Aubrey, they're MiG-23s, interceptors. The flight leader demands to know our mission and the reason for our invasion of sensitive airspace.'

'What is their intention, would you say?' Quin was staring out of the window of the Nimrod, watching the slim, shark-like silhouette that had begun to shadow them.

'Shoo us away.'

'What course of action do you — ?'

'Just a minute, Mr Aubrey. I've got the Norwegian flight leader calling me. Do you want to listen into this?'

'I don't think so,' Aubrey replied wearily. 'I am sure I already know what he wishes to say.'

'Very well.'

The headset went dead, and Aubrey removed it. It clamped his temples and ears, and seemed to cramp and confine thought. He did not like wearing it. Quin did not seem disappointed at Aubrey's decision.

There was another flash of lightning, streaking like bright rain down a window towards the sea. The blare of unreal light revealed the closest of the Northrop F-5s turning to port, away from the Nimrod. Their Norwegian fighter escort had been recalled to Kirkenes. Norway's unwritten agreement, as a member of NATO, with the Soviet Union was that no military exercises or provocative military manoeuvres were undertaken within a hundred

316

miles of the Soviet border. Evidently, the Russians had registered a protest, and their protest had been accepted.

Aubrey replaced his headset. 'Has our Norwegian escort gone?'

'Yes, Mr Aubrey. We're on our own.'

'Very well. Our signals cannot be intercepted, nor their origin traced so far as Clark is concerned?'

'No. Mr Aubrey, how long do we need to hang around?'

'For some hours yet.'

'Very well.' Eastoe sounded grim, but determined. 'We'll do what we can. I'll try not to get shepherded out of range.'

'If you would.'

Aubrey stared at the console on the table between himself and Quin. The hull sensors had been inspected and repaired, yet the achievement of that task had been the completion of the easy and least dangerous element. Clark now had to inspect and, if necessary, repair the back-up system of 'Leopard'. Aubrey suddenly felt alone, and incompetent.

Eastoe spoke again in his ear. 'They're demanding we leave the area. They'll see us off the property.'

'You are on our eastbound leg at the moment?'

'Yes. But that won't fool them. They'll have been watching us on radar for a long time. They know we're flying a box pattern.'

'But, for the moment, we're secure?'

'Yes – '

The window seemed filled with the belly of the MiG-23. The sight was gone in a moment, and might have begun to seem illusory, except that the nose of the Nimrod tilted violently as Eastoe put the aircraft into a dive.

'Shit – ' the co-pilot's voice cried in Aubrey's ear. The Nimrod levelled, and steadied.

'They're not in the mood to waste time,' Eastoe commented. 'You saw that?'

Aubrey remembered the underbelly, almost white like that of a great hunting fish, and even the red-painted missiles beneath the wing.

'Yes,' he said. 'What happened?' He ignored Quin's worried face, the man was frightened but there was a determination in him now, replacing the former cunning that had sought only escape.

'One of them buzzed us – and I mean buzzed. Crazy bastard!'

Aubrey paused for a moment. 'The aircraft is in your hands, Squadron Leader. All I ask is that we never pass out of range of Clark's transceiver. The rest is up to you.'

'*Thank you*, Mr Aubrey.'

The MiG – perhaps the one that had buzzed them – was back on their port wing, slightly above and behind. Shadowing them. It was, Aubrey considered, as unpredictable as a wild creature.

Tricia staggered under Hyde's weight, slipped, and fell against the long, high bank. Her breath roared in her ears, but she could feel it in her chest – ragged, loud, heaving. Hyde, unconscious, rolled away from her, slid until he lay at her feet looking sightlessly up at her and was still. Tricia was simply and utterly relieved that she was no longer bearing his weight against one side and across the back of her neck where she had placed his arm. She loathed and hated Hyde at that moment, and even feared him; as if he might wake and attack her himself. She blamed him totally, for every fragment and element of her predicament.

Her body was bathed in perspiration, and her limbs were shaking with weakness. Hyde continued groaning, like a murmured protest at his pain.

'Oh – shut up,' she whispered fiercely. 'Shut up.' The repetition was bitten off, as if she admitted he was not to blame.

She had helped Hyde, often supporting his unconscious weight when he slipped once more from pain into stillness, as they moved north, then west. There had been no effective pursuit. The helicopter had lost sight of them after she had half-dragged, half-shouldered him away from the rise where he had first passed out, into a small copse of trees. A tiny dell, where the dead ferns were long and curving, like the roofs of native huts, had concealed them. Terrified, she had heard legs brushing through heather and ferns, voices near and more distant, the crackle of R/Ts. She had kept her hand over Hyde's mouth, in case he babbled in delirium.

The wound had been ugly, and she knew nothing of medicine or nursing. It had bled a great deal. It seemed that the bullet had not lodged in Hyde's shoulder or chest because there was a small hole near his shoulder blade and a larger hole near his collar-bone. She had seen sufficient television wounds to assume that the bullet had passed straight through. Her knowledge of anatomy was sketchy, and she watched anxiously for blood to appear around his lips. When it did not, she assumed the lungs were undamaged. She did not know what other bones, muscles or organs might reside in the area of the wound. She bound the wound with a torn length of Hyde's own shirt.

Now, under the looming shadow of the long, high bank, she knew she could go no further. Hyde's weight had become intolerable. She could bully him no more, support him no longer. She was hungry, and cold, and impatient of Hyde's helplessness. His repeated groans of pain enraged her.

She knelt by him because he would not quieten. She shook his head carefully, as if it fitted only loosely, her fingers holding his chin. His eyes flickered, but then closed again, as if he wished to exclude her and what she represented. She shook his head more violently. A great weariness possessed her, and she sat instead of squatting on her haunches.

'For God's sake, wake up,' she pleaded.

'Uuh,' he grunted. She looked at him. His eyes were open.

'You're awake.'

'Oh, *Christ*!' he cried in a broken voice, his breath sobbing. 'My bloody shoulder.' He groaned again.

'You're not delirious?'

'My bloody shoulder won't let me. Where – where are we?'

'Behind the rifle ranges. Are we going to stay here?'

'I'm not going anywhere.' Hyde looked at the stars. 'I can't go anywhere, Tricia.'

'I know.'

'Have a quick look around. See if you can find some dense undergrowth, a ditch, a trench, a hole in the bank, anything. If we can get under cover, we – ' He groaned again.

319

'Where are the police?' she asked plaintively.

'Searching Cheshire probably,' he replied, coughing. She looked anxiously for signs of blood as he wiped his lips. There were none. 'Trouble is, we're in Staffordshire. They'll get round to us. I hope.'

'They must be looking, surely?'

'I bloody well hope so, darling. I pay my rates and taxes so they can pull me out of holes like this. I'll be writing to my bloody Pom MP if they don't turn up.'

She almost laughed at the pronounced accent and the sentiments it expressed. Something lifted from her; not her weariness, but something of her isolation. Hyde sounded more like a human being, less like a liability.

'I'll look,' she said, and got up. He turned his head slowly and watched her. He felt tears in his eyes which might simply have been the result of pain and weariness. He did not understand them, and for a few moments he could not prevent them. The pain in his shoulder subsided now that he was resting, but he felt his body could make no further effort, not even to defend itself or the girl. He needed to hide.

The girl came back quickly, almost running.

'No – ' he protested, sensing her pursued.

'What? No, it's all right, I've found a hollow, scooped out of the bank. It's almost masked by a bush. Can you come?'

He sat up, rocked, then steadied himself. 'Give us a hand, mate.'

She tottered, but pulled him to his feet. She hitched his arm across her aching shoulders again, and dragged him along the gully behind the bank, which loomed thirty feet or more above them.

It was less than fifty yards, but she was staggering with tiredness when they reached the bush growing out of the bank. Hyde felt its stiff, resisting branches, the sharp ends and points of old thorns. It had spread and flourished for many years, but he could see behind its present leaflessness the outline of a hole in the bank.

'How far in does it go, do you think?' she said, shivering as she realised she would have to investigate.

'It's all right. No bears left, and no wolves. And no bloody snakes like we've got in Aussie biting your arse

320

when you climb in. Go on, then.' He sounded genuinely impatient.

She heaved and struggled with the branches of the leafless bush, then went head-first into the hole. 'It smells,' he heard her call hollowly.

His cackle degenerated into a cough. 'It's those bloody rabbits from Watership Down,' he said. 'How big is it?'

Her head emerged. 'Just big enough for two, if you don't mind a crush.'

'You'll have to push me in,' he said.

She climbed out, snagging her jacket on thorns, then she helped get him to the bush, lifted some of the whippier branches aside like a curtain, then got her shoulder beneath his buttocks.

'Ready?'

'Yes.'

She heaved, and he disappeared into the hole.

'Are you all right?'

'Yes,' he answered faintly. 'Rearrange the bush when you climb in.'

She squeezed into the hole, then turned with difficulty, putting her foot into his back at one point, and reached out, tugging and pulling the bushes back into place as well as she could. Then she slithered backwards until she was bunched up against him.

'Wait a minute,' she said, and fumbled in the pockets of the donkey jacket. She rattled the box of matches, fumbled with it, then struck one. 'There you are.'

Hyde's face looked grey and ill, but he managed to say, 'Now I get you alone at last, some bloody Russian puts a contraceptive through my shoulder.'

'Yes,' she said thoughtfully, already finding the light of the match much too bright and wanting to close her eyes. She shook it out and dropped it. 'Are you all – right?' she asked faintly. The darkness closed satisfyingly around her. She was not certain whether his reply was positive or negative, and she did not really think it mattered. She heard him groan once before she fell asleep.

Clark closed the tiny hatch into the space between the outer and the pressure hulls, leaving his helical aerial attached to

321

the surface of the outer hull. The darkness was sudden and intense after the hard lighting from the roof of the pen. He could not stand upright, but bent his head and hunched his back as he waited for his breathing to return to normal, or to an approximation of normality.

He emerged from the aft escape chamber knowing that the new guards on either side of the submarine would be self-consciously, fearfully alert for any and every unexpected noise and movement. Their peripheral vision would be enhanced by the threats of the senior *michman*, and they had been on duty for only twenty minutes. Yet he had to risk it.

When he recovered in the escape chamber, his arms full of cramp and pain, his whole body exhausted with the effort of abseiling down the hull and climbing it again, he first collected the second pack – left hand bad – from the electric motor room and took it into the chamber. He would have to take both complete packs with him. He was on the point of incarcerating himself between the twin hulls of the *Proteus* until he either repaired the back-up system or was forced to abort and plant the explosives which would melt it into a lump of useless metal.

The hatch fitted to the *Proteus* which allowed access to the inner hull where the blister containing the back-up system was fitted lay thirty feet from the aft escape hatch. He had eased open the hatch a matter of inches, listening with his whole body. When the guards' footsteps moved out of range, precise and regular and unconcerned as clockwork, he opened it fully, climbed out, closed it again, and moved along the hull. He had opened the other hatch, and lowered the first pack in. Then he had closed it and returned, waiting until the next patrol of the pen took the two guards towards the bow before moving the second pack along the top of the hull, dragging it after him as he slithered on his belly, into the space between the hulls.

In the darkness now, the two packs rested at his feet. He was aware, as his breathing calmed, of the way in which the pressure hull curved away on either side of him. He was on a narrow ledge, a metal bridge across a chasm, and he must never forget the fact.

He paused for another moment, his bearings uncertain

then assured, and then he hefted the two packs until they no longer dragged on the pressure hull before moving forward. He pushed his feet forward, disregarding the lamp for the moment because his hands were full and because it seemed necessary to establish some sense of mastery over his new and alien environment. Behind him, he paid out the wire from his transceiver to the aerial outside the hull. He felt the hull slope slightly upwards, in ridged steps. Unlike the smooth outer hull, the pressure hull of the *Proteus* did not follow exactly the same outline or shape. His shoulders bent lower as the two hulls narrowed the distance between themselves. Another three steps, and he dropped lightly to his knees. The outer hull seemed to press down upon him in a moment of claustrophobia, and the pressure hull beneath his knees and toes seemed thin, uncertain, narrow. The chasm waited for him on either side.

He switched on the lamp. Ahead of him, where the space between the hulls narrowed like a thin, deep shaft where a miner would have had to work on his back or his stomach to dig the coal, he could see, like the pit-props appropriate to the analogy his mind had discovered, the stanchions growing like grey metal trees between the two hulls, separating and binding them. He moved the torch around him, pressing back the thick, blind darkness. It smelt old, and damp, and empty. The sounds thrumming lightly and occasionally through the pressure hull, the murmur of machinery and air-pumps and filters and voices and electrics and ovens and toilets, seemed completely removed from him and not of human origin.

The outer hull sloped away like the roof of a dome to either side, falling sheer out of sight. He could see the lip where the pressure hull followed its shape on either side. The ledge seemed narrow and fragile. He flicked the torch's thin beam deliberately forward again. A hump like a turtle shell or the scaled back of an armadillo hunched in the shadows beyond the stanchion trees. The sight of it relieved him. He fixed the packs to his belt by their clips once more, and lay flat. He began pushing the packs in front of him, slithering awkwardly forward, alarmed by the noise he seemed to be making.

He began to weave through the stanchions, thrusting

323

and pushing the packs in turn ahead of him, then using his elbows and knees to move his body forward behind them. Whenever he flicked on the lamp – needing its light now as reassurance as well as a guide – the grey humped back of the turtle shell remained ahead of him in the shadows at the edge of the pool of light.

Push. The left-hand pack was fumbled round the next stanchion. Push. The right-hand pack moved. He then moved his body forward. His cheek rested for a moment against the cold, wet-seeming metal of the stanchion, then he pushed the left-hand pack forward again. His lamp clanged against the pressure hull. He cursed the noise, momentarily distracted, and the left-hand pack slid away from him. He felt it tug at his body, urging it sideways. The pack slithered into the chasm. His right hand grabbed the stanchion, and his arm was almost jerked from its socket. He suppressed a cry of pain and held on, reeling in the heavy pack with his left hand. He gripped it to him, shaking.

When he had swallowed the fear in his mouth, and his legs had seemed to recover some of their strength, he moved on, passing the last of the stanchions, slithering more quickly the last few feet to the shell of grey metal, the tumour on the pressure hull.

He was able to kneel, just, with his back arched like a frightened cat's, and shine his lamp over the surface. His first task was to remove it. He placed the packs carefully beyond it, where he would not disturb them accidentally, and began removing the bolts from the sealing gasket of the grey carapace. He was aware that he was above the ceiling of the turbine room, crouching in shadow, alone and even ridiculous, taking his first steps to cure an illness he was unlikely to be able to diagnose. Below him, from what he had seen when aboard the *Proteus*, it was likely that engineers and technicians from the naval base would be inspecting the giant turbines. He had to presume that they were there, assume that the slightest carelessness with regard to noise would betray his presence to them.

'I'm in the tunnel,' he said softly, aware of the point on the relief map which Pasvik had pointed out and where he now hid. Pasvik was in the bushes with his dish aerials, the one fragile link between himself and Quin aboard the Nimrod.

'Good.' Aubrey's voice.

'Beginning to remove the cowling,' he said.

He reached into a pocket of his immersion suit and removed a rubber suction cap. He fixed it to the lamp, and pressed the other side against the outer hull. He jiggled the lamp, but it remained fixed. The pool of light fell upon the grey metal shell.

He loosened the final screw, pocketed it, and lifted the carapace away. Inside it were the carbon fibre braces to withstand pressure at depth. Beneath the carapace were a number of further box-like housings with neoprene seals. He half turned a spring-loaded catch, then lifted the first of the inner covers. What he saw, as he had suspected from the diagram but which still surprised and daunted him, resembled a dug-out, exposed telephone junction box he had once seen beneath the sidewalk of Pennsylvania Avenue in Washington. The telephone engineers had exposed a mass of bright, spiderish wiring, incomprehensible, baffling. He shook his head, and began to learn the nature of what he looked at, remembering Quin's voice guiding him through the wiring diagrams and the 'Leopard' manual. Printed circuit boards, a sickly grey-white and green where the copper was coated with anti-corrosion varnish; on the boards, resistors with bright bands of colour in the lamplight, capacitors in tubes of various sizes, some sheathed in coloured plastic, some like sucked cough lozenges. He nodded to himself. His eyes recognised the number of small boxes set out as regularly and rigidly as units of some eighteenth-century army drawn up for battle. Pins like defences protruded from the boxes, glinting gold. Microprocessors.

It was no longer mysterious. Merely a collection of components. He breathed easily, with satisfaction. He was now the telephone engineer, not the passer-by. The sheer mass of wiring, however, prevented complacency; all colour coded, lashed into ropes with fine cords. Each circuit board had a serial number, which he would read to Quin or Quin would instruct him to test, and each component, however tiny it might be, fitted in its place in company with a reference number.

His finger traced across the bulk of large power

325

transformers, mounted on blocks of metal and used to dissipate heat from the system. Then his eye began to register the miniature switches labelled *Self-Test Facility* and the multi-pin sockets labelled *Input Tester Socket Type 27 P3D*. They were his heart of the matter, all he really needed to recognise.

He hefted the carapace away from him, together with the inner cover, and placed them gingerly in the pressure hull beyond his packs, steadying them until he considered neither of them would slip into the chasm. Then he removed his special test kit from the pack, and clipped it to his belt. A bead of wetness ran down his cheek, then dropped from his jaw. It would take hours, just the checking. The thought made his hands almost nerveless and caused a cramp in his arched back and neck.

'Okay,' he said in a whisper.

Quin was back almost immediately, the eagerness evident in his voice. 'Begin with the Opto-Electric Converter,' he said. 'You can identify that?'

Clark studied the exposed boards. 'Yes, got it.'

'Good. Switch SW One off, and SW Two on.'

'Right.'

' Rotate SW One to Test.'

'Yes.'

'Look at the two rows of LEDs – describe the sequence of lights to me.'

Clark watched the two rows of light emitting diodes. The top row lit up one by one, accompanied by a low hum. As the last one illuminated, the first light of the lower row lit up, followed by its companions, the top row of lights going out immediately. When the second row was complete it, too, went out, and the first light of the top row lit up once more, repeating the sequence.

When Clark had reached the end of the sequence in his description, Quin interrupted him.

'Switch off. Everything's working properly there. The transducers, the wiring, the fibre-optics and the connectors are all working as they should.'

'Uh,' Clark grunted, disappointed in a childish, impatient way. Nothing wrong. He sighed.

*

The Nimrod banked sharply to starboard. Eastoe was trying to come round on to the northern leg, across Varangerhalvöya, and two of the MiG-23s had crossed the nose of the aircraft as soon as he began to change course. Aubrey gripped the sides of his seat fiercely, but he did not allow any expression to appear on his face. He could hear the Russian flight leader, speaking in correct, unemotional English, demanding that Eastoe continue on his former course, west along the Norwegian coast towards North Cape. Eastoe remained silent.

The Nimrod, however declared his intention. It dipped violently as the two MiGs banked up and away, flicking with the agility of flies across the darkness, illuminated by a flash of lightning only when they were already more than a mile away, and beginning a turn to bring them back alongside the Nimrod. Eastoe levelled the big aircraft below the flight level of the Russian interceptors.

'Everyone all right – *you*, Mr Aubrey?'

'Thank you, yes. No more than unsettled.' The console in front of Aubrey crackled, and what might have been a voice tried unsuccessfully to communicate something to them. Quin had turned up the volume to maximum, and was leaning forward.

'What did you say, Clark? Clark, I can't hear you.'

'What's the matter?' Aubrey snapped fearfully. 'What's happening?' Quin shook his head and shrugged. 'Eastoe – we can't hear Clark.'

'I'm at the limit, Mr Aubrey. Over a hundred miles out. I'm sorry, but I'm trying to shave the corner off the northbound leg. You'll have to bear with me.' There was no satisfaction in the voice. Eastoe had suspended his personal feud with Aubrey.

'Very well.' The storm filled the empty ether that was being amplified by the console. A MiG popped into Aubrey's vision, below and almost beneath the port wing of the Nimrod. It had bobbed there like a cork tossed on rough water. There was only the one. Aubrey bent his head and stared through the starboard window opposite him. He could see two more of the Russian interceptors. They were close in, as if juggling for position in order to refuel from the Nimrod. Dangerously close.

Drawn to what he suspected was happening, Aubrey left his seat and crossed to the starboard side of the Nimrod. The aircraft was sliding into a turn, banking slightly and nose-down so that the metal floor had tilted like the floor of some disorientating fairground tunnel. The closest MiG was edging into the Nimrod like a smaller animal ingratiating himself. Its speed had matched the Nimrod's and Aubrey could already see the helmeted head of the pilot within the bubble of the canopy. The flying was skilful even as it was threatening and dangerous. The Nimrod was being headed off, a sheep being directed by a sheepdog. A collision appeared inevitable as their paths converged. Aubrey could do nothing except watch with an appalled fascination. His old frail body trembled with its sense of mortality.

He dimly heard the Nimrod's four Spey engines increase their power, and he felt the nose tilt upwards suddenly. He hung on to a bracket like a straphanger in a tube train, his body wanting to lurch towards the tail of the aircraft. The MiG-23 appeared, then whisked away from the window, like a fly that had been swatted. Even as the Nimrod climbed it began to bank to starboard, pushing Aubrey against the fuselage and his face into the double window port. He felt the glass against his cheek, and his arm aching from its hold on the bracket. The MiG was below them, the other Russian interceptor above, at a distance that implied respect or nerves. Aubrey felt himself hanging over the chasm of thirty thousand feet, imagined the rocks and the landscape below them.

He heard Clark's voice bellow behind him, reporting a stage of his inspection. Then two hands moved his small, frail body, and he was able to let go his hold on the bracket. He looked round into the face of the young flight-lieutenant who was in charge of communications.

'Please don't leave your seat again, Mr Aubrey.'

Aubrey shrugged his clothing to greater tidiness on his form. 'I'm sorry,' he said. 'What did Clark want, Quin?' Aubrey sat down heavily.

Quin shook his head. 'Nothing so far,' he said.

'He is performing the check correctly?'

'He is.'

A livid flash of lightning in the distance. The storm was behind and to the north of them now.

'Mr Aubrey?' It was Eastoe in his headphones.

'Yes?'

'I'm sorry, Mr Aubrey, I'm not going to be allowed to fly the eastbound leg. They won't stand for that.'

'What can you do?' Aubrey asked in utter exasperation.

'Fly a north-south course, over and over – if we can get away with it.'

'You're not hopeful.'

'No, I'm not. Our time here is strictly limited, I'm afraid. they're determined to get rid of us, one way or another.'

'Section completed. All readings positive,' Clark's voice announced ominously from the console.

'Damn,' Aubrey whispered. 'Damn.'

They were all drunk now, yelling, bellowing, fighting drunk. Falling down and laughing drunk, too. Disrespectful, abusive, coarse, uproarious. Ardenyev enjoyed the noise, the swirl and shudder of the vodka in his veins and head, while one still sober, cold part of his awareness perceived where their laughter and taunts were leading, and anticipated with nothing more than a shudder of self-consciousness the nature of leadership and what he would now have to do to fulfil their expectations and to maintain his grip on their affection and respect.

And also, he concluded, the drinking party had to end with buffoonery, with the game of the ego and the shallowly physical prowess they required to perform their duties. After the death of Blue Section and the others of his own team, the three survivors had been absorbed and ingested as they drank and ate into the cameraderie of the men from the rescue ship *Karpaty*. Balan had understood the necessity of the merger. So Balan's challenge now to him to demonstrate how he boarded the *Proteus* was that of a shrewd drunk. His men wanted it, a boast and valediction. *He* had survived, become more than ever a necessary figurehead, even to the salvage men. In the absence of an athlete, a football star, an actress, he had to submit himself to their fuddled worship, their drunken amusement.

He was drunk, though. He knew that as soon as he stood up, and swayed as if the vodka had punched him in the temple. Teplov was watching him, he could see, as if weighing whether he should let his officer proceed. Viktor Teplov appeared sober, as ever.

Ardenyev looked up, the two images of the wall and the ceiling of the officers' mess coming together, as if he had correctly, though slowly, adjusted a pair of binoculars. He held the new and single image with an effort of concentration. Teplov nodded at the fuzzy corner of his vision. He was prepared to extricate his officer from whatever situation he found himself in.

'Come on, then!' Lev Balan roared, pointing up at the air-conditioning grille. 'From that one, right round the room to that one!' His arm swept round the officers' mess, now deserted save for their own noisy group. The two grilles were on opposite walls. Ardenyev was being challenged to clamber and push his way through the duct until he could emerge with honour. Two of Balan's team were busy, balancing with difficulty on chairs, unscrewing the two grilles. Ardenyev looked at Balan, and then at Teplov, and Vanilov. All that remained of the Special Underwater Operations Unit. Teplov had the face of a stoical peasant in which his eyes gleamed with memory and with a strange amusement, perhaps even with approval. Vanilov looked as if he had drunk too much to forget. He wanted Ardenyev to prove something, perhaps only to be the adult coming into his child's bedroom, easing away the threatening shadows that had gathered around the cot.

'Okay. You're on. Two hundred roubles it is.'

'One hundred – !' Balan protested.

'Two.'

'All right, two. That means a time limit. Okay?'

Ardenyev hesitated for a moment, then he nodded. Balan's man stepped down off his chair, the grille in his hand. Ardenyev flicked the remainder of his drink into his open mouth, feeling it burn the back of his throat, then he reached up and took hold of the rough plaster edges of the square hole where the grille had been. He felt mouse droppings under his fingers.

'One minute,' Balan called. 'You've got one minute to

get at least your head out of that other hole. Five, four, three, two, one – *go!*'

The cheering was deafening. Ardenyev pushed himself up level with the hole, ducked his head into it, and then heaved himself half into the duct, which bent immediately to the left. His shoulders rubbed against the plaster, and he found he had to angle his body in order to be able to move at all. The cheering behind him was muffled by the bulk of his body and by the plaster wall and the metal. He kicked, and his legs followed him into the duct. Immediately, Balan's voice came from behind him, counting.

'Eleven, twelve, thirteen . . . '

Ardenyev shook his head to clear it. Then he began scrambling, leaning to his left, his body rubbing along the metal channel. The cheering was dim and wordless now, falling away into silence. He reached the corner of the room. The duct was a severe right-angle. He squeezed his head and shoulders around the angle, then tried to bring his thighs and knees after his upper torso. He found himself wedged immovably. He struggled as if panicking, and sweat broke out all over his body. He cursed in a yell, and then lay still. Balan's head appeared further down the duct, in a shadowy patch of light. There was a noise that no longer interested Ardenyev coming from behind him.

'Forty-seven, forty-eight, forty-nine . . . '

'Piss off!' Ardenyev yelled, not even attempting to move again. 'I'm bloody stuck!'

Balan's head disappeared with a shriek of laughter. Teplov's head appeared in its place. At the same moment, a huge cheer went up as the minute ran out. 'All right, sir?'

'Yes, thank you, Viktor.'

'Bloody silly game, sir.'

'Yes, Viktor.'

'I'll come in the other side and give you a shove, sir.'

'Thank you, Viktor.'

Ardenyev smiled, then relaxed. It didn't matter. Nothing did. The air conditioning duct enclosed him more surely and tightly than the aft escape chamber of the *Proteus*, but there was similarity of darkness and confinement that pressed itself upon him. He allowed a congratulatory sense

331

of memory its place in his fuddled awareness. He'd done it, he'd done it –

No one else, he told himself. No one else could have done it. Then, more sharply, he thought, if I could, someone else could. Most of the team, the dead team –

His thoughts had swung towards a maudlin, drunken horizon. He heard Teplov moving along the duct behind him, grunting with effort. He giggled drunkenly. Anyone could have done it, he affirmed in a mood of quick and sudden self-deprecation as he imagined those who had died. It wasn't anything. Then, through a connection of which he was not aware, he wondered: why is that Nimrod hanging around? What is it doing?

Teplov's hand tapped his calf. He called back to the *michman*: 'What's that Nimrod doing up there, Viktor?'

'Beg pardon, sir?'

'That Nimrod – they were talking about it earlier.'

'Oh, that one,' Teplov said indulgently. 'I wouldn't know, sir.'

If I could do it, he thought, anyone could. That Nimrod –

He was aware of himself, stretched out on the pressure hull, held there by the mesh of nerves that covered his body. He had heard the footsteps clattering along the hull from the stern. The boots had stamped to a halt directly over the hatch through which he had entered the space between the two hulls. He had immediately switched off the lamp, as if the outer hull had been no more opaque than a curtain, and he had turned on to his back, He seemed to himself to be less vulnerable, facing the direction of the noises. Evidence, evidence? he asked himself repeatedly. Why? Why now? Noise, suspicion, *evidence*?

He stared up at the outer hull as if he could really see it, almost as if he could see the armed man whose boots had clattered up on him. He listened. Tiny noises now, almost mouse-like. The irresolute shuffling of feet, the claw-like scratching of nails and metal heel-tips. The darkness pressed in, unwelcome, bringing its unexpected and disturbing claustrophobia with it. He reached up and flicked on the lamp. It shone in his eyes. He inspected his watch. Six o'clock, almost. He had been working on the back-up system for over two hours. And he had found nothing. Every circuit, every resistor, every capacitor and microprocessor and wire and pin *worked* –

There was nothing wrong with it, at least not with the sixty-five per cent of the back-up system that he had checked. There was something less, or something more mysteriously, wrong with the complex lump of junk near his head than was the matter with the Nimrod. Sure, Aubrey kept reassuring him, but the communications black-outs and the poor reception and the constant re- requests and repeats of instructions told him everything.

The boots shuffled, then moved, on the hull. They were over his face now, only a couple of feet from stamping on it.

The Nimrod was at the fringes of, and at times beyond, the communications range. Which meant that the aircraft had company, Soviet company. MiGs were shadowing the Nimrod, maybe even playing shepherd games with her –

As he rehearsed the conclusion once more, a chill coldness seized him. They suspected, even knew, about him. The boots on the hull, and the silence which he had noticed from the turbine room beneath him. They were listening, too. Everyone was listening for him, waiting for the mouse behind the wainscot to move again. He held his breath, one part of his mind explaining with a weary patience that he was behaving ridiculously, the remainder of his consciousness believing that the hull above him and beneath his back and head and legs was no more than a sounding-board, a corridor of whispers eager to betray his whereabouts.

The boots moved away, forward along the hull towards the sail. Almost immediately, Lloyd was speaking in a voice muffled by the pocket of his immersion suit, through the tiny R/T Clark had left with him. Relief overcame Clark, and he felt the renewed perspiration cool almost at once on his skin, making his flesh shudder.

He removed the R/T from his pocket and pressed it to his cheek.

'Yes?'

'I've seen Hayter and Thurston. They know what to do.'

'Good.'

'Any luck?'

'None.'

'It's six now.'

'I know.'

'Is it still on?'

'Eight o'clock, on the button.'

'I heard my guard and another talking. The man from Novosibirsk has arrived in Murmansk.'

'Damn. Is he on his way?'

'I don't know.'

'Okay – I'll call you.'

Clark replaced the R/T set in his breast pocket, and zipped the pocket closed with a real and savage anger. He rolled on to his stomach, and the turtle without its shell was humped on the edge of the pool of light from the lamp, still baffling him, still apparently undamaged.

'You heard that?' he whispered. There were noises now from the turbine room. He had imagined the silence.

'Yes,' Aubrey replied. His voice was gauzy and faint, a smear of distant sound. Flying on the limit again.

'What trouble are you in?'

'None.'

'Tell me.'

'Four MiG-23s. They're keeping us as far away from Soviet airspace as possible – ' The voice blacked out, then Clark heard an additional smear of sound some seconds later which he could not decipher. Then two more spits of sound which the cassette recorder slowed down and replayed. He could understand neither of them. The cool part of his brain suggested a storm might be adding to the difficulties, but the remainder of his awareness was raging with the same kind of helpless, impotent fury his body felt. He was shaking as he knelt in front of the 'Leopard' back-up system. He was in a mood to break, damage, throw. The rational part of him understood, and mocked at, the emotions he felt and his desire for their expression, and gradually he calmed himself. Then, suddenly, Aubrey was speaking again, clearly.

'Can you hear me now?'

'Yes.'

'Eastoe has dodged them, ducked inside,' Aubrey said. Clark could even pick out the irony of the old man's tone.

'Quin suggests it will take only hours to dismantle "Leopard", if that is what they intend, and the same amount of time for a full analysis, with the resources they have available. Once they begin the work, they will be searching for the back-up system. You must not be where you are when that happens. "Leopard" must not be intact when this expert steps aboard. Do I make myself clear?'

'Yes.'

'It will take an hour from Murmansk by helicopter.'

'All right, all right. I'm moving on – what next?'

'Very well. You have *both* packs with you?'

Clark looked up and into the gloom beyond the lamplight. 'Yes,' he replied with a sense of defeat. 'Both of them.'

'Keep me informed.'

'Clark?' It was Quin's voice now, not so irritating, not so pessimistic as that of Aubrey. Quin allowed the fiction of success to be entertained. 'You should move on to the spectrum analyser, noise generator and phase reverser unit.'

'Right.'

'You need the special test kit.'

'Sure.' Clark unclipped it from his belt. A dial, various scales, a rotary switch, buttons, a small grille. Quin had to instruct every step of the way: every switch, every light, every reading. 'All right, I'm ready.' He studied the exposed maze of wiring, microprocessors and circuits in front of him. For a moment, his mind was a blank and the system before him was a puzzle to which he had no clue. Then, sighing, he shrugged off his numbing reluctance, and reached out and waited for Quin's instructions.

It was six o-five.

'It's almost six, Admiral – perhaps we can now be leaving for Pechenga. Too much time has already been wasted.'

'Comrade Academician, you say it will take a matter of no more than three or four hours to complete your work on "Leopard". What is your hurry? You waited at the airport in Novosibirsk for almost three days.' Dolohov was expansive, and mocking. He was almost drunk, Panov decided, and had abandoned most of his dignity. Panov did not like the military, especially the older representatives, the officer caste. As a man who was an honoured member of another élite, one without the stain of imitating those that existed before the Revolution, Panov disliked, even loathed, the upper echelons of the military.

Panov glanced again at his gold Swiss watch. He had purchased it in Paris, while attending a scientific congress, and that had added to its potency as a reminder of his identity. The large-faced clock on the wall behind Dolohov, which Panov would hardly have admitted to his wife's kitchen in Novosibirsk, jerked its hand past another minute. The drunken old fool remained in his chair.

'Admiral – I must insist that we leave for Pechenga at once. My colleagues will be waiting for me. I must study their preliminary findings before I can specify what needs to be done.' Panov stopped at this point, feeling the asperity in his tone raising his voice beyond the point of acceptable masculinity. He despised his own too-high voice. The admiral growled and huffed like a bear.

'I see. You insist?'

Panov cleared his throat. 'I do.'

Dolohov reached across his desk and flicked the switch of his intercom.

'Get my car to the door at once, and warn the tower I shall want an immediate take-off.' He switched off, and stood up, his arms extended in a bear-like embrace. The image made Panov suppress a shudder, and smooth dislike from his bland features. 'Come, Comrade Academician Panov – your carriage awaits.' Then Dolohov laughed. Panov had to endure a large hand slapping him on the shoulder, and the log-like fall of an arm across his neck, as he was ushered to the door. Dolohov's voice was like a caress when he added: 'Don't you think *I* am anxious to see our prize, too?' Then he laughed again.

The hand of the clock on the wall clicked again. Six o-five.

Clark moved the rotary switch on the test kit for the final time, the needle on the dial flickered away from zero, and he cursed as he unclipped the kit's leads from the last of the test pins on the power supply units. Each and every one of them worked, gave a positive reading, had nothing wrong with them.

'Okay, that's it,' he said, glancing at his watch. Seven o-two. Another hour had passed, and he was still at the moment before beginning. Everything he had done during the past three hours had been necessary, and pointless.

'Very well, Clark, you'd better run a check on the power lines, from TP Seventeen, Eighteen and Twenty-Four, using the cable adaptor with the yellow sleeve, marked BFP 6016 – '

'I got that,' Clark snapped, wiping his forehead, then letting his hand stray to his eyes. He rubbed at them. They felt gritty with tiredness and concentration. He squeezed them shut and opened them again. He wanted another perspective. 'Hold it, I want to talk to Lloyd again.'

He took the R/T from his pocket, and pressed its call button.

'Yes?' Lloyd said quietly a moment later. Clark pressed the R/T to his cheek.

'What's happening?'

'I've just been on my rounds.' Lloyd almost chuckled. There was a crackling, electric excitement in the man. He had swung away from the helpless depression of the prisoner. Now he was the schoolboy escapee. 'I managed to brief one of my chief petty officers while I was doing it.'

'What about the gates?'

'There's a minimal guard outside, always has been. The repair crew won't be here before eight. The gates can be opened by two men, one to throw the switches, the other to guard him. I'll detail men as soon as we free the wardroom. Then they can smash the switches so the gates can't be closed again.'

'I agree.'

'Clark – can you give me "Leopard"? I can't risk my men and my vessel unless you do.'

'Can you kill the first guard, Lloyd, the one outside your door?' Clark snapped back at him. 'Because if you can't, then *Proteus* goes nowhere!' Clark, in the silence which followed, imagined Lloyd reaching under his pillow for the tiny Astra pistol he had left with him. Everything depended on Lloyd being able to kill the guard outside his cabin, retrieve the man's Kalashnikov, and release his officers from the wardroom along the corridor from his cabin.

'I – think I can,' Lloyd replied eventually. 'I'll have to, won't I?'

'And I have to repair "Leopard", don't I?'

'Very well. Rumour has it that Panov, the scientist, is expected at any moment. The technicians on board have been informed to that effect. No later than eight o'clock.'

'It's all coming right down to the wire, uh?' When Lloyd did not reply, Clark merely added, 'I'll call you.' He replaced the R/T in his pocket. Even as he did so, he heard Aubrey's voice in his ear.

'Clark, you must begin preparing to abort "Leopard". It will take you at least thirty to forty minutes to place the charges. You must begin at once.'

'No, dammit!'

'Clark, do as you are ordered.'

'Mister Quin gave me a job to do – maybe after that.'

'*Now!*'

'Not a chance.'

Rapidly, he fitted the cable adaptor to the first of the power lines Quin had designated. Positive. He cursed under his breath. Then the second. Positive. Then the third. Positive. He sighed loudly, in anger and frustration.

'Fit the charges, Clark – please begin at once,' Aubrey commanded with icy malice.

Ardenyev watched the MiL-8 transport helicopter sag down towards the landing pad. The down-draught, exceeding the wind's force, stirred the dust on the concrete. Behind it, the sky was beginning to lighten, a thin-grey blue streak above the hills, almost illusory beyond the hard white lighting of the helicopter base. Ardenyev glanced at his watch. Seven-ten. The admiral and Panov were almost an hour early. Viktor Teplov – face-saving, loyal Teplov – had picked up the information somewhere that Dolohov was on his way, and revived his officer with coffee and one large vodka, which Ardenyev had felt was like swallowing hot oil. Then he had commandeered a staff car and driver and accompanied Ardenyev to the helicopter base.

The MiL-8 hovered like an ungainly wasp, then dropped

on to its wheels. Immediately, ducking ground crew placed the chocks against the wheels, even as the noise of the rotors descended through the scale and the rotor dish dissolved from its shimmering, circular form into flashes of darker grey in the rush of air. Then they were individual blades, then the door opened as the rotors sagged into stillness. Dolohov's foot was on the ladder as soon as it was pushed into place for him. He descended with a light, firm step, inheriting a kingdom. Men snapped to attention, saluting. A smaller, more rotund figure in a fur-collared coat stepped more gingerly down behind him. Panov. Dolohov waited for the scientist, then ushered him towards Ardenyev.

Ardenyev sucked spit from his cheeks and moistened his dry throat. He saluted crisply, then Dolohov extended his hand and shook Ardenyev's warmly.

'May I introduce Captain Valery Ardenyev,' he said, turning to Panov. The scientist appeared intrigued, his face pale, almost tinged with blue, in the cold lighting. He shook Ardenyev's hand limply.

'Ah – our hero of the Soviet Union,' he said with evident irony. Dolohov's face clouded with the insult to Ardenyev.

'Thank you, Comrade Academician Professor Panov,' Ardenyev replied woodenly. He was enjoying fulfilling Panov's prejudices, meeting one of his stereotypes. 'It was nothing.'

Dolohov appeared bemused. 'Shall we go?' he remarked. 'Directly to the submarine pen, I think?'

'If you please,' Panov said primly.

'This way, Admiral – Professor. The car is waiting.'

'I'm sorry you lost so many men,' Dolohov murmured confidentially as they walked towards the car. Panov, who was intended to overhear the remark, appeared at a loss, even embarrassed.

'So am I, sir – so am I.' Teplov came to attention, then opened the rear door of the Zil. Ardenyev smiled wearily. 'A ten minute drive, sir, and you'll be able to see her: HMS *Proteus*, pride of the fleet!'

Dolohov laughed uproariously, slapping Ardenyev on the back before getting into the car.

Fourteen: RUNNING

Hyde woke, and reacted instantly to the cold air that had insinuated itself into their burrow. It was damp. He knew there was a fog or heavy mist outside, even though he could not see beyond the bush. There was greyness there, which might have been the dawn. He felt his shoulder protest with a sharp pain as he tried to rub his cold arms, and he stifled his groan as he remembered what had roused him. The running feet of deer along the track behind the rifle range, past the bush and the entrance into their hole. He looked immediately at the girl. She was soundly asleep.

He listened. And tested his shoulder, moving fingers and wrist and elbow and forearm. Slightly better. He touched the crude, dirty bandage. Dry and stiff. He investigated his resources. His body felt small, shrunken, empty and weak. But not leaden, as the previous night. His head felt more solid, too, less like a gathering of threads or misty tendrils. There was some clarity of thought, some speed of comprehension. He would have to do as he was. He was all he had, all they had.

The hoofbeats of the three or four deer who had fled past their hiding place died away, swallowed by what he was now convinced was a heavy mist. He listened to the silence, slow and thick outside the hole. He stretched his legs carefully, not disturbing the girl, felt the expected cramp, eased it away, rotated his pelvis as well as he could while hunched in a seated position. His back ached. He flexed his fingers once more, aware of the small of his back where the gun had been. Having completed his inventory, he pronounced himself incapable, with a slight smile. Some stubbornness had returned during the few hours' sleep he had had.

Noises. Slow, regular, cautious footsteps outside. He reached up and pressed his palm flat against the roof of the hole. The sand was damp. He levered himself out of his sitting position, and stepped over the girl's drawn-up knees. Her head rested on her chest, and her blonde hair, dirty and hanging in stiff, greasy tails, was draped like strands of cloth over her knees. He leaned forward, then slid towards the entrance to the hole. The branches of the bush became clear, as if he had focused an inward lens on them, and beyond them the heavy mist was grey and impenetrable. One chance. Don't wake up, darling –

The figure of a man emerged from the mist, bent low to study the track, the slim, pencil-like barrel of the rifle he carried protruding beyond the bulk of his form. He was little more than a dark shadow in the first light seeping into the mist. Then he saw the bush, and might have been staring into Hyde's eyes, though he registered no sign of having seen him. The gun moved away from his body, and Hyde recognised it, with a chill of danger and a strange greediness, as a Kalashnikov. Stubby, with a folding steel stock and plastic grip and the curving thirty-round ammunition box beneath the magazine. It was infinitely desirable, and deadly. The small R/T set clipped to the pocket of the man's anorak was similarly desirable and dangerous. Hyde coveted them both.

He held his breath as he felt one of the girl's feet touch his shin. Don't let her wake up, not now –

The man moved closer to the bush, the Kalashnikov prodding out in front of his body. Hyde flexed his fingers, keeping his head as close to the lip of the hole as he could, watching the man intently. The girl's foot stirred again, and Hyde prayed she would not make a noise in the last moments of her sleep. He felt her foot shiver. The cold was beginning to wake her. The stubby barrel of the rifle moved among the leafless branches, disturbing them, brushing them to one side. He squashed himself flat against the damp sand. He felt, through her foot, the girl's whole body stir, then he heard her yawn. Immediately the man's head snapped up, alert, cocked on one side as he listened, attempting to gauge the direction of the sound, waiting for its repetition. His eyes glanced over the bank, the rifle's barrel wavered in the bush, pointing above the hole. The girl groaned with stiffness. Hyde reached out, grabbed the stubby rifle, one hand on the barrel the other on the magazine. The man jerked backwards in surprise and defence, and Hyde pushed with his feet and used the man's response to pull him out of the hole and through the bush. He cried out with the sudden, searing pain in his arm and shoulder, but he held on, twisting the barrel of the rifle away from him, rolling down the sand to the track, pulling the man off balance.

The man almost toppled, then jerked at the rifle. Hyde had to release the grip of his left hand because the pain was so intense, but he had rolled almost to the man's feet. He kicked out, using his grip on the rifle as a pivot, and the man overbalanced as Hyde's shins caught him at the back of the legs. The Russian held on to the rifle, and Hyde felt the heat before he heard the sound of the explosion as a round was fired. Hyde used the rifle like a stick, an old man assisting himself to rise from a deep armchair, and as the man made to turn on to his side and get up, Hyde kicked him in the side of the head. The grip on the Kalashnikov did not loosen. Hyde, enraged and elated, kicked the man once more in the temple, with all the force he could muster. The man rolled away, his head seemingly loose on his shoulders, and lay still. Hyde could see the man's chest pumping. He reached down for the R/T, and a hand grabbed at the rifle again as Hyde held it still by the barrel. The man's eyes were glazed and intent. Hyde staggered away, taking the rifle with him. He had no strength, he should have killed the man with one of the kicks, it was pathetic –

The man was sitting up. He heard Tricia Quin gasp audibly. He fumbled the rifle until it pointed at the man, who was withdrawing his hand from his anorak and the hand contained a pistol, heavy and black and coming to a bead. Hyde fired, twice. The noise of the shots seemed more efficiently swallowed by the mist than the cries of rooks startled by the gunfire. The man's pistol discharged into the earth, and he twitched like a wired rabbit. Hyde, angry and in haste, moved to the body. He swore. One bullet had passed through the R/T set, smashing it. Tricia Quin's appalled groan was superfluous, irrelevant.

Hyde knelt by the man's body, searching it quickly with one hand. He had had to lay the rifle down. His left arm was on fire, and useless to him. He hunched it into his side, as if he could protect it or lessen its pain by doing so. He unzipped the anorak. No papers. The man didn't even look Slavic. He could have been anybody. He patted the pockets of the anorak. Yes –

Triumphantly, he produced a flask of something, and a wrapped package of sandwiches.

'Food!' he announced. 'Bloody food!'

The girl's face was washed clean of resentment and fear and revulsion. She grabbed the package eagerly. The sandwiches had some kind of sausage in them. She swallowed a lump of bread and sausage greedily, then tried to speak through the food.

'What – ?' was all he heard.

Hyde looked around him. 'Help me get this poor sod into the hole. It might hide him for a bit. Come on – stop stuffing your face, girlie!'

Tricia put the sandwiches reverently, and with much regret, on the track, roughly rewrapped. He took hold of one arm, she the other, averting her eyes from the man's face, which stared up into the mist in a bolting, surprised way. They dragged the body to the bank, hoisted it – Tricia would not put her shoulder or body beneath the weight of the man – and Hyde with a cry of pain and effort tumbled the body into the hole.

'His foot,' the girl said as Hyde stood trembling from his exertions. Hyde looked up. The man's walking boot was protruding over the lip of the hole.

'You see to it.'

Reluctantly, the girl reached up, and pushed. The man's knee seemed locked by an instant rigor mortis. The girl obtained a purchase for her feet, and heaved. The foot did not move. She cried with exasperation, and wriggled and thrust until the foot disappeared.

'Bloody, bloody *thing*!' There was a crack from inside the hole. She covered her mouth, appalled. She turned accusing eyes on Hyde.

'We can all be shitty when we try hard,' he said, eating one of the sandwiches. Then he added, 'Okay, pick the rest of them up – ' He thrust the Makarov pistol into his waistband, and hefted the rifle in his good hand. The girl pocketed the sandwiches, looking furtively sidelong at him as she ate a second one. 'Come on, then.' He looked around him. 'Bad luck and good luck. No one's going to find us in this.'

They walked up the track behind the bank. The girl

looked guiltily back once, still chewing the last lump of the second sandwich.

Clark ground his teeth in frustration, and clenched his hands into claws again and again as if to rid them of a severe cramp. The sight of what he had done enraged and depressed him. The plastic charges were taped and moulded to the back-up system, lying across the wiring and the circuitry like slugs, the detonator wires like the strands of a net that had dredged up the equipment from beneath the sea. He had done as Aubrey asked – commanded – and then he had requested Quin to set him another task, like an over-eager schoolboy. More power lines, and still nothing.

'Clark?' For a moment, he was tempted to curse Aubrey aloud. Part of him, however, admitted the correctness of Aubrey's decision.

'Yes?'

'It's time for you to rig the main "Leopard" system. Good luck.' There was no sense of possible argument or disobedience. Aubrey assumed he would behave like the automaton he was intended to be.

The bleeper on the R/T in his pocket sounded. He pulled the set out and pressed the transmit button. 'Yes?'

'Clark? I think Panov's about to make an appearance. The technical team are streaming out of the *Proteus*, lining up like a guard of honour. I've just seen them.'

'Where are you?'

'Hurry, Clark. You do not have much time – ' Aubrey said in his ear.

'The officers' bathroom.'

'Your guard?'

'Clark listen to me – '

'Outside.'

'Mood?'

'Pretty sloppy. He's waiting for his relief at eight.'

'Clark, you will abort "Plumber" immediately and proceed to destroy "Leopard". Do you understand me?'

'Well?' Lloyd asked with a nervous edge to his voice.

'Get as close to him as you can, preferably the side of his head or under the jaw, and squeeze the trigger *twice*.'

344

'Clark, you will rescind that instruction to Lloyd – '

'What about "Leopard"?' Lloyd asked.

'I'll give you "Leopard" in working order!' Clark snapped. 'Where is Thurston, where's Hayter?'

'The First-Lieutenant's in the cabin next to mine, Hayter's in the wardroom with the others.'

'Then – '

'Clark – !'

'Time for Quin to earn his money!' Clark almost shouted, with nerves and relief and the adrenalin that suddenly coursed through his system. 'Help me get this fucking back-up working, Quin!'

'Clark – *Clark!*'

'Go or no go?' Lloyd asked.

'Go – *GO!* Kill the bastard!'

'I'll be in touch.'

'Clark – you are insane. You will never get out of Pechenga without "Leopard". You have not, you *cannot* repair it. You have just sentenced Commander Lloyd and his crew to imprisonment, possibly even death. You are *insane*.' The last word was hissed in Clark's ear, serpentine and venomous.

Clark felt a heady, dangerous relief, and a pressing, violent anxiety. 'For Chrissake, Quin – help me get this fucking thing to work! *Help me!*'

Aubrey stared at Quin. He could not believe in what Clark had put in motion, could not apprehend the violent and dangerous half-motives that had prompted him. In its final stage, the *Proteus* business was escaping him again, running on its own headlong flight unhindered by reason or caution or good sense. In a split-second over which he had had no control, Clark had made the decision not to abort. Now, everyone would face the consequences of that decision.

'Quin? *Quin?*' he snapped at his companion. The scientist tossed his head as if startled from sleep.

'What?'

'Can you help him?'

Quin shrugged. 'We've tried everything we can. There's nothing wrong – '

345

'There must be, dammit!'

'I don't know what it is!' Quin almost wailed.

Aubrey leaned towards him. 'That bloody American has set the seal on this affair, Quin. Lloyd will either kill his guard, or be killed. If the former, then they will kill others, picking up weapons at each death, until they can open the gates and sail *Proteus* out of Pechenga. Without "Leopard" in an operational condition, they will be a target for every naval unit in the port. I would not wish to assume that the Russians will be prepared to let her sail away scot free! What can you do? Think of something!'

Quin began flipping through the 'Leopard' manual, most of which he had written himself. Aubrey recognised an unseeing, desperate gesture. Quin *knew* the manual, nothing would come from it. The man's hands were shaking. He had collided with a brute reality. Aubrey shook his head with weariness. Tiredness, the sense of being utterly spent, seemed the only feeling left to him. Clark had renegued on reason, on authority. He could understand how it had happened. The American had simply refused to acknowledge defeat.

He heard Eastoe's voice tinnily in the headphones resting around his neck. He placed the set over his head. The microphone bobbed in front of his mouth.

'Yes, Squadron Leader?' He had not meant his voice to sound so waspish and dismissive.

'Mr Aubrey. We're out of range again. I can try to get back, but I won't be able to hold station for very much longer. I can give you a couple of minutes, perhaps.'

Aubrey wanted to rage at the pilot, but he acknowledged the weariness in the man's voice. The MiGs – there was one on the port wing again, turning silver in the beginning of the day – were making patterned flying impossible. Slowly, inexorably, the Nimrod was being shepherded away from the Soviet border.

'Do what you can, Squadron Leader. We're in your hands.'

'Very well, Mr Aubrey. I'll give you as long as I can.'

The nose of the Nimrod dipped, and then when Eastoe judged he had lost sufficient height, the aircraft banked savagely, rolling away towards the east and the sun. The porthole in the fuselage became a blaze of gold, blinding

346

Aubrey. He felt as old and thin and stretched as a ghost. Transparent in the sudden light.

'Quin, come on, man – suggest something. We don't have much time.'

Quin groaned aloud, and rubbed his face with his hands, washing off his present circumstances. He looked blearily at Aubrey, and shook his head.

'There is nothing.'

'There must be. Some faulty system, something you disagreed with Plessey about, something you've always suspected or disliked about the system – anything!' Aubrey spread his hands around the communications console, which hissed at him. It was as if he were about to jettison it as useless cargo. A MiG, gold-bright, popped into his view, just off the port wing. Craning his neck, Aubrey could see the grey sea, the misted coast below them. The MiG ducked beneath the Nimrod, and Aubrey saw it bob like a cork into the starboard porthole opposite him. 'Something – *please*?'

The console crackled. Clark's voice was faint. The coast and sea below moved, and Aubrey could hear the Spey engines more loudly. Eastoe was running for the border with the Soviet Union in a straight, desperate line.

'You must help – '

'For Chrissake, Quin – say something!' Clark bellowed from the receiver.

Quin's face was an agony of doubt.

'Come on, Quin, come on, come on,' Aubrey heard himself repeating.

'I can hear shooting!' Clark yelled. Aubrey knew it was a lie, but a clever one. And perhaps it only described events that had already occurred. Lloyd dead, a guard dead, two guards, three?

'Change-over – automatic change-over,' Quin murmured.

'What's that?' Clark snapped.

The MiG on the starboard wing – two of them now, one above the other, moving on a course to head off the Nimrod. There was a slim shadow taking and changing shape on the port wing. One of the MiGs was above them, appearing almost as if it might be lowering itself on to the wing, to snap it in half. Eastoe dropped the nose of the Nimrod again, dropping towards the sea and the rocky coast that seemed to lurch up to meet them. The port wing and the starboard window were swept clean for a moment. Aubrey felt Eastoe begin to turn the aircraft. He'd given up. They were on their way back, and out of range.

'The automatic change-over from the main system to the back-up. I argued time and again, with the Admiralty. No trust in completely automatic systems. They insisted – '

'Tell him!'

Quin leant towards the console. 'Clark,' he began, 'you must check the automatic change-over on the power supply from the main system to the back-up. Locate the power supply box . . .'

Aubrey ceased to listen. The Nimrod had completed its turn, through the brief blinding sunlight on the porthole, and was now heading west once more. Eastoe had dropped the aircraft's speed, but it was a matter of mere minutes until they would no longer be able to talk to Clark.

And, in Pechenga, with whatever outcome, the killing had undoubtedly begun.

One of the MiGs bobbed back into view, off the port wing. The Russian interceptor appeared to be flying a little further off, as if its pilot, too, knew that the game was up.

Lloyd hesitated for a moment, on the threshold of the bathroom, straddling the body of the guard who had only had time to half-turn before the small Astra, pressed against his side, had exploded twice. Lloyd had had to take him into an embrace, feel the man's final shudder against him, and lower him to the deck. One guard only in the corridor. Lloyd had been surprised at the small, muffled sound the gun had made when pressed into the spare flesh the man was carrying. It was as if the pistol had been fitted with a silencer.

He saw the guard outside the wardroom door at the end of the corridor, and hoped, as he studied the man's movements and saw the Kalashnikov turn in the guard's hands and draw a bead on himself, that Thurston would not blunder into the line of fire out of the cabin next door to his own. Then he prayed his hands would move more swiftly to bring the small pistol up to the level of the guard's trunk.

348

He could not believe that he would move more quickly than the trained marine, but some realisation that the clock was ticking away precious seconds only for him, came to him as he fired. He had moved inches faster, reaction had been milliseconds quicker, because he had an imperative the Russian did not share. The guard thudded back against the wardroom door, and slid down, feet out, to a sitting position with his head lolling. The pistol now made much more noise, and would have attracted attention.

'Come on, come on!' he yelled, banging on Thurston's door as he passed it. Then he was stooping to retrieve the Kalashnikov, which felt immediately bulky and menacing in his grip. He flung open the wardroom door. Surprised faces, half a dozen of them, mostly unshaven, were grouped around the table above mugs of steaming coffee. Thurston was behind him now. He passed the Astra back to his first-lieutenant. 'Get the others out – *now*!' he snapped, feeling the dangerous, elating adrenalin running wildly through his body.

Seven twenty-one. Clark had recognised, almost subliminally, the two shots, then the third after a slight delay. He imagined that the same small Astra pistol had made all three reports, but he could not quite believe it, until Lloyd's voice could be heard plainly, coming from the R/T which was clipped to the breast of his immersion suit, ordering his officers to remain in the wardroom until the control room had been recaptured. Then there was the awful, cloth-ripping stutter of the Kalashnikov on automatic – Clark presumed feverishly that it was the one Lloyd had taken from the wardroom guard. It was. Lloyd yelled at Hayter to recover the gun of the man he had just killed. Clark nodded to himself. Lloyd would go on now until he became exhausted or until someone shot him. He was high on escape, even on death.

Clark lifted the lid of the power supply box, as Quin had instructed him. LIFT HERE ONLY. He had unclamped the lid, and obeyed its command, stencilled in yellow.

'Clark?'

'Yes. The box is open,' he told Quin. Communications were already weakening as the Nimrod moved towards the fringes of reception. Aubrey had told him what was happening, then patched in Eastoe. The pilot did not enjoy admitting his weariness, his loss of nerve, his failure, but he had done so. The Nimrod was shot, finished. It was on its way home. Eastoe had dropped the airspeed as much as he could, but they were gradually moving out of range, taking Quin with his manual, his diagrams and his knowledge with them. He had, at the Nimrod's present speed, no more then five minutes. Seven twenty-two.

'Switch SW-Eight-R should be off.' Clark followed Quin's instruction. Lloyd's breathing was audible to him in the confined, lamplit darkness from the R/T against the submarine captain's chest. Running – ? Cries, yells – ? *Come on, Quin –*

'Okay.'

'Press the yellow button marked PRESS TO TEST. Have you got that?' A faint, weak voice, like a man dying in the next room.

'Okay?'

Firing.

'Lloyd, what's happening?' He knew he should not have called, that it might be fatal to distract Lloyd now. Yet the sounds tormented him, made his body writhe with an uncontrollable tension and anxiety.

Firing.

Quin said something he did not catch. He prayed it was only his inattention. ' . . . through top . . . cover?'

'Repeat, please,' he requested loudly, holding his breath. Lloyd's breathing roared on his chest like an illness he had contracted.

' . . . contacts move . . . clear top . . . ?'

'Repeat, repeat!' Clark shouted, almost as a relief for the hours of whispering and silence he had endured and partly because he was panicking. The irreversible had begun. Lloyd had killed, the officers were armed with two Russian Kalashnikovs and were in the control room of the *Proteus*. He had begun it – *he* had. 'Repeat. I say again, repeat your message.' The words were formal, the voice running out of control.

'Right. Hold them over there – no, get them off my ship, *now*!' Lloyd's elation, his success, drummed in the cramped

350

space between the two hulls. 'Clark?'

'Yes?'

'What's wrong?' Even in his excitement, Lloyd was responsive to tone, to nuance.

'Nothing.'

'We have the control room in our hands again.'

'Good – ' Clark paused. There was a spit of sound, but when the tape had been slowed, there was only the ether, mocking him. A gauzy, sad, distant voice mumbled behind it. *Christ, what have I done?* 'Outside?'

'Thurston's taking a look. I've despatched three men, two of them armed, to the control booth for the gates. A couple of minutes now – ?' the statement ended as a question. Another spit of sound, Clark's heart pounding as he waited for it to replay more slowly in his earpiece, Quin's voice broken and racked by the interference.

'Can you see . . . through top . . . moving?'

Contacts, *contacts,* he recalled. Can you see the contacts moving through the clear top of the cover?

'Got you!' Then, immediately, he cried, 'They're not moving!'

'Clark, what the devil's wrong?'

'I *can't* –!' Clark cried despairingly. 'I don't know what's wrong!'

'For God's sake . . . ' Lloyd breathed. 'Oh my God!' Clark stared desperately at the contacts, which remained unmoving. Then he jabbed his finger on the test button again and again.

Spit of sound in his ear. What is wrong? What is the matter?

'Examine the relays,' he heard Quin say quite clearly in a calm, detached voice. Then the interference rushed in to fill the small silence after he had spoken.

Relays, relays –

'What do I do?' Lloyd asked peremptorily, a sense of betrayal in his voice.

'Open the fucking gates!' Clark snarled. 'You got nowhere else to go!' Relays, relays –

One of them is unclamped, *one of them is unclamped*!

'Chief – get the men to their stations, immediately. Engine room?'

351

'Sir, we're clear down here.'

'Run up electric power. Well done, Chief!'

'Thank you sir.'

'Sandy, clear the ship of all Soviet personnel – all of them, mind you.'

'One of them is unclamped!' Clark yelled into his throat-mike, as if he expected Quin to be able to hear him in an identical freak reception spot.

'What?' Lloyd asked.

'You do your thing, Lloyd – let me do mine!'

'Is it go?'

'It was go a long time past! Let's get out of here!'

'What about "Leopard"?'

'I'll give you "Leopard", dammit!'

'What about you? You can't be outside the pressure hull when we dive.'

'You worry about your business, I'll worry about mine.'

'Very well. Thurston's opening the gates now.'

'Get with it.'

Faulty fitting, he told himself. The relay, one single fucking relay, lying there on the base of the case. His fingers trembled as he reached down to it, touched it almost reverently, fearfully. His fingers stroked, embraced, lifted it. The vibration caused by the torpedo damage had shaken it out of place, disabling the back-up system, preventing the automatic change-over from working.

There was another spit of sound in his ear, but he ignored the slowed-down, true-speed voice of the storm and the air. Quin was invisible, inaudible somewhere behind it, but he no longer mattered.

Clark pressed home the detached relay, flipped over the retaining clamp, then removed his fingers from it. They came away clammily. The electric motors of the *Proteus* thrummed through the pressure hull.

His back ached. He groaned with the sudden awareness of it and of his cramped and twisted body and the rivulets of perspiration running down his sides and back.

Lloyd's stream of orders continued, murmuring on his chest like the steady ticking of his heart, slower and calmer and younger then his heart felt.

'Slow astern.'

'Slow astern, sir.' Thurston's voice was distant, but Clark could still hear it repeating the captain's instructions. They'd got the gates to the pen open, they'd cast off their moorings at bow and stern. How many men had they lost, just doing that?

'Clark?'

'Yes.'

'Have you finished?'

'Yes. I hope to God, yes.'

'Get back in here – now.'

'Aye, aye, sir.'

Clark turned, still on his knees. He could hear a siren through the outer hull of the *Proteus*. 'Leopard' had to work –

He turned to look at the back-up system – the grey carapace lay behind it. He tore at the wiring and at the wads of explosive, huddling them into his chest then thrusting them back into the pack in pure elation. Then he lifted the grey metal casing, fitted it, fidgeted in his pocket for the screws, fixed them one at a time, feeling the submarine moving slowly backwards on her batteries, out of the pen. Yes, yes.

Pack, pack – left hand bad. The other could stay. Whatever happened, he would not be coming back. He took hold of the pack, and turned once more to make his way back to the hatch following the wire of his aerial. He shunted the pack and his lamp in front of him, hurrying now, winding through the tree-like stanchions like an obstacle course.

The *Proteus* lurched forward, as if freed from some constraint.

Clark slipped, and began to slide into the abyss, into the dark. His lamp slid away, wobbling its light back at him for a moment before leaving him in entire darkness, his body weighted by the pack in his right hand – left hand bad – beginning to pursue the fallen lamp. He crooked an arm round one of the stanchion trees; heaving his body into stillness, into a quiver that was devoid of downward movement. He felt sick. He felt exhausted.

'Clark – Clark, where are you, man?'

Clark groaned. He swung the pack until it rested on the level top of the pressure hull, then grabbed the stanchion

353

with his right hand, changing the agonising hold of his crooked arm for a two-handed grip. He heaved at his leaden body, feeling the revolutions of the motors rise in speed. *Proteus* must be almost out of the pen.

He pulled himself up, aided by scrabbling feet and knees, and lumbered along the top of the pressure hull, reached the hatch and thrust it open. He hefted the explosives through, and let them roll away down the outer hull. Then he clambered after them, closing the hatch and locking it behind him.

The stern of the submarine had already passed into the concrete tunnel leading to the harbour. On her docking prop, *Proteus* was sliding through the tunnel, out to sea.

He watched as the sail of the submarine slid into the shadow of the tunnel. Above the bellow of the siren, he could hear shooting in the distance, like the pinging of flies against a windscreen. Then he ran crouching along the hull, almost slipping twice, until he reached the aft escape hatch, lifted it, stepped on to the ladder inside the chamber, closed the hatch and locked it. Then he felt his legs go watery and he stumbled to the bottom of the escape chamber, bent double with effort and relief.

'Prepare to dive,' he heard Lloyd saying, then: 'Clark? Clark, where are you?'

'Inside.'

'Thank God. Well, does it work?'

'Switch on, and pray.'

'You don't sound too hopeful – '

'Switch the damn thing on!' Clark bellowed with rage and relief and tiredness.

Valery Ardenyev instinctively placed himself in front of Dolohov and Panov. The scene in the pen had no precise focus, nor did it possess a great deal of movement – certainly not sufficient to suggest panic – yet Ardenyev knew what was happening. One guard was firing, the technicians who must have been lining up like an honour guard to await Panov's arrival were shuffling like a herd smelling the first smoke of the grass fire. Also, there was someone clambering up the side of the *Proteus*'s sail, making his way back into the submarine. Ardenyev had the immediate sense that events were already minutes old, even though the white-coated group of figures seemed only now to be reacting to them. Yes. The gates were wide open, and there were two uniformed bodies lying dead on the concrete, alongside the *Proteus*,

He heard Dolohov say, in a strangled old voice, 'No – !', and then he ushered them back through the door by which they had entered the pen, pushing them against the officers who had accompanied them, then had stood deferentially aside so that the three of them might be the first of the party to see the captured British vessel.

'Close the door – give the alarm!' he snapped, then he was pushing through the jostle of technicians towards the submarine.

The *Proteus* slid away from him. As he passed the huddled bodies he believed he recognised the face of the guard on Lloyd's cabin, the man who had patrolled behind the British officer when he had brought Lloyd lunch and told him about Panov.

He ran faster. The *Proteus* shuddered against the side of the pen, then was free. The bow was still moving away from him as he raced to overtake it. He could not believe the panic appearance of the breakout. There had to have been help, and hope. Lloyd or someone else had been given a gun. He *knew* 'Leopard' must have been repaired. Lloyd would not have risked lives, and his submarine, without knowing he could rely on the protection of the anti-sonar equipment.

The bow was behind him now. He ran closer to the hull. It rose smoothly above him. He was half-way down the pen, the only moving figure. There was rifle fire behind him, pointless but noisy. The *pitons* of a ladder climbed away from him. He reached for the lowest one, felt his feet lifted and dragged, his stride extending to great lunar bounds as his arms protested. Then he was pressing himself against the side of the submarine, watching the concrete wall of the tunnel approaching. He might have been half-jammed into the door of a metro train, watching the end of the platform racing at him.

He clambered up the hull, feet slipping, hands sweaty, on to its upper section. He climbed the last few *pitons* and stood on top of the hull as it slid into the tunnel. He ran to the forward escape hatch, unlocked it, lifted it, and clambered down into the chamber, closing the hatch behind him.

'Did he hear you, man? Did he?'

Quin shook his head. 'I don't know,' he admitted. 'I really don't know.'

Aubrey looked at his watch. Seven twenty-seven. They were out of range. The link between Clark and the Nimrod had been broken as certainly as if Pasvik had been shot, and his dish aerials smashed. There was nothing more to be done. As if he saw clearly into Aubrey's mind, Eastoe's voice sounded in the headset.

'That's it, Mr Aubrey. Sorry.'

Aubrey looked through the porthole, out beyond the sun-tipped port wing. Ahead of the Nimrod, the sky was darker, and the land below them was tumbled and cracked in shadow. Cloud and mist wound like white, unsubstantial rivers through the peaks and the fjords. The MiG-23 on the port wing waggled its body like an athletic silver insect, dipping its wings in turn, and then it dropped away and out of sight. The Nimrod was more than a hundred and fifty miles from the Soviet border, making for North Cape.

Aubrey groaned with disappointment.

'I'm sorry,' Quin said.

'Do you think he would have found anything?'

'There seemed no other place to look –' Quin shook his head and stared at the still-open manual in front of him. He closed the wirebound book. 'I don't know. I could think of nothing else,'

Behind them, *Proteus* and her crew would be breaking out – to what purpose? With what reprisals? There was blood now, instead of diplomacy or an intelligence game. People had been killed, Soviet citizens. It did not bear consideration. Aubrey surrendered instead to his utter and complete weariness of mind and body; a comforting numbness.

Seven twenty-nine.

Then the signal, in clear, that he no longer believed to be possible.

'Mr Aubrey?'

356

'Yes?'

'A signal from *Proteus*, in clear.'

'No – '

'It reads – "At one stride comes the dark" – end of message. Do you understand it? Shall I ask for a repeat?'

'No, thank you, Squadron Leader. Let us go home.'

'Very well, sir.'

A beatific smile wreathed Aubrey's features, inflating his grey cheeks, forming his lips, screwing up his eyes. Coleridge's *Ancient Mariner*. 'At one stride comes the dark'. The signal he had told Clark to make in a moment of amusement, a moment of looking for the right, witty, portentous thing for Clark to say if and when he repaired 'Leopard'. Somehow, he had done it.

'What is it?' Quin asked.

'It's all right. It's all right,' Aubrey repeated, opening his eyes, slouching back in his seat, almost asleep already. 'Clark has done it.'

'Thank God,' Quin breathed.

The man's daughter, Aubrey thought, his body immediately chilled. Tricia Quin and Hyde. What of them? Alive, or dead? If the latter, how would he tell Quin?'

'Admiral, we have no units capable of detecting and stopping the British submarine – not in the inner harbour,' the officer commanding the defences of Pechenga explained to Dolohov, nervously standing to attention before the older, more senior man. Inwardly, he wished himself a great distance from the defence control room, set beneath thick concrete and lit by strip-lighting, but he struggled to preserve a form of dignity and an impassive expression on his face. Dolohov was evidently beside himself with rage.

'Nothing? *Nothing?*' Turning, Dolohov waved at the sheet of perspex marked in a grid, displaying coloured lights and chinagraph markings. The two anti-submarine nets were bright red strings of beads, the mines, represented by colours according to type, were like the knots in a fine skein, ready to be drawn about the *Proteus*. Beyond the first net, the units of the Red Banner Fleet at present in Pechenga appeared as a host of bright lights.

'Everything is cold, Admiral – reactors, diesels, turbines

all need time to run up to operational readiness. We have been caught flatfooted – ' He cut off his explanation as Dolohov turned to him again.

'Where is she? *Where is the submarine?*' he bellowed.

'She disappeared from our screens two minutes ago – here.' The defences commandant hurried to the perspex screen in the centre of the operations room and gathered up a pointer that rested against its base. The perspex flexed and dimpled as he tapped with enthusiasm at it. A chinagraphed dotted line ran from the fifth of the submarine pens to a point marked with a circled cross, in the inner harbour. 'We think she was already turning at this point – ' A junior officer beside the perspex screen nodded in agreement.

'What do you intend to do about it?'

'There are two patrol boats in the inner harbour now – the mines, of course, are all activated. However, the inertial navigator memory aboard the submarine may have tracked their course when they entered the harbour, if it had been left on. Even so, it is unlikely they will be able to avoid the mines with any degree of success – '

'Switch them off! Switch off all your mines, at once!'

'But Admiral – '

'Do as as I order! That submarine must be stopped, not destroyed. We cannot take the risk of doing permanent or irreparable damage to her.' Dolohov paused. The political consequences would be enormous, and possibly violent, he considered. In making that judgement, he gave no thought to London or Washington or Brussels, only to the Kremlin. His political masters would not forgive the international repercussions of the destruction of the British submarine in Soviet territorial waters. That had been made clear to him, from the outset.

The commandant nodded to one of his juniors, and the order was given. Almost immediately, the fine skein of lights blinked off, leaving great areas of the perspex screen blank and grey. Every mine in the inner harbour and in the outer basin was now disarmed. The fleet vessels which had before glowed in tiny pockets of greyness, their safe anchorages clear of the mines, now beamed out in isolation; single, unmoving lights. Dolohov hated the blank areas of the screen, like areas on a map still to be explored.

'Now,' he said heavily, 'I want every unit in the outer basin to be prepared. You have a minelayer in port?'

'Yes, Admiral.'

'With low power mines?'

'Yes, Admiral.'

'Then they must be instructed to sow fresh mines along the seaward side of the inner net. Proximity fuses, or magnetic. But they *must* be of sufficient strength only to cripple, not destroy. Understand?'

'The inner net, Admiral, will not be opened?' The man evidently did not understand.

'You will lay the mines, by aircraft if you have to, and you will do it at once,' Dolohov said with a passionate calmness. 'The British captain has torpedoes, wire-guided with television cameras. He can blow a hole in the inner net. If there are mines waiting for him when he escapes through his own hole, he will go to the bottom, or be slowed down, or be forced to the surface. Now do you understand?'

'Yes, Admiral. I will issue the orders at once.'

'Good.' Dolohov thought once, and briefly, of the fact that Ardenyev was aboard the *Proteus*, and then dismissed his image in favour of self-congratulation. In the midst of his fierce rage and disappointment, there was room for satisfaction. He had anticipated what the British captain would do to escape, and he might already have made the move that would frustrate his efforts.

He studied the perspex screen intently.

'Torpedo room— stand by.'

'Aye, aye, sir. Standing by.'

Lloyd studied the sonar screen in front of him. As its arm circled the screen, washing the light-pattern behind it, the bright spots and lines of the submarine net appeared on the screen. It was, as Clark had originally outlined, the only way out— through both nets.

'Range?' he said.

'Eight hundred, sir.'

'Torpedo room— load number one tube.'

'Number one tube loaded, sir.'

The Tigerfish wire-guided torpedo was ready to be fired. Lloyd looked at his watch. Four minutes and thirty-six seconds since they had cleared the pen. Speed was the essence, Clark had said. Just like killing the two guards, he reminded himself with a sick feeling in the pit of the stomach. Speed, surprise. And the gamble that Pechenga would switch off and disarm its minefield in order to preserve 'Leopard'.

'Range seven-fifty, sir.'

'Torpedo room – fire one!'

'One away, sir.'

Lloyd crossed the control room to where Thurston was studying the tiny, blank television screen set alongside the fire control console's other screens and panels of lights. The screen flickered on. Both men ignored the voice over the intercom calling the range and speed and functions of the wire-guided Tigerfish. They seemed mesmerised by the stir and rush and billow of grey water illuminated weakly by the light on the torpedo. Lloyd's wrist with its curling, dark hairs was at the edge of his eyesight. He saw, conjointly with the image on the screen, the second-hand ticking round, moving up the face of the watch, a red spider-leg.

The flash of something, like a curtain or a net though it might only have been an illusion created by the moving water. Then the screen blanked out as the torpedo operator registered the correct and chosen proximity to target and detonated the warhead of the Tigerfish. The shock-wave was a dim, rumbling shudder along the outer hull a few moments later. Lloyd grinned at Thurston.

'Let's see if you can find the hole, John, mm?'

Aye, aye, sir.'

The mist had lifted, remaining in small, thin pockets only in hollows and folds of the ground. The sun had resolved itself into a hard, bright circle, and the sky was palely blue. Hyde was sweating with effort and the rise in temperature as he pulled the girl up the steep bank behind him. When they stood together on the top of the bank, Hyde could see the Chase sloping away from them. He pulled the girl down beside him, and they lay on the wet, dead ferns, staring down through the silver-boled, bare birches towards the tiny figures making their way with laborious effort up towards them. The rifle ranges were behind them, the line of huge, numbered targets perhaps six hundred yards away.

Three of them – no, four. Somehow, Hyde knew there were no others. He checked the magazine, weighing it. Perhaps ten rounds left of the thirty it had originally contained. He thrust the folding double-strut stock against his good shoulder, and looked through the tangent rear sight and the protected post foresight. The action gave him confidence. The mist had been their patron, then their betrayer. Now, the clear air and the bright, warming sun were on their side. Hyde held the high ground. The effective range of the AK-47 was three hundred metres. The four men were at twice that range. He was required to wait.

'You all right?'

'Yes.'

The situation became increasingly unreal the more he considered it, the closer the Russians drew. He was in the middle of Staffordshire, these men were either accredited diplomats of the Soviet embassy or they were casuals called out from the woodwork to assist Petrunin. They were the ones on alien ground, and only now that he looked down on them, armed with one of their rifles and with the mist evaporated, could he perceive the situation in those terms. He had already won. The men down there pushed other men under buses, poisoned them with tiny metal pellets in the tips of umbrellas, pushed them on to the live rail of the underground. Maybe in the north of Scotland they could go on playing this hunting game, but not here. In a minute, a portly matron would appear, exercising a small dog, or someone from the Forestry Commission would pass them in a Land-Rover.

Stop it, stop it, he instructed himself. It was still four to one, and the police would be out in force on the M6, but not necessarily on Cannock Chase. Perhaps four hundred yards now. The four men had spread out, but until they reached the trees on the slope below they had no cover. They moved more cautiously now, probably afraid.

'Not long now,' he offered to Tricia Quin.

'What isn't? What won't be?' she asked in a sullen, tired voice. 'Christ, I'm tired and scared and hungry.'

'That's two of us.' He opened his squinting eye, and

removed the gaze of his other eye from the sights of the Kalashnikov. He studied her. She had become girlish again, and his attitude to her hardened. The rest of it, anything warmer, belonged in the burrow where they had hidden and in his disordered imagination as he half slept. Now, he could not say that he even liked her particularly. She, evidently, disliked him. Their former attitudes had re-emerged, as if they both understood that they were already on the other side of their experience. 'We've got the advantage now.'

She shook her head, staring at the rifle. It alienated her from him. He accepted her distance. She was about to climb back into the feckless skin which he had forced her to shed. She already resented the sloughing of her past self for the last few days.

He looked back. Still the four men, clambering through the wet ferns and the dead heather. A Land-Rover passed along a distant, open track behind them, and he grinned. He put down the rifle and cupped his hands.

'Petrunin! Can you hear me, Petrunin?' he bellowed. The men stopped immediately.

'Yes,' came the faint reply. Petrunin remained just out of effective range of the Kalashnikov. And he knew he was out of range.

'I've won, you stupid joker!'

'Not yet.'

'Admit it. You're finished. You'd better start making arrangements to fly out before they catch you. You're finished in England, mate!'

The four men remained standing, like an irresolute group of hikers. Just over three hundred yards away. There was nothing they could do, no way in which they could move forward into the trees without coming into range. Stalemate. Stand off.

'I think not. We are four to one.' Petrunin's voice was faint, unthreatening. The Forestry Commission Land-Rover had turned into a wide, sunlit ride, and was moving away. The normality it represented did not, however, diminish. Petrunin was bluffing, his words empty.

'Piss off!' Hyde yelled with a quick, sharp delight. 'You're beaten and you know it! Go home to Mother – '

The girl's gasp was inaudible, the begging of her scream merely scratched at his attention, far below the volume of his own voice, but the slump of her body at the corner of his vision attracted him, caused him to turn, his hands reaching instinctively for the rifle. It was kicked away from him, and then a second kick thudded into his wounded shoulder as it came between the walking boot and the side of his head. Tricia Quin, he had time to see, had been struck by the man's rifle stock on the temple, and her head was bleeding. He heard himself scream with pain, his whole body enveloped in the fire which ran from his shoulder. He raised one hand feebly as the man kicked again, them drove the wooden stock of his AKM rifle down at Hyde's face, an action as unemotional as stepping on an insect. Hyde attempted to roll away, but the stock of the rifle caught him between the shoulder blades, winding him, forcing all the air from his lungs so that he fell transfixed to the ground.

He went on rolling, and the man who must have doubled around behind them before they had reached the top of the slope came after him, rifle still pointed stock-first towards the Australian. There was a set, fixed smile on the man's face. The man wasn't going to shoot him, he was going to beat and club him to death. Petrunin and the others would already have started running, reaching the bottom of the slope, beginning now perhaps to labour up it to the top, through the birch trees.

Hyde kicked out, struck the rifle but not the man, who stepped nimbly aside and then came forward again. Hyde tried to get to his knees, aware of himself offering his back and neck for more blows, for execution. He could not catch his breath, which made a hollow, indigestible noise in his throat. The rifle swung to one side, then the stock swung back. Hyde fell away from it, and kicked out, catching the man on the shin, making him exclaim with the unexpected pain. The rifle stock sought his head. He pushed himself half upright on one arm, and dived inside the intended blow. His head snapped up into the man's groin, making the man's breath explode, his body weakly tumble backwards. Hyde grabbed the man's legs, squeezing them together, aware of his back exposed to the next blow. Broken back, his imagination yelled at him. Broken back, lifelong cripple in a chair. He heaved at the man's thighs against his shoulder, and they tottered in that supplicatory embrace until the ground dipped and the Russian lost his balance and fell on to his back. Hyde clambered along the man's body, aware of the shadow of the rifle and the man's arm moving to his right, holding his belt, then his shirt, then his throat as if he might have been ascending a sheer slope. He raised himself above the man, blocking the swing of the rifle with his shoulder and back, pressing down as he levered himself up on the man's windpipe. Then he released his grip, bunched his fist, and punched the man in the throat. The man's tongue came out, his eyes rolled, and there was a choking, gagging sound from his open mouth. His body writhed as if at some separate pain.

Hyde scrambled back to the lip of the slope, dragging the man's AKM behind him by its strap. He fumbled it into his hands, and flicked the mechanism to automatic. He knelt, unable to climb to his feet, and squeezed the trigger. The noise deafened him. Bark flashed from the scarred birches, ferns whipped aside, one man fell just as he emerged from the trees, twenty yards from Hyde; a second man was halted, then turned away.

Hyde released the trigger, and inhaled. His breath sobbed and rattled, but it entered his lungs, expanded them, made him cough. He swallowed phlegm, and crouched down breathing quickly as if to reassure himself that the mechanism of his lungs now operated efficiently. When he could, he yelled at the hidden Petrunin.

'Tough shit, mate! Nice try!"

Silence. He waited. The man behind him was making a hideous noise that somehow parodied snoring, or noisy eating. Otherwise, silence. He looked at the girl, and thought he could see her breasts rising and falling in a regular rhythm. He hoped it was not an illusion, but he could not, as yet, summon the strength or the detachment to investigate. Silence.

Eventually, he raised his head. Beyond the trees, three tiny figures were moving away. One of the dots supported a second dot. The one in the lead, striding ahead, Hyde took to be Petrunin, his mind already filled with images of his skin-saving passage out of the country. A small airfield in

Kent, after he had arranged to be picked up by car and driven down the M1. Hop across the Channel, then Aeroflot to Moscow direct.

Hyde lay back exhausted, staring up at the bright sun in the almost cloudless, pale sky. He began laughing, weakly at first, then uncontrollably, until his eyes watered and his back and ribs were sore and his shoulder ached.

He heard a noise, and sat up. The girl was wiping her head with a dirty handkerchief, pulling grimacing faces, seeming surprised at the blood that stained the handkerchief. Hyde wiped his eyes, and lay back again. The sky was empty, except for the sun. He waited – he decided he would wait until he heard a dog bark, and then raise his head and check whether it was indeed a portly matron out exercising a runt-sized, pink-bowed dog in a tartan overcoat.

Clark looked up at the ceiling of the wardroom pantry with an involuntary reaction. A forkful of scrambled eggs remained poised an inch or so from his lips. The cook had disliked his insistence on eating in the pantry rather than the wardroom proper, but the rating now seemed almost pleased at his company. What was it Copeland had said? *They'll have to be careful, like small boys scrambling under a barbed wire fence into an orchard. Lloyd could get his trousers caught.* Clark smiled. Evidently, they had found the hole they had blown in the net, but not its exact centre. The starboard side of the *Proteus* had dragged for perhaps a hundred feet or more against some obstacle, some bent and twisted and sharp-edged remnant of the net, and then the fin had clanged dully against the net, jolting the submarine, which had then altered its attitude and slipped beneath the obstruction.

Clark registered the scrambled egg on his fork, and opened his mouth. He chewed and swallowed. The food was good, and it entirely absorbed his attention and his energies. He picked up his mug of coffee, and washed down the mouthful of egg. He was eating quickly and greedily and with an almost sublime satisfaction. The responsibility was no longer his. 'Leopard' worked. Immediately, his concussive readiness had drained from him while he lay slumped in the aft escape chamber, and he had gone into a doped and simple-minded superficiality of awareness and sensation. He realised how dirty he was, how much he smelt inside the immersion suit, how hungry and thirsty he was, how tired he was. A junior officer had escorted him to the wardroom. By that time, food had become the absolute priority, after removing his immersion suit. They gave him the disguise of his overalls to wear until he had taken a shower.

What was happening, in the control room and outside the submarine, was of no interest to him. He could not, any longer, have recited the instructions he had given Lloyd when he first boarded the *Proteus*. Some tape in his mind had been wiped. He could not have seen the loose relay in the back-up system now, without having it pointed out to him.

'Like some more, sir?' the cook offered, holding the saucepan out towards him.

Clark grinned, and patted his stomach. 'That'll do, I think, don't you? Very good.'

'Thank you, sir. More coffee, sir?'

'Please.'

The senior rating brought the jug of coffee towards the table where Clark sat. Then he seemed to wobble sideways and lurch against the stove. A stream of dark coffee flew from the jug, cascading down one of the walls – at least, Clark knew that would be what the coffee would do, but the lights went out before he could observe it happen, and he was flung off his chair and bundled into one corner of the pantry. His head banged sickeningly against some jutting piece of kitchen furniture, and he rolled away from it, groaning. He sat up, rubbing his head, his ears ringing with the concussion and the noise that had accompanied the shudder of the submarine, as the emergency lights flickered on, then the main lights came back almost immediately after.

'All right?' he asked.

The cook was wiping coffee from his apron, and rubbing his arm. He still had the empty jug in his hand.

'What happened, sir?'

The *Proteus* was maintaining course and speed, as far as Clark could apprehend.

'Mine.' Someone in Pechenga was thinking fast. He got to his knees, head aching, and the second mine threw him forward as the submarine rolled to starboard with the impact of the explosion. Darkness, slithering, the clatter of utensils, the groan of the hull, the terrible ringing in his ears, the thud of the cook's body on top of him, winding him, then the lights coming back on. He felt the *Proteus* right herself through his fingertips and the rest of his prone body. Over the intercom, Lloyd requested an all-stations damage report immediately. The senior rating rolled off Clark and apologised.

'Okay, okay. I think I'll just go see what's happening.' The cook appeared disappointed at his departure. 'You okay?'

'Yes, thank you, sir.'

Clark left the wardroom pantry, his body tensed, awaiting a further explosion. He entered the control room at the end of the short corridor from the living quarters, and immediately sensed the mood of congratulation. *Proteus* had not been seriously, hamperingly damaged.

'Contact at green three-six closing, sir.' Someone had got the Soviet ships moving in double-quick time.

'Increase speed – nine knots,' he heard Lloyd say.

'Nine knots, sir.'

'Net at two thousand yards.'

'Contact at red seven-zero also moving. Range one thousand.'

'Contact at green eight-two closing, sir.'

The hornet's nest had been poked with a stick. Clark realised that the Russians needed less luck in the confined space of the harbour than they needed out in the Barents Sea, and then they had found a crippled *Proteus*.

'Contact at red seven-zero making for the net, sir.'

'Contact at green three-six closing, sir. Range seven hundred.'

Lloyd saw Clark from the corner of his eye. Clark waved to him, and grinned. Lloyd returned his attention at once to the bank of sonar screens in front of him. Moved by an impulse to see the equipment he had repaired actually functioning, Clark crossed the control room softly, and exited through the aft door. The

'Leopard' room was directly behind the control room.

As he closed the door, he heard Lloyd speak to the torpedo room after ordering a further increase in speed.

'Torpedo room – load number two tube.'

They would make it. Just, but they would make it.

The door to the small, cramped 'Leopard' room was open. Clark, as he reached the doorway, was instantly aware of the rating lying on the floor, and the officer slumped against one of the cabinets containing the main system. And he recognised the dark-jerseyed man who turned towards the noise he had made, knocking on the door-frame in the moment before he had taken in the scene in the room.

Valery Ardenyev. It *was* him. Clark knew he had killed Hayter and the rating.

Seven forty-three. He saw the clock above Ardenyev's head as he took his first step into the room and the Russian turned to him, a smile of recognition on his face. Ardenyev's hand moved out, and threw the switch he had been searching for before Clark disturbed him. As the switch moved, Clark knew that 'Leopard' had been de-activated. The *Proteus* moved through the outer harbour of Pechenga, registering on every sonar screen of every Soviet ship and submarine.

'I knew it had to be you,' Clark said in a surprisingly conversational tone, warily skirting the rating's body near the door. Ardenyev had apparently killed both of them without a weapon.

'I didn't reach the same conclusion about you.' Ardenyev's back was to the control console of the 'Leopard' equipment, protecting the switch he had thrown. 'Perhaps I should have done.' The Russian shrugged, then grinned. 'It won't take long. I only have to keep this stuff –' he tossed his head to indicate 'Leopard', – 'out of action for a few minutes.'

'Sure.' Clark shook his head, smiling. 'You're beaten. We're on our way out, you're alone on an enemy submarine. What chance do you have?'

'Every chance, my friend. That's the Soviet Union a few hundred yards behind you – '

Clark sprang at Ardenyev, who stepped neatly and

swiftly to one side, bringing his forearm round sharply across Clark's back. The American grunted and collapsed across the console, his hand reaching instinctively for the switch above him. Ardenyev chopped the heel of his hand across Clark's wrist, deadening it, making the hand hang limply from his forearm. Then Ardenyev punched Clark in the kidneys, making him fall backwards and away from the control console, doubling him up on the floor. Ardenyev leaned casually against the console, watching Clark get groggily to his knees, winded.

'You're tired, my friend,' Ardenyev observed.

Mistily, Clark saw the red second-hand of the clock moving jerkily downwards. Fourteen seconds since Ardenyev had thrown the switch. He staggered, then tried to lean his weight against the Russian and hold on to him. Ardenyev rammed his knee into Clark's groin, and then punched him in the face. Clark fell backwards again, groaning. He did not want to get up, and did not feel he had the strength to do so. The clock just above Ardenyev's head obsessed him. Twenty-two seconds. *Proteus* must almost have reached the net.

He seemed to feel the submarine hesitate, and saw the attentiveness on Ardenyev's face. He heard a noise scrape down the hull. The net—

The mine exploded beneath the hull, rocking the submarine, blinking out the lights. In the darkness, Clark struggled to his feet and groped for the Russian, feeling his woollen jersey, grabbing it, striking his hand at where the Russian's face would be. He felt the edge of his hand catch the man's nose, below the bridge, felt Ardenyev's breath expelled hotly against his cheek as he cried out in pain, and grabbed the Russian to him in the dark. The room settled around them.

Ardenyev thrust himself and Clark against one of the cabinets. A sharp handle dug into Clark's back, but he hooked his leg behind Ardenyev's calf and pushed. The lights came on as they rolled on the floor together. Clark drove his head down into the Russian's face, but the man did not let go of his neck. Clark felt his throat constrict, and he could no longer breathe. He tried to pull away from the grip, but it did not lessen. Blood ran into Ardenyev's mouth and over his chin, but he held on. The fin of the submarine scraped beneath the holed outer net, the submarine jerked like a hooked fish, shuddering, and then *Proteus* was free.

Clark's thoughts clouded. Ardenyev was interested only in killing him. Nothing else mattered. He beat at Ardenyev's face and neck and shoulders, his punches weak and unaimed and desperate. Consciousness became more and more fugged and insubstantial, then Ardenyev's grip on his throat seemed to slacken. Clark pulled away, and the hands fell back on to Ardenyev's chest, lying there, curled like sleeping animals.

Clark looked at his own hands, covered with blood, bruised, shaking. In one of them he held something that only slowly resolved in his watery vision until he was able to recognise it as the R/T set from his overalls pocket, the one he had used to communicate with Lloyd. He leaned down over Ardenyev's chest, listening. He avoided looking at the man's battered face. He had slapped the R/T set against Ardenyev's face and head time after time with all his remaining strength, as if the movement of his arm would pump air into his lungs.

Ardenyev was dead.

Clark clambered up the cabinet, then lurched to the control console, flicking the switch back to 'On'. 'Leopard' was activated. It was seven forty-five. 'Leopard' had been switched off for almost two minutes. Long enough for *Proteus* to have been spotted, not long enough for her to be attacked.

He sensed the increased speed of the *Proteus* through the deck, as she headed for the open sea. He avoided looking at Ardenyev's body. He dropped the blood-slippery R/T to the floor and hunched over the console, wanting to vomit with weakness and disgust and relief. He rubbed at his throat with one hand, easing its soreness. He closed his eyes. Now, he wanted only to sleep, for a long time.